A SACRED STORM

Theodore Brun

CORVUS

First published in Great Britain in 2018 by Corvus, an imprint of Atlantic Books Ltd.

This edition published in 2019.

10 9 8 7 6 5 4 3 2 1

A CIP catalogue record for this book is available from the British Library.

Paperback ISBN: 978 1 78649 003 2
E-book ISBN: 978 1 78649 000 1

Printed and bound by CPI Group (UK) Ltd, Croydon, CR0 4YY
Corvus
An imprint of Atlantic Books Ltd
Ormond House
26–27 Boswell Street
London
WC1N 3JZ

www.corvus-books.co.uk

A
SACRED
STORM

Also by Theodore Brun
A Mighty Dawn

Theodore Brun studied Dark Age archaeology at Cambridge. In 2010, he quit his job as an arbitration lawyer in Hong Kong and cycled 10,000 miles across Asia and Europe to his home in Norfolk. *A Sacred Storm* is his second novel.

This one's for Tash.

N

SVEÄLAND

UPPLAND
• *Uppsala*
Sigtuna

VESTMANLAND

← The Throat

NAIRKA

← The Great Bay

SODERMANLAND

← The Kolmark Forest

WESTERN
GOTARLAND

Bravik ✕

→ Fjord of Braviken

• *Dannerborg*

Vendlagard •

EASTERN
GOTARLAND

GOTLAND

ÖLAND

JUTLAND

EAST SEA

DANMARK

• *Leithra*

SKANIA

**Southern Scandinavia
in
Early 8th Century**

CAST OF CHARACTERS

AT THE HALLS OF UPPSALA, SVEÄLAND:

Sviggar Ívarsson – King of the Sveärs

Lady Saldas – Queen of the Sveärs and Sviggar's second wife

Svein & Katla – their infant children

Sigurd Sviggarsson – Prince of Sveäland and heir apparent

Vargalf – his personal oathman

Aslíf Sviggarsdottír, known as Lilla – Princess of Sveäland

Erlan Aurvandil – the king's bodyguard and member of the Council of Nine

Kai Askarsson – his servant

Huldir Hoskursson – Earl of Nairka and member of the Council of Nine

Gettir Huldirsson – known as "the Black" – one of Huldir's two surviving sons

Gellir Huldirsson – known as "the White" – his twin brother

Bodvar Beriksson – Earl of Vestmanland and member of the Council of Nine

Bara Ballirsdottír – handmaiden to Queen Saldas

Einar the Fat-Bellied – a king's karl

Jovard – a king's karl

Aleif Red-Cheeks – a king's karl

Vithar Lotharsson – a goði and member of the Council of Nine

Rissa – a serving-thrall

AT THE HALL OF DANNERBORG· EASTERN GOTARLAND:

Ringast Haraldarsson – Lord of Eastern Gotarland, Prince of Danmark and eldest son to Harald Wartooth, King of the Danes

Thrand Haraldarsson – Prince of Danmark and second son to King Harald

Rorik Haraldarsson – Prince of Danmark and third son to King Harald

Sletti – the steward of Dannerborg

Ubbi the Hundred – a warrior mercenary from Friesland and Prince Ringast's guest at Dannerborg

Visma – a Wendish shieldmaiden

Duk – her husband

Gerutha – a servant-woman

Grim & Geir of Hedmark – cousins and mercenaries

AT THE HALL OF LEITHRA· DANMARK:

Harald Roriksson – known as "the Wartooth" – King of the Danes

Branni – his oathman, councillor and oldest friend

PROLOGUE

He is dying and he knows it.

In the slanting rays of a falling sun his horse's shoulder glistens with blood soaked through his breeches.

His comrades are dead. But somehow he got away. Got this far.

He feels cold, despite everything around him signalling a warm spring evening. Golden light, foliage erupting, mocking the numbness creeping through his bones. All the while he hears the whisper of Hel, her breath soft beside his ear. He will slide back into her embrace soon enough, but not before he has done this last service to his king.

He glances down at his wound: an ugly gape in the left of his abdomen. The leather byrnie is torn and through the oozing blood he glimpses the slick greyness of his own entrails. The sweet scent of spring is soured with the reek of open viscera. He has smelled it before – many times in battle, amid the roil of Skogul's Storm, when the *Valkyries* ride to carry off the fallen heroes – the *einherjar* – to Odin's hearth in the Hall of the Slain.

1

Valhöll.

Is that to be his glorious reward?

There was nothing glorious about that savage skirmish under the gloomy boughs of the Kolmark forest. Screams of terror, desperate pleas for mercy, bowel-emptying shrieks of pain. There was hardly time to snatch their weapons before half of them were butchered.

How did I get away?

The question haunts him. Perhaps he didn't. Perhaps he died with the others and Odin has chosen him to deliver this message – has sent him back from the dead, a *draugr*. A harbinger of death to the living.

There is a rustle in the undergrowth to his right. He looks and sees something moving. A shadow lurking beside him. Is it following him?

He stops. The shadow stops. And then he sees. A wolf? No. A dog – a hound, staring at him with one wide, unblinking eye. The other is an empty socket. A doorway into darkness.

The horse moves on, unbidden. Its sudden movement jars him. When the wave of pain has passed he looks back. But the hound is gone.

Perhaps it was another *draugr*-spirit, sent by Odin to watch him to his doom.

One eye.

The eye that sees. The eye that calls...

He lifts his own. Their lids are heavy. Through the last of the beech trees, he can see smoke-wreaths swirling into the purpling sky, risen from the hearths of the halls of Uppsala. One roof towers above the others: the Great Hall of Sviggar Ívarsson, the seat from which the old king has ruled over Sveäland for thirty years. The Bastard King, his enemies call him, although to him, Sviggar has been a faithful lord. Honest and generous.

Yet now all his gifts will be paid for in full. Paid with the last drop of blood.

The Great Hall looms like an oak mountain, propped by vast buttresses, each thick as a giant's forearm. Through the foliage of the Sacred Grove he spies the carving that crowns the gable: a black eagle with a wolf's head – symbol of Sviggar's line and now the Sveär people also.

How many feasts have I enjoyed under that roof? How many toasts have I drunk? How many songs have I sung? And the women...

There will be no more of them. Not in this life.

The sun is kissing the horizon. Looking west, he sees the three familiar domes of earth: the King Barrows. Under each is buried an ancient king of the Yngling line. The western half of each mound is bathed in copper light, their eastern halves swaddled in shadow. The first midges of the year dance on the air like sparks from the hearth of the sun. The sparks smear and he realizes his vision is blurring.

A beautiful day to die.

His breathing is a shallow rattle. His horse suddenly lurches into a trot, each rise a stab at the wound in his side. Perhaps the animal senses its home and hay are near; or that its master's final breath is nearer still. But he mustn't die yet. Not until he has reached the shadow of the Great Hall. Not until he has found someone.

Not until he has delivered his message.

3

PART ONE

DAUGHTER
OF A KING

CHAPTER ONE

The apple was gone in a blink.

The horse nuzzled his other hand, expecting another.

'You're not an easy girl to please, you know that,' said Erlan Aurvandil, tickling her hoary chin. But Idun loved apples, just like the goddess she was named after.

Gods, but she's a grumpy-looking beast, he thought. Still, she looked a sight healthier than the bag of bones he'd ridden in on when he first arrived at the halls of the Sveär king. Good eating and rest had seen to that. And the odd apple.

Erlan produced another from his pouch. Idun gobbled it down.

'Off you go, you old mule,' he said, thwacking her rump. The horse plodded off to a clump of grass nearby. Erlan, meanwhile, began limping back towards the halls and smaller dwellings, inhaling the sweet, green air. It was one of those evenings that seemed swollen with life, a foretaste of summer, when even the pain in his ankle felt not quite so sharp. As if, one day, it might heal.

Of course, it never would.

The limp was his father's mistake. He hadn't known the rock lay under the sand waiting to change his son's destiny. 'Jump. I'll catch you,' he had laughed. A test of trust: at least that was what Erlan thought it was. He had jumped. His father stepped aside. The rock did the rest. No test then, just a lesson: that you can't trust anyone in this world, least of all the ones you love. Aye, he had learned that lesson well. That was why his father, his home, his inheritance – his very name – were all buried under an oath. Buried with *her*.

Because of his father's lie, she had had to die. Inga – his first love. Inga – the ghost in his soul. She had cut her own throat and with the same stroke cut him loose from all that he knew and loved. So he was here, and she was there, lying under some barrow in the land of his birth. A land he had sworn never to see again.

He spat into the dust, as if that could expel the bitterness that rankled in his blood. Here, he was an exile. An outlander. Yet this was where he had found a new home and a new life after that other life had ended.

A cuckoo's call floated down out of the treetops of the Kingswood.

He sighed, shaking off worn, old thoughts. Surely even a cripple couldn't feel bitter on an evening like this? After the long winter the beech trees were in full garb, bulging in on the Uppland halls while the last of the sun splintered through their branches. His nostrils filled with the scent of the woods and meadows. Laughter and shrill voices tinkled on the twilit air as mothers called their children home. And with the dusk-dew, a kind of peace settled over the shingled roofs around Uppsala.

Maybe this was enough. Maybe this was his reward after enduring that dark and savage winter. He had arrived no better than a beggar, but King Sviggar had accepted his oath in return for salt and hearth. And afterwards came those mysterious deaths. Sviggar's daughter, Lilla, had disappeared. Erlan had stepped forward. He had followed the trail into a vast, cold wilderness until it led him down into the dark depths under the earth. He entered seeking death. Instead he found life, and her. And he was a different man when he restored her to her father. The grateful king had honoured him, given him gold and a place on his council, even given him a new name: *Aurvandil*. It meant 'shining wanderer'. But for now he had no need to wander.

Now? Why not for ever?

He crossed the expansive yard of the Great Hall. All was quiet. Most folk would be settling down to supper around one of the many hearth-fires. His belly grumbled in anticipation, hoping Kai had cooked something good.

Kai Askarsson was his servant, at least in name. Erlan had rescued Kai from a whipping post in a lonely corner of Gotarland, many leagues to the south. At the time it had been against his better judgement to let Kai tag along, but since then the Norns – those ancient spinners of fate – had woven together their paths tighter than the great wolf Fenrir's leash.

Kai was fearless, reckless, irreverent, irrepressible, mischievous, garrulous, sneaky and downright mad at times. In short, about as different from Erlan as a man could be. But Erlan liked him better than any other, too.

He set off down the slope towards the scattered halls and houses that lay to the east of the Great Hall, eager to discover what Kai would conjure from their pot tonight.

That was when he heard a strange noise.

It stopped him at once.

He turned and shaded his eyes against the sunset, judging the sound to have come from back towards the Sacred Grove. Seeing nothing, he was about to shrug it away, when out of the haze emerged the silhouette of a horse and its rider. Even from there, he could see the rider was slumped over the horse's withers.

There was another sound, halfway between a strangled salutation and a wail.

'You all right there, friend?' he called as the horseman drew closer.

No answer. And the horse kept on, so that Erlan was forced to lurch aside. Before he had time to object, the rider had collapsed on top of him.

They hit the ground hard, Erlan winded under the man's full weight. The rider was groaning like a stuck boar. He was wounded, clearly, but only when Erlan slithered out from under him and saw his own tunic soaked with blood did he realize how badly.

He rolled him onto his back. 'We need help here, now!' he yelled. A stable-thrall appeared from under a byre and came running. Then a woman in a head-cloth emerged from a smithy. When she saw the blood-soaked rider she screamed. That brought others.

The man's breath was grating like a saw. Erlan smelled the stink of punctured bowels and peered at his wound. It was an ugly gash caked black around its edges. Blood still welled from inside. His cheeks were deathly pale. Still, his face was familiar. Another of the king's house-karls, Erlan thought, named Uttgar or Ottar, maybe? There were so many of the buggers it was impossible to remember all their names. 'He needs water.'

The stable-hand rose and pushed through the gathering crowd. Meanwhile the rider was gulping at the air, bleeding.

Dying.

More folk were arriving, crowding round. 'Give him some room, damn you!' Erlan shifted, trying to cradle the karl's head in his lap.

'That's Ormarr,' said a thrall-girl.

'Poor bastard,' said a smith. 'Look, he's trying to say something.'

Certainly his lips were moving. Erlan put his ear to the tremulous breath.

'The... Kolmark.' Hardly a whisper.

'The forest?'

'Slain... all of us, slain.'

'What's he saying?' the thrall-girl demanded, plucking at Erlan's elbow.

'If you shut up, I could tell you... Go on.'

'War— tooth... War— tooth...'

'Wartooth, he says. He must mean King Harald!' declared the smith, who was leaning over Erlan's shoulder. The name buzzed around the gathering. None was more hated or feared in all of Sveäland than Harald Wartooth, King of the Danes.

'What's the old bastard done now?' growled someone further back.

Ormarr groaned.

'He's dying,' the smith said, prodding a bony finger in Erlan's ribs. 'Ask him again.'

'Look at me.' He tried to brush Ormarr's sweat-slicked hair out of his eyes. 'What about the Wartooth? Who is slain? Speak, man.' But the karl only rolled his eyes. 'Where's that bloody water?' Erlan yelled, looking round for the errant stable-thrall. The nearest water butt was not thirty yards away but there was no sign of the fool. Not that a gulp of water would do much good now.

With a sudden surge of strength, Ormarr seized Erlan's tunic and pulled him close. His eyes were burning with fever. He put his lips to Erlan's ear and uttered his last words, so faint Erlan could barely hear them. Then his grip slackened, his eyelids drooped, his head fell back. Dead.

Erlan slumped back on his heels.

'What 'e say?' asked the smith.

But Erlan was staring at Ormarr's lifeless lips.

'He whispered something. Was it about the Wartooth?'

'What did he say, damn it?' demanded another.

Erlan rose to his feet, glaring right through the wall of eager faces, deaf to their questions, his mind fixed on one object and one alone. He had to see the king.

Because war was coming.

CHAPTER TWO ☉

S viggar Ívarsson, King of the Sveärs, sat on his oak-hewn throne tugging at his grey and white beard, glowering like a dwarf who'd lost his gold.

Behind the old king hung dusty tapestries – some depicting great deeds of his war-mongering father, Ívar Wide-Realm; others, scenes from older sagas of heroes long dead or tales of the ancient gods who still haunted the reaches of the north. The hour was late, the air fragrant with the scent of pine resin burning in stone-dish lamps. Around the chamber shadows danced, leaping with each flicker of the torches on the walls.

'Confused words from a dying man,' said Sviggar at last. His voice, though hollowed by age, still carried the weight of authority. When he spoke, men listened, and obeyed. 'A man says wild things at death's threshold. His words tell us nothing.'

'His words are clear enough,' exclaimed his son Sigurd, rising from his seat. 'And *someone* put a blade in his belly!'

'Sit down!' Sviggar hauled himself to his feet. He was tall still and once must have been an imposing figure. But age, ever the vanquisher of great men, had reduced his long limbs to brittle sticks.

With a scowl, his son flung himself back in his chair and went back to tugging at the corner of a dark eyebrow. Erlan had witnessed this cavilling between father and son a dozen times at least since his appointment to the king's council. More often the older, wiser head had the right of it, but this time Erlan wasn't so sure.

Upon hearing news of this strange death, Sviggar had summoned an immediate council. However, only five members of his Council of Nine could be found just then: his son Sigurd, the white-haired goði Vithar, a pair of earls – Bodvar and Huldir – and Erlan himself.

These five were arranged around the council table according to their rank. The guards had been dismissed, all except Gettir, the son of Earl Huldir, who hovered in attendance of his father. There was only one other, gliding back and forth behind the king's throne like some beautiful spectre, caressing a wine cup in long, slender fingers.

Perhaps it was natural that Queen Saldas was there: she had been present when Erlan brought word to her husband. Erlan, however, wished she wasn't. Of course, with her raven-black hair, the smooth fall of her robe over the curves of her body and those restless emerald eyes, she was a distraction to any man. But Erlan had more reason than other men to keep his mind from wandering.

At the great feast that winter there had been certain words exchanged. A certain look in those green eyes. Now Erlan knew only a fool would set about cuckolding a king. Of course, if the prize were tempting enough, a man might hazard it. Saldas was undoubtedly that – Sviggar afforded himself the best of all things and his second wife was no exception. But there was something dangerous about her, something Erlan didn't trust. He had decided to give her a wide berth.

She was looking at him now, a faint crease at the corner of her mouth. He took a swig of ale to break her gaze and the almost-smile curdled into a sneer. She turned away. 'The message may be unclear, my lord husband, but some things are fact. A man arrives. He is wounded. He utters the Wartooth's name and the Kolmark forest. He says war is coming. And then he dies.'

'Exactly!' cried Sigurd. 'It confirms the rumours we've heard all winter.'

'Rumours are like clouds on the horizon,' his father growled. 'Not every one brings a storm.'

'We're not talking about a few drops of rain, are we? All over the southern marches, it's the same. Merchants from the south say Skania and Gotarland are bristling with spears. Have I not been saying so for months?'

'Aye. To anyone who would listen,' Earl Bodvar observed drily. Earl Bodvar was a dry man, with a voice so hoarse he might have swallowed a horn full of dust.

'Fine. Mock me, Bodvar,' Sigurd replied indignantly, 'but this proves me right. Why else would the Wartooth be gathering men if not to bring war on us?'

'Harald Wartooth would never do that,' said his father. 'He knows it's a war he could never win. He's no fool. It's been thirteen years since the last blood was spilled. What could he gain by bringing war now?'

'Vengeance,' snarled Earl Huldir ominously. 'Vengeance is what he seeks. And it's what I will have from him and his seed one day.' No one needed reminding why. Earl Huldir's face bore a terrible scar that fell from his hairline, slitting his eyebrow, blinding an eye and leaving a purple seam across his left cheek. 'The Wartooth owes me one eye and two sons. I mean to have them all before I join my fathers at Odin's table. If that day is drawing nearer, I say let it come.'

'No one denies your grievances, Huldir,' said Sviggar. 'This feud has cost us all much.' His gaze happened to fall on Erlan. 'Well, most of us. But if Harald is looking for vengeance, my father is already dead.'

'The blood feud is not over until *all* debts are paid,' replied Huldir. 'While any of your line still lives, so the feud lives.'

'This I know well,' murmured the king in a weary voice.

This wasn't the first that Erlan had heard of the feud between the houses of these two great kings. Princess Lilla had told him of it once before. But he had had no cause to think any more of it until now.

'I hate to see this noble brow so troubled,' soothed Queen Saldas, laying a hand against Sviggar's forehead. 'This talk is idle until we know more. Let me consult Odin. He is the giver of wisdom.' She gestured at the aged goði leaning on his crutch. 'Vithar and I will make the necessary offerings. The Hanged Lord will show us the course we must take.'

'No one can deny your sacrifices are effective, my lady,' the white-haired goði croaked, with an obsequious bow.

Erlan recalled the nine corpses hanging from the Sacred Oak that winter, sparkling under their veil of hoarfrost, each face frozen, each more beautiful than the last. Such were the sacrifices Saldas was only too willing to make to win the gods' favour.

16

'No,' Sviggar replied at length. 'Not that way.'

'If war is coming—'

'Aye, if!' the king shouted.

His outburst was followed by an awkward silence. It was Earl Bodvar who eventually broke it. 'My lord, I have a suggestion which you may find more practicable.'

'Go on.'

'This Ormarr was part of a shieldband that was scouting the southern marches. They weren't due to return for another five days, but we've heard nothing else from them. My guess is we won't. Ormarr mentioned the Kolmark forest—'

'You want to send another shieldband to investigate?'

'It would seem an obvious measure.'

'Except that our border through the Kolmark is fifty leagues long! *If* he came from there – and it's possible he did not – then it could be almost anywhere. It might take a shieldband weeks to find anything.'

'Send two, then,' boomed Earl Huldir, standing and pulling his son out of the shadows. 'Gettir and his brother can lead a band of my men to scout the southern boundary of our lands in Nairka. No one in the kingdom knows that part of the forest better than them.'

Gettir Huldirsson looked straight ahead, offering himself for the king's inspection. He was a lean, dark lad of eighteen or so, not much younger than Erlan himself. And thanks to Kai's talent for gossip, Erlan happened to know he wasn't a man to steer clear of a fight. The king eyed him doubtfully. 'He's very young.'

'So he is,' conceded Huldir, 'but he's capable. And my men obey him and his brother as they would me.'

Sviggar looked unconvinced.

'Surely it's at least worth looking, my lord?' Earl Bodvar suggested.

Sviggar scraped a bony finger down his cheek. 'Very well. We will send two scouting parties. One by the western road through Nairka, the other through Sodermanland.'

'Thank you, my lord,' replied Bodvar. 'Would it also be prudent to send word to the other earls to make ready to raise their levies? If the worst should prove true.'

'Of course it would,' said Sigurd excitedly. 'We're wasting precious time even now. We should summon the levies at once, Father.'

When Sviggar still hesitated, Earl Huldir lost patience. 'Gods – what are we? Old women! We should be bringing war to the Wartooth and his lands, not sitting here like a flock of hens waiting for him to come to us!'

'Silence!' cried the king, smashing a bony fist on the arm of his chair, making it shudder. 'You're all in such a fine lather to throw yourselves into the abyss.' His eyes ranged over his councillors, grey and sharp as a well-honed blade. 'I've seen war. Seen death and an ocean of blood. Wasn't half my life given over to it? And did it ever bring my people any good? Wasted lives and wasted silver. But I did my duty to my father, all the same. When he died, that was the end of it. Instead I've built something that will endure. I will do nothing to provoke another war and put my kingdom at risk!'

'Do nothing and your precious kingdom may be taken from you all the same,' answered Sigurd in a quiet but firm voice.

'A man is dead,' Bodvar interjected before Sviggar could unleash more invective on his son. 'As Lord Sigurd said:

someone killed him. Even if you want to avoid war, surely it's unwise to make no preparations.'

The old king grunted, his brow twitching like scales in the balance. After a while, he shook his head. 'No. I'll not be goaded into fanning the flames of war, nor stir up needless panic among these halls. We will dispatch these two shieldbands and they will find out more. But,' he added, fixing Huldir's son with a hard gaze, 'you will keep within our borders. I'll not give the Wartooth and his sons any provocation for war. Do you understand?'

Gettir said nothing, only bowed his head obligingly.

'*Do—you—understand*?' the king repeated.

'I do, my lord,' Gettir murmured, a grin ghosting about his lips.

'Good. Now – who shall lead this second shieldband?'

'I will lead it,' said Sigurd.

'Out of the question.'

'What? But why, Father?' Sigurd was a man of twenty-eight winters. Just then he sounded like a little boy.

'I've lost one heir. I'm not about to lose another.' Sviggar's firstborn Staffen had been murdered the previous autumn. It was common knowledge that Staffen had been the son Sviggar had wanted for his heir. And none knew it better than Sigurd.

'You can't keep me from—'

'Enough,' Sviggar interrupted, waving him down. Sigurd slouched back onto his seat.

'I will go, lord,' said Erlan, earning himself a hostile look from the prince.

'You? Erlan *Aurvandil*.' Sviggar eyed him up and down. 'No. Your place is here, beside me.'

19

'Ormarr delivered his message to me. Am I not responsible for finding out the truth of this?'

The queen appeared at her husband's shoulder. 'Perhaps it's no accident that the dead man found the Aurvandil,' she said in a soft voice, never taking her eyes off Erlan. 'A man's fate finds him out.'

The old king regarded his wife, smoothing down his beard with brittle fingers. 'Hmm.' He suddenly chuckled and lifted his wine cup to Erlan. 'Very well. It seems the Norns point their finger at you once more, my young friend. I trust you'll be as lucky as you proved the last time.'

Erlan bowed low.

Lucky? If I were lucky, I wouldn't be here.

CHAPTER THREE

It was already far into the night by the time they were dismissed, though Erlan doubted any of them would sleep much. Sviggar, perhaps, least of all.

Outside, under the vastness of the northern sky, Earl Huldir pulled up with a curse. 'The man's a mule-headed old fool!' His milky eye glared fiercely in the gloom.

'He's no fool,' returned Bodvar. 'He's just a cooler head than you, old friend.'

'His indecision will get us all killed – whether he wants the fight that's coming or not.'

'We don't know what's coming.'

'Horseshit, Bodvar! This thing has to play out. The Wartooth knows it. So do you.' He pressed a massive thumb into Bodvar's chest. 'And I for one intend to make that son of a bitch pay.' He nodded grimly at his son. 'We'll be ready.' With that he stomped off into the night, his son Gettir following at his shoulder.

'You think he's right?' said Erlan, looking after them.

'That's what you're going to find out.' Bodvar laughed – a short, sharp bark. 'Count yourself lucky. You're young. You're an outlander. You have no blood debts to pay.'

'Not here, anyway,' muttered Erlan.

'H'm,' grunted Bodvar. 'Maybe. But Huldir there – he's been carrying the weight of those dead sons half his life. A man gets sick of a weight like that.'

'Are there many like him?'

'What a question!' exclaimed Bodvar. 'Hel, do you even know what this is about?'

'Some. The princess told me once. Something about a disagreement between the old King Ívar and his daughter.'

'You could call it that. Sviggar's father was a mean old wolf. They called him Ívar Wide-Realm because no man before him had ever ruled over a kingdom so vast. He stole the Sveär crown from the last of the Yngling kings. The few surviving nobles loyal to the Ynglings escaped west into Norway. So Ívar made his own earls and gave them land. My father was one of them. Anyhow, things settled down. But Ívar's ambition wasn't sated. He fancied himself a piece of Danmark too and figured a way to get it. By then, he had a daughter. A handsome creature, by all accounts—'

'Autha?'

'So you know her name, at least.'

Erlan shrugged.

'Aye. She was handsome. And clever, too. Far cleverer than her father. Maybe too clever for her own good. She liked to make a fool of him, especially in front of his own household, thinking she could get away with it. But he held scores, did Ívar, even against his own kin, and he found a way to use Autha to get what he wanted and see her sorry for it.'

'How?'

'By marrying her to one of the sons of the King of Danmark. The wrong son, so Autha reckoned.'

'What do you mean?'

'This king had two sons – the older was called Rorik and his brother, Helgi. Rorik was set to succeed his father but he was ugly and awkward. His brother Helgi was silk-tongued and fair as Baldur. Naturally, Autha wanted to marry Helgi, but instead her father gave her to Rorik, who was soon wearing the Danish crown after his father died.'

'So Autha became Queen of Danmark.'

'Aye. But then Ívar starts his scheming. He sets rumours flying that his own daughter has been sharing Helgi's bed. Of course, King Rorik doesn't fancy that, so he has his brother murdered. There's an outcry, and the accusation of Autha's infidelity is there for all to see. And so, humiliated, Autha sends word to her father, begging him to avenge her honour – aye, and the man she truly loved. And old Ívar was only too happy to oblige. He sent an army south, routed the Danes and slew King Rorik.' Bodvar gave a low chuckle. 'It was only then that Autha realized her father had only ever meant to steal Danmark for himself and that she'd been used.'

'What does any of this have to do with Sviggar?'

'Sviggar was Ívar's only other surviving child. Bastard-born, but still... He was a lad when all this caught fire. Autha rallied support to throw her father out of Danmark, but he soon defeated them and she fled with her own son, Harald.'

'The Wartooth?'

'Aye. The Wartooth.' Bodvar grinned. 'Keeping up?'

'Just about.'

'Good lad. Of course, Harald was just a boy then, too. Autha took him east, made alliances, raised an army. And Ívar couldn't let it lie. He went in pursuit of her. The wars between them flared up now and then. Harald grew to manhood and took up his murdered father's claim over Danmark. So it went on.'

'Those were the Estland wars?'

'Aye. Many of us cut our teeth there, myself included. And Sviggar... He made a name for himself over there. He was a Hel of a man to follow into Skogul's Storm, I tell you...' Bodvar looked up into the night, presumably recalling battles past. Suddenly his eyes snapped down. 'Anyhow, by the end Autha claimed both Danmark and Sveäland as hers by right, saying no bastard-born son could deprive her of her inheritance. She died making her son Harald swear he would recover both. And then old Ívar died, too – drowned off the Estland coast.'

'And that was the end of it?'

'For a time. Harald Wartooth raced back to Danmark to secure his claim there, and Sviggar did the same here. That's how things lay for a long while. Sviggar here in Uppsala, ruling the Sveärs and a few other tribes. Harald Wartooth, ruling Danmark and a few other lands from his hall at Leithra on the isle of Zealand. Neither was strong enough to uproot the other. Although they tried a few times.' He winked. 'Usually it was the Wartooth flexing his muscles.' Bodvar nodded in the direction Earl Huldir had disappeared. 'That's when two of his sons were slain. Eastern Gotarland saw many battles but they only served to prolong the feud and deepen the debts of blood. So that's how it stands. The Wartooth holds sway over the Eastern Gotars, from Skania in the south all the way north to the Kolmark.'

24

Erlan scratched at his scrub of a beard. 'I guess that's where I come in.'

'I guess it is,' said Bodvar, slapping him on the shoulder.

'Think we'll find anything?'

'Who knows? The forest is vast and thick as the hair on a bear's backside. But maybe the gods want to see this feud played out, like Huldir says.'

Erlan nodded. 'And what about you?'

'What about me?'

'Don't you have blood debts to settle?'

The lines of Bodvar's craggy face cracked into a broad smile. 'I have no brothers, no sons. Only daughters. Three of them, and a giant thorn in my arse they are too. But at least they're alive.'

Erlan laughed.

'Well, my friend, I'm to bed. Meet me here tomorrow at the Day-Mark and I'll pick you a good crew. Something tells me you're going to need it.'

A short walk later Erlan was pushing aside the hide-skin drapes that kept the heat inside the house where he lived with Kai. It stood among the smaller barns and dwellings that lay to the east of the Great Hall. A modest place, with a turf roof and strong timber walls – easy to keep warm if there was a chill in the air.

Erlan slept on the bench near the hearth-fire, but Kai preferred the loft, apparently unfussed by the smoke that gathered in the rafters before it found its way out of the smoke-hole. He maintained anything was better than sleeping near

Erlan, who, he claimed, snuffled like a boar digging for acorns all night long. Of course, Erlan denied it.

He shuffled inside and let the drape fall.

'Frey's fat cock,' exclaimed Kai in a loud voice. 'You took your sweet time!'

'Aren't you asleep yet?'

'How am I supposed to sleep after the hornet's nest you've kicked over?' A mess of blond hair appeared over the edge of the hayloft. Kai pushed his fringe out of his eyes and swung his legs onto the ladder. 'What's it to be, then? A spear for every man, set sail for Danmark and bugger the consequences?'

'Not exactly.' Erlan slumped on the sheepskin that lay along the bench and began pulling off his shoes. 'I'm to lead a shieldband into the Kolmark and see what I can find out.' He leaned back and set about kneading the soreness out of his aching ankle.

'What's to find out? It's war, ain't it? The whole place is saying so.'

'Well, they can unsay so. Sviggar'll cut the tongue out of anyone who goes spreading talk like that. Not till we know more.'

'The Old Goat's a bit late for that! He might as well try and push a fart back up the Fat-Belly's arse. They're damned windy these Sveärs, you know.' Being Gotar-born himself, Kai was happy to cast aspersions. 'They're all croaking away like a sack of frogs.'

'They might have good cause to croak. We'll know soon enough.'

'By the way – there's ale in the jug if you want it.' Kai jerked his head at the smoke-stained pot hanging over the embers in the hearth. Erlan grabbed an ox-horn mug and ladled some out. Meanwhile, Kai had shinned down his ladder and begun rummaging about under the loft.

'What the Hel are you doing?'

'What do you think? Sorting my gear. I suppose we're riding out early, eh?'

Erlan realised he should have anticipated this. He sighed. 'No. *I* ride out. You're not going anywhere.'

'What? Why not?'

'Because...'

'Well?'

'Because I say so. You're not fully trained yet.'

'Not fully trained! Then what the Hel have we been doing all these months?'

'Look, if something happens, I don't want to be worrying that some oversized Danish troll is about to knock that empty head off your shoulders.'

'You do talk horseshit sometimes, master. Have you forgotten last winter – when the Vandrung came? I killed as many of those things as any of us. And two wolves 'n all!'

'That was different. We had no choice.'

'You've got no choice now, either. Need I remind you that we're blood-sworn, you and I?' Kai pulled up his sleeve to show off the thin scarlet seam across his forearm where he'd cut himself and made his oath. A gesture he used to dramatic effect about five times a day. 'Where you go, I go.' He gave a nod, as if that was an end to it.

'Not a chance. Next time... maybe.' Erlan smiled and got a scowl for his pains. 'Anyhow, the whole thing could be a fool's errand.'

'You don't believe that. And you know I'm worth five of any of those halfwit karls that'll ride with you.'

'You're worth fifty,' snapped Erlan, losing patience. 'That's why you're staying here.' Kai frowned, unsure of the comeback to that. 'Listen, you mad little bastard. If there is a war coming I promise you aren't going to miss out. This way at least I'll have time to finish your training. The shieldwall is savage. Others can fall cheaply if that's their fate, but I'm going to make damn sure you aren't one of them.'

Kai slouched onto the bench and helped himself to a mug of ale. He gazed dejectedly into the amber liquid. 'Bara says, till I've proved myself as one of the king's hearthmen, I don't stand a chance. Those were her exact words.'

Erlan burst out laughing. 'Is that all this is about? Bedding Bara?'

'What do you mean, *all*? That's about the best reason there is!'

These days it seemed whatever the starting point, their talk always led back to Bara. To say Kai was besotted was a blistering understatement. And if the servant-girl had been elusive before, since she had been appointed handmaiden to the queen she had made it very clear that she was now utterly beyond Kai's reach. Elfin pretty, fire-headed, fire-tempered, lissome as a wildcat, conceited as the day was long, she was no easy tree to fell. And by the gods, Kai had put in some axe-work.

'Well, here's to the chance to prove yourself.' Erlan raised his cup. 'Might be that day's coming sooner than you think.'

'No thanks to you.'

Erlan shrugged and drank anyway. Eventually, moodily, Kai joined him.

'You're sure I can't tag along?'

'Next time.'

'Piss on it then! And piss on you!' Kai stormed off to his ladder. 'Still,' he added on his way up it, 'there's many a rung in war for a man to climb to higher stations in life.'

'For a resourceful fellow like you – no doubt.'

'Exactly! And you too, master. I mean, this place is all well and good but we hardly want to live here for ever. You being destined for great things and all!'

'Great things?'

'Undoubtedly, master. And Kai Askarsson is going to see that you get 'em.'

'What kind of things?'

'Land. Silver. A buxom wife. Four square walls, and big ones too. Oh, I've got plans for us. Don't worry about that. It's all in hand.'

Erlan heard Kai settle into his nest of straw and blankets. 'You dream on, my friend,' he called up. 'I'm going for a leak.'

Is that what war will bring? he wondered, as he unlaced his breeches outside. Land and wealth and fame. The love of his lord and king.

No. War might bring him a lot of things. But it couldn't bring him the one thing he wanted.

Because no matter how many men you kill, you can't unstitch the past.

CHAPTER FOUR

Princess Aslíf Sviggarsdóttir swept towards the queen's chamber with the ease of one long familiar with the blackened sconces on the wall, the shuffle of rushes underfoot, that rugged smell of ageing oak in her nostrils.

Her earliest memories whispered like ghosts in these shadows, when it was her own mother she rushed to see, her own childish squeals of delight as she was swept up and swung around in those comforting arms. That was long ago. She remembered how her mother would whisper her name close to her ear like a secret. 'My little Lilla. My little Lilla.'

'Lilla' was the nickname her brother Staffen had given her. It meant simply 'purple' – chosen, he said, because her legs were always turning that colour when she was a baby. But like all silly names, it had stuck. She didn't mind. She preferred it to Aslíf anyway.

But now her mother was gone and the chamber belonged to another. To this Saldas, her father's second wife of four years past. And instead of her own infant footsteps, it was those of Saldas's children that rattled the floorboards beside her.

Every day she would bring her half-brother and half-sister to the queen's chamber to say 'good day' to their mother. Afterwards she would take them to the Kingswood where they helped her find herbs and seeds, and she would teach them about the flowers and plants that grew there and the healing lore that her mother once taught her.

But today was different. Today her steps were urgent as she half-dragged the children along the corridor by their little fists. Because yesterday the halls had been turned upside down. Someone who had watched that poor man die had told her maidservant what had happened. It sounded grim, and grimmer still the words of foreboding the man had spoken.

As soon as she heard it, Lilla had dressed and sought out her father, only to discover he was already in council. There he had remained. The night had worn on until Lilla grew weary of waiting and had retired to her bed where she had been troubled by a swirl of dreams. Somewhere within them, she had seen that dark place again, and shivered with the memory of the cold. And afterwards another dream, in which she saw a wolf snarling at a wolfhound, ready to fight. The hound had only one eye and seemed from its movements to be lame. But it was fearless and stood its ground, unafraid of the wolf with its fierce fangs. Before they fought, her mind had drifted on. Several times she had seen Erlan's face as it had been in that dark place, filthy, gaunt, urging her onward, mouthing something, some warning perhaps. Only when she awoke did she wonder whether the lame dog was connected with him. If so, it was a strange image indeed.

While she had passed a fitful night, she knew her stepmother had been admitted to the council. That was why she hurried. Saldas would be able to tell her all that had been said.

'Good day, Mother,' she called through the curtain. *Mother*. The word was a joke. Saldas was hardly ten summers older than her – but she insisted Lilla use it. 'May we come in?'

'Enter,' came the reply, in a low, melodious voice. Lilla pushed aside the drape and hustled in the children.

Saldas was seated before the tall mirror propped against the wall, its silver surface polished to a shine. She was wearing a flowing white robe and, unusually, was combing out her long black hair herself. She rose to greet them.

There was the usual awkwardness as first Svein and then Katla embraced their mother. For all the queen's grace, Lilla had never seen a mother less natural in handling her own offspring. She kissed each child in turn, smiling – though her eyes stayed cool.

'You slept well?' asked Saldas.

Svein was already busy pulling out a chest from the corner and began unpacking his collection of wooden toys in front of his little sister.

'Not really. I don't suppose many did.'

'A little soon to be losing sleep, I think,' Saldas said with a note of contempt. She wafted a hand at the edge of her bed.

Lilla took the seat, glimpsing a flash of honey-blonde hair above the pale russet of her dress as she passed the mirror. 'Are you not anxious about what is to come?'

'Why fear the future?' Saldas smiled mysteriously. 'Better to control it.'

How could one control the future? Lilla wondered. Especially in war. 'I suppose the Norns weave all of our paths.'

The bridge of Saldas's nose wrinkled. 'An obvious thing to say, my daughter. I should have thought better of you.' She chuckled as though it were a shared joke, but the condescension in her eyes nettled Lilla. 'I prefer to weave my own,' Saldas added. 'Anyway, we know next to nothing about this supposed threat. And your father seems reluctant to learn more.'

'Something must have been decided. The council talked until late.'

'You know how it is with men, my dear. Each one must be heard five times over and none is ever persuaded. So round it goes.'

'Father must have settled on doing something. His folk need reassurance at the least. I should speak with him. Perhaps there's something I can do.'

'I fear not. The best you can do is make sure this beautiful face keeps its composure.' Saldas stroked a fingertip down Lilla's cheek. 'So lovely...' She sighed. 'If you must know, your father has sent two patrols south. They may find something.'

'Who is to lead them?'

'Gettir Huldirsson leads one. And the other is—'

'Erlan,' Lilla said without thinking.

'Why, yes! How did you know?'

'I didn't,' said Lilla, although she must have. She thought of the dream and her belly tightened.

'Hmm. A premonition then,' Saldas replied casually, inspecting some detail in the mirror a little closer, flicking at her hair with her comb. When she looked up, her expression changed. 'Why, my dear, you've gone quite pale. Are you unwell?'

'No. I— I'm fine.'

'Ah.' The queen's frown slid into a knowing smile. 'I see. You hold a secret affection for him.'

'No! I—'

'It would only be natural after all he did for you. But you mustn't fret on his account. He's a most able young man. Despite his... affliction.'

'It's not that. I just...' Lilla trailed off, feeling miserably transparent. 'When do they leave?'

'This morning, I think. Perhaps they've left already.'

Lilla was on her feet immediately. But then she stopped. Now it was her being awkward. She felt her cheeks burning. Her eyes flicked between the door and the children, caught between staying and going.

'Go on,' said Saldas languidly, turning back to her reflection. 'Though I fear you may be too late—'

Lilla didn't wait to hear more. She was at the door and through the drapes, hurrying along the corridor and outside into the crisp morning air. She felt stupid. She hated her stepmother to see more than she meant to show her, and she had let her guard down. In truth, her reaction was a surprise even to herself. But she couldn't think about that now. It was more important to see him if she could.

The day had started brightly, but there was a thin skein of cloud forming high above. Once the sun climbed up there, it would be a dull day and already, as she hurried towards the scattered dwellings to the east, she felt the coming gloom infecting the folk that she passed.

She had no idea what she wanted to say to him, but the threat of war seemed to lend urgency. Instinct told her she must see him. But why? She couldn't say.

Maybe Saldas was right. Maybe it was only natural that she should fear for him. After the dark terrors of that winter he had been much in her mind. Only he understood what she had endured. Only he had followed her down into the dark heart of the earth where they had carried her, only he had seen those terrible things that still filled her mind with horror.

The memory of it all was more like a nightmare than something real. Those fearful creatures that had snatched her from the Kingswood, dragging her a hundred leagues or more across a snowbound wilderness, and then plunging her deep down under the earth. She had thought herself lost for ever... *until she saw his face*. Somehow he had come for her. Somehow he had got her out. They had got each other out, for she had killed too. And they had escaped to the light, no longer the same people.

How could they be after that?

But there was something else that drew her to him. He was an outsider like her. He had come to her father's hall in bonds, together with that odd friend of his. He had been a stranger with a clumsy way of speaking. Yet surely some favourable wind of fate blew at his back. From a beggar's rags, he had risen to the high council. More, her father now saw him almost as a favourite.

She passed a smith's forge and caught snatches of talk from some hall-folk gathered there. Words like blood, steel, slaughter. It would be the same all over Uppsala. Words uttered like poisonous invocations, their dark magic summoning death ever closer. She glimpsed the grindstone whirring, sparks flying. Already men were sharpening their killing edges.

So it had begun. And what could she do to stop it?

She hurried on, her thoughts returning to Erlan.

The king's favourite... Her father's last favourite, Finn Lodarsson, had met with a bitter end, murdered in her father's mead-hall in plain sight of everyone. He had died choking, death gurgling in his throat.

A horrible sight.

Traces of wolfsbane were found in his cup. Suspicion fell first on one man, then another. Men were tortured. But nothing came of it. No motive. No reason. Only silence, until eventually folk stopped talking of it. Or if they did, they began to doubt Finn was murdered at all. Just one of those things, they said. He was ill-fated.

Aye, thought Lilla. *In the end, fate is guilty of all things.*

She stopped. There in front of her was Erlan's squat little home. She was breathless from her hurrying and, she realized, probably flushed too. She felt foolish. She took a moment to straighten the brooches pinning her robe and apron, then smoothed out the strings of amber beads hanging between them, pushed the wayward strands of hair behind her ears and re-tied the ribbon at the nape of her neck. All of a sudden the door flew open and a warrior, looking like Tyr himself, stepped outside.

He was so wrapped in gear, it was a moment before she recognized him. His helm hid his tousled black hair, but the dark grey eyes shining out either side of a long nose-guard were unmistakably his. Over his tunic he had a leather byrnie crossed with belts and slings supporting a small armoury: a hand-axe, a couple of seax fighting knives, a limewood shield slung over his back and of course his precious ring-sword, sheathed in an ox-hide scabbard, at his hip.

She realized she was staring and looked away.

'What are you doing here?' he said.

She opened her mouth but just then Kai appeared, carrying a cloak and a sort of knapsack, presumably his master's.

'Lady Lilla!' he exclaimed. 'A fine day for a ride, don't you think?'

She looked up, as if noticing the sky for the first time. 'I fear it won't last,' she replied distractedly. She turned to Erlan. 'I need to speak with you.'

'They'll be waiting for—'

'Alone.'

Erlan shrugged in acquiescence and sent Kai off to fetch his horse, sniggering. 'So...?'

'I had a dream about you.'

'A dream? I'm flattered.'

'You were in danger.'

'Well, all of us may be in danger.'

'This was different.'

'How?'

'I don't know exactly.' She described her dream to him, the wolf and the wolfhound. He listened carefully.

'That could be anyone,' he said when she had finished.

'But I kept seeing your face in those black caverns. And there was another.'

'The Witch King?'

'No.'

'Who?'

'I— I couldn't make it out.'

A shadow fell across his face. 'Those were dark things, Lilla. They're best forgotten.'

'How can I forget?' she exclaimed. 'How can you?'

'Listen, Lilla. I'm sorry. I can't help every dream you have.'

'But don't you see? After what we went through... We're... connected. After what we endured together.'

'Are we?' he said coldly. 'Granted, we both endured. We both lived. But that's all. You're the daughter of a king. And me...' He shook his head.

'You're wrong, Erlan. The dream means something. It was a warning.'

'A warning? Of what?'

'I can't say. Please, Erlan – I need you to be careful.'

'What need have you! Your father has a hundred other men here to protect you. He could call upon a thousand more. Why do you care what happens to me?'

'I don't know.' She looked up at him and saw his dark eyes soften a little. 'I do, though.'

'Fine. I'll be careful. But if we run into the Wartooth's men—'

'It's not the Wartooth that I saw.' She seized his hand. 'Promise me you'll be vigilant.' He said nothing. She squeezed his hand tighter. *Promise me.*'

'All right... I promise.'

She smiled but he was looking over her shoulder. Kai had returned with one of the large scout-horses from her father's stable. 'The gods go with you,' she said, and stretched up to brush her lips against his cheek. She felt him start, but before he could answer, she was already hurrying away up the hill, the imprint of his stubble prickling her skin.

CHAPTER FIVE

I t was nearly noon by the time they rode away. The crowd of onlookers parted like a bow-wave as they took the road east.

Most of the horses were strong and fit although Erlan had his doubts how Einar Fat-Belly's mount would fare. Gloinn was another, with limbs so long that, sat on his horse, he looked like a spider riding a woodlouse. The rest of them were a decent enough crew. Jovard he trusted, having fought with him before. Jari Iron-Tongue was a beefy lad, useful in the training circle, but never seemed to give his mouth a rest.

He was less sure of some of the others. Aleif Red-Cheeks was a churlish bastard at the best of times, and argumentative too, with a face full of sores. He had taken an instant dislike to Kai when they arrived in Uppsala and he wasn't too keen on Erlan, either. The feeling was mutual. His friend Torlak the Hunstman was another Erlan might have done without, but the choosing had been Earl Bodvar's. He had assured Erlan that Torlak was one of the best trackers in Sveäland and a useful man to have on your elbow if things got savage. Erlan trusted

Bodvar's judgement. Then again, he didn't have much choice.

There were others – Eirik Hammer and a couple more. Ten in all, and they had a fair distance to go. It would take them the better part of two days' hard riding, heading first south-east towards the ferry crossing at the neck of the Great Bay. On the south side, they would cut south-west across the Earl of Sodermanland's estates until they came to the northern edge of the Kolmark forest. There, the road turned south, driving straight as an arrow through the forest until it reappeared in Eastern Gotarland, the northernmost territory under King Harald Wartooth's rule.

But all this lay far ahead.

The men were in high spirits. It was a pleasant enough day and what wind there was had swung round to their backs. Erlan relaxed his reins, letting his horse find a rhythm it could sustain for most of the day.

Ten men. Either this was a waste of ten men's time, or else... Would ten be enough?

He shelved his doubts. He was glad to be going. This mystery had landed in his lap – literally – and he could at least admit to himself that he was curious to know the truth of it.

The road skirted the southern edge of the Kingswood. The lead riders had just reached the place where the road split from the trees when two horsemen suddenly appeared and stopped beside the track.

Erlan called a halt.

'Good day, Erlan Aurvandil!'

'Lord Sigurd,' returned Erlan, warily.

On the second horse sat the prince's oathman. 'Vargalf,' nodded Erlan. The servant's gaunt features flickered, apparently all Erlan would get for a greeting. The pair were in full war-rig, leather greaves on their forearms, shields on their back and twin-ringed swords at their hips. Erlan noticed a ring-mail shirt rolled up behind Sigurd's saddle. An expensive item, and heavy too. Not something to carry about without good reason. 'Come to wish us good fortune, my lord? I'm flattered.'

'Don't tell me you've developed a sense of humour, cripple.'

There were a couple of laughs behind him, but Erlan didn't care. He had heard that taunt all his life. 'Is there something you want to say then, my lord? Or are you going to stand there blushing like a maiden on her first night?'

The smirk fell from Sigurd's face. 'We ride with you. No questions.'

Erlan glanced at Vargalf's deep-set eyes, flat and grey as slate. 'Suppose there's no point reminding you that your father forbade it.'

'Younglings obey their fathers. Men make their own choices.'

'Let's be clear then. You want to lead this patrol?'

Sigurd smiled – a strangely unpleasant sight. 'Don't fret, cripple. I haven't come to steal your little moment. I'm merely curious. If the Danes intend war, I mean to see how things lie for myself.'

'As an observer?'

'You could say that. Let's see what happens, eh, cripple?'

'One thing I know *will* happen, my lord.' Erlan touched the hilt of his sword. 'Call me cripple again in front of these men and you'll find this blade so far up your princely arse you'll choke on it.'

'It isn't wise to threaten your future lord and king,' snarled Sigurd.

'No threat,' smiled Erlan. 'Are we agreed?'

Sigurd's eyes flicked from Erlan to the other men. 'Agreed... Erlan *Aurvandil*.'

'Erlan'll do.' He leaned forward and spat into the grass. 'And you?' This to Vargalf.

'He rides with me,' Sigurd answered.

'Can't he speak for himself?'

'Just what would you have me say, Aurvandil?' Vargalf said in a soft voice, calm as a windless sea.

'Are we agreed?'

'If a word makes you feel better – aye. Agreed.'

'H'm.' He turned back to Sigurd. 'And when your father finds out, you'll own it?'

'You needn't fear, Aurvandil. My father will remain as fond of his little pet as before.'

Erlan couldn't be bothered to rise a second time. Besides, it wasn't his place to keep the peace between the king and his son. And two more swords might be no bad thing.

'Away then!' he cried, and put his heels to his horse's flank.

The journey took them south and east towards the narrow channel of salt water called the Throat – so-called because it was the way out of the Great Bay into the open waters of the East Sea. Trade-ships had to pass through this strait before they entered the Great Bay's calmer waters, which stretched away west, carrying any vessel deep into the heart of Sveäland. The shores of the Great Bay were littered with little trading villages and market harbours. A few like Sigtuna or Helgö were bigger. Control of the Throat had made Uppland the most powerful region of Sveäland, and the richest. Long ago the lords of Uppland had risen higher than those of the surrounding provinces on a tide of merchant gold. Earls had sworn oaths to the Uppland lords. And so it had gone until Uppsala had become a seat for kings. A seat worthy of the gods, even. And eventually folk forgot that it had ever been any different.

With the wind in the north, the ferry crossing was uneventful. They loaded the horses onto two flat-bottomed *karvar* that ran with the wind across the Throat to the southern shore under the mournful shrieks of the gulls and shearwaters turning in the sky. By the time they remounted, dusk was settling. Erlan pushed them on another league or so, but as the wind brought on its back a blanket of cloud, the night fell darkly. They made camp in a wood set high on a rise to the east of the road.

The fire was lit, food prepared and eaten, ale poured and drunk. Erlan ate in silence, enjoying the fire's warmth, listening as the talk moved around the men. Gradually it grew quieter as each drained the dregs of his cup and curled up under his cloak.

Sigurd and Vargalf had placed themselves at a little distance. Erlan had half an ear on their conversation while they ate Einar Fat-Belly's stew, but not much passed between them. He was curious about their arrangement. Vargalf was a riddle to him. The only thing he knew of him was that he had sworn no oath to the king, only to his son Sigurd. And he seemed remarkably attached to the prince, though he rarely looked at ease, his eyes always moving. In contrast, his lips seldom moved. Erlan supposed the prince took some enjoyment from his company since the two men were rarely seen apart. He might have suspected the two were more than mere companions, but that he'd heard the other karls joke how Sigurd liked to throw his silver at the mud-whores who came to peddle their wares on feast days.

Erlan took the first watch. He bid the last couple of men still awake put their heads down. And soon the only sounds over the wind were the sighs of the sleeping riders, now and then the crackle of the fire or a whicker from the horses.

Feeling his own eyelids grow heavy, he rose and picked his way to the edge of the wood. The crack in his ankle-bone was always sore after a day on horseback. He figured it should have been otherwise, but so these things went. He leaned against a beech tree and took the weight off his left leg, gazing south, trying to imagine what lay out there in the night, waiting for them.

Perhaps nothing. Perhaps a massive army. Perhaps the mistlands of death itself. But all he could see was darkness. His mind drifted back to the morning – to Lilla's words. Her warning. He wondered what it was about. Maybe she believed he really was in danger. Then again, she believed a lot of strange things, and saw yet stranger things where others saw nothing. He found himself remembering the brush of her lips against his cheek, the concern in her eyes—

'Not falling asleep, are you?'

Erlan jerked round. It was a moment before he recognized the outline of the prince, his curly hair and square shoulders silhouetted against the fire. Erlan turned back to the darkness. 'I'm fine.'

'Not much to look at on a night like this,' Sigurd muttered. 'My mother used to try to scare us with all kinds of nonsense when we were children. About fetches and evil spirits and trolls and killer-wolves. They all lay out there... In the shadows. I suppose she was trying to make us behave – or stay in bed.' He snorted. 'She'd scare my sister witless. Give her nightmares. I'd hear her snivelling under her covers, trying to count herself to sleep so she wouldn't have to think about the things my mother had put in her head. But me – I'd lie awake imagining what it would be like to run with the wolves, or to come back as a *draugr* or a ghost and creep up on my brother and scare him to death.' He chuckled. 'Have you ever sat in the darkness, Wanderer... and just waited?'

Erlan shrugged. He'd had a belly-full of darkness in the caverns of Niflagard.

'Your senses become sharp. You hear things. Smell things you'd never notice in the day—'

'Where did you meet him?'

'Who?'

'Vargalf.'

Sigurd chuckled, apparently not minding this change in direction.

'Is he a Sveär?'

'No. In fact, I don't know where he was born. He's not a man to talk of such things.'

'How did you come by him? Was he a slave?'

'No.' Sigurd smiled. 'When I first saw him he was a dead man. At least so he seemed to me. He came to Uppsala one spring, about five years ago now. He was a stranger, like you. A few karls didn't like the look of him, picked a fight, blades were drawn. Five of them surrounded him. I was there myself. Gods, I tell you he was a dead man! But when they set to it you never saw anything like it. Five of them. One of him. And before you could sink a horn of ale, all five lay dead as Baldur.'

Erlan grunted. 'And you just let a stranger like him slay your father's karls?'

'Well, I had more sense not to step in than the five of them. Besides, he turned himself over to my father's justice. The dead men's kin demanded *wergeld* from him or else his head, but the way my father saw it, the other men bore the blame for the fight. They'd provoked Vargalf, he said. So he forced their kin to accept *wergeld* from him and let Vargalf go free.'

'Mighty generous, your father.'

'Aye. He always was a stickler for fairness. It'll be his undoing one day.'

'And you?'

'I figured I could use a man who could fight like that. I asked Vargalf. He agreed. So he swore an oath to me.'

'He doesn't speak much.'

'Maybe. But he has sharper wits than any man at my father's seat. Oh, he's a cold son of a bitch, but that's what you want from any tool worth its metal. An edge that's cold and hard and sharp. Vargalf will be very useful in the time to come.'

'If there's a war, you mean.'

'That, for a start. And afterwards, when my father is... well, when his time has passed.' Sigurd's close-set eyes suddenly glowed with passion. 'Fate has now shown that I was always destined to be a king. My brother got himself killed, one way or another. More fool him. And what fame did he ever make for himself for all his boasting?' Sigurd scoffed. 'But me... I'll make my mark all right.'

'How do you mean to do that?' Erlan was sceptical. He'd always reckoned Sigurd's mouth stretched further than his stride.

'The Wide-Realm,' whispered the prince.

'The Wide-Realm? You mean old Ívar's kingdom?'

'Aye. All the lands that my grandsire ruled. Twice the land and wealth of my father's kingdom. Twice the power. My grandfather held all of Sveäland, Gotarland, Danmark and the Estland marches. He even held estates in Northumberland across the English sea. One day I will win it all back.'

'I can't see your father rousing himself for that.'

'H'm... I fear our noble king is fading. Gods, even if the Wartooth came and lit a fire under his chair, it wouldn't get him off his bony arse. No. His time is passing. Soon it will be gone for ever.'

'I saw him fight like one of Odin's heroes against the Vandrung.'

'A skirmish,' said Sigurd, dismissively. 'And look where it left him. He's been little better than a corpse ever since.' That was true enough. The long exposure of those cold winter nights had weighed heavy on the old king's health. 'No – you mark this well, Wanderer. He's your lord, I know, but no lord lives for ever. So think on what I said. We've traded words before, you and I. But I know your value. I'm prepared to overlook past disagreements if you pledge yourself to me, when my time comes. The Wide-Realm promises much to a man like you.'

Erlan nodded, but made no reply.

'Come on, man – what do you say?'

Erlan smiled. 'I say my watch is over. Sleep well, my lord.'

CHAPTER SIX

The rain began to fall before dawn.

It continued most of the day in a ceaseless drizzle, soaking mounts and men, dampening the talk to the odd joke about chafed backsides or curses about the weather. Still, they made good progress since there was little point in resting when there was no hope of getting a fire lit or cloaks dry.

Around the middle of the afternoon, the road slipped under the northern edge of the Kolmark, its ancient spruces engulfing them in gloom.

Erlan felt his men's unease rise a notch, noticed a few hands move from reins to hilts, a few fingers touch amulets around their necks, or twist the silver rings plaited into braids and beards. He touched his own amulet – a little replica of *Mjöllnir*, Thor's hammer, crudely fashioned in silver. It had been a gift from Inga, his first love. A peace offering to heal a lover's spat. But there had been no healing the wound she had inflicted on herself.

'Hey, Jo – how far to the border from here?' he called to distract himself from darker thoughts.

'Another league and a half,' Jovard answered, flicking back his sodden hood to reveal his white-blond braids, dyed darker by the rain. Under the forest canopy, the drizzle had thinned almost to nothing.

'There's still light enough to make it before night falls.'

'It'll be dark as a giant's arse-crack when it does,' Einar Fat-Belly observed.

'You know how to make a fire, don't you, fat man?' Jovard replied.

'Sure he does,' Aleif Red-Cheeks chuckled. 'Just strike firesteel near one of his farts and the whole damn forest'll go up!'

A few others laughed.

'There'll be no fire tonight,' said Erlan.

'What? Why the Hel not?' squawked Jari Iron-Tongue, the youngest of the crew.

'A fire'll bring anyone out there on top of us quicker than flies to a shit-heap.'

There was some grumbling at that but Erlan was adamant. If they were going to encounter the Wartooth's men, or anyone else for that matter, it would be on his terms. Not that he relished the prospect of a damp night, but it was better than waking up with six inches of steel in his throat.

The Kolmark spread south – a dense forest of mostly pine and spruce trees with a few gnarled old ash and oaks among them, carpeting a series of folds in the land that eventually rose to a long ridge. On the other side of that lay Eastern Gotarland, the first of the lands under the Wartooth's rule. As they crested the first rise, Erlan let some of the others pass him while he scanned the woodland below. The wind had swung to the south. Perhaps they could hope for better weather the next day.

'Gaagh! Thor's balls, fat man!' growled Gloinn, ridden on ahead. 'What the Hel have you been eating?'

But Einar didn't answer. Instead he covered his mouth. Then the stench hit Erlan like a stone wall. He pinched his nose but the foulness was overpowering, invading his nostrils like blunt fingers.

'By the hanged, what is that?' said Jari Iron-Tongue.

'Could be a dead wolverine,' Jovard answered through his fist.

Erlan gagged. But he knew that was no wolverine. He drew his sword. Others did the same.

Riding on, the air became even more rank. The rain had stopped. The light was fading. As the horses followed the track downhill, the soil, sticky from the rain, sucked at their hooves.

'Down there – do you see?' Jari Iron-Tongue was pointing excitedly ahead. Before Erlan could make out anything, the brawny lad had jumped down and pulled out his hand-axe. The others began to dismount. Erlan did the same, too hastily, jarring his ankle. He cursed and limped after the others.

Everything was blurring with the thickening dusk. Some of the men advanced in a line ahead of him. Jari had run on, but he suddenly stopped and swore, burying his nose in the crook of his arm.

Beyond him, Erlan saw two shapes on the ground.

'Bastards,' someone muttered.

Even in the gloom, it was a sight to turn the stomach. Two bodies, their eyes unnaturally swollen, faces and necks darkened to a greenish hue, black tongues protruding. If possible, the smell was even worse. Innards had spilled from one corpse through a slash to the belly. They glistened wetly from the rain, but some beast – a wolf or wildcat maybe – had been gnawing at them. The second body had a half-severed arm, flung grotesquely over its head. A dark stain fanned outwards from the wound. There were flies crawling all over the bodies. The air was thick with them.

He tore away his eyes. Some of the others had begun hunting along the roadside and in the undergrowth.

'There's another over here,' Aleif called, prodding the butt of his spear in the bracken beyond the road. 'It's that kid Rolf with the rotten teeth. Poor fucker.'

Rolf. He was one of the karls assigned to the same scouting party as Ormarr... It seemed they had found what they were looking for.

'Spread out,' Erlan called. 'See if there are any others.'

They found eight in all. Three fallen together at the foot of a thick old oak tree. A last stand, perhaps. Not that it had earned them a fate any different from the others. The bodies had been stripped of their war gear and anything else of value. Arm-rings, belts – even the ornaments in braids and beards which had simply been cut off. Some of the bodies were not even whole. They found an arm severed above the elbow, three hands – one still holding a seax – a leg hewn off at the knee.

All were in an advanced state of decay. Most were beginning to bloat.

'They must have lain here five days,' Vargalf said in his soft voice. 'No more.'

'Any longer and they'd be putrefying,' agreed Sigurd.

Five days or something close made sense. Anyway, they had already been identified as several of Ormarr's comrades. 'There's still two missing.'

'Perhaps they took them prisoner,' Sigurd suggested.

But there was a sudden shout from deeper in the forest. 'Over here!' Jovard appeared out of the gloom. 'There's something you should see, Erlan.'

They followed Jovard under the dripping branches another twenty yards into the trees where the canopy suddenly opened out into a small clearing. There, the last of the daylight was clinging on.

Jovard pointed across the glade. 'There.' Erlan's eyes had to adjust to the diminishing light. After a few moments he made out two shapes suspended from a tree.

The last two men.

They were roped to the same branch of a large ash tree, stiff as idols, faces white and bloodless. But Erlan didn't look at their faces. His gaze fell to the gaping holes where their abdomens should have been, and the ropes of intestine hanging tumbled to the ground in a grisly cascade.

The others had all now followed them into the clearing.

'By the hanged!' cursed Jari, eyes wide with horror.

'Poor choice of words,' said Erlan. 'Cut them down.'

Whoever had done this had meant to leave this message, had meant to make these men suffer. 'Do it quickly.'

Jovard's axe sank into the bark. The ropes snapped and the dead men crumpled to the ground in a heap of limbs and viscera. The other karls crowded in to see who had suffered such a grim fate. But if they did recognize them, no one said their names.

Perhaps they had been struck dumb, like Erlan. Because on each forehead, stark against their deathly pallor and carved deep into their flesh, was a rune.

An arrow shape. Tyr's rune. The rune of victory.

The rune of war.

In the end, they burned them, despite Erlan's misgivings about fire.

He had tried to insist they at least drag the bodies over the hillcrest behind them, out of sight of the rest of the valley. But Vargalf had shown the futility of that, dragging one of them a few feet, which then burst like rotten fruit, to groans of disgust. The clearing was the furthest his men were prepared to drag the dead.

The fire blazed high. Erlan watched with a lump like flint in his gullet while the flames coiled round each body. Jovard said words for each man before they flung him on the pyre. By his reckoning they had died in a fight and that meant they had a chance of being one of the *einherjar* – Odin's chosen heroes – with a seat at a bench in the Hall of the Slain. So he sang songs into the night, asking the All-Father to open his gates.

Erlan doubted it would do any good. But Jovard was a decent man and so he sang.

Afterwards, Erlan ordered them back up the hill to make camp north of the rise, a good distance from the pyre of the dead. His men bedded down without fire, grumbling that the fetid reek of death still lingered in their nostrils.

Tomorrow they would hunt whoever had done this.

Tomorrow...

Far away a wolf cried, its sad voice riding the wind across the sky. Erlan closed his eyes. Then again, he thought, maybe there was no one out here any more. Nothing but the wild forest and its shadows.

CHAPTER SEVEN

Erlan awoke. Slowly his eyes adjusted to the darkness, but even then there was little to see. A slender moon was hidden behind a blanket of cloud.

He wondered what had woken him. Then he heard it again. The snap of burning wood. He cursed, looking round. Close by were the sleeping silhouettes of Sigurd and the other karls. But no sign of a fire. Stiffly, Erlan got to his feet and scanned the trees. Suddenly he saw it: a tiny beacon of light, a stone's throw away.

What fool had lit that now? He tried to think who would be on watch: Einar or Aleif maybe? He snatched up his sword and stalked off towards the flame-flicker.

There were two of them, cross-legged by the fire, conversing in low tones. One had a spear across his knees, the other a hand-axe. Both looked up when a twig snapped, announcing his approach.

'I said no fires,' Erlan hissed, recognizing Aleif and opposite him the large, dished face of Torlak the Huntsman.

'Couldn't sleep,' Aleif answered. 'Too bloody cold.'

'I don't give a rat's turd how cold you are. I said—'

'Ain't no one out there,' Aleif drawled. 'Them poor bastards been dead for days.'

'Whether there is or there isn't, you'll do what I damn well tell you.'

'Will I? You know, I remember the day you turned up, *boy*. You and that scabby runt of yours. And now you think you're better than the rest of us, just because you've managed to wiggle your snout up Sviggar's arse.'

Torlak chuckled.

Anger flushed hot at Erlan's temples but he held it in. 'Get back over there and keep watch like you're supposed to,' he said in a steel-edged whisper. 'You're no fucking use to anyone over here.'

The two men exchanged a dark look but grudgingly got to their feet and picked their way back towards their sleeping comrades. Erlan, meanwhile, kicked damp pine needles onto the flames until there was nothing left but smouldering embers. He let them cool, then spread the last of them in a smear of charcoal and ash.

'Halfwits,' he muttered, and something whipped past his face.

There was a sound like a cough. A long, thin shape had suddenly appeared, shuddering in the spruce beside him. For a second he gawped at it stupidly, seeing shaft and fletching. Then raw instinct kicked in. He ducked and rolled left, already bellowing an alarm loud enough to rouse the dead as a second arrow hissed over his head. He threw off Wrathling's leather sheath and swore because he was nowhere near his shield.

Other voices echoed his shout – some in the camp; others, ominously, in the surrounding darkness. He heard someone running through the brush and to his left the scrape of Sveär blades, more confused shouting, the clatter of shields. He had to reach the others. If they were under attack, their best chance was to stand together. Then he remembered the prince.

Damn him! Why had Sigurd come along? Sviggar would hardly thank him for getting his son and heir slaughtered like some hind. Then again, come dawn there might be no one alive to tell the tale.

He lurched forward off his hobbled ankle through the shadows. They needed to form a *skjaldborg* fast. In the confusion of night, the shieldwall would at least give them something solid to defend. Every karl was trained to form a shieldwall, with three men or fifty. To form, fight and, above all, stand. Though without his shield, he'd be about as much use in the shieldwall as a bull with a broken cock.

He changed direction, arcing through the trees towards where he'd been sleeping, best he knew. But other figures were stealing closer, hunched shadows carrying spears or axes. He glanced ahead where his comrades were lining out, their limewood shields banging together.

'I'm here,' he yelled, giving up on his shield. 'It's Erlan!' A couple of faces turned towards him, beaming like moons in the dark. There was a flash of movement in the tail of his eye. By pure reflex his arm snapped up, the blow jarring his shoulder to the bone as an axe-shaft grated against Wrathling's twin-ringed hilt.

There was a snarl, a curse, the stink of sweat. Then the forest came alive with fierce shrieks. He saw pale eyes in a blackened face and shoved the axe aside as his hand found the seax at his belt. His attacker flailed backwards, tripping, and a moment later Erlan's knife was buried to the haft in his neck. He twisted the bone handle and ripped it clear. The man slumped to the ground.

One finished. But how many were out there?

He sheathed his blooded seax and snatched the dead man's shield. He had to get behind that bloody shieldwall. He ran at it, screaming all the names that came to mind, hoping they wouldn't greet him with a spear in the guts.

'Erlan?' someone yelled.

'It's me! It's me! Let me in!' He skidded the last yards on his arse, sliding through the gap that opened for a second, then slammed shut behind him.

'Where were you?' Sigurd demanded.

'Ask that cocksucker Aleif,' Erlan replied fiercely, catching his breath.

'A fine time to be off dropping your guts,' smirked Gloinn. Erlan scowled up at the lanky karl. There was a sigh above him and then an arrow-shaft sprouted from his eye-socket, showering blood into Erlan's open mouth.

'Behind your shields, now!' screamed Einar Fat-Belly as Erlan scrabbled to his feet and locked his shield into line, spitting the iron taste of Gloinn's blood into the dirt.

The big lad Jari was muttering prayers under his breath.

'Look forward. Here they come, lads!' Jovard cried.

Erlan shook himself. He was supposed to be leading this band of misfit raven-feeders and already one of them was on his way to Odin's hall.

'Close up,' he shouted as another arrow whipped between him and the fat man. He saw shadows running in a ragged line, screaming like Hel's hearthmen. He counted five, then a sixth, saw shields and axes and spears, the steel pale in the gloom. In the middle of their line, a man, likely their leader, was shouting to hit the wall hard. 'For the Wartooth! For the Mighty Boar!' he roared.

'Hear his accent?' Einar muttered grimly. 'They're Gotars.'

'Gotar timber falls to an axe like any other,' Aleif growled.

'Aye – well, see it does,' Erlan snapped, then filled his lungs and screamed, 'For Sviggar Björnabani! Send his foes to Hel!'

The first of them hit. Immediately there was a frenzy of shoving and stabbing and snarling, axes crashing from above, met in a grind of iron and wood. Erlan saw no faces, only shapes, streaks of steel, grunts and curses and panting breath, war-braids flailing like whips. He stabbed and cut, grinding his heels into the soil, bracing his shield arm against the weight of the attacking wall. The Gotar leader was half a man to his left. Metal glinted behind his shield. He was wearing ring-mail. Erlan stretched for him, gulping back the fear his hand might be chopped like firewood, but instead felt Wrathling's edge scrape the man's helm. The Gotar's eyes darted left, his mouth gaping. A fatal hesitation: a Sveär spear jabbed up, ripping through the side of his jaw in a splay of blood and bone.

The man sank like a sack of stones.

'Their leader's dead! Now drive them back!' Erlan screamed, wanting the Gotars to know as much as his own men. It worked. Doubt shivered along their wall. For a second Erlan hoped they would fall back into the night as fast as they had appeared. But one at least had some fight in him. A hulk of a man, his shoulders shaggy with a sheepskin cloak, stinking of ale and leather. He roared, slamming against Einar's shield. The fat man slipped a step, growling like a bear. Erlan felt his face flecked with sour spittle.

'Push, you fat bastard!'

'Since you ask so nicely.' Einar shoved his considerable body-mass into his shield, somehow sealing the gap. The sheepskin warrior was leaning over the top, darting his spear-point like an adder's tongue. Erlan dropped and hooked Wrathling's point, aiming to sickle his legs. His edge bit sinew and the Gotar staggered backwards. An axe fell after him – whose, Erlan could only guess. All he saw was more blood, felt the red rain spatter his face as the man crashed at his feet.

'They're falling back! They're beaten!'

It was true. As suddenly as it had started, the skirmish was over. Erlan wasn't so surprised: with a leader fallen, most men soon lost their stomach for a fight. He kneeled in the dirt, panting, watching the retreating enemy melt back into the shadows. There were bodies strewn in front of him. Someone was groaning loudly on his side of the wall.

'After them!' That was Sigurd's voice.

'Wait!' screamed Erlan, climbing to his feet. 'We should hold the wall.'

'Bollocks to the wall – we need one of them alive! Follow me, men!'

'No one moves,' countered Erlan. The other men stayed put, but Sigurd had already broken formation and gone haring into the darkness. Two steps behind him went his oathman, Vargalf.

Erlan swore. This was exactly what he had feared when the prince and his pet wolf had tagged along. They were almost out of sight. He could feel the men beside him, taut as a bowstring ready to be released, the battle-fire still boiling in their skulls.

But if they scattered now, who knew how many would survive the darkness?

'What do we do?' Jovard hissed.

'Stay here. Keep your eyes open – and keep this damn wall up!'

Then he launched after Sigurd.

The shadows were thick. Using his ears as much as his eyes, he chased the prince. And Sigurd was no lame-foot. Erlan cursed his ankle. He needed speed now more than ever.

They were running for the road. There, the gloom didn't hang quite so heavy. There was a flurry of noise ahead, then other sounds – buckles and bridles, maybe – then Sigurd's yell. But the only answer was drumming hoofbeats, which quickly faded into the forest.

He saw the fugitive figures halt by the roadside, and a few seconds later he had caught them up. They turned, points raised.

'Oh. It's you,' Sigurd grunted dismissively, lowering his sword. 'I'll say one thing for that limp of yours, Wanderer – you could never be mistook for anyone else... As you can see, our friends have already taken their leave.'

Erlan stabbed Wrathling into the ground, catching his breath. 'Just what the Hel are you doing?'

'What do you think I'm doing?' rejoined Sigurd. 'This whole scouting mission is a waste of time unless we take one of them alive.'

'Not at the cost of the king's heir, you selfish prick.'

'Balls to that! I can look after myself.'

Erlan stepped in, seizing Sigurd's collar. 'Listen, *my lord*. If you jeopardize your life or the lives of my men again, I'll gut you like a—'

Suddenly he felt steel, cold and sharp, against his jugular. 'Let him go.' The voice in his ear was calm as death. 'Now.'

Sigurd grinned past Erlan's fist. 'I'd do as he says, cripple. Vargalf isn't known for his patience.'

Erlan felt Vargalf's knife press closer. Any harder and it would draw blood. He didn't doubt Vargalf would slit his throat soon as look at him. Come to that, it would be easy for them to explain away his death. With a scowl he shoved Sigurd away but the knife didn't move.

'You know your problem, cripple,' sniggered Sigurd. 'You're more interested in doing things right than doing them effectively.'

Just now Erlan was more interested in the steel edge still at his throat than anything else. But then Vargalf's arm stiffened. 'Don't think there's any need for that, is there?' said a new voice. 'Ain't we all friends here?'

'Put that down,' Sigurd ordered, looking past Erlan.

'Oh, I will. Soon as your man does the same.' Erlan recognized Jovard's laconic voice this time. A second later the steel edge vanished and relief flushed through him. He turned to see Jovard, grinning wolfishly with his axe-blade pressed high under Vargalf's jaw. Slowly, he eased the pressure, then let his arm fall and pushed Vargalf clear.

'Thought you all might like to know,' he said. 'We've taken one of them. Alive.'

'The bugger won't talk,' Aleif said when they returned to the camp.

The place was scattered with the detritus of battle: bodies and war gear strewn among their knapsacks and cloaks. In the middle of the other karls, a man was kneeling in front of Aleif. He had a thatch of blond hair and he was shivering and cradling one arm that ended at his wrist. Someone had wrapped a belt around the stump to stem the blood.

'Let's get a fire lit,' said Erlan.

'Thought you said no fires,' Torlak sniggered.

Erlan glowered at him. 'So I did. But thanks to you and your idiot friend there, it's a bit late for that.'

Jovard began scraping together some wood. 'What do you want to do with him?'

'Let's gut the bastard.' Aleif gave the prisoner a shove.

'No one is gutting anyone.'

'Ain't nothing less than the fucker deserves. Nothing less than he and his mates gave Ormarr's crew back there.'

'We need him alive. We're taking him to Uppsala. The sooner we're gone the better.'

'We don't need him alive,' said Sigurd, leaning casually against a tree. 'We just need what's in his head.'

'Let's open it then, eh?' Torlak smirked, grabbing the blond shag of hair that covered the prisoner's face.

Erlan shoved him away. 'Back off, you big troll.' He glared around the circle of faces. 'Now we have him, we keep him alive. His friends could be back any moment – and a lot more of them for all we know.'

'Them piss-livered færies are long gone.' Aleif spat

disgustedly. 'You can smell their soiled breeks from here.'

'Sure that ain't your own, Red-Cheeks?' Einar drawled, one finger absently digging in his nostril.

'Maybe they are gone,' said Erlan. 'Maybe not. But we can't take that chance. And the king will want to see this prisoner as soon as possible.'

Sigurd snorted. 'My father will have no interest in this piece of dog-dirt beyond what he has to tell. After that, he's a dead man.' He yanked back the prisoner's head. 'You hear that, Gotar? You're a dead man.' He spat in the man's face.

Erlan watched spittle slide down his cheek in the light of Jovard's fire. 'Look at me.' The prisoner's eyes shifted to his. 'Will you tell us what we want to know?'

A shallow smile crept across his pain-drawn features. 'Dead men don't speak, do they?'

'Vargalf could have him singing like a lark in the time it would take you to sharpen that knife there.' Sigurd pointed at the seax on Erlan's belt. 'Couldn't you?' Vargalf was standing a little back from the circle. He looked from the prince to the man on his knees, then nodded.

'We're wasting time,' Erlan replied. 'The longer we stay here the more we risk the lives of these men.'

'And if we drag him all the way to Uppsala, what are the chances the fool dies on us on the way? Then what? All this will be for nothing. Do it now and the job's done.'

'But the men—'

'They don't care! If you doubt me, put it to a vote.'

Erlan looked from face to face. A couple were missing now. Gloinn Short-Shanks, Eirik Hammer. He looked at the prisoner. Even in the half-light, his face was pale and bloodless. If he did die on them, Gloinn and Eirik would have died for nothing. Erlan spat into the dirt. 'Piss on it then. Who wants that we stay and do this now?'

There was a rattle of war gear. Except for Jovard, everyone had raised a shield or an axe. Even Einar. 'You too, fat man?'

Einar shrugged. 'Reckon toting his sorry carcass halfway across Sveäland ain't worth the bother. I don't suppose his crew would return the favour if it was one of us.'

'That's settled then,' Sigurd said, grinning. The prisoner stirred uneasily. Vargalf stepped forward.

'No.' Erlan palmed his chest. 'I'll do it.'

'You?'

'Tie him up.'

The prisoner was soon bound with his back to a beech-trunk, arms pinioned at the elbow to his side. 'First we need to seal that.' Erlan pointed at the stump of his severed hand, from which droplets of dark blood still dripped. 'Ready?'

The prisoner said nothing. His mouth was a weld of hate and fear. Erlan went to the fire and put his seax in the flame. It soon began to drink up the heat, the patterns in its spine shimmering and shifting in colour. He removed it just before it began to glow red.

'What's your name?'

'Arn Skytja.'

'You're an archer then?'

The prisoner scoffed. 'Not any more.'

Erlan picked up a stick and told him to bite down on it, hard. Arn obliged, and when the blade touched he gave a long, deep moan, clamping his jaw against the wood. Soon as he caught the whiff of burnt flesh, Erlan snatched his knife away.

He wanted to seal the wound, not roast it. Still, he couldn't help thinking this was all upside down – trying to save a man's life only for as long as it took to get out of him whatever he knew.

After that...

'You're going to give me answers, you understand?' Arn's eyes were still half-closed from the pain. 'Who is your lord?'

Arn tipped back his head and smiled. 'Go fuck a goat, Sveär.'

Erlan buried his fist in Arn's stomach. The prisoner bucked forward. Erlan grabbed his throat and banged his head back against the tree. 'I'm no damn Sveär.'

'One turd stinks like another.'

Erlan stepped back, then punched him as hard as he could in the jaw. There was a crack. Arn's head slumped forward. When Erlan pushed it back blood was streaming from his mouth. 'Now – again. Where do you come from?'

Arn laughed, making the blood on his lip bubble. 'From Freyja's wet cunny.'

Erlan grimaced. He had never had to break a man before. It suddenly occurred to him he didn't know how. Killing a man was simple enough. But to make a man talk...

He seized Arn by the throat and squeezed, tighter and tighter. 'You're going to tell me who sent you here, or else you'll never see another dawn.' There was a rasping sound in Arn's gullet. Erlan held on a little longer, feeling his nails dig deep into the man's flesh. Then he released him.

Arn sucked down a few gulps of air. 'I've already seen my last dawn, you limp-prick fool. Are you the only one here can't see that?'

'Enough of this damned foreplay!' Sigurd exclaimed, losing patience. 'You talk about wasting time, then expect us to listen to this stinking worm throw insults at you. Vargalf – find out what he knows.'

His oathman drew a knife from his belt. It was narrower than a normal seax, double-edged, with a point that glinted needle-sharp. He looked at Erlan, waiting patiently for him to step aside. 'This is man's work,' he murmured.

Erlan moved away, feeling his humiliation flush up his neck. But he also felt relieved. Man's work or not – he had no taste for it.

Without another word, Vargalf took hold of the man's collar and cut through his quilted corselet and the tunic below. Once through, he pulled aside the two halves, exposing Arn's naked torso. The bowman's skin flickered gold and black and yellow in the flame-light.

Vargalf nodded to Sigurd. 'Ask your questions, lord.'

If there had been any other men lurking in the darkness – or wolves or bears or trolls or foul spirits of the night – the screaming would have sent them running far, far away. At times the sights and sounds were more than Erlan could stomach. Several of the other men turned away despite that, between them, there was little in the way of woundings and inflicted pain that they hadn't witnessed before.

And piece by bloody piece, Sigurd got his answers. At first, Arn was iron-hard – harder than many men would have been in his position. But true to Sigurd's boasting, it didn't take long for Vargalf to pry his stubborn mouth open. This is what came out.

Arn was an Eastern Gotar. Most of his war band were, though some came from further south in Skania. They were sworn, he said, to the dead man in the ring-mail – an earl called Thorgil Thorinsson – who in turn was sworn to Ringast Haraldarsson, eldest son of the Wartooth and the man King Harald had appointed lord over all Eastern Gotarland in his stead. Sigurd had leaped on this like a dog on fresh liver, demanding to know more about the Wartooth. But Arn gave up little, except that he'd heard the Wartooth was bent on settling some old scores with the Bastard King – so they called King Sviggar – but he didn't know the reasons why.

To drag even this much out of him left Arn mutilated beyond recognition: an eye was gone and one ear – its twin spared only so that the wretched man might hear Sigurd's questions. His torso was a web of bloody slashes, exposing sinew and muscle beneath. He had only two fingers left on his good hand. His tongue, of course, was untouched. And still Vargalf had not uttered a single word.

But Sigurd wanted more. More about this score the Wartooth intended to settle. So on it went. In a faltering stream of agonized whimpers, Arn confessed that there was talk of an invasion this summer, though none but the Wartooth knew exactly when, not even his son Ringast. All Arn knew was that King Harald and his sons were gathering two armies: one at the hall of Leithra, on the isle of Zealand in Danmark. The other was at Dannerborg, his son Ringast's stronghold in Gotarland.

'How many at Leithra?' Sigurd demanded.

'I— I don't know,' Arn sobbed between blood-encrusted lips.

Sigurd nodded to Vargalf. 'Again.'

'No! I beg you. Please!... I swear I've never even been there.'

'What of Dannerborg then? You know that place well enough.'

'Aye—I do...'

'Well then – how many there?'

'Truly, my lord, I don't know. Please.' He was staring out of his one eye with horror at the blade dangling languorously from Vargalf's hand.

'You will tell me the truth. And soon.' Sigurd smiled maliciously. 'Cut him there.'

Seeing where he was pointing, Arn started babbling. 'I swear, my lord! I would tell you if I knew. There are many men, but I know not what numbers... Please!' He continued pleading while Vargalf approached. With grim resolution, he removed Arn's belt and unceremoniously pulled down his hoes. Arn sagged against the ropes, a pathetic half-skinned carcass, shivering with pain, his manhood slack as a dead stoat.

'I'll give you one more chance. Although I am curious to see what Vargalf can make of that,' said Sigurd with a chuckle.

'He doesn't know,' said Erlan.

'Of course he knows! Just as he knew all the rest!'

'Look at him, for Frigg's sake! If he knew, he'd have told you already.'

'That's right, lord,' Arn whimpered. 'I swear I know no more!'

'You've had your chance.' Sigurd's mouth was a cruel line. 'But I promise you, we soon will know how many spears these Danish dogs have gathered. Vargalf!'

Arn released a long, mournful howl as Vargalf set about fresh butchery. But suddenly something streaked through the air, landing with a thud that cut the scream dead. There, buried to the haft in the Gotar's heart, was a seax. Vargalf jerked round to see who was responsible.

'Enough now.' Erlan nodded. 'That's enough.'

Arn had died instantly. No one said a word, not even Sigurd. Erlan went to Arn's lifeless body and pulled out his knife.

'Now,' he said, 'we ride for Uppsala.'

CHAPTER EIGHT

I t was a brooding return to Uppsala. They had some certainty now, but little in the way of detail, and Erlan's first taste of authority had been sour as rotten milk.

On arrival, of course, they took what they knew straight before the king. He was out on the meadows to the north of the halls.

'You must raise the levies, Father,' Sigurd had insisted after his breathless report. 'You must do it now.'

But his father's answer was a weary snort. Then he pulled his bowstring a little tighter, making the yew-wood yawn.

For a change, Erlan had some sympathy with the prince. The king's intransigence apparently knew no bounds. But it wasn't his place to say that. Not yet. Instead he watched the old warlord still his breath, narrow one eye and release his bowstring. A second later the shaft slammed into a linen target fifty paces off with a satisfying *thtuck*. This one had strayed left, outside the cluster of arrows already shot.

'Bah!' Sviggar scowled. 'These damned old fingers.' He

gazed up at the bright clouds scudding west. 'The wind's picked up.'

Erlan had already noticed it, feeling the stronger lick of air cool against his face, carrying with it the scent off the patchwork of hayfields to the north-east.

Sviggar smiled at him over his shoulder. 'Young Erlan – time was I would have felt the change on my cheek without even thinking. Back then I never used to miss.'

'Are you even listening to me?' Sigurd gripped his father's arm. 'Perhaps I wasn't clear. The Wartooth is raising an army against us!'

Sviggar shrugged off his son's hand and turned back to his target. 'Your brother would never have sounded so shrill.'

Sigurd glowered, as he always did at mention of his dead brother. 'By all the gods, tell him Bodvar!'

The Vestmanland earl obliged him. 'I fear the prince is right, my lord. Summoning the levies is the best course. That much is clear.'

'Is it?' Sviggar took another arrow from his attendant and nocked it to his bow. 'Then tell me, my worthy earl, how many spears are there in this army of his, heh?'

'Well...' Bodvar faltered. 'Knowing King Harald's strength—'

'We do *not* know it.' Sviggar loosed his shot. This time, the arrow hit among the main cluster. Sviggar smiled to himself and held out his hand for another. 'There, you see. It was the wind.'

'We would have known it,' Sigurd shot Erlan a scathing look, 'were it not that this man couldn't stomach a few drops of blood.'

'He told us everything he knew,' replied Erlan.

'So *you* say... You know, perhaps you'd better serve the queen. I hear she takes a keen interest in needlework. That may be more to your liking.'

'Enough of this foolishness,' Sviggar snapped, rounding on his son. 'So, my fine prince, I've listened to you. Now you hear me. Suppose an army *is* gathering somewhere beyond the Kolmark. What would you have us do? Must we ride into Gotarland, yelling like berserks, ready to put every man and boy to the sword?' He glared at his son. 'What then would come of my kingdom? Eh?'

Sigurd didn't answer.

'Oh, we might win a famous victory!' Sviggar continued. 'Danes and Gotars and the whole pack of them might kneel to me as overlord. Perhaps... Or perhaps I'm marked for death. Perhaps we all are – and after we've rushed headlong into the battle-storm, my kingdom will be lost between the rise and fall of a single sun. Tell me, my son, are you so sure that's not our fate?'

'I know not.'

'*You – know – not*... And nor do I. And, I wonder, would our good Sveär folk thank us for rushing them to the brink of destruction? After all that I've striven to do for them? To be raped and robbed by that merciless son of a whore?' Flecks of spittle were gathering at the corners of his mouth as his temper rose. 'All that I've built here fallen into the hands of the Wartooth and his kin. Hands that my own father swore would never touch the Sveär crown!'

His burst of anger was curtailed by a fit of coughing that went on almost as long as he had been speaking. Meanwhile, his son looked on with eyes barely concealing his contempt.

'It's well you speak of your father's vow,' Sigurd said, once Sviggar had recovered himself. 'But what of *his* kingdom – the true kingdom that was lost, which you haven't lifted a finger to recover? The Wide-Realm.'

Sviggar glared at his son under hooded eyelids, wiping spittle from his mouth.

'Hasn't the moment come to take back what's ours by right? To re-establish our lordship over the southern lands your father once held?' Sigurd said, suddenly animated. Erlan had already seen for himself that this was the prince's favourite passion, this Wide-Realm.

'You don't know what you're saying.' Sviggar turned back to his target.

'You want prosperity for your people. What could prosper them more than making this the most powerful kingdom in all the north?'

Sviggar suddenly rounded on him. 'You do have grand visions, don't you, my boy? But they are born of your ignorance.' He jabbed a bony finger at Sigurd. 'What do you really know of the Wide-Realm, heh? There's a reason it did not last. It *could* not be held. It cannot be. And I'm not stupid enough to try.' He flung his arm in a great arc. 'Why, it's too vast! One king cannot hold such far-flung lands for long. Loyalty wanes too thin. Ambition and greed wax too fat. Even when oaths have been sworn.'

'Perhaps,' Sigurd returned. 'If the hand of the king is weak.'

'You dare to speak to me like that,' Sviggar snarled. 'You don't know what strength is, you – you damned puppy! Get out of my sight. Go on! Back to those mud-whores you find so much to your liking.'

Sigurd didn't move. Erlan could see him struggling to bridle his anger, apparently preferring to stay and be heard than give full vent to it. At last he answered. 'Forgive me, Father. I spoke too strongly. I merely want what's best for the kingdom.'

'Well, then,' his father growled, 'I'll be the one to decide what that is.'

There was a flutter in the tops of the oak trees at the edge of the Kingswood. A pair of pigeons took to wing and circled round to the north. One of them, continuing its arc, caught a gust of wind and came sailing straight towards them high over their heads. Sviggar had tracked it and, with a smooth roll of his shoulders, brought up his bow.

Erlan's eye flicked from the taut old forearms to the grey wings above. There was a soft *thrum*, a thud and then bird and shaft plummeted to the meadow.

It would have been an exceptional shot by anyone, but from this old man, who these days struggled to pull himself out of his chair, it was as surprising as anything Erlan had witnessed in Sveäland. The attendant let out a yelp of admiration.

'Well, don't stand there gawping, lad!' Sviggar cried, evidently pleased with himself. 'Off and fetch it.'

The servant launched across the meadow and soon returned with the pigeon, its body perfectly impaled on the shaft. He gave it to the king as reverently as if the thing were made of gold.

'Ha! What do you make of that?'

'A remarkable shot, my lord,' Bodvar answered gruffly, as though the role of sycophant didn't sit well on his shoulders.

'So it was.' Sviggar handed his bow to the servant. 'But see here.' He turned the dead bird over in his hands. 'If I were to pull out this shaft and somehow breathe life back into this lifeless thing and fling it back into the sky and see it soar once more on the wind... Tell me, which feat were more remarkable?'

He looked from face to face. No one answered. Sviggar smiled. 'It's easy enough to destroy – even when it takes great skill. It's much harder to create. And much better, too. This kingdom is my creation. I've raised it up from the wreck my father left me, defended it from troubles inside and out. I don't intend to see it destroyed now.'

Bodvar cleared his throat. 'With respect, my lord, what if someone else wields the bow? Even if you had the power to give life to something dead, another might be set on killing it. So too with the kingdom. Even if your wish is to avoid war, you must take measures to defend your realm.'

Sviggar's nose wrinkled with irritation. The earl's argument clearly had weight. 'So you truly believe this threat to be serious, Bodvar?'

'I do.'

'And what measures – as you call them – do you counsel?'

'At least raise the southern levies. Send word to the Earl of Sodermanland and Earl Huldir at Nairka. Even without a full muster, you must alert the southern lands. And seal the border. None shall pass into or out of the kingdom. Not until we know more.'

'Even that much will spread panic.'

'Not if you speak to the people yourself. Tell them war is not your aim. Panic will spread much faster if you do nothing while rumours ripen and grow. This way your folk will see you act and feel secure, even if – should the threat prove real – they may yet suffer war.'

The king rubbed at his temple. 'Very well. Send word to the southern lords.'

'I'll see it done.'

'And announce a decree sealing the borders. No one is to cross into Gotarland. I want to give them no provocations.' Sviggar seemed satisfied, though his face looked grim. 'Although, in truth, we still know precious little.'

'We know he's raising spears at Leithra,' Sigurd countered. 'And at Dannerborg.'

'But how many? Someone tell me that?'

'Find out for yourself.' It was the first contribution Erlan had made to the meeting.

Sviggar stared at him. 'Myself? What do you mean?'

'Send a man to this Ringast's hall at Dannerborg. A pair of eyes and ears you trust. You'll soon know the truth of it.'

'I suppose you're offering yourself for this service?' Sigurd sneered.

'Maybe it is better an outlander goes. A Sveär would only arouse suspicion.'

'A Gotar would be better still,' said Bodvar, his rugged face creasing into a smile.

'What Gotar?' demanded Sviggar.

'Why, one who wouldn't draw a second glance!' Bodvar exclaimed.

Erlan knew of only one Gotar living among the Uppland halls, and suddenly he saw what Bodvar was driving at. 'No. Not a chance.'

'But he's perfect,' Bodvar grinned.

'Who's perfect?' croaked the king impatiently. 'Damn it – what are you on about?'

'That one's servant boy!' Bodvar jabbed a finger at Erlan.

'This is folly, my lord,' protested Erlan. 'Kai is hardly more than a boy.'

'Nonsense! He's not much younger than you.'

'Maybe. But I've been trained for combat. Hel, Kai has never even learned how to hold a shield. Not properly, anyhow.'

'Bah! If he needs use of his shield, he's already failed.'

'But you've seen him. He's so... scrawny.'

'All the better! The whole point is no one should notice him.'

Sviggar began to chuckle, too. 'Erlan, I sympathize with you. Truly, I do. But we must all fill the boots of manhood one day. Besides, I like the lad! He's got guts and his wits are sharp. I've seen that for myself.'

Aye, too bloody sharp for his own good most of the time, thought Erlan. 'Lord, I grant you, Kai is resourceful in his way, but he's not... How can I put it? He's not reliable. You'd be putting the fate of the kingdom in his hands. It's not exactly the safest place for it.' That was putting it mildly.

Sviggar waved away Erlan's excuses. 'My mind's made up. Just tell me this – would he agree to it?'

Erlan considered the question, his heart sinking. The fact was the mad little bastard would probably like nothing better. Erlan sighed. 'I guess he would.'

'Then see that he does. The sooner he leaves the better. Certainty, Erlan, certainty! Then we can act. The boy shall be my eyes!' The old king's face was absolutely glowing with the idea.

'Lord, if this is your wish then I have two requests.'

'Go on.'

'Give me two days to hone his training.'

'Two days!' scoffed Sigurd. 'What can you teach him in two days?'

'I guess I'll find out.' If the boy would listen for a change, perhaps enough.

'Granted,' Sviggar said impatiently. 'And the second?'

'That if you want me to remain here with you, at least send someone with him who knows how to fight.'

'It may be wise,' Bodvar conceded. 'It'd be a shame if the boy succeeds, gets clear of Dannerborg, and then falls prey to brigands on the road.'

Sviggar was reluctant at first but eventually he agreed, and after more discussion, they settled on Einar Fat-Belly as Kai's protector, whom Bodvar happened to know was half-Gotar by blood.

Gods, the fat man will be delighted, Erlan thought to himself. But secretly he was pleased. He trusted Einar more than most of Sviggar's hearthmen.

That brought the audience to an end. Sviggar resumed his archery while Erlan set off for the small halls to find Kai and tell him the news. He was surprised when Sigurd fell in beside him.

'None of this would be necessary if you had let Vargalf finish his work.'

Erlan halted and turned to him. 'You call that work?' he snarled. 'Your man is a fucking animal.'

'Well, we're all of us animals,' the prince smiled. 'The only question is which of us will survive.'

CHAPTER NINE

Erlan was right, of course.

Kai leaped at the idea. 'There you go! That'll learn you to leave me out of your patrol. I told you the gods love me.'

'You do realize what this involves?'

'Course! Bit of sneaking around. Keep the old flappers open. No problem. What's a few Gotars anyhow, after what we faced last winter?' He took a couple of heroic cuts at the air. 'Ha! Now I'll show you all the stuff Kai Wolf-Hand is made of! Let's see what Bara has to say then, eh?'

'Hey.' Erlan caught his arm. 'This is about more than impressing some wench. This could mean war. And your neck with it.'

'I know.' Kai blinked up at him with guileless blue eyes.

Erlan shook his head. 'You're crazy, you know that?'

The next morning, he kicked Kai out of bed early and dragged him off to the training circle that was marked out a stone's throw east of the Brewers Hall. Both of them were laden down with gear – some steel, some wooden for practice.

'This is going to be a long day,' Erlan warned. And so it was. He'd seen Kai fight – seen him do some remarkable things, in fact – but he wasn't taking any chances. He stripped it all back to the bone. Wooden sword – light shield – mouth shut and listen.

They sparred all morning, sweating till their tunics were soaked through. After each bout Kai's question was always the same: when could they use the real steel, as he called it. 'When I say so,' was always Erlan's reply.

By early afternoon he'd given Kai a proper limewood shield, bound with leather and sealed with an iron boss. At first this slowed Kai down, but as the sun went on its course Erlan fancied he saw some improvement. By the time their shadows were lengthening in the dust, he finally let Kai have his way and moved them on to metal blades, albeit ones with blunt edges. Fatigue was beginning to dint even Kai's boundless enthusiasm and he grew more and more frustrated with Erlan's badgering.

'Looks bloody exhausting,' said a languid drawl that turned their heads, sparing Kai from another of Erlan's long explanations of what he'd been doing wrong. Einar Fat-Belly was draped over the rough-plank fencing that marked out the training circle. Seemed he'd swiped a drinking cup from the bucket of beer that had been their refreshment all day. He took a swig and immediately spat it out.

'Urgh! Fenrir's fangs! What *is* this? Goat's piss?'

'It's watered down,' explained Erlan.

'Water! Gods, do you want to poison me?'

'Well, we can't have him fighting drunk, can we?'

'Best way for it, if you ask me.'

'I take it you've heard the news.'

'Oh, aye.' Einar scratched noisily under a braid.

'And?'

'And I'm over the fucking moon. Can't you tell?'

Erlan chuckled. 'Well, time's coming when we'll all have to make sacrifices.'

'Aye. Some of us sooner than you other bastards.'

'Fancy a turn?' Erlan proffered the hilt of his training sword.

'You must be joking. It's making me break sweat just watching you.'

Erlan shrugged and turned back to Kai while Einar peered dubiously into his ale-cup and hazarded another sip.

'Where was I?'

Kai rolled his eyes. 'You were saying in a fight between two men, one of 'em loses it but the other one doesn't win it. Which doesn't make a lick of sense, but there you go.'

'No, I said a man loses a fight more often than his opponent wins it.'

'And what's that supposed to mean?'

'It means people make mistakes.'

'Of course they do. So what?'

'So make damn sure it's not you who's making them.'

'Phuh! Surely you've learned by now, master? I don't make mistakes.'

'Really?' Erlan beckoned to him. 'Again. Your strike.'

Kai squared off and began to lift his sword, but his hand had hardly moved before Erlan stepped in, knocked the blade left and cut down till his sword edge touched Kai's neck. 'Dead. Sword too wide. Again.'

Kai snorted, took his guard and tried again. This time he jabbed from below, but Erlan's shield met the point, there was a streak from the right and a clang as his sword clipped Kai's half-helm. 'Dead. Shield too low. Again.'

Kai huffed, rolled his shoulders and swore.

'Don't lose your temper. Just think.'

This time Kai cut across at Erlan's sword arm, but before the blade was halfway down, Erlan hefted his shield, crouched low and in swept his edge to knock out Kai's knee. The lad was on his arse in a cloud of dust before he knew what had happened, with Erlan's point under his chin. 'Dead! Shield too *high* this time. Back on your feet. Let's go.'

So the refrain went on. 'Dead. Too slow turning. Get your bloody shield round. Again!'

'Dead.' This time Erlan punched Kai's shield flat with his own shield-rim, exposing Kai's head and neck. 'I've told you before. Hold onto the thing tight as a rivet. Your shield is a weapon, too.' The final time Erlan allowed Kai to bat at his shield a couple of times, while he shuffled left with his back to the falling sun. Suddenly he dropped left, spilling sunlight into Kai's eyes. The boy yelped, Erlan stepped wide, backhanded a cut from above and the blunted edge stopped an inch short of the back of Kai's neck. 'Dead,' he said, with grim finality.

'That was cheap.'

'No move is too cheap when you're up against someone who knows what he's doing.'

'You know something, Erlan,' mused Einar from his fence, a finger idly foraging in his ear. 'You move pretty fast... considering that leg of yours.'

Erlan hadn't thought about his ankle once the whole day. The pain was just there, like the ground or the sword in his hand. He shrugged. 'My father used to tell me, if you can't run, you have to learn to stand and fight. So I did.'

Einar raised his cup in mock toast. 'Well, well. So the man does at least have a father.'

Erlan frowned, reminded of his oath. He had sworn his past would remain sealed up in a barrow-grave of silence. Yet here it was, seeping back into his present like sea-water into the bilges of a leaky hull. He turned back to Kai with a scowl. 'Let's go again.'

But Kai refused his guard. 'I've had it with these stupid toys.' He flung down his training sword. 'When do I get my hands on that proper gear, eh?' He jabbed a finger at the assorted weapons propped against the fence. There was a long-spear, a double-handed axe, a war-hammer, a couple of hand-axes and a shorter throwing spear.

'Not yet.'

'Come on, master. Don't be such an old fart. I'll soon have to stand in the shieldwall tooled up like everyone else.'

'You've got plenty to worry about before that happens. Besides, that stuff's too big for you.'

'Balls to that! Let me try.' His eyes twinkled with desperation. 'Please!'

'Humour the lad,' Einar said. 'Gods, I'd like to see it for myself.'

'Fine,' sighed Erlan, relenting. 'But you'll be needing this, too.' He threw down his gear and pulled off his leather byrnie.

It took a while to load up Kai and when he was done Erlan stood back to admire his handiwork. Kai stood there, grinning like a happy pig, byrnie gaping at his sides, a seax sheath hanging to his knees, the hilt of Erlan's ring-sword prodding at his nipples. On his left he had a shield and gripped behind it a hand-axe. Last of all, in his right hand, he clutched a long-spear that towered over him like a banner.

'One final touch.' Erlan swapped Kai's wood and leather half-helm for his own metal helmet. It dropped onto Kai's unruly mop of hair, squashing his fringe over his eyes.

Kai shook his head till he could see out again. 'How do I look?'

'Ridiculous,' said Einar.

'Shut your hole, fat man! No one asked you.' Kai looked hopefully at Erlan. 'Well, master?'

Erlan frowned doubtfully. 'It doesn't matter how you look. What matters is what you can do.' He crossed to the other side of the circle. 'All right – run at me.'

'What?'

'You heard – run at me!'

Kai shrugged, took a mark, dropped his spear-point and ran, buckles jangling, seax bouncing, helmet rattling on his head. Before he'd got halfway the hand-axe slipped from his grasp and thudded to the ground. Kai swore, stopped to pick it up, got a hold on it and set off again, only for his spear to drop and skewer the dirt. He tripped, flipped and ended up in a cloud of dust and steel and curses on his back.

Einar fairly bellowed with laughter, his belly shaking like rotten rafters in a storm. Kai sat in the dirt, scowling.

'I don't know why you're laughing, fat man,' said Erlan. 'He's all you've got once you cross the Kolmark.' That shut Einar up pretty quick.

Erlan offered Kai a hand but he knocked it away. 'I can manage,' he growled, peeling himself off the ground.

'Tell you what, runt,' said Einar, climbing through the fence, 'try this one. More your size.' He plucked the throwing spear off the ground and tossed it to Kai. The lad caught it, his face still boiling with fury.

'A little spear for a little man.'

Even Erlan laughed at that.

'Bollocks to the lot of you!' Kai flicked the javelin over his wrist and hurled it hard as he could. The thing flew straight as a comet, slamming into one of the fence posts so that the whole training circle shuddered. The other two stopped laughing.

'By the hanged, boy,' Einar gasped. 'That one shook the World Tree to its bloody roots!'

'Where did you learn to throw like that?' demanded Erlan, no less amazed.

'I don't know,' Kai shrugged. 'Back home, I suppose. I didn't have one of those things, of course, but I used to kill rabbits with stones from the lakeshore. You get pretty good when no one gives you bugger all else to eat.'

Einar had gone to inspect the javelin. 'Not bad, at all... Could've gone in a bit further, mind.'

'What are you talking about? It's sticking straight out!'

'Let's see you do it again,' said Erlan.

Einar yanked it free and drew out his knife. 'Aye. Only this time, see if you can hit this.' He marked a cross in the wood a little higher up the same post.

'Easy,' said Kai. 'Toss it here.'

This time he put down his shield and took careful aim while the other two watched him. He planted his foot, drew back his arm and flung it.

'Bang on the nose!' Einar cried in delight. 'The lad's a natural!'

'Well done, little brother,' Erlan exclaimed, and gave him an affectionate thump on the back.

'That's a neat trick,' said a woman's voice.

They all turned to see a girl with flaming red hair and flouncing curves approach the fence. Bara, the queen's hand-maiden, and the object of Kai's salivations for months now, despite the fact that she was probably the most conceited woman in all of Sveäland. If you didn't count her mistress.

Kai gave a nonchalant glance at the javelin. 'Oh, that? Just one of my many talents. I could show you a few others if you like.'

'I'm good, thanks.' Bara smiled. 'Still, that was impressive.' Kai beamed. 'Just a shame about the rest of you,' she added.

'What do you mean?'

'Well – look at you. You couldn't fill a pail of milk, let alone that thing.' She pointed a lithe finger at Kai's oversized byrnie. Erlan watched the bounce leak out of his friend like piss from an old man's bladder.

Kai threw Erlan's helmet moodily at the fence. Bara giggled. 'Temper, temper.'

'What are you doing here?' said Erlan.

'Jo said I'd find you here. My mistress wants to see you.'

'Me? What for?'

'How should I know?'

'She must have given you some reason.'

'I don't know. Something about some dispute or other. Why don't you go see for yourself?' she pouted. It had to be said, no one pouted quite like Bara. But Erlan wasn't much the wiser. Now and then, Sviggar had given him authority to settle some of the petty disputes that arose around the halls, but he didn't see what that had to do with Queen Saldas.

'Can't it wait till morning?'

'What do you think?' Bara arched an artfully plucked eyebrow.

'Fine.' He dusted off his hands. 'I guess we're done here. Kai, clear up this lot and I'll see you back home for supper.'

'What are the pair of you up to, anyhow?'

'Haven't you heard? The king's fingered this one for an important mission.'

'What mission?'

Erlan winked at her. 'If you ask nicely, maybe he'll tell you.'

Bara glanced uncertainly in the direction of the Great Hall while Erlan climbed through the fence. 'Well?' he called. 'Are you coming back or staying here?'

'What, you need me to hold your hand, do you, hero?' Bara gave him a coquettish flick of her shoulder and turned back to Kai. 'All right then, shorty – what's this all about?'

Ambling through the small halls towards the looming shape of the Great Hall, Erlan was almost grateful for Bara's interruption. The day had softened into a windless evening. Almost peaceful... Aye, he wondered, but how long would such a peace last? Till midsummer? Till the corn was cut? The gentle quiet as evening settled seemed a world away from the horrors of the Kolmark, but like the shadows lengthening over barn and byre alike, a darkness was coming. He felt it in his bones.

He looked up at the last streaks of light and thought of his own kin, far away. Right now, they would be sitting down for their supper after a long day in the fields – pulling weeds, putting in the second sowings of barley and rye.

A memory came, unbidden. Of Inga, flinging joyous arcs of seed across dark furrows. He tried to picture her face and found he could not. Only her hair. The taste of her lips, the feel of her fingers laced among his—

He recoiled, the memory suddenly pricking like a knife, too close. He forced his mind back to the present business.

Why the Hel was the queen troubling him with someone's quarrel now? They had hardly exchanged a word since the Yule feast. What had been said then seemed unreal now. Perhaps he had imagined it. All of it. The lingering scent, the spark in her fingertips, the suggestion in her whispered words. Some ephemeral dream that lurked in the shadows of his mind... *No – it couldn't be that.*

By the time he reached the north end of the Great Hall, darkness had cloaked the surrounding buildings, sharpening the flares sputtering overhead.

He thumped on the door.

Moments later he was following the flickering sconces down the corridor, his lopsided gait reverberating dully off the walls. There wasn't a servant in the place. But then, never having been in that part of the hall, he thought perhaps that was normal. At length, he reached the queen's chamber and knocked.

'Who is it?' came the queen's soft burr.

He stated his name. There was silence, then, 'Enter.'

He went in.

In one corner stood a brazier, the air above it rippling with heat. Against another wall was a silver mirror, tall as a man, and opposite, a bed-closet fashioned from rough-hewn timber framing the bed, which was covered with thick white furs. But of Saldas, there was no sign. At least none but the scent filling his nostrils, rich and subtle as a summer twilight.

'Close the door.'

He turned and there she was, appearing from a curtain that screened one corner of the room. Her black hair, normally combed straight, was a little tousled and fell loose about her shoulders. She wore only a plain white shift cinched at her waist with a pale ribbon and clasped a small bronze mirror to her chest. Her eyes seemed to sparkle as if jealous of the torch flames. Altogether the effect was most striking. She was a woman of a little over thirty summers – perhaps twelve years older than he. Seeing her like this, he couldn't deny her reputation as the greatest beauty in all of Sveäland was well deserved.

None knew it better than her, of course.

'You know why you're here?'

'Bara said something about a dispute. Does the king wish to speak with me?'

'The king is indisposed.'

'He seemed well enough yesterday.'

'And this evening he is not.' The glimmer of a smile passed over her lips. 'Do you doubt me, Aurvandil?'

'No.'

'Good.' She looked him up and down. 'Have you been fighting?'

Erlan was suddenly conscious his tunic was covered in dust and still damp – and stinking – with sweat. 'I have, my lady.'

She seemed amused. 'Other men might have made themselves more presentable before an audience with their queen.'

'Forgive me, I—'

'No matter,' she interrupted. She took a step closer and he watched her slim nostrils flare. 'Perhaps you have a thirst.'

'As it happens, I do.'

She went to the table and filled two ox-horn cups from a silver jug.

'What shall we drink to?' She handed him one.

'To the health of the king, I suppose.'

She lifted her cup and smiled. 'Naturally.' She took a languorous sip while Erlan slugged back his wine. It tasted sweet and heavy.

'Now then,' she said, her tone become business-like. 'Some folk arrive tomorrow. The cousin of the Earl of Sodermanland. He appeals to my husband as kin – though in my opinion he presumes far too close a connection.'

'What's it about?'

'It concerns his daughter. She's to be divorced and there's some disagreement over the property her father gave as dowry. It seems the husband has dropped his wife and is keeping the dowry for himself.'

'A worthy man.'

'Things are never simple. I'm told he paid a considerable bride price for her only to discover she's of feeble health. Apparently she told her husband to find himself another woman. Sentimental little fool! Now her father is spitting because her husband took her at her word. Anyway, it's all rather absurd. The king wants you to deal with this man while he is unwell.'

'Are they feuding?'

'Not yet. But that's the point, isn't it? The king wants none of this to escalate – especially not in Sodermanland and especially not now. Not with our current... preoccupations,' she added. 'You're to convince him to do without his silver until it can be settled at the Summer Throng.'

She meant the annual assembly of Sveärs, which every freeman in the realm was entitled to attend, where disputes would be judged, debts settled and deals struck.

'And if he can't be convinced?'

'See that he is.'

'I'll do my best. Though if you ask me, sickness seems a weak reason to put away a wife.'

'Nonsense. It strikes me a very good reason. Why, I've known a woman divorce her man because drunkenness deprived her of her womanly dues once too often. Another man became a laughing stock when he was wounded across his buttocks. In battle, true,' she shrugged. 'He reckoned himself a hero, but his wife divorced him within the week!'

At this Saldas laughed, throwing back her head and shaking out her long, dark hair. Erlan watched the shadows play about the contours of her throat, feeling a stirring that had very little to do with legal disputes.

'There seems small point in making a marriage vow if it can be undone so easily,' he said to distract himself.

Saldas pouted. 'How serious you sound! And how young! Have you not been married?'

He hesitated. He had made a promise once. Not a marriage vow, but words as solemn. 'I can't say.'

'Ah! Of course. Our mysterious stranger who refuses to speak of his past. Come to save us all, and yet we know nothing of you.' She moved closer, took another sip of her wine, eyeing him over the rim of her cup. 'Nothing at all... Well, one day you'll marry – again or for the first time – and you may come to appreciate the freedom of a vow that's easily undone.'

'Perhaps you're right.' He took another swig to break her disconcerting gaze.

'Count yourself fortunate. I am not so free. A king may cast aside his queen, but no queen can spurn her king.' She scoffed. 'Anyway, she'd be a fool to.'

Saldas moved still closer. He could almost feel the heat off her body, but he said nothing, only watched a slender finger trail along her collarbone.

'Then again, power isn't everything,' she murmured. Her hand fell to her shift, teasing at the flimsy material, drawing his gaze to the plunging shadow beneath. 'Sometimes even a king and queen are ill matched. And what's a queen to do then, stranger?'

Erlan's throat was dry as dust, despite the wine. Her breathing seemed to deepen, swelling her breasts towards him. He could see the shadow of a nipple, dark and firm beneath the linen. She took his cup and set it down beside hers on the table. She didn't say a word. Didn't need to. It was all very clear.

And yet he hesitated. This was a line only a very brave or a very stupid man would cross. But she wasn't going to wait for him to decide which he was. Suddenly there was nothing between them. She ran a finger down the line of his jaw, then looked at her fingertip, rubbed away the salt of his sweat. 'You've worked hard today. I wonder what strength you have left for the night.' She smiled and let her hand drop. He felt fingers, light and sinuous, trace the hardening heat in his loins. She glanced at the mirror and he followed her gaze. In it he saw the slender figure in white pressed against him, watched what he could feel as her hand moved up and down.

Something in him snapped. He suddenly seized her waist, pulled her against him, heard her gasp as he bit her neck, his hand fumbling for her breast and finding a nipple, already hard as a bead of amber. Then his face was in her hands, her tongue in his mouth, wild and hungry, its taste indescribably sweet.

All of it, impossibly sweet...

Except that a voice crackled like lightning through the clouds of intoxication billowing in his mind. *Beware another man's wife. Her bed is a road to trouble.* He recognized the words, and the voice. Both were his father's, pounded into his head since he was a boy. He cursed that voice because his father was a hypocrite. Cursed the words because he knew they were true. Sviggar was an old man, an ill-matched husband maybe. But he was also Erlan's lord.

He pushed her away.

'What is it?' she gasped.

'I can't do this.'

'What?'

'I'm sworn to your husband. I can't love you.'

She threw back her head and laughed. 'Who said anything about love?' Teasingly she bit her lower lip while her fingers slipped through his hair and pulled his mouth down a second time. He felt her body enveloping him like a mist, her hand searching for his buckle.

But the thought was in his skull now, beating at it like Thor's hammer. 'I can't.' He jerked away.

'No one will ever know.'

Erlan wished he could believe that. But there was some deeper instinct telling him to leave, to have nothing to do with this woman. He tried to push her away, but she wouldn't let go. Then he shoved her, harder than he meant to, harder than was wise. She stumbled backwards, butting the table and upending a cup. Wine splashed down her shift, staining the white linen red.

For a moment she was stunned, looking down at herself as if she couldn't believe what had just happened. But when her eyes rose to meet his, they were bright with anger.

'What do you think you're doing?' she whispered, in a voice harsh as winter.

'The only thing I should do. I'm leaving.'

'Should?' She scoffed. 'Slaves live by "should". Is that all you are, Erlan Aurvandil? A slave?'

The thought occurred to him that, if ever he were, it would be to her. That was exactly why he had to get out.

When he was at the door, she called his name, her voice now smooth as silk. 'Look at me.' His hand was on the latch but still he turned. She was a terrible sight. Terrible and beautiful as Freyja – if the goddess had happened to be in a particularly vengeful mood – with her black hair, her fierce eyes, and her white gown daubed red as blood. 'Go, if you must,' she smiled. 'But know this. I mean to have you. And sooner or later, I will.'

Erlan let the drape fall and closed the door behind him.

CHAPTER TEN

Gerutha was naked.

That's what she noticed first – the night air washing cold over her skin. Then she heard shouts, shrieks, the crackle of fire.

She opened her eyes, pain pounding her skull like a cudgel. Someone had hit her, hard.

It took a few moments to remember. The men had come by stealth. There had been wailing and the warning bell. Voices screaming in the night.

She had rushed outside, but already it was chaos. Shadows were breaking between the thatched houses in a swirl of fire and steel. A ghostly howling danced on the air. She remembered her first crazed fear: that the dead had returned to carry off the living – remembered turning to retrieve her boy, to keep him safe, and then the blow. That was all.

She tried to rub her eyes but couldn't move her arms. She felt hemp bite at her wrists and realized her hands were tied behind her back. Why did her head feel so heavy? She looked down at naked feet. They too were lashed together. Beyond them, she could see a branch. She tried to wriggle loose, but only ended up flapping like a herring on a hook. Finally she understood: she was upside down.

Someone beneath her laughed. She felt a slap to her buttocks. 'Patience, sister! Your turn will come.'

Gerutha twisted her head and saw a sneering face, smeared with grime.

I'm too old for this. But what surety was age against men like these? These killers didn't care. She wanted to scream, like so many others were screaming, but what good would it do? Instead she hung, limp as a sack of seed, trying to make sense of what she could see.

Flames were everywhere. Blisters of black smoke billowed downwards into the abysmal dark. Shadows rushed, appearing to her like cockroaches scuttling across a ceiling. She saw blades fall and rise, heard whimpers and cries, animal yells and whoops. A man collapsed, but upwards, found his feet again, staggered, only for two shadows to pounce on him, scything him down like barley.

She didn't want to see any more. Didn't want to witness the destruction of everyone and everything she held dear. A man was gibbering prayers beside her. She turned her head and saw a line of bodies strung along a bough of the gnarly old oak that marked the village centre.

Every one was naked.

The screams were now dying away like an ebb tide, leaving only the wails of womenfolk being put to shame. The killers weren't running now. They could take their time, stalking with horrible deliberation among the corpses that, until tonight, had been her kith and kin.

She hoped it had been quick for her boy. Hoped he hadn't suffered.

She was about to utter a prayer to Hel, the two-faced guardian of the dead, but something caught her eye that killed the words in her throat: two figures approaching, silhouetted against the flames. Something about them seized her, something uncanny.

'Well, well! You folks are in for a treat,' crowed the man who had slapped her rump.

She paid him little heed. She was watching these other men, each an exact imitation of the other, except one wore a black wolf-skin, the other white. Both faces were obscured behind metal eye-guards. They halted before the captives. Then, as one, they removed their helms.

'The White and the Black!' moaned someone along the line. A woman began to blubber.

'Sveär butchers!' cried another.

'Watch your filthy Gotar tongue,' snarled the guard. There was a shriek as he prodded the offender with his spear-tip.

Gerutha was rigid with fear. Even upside down, their faces were all hard-set brows and noses cruel as daggers, mirrors of each other. Except the twin on the right had dark hair, dark eyes, dark beard. Everything dark as death. And the other... the other was a ghost. His hair and beard white as milk, his skin pale as a corpse. Only his eyes had any colour at all, glowing pink and pitiless in the reflected flames.

The White and the Black.

These last days their reputation had spread like a straw fire throughout the farmsteads and villages that bordered the southern edge of the Kolmark Forest. At first, the stories had been confused, exaggerated, too horrible for anyone to believe. But the reports grew, the details always the same, each affirming the last like some awful refrain. *Wolf-warriors from north of the forest. Sveär bastards who wouldn't keep to their own lands.* The deaths were bad enough, but it was *how* they died. Men flayed alive, women butchered beyond recognition. They struck like a hammer-blow, then slipped back into the forest, leaving everyone dead. All except one. There was always one survivor, and the survivor's story always the same: two men with the same face. One white as a *draugr*. One black as Hel.

Their eyes flicked up and down the line of wretched villagers like wolves salivating over their prey. She recognized the voice of Klep the blacksmith, babbling for mercy. But she couldn't speak, couldn't take her eyes off those two faces that were one.

They looked at one another and seemed to smile. In her upside-down world, their faces looked like grimacing idols.

'Well, brother,' said the Black, 'shall we begin?'

The White didn't answer, only uttered a laugh so hollow it could have come from the gullet of Garm himself, Hel's hound. He lifted his blade, already fouled with its night's work. The villagers began to scream.

Gerutha swore an oath to herself: that she would not look. Not if they flayed the lids off her eyes. Nor did she. But she couldn't shut her ears to the fearful sounds that rushed about her like the winds of *Ragnarök* while these brothers went about their work. She tried to think of better times, times with her son, who now, surely, was walking the Hel-road ahead of her. He wasn't much younger than these two devils. She thanked the white god Heimdall that her son would never live to become like these.

She was shaking, her body no longer hers to control – except for her eyes, which she welded shut against the horror, though she knew her time was coming. She heard the man next to her uttering sounds no human should ever make, nor ever hear. On and on until at last there was a splattering noise. Then silence.

She was almost relieved. Hoped the pain would not be too unbearable. Nor too long. That her reward would be to see her son again, and soon.

'Open your eyes.' It was the smoother voice of the Black twin.

She refused. She thought of her son instead. His would be the last face she saw, not this monster's.

'Stupid bitch,' the voice said, its tone unhurried. 'Go on, open them.'

Someone stepped forward. She felt rough fingers pinch her neck. There was a chuckle and she recognized the guard's laugh. Nails dug into her eyes. She tried to screw them shut, but the fingers were too strong, prising open the lids until she saw she was face to face with the brothers.

Except now White and Black were daubed chin to toe with her kinsmen's blood, each glistening red as a butcher's bib. She tried to look away but the guard held her neck firm.

The White stepped forward, gazing at her wonderingly with those uncanny pink eyes. He lifted his sword-point, his upside-down smile a gash across his blood-spattered face. She felt the steel tip rest coldly on her sex.

'I anoint you with the blood of your kin,' the White murmured hoarsely, with another slow, guttural laugh. She stiffened, then shuddered with revulsion as he traced the steel through her triangle of hair. The point came to rest over her womb. That was when she realized she despised these devils as much as she feared them. She remembered what she had done, right there under that bloody blade. She had made life, grown it within her. She had created. These brothers knew only how to destroy.

The pressure increased. She sucked a breath, feeling the tip break skin.

'Do you know who we are?' His voice was hardly a whisper.

She gave a clumsy nod, watching a droplet of blood fall from the White's hilt.

He whipped the sword away.

'This one lives,' the Black said. Someone started laughing. 'Cut her down.'

And before Gerutha could make sense of the words, the rope had snapped and she crumpled to the ground, relief and fear flooding warm and wet over her thighs.

CHAPTER ELEVEN

On the morn of their departure, Einar and Kai made an underwhelming sight – Kai looking like a badly made scarecrow, albeit one weighed down with razor-sharp steel, and Einar balanced precariously on his horse, big belly resting on his thighs like a barrel of butter, slowly melting in the spring sunshine.

'It's so damned hot,' Einar grumbled. It wasn't, but the fat man's cheeks were already glistening with sweat. 'At least give me an ale-skin. You can't expect me to listen to the runt's drivel all the way to Dannerborg and stay sober.'

'Sorry, friend,' Erlan replied. 'You need a clear head. Orders straight from the king's mouth.'

'The king's arse, more like. Anyway, the king's dying – hadn't you heard?'

'He'll mend,' Erlan replied firmly, as much to reassure himself as the fat man.

'Huh! I guess he usually does.'

Kai, on the other hand, was happy as a flea. 'Cheer up, fat

man. They say a journey never took no hurt from a story of two. Did I tell you about that time last winter when Erlan and me were—'

'Gods – spare me!' Einar groaned.

'Just keep your ears open and give that tongue of yours a rest.' Erlan was more worried about Kai than he cared to admit. But it was out of his hands. It was Einar's job to protect him now.

'All ears. No tongue.' Kai leered past Erlan at Bara who, to his delight, had come to see them off.

'Take care of yourself, pup,' she said, shading her eyes against the morning glare. 'And keep your hands off those Gotar girls. They're pox-riddled sluts, every one.'

'I'll bear that in mind,' Kai grinned.

'I'll keep the runt out of trouble,' said Einar.

Somehow Erlan doubted that.

'So long then!' Kai cried and he was off in a clatter of hooves, yelling over his shoulder, 'Back before you know it!'

'Aye – make sure you are!' Erlan called after him, adding in a murmur, 'Sveäland is counting on you.'

Einar grunted. 'That's what worries me.' He gave his grey a kick, rousing it to an unenthusiastic trot and away he went, joggling like a sack of turnips.

Erlan and Bara watched as the figures grew smaller until the distant woods finally swallowed them completely. Erlan wondered whether he ought to say something vaguely encouraging, though the gods knew he wasn't feeling encouraged. But she beat him to it.

'Well then, hero, guess you'll have to do your own damn cooking now, won't you?'

In the days that followed, talk among the halls was all of the coming war. A little hasty, by Erlan's reckoning, but then it didn't take more than a spark to burn a hayrick to dust, and even he had to admit what they knew already was more than a mere spark.

He could see the worry in their faces, specially the womenfolk – could hear it in their voices when they called to their young. Fear was seeping through them like a flood tide, rising higher each day. *There are always shadows that roam*. Inga had said that, and how right she was proved. Still, whatever shadows were out there hadn't swallowed them yet.

Of course, the smiths and fletchers and leathermen were content enough. It was a good time to be in that line of work. But even their faces grew etched with apprehension when news filtered back to Uppsala that the southern earls had begun to call their levies. Each new wrinkle a mark of the fear that gnaws at a man's belly when he wonders what fate the Norns have spun him.

Nevertheless the hall-folk cheered themselves with the prospect of the horse fair held each year on the feast day of Idun, the goddess of spring. It met about six leagues south of Sviggar's Seat, at Sigtuna – the little market village nestled against the waters of the Great Bay. Cargo boats could land there, many from faraway Gotland, laden with horseflesh. Finnish traders came too, from across the East Sea with their furs and amber, and Sami from the north bringing reindeer skins and a thousand trinkets and tools fashioned from bone or antler – all of them looking for a ripe deal and a little amusement on the side. Gotlandish horses might be the finest around the circle of the East Sea, but every trader knew the best whores and the best ale were to be had in Uppland.

With the fate of his friends still on his mind, Erlan hadn't planned to go along, but on the eve of the feast day, Sviggar summoned him to his chamber. Erlan approached, dread tickling his conscience, half-expecting some accusation or worse. But apparently the queen had kept their indiscretion to herself. Instead he found the king in better health and a fine mood and with a quite different reason for summoning him.

'My daughter tells me her horse has been lame for weeks,' Sviggar explained. 'I want you to help her buy another and see she returns safe before sunfall.'

'The princess asked for me?'

'Of course she didn't!' Sviggar cried amiably. 'She insists she needs no escorting. But I've suffered too many new grey hairs on her account, and with all this other business... You understand.'

'Yes, lord.'

'Besides, a woman with a pouch full of silver needs watching! You ride with her in the morning.'

'Very well.'

Sviggar gave a hoarse laugh. 'She should count herself lucky. I'm sure there isn't a safer pair of hands in the kingdom.'

A safe pair of hands?

The irony cut like a blade.

Dung and horsehide.

The place reeked of it, and hovering over it all was a haze of dust. Naturally, the animal enclosures were filled mostly with horses, but folks had also brought oxen and goats and sheep, even hunting dogs, to trade.

'Four ounces.' Lilla folded her arms defiantly.

'Four ounces of silver for my best mare?' screeched the Gotlandish woman. 'Why not have the clothes off me back while you're at it?' She tugged at her smock. 'Here – go on!'

But that only made Lilla giggle. 'Four is fair. You know it.'

The woman had named a price three times that. The tall black mare gazed down on them with bored disdain, as if haggling was a thing far beneath her. And there was no doubt, she was a noble-looking beast. Her coat shone like warm tar. But a mark and a half of silver was a Hel of a price for one horse.

'My husband would divorce me on the spot if I took less than ten ounces.' The older woman scanned the faces behind Lilla. 'Curse the man, where is he? Probably sucking on the end of an ale-skin if I know him.'

'Come on – what's your best price?' Lilla grinned. She enjoyed this game. She was good at it, too. They had been through this five times already, each time Lilla screwing down the price till the seller was gnawing their knuckles off, only to walk away on the flimsiest pretext: a phantom swelling of a tendon, some invisible crack in a tooth.

Erlan palmed the sweat off his brow, feeling his temper fraying. Surely there was nothing wrong with this one? Far as he could see, the mare was as fine a beast as silver could buy.

But apparently there was a lot more haggling to be done: Lilla pretending to drag him away, only to be called back; poking and prodding till there wasn't an inch of the mare hadn't been

106

argued over at length. He wondered if Sviggar appreciated how tight-fisted his daughter was with his silver.

'For the love of Freyja,' he whispered at last, 'I think you can spare another ounce.'

'It's the principle. Besides, you know I like to win,' she whispered back, flashing a smile.

At last, they settled on six and a half ounces. The Gotlander weighed out Lilla's hacksilver, grumbling all the while.

'A pleasure doing business with you,' Lilla said.

'Oh, I'm sure it was.' The woman untied the mare and passed Lilla its halter with a forced smile.

'Can you believe it?' Lilla cried when they were out of earshot.

'I'll believe anything so long as you're happy... You *are* happy, right?'

'Wouldn't you be? She's worth a mark at least!'

'Good. So we can head home?'

'Home? There's still so much to see!' She patted the mare's neck. 'We'll leave her with the watchman and look around.'

'I told your father I'd have you back before dusk.'

'It's not even noon.' She smiled at him mischievously. 'Don't you trust me?'

'Not even slightly.'

She laughed and looped her arm through his.

They wandered among the stalls with Lilla insisting they try everything on offer – a wedge of Varmland cheese, a strip of dried cod from the Botten Gulf, skewers of spiced reindeer meat roasted almost black, straight from the Sami herds. She made him taste the Finns' favourite drink, a clear liquid they called 'little water' but the stuff burned like fire, as

Erlan discovered to his cost when he gulped it down in one.

'You could have warned me,' he choked while Lilla fell about laughing.

They drifted along a row of booths selling cloth, Lilla dawdling at each, fingering bolts of linen or homespun or felt, and some of the more exotic materials that had found their way to Sigtuna from distant lands across the sea. If the trader was an outlander, Lilla wanted to know all about their homeland and how they had journeyed to the shores of Uppland. Erlan followed along, happy to listen, though often his mind strayed back to Kai who, he knew, must be somewhere south of the Kolmark by now.

Lilla was picking her way through a pile of homespun, chatting to the stall-keeper, a local woman of middling age, when a boy of ten or so ran up.

'Mother, mother,' he gasped, 'the horse fights are about to begin. Can I go? You promised I could this year. Please!'

Erlan noticed a couple of other boys lurking nearby. The woman looked from them to her lad and must have read in his face the silent plea not to humiliate him in front of his mates. She smiled. 'The promises we make, eh? All right, off you go. But no betting, mind, or your father'll have something to say about it.'

The boy garbled his thanks and raced off with his pals towards two large mounds set back from the shore.

'Most sons wouldn't be so respectful,' said Lilla. 'You must be proud.'

'He's a good boy,' the stall-keeper replied. 'Still, I worry for him. Especially now.'

'Why?'

The woman peered at Lilla as if she were simple. 'Why do you think? I can't be sure he'll even outlive the summer. Who can be when they look at their younglings these days?'

'Surely you needn't always fear the worst?' said Lilla, trying to sound encouraging.

'There's a war coming, girl! Haven't you heard? And I wouldn't take no odds of my boy living through it.' She pointed out a gaggle of young men nearby. Two were stripped to the waist and going at it, sparring fist for fist, while their mates cheered them on. 'All of them lads – how many do you reckon will be alive to see next year's fair, hey?'

'It's not certain there'll be war,' said Erlan. At least, that was the line Sviggar wanted his counsellors to take.

'Oh no? My brother got it from that Jari Iron-Tongue who says it's already started. Men have died. And I'll tell you why.' She beckoned Lilla closer. 'All because of those damned high folk up at Uppsala. A curse on their heads! They don't know the trouble they cause. It's their disputing going to put my husband behind a shieldwall and, gods forbid, my boy too if things go bad. That ain't right, is it? What's it to do with us low folk?'

Erlan was about to suggest she watch her tongue given her present company, but he felt Lilla squeeze his hand to silence.

'I heard the king doesn't want war,' Lilla said.

'What he wants and what he gets might not be the same thing. But who has to pay to protect the king's honour and the king's land, hey?' She jabbed a finger at Lilla. 'Your kin and mine, that's who. And all these folk!'

'Maybe,' said Erlan. 'But doesn't each man have a duty to defend his own kin? Honour demands it.'

'Honour? Pah – here's to your honour!' She made a rude gesture. 'Next you're going to tell me all is fine because a dead husband and a dead son will end up in Valhalla. But what bloody use is either of them to me there?'

'Let's pray it doesn't come to that,' replied Lilla.

'Oh aye, the gods'll want their cut. But if the Gotars and Danes and gods know who else do come, how many of these mothers will be weeping?'

'The king won't let that happen.'

'You're naive if you think that, my girl,' the woman scowled.

Lilla just smiled and pressed her hand. 'We must be getting on.'

As they walked away, Erlan could see she was shaken. 'She's right,' she said. 'Why should all these folk have to suffer because of my family's mistakes?'

He didn't have an answer to that.

They strolled on in silence. The air was full of chatter. A gentle breeze mingled the smells of mead brews and hot berry juices and newly baked bread with the stink of fresh dung and the musky tang of fox skins. Traders meandered among the crowds peddling amber stones from shallow baskets, some with jewellery fashioned from antlers or bead-stones, others hawking mushrooms and forest-herbs. Old men huddled in circles, shuffling tafl-pieces around gaming boards, while the younger men proved their mettle in wrestling bouts, to the cheers of their friends. Youngsters splashed in the shallows. Skaldmen earned a few slivers of silver, singing lays or sagas or drapas, plucking at lutes or blowing mournful melodies on goat-horns. Whores lounged beside their booths – those not already occupied – sizing up passing menfolk like cattle. Benches were lined with drinkers while their wives and daughters clustered nearby, chattering like starlings.

But in spite of the air of merriment, the delight had gone out of it for Lilla, and every time they passed talk about the possibility of war her despondency deepened.

As if to match her mood, the southern horizon grew murky, clouds towering high above the water, portending a storm. Watching it, Erlan knew she was thinking the same as him. What would happen to all these folk if the Wartooth came?

The sun was well past the midday mark when Erlan noticed a swell of folk making their way towards the two mounds where the horse fights were to take place. He was about to suggest they take a look when a voice called, 'Good day, sister.'

They turned to see Sigurd emerging from a nearby booth, fastening his belt. A young woman in a shift slit to her thigh followed him out, her hair dishevelled and turning a silver ring in her palm. She went to talk to her friends.

'Enjoying yourself I see, brother.'

Sigurd stooped to a bucket and sluiced water over his face, then took a long swig from a nearby pitcher. 'Ahh! Nothing like ale and a good fuck to refresh the spirit.'

'Mother would be so proud.'

'Mother's dead. Or hadn't you noticed?' His eyes shifted to Erlan. 'I see you've found yourself a bit of flesh, sister. How much did he cost you?' When Erlan bristled, he laughed. 'Oh lighten up, cripple. You take yourself so *bloody* seriously.'

'You've been drinking,' said Lilla.

'Who the Hel hasn't! I suppose you're going to chide me for that as well?'

'No. You can please yourself.'

'Oh, I intend to… while I still can,' he added, with a scornful look at the crowds flocking towards the mounds. 'There's so much damn croaking round here, you'd think we'd already lost a war.' He turned back to his sister. 'Let them come, I say! The sooner they do, the sooner they'll be sorry for it!' He threw back another swig of ale and then tossed the pitcher back on the table. 'Well, sister, are you coming to watch the fun?'

'You go ahead. We've other things to see.'

'Oh, that's right… Couldn't sully those pretty eyes with a drop of blood, could we?'

'It's not the blood that's not to my taste. It's the faces. Folk need no encouragement to be cruel.'

'Bah! And you, Erlan *Aur—van—dil*?' He slurred the name like a curse. 'I suppose you think a bit of sport between dumb animals is cruel too, hey?'

'If a man wants to see his best horse come to harm that's his business.'

'I've a horse in this myself, and I promise you, with Vargalf handling him, he comes to no harm at all. In fact, he's about to challenge last year's champion.' A loud cheer erupted from beyond the mounds. 'Hel, that must be it now! Well, are you coming or not?'

Erlan hesitated, casting a diffident look at Lilla.

'Gods, don't let her stop you! This'll be a sight worth seeing, I promise you. It won't take long for Vargalf to finish him.' As if to make his point, another cheer rose from the crowd.

'Go, if you want,' said Lilla, but he could see the distaste in her eyes. Even so, it wasn't that which stopped him. To his surprise he found, now given a choice, he didn't want to leave her company.

'You go,' he told Sigurd. 'Your father charged me to watch over Lady Aslíf.'

'Did he now? I guess you'd better see to that then, cripple. Just be sure to watch your step!' With that he feigned a stumble and set off, laughing, for the arena. Erlan let the slight pass. Flies were but flies, after all. Instead he turned to Lilla but she looked far from happy.

'If it's only my father's *charge* that keeps you with me, then please yourself. I didn't ask for your company.'

'I am pleasing myself.'

'Oh.' She seemed surprised by that answer. Perhaps as surprised as he was to give it. Her frown disappeared.

'Are we done here?'

She nodded up at him. 'Yes. Take me home.'

CHAPTER TWELVE

She had got what she came for, but as they rode away from the fair, Lilla's heart was restless as an autumn sea. She knew why, too. It was him. There was something unsettling about *him*. This closed man. And try as she might, she couldn't turn her mind away from him, as if he were a door that she sat beside, waiting for it to open, unable to leave it alone, too curious to know what was inside, too convinced that what lay behind it was hers. But why?

Maybe she was wrong.

She watched the back of his head, wondering what he was thinking, his tousled hair hanging loose, rocking with the motion of his horse, his shoulders broad and strong, telling her no more than a stone wall.

Maybe if her mother had lived, she could have explained what she was feeling, could have shown her how to understand this man. But her mother was gone.

They had ridden perhaps three leagues since Sigtuna. Afternoon was spreading into early evening, the warm southerly wind carrying with it a bank of cloud. It soon overtook them and the air grew thick and humid.

Erlan looked up. 'We're going to get a good drenching by the look of things.'

There still lay a fair distance between them and the shelter of her father's hall. 'There's another way.' Through some woodland and it would take a little longer, she explained, but at least there would be cover if there was a real downpour.

Erlan followed her off the main pathway, leaving behind the column of stragglers trudging their way home to Uppsala. They were soon alone, riding across open country, only slipping under the trees as the first raindrops fell.

They'd hardly spoken since setting out and under the damp foliage the silence between them seemed to grow louder. The only sounds were the rain above, the drip of water off the leaves and the soft pad of the horses' hooves, side by side. The more she listened, the more oppressive they became.

'Do you agree with her?' she suddenly blurted.

He turned to look at her. 'Agree with who?'

'The woman at the stall.'

'Your conscience bothering you, is it?'

'I'm serious. It's hard not to feel responsible in some way. Or at least complicit. The fault lies all within my family.'

'No one's dead yet. At least, none of that crowd anyway,' he corrected himself.

She closed her eyes, but all she could see were faces of the fair-folk, their merriment worn in mockery of the horrors she feared were to come. 'I can't bear to think of it. Those children. All those young men.'

'They're not your responsibility. None of it is.'

'That's no reason not to want to help. Every life is worth saving, isn't it?'

'To save a life means being willing to fight. Willing to take another life, come to that. How else could it be if someone's bent on killing those you care about?'

'I don't know. There must be other sacrifices that could be made, besides more killing.'

His brow furrowed. 'You mean like your stepmother's sacrifices?'

'No. I don't mean that,' she replied quickly. 'Just that there must be another path to peace that doesn't plunge us into war.' She shook her head. 'What would all that killing serve anyone anyway?'

He shrugged. 'Blood debts are repaid. Vengeance is satisfied.'

'Vengeance is *never* satisfied. It's a spiral that never ends, driving us all to Hel. Blood only breeds blood. I *hate* it.'

'You may hate it. But it's the way of men. You can't change that. No one can.'

'What a dismal thought,' she murmured. She almost felt sorry for him, believing that. It left little room for any hope. They rode on in silence for a while. Her thoughts returned to the horse fair – to the boys wrestling, how they strove so hard to do each other harm, and then the whoops of delight from the crowd at the horse fights when one horse blooded another. 'Why do men so love cruelty?'

'If the world is cruel, why should the men who live in it be any different?'

'The world isn't cruel. It's full of life and light and beauty. Just look around you. Only men make it cruel. You have to tear things down. To destroy them.'

'That's a little harsh,' he chuckled. 'Don't we build things, too? We build halls, we sing songs, we raise crops. Raise children, come to that.'

'Yet it's the names of the most deadly killers among you that are raised the highest. Vengeance is esteemed more than love. Death more than life.'

'Sometimes a man has good reason to seek vengeance. Good reason to seek death over life.' She noticed his gaze drift away into the distance. Remembered how he'd spoken like this before, in the frozen forest. 'Anyway,' he added, 'I dare say you're right about most men. But it's not true for me. Not any more.'

'Then what about love?'

'Love! You're speaking to the wrong man. I've nothing to say about love. Nothing good anyway.'

'Say something bad then.'

'Better to say nothing at all.'

She gave him a quizzical look. 'That's all you ever do, isn't it? You hold everything in, guarding your thoughts jealous as Fafnir's gold. Don't you ever *feel* anything?'

'Who cares what I feel?'

'I do,' she said, and immediately regretted it. As usual she had given away more than she meant to. But it was out there now.

'Well, you shouldn't. It won't do you a lick of good, anyhow.'

'Why not?'

He chuckled and turned away. 'Just wouldn't.'

But her curiosity wouldn't let that lie. 'There's a sadness about you, you know that? You wear it like a mantle. Maybe even like a shield.' She hesitated but he didn't answer. 'You must have lost something very precious to you.'

'I can't speak of it... I swore,' he added softly.

'Has it ever occurred to you that everyone has lost something they once loved? Do you really think you're the only one?'

He suddenly rounded on her. 'Lost something, maybe! Not *everything*.'

She waited for the wave of anger to ebb from his dark eyes. She had to be delicate. That was obvious. But she was determined to hunt him down. 'My mother used to say self-pity will suck you down like a mire. And she was right. Believe me, I know. I've tried to walk that way, but it's a short road to suffocation.'

'You don't know me.'

'I know you well enough to know your problem. You're so blinded by your own pain you can't see anything else, even when it's right in front of you. You should let it go.'

'You have no idea what brought me here, Lilla. To lay it down... That would be an even greater betrayal...' He trailed off with a shake of his head. 'Never mind.'

'I understand,' she said gently. 'I do. It's the last link to your home. That's why you can't let it go.'

'No. I have no home.' He shook his reins and his horse moved ahead. Apparently he was done talking.

Well, that went well, she thought irritably. From that angle, she could see the sharp line of his jaw, clenching, unclenching... Why couldn't she just let him stay behind the wall he'd built around himself? Wasn't that where he wanted to be? Wasn't that where he belonged?

They rode on. She closed her eyes, feeling the rain running down her face, as if it could wash away her frustration. Why was nature so simple, yet people so complicated? She ran her tongue over her lips. The rainwater tasted sweet. There was no wind in the wood. The air was warm. Overhead, the rainfall grew louder.

'We'll be soaked through if we stay out in this.'

'I am soaked,' she said. He didn't seem to hear. Or else he was no longer listening.

'We can wait out the worst of it under there.' Just ahead stood an old blood-beech, its branches spread above them in a thick canopy of deep purple. They dismounted and led the horses off the path just as the first thunder rolled overhead. Erlan tied their halters to a young sapling that was struggling its way through to some light in the shadow of its ancient rivals. Then he unrolled his cloak and led Lilla to the trunk of the blood-beech. There the rain was at least tolerable, certainly more sheltered than the path.

He passed her two corners of his cloak and they pulled it taut over their heads and then, with their backs to the trunk, they gazed out at the dismal cascade leaking through the canopy.

There was no birdsong, not even a whisper of wind. The rain muffled all. Lilla breathed in and breathed out. The air smelled damp and earthy. She listened to Erlan breathing beside her – steady, slower than her. She could smell him, too. A slight tang of sweat, the wet wool of his clothes, that indescribable scent underlying them both that she had noticed before. The smell of *him*.

She wondered whether he was angry with her. She didn't blame him. She was angry with herself. She should learn to keep her thoughts hidden, her mouth shut.

'Erlan.' He looked down at her. Strands of wet hair clung to his temples. 'You do have a home, you know. It's here. With us.'

His eyes smiled. 'It's no good, Lilla. I wish I could be whatever it is you think I should be... But I can't.'

'I don't want you to be any different. I just want you to be happy.'

She wasn't exactly sure why but suddenly her hand was against his cheek and she was wiping the rain off his eyebrow with her thumb. In fact, it was more of a caress than a wipe. Perhaps that was why he caught her wrist. She thought he would push it away, but instead he held it there. Closed his eyes. And then he kissed the palm of her open hand. His lips felt warm.

Almost without her noticing, the cloak slipped from her fingers and slid to the ground. She stood before him, rain plastering her hair to her head, still confused, her mind catching up with what was happening. But in his eyes, she suddenly saw a longing that caught her breath, that seemed to have snuck up on her too, like a thief with a knife at her throat. And inside she felt a dam breaking, filling her body with desire, and in his eyes she saw the same desire reflected. He pulled her closer, lifted her, kissed her, softly at first and then harder. At first it was a shock. But soon she found herself responding, pressing against his chest, almost crushed against him, feeling the flicker of his tongue in her mouth.

Just as suddenly he drew away.

'I'm sorry. I shouldn't. Your father—'

'This isn't about my father. It's just you. And me.'

'I'm sorry,' he repeated in a murmur, 'I'm sorry.' It was strange. Like he was speaking to himself, or to someone else. He bent down and picked up the cloak at their feet. 'I should get you home.'

The rain continued to fall.

CHAPTER THIRTEEN

'Dannerborg,' Kai said.

Einar nodded.

'So we're agreed? Not a word past those lips, fat man, or it'll be both our necks.'

'It's my neck I'm worried about. You watch out for your own.'

Kai grunted. That went without saying.

'Can't say I care above half for all this sneaking about.' Einar fidgeted with his buckle.

'We'll be fine.'

'Just remember, lad, the less bollocks comes spilling out of that mouth of yours, the less chance we'll end up the wrong side of Odin's necklace.'

'Bah! The noose hasn't been made that Kai Askarsson couldn't talk his way out of.'

Einar jutted his whiskery jowls up the hill. 'Let's hope it's not waiting for you up yonder.'

It looked impressive enough, the high stockade around the

mead-hall and its outlying buildings an imposing presence over the landscape, built for defence to serve as stronghold for a lord. The hall was big and dark, clad in stone with a thick turf roof, although hardly a match for the sheer majesty of Sviggar's Great Hall.

But what caught Kai's eye was the bustle around it. So many *people*. Many more than you'd expect in a place like that. Outside the stockade was a scattering of rough-timber booths for tradesfolk and a few livestock, though by now most sheep and cattle would be out in the pastures.

'See there.'

Kai looked where Einar was pointing. The ground sloped away west, flattening into an area of reedbeds skirting the edge of a piece of water – some shallow-bottomed lake or perhaps an inland fjord. Carpeted over the slope were dozens of small tents, a good number of folk, mostly men, moving among them.

'Someone's hosting a lot of guests.'

'Food for ravens,' Einar grunted.

Kai's blood tingled. This was the first sign of anything out of the ordinary since leaving Uppsala. The ride through the Kolmark had been anything but eventful. Of course, crossing the forest they'd had an eye out for the usual. But even bears and wolves didn't hold the same terror for him they once had. Not for old Kai Wolf-Hand. Nevertheless, they had taken extra precautions when they crossed into Eastern Gotarland proper, travelling by night, tracking away from the road and only returning to the main route south four or five leagues into Gotar territory.

By then, they had their story straight.

It had been decided – mostly by Kai, admittedly – that however well Einar knew the idioms of the Gotar dialect, his accent marked him out as a Sveär without any shred of doubt. Kai insisted it was better he said nothing at all. Instead Einar would pose as Kai's mute protector, with Kai the younger son of a freedman on his way to become heir to a childless uncle living on the shore of the Lake of Two Forests. Kai had suggested he style himself son of a lord, but Einar pointed out that most lords of the land would be known to Prince Ringast. Besides which, the fat man observed, he'd met swine who looked more lordly than Kai.

'Come on, come on!' a voice croaked behind them. It belonged to an old man pulling a ramshackle handcart up the track. 'What's the hold up, you dozy dungheads?'

Kai was so surprised he forgot to speak, forgot that Einar wasn't to speak.

'One of them foreign buggers, heh? Can't understand a word I'm saying.' The carter jabbed Kai's thigh with his stick.

'Cut that out! I am too a Gotar.'

'Well then – what're you doing standing like some arse-head mule taking up the road? Out the way, man!'

Kai moved his horse off the track and the shrivelled old man ploughed on up the slope. Watching him, Kai had an idea. He jumped down, tossed Einar his reins and ran on to the handcart.

'Need a hand, old father?'

The carter snorted, sniffed and spat. 'Huh! First finger any of you outlanders has lifted for me.'

'I told you, I'm a Gotar.'

'So you are then,' he said, ceding the handle to Kai. 'Guess I'm obliged to you.'

123

'Enough for a favour in return?'

'Depends.' The carter's nose wrinkled with suspicion.

'Won't cost you a thing. Just want to know who's in charge up there.'

'Lord Ringast Haraldarsson. Any halfwit knows that.'

'I mean who runs his household?'

'Ahh,' croaked the carter. 'You'll be wanting Sletti the steward. They call him *Smjörreðr*.'

Kai chuckled. *Smjörreðr* meant 'Butter-Cock' in the Gotar tongue. 'What the Hel for?'

'Ask him!' he smirked. 'Anyhow, he's the smooth-faced bugger with the big mouth and skin the colour of pig-piss. Can't miss him.'

Kai pulled the handcart to the top of the slope, only passing it back once they were through the gate. Einar had dismounted and was leading the horses behind. Kai flashed a grin. The fat man rolled his eyes in reply.

Inside the stockade the atmosphere was an odd mix of idleness and bustle. Those idling were mostly warriors, it seemed. House-karls, or hearthmen maybe, chatting, drinking, leering at passing thrall-maids, who hurried about like Garm himself was snapping at their heels.

It took only a moment to pick out the steward, Sletti. Hall-folk were buzzing round him likes flies round a fresh turd, while the man himself was embroiled in a heated exchange with a servant-girl.

As the carter had said, his face was oddly smooth and tanned. He wore a long tunic – so long it looked more like a woman's dress. In fact, altogether the impression was of someone neither all man nor all woman. His voice carried higher than an ordinary man's too, yet there was no mistaking its assurance.

Kai always thought it best to go straight in. He laid an arm across the girl's shoulder and grinned at the steward. 'Good day to you, Master Sletti!'

'Do I know you?' the steward replied irritably.

'Not yet, but I'm glad to make your acquaintance.'

'I'm in the middle of something.'

'Sure, sure. We're happy to wait.' Kai gave a courteous nod and winked at Einar who stood by, red-faced.

'Oh gods, very well,' Sletti scowled. 'So what are you?' He peered down a long straight nose at Kai. Only then did Kai notice the rope necklace tied tight round his neck: the mark of a thrall. 'Let me guess. Another brace of swords for Lord Ringast?' He raised a sardonic eyebrow. 'Impressive ones too, I see.'

'Not us, Master Sletti! We need a roof for a night or two, then we'll be moving on.'

'On where?'

'I'm off to inherit my uncle's farm beside the Lake of the Two Forests,' Kai beamed proudly.

'How wonderful for you,' Sletti replied drily. 'And you?'

'He's my protection. Not that I can't look after myself, mind, but my father's always been a cautious man. And you can't be too careful these days.'

'Can't he speak for himself?'

'Happens, no. Poor bugger! Not so much as a whisper comes out of those fat chops, alas. But as you can see,' he gave Einar's belly a slap, 'plenty goes in.'

Sletti looked doubtful. 'What makes you think we have food to spare for his belly? Or yours?'

'We're reasonable men. We're happy to work for our supper.'

'Hmm. Very well. Two nights for two days' work.'

'Much obliged. Ain't we, fat man?' Einar grunted his assent, after a jab in the stomach.

'Gerutha, come here.' Sletti signalled to a tall woman who stepped out from the crowd of hall-folk waiting to see the steward. Kai tipped her a friendly nod which she didn't return. 'Take them to the Back Barn and show them where they can leave their horses and stow their gear.' Sletti eyed Kai up and down. 'After that, the boy can help Snorri. The mute can go to the tannery.' He looked at Einar. 'And not a word of complaint, you hear?' he added, with a feathery snigger.

Einar bristled, though he could hardly raise an objection now. The tall woman gestured to follow.

'What's his story then?' Kai asked when they were clear of the steward's earshot.

'I don't gossip about folks that give me orders,' she replied. She had a warm husk to her voice, and though she had a fair few years on him, she wasn't *that* old. Kai guessed a couple of summers shy of forty.

'Go on, you must know something. He's a queer fish to look at – that's for sure.'

She turned her head and for the first time he noticed the shock of white that ran down the middle of her rust-brown hair. 'Truth is, I ha'n't been here so long myself. But I gather his mother was one of King Harald's women in Leithra. A bed-slave from the south shores of the Black Sea, someone said.'

'That explains the skin. And if he's a king's bastard that explains the rod up his backside.'

'I didn't say that.'

'You didn't have to. Anyhow, what about you?'

'What about me?'

'You said you're new yourself.'

'You're a curious one, ain't you?'

'Nothing wrong with that.'

'H'm.' She walked on a bit, apparently deliberating whether she would give him an answer or not. 'There was some trouble,' she said at length. 'Along the edge of the Kolmark. Nearly every village has been burned to ashes, or ha'n't you heard?'

This was news to Kai. 'Not us. We came up from Skania,' he lied.

'Aye, well, the stories have spread far enough. There's been a heap of raiding these last days. Sveär wolves.' Her nose wrinkled. 'My village was... well, there wasn't much to stick around for. Afterwards. So I came here. Lord Ringast took me in when he heard what I was.'

'What are you?'

'A survivor. A witness.' She pointed to her eyes. 'I *saw* 'em.' Kai noticed they were the colour of ripe corn, dotted with dark flecks. Pretty, in their way. Though just then they looked a bit alarming.

'Saw who?'

'The White and the Black.' From the look on her she expected him to be impressed.

He shrugged. 'Never heard of 'em.'

'A pair of Sveär butchers. And two faces I couldn't have conjured in my worst nightmare.' Her hand rose absently to the white streak in her hair. 'Anyhow, my luck was better than plenty other folks so I ain't complaining.'

They happened to be passing a crew of karls sprawled in various states of indolence over a pair of benches and the back of the hay-cart. A couple were crouched over a tafl board, intent on their game. Another pair were chatting over a skin of ale. The fifth man was lazing on the hay. It was him who sprang to life.

'Hey, porky! Hold up there!'

His friends looked up. The man was a sinewy bastard with malice in his eye and doubtless not a little ale in his belly. Kai suddenly had a bad feeling. He would have kept walking but the man leaped off the cart with surprising agility and blocked their path.

'I'm talking to you, butterbelly.'

Einar had halted and was staring the man down.

'Nice piece you're carrying,' said the karl, gesturing at Einar's hilt. 'Mind if I take a look?'

'Let him be, Geir,' said one of the tafl-players in a bored voice, as though this scene had been played out a hundred times before.

'Nah. I don't think so.' The man called Geir chuckled and reached for Einar's hilt. But Einar was quicker, gripping his blade and shoving him. Geir stumbled backwards.

'Hohoooaa!' crowed one of the drinkers. 'You shouldn't have done that, friend!'

In an eye-blink Geir was back in their faces. 'No one fucking pushes me.'

'Not quite true that,' Kai chuckled nervously. 'Still, no harm done, eh? We'll be on our way.'

'Shut your mouth, worm. I'm talking to this fat fuck.'

'Sadly this particular fat fuck can't say a word.'

'What's wrong with him?'

'Mute from a lad. It's a tragic tale.'

Einar was standing like a stone pillar, his face a few inches from the karl's. Geir looked him up and down, licking his teeth. 'Is he simple or something?'

'Hmmm,' mused Kai. Einar shot him a thunderous look. 'I mean, no. *No!* Far from it!'

'Bet he's a coward. Soft as he is flabby. He looks like a coward.' Geir sucked on his nostrils. 'Smells like a coward.' He leaned in closer. 'Is that what you are? A piss-breech yellow-livered coward?'

'Oh, no,' cried Kai, 'brave as Baldur, this one. Now we'll just leave you to your ale, shall we?' He tried to pull Einar away but the fat man wasn't budging.

'Prove it,' Geir said.

The ale-drinker clapped his hands with glee. Einar shrugged and glanced at Kai, who supposed the flick of his eyebrow was meant to be reassuring.

Geir beckoned him forward from his horse. 'We have a little test we do round here. We use it to see whether a man's got the backbone to stand in the 'wall.'

Einar reached for his hilt.

'Nah.' Geir shook his head. 'You don't need to do a thing. Just stand there.'

'Hang on, cousin,' said the tafl-player languidly, getting to his feet. 'You have to show him how it's done first. Fair's fair.'

'As you like, Grim. Who's going to go then? You?'

'Sure.'

Geir went and pulled out his sword from under the pile of hay. Grim stood. The blade was drawn. The cousins stood facing each other.

'This is what happens when men have too much time on their hands,' Gerutha muttered.

Geir lifted his sword, straight-armed, to eye level. Grim came closer, so close the point was hovering hardly the length of a fingernail from the bridge of his nose.

'Ready?'

'Ready.'

Kai barely had time to blink before Geir had wheeled the blade and slashed it with full force at his cousin's head. The point shot past Grim's face faster than a whip-crack, passing a hair's breadth from his eye. But he didn't flinch. Didn't move a muscle.

Kai released his breath. The five karls fell about laughing.

'Your turn, butterbelly,' Geir growled.

The other tafl-player stood up to pull Einar into position, but the fat man shook his head and stepped forward. This was all a bit alarming to Kai's mind. He was pretty sure this wasn't what Erlan had meant when he had told them to keep a low profile.

A few other karls had gathered now, taking bets on whether the fat man would flinch. Meanwhile Einar took his position. Geir held out his sword again, measuring the distance so the tip was barely a whisker from his eye. Kai thought he noticed something – Geir's arm wasn't quite as extended as the first time. But before he could say anything, Geir drew it back and grinned. 'All set?'

Einar nodded.

Geir gave a chuckle and his blade whirled. Kai watched the point snap past. Einar stood still as death. At once, there were groans and cheers as bets were won and lost. Geir was looking mighty peeved – as if something had gone wrong.

'Look – he's bleeding!' someone yelled suddenly.

It was true. Einar still hadn't moved but a red seam of blood appeared across one eyebrow.

'By the hanged! He's cut and didn't move a bloody muscle!' cried the ale-drinker. Einar, of course, said nothing, only touched his brow and examined his fingers. They were wet with blood. He looked up, grinned, then flicked his thumbnail. The others watched in stunned silence as a single drop of blood arced high through the air and landed square between Geir's eyes.

The other karls broke into gales of laughter. Geir slowly wiped the spot, leaving a red smear across the bridge of his nose. 'Why, you cheeky son of a whore,' he snarled, raising his sword.

But Grim stepped in and held him. 'Think the game's over, don't you, cousin?'

Einar turned back to his horse as the rest of them crowded round Geir, laughing and joking and joshing him till they had bundled him back into his hay-cart.

Gerutha shook her head. 'I can see you two are going to fit right in.'

She led them to the Back Barn, a small building stood behind the main hall that was gloomier than a barrow-grave and smelled of dung. A row of animal stalls ran along one side and above them a bower strewn with old hay.

'You can sleep up there,' said Gerutha, leaving Kai to wonder how the Hel they were supposed to discover Lord Ringast's or indeed his father's plans if they were lodged with the farmhands. Still, he resolved to stay hopeful. Something would turn up. It usually did.

However, once Gerutha had showed him where he was to work for the next two days, his confidence dwindled some.

Snorri the smith looked like a bird, squawked like a bird, walked like a bird and, Kai was fairly sure, didn't have much more brain than a bird rattling inside his skull. The stream of meaningless blather out of his mouth never seemed to stop. Kai began to think the smith was suffering from some kind of brain-rot, or madness even.

When Kai managed to get a word in and asked who all the warriors were and what was their business, Snorri replied: 'If a man comes and says, "Make me a sword," I make him a sword. If he asks for a knife, I make him a knife. He might use it to skin a weasel or slit his brother's throat. It ain't my business. I just make 'em strong and sharp. Now you get on with polishing that axe till you can see your face in it and never mind what it's for.'

Thereby demonstrating an unforgivable lack of curiosity, at least in Kai's opinion.

Worse, Snorri worked him damned hard. By mid-afternoon, his arms ached with hours of scrubbing newly tempered blades till they shone like silver.

Still, he had it better than Einar. Gerutha had taken him to the tannery where, unable to offer any protest, he had been given the very worst tasks: plunging hides into a barrel of urine to loosen the hair, so he could scrape them clean and then bate them – a hideous process involving squelching around in a vat of liquid dog-dung, kneading the hides with his feet till they were good and supple. Needless to say, the fat man's mood hadn't improved much.

A grey afternoon darkened towards a gloomy dusk. Kai's belly was grumbling and he was cursing himself for not choosing a better cover story – one involving more drinking with house-karls and less muscle-wringing labour – when there was a commotion at the gate.

Men were shouting. There was a sound of hoofbeats and suddenly a troop of riders burst into the yard.

More cheers, more shouts. Folks were leaving their work, curious to know what was afoot. The brewer's boy ran past Snorri's forge, face beaming with excitement.

'Hey, kid! What's all the racket?'

'They've caught 'emselves a Sveär!' he cried.

He ran on. Kai followed him, deaf to Snorri's bleating protests. People were streaming towards the riders who'd halted in front of the main hall. They were a grim-looking crew – sweat-stained and covered in dust. Looked like they'd been in a fight too, judging from a few cut faces.

But the hall-folk's attention was focused mainly on the man slung across the rump of a chestnut horse. He was trussed up like a sheep for market, stripped to his waist with his hands bound at his back. But that didn't stop him lifting his head to look about.

Kai shoved and slithered his way through the crowd till he was quite close and could see the man's face. He was a fierce-looking bastard – a lot fiercer than Kai would have looked in the same predicament. His hair was black as pitch and his eyes sunken, and he'd taken a beating or two. But he wasn't broken yet.

'Fetch Lord Ringast,' yelled one of the riders.

'We've brought him a little gift,' cackled another. 'Eh, Sveär pig?' He rode alongside and gave the man a kick. The prisoner didn't make a sound. The bolder ones in the crowd scuttled forward, spat at him, then retreated. But nothing seemed to dim the scorn in the man's eyes.

Another rider dismounted and drew a knife. Moments later the rope was cut and the prisoner was sprawling on the ground. He tried to get up, but the rider pulled the rope binding his neck, hands and feet, and he fell back down.

'Stay in the dirt where you belong, dog!'

'Make way! Make way!' cried a new voice. The crowd parted to reveal three men striding down from the hall.

From their dress, Kai marked them highborn – embroidered shirts, silver cuffs, studded belts. From the bowing and scraping of the crowd, he figured them lords even. They were strikingly different in appearance, though. The one nearest was slim and surely the youngest – russet-haired with barely a whisker, almost girlishly handsome. He hung back from the other two – one a bear of a man, the other an eagle. At least, that was Kai's impression.

'Silence!' cried the eagle. The insults and curses ceased at once. Kai judged this must be Ringast, the Lord of Dannerborg and the Wartooth's heir. His blood prickled with excitement. 'Put him there.' Two of the riders hefted the prisoner onto his knees.

Ringast circled around him. 'Who is he?'

'The Black, my lord,' answered a rider, with evident pride. A gasp rose from the crowd, followed quickly by a cheer. The rider's soiled face fairly glowed.

'Silence!' Ringast shouted again, irritated by the interruption. 'Where did you find him?'

'We surprised his shieldband in the woods west of Ravenstorp.'

'Aye,' added another, 'before the whoresons torched the place!'

Ringast grunted. 'Well done. If he is the Black, he has burned enough.'

'What do you mean, *if* he's the Black, brother?' roared the bear. 'Who else could he be?'

'Peace, Thrand.' Ringast raised a hand – apparently enough to check his brother's tongue and the murmurs of the crowd. 'You're all of you in such a hurry to tear him apart. But every man deserves justice.'

'Justice for this one is a knife in his throat,' growled Thrand.

'We'll see.' Ringast turned to the rider standing over the prisoner. 'Where's the other?'

The man exchanged glances with his companions. 'The White broke clear with a few of his men. Last we saw they were heading north into the Kolmark.'

The Black sniggered. It was an ugly laugh. Ugly and irritating. Something about it jogged Kai's memory. But before he could fix on it, Thrand had put a boot in the man's chest. The Black went sprawling in the mud. 'We should just kill him now. Those bastard twins have butchered half the folk along the Kolmark. He deserves the same fate he dealt them.'

At the mention of twins, Kai suddenly recognized who this was. *The Black and the White.* Two brothers, the twin sons of Huldir, the Earl of Nairka – as malicious a pair as any living north of the Kolmark, although they didn't often show their faces at Uppsala. This one's name was Gettir.

Ringast shoved Thrand back. 'If we do this, we do it according to our father's law.'

'Fenrir take the law!' snapped his brother. 'This man needs killing and that's an end to it.'

'No. We have someone who has seen what the Black has

done. If indeed this is him. Where's the witness?' Ringast cried abruptly. 'The woman Gerutha – where is she?'

At Gerutha's name, Kai's ears pricked up. He scanned the faces for the servant with the white streak of hair. Then he saw her being half-dragged almost through the eager crowd. Her face was composed but he could see she was steeling herself, too.

'My lord,' she said huskily.

'Is this one of them?'

She looked at the prisoner. Gettir looked back. A smile crept over his face, almost as if he were recognizing an old friend. A kind of shudder passed through her. Suddenly the prisoner jerked his head at her and she fell back a step. He laughed – that irritating snigger again.

'That's him. That's the Black,' she said. A cacophony of jeers swallowed up her last words, but Ringast waved the crowd to silence. His voice was calm. 'What did he do?'

'It was just as I told you, my lord.'

'Tell it again so all may hear.'

And so she did, in all its gruesome horror, her description punctuated with gasps from her audience. Of course, they'd heard it all before, doubtless a dozen times or more. But Kai had to admit, it was a tale to put a man off his supper. When she was finished, Ringast thanked her and let her escape into the crowd.

'Well, Sveär. What have you to say for yourself?'

At first the Black said nothing, just leered up at the Danish prince with that half-crazed grin. Then he started sniggering, on and on, till his whole body shook.

Ringast had no patience for this. He seized him by his hair.

'Answer, Sveär. Why did you this crime and many others? *Why?*'

The Black stopped laughing and smiled. 'Because it's – *so* – *much – fun.*' Then he spat in Ringast's face. There was a gasp from the crowd and Thrand stepped forward so enraged Kai thought he might tear off the Black's head there and then. But Ringast blocked him, calmly wiping the phlegm from his beard.

'Then hear my judgement.' Ringast raised his voice. 'Wound for wound. Death for death.'

The Black's smile slanted into a cold sneer. 'My brother will be revenged on you. On all you southern pigs!'

Ringast peered down at him, unimpressed. 'If you are the Black I know your name. Gettir Huldirsson. Your father made quite a name for himself in the Eastern wars.' His jaw tightened. 'I think it's time we sent him the same message you've been sending us. Perhaps then your brother will stop.'

'You started this war, Dane. But we will finish it.'

'I think not.' Ringast turned to the crowd. 'Wound for wound. Death for death!' The crowd fairly bellowed with delight. 'Take him.'

The men flanking Gettir hauled him to his feet and dragged him down the slope towards two weathered stakes. Kai gave a rueful snort when he saw them. He was only too well acquainted with flogging posts. But he suspected Gettir was in for something far worse than a few lashes.

'Mark well the fate of any Sveär who crosses us!' cried Ringast.

Once his mind was made up, it seemed to Kai, this Danish prince was as bloodhungry as the next man.

The crowd cheered. Kai felt their bloodlust swirling round him, heard house-karls yelling drunken curses and death to all Sveärs. Instinctively he looked for Einar but couldn't see him. Savagery was stalking among the crowd and he wasn't the only one feeling it. Thrand's voice boomed above the clamour. 'See the dogs that dwell beyond the Kolmark! There are thousands more like this one! We should ride now and bring death to them all! Death and slaughter!'

'Patience, brother!' rebuked Ringast. 'We need more men. But the time is near.'

'Cowards are patient!'

'And fools are impetuous. Enough of this, I say.' Ringast turned to the flogging posts. His men already had Gettir stripped, spread and bound. 'Now – begin.'

The crowd howled as the riders began meting out their lord's hard justice.

Kai watched, his mouth a long grimace. But he was suddenly distracted by a smell that made him gag. He turned and there were Einar's ruddy features at his shoulder, one eyebrow a line of dried blood. Kai looked down. Einar's feet were bare and caked with brown smears.

'Sorry to be the one to tell you this, my fat friend. But you stink.'

Einar paid him no heed. Instead Kai saw on his face an expression he'd not marked there before. *Fear.*

Kai clapped his shoulder. 'I reckon I've seen enough for one day. Ain't we got work to do?'

Not waiting for an answer, he turned Einar around and led him back through the crowd towards the forge. Einar followed, meek as a lamb. But Kai couldn't resist one last look back. Through the welter of angry faces, he glimpsed the Black hanging there, body shuddering, features hard as granite.

And amid all those blood-chilling cries, he uttered not a sound.

CHAPTER FOURTEEN

Kill enough people and sooner or later the most powerful lord in the land is going to learn of it.

Erlan was in attendance when tidings of the great scathe wrought by Huldir's sons reached the ear of Sviggar. It arrived in the mouth of a young cowherd who lived in the south. The boy's appreciation of the boundary between Sveäland and Gotarland was vague at best or, more likely, a matter of total indifference to him. Sviggar's decree that none should cross the boundary in either direction had not reached him and his herd. If it had, he would likely have turned a deaf ear. At that time of year the best grass was south of the Kolmark, so south he went. And there, he gathered from the few encounters he had that all was not well in those borderlands. Death, destruction, rape and pillage more brutal than any had ever known. And all of it the work of cursed Sveärs. (The cowherd was sharp enough to keep his mouth shut when the talk took this turn.) He soon began to piece together the picture, and smart lad that he was, he saw it was worth the journey to bring word back to the lord of his land, especially if it meant a pouch full of silver for him, as he hoped. Thus, the news came to the king's halls.

This is what he told.

A band of Sveär warriors, merciless killers, led by two brothers. Twins. One dark as the night, the other white as a new snowfall. Sviggar needed to hear no more. He paled with anger.

Earl Huldir was summoned at once, and with him his sons. Only one accompanied him, however. The ghost-man, as Kai called him. In truth, he hadn't shown his face around Uppsala much in the time Erlan had been there. He didn't speak much either, and what he did say was uttered in a low hiss, almost unintelligible unless he was looking you straight in the eye with that limpid stare of his.

He was peering at Sviggar now with the same smile bowing his mouth as had his brother's, despite the fact that Sviggar was launching gouts of invective in his direction. But it all ran off Gellir the White like water off a moorhen's back.

His father took it rather worse. Every man's pride has a limit, and by Erlan's reckoning, Sviggar was running Huldir pretty close to his.

'I told you, my lord – it's no slight against you that Gettir is not here before you now. We don't know where he is.' Huldir nodded at his son. 'Gellir will tell you. They lost contact in the forest. After that, he's heard nothing.'

'Then we can assume he's dead.' Erlan thought it might have been prudent of Sviggar not to look quite so happy about it. 'He's a damned renegade! And a fool! You both are. None of this would have happened if you had done as I ordered. Do you have anything to say for yourself?'

He left a space of silence for Gellir to fill. It stretched and stretched. Eventually Gellir's long tongue emerged, but only to wet his lips and retreat again. The fact was he didn't need to say anything. He was practically glowing with insolence.

'You're a disgrace,' the king muttered. 'You and your brother. There was to be no provocation of the Wartooth's hand, no cause for war given—'

'The Wartooth makes his own cause,' Huldir growled.

'Hold your tongue, damn you!' Sviggar pointed a long, brittle finger at the earl. For the moment Huldir backed down. 'There was to be no cause of war given,' Sviggar repeated. 'Instead you have lent justice to their cause and doubtless put a surfeit of hate in their hearts.'

'No more hate than burns in my heart already.'

'I told you to be—'

'I will not be silent! I cannot be! Not when I hear these words you speak. They're the words of a coward. A craven! Since when did the king of Sveäland become lickspittle to that pile of excrement steaming on the throne of Leithra?'

'You forget yourself, my old friend,' hissed Sviggar.

'No, it is *you* who forget yourself, my lord. You! The man I swore fealty to thirty years ago would never speak like this. That man would never cringe in his hall like some whipped cur in his kennel. Why would you dishonour me and my kin now?' Huldir's face was thunder. 'It's you who owes the explanation, not my sons. You! For trying to appease that murderous boar. He and all his kind deserve death. My sons have delivered no more than that.'

Huldir's meaty fists were bunched on the table, the scar that ran across his grizzled face pulsed purple, his blank eye fixed in challenge upon his king.

Sviggar rose and nodded. 'You've had your say. Now you hear me. Your sons are rabid dogs. Nothing more. Whatever fate has befallen the other, this unruly boy and you are banished from these halls forthwith. Banished – you hear! Go back to Nairka and think about that oath you swore. Think about those thirty years of loyalty. It's because of them that I let you leave here with your tongue. Go! And wait there for my instruction.'

Huldir's jaw was grinding like a bondsman's millstone. Erlan wondered whether a fresh outburst might erupt from his bush of a beard. Instead his reply was soft, almost sorrowful. 'Your father would be ashamed to see this day.'

'Get out.'

For a moment, Huldir seemed to remember his place. He drew himself up to his considerable height and bowed his head respectfully, as if there wasn't a more devoted man in the kingdom. Then he signalled to his son and they marched out of the chamber.

Erlan watched as they swept past him. Huldir's eyes were fixed ahead. Gellir, however, glanced at him as he passed. His pale eyebrow flickered, his mouth curled in a sneer.

Doubtless Sviggar had the right of it, as far as it went. But by Erlan's reckoning he had just made an enemy he might come to regret.

'That boy of yours needs to come back with some answers,' Sviggar said to him when they had gone.

'He will.'

'*If* he comes back.'

Erlan said nothing, refusing to entertain that notion.

'You see it, though, don't you?' Sviggar waved his hand after the banished earl. 'I'm surrounded by incompetents and traitors.

143

Men I used to trust with my life, I can't even rely on to follow a simple command.' His craggy frown softened and he smiled at Erlan. 'I can trust you, though, can't I?'

'Of course, my lord.'

'Yes. You must stay close, Aurvandil,' he muttered, his eyes glazing. 'I need you close to me.'

And suddenly he seemed very old and frail.

CHAPTER FIFTEEN

Lilla's head throbbed like a dragon's heart.

She had gone deeper this time and for that there was always a toll to pay.

Seeking answers, she had gone to the ancient ash tree at the heart of the Kingswood, impatient to know what would be. To know what truly lay in Erlan's mind. But when she sank back into the smoke-wreathed embrace of Urtha's Weed and tried to conjure his face, he was elusive, unreadable. And now, having returned to her chamber, the pounding in her skull only made the wheel of thoughts in her head so much the worse.

She called in a servant and summoned water. The thrall-boy soon returned with a brimming basin. She plunged her face into it, enjoying its cold caress against her throbbing temples.

She looked into the bronze mirror and sighed. The smoke of Urtha's Weed still tasted dry in her throat. Her mind wheeled again and she saw his face, remembered that look of longing in his eyes. But somehow, instead of the thrill of that moment, she felt embarrassed. The way it had ended had confused her. His stuttering apologies. What did it mean?

The boy was still standing by the door, shuffling from foot to foot.

'Was there something else?'

The queen wished to see her, though about what, the boy had no answer. Only that she would find her bathing in the river.

She sent him away, fussed a little with her hair in the mirror, but soon gave that up for a bad job. Her tresses were an unruly muddle. Much like the inside of her head, she thought ruefully. Instead she went to find her stepmother.

Saldas had a favourite spot in a crook of the river where the waters of the Fyris ran a little slower and the branches of a weeping willow protected her modesty from the gaze of any hall-folk who happened onto the flood meadows. In any case, she was easy to find. Bara, her handmaiden, was standing on the bank holding her robe, gazing up at the clouds, her hair a splash of rust-red in all that green. Nearby Svein and Katla were foraging along the riverbank like a pair of terriers. When they saw her coming, they squealed with delight and ran to her.

'We're hunting grasshoppers,' cried Svein.

'How very brave of you!' Lilla stroked each face in turn. 'Can you catch one for me?'

'What colour would you like?' asked Katla earnestly.

'They're all green, stupid. Come on!' Svein raced off along the rushes, leaving his little sister looking deflated. Lilla caught her hand and crouched down, level with her face. 'Find me a blue one,' she winked. Katla beamed and trotted off after her brother.

'There you are,' Saldas called up when Lilla appeared by the river's edge. 'I was beginning to think you wouldn't come.'

'I went for a walk,' Lilla lied. She never spoke of what she did in the Kingswood to her stepmother. And if Saldas knew, she never mentioned it.

'Why don't you come in?' Saldas swirled her arms.

'It looks cold.'

'Of course it's cold. That's the point.' Cold and clear. Lilla could see beneath the surface the wavering image of Saldas's body, pale against the dark green of the Fyris.

'I just washed.'

'Your loss.' Saldas sighed, a cloud of dark hair eddying about her shoulders. She ducked underwater and swam a couple of strokes towards the bank. Re-surfacing, she slicked back her hair, then rose out of the water. She was naked. The cold water had stretched her skin somehow, seeming to exaggerate the curves of her body – her rounded hips, the smooth orbs of her breasts. Her limbs were lithe and strong and, despite bearing two children, she had the figure of a much younger woman. Lilla was slightly in awe of her beauty and she found herself thinking, not for the first time, that her father must enjoy his young wife's body. Not that she knew much about love-play herself. But looking at Saldas anyone could see that her father must be the envy of all the menfolk thereabouts. It was a strange thought. That this woman – who would have no business being in her family if it weren't for her mother's death – was now much closer to her father than Lilla ever would be. And looking at all that glistening flesh, she knew she could never offer him what Saldas could.

'Help me out.' Saldas reached for Lilla to assist her up the bank. Bara was waiting to wrap her mistress in an expansive blue cloak.

'What did you want to see me about, Lady Saldas?'

'Mother,' Saldas corrected her.

'Sorry... Mother.' *Bitch,* Lilla thought, then felt guilty.

'Bara – would you mind? The children...' Saldas wafted a hand in the direction of the little ones, who were playing upriver. 'They can stay a little longer, then bring them back to the hall.' She turned back to Lilla. 'Walk with me.'

Without waiting for her assent, Saldas set off across the meadow, her feet padding soundlessly through the tufts of grass. Lilla hitched her skirts and ran to catch up.

'I've been thinking about something.' Saldas turned to look at Lilla directly. 'Someone, in fact.'

'Who?'

'Erlan, of course.' Lilla said nothing. 'I've been thinking about your reaction the other morning. About those other times I've seen you together. Even just yesterday—'

'It hasn't been so often, has it?'

'It's fine, my sweetling. There's no need to deny it.' Saldas reached out and squeezed Lilla's hand. 'I merely want what's best for you. You know that.'

Did she? She hadn't ever noticed Saldas wanting anything much for anyone but herself.

'Anyway, it's been turning over in my mind,' she continued. 'I feel it's my place to warn you about letting your feelings run away with you.'

'My feelings?'

'I know you try to conceal the fact but you must remember

I see more than other people.' She smiled, touching Lilla's arm. 'You like him. Do you deny it?'

The pulse in Lilla's temple seemed to beat a notch faster. Gods, but her head ached. And now she felt like a rabbit scurrying for cover under the shadow of a hawk. But it was too late. The warmth in her cheeks had already betrayed her. 'I suppose. I like him well enough.'

'Is it a passion?'

'A passion – gods, no! It's— just a passing thing. Silly, really.' Another lie?

Saldas gave a faint snort. 'Of course, I remember how it could be at your age. So easy for the heart to get carried away. And if you're not careful the body with it.'

Lilla blushed, embarrassed to speak of such things with her stepmother.

Saldas levelled her green eyes. 'Erlan is an attractive young man, I suppose, in his way. But he's an outsider. He's not one of us, and certainly not for you.' She scoffed. 'A man like that – I mean! Come day's end, what is he but a killer? In any case, a man of his unvarnished nature would never be interested in someone like you.'

'What do you mean?' asked Lilla, a little too sharply.

'Well, I—' Saldas's mouth curled, half-amused. 'I don't wish to be indelicate. But it would take a woman of altogether more experience than you to satisfy a man like Erlan. No. You're destined for a different sort of man, one with a tender heart to suit your nature.'

What she means is someone insipid and weak, thought Lilla, her temper rising. 'Maybe there's more to Erlan than you know.'

'That's beside the point. And anyway, I don't think so,' Saldas added. 'When a man kills as much as he has, his heart becomes hard. Incapable of love. He wants a woman only to satisfy his baser needs.'

Perhaps Saldas was right. Perhaps his 'baser needs' were all she had seen in his eyes.

'Oh, there's no need to look so disappointed, my dear. I'm simply trying to counsel you. Besides,' she leaned a little closer, 'he hasn't given you any reason to think that he likes you in the same way, has he?'

Lilla hesitated, remembering the kiss, the flick of his tongue, sweet and alive in her mouth, how he had seemed to want to crush her against him. 'No,' she lied. 'He hasn't.'

Saldas observed her closely. Lilla wanted to look away. Wanted to flee, in fact, but instead she forced herself to hold the queen's gaze. The lines either side of Saldas's mouth tightened a fraction, but then her features softened, blooming into a radiant smile. 'There, you see.' She nodded, satisfied her point was proven. 'You mustn't worry, my dear. These girlish fancies soon fade. And you can help them on their way by keeping your eyes set on your destiny. Your father reminds you of it often.'

Saldas was certainly right about that. *You are the daughter of a king. One day you will be the wife of a king and in time the mother of kings.* How many times had she heard that? It had become a kind of refrain, a dirge chanted in the background of her life. She couldn't deny it was a noble destiny, just that somehow it didn't fit. 'I know what my father wants for me.'

'Of course you do. But for every fate, there is a cost. You are not free, as other women are, to give your heart full sail and follow after any man who takes your fancy. Your virtue is a precious thing. You must guard it wisely. Because it will be required of you one day. And you must still have it to give when your father chooses you a husband.'

'I know what's required of me.' She certainly didn't need Saldas reminding her of that.

'Good. Then remember, the daughter of a king may lose her honour only once. Too soon and I'm afraid she is quite lost.'

When Lilla didn't answer, Saldas laid a hand against her cheek. 'Gods, don't look so troubled, girl! You know I warn you only to protect you.'

'I know. It's just that—' That throbbing in her head again.

'I understand.' Saldas's voice softened. 'Your heart suffers.'

Lilla palmed her brow, feeling a little dizzy.

'It will pass. I promise you.'

'If you say so.' Lilla forced herself to smile.

'That's better.' Saldas suddenly sighed. 'Of course, it would be a terrible thing for your father to learn of this. I fear he would not be so understanding. Likely he would take it as a most vile betrayal on the part of Erlan. And then, alas, the stranger's days as your father's favourite would be few indeed.'

'You won't tell him, will you?'

'Sweet Lilla. Do you really think I would?' She laughed gently. 'After all, if I could not keep the confidence of my daughter, what kind of a mother would I be?'

The queen was still smiling. But somehow Lilla found cold comfort in her words. They had crossed the meadows and almost reached the first of the halls. Just ahead, on the edge of the flood-meadow, a man was waiting, gazing high into the morning sky.

'Ah! There's Svenning now. That means Freki must be near. What perfect timing the man has!' Saldas bade him good morning. He returned her greeting. He was wearing a huge leather gauntlet on his hand.

'Where is he?' Saldas called, already scanning the sky.

'Out yonder,' nodded Svenning, pointing east.

Lilla looked too, though without her stepmother's enthusiasm. She didn't particularly like Svenning. She liked his charge even less.

'I see him!' exclaimed Saldas. Lilla shielded her eyes. High above, she could make out a shadow in the sky, banking and turning on the breeze. *Himinns Freki*: the wolf of the skies. That was the name Saldas had given him.

'Call him back.'

Svenning reached into a pouch at his belt and fished out a strip of meat, bloody and raw. Then he whistled, loud and long. A sharp screech sounded in reply and the shadow swooped down.

Within seconds the eagle had landed on his arm in a squall of flapping wings, darting its head at the piece of meat in his glove. Up close, it was enormous, much larger than any bird of prey native to her father's kingdom. While Freki ate, Saldas stroked a fingertip down the length of its spine, over and over. There was something disturbing about the way she touched the creature, so tenderly, with a kind of intimacy that Lilla had never seen pass between her father and his queen.

The eagle had been his wedding gift to her four years earlier. A plaything, although to Lilla's mind, there was nothing playful about those flaming orange eyes with their jet-black pupils. She saw in them something pitiless, something untameable.

The merchant who had sold Freki as an egret to her father said he came from thousands of leagues away, from a burning hot wilderness far beyond the Great Rivers and the Black Sea. Lilla found it difficult to imagine, but looking at Freki's stone-hard gaze, she thought it must be a cruel place.

When the eagle was done eating, his head came up. Svenning lifted his arm and in an instant Freki was gone again, climbing higher and higher on his dark wings, their tips curling in the rush of air.

'Magnificent, don't you think?'

'Undoubtedly,' said Lilla, then added, 'I should go... Mother.' She'd say anything to get away now. Even that.

'As you wish.' But instead of bidding her farewell, Saldas suddenly took her elbow and steered her clear of Svenning's hearing. 'Stay away from him. It's for the best. And if you suspect he has any designs on you, you must tell me at once. Do you understand?'

Lilla nodded.

'At once.' She touched her thumb under Lilla's chin and tilted her face. 'So beautiful,' she murmured. 'You must trust me. I will protect your heart as if it were my own. Now come, kiss me before you go.'

But despite the warmth of her stepmother's smile, her lips were cold as stone.

CHAPTER SIXTEEN

The second day Kai awoke frustrated. That there was a boatload of bad feeling towards the Sveärs here was beyond doubt, but that would hardly be news to Sviggar, and aside from the Black's grisly dispatch, so far they had precious little detail to offer the Old Goat.

In hushed whispers, Einar had cursed their decision to pass him off as mute. 'How in the name of Baldur's bollocks can I find anything out if I can't speak?' After a day of listening, he'd heard not much more than the squelch of shit between his toes.

Kai reminded him that if his Sveär accent gave him away, the Dannerborg folk would make short shrift of his own bollocks. Einar didn't look any happier. But he had a point. They needed something solid and it was down to Kai to find it out.

After several hours at Snorri's forge, Kai was no more hopeful. A handful of warriors had come and gone – some to collect weapons, some to drop them off – but none took the bait when he tried to engage them in talk. Only one had lingered at all. At first he'd thought him an odd-looking lad – smooth-faced, splayed hips, an enormously fat chest – until he realized the lad was a lass, albeit a terrifyingly large one.

She called herself Visma and hailed from Wendland, she said in an accent blunt as a cudgel, handing over a double-handed sword Kai could barely lift.

'You're a long way from home.'

'Word has spread far from Leithra that Harald is gathering warriors. Both there and here. I came with my husband, Duk. We are here to fight. Together.'

'Sounds charming,' Kai said, as he put the massive sword to the grindstone.

'Something amuses you?'

'Me? Not a thing! I'm sure there's nothing finer than knocking off a few heads with your lord and love. I expect he likes a good supper when you get home.'

'You are mocking me.'

'Gods forbid it! I'm sure you make a terrifying pair.'

For some reason the woman laughed like a tickled troll. 'You are a funny fellow!'

'If you say so,' he said, somewhat disconcerted by the way she was eyeing him. 'How long have you been here?'

'Three weeks only. Others have been here months.'

Kai grunted and went on grinding.

'If it were my decision, we wouldn't wait at all. But Danes are cautious. Ringast Haraldarsson, most cautious of all.'

'Didn't seem too cautious yesterday.'

'Well... that man was a Sveär murderer. He deserved it.' Seemed that was explanation enough for her.

'So what's he waiting for?'

'More spears. Always more. And always more come.'

Her sword was ready. Kai handed it over, resolving to stay well clear of its wickedly sharp edges.

'How many does he want, by the way?'

'You ask a lot of questions, little man,' she said, slipping the blade back into its sheath.

'You seem to have a lot of answers.'

She looked at him, curious. 'Well, if you want more, come find me later. We'll drink. We'll talk.' She patted his cheek. Her palm was rough as splintered wood.

'Askar!' someone yelled.

'I think you're wanted,' Visma nodded as she left with her sword. Kai suddenly remembered the name he had given as his own – his father's, in fact – and turned to see Gerutha hailing him from across the yard.

'Sletti says you're needed at the hall. Another party arrived today and we're short of hands.'

'You want me to serve supper?' They must be damned stretched if they needed him to play hall-maid.

'Just do what you're told like the rest of us.'

After a moment's reflection, a bit of woman's work wasn't a bad prospect if it meant being spared Snorri's incessant drivel and more aching arms. But more importantly it would get him inside that hall.

'Well, old man, a woman's wish must be obeyed.' And with that, he pulled off his apron and flung it at the bony old bird.

Kai had known some unruly feasting but for sheer, unfettered gluttony, he'd seen nothing like the benches of Dannerborg. He became quite worn out carrying cauldrons and kettles and platters piled high with bread and boiled beef and hard cheeses and the gods knew what else. It all sailed down the gullets of this ravenous mob.

The loudest and greediest of them all was Prince Thrand, the middle-born of the Wartooth's sons. When he wasn't filling his face, his booming laugh reverberated off the walls. Everything, apparently, amused him, although the compliment wasn't returned. All evening Kai overheard ale-wenches complaining of his groping hands and lewd suggestions. But no one seemed more irritated by him than his older brother.

As for him, Lord Ringast was a thinker. That was obvious. Not brooding exactly, but serious. He wasn't old – thirty winters maybe – with the crook-nose that had minded Kai of an eagle the day before. He knuckled the crook repeatedly as he listened to the man next to him, a grizzled warrior with a scar running from the corner of his mouth, who looked as though if you tapped him, he'd ring like iron.

Kai was loitering in the shadows with an empty platter, hoping to hear some juicy morsel when Thrand lurched to his feet. 'To the death of that black twin!' He raised his cup. 'On your feet, brothers! Drink, damn you!'

Rorik, the third and youngest brother, obliged but Ringast left his cup untouched. 'Do you never tire of making a fool of yourself?'

'Hel piss on you then!' Thrand was swaying. 'What about you, Ubbi? Show us how a Frieslander can drink!'

'If it'll shut you up, I'll match you,' the old warrior growled. Like Visma, he had a thick southern accent.

'Good man! And you, Rorik!'

The fair-faced brother got to his feet.

'There's a lad!'

All three emptied their cups.

'Snaring the Black was a sign, brother,' slurred Thrand, wiping his beard. 'We've waited long enough. The road through the Kolmark lies open. It's time to make Sveäland burn.'

'Patience was never your strength, was it?'

'What fucking use is patience after such provocation?'

'The White and the Black are not our main concern. They're dogs that want destroying, but Father's plan is bigger.'

'How much bigger does he want? We have hundreds already. Thousands, with the spears at Leithra.'

'The time isn't yet ripe.'

'When the Hel will it be?'

'What are you doing here?' said a thin voice at Kai's elbow. He looked to see who it belonged to. Sletti the steward was glaring at him, waiting for an answer. 'Get your lazy carcass back to the kitchens.'

'Charming way to speak to a guest.'

'Now!'

Kai went, cursing his luck, wondering what talk he was missing. Halfway down the corridor, he passed an ale-maid clutching a frothy pitcher on her way in. 'Slow up there, sister. Fancy a trade?'

'You, serve ale? Are you mad?'

'Some reckon so,' he grinned. 'Now take this, my lovely, and I'll make sure everyone has a full cup.' Before she could protest, he'd swapped his platter for her pitcher and gone back into the hall.

When he re-entered, Thrand was gnawing moodily on a mutton joint. Kai guessed the argument between the brothers was old ground. Meanwhile, Ringast was deep in conversation with the Frieslander, Ubbi. From the look of him, the old battle-axe knew the sharp end of a spear all right, but from the respect Ringast gave him, he was also someone of consequence. Kai went to the end of the table and began refilling cups, slowly as he dared without drawing attention.

'I saw more riders arrive today,' he heard Ubbi say.

'Ruslanders.'

'Seems your word carries far.'

Ringast swigged his ale. 'Ruslanders love a fight.'

'How many?'

'Another ten.'

'Any good?'

'I'd take five, maybe six of them. The rest are green. But we need the numbers.'

'Any word from your father?'

'Aye. We had a rider two days ago.' He knuckled the crook of his nose.

'Well?'

'It wasn't what I wanted to hear. Only that he'd received my message about the raids along the Kolmark. That we are to wait as before. He wants more men. He thinks Starkad the Sea-King will follow him.'

'Starkad?' The name evidently impressed Ubbi. 'With him and his spears, victory must be certain.'

Ringast growled doubtfully. 'We'll see. Anyhow, my father has sent word even to the Irish tribes now. Oh – and he had another dream.'

'Oh, yes?'

Ringast gave a rueful snort. 'When my father dreams, Hel rubs her hands.'

'What was it this time?'

'A great battle. *The* greatest battle, he says.'

'*Ragnarök*?'

'If not, something like it. A battle where the gods themselves fight among us, so he says.'

'The Sveär are strong. Perhaps it'll be like that.'

'Maybe. But this is about more than a final reckoning with Sviggar and his kin. My father has a kind of vision... If you ask me, it's more like a madness.'

'Yet you do his bidding,' Ubbi chuckled.

'I am his son. But if he wants more numbers, we must delay.'

'You fear that?'

'I *fear* nothing.' Ringast shot him an emphatic look. 'But if we don't move soon, how long before these warriors turn on each other? Frieslanders and Danes, Gotars and Wendish, Irish, Rus... My father will have a battle, all right – just not the one he intends.'

'Has there been trouble?'

'Some. Just drunken brawls so far. But brawls can grow to feuds, feuds to bloodbaths. And if we delay much longer, we risk some leaving.'

'Only those who wish to bear the name coward.' Ubbi tipped his horn against Ringast's. 'Be sure, I'll not flee the coming fight.'

Ringast suddenly looked round. Kai was hovering a couple of places along the table. A perplexed look flashed across the prince's face but then he beckoned Kai forward. Kai hurriedly obliged, charging their cups, before melting out of sight. But not out of earshot.

'Your patience deserves its reward, my friend. You've come to know my table far too well.'

'Aye. It's been a long winter and a longer spring. But if Odin still hears an old friend's prayers, my sword will not go thirsty beyond the cutting of the corn.'

'Vision or none, I'll not let my father delay beyond then.' Ringast drained his cup in one long, decisive gulp. 'Meanwhile, we keep gathering spears.'

'How many till he's satisfied?'

'The number he saw in his dream... Fifteen thousand.'

Kai nearly dropped his pitcher, a thrill of terror and triumph shooting through him. *Fifteen thousand spears!* These were tidings the Sveär king would pay handsomely to hear. Not that it would bring a smile to the Old Goat's face. But that wasn't Kai's problem. At least, not yet.

It was time to make himself scarce, only Thrand was banging the table, bawling for ale. Kai scurried forward to his shoulder and began filling his cup.

'You took your sweet time. Go ahead – fill it up. And maybe I'll fill you up later, you little vixen!'

'You'll have to catch me first,' chuckled Kai.

Thrand's big head shot round. 'Who the Hel are you? Where's that little piece was here earlier?'

'Taken the evening off, my lord. Something about a headache.'

'Are you mocking me, boy?'

'Leave him alone,' Ringast called down the table. 'Let him do his job.'

'His job! It's woman's work to wait on a man. Well, boy – you got a pair of balls in them breeches or not?'

'Finest pair you ever saw. Now if you'll excuse me, my lord.' He moved along the bench, but suddenly a hand caught his collar.

'I was talking to you.' The big Dane levered himself out of his seat. At full height, he was a good six and a half feet tall. He shoved Kai against the wall, towering over him like an angry bull-bear.

'Now you go back there and tell that plump little bitch to get her pretty tits out here before I drain that cup or I'll geld you myself, you hear?' Rancid breath billowed in Kai's face. 'We'll see who's got the finest pair of balls then, eh?'

Half a dozen witticisms leaped to Kai's mind, but he figured now wasn't the time. 'Whatever you wish, my lord,' he mumbled and escaped under Thrand's arm. He was about to flee for the obscurity of the kitchens when a boot slammed into his back, sending him flying. He landed with a crash in a heap of beer and broken potsherds.

The benches around him erupted with laughter, Thrand's bellow the loudest of all. Kai wasn't enjoying this any more. He scraped himself off the floor, along with the biggest shards of the pitcher, and limped off towards the passageway and the kitchens beyond.

'Hey, you!'

He turned and was surprised to see the youngest of the three brothers, Rorik, had followed him into the passageway. 'Are you all right?' The man actually looked concerned. Well, he was a boy really, not much older than Kai.

'Nothing I can't handle.'

162

'My brother's an ogre. Always has been.'

'And I'm a cheeky bastard. Always have been. I should know better than to cross one of Harald Wartooth's sons.'

'We're not all the same.'

'Father's seed, father's fruit. That's what they say.'

'We have a mother, too.' Rorik's voice was soft, not like the others at all. He reached out and laid a hand on Kai's chest. 'You're all wet.'

'Yep. A puddle of beer'll do that to a man.' Kai chuckled awkwardly. Rorik didn't take his hand away. Instead he slid his fingers inside the neck of his tunic and stroked Kai's chest.

'You should get out of these wet things.' Rorik's eyes suddenly seemed round as moons. 'I know somewhere we could go.'

'Woah-woah,' said Kai, checking his hand. 'I think you've got the wrong end of the spear, my friend.' Hmm. Poor choice of words, that. 'Listen, if you figured any man willing to play hall-wench would play soft cat too, I'm afraid—'

'Actually it's me likes to play soft.' All of a sudden, Rorik's other hand was between his legs.

'Gods! You could do a man an injury like that!' He shoved Rorik so hard the prince stumbled backwards. 'What is it with you Danes? You all want to get your hands on my bollocks.'

Rorik was suddenly embarrassed. 'Never mind. I just thought—'

'Hey, look! No harm done, friend. Just ain't my game. There must be plenty of other lads round here who like to play kitty.' Hel, they seemed willing to do almost anything else, so why not that?

But Rorik didn't linger for consolations. He mumbled an apology and disappeared back into the hall, leaving Kai to flee to the kitchens. His escape was short-lived, thanks to the ever-watchful eye of Sletti, who collared him for more unpleasant tasks in the kitchens.

The hour was late by the time Kai was finally released. Most of the household, including the three princes, had retired to their beds. Exhausted, Kai wove his way through the empty benches and tables towards the hall-door. The last of the drinkers sat in huddles, talking in whispers. As he was passing one group, someone broke off and crossed towards him.

He recognized the long-limbed shield-maiden, Visma, her short-cropped blond hair sloping across her eyes. She sauntered over, swinging a mead-skin in one hand, a couple of drinking horns in the other.

'I thought I told you to come and find me.'

'It's been a busy day.' Judging from her drink-glazed eyes, this woman had already sunk a skin-full, and then some.

'The day is over now. Drink with me.' It was less a request than a command. He hesitated, knowing he should get clear of the hall and steal off to his bed, safe with Ringast's words in his head.

'Come, drink! What harm could it do, little man?'

Then again, this ale-soaked giantess seemed friendly enough. Maybe she had some gem of information for the Sveär king. And his throat was parched.

'What are we drinking?'

'Excellent!' She pulled him down onto an empty bench. 'The horns shall never be empty – yes?' She filled them up with a golden brew. Mead – the drink of skalds.

'If you say so.' Kai steeled himself for an onslaught.

'What do we drink to?'

'You're the one pouring.'

'Very well. To victory – or death!'

Kai scoffed. 'Drink to your own death if you like – that ain't for me.'

She sniggered. 'Are you afraid to die, little swordsmith?'

'Don't care for it above half, no. I intend to do a good deal more living.'

'So then – to victory and to life!'

'That'll do.'

Their horns clattered and Kai drained his to the last drop. Mead was always too sweet to his mind, but somehow he doubted this brawny bitch would accept any excuses.

'Again!'

'Give a lad a chance.'

'Come on – this will loosen your tongue.' She refilled his cup.

'My tongue's loose enough.'

'So it will loosen your belt then!' She brayed like a pony. 'Oh, don't look so alarmed, little man. I saw you flirting with me today.'

'Flirting?'

'*Shhshh,*' she hushed, drowning him in spittle. 'It's all right. Besides, I'm too old for you. What are you, sixteen?'

'Seventeen,' Kai corrected.

'Still a boy! And so low born. Such a worm!'

'Steady on.'

'No. It could never be,' she insisted, grinning like a halfwit.

'Bad luck that.'

'Still – there is something about you that makes me so *very* curious.' He could see the hunger in the great lust-bag's eyes.

And he had to admit that she didn't have a bad-looking face. It was just twice as big as any other woman's he'd ever seen.

'Curiosity only leads to mischief and mischief to a bad end, as my ma used to say. Let's have another drink instead.'

'Yes.' She smiled, her lower lip shining in the firelight. 'Another drink. Before my desires run away with me.' She downed hers straight and made him do the same.

He was definitely feeling the drink, but figured that her tongue must be good and loose by now too.

'This blood feud then, between this pair of kings. Ain't got much to do with you Wendish folk, has it?'

'It has now.'

'But why fight for a Dane?'

'The Wartooth has a favour over my husband. A favour or two, if truth be told.'

'And you?'

'I follow him. He fights, I fight.'

'Must be a Hel of a man.'

'Bah! My husband is a noble ass, but an ass nevertheless. He's probably off in some corner with one of Ringast's bed-thralls now.'

'You don't care?'

'Why should I? If it means I can enjoy the company of younger men like you.'

'Cosy arrangement.' Visma poured another drink, tipping his elbow till he'd seen it away. He felt dizzy. *Information*. He was supposed to be squeezing her for *information*, but he was struggling to see beyond the ogrish leer on her lips.

'So this Wartooth – have you been to his hall?'

'Leithra? Of course! We've been honoured guests there

many times. We were there not one month ago.'

'That a fact? And how many spears does he have down there?... Roughly.'

She suddenly snatched the scruff of his tunic. 'How many questions you ask, little man! But there are far more interesting things to talk about.'

'Such as?'

She beckoned him closer. 'Secret things,' she whispered and before he knew it her enormous mouth was locked over his. He stared wide-eyed, struggling for breath.

'Hel's tits, woman! Do you want to suffocate me?' he gasped when she finally came up for air.

'That's exactly what I want to do,' she slurred. 'But if you have more questions, let's find somewhere more comfortable and I'll give you some answers.' She pointed to the sleeping bower over their heads, then hauled herself up and offered an empty hand.

Kai's mind was a fog of drink and doubt and terror. And – he had to admit – excitement. Seemed he was about to become a late-night treat for this bloodthirsty boozer. If Bara ever found out, he could kiss goodbye to any hope of her favours.

Then again, wasn't he here for a moment just like this? On noble service to his king? So then, this was a sacrifice he had to make. He had to think of his friends back in Uppsala.

They were counting on him.

Visma led him up the stairs. He followed, feeling like a man who has cut too big a hunk off a roasted hog and knows it. The bower was swathed in shadow. Ahead of him, Visma picked her way unsteadily over bodies either asleep or ale-sodden, though somehow she only roused a grunt or two.

Suddenly she dropped to the floor, pulling him down with her, apparently satisfied she'd found her place. And before he'd had time to think, her hand was clamped round his head and her tongue was thrashing in his mouth like a demented eel.

Fighting for breath, he managed to pull away for half a second. 'What about these questions, eh?'

'Hel take your questions, little man!' she moaned and began chewing on his ear. He was trying to remember what it was he wanted to know, but it was hard to concentrate with a tongue burrowed halfway into his skull. Her hands were all over him, pawing at his clothes. The gods knew he was no prude, but this was too much. He was the first to admit his experience was limited, but usually he played a more active role when it came to this sort of thing. In Visma's case, he hardly knew where to begin. Somehow she had hold of his feet, was pulling off his shoes and flinging them into the shadows. Someone cursed, but nothing daunted, she rolled her hips and suddenly was astride him, tugging at his belt.

A grin flashed madly on her face as she finally worked it loose and shoved down his breeches. Once she'd got him free, she stopped, gazing down on him with that monstrous smile. 'My little man,' she mumbled dreamily, then whipped off her tunic, showing herself in all her naked glory.

It was a Hel of a sight. *If a Valkyrie ever comes for me*, thought Kai, *she can't be more terrifying than this.* Towering above him, mouth agape, eyes slavering with lust, breasts swinging like sacks of flour...

She fell on him.

He lay, pinned like a weasel in a trap, under her slather of kisses. He had a fleeting memory of an old tale about a she-wolf licking honey out of a hero's mouth. *Now I know how the poor bastard felt.* Her thighs were thrashing about, trying to work his breeches lower, when suddenly, before he could even recall the name of the honey-slicked hero, a stray knee drove into his groin.

He groaned in agony, his loins dissolving into a lake of fire.

'Oh, my sweet loveling – what have I done?' Kai only groaned some more, the pain now spread to his belly. Meanwhile, the clumsy giantess bent over, kissing his cheek, murmuring tender apologies. He tried not to move. Everything below his navel was hollowed out with pain. All he could do was listen to her slobbering as she nuzzled his neck and hope for the pain to ebb.

Soon, though, he noticed her body was growing heavier – so heavy he was struggling to breathe – and her muffled endearments had blurred into a succession of long sighs.

She had fallen asleep.

If she hadn't been so damn heavy, Kai might have been relieved, except just then a voice erupted up the stairway.

'Visma! Are you up there?'

Heavy footsteps on wood.

Kai peered out of his fleshy prison. Through the gloom, he saw the shape of a bull of a man peering along the row of sleepers. 'Visma?' There were some disgruntled moans.

'Wake up! Wake *up*!' Kai whispered, desperately shaking her.

She only sighed in reply.

'Someone's coming.'

'Visma?' the man thundered. Others were waking now, telling him to shut up.

She lifted her head a fraction and giggled. 'Oh him? Forget

about him! It's just my silly husband.' With another long sigh, she sank even heavier onto Kai's chest.

'Your husband?' In panic, he writhed and heaved but she wouldn't budge. He glanced over. Her husband was picking his way over sleeping bodies a sight less carefully than they had.

'Just move, you silly bitch, can't you?' he pleaded, nearly weeping with frustration. 'You're going to get me skewered like a hog.' He gave one final heroic heave and at last she slipped a few inches.

It wasn't much but it was enough. He wiggled and wriggled until he could slide out from under her. Her head hit the floor with a bump. He dragged himself clear and felt the surge of his luck returning when his hand fell on his belt in the darkness. Then he rose like a *draugr* from the grave.

Visma's husband froze in surprise. 'Who the Hel are you?'

Kai wondered whether he could pretend he was a hall-guest on his way to take a piss, but the breeches round his ankles weren't helping.

'Is that you, my noble husband?' drooled Visma. 'Come to join our fun?'

That helped even less.

Kai flashed a rueful grin, hauled up his breeches and then was away, hopping over bodies like a rabbit through clover. There was a roar behind him and suddenly all bloody Hel broke loose. He could hear Visma's bull blundering after him, shapes were rising ahead, threats filling his ears, but he wasn't about to loiter. He fancied he was roaring himself now. (Seemed like the opportune moment for it.) The end of the bower was approaching fast. Without a second thought, he vaulted the last of the waking sleepers and flung himself over the edge, slamming against the massive door.

There was a terrific thump. His bones jarred. Then he half-fell, half-bounced down the crossbeams, hitting the floor in a heap. He looked back up and saw a tangle of shadows and limbs and curses, but happily no sign of the big Wendish brute coming after him.

With a chuckle, he tugged open the door and slipped outside. The night was cool. His head was fuzzy to say the least, but with a bit of luck he could sneak back to his bed and no one would be any the wiser. He doubted that girning she-cat Visma would remember much of the evening's events.

He began to breathe a little easier. There was still a Hel of a racket in the hall, but he was well clear now and no one seemed to be coming after him. At least, that was his last thought before fingers closed round his neck. He jerked away, but this fellow wasn't for letting go.

'Quit your wriggling,' said the shadow. Kai twisted his head and saw moonlight glint off a smooth face.

'Master Sletti! Fancy meeting you here!'

'Shut it!' The blade suddenly at Kai's throat made the steward's point admirably. Inside, the noise was abating. The thumping pulse in Kai's ears, not so much. 'Where are you going in such a hurry?'

'To bed, naturally.'

'Liar. I've seen you one too many times today, lad. Just who are you?'

'I told you. I'm a landed man on my way—'

'You're no landed man. If I had to bet, I'd say you were a thief – you and that fat man you say cannot speak.'

'That's a bit unkind. I mean, he's on the porky side, to be sure—'

'Silence!' The knife moved a fraction. Kai yelped as he felt it bite. 'Whatever you are, you're lying. But I'm going to find out the truth. Lord Ringast has a particularly severe sense of justice, as you might have noticed. I think it's time you and he became properly acquainted.'

'I don't know what you mean, master.' At a loss how to get out of this one, Kai thought a bit of abject pleading was always worth a shot. 'I'm no thief. *Please!*'

'It's no use whining— oh gods, you've soiled yourself! You filthy little coward!'

It was true. There was a definite foulness on the air, but – as far as Kai could tell – it had nothing to do with the contents of his breeches. The smell grew even stronger and suddenly there was a thud, the knife fell away and something crumpled to the floor.

Tentatively, Kai looked round. Einar was standing there, a short cudgel in his hand, shaking his head and reeking of shit. 'Why did I ever listen to you, runt?'

'Cause I'm a bloody genius, fat man, and you know it,' Kai grinned.

'What's all the fuss in there?'

'Oh, that. Well, just so you know, I *think* we may have overstayed our welcome.'

'About bloody time.'

· · · · · · ·

At Dannerborg next day, two fine mares were found missing from the stables. And Snorri the smith was late to his forge. For years afterwards, he would bore anyone who'd listen about how one dark night in the springtime, *draugar*-spirits came and stole his boots.

CHAPTER SEVENTEEN

Kai should have known better.

After all, the king himself had been waiting for their return. He wasn't known for his patience. Kai had hoped for some hot vittles before they had to report but he soon discovered there was slim chance of that.

'The king's orders,' insisted Erlan, after he had overcome his delight at seeing Kai safely home. 'Straight to his chamber the second anyone lays eyes on you.'

'All I want is a bowl of something hot.'

'The sooner you get moving the sooner you can have it.'

By the time he got something into his belly, he'd put the noblest heads in the land in a spin. Sviggar had hung off every word, firing question after question until Kai was so squeezed of information he felt like a bag of curd.

How many warriors at Dannerborg? How many at Leithra? Which named champions had they seen? How many men were high-trained karls, how many mere levied bondsmen? How many horses did they have? When neither Kai nor Einar could answer every question, Sviggar railed at them for wasting their chance – which, given all they'd been through, Kai reckoned a bit off, to say the least. Still, they recounted everything they had seen and heard best they could, Kai leaving out only the odd detail, for discretion's sake.

Eventually Sviggar released them. Servants were sent to summon those of the king's counsellors in residence. Erlan told Kai to wait for him at home.

Kai slouched his way home, kicking at the dirt, feeling damned unappreciated. But he had hardly sat down when there was a knock at the door.

He opened it. There was Bara.

Perhaps the evening wasn't going to be a dead loss after all. She looked delightful, all fiery hair and fulsome curves. Less delightfully, she set about interrogating him almost as harshly as the king, demanding to know exactly what he had been up to in that land of 'pox-addled sluts', as she called it.

'Swear there was no fooling with them Gotar hall-maids.'

'No hall-maids, I swear,' he cried.

'Nor anyone else!'

'None at all,' he lied.

'No kissing, no fleshy fun and games.' She poked his chest – quite hard, he thought. 'And absolutely no fucking!'

For a brief moment he considered whether a blood-crazed giantess trying to drown him with spittle counted as kissing, but, deciding the case in his favour, he was happy to swear. Indeed, he would have sworn away his own mother just then if Bara had demanded it, being rather absorbed by the ample bosom stirring within reach.

'You've no idea how I've missed you.'

'Oh, you have, have you, pup?'

'Aye – something awful.'

She cocked a doubtful eyebrow. 'How much?'

'Let's see now.' If there was a girl who enjoyed hearing her own praise more than Bara, he'd yet to meet her. 'I've missed you like a ship-wrecked man longs for the shore-sands, like a northern huntsman longs for the sun, like a—'

'All right, all right.' She gave a pout and shook out her long hair. For a second, it dazzled Kai like a cascade of fire. 'So, Kai Askarsson,' she said with a wicked smile. 'If you've missed me that much, let's see you prove it.'

By the time Erlan returned Kai was a spent man and Bara had left with convincing proof of his unswerving devotion. At least by Kai's reckoning. Although the council had run long into the night, Kai had been too curious to sleep.

'So what's been decided?'

'You've stirred up a real wasp's nest, I'll give you that.'

'Is it war?'

'War within the council – aye.' Erlan went to the table and took a swig from the pitcher. 'If Sviggar had his way, nothing would be decided.'

'But Harald and his lads are coming. That's certain!'

'Apparently not,' Erlan shook his head. 'The king says the numbers are too vague.'

'What the Hel?'

'You did your best but you couldn't give him a clear number, could you? Even at Dannerborg. And as for Leithra—'

'Bollocks to the numbers! Surely he accepts the Danes, the

Gotars, the Wends – gods, the whole pack of 'em are coming! Fifteen thousand spears, Ringast said!'

'Sviggar reckons it'll all break up before summer's done. He thinks with so many different tribes and clans, it'll split apart like an over-ripe marrow. Especially after what you told him Ringast said.'

'But Ringast promised that Ubbi fella that they would come.'

'Maybe. But he also had fears, didn't he?'

'Doubts, maybe.'

'Fears, doubts? It's all the same. The fact is even Ringast reckons their plan may go awry if they delay too long. Sviggar's nailed himself to that for now. He says if they've been delaying since the winter and not yet come, they never will.'

'What about Ormarr's patrol? And what they did to Gettir the Black?'

'The way he talked, it seemed he thought Ringast had done everyone a favour. He said those twins were worse than a pair of rabid wolves.'

Kai whistled. 'I don't expect old Huldir sees it the same way.'

'Fortunately he's back in Nairka for now.' Erlan unfastened his belt and flung it on the table. 'Anyway, Sigurd took Huldir's part.'

'Gods, yes! What does he make of it?'

'He's crowing of course, since everything you reported proves what he's been saying since the Yuletide.'

'What does he want?'

'War. Same as before. War on Dannerborg. War on Leithra. And the sooner the better, since there'd be more chance of destroying each army before they can unite.'

'Does anyone support him?'

'Vithar. I'd guess Huldir would too if he were here.'

'What about Bodvar?'

'He seems to be the only one Sviggar is willing to listen to. He's not for all-out war like the others but he insists the king orders a full levy and fast – every vassal lord that's sworn to him – and that Sviggar sends word to his allies. To Finnland and the Western Gotars. Even to the Estlanders.'

'For what?'

'For men, of course! But Sviggar thinks that will only precipitate war the faster.'

'Well, he's probably right. But I don't see how he can avoid it now. Better to be at full strength, surely?'

'Exactly.' Erlan raked his fingers through his hair. 'He talks on and on about his realm and what he's built. It's as if he feels death's shadow creeping over him and he's worried about all he leaves behind. I don't know. And then he talks about a treaty to preserve it all. He's clutching at straws.'

'So what we saw at Dannerborg changed absolutely fucking nothing!'

'No. It's brought urgency, at least. Sviggar knows he must act.'

'By sitting on his arse?'

'Not quite. Bodvar at least persuaded him to increase the levy to include the northern clans. But he still talks about parleying with the Wartooth.'

'He's crazy! The Wartooth wouldn't agree to any treaty, would he?'

'Not if what you heard at Dannerborg is true. At least, *I* don't think so. But Sviggar is looking for any way out he can find.'

Kai sighed. This certainly wasn't the outcome he and Einar

had expected. He leaned back against the wall and slung his feet on the table. Then again, things were rarely so black that, if you looked hard, you couldn't find some glimmer of light. 'Well, master – it's not all bad news.' He couldn't keep the grin from his face any longer.

'Why, what have you done now?'

Kai chuckled and grabbed the pitcher. 'You'll need a drink for this one, master. For I have a wondrous tale to tell.'

Queen Saldas glided towards her husband's chamber smoothly as a cloud across the night sky. But her heart was full of bitter thoughts. She hated being summoned from her sleep by one of Sviggar's bootlicking servants. Hated even more the prospect of his mottled hands all over her. The contrast between her flawless skin and his gnarled old knuckles, that stump of a thumb prodding at her, the wheeze in his lungs as his shrivelled passion tremored through his body – it was all of it too revolting.

Of course, her mood had been bad enough since the discovery that there was some kind of passion budding between her bloodless stepdaughter and the stranger. What a fool he must be! *A conceited fool.* That he should reject her for that... that *girl*! The experience was not one she had known before, and not one that would ever be repeated.

But she would see to that in its time. Instead she resigned herself to the unpleasant ritual to come. However, when she arrived at her husband's chamber, she found he only wanted to talk. His brow was creased with disquiet, the flame-light deepening each wrinkle.

'You summoned me, my lord, and I am here.'

Sviggar lowered himself between the arms of the ornately carved oak chair beside his bed-closet. He extended his hands to her. 'Come.' She took them and smiled. Her eyes were still cold. She could feel it. But with his fading sight, he wouldn't notice. He never noticed. 'The goddess Frigg blessed me richly when she gave me you.'

'You flatter me, my lord.'

'You know I do not. Alas, I'm only too conscious of your youthful beauty while I slip further into old age.'

'Long years carry with them wisdom and splendour.'

'Now it's you who flatters.' He shook his head. 'But I didn't call you here to talk of such things.'

'How may I serve you?'

He gazed at her fondly. 'I need your counsel, my love. There are roads before me – I confess, they are shrouded in mist. I know not which to take.'

'I heard the news that came with the Gotar boy. It's bound to trouble you. It troubles us all.'

He stroked the back of her hand with his nub of a thumb. She felt the corners of her mouth tighten. 'All things come together in this moment. My own fate. The fate of my kingdom.'

She knelt before him. 'Unburden yourself. Tell me all that is on your heart.'

He smiled. 'We have had our differences, my love, have we not? But I know in your heart you are true to me. My body is tired. I feel the wind of Hel's breath ever closer, ever colder each day.'

'You are yet strong in mind and body, husband.'

'Not as I was. And I ask myself – have the Norns brought on this threat of war to steer me to the climax of my fate? To meet my doom in battle, to fall beneath the sword of Autha's son? To ride at last on a *Valkyrie*'s steed to take my place at the All-Father's table? It would be a worthy death.'

'It would indeed.' She sneered inwardly. How men loved to talk like this, yet how little they understood of destiny or how to control it.

'If I thought only of myself, it would be the fate I would choose. But I *cannot* think of myself alone. A man's name shines down the generations with more than how he meets his death. His life *must* amount to more. What he did, what he *made*... If my heirs are to sit long on this throne, then the kingdom must be preserved.'

'Is a kingdom not best preserved with the sword?'

'Sometimes. But I feel now is not that time. I don't know why. Call it a king's intuition. If I can only get Harald to parley... But already it may be too late. Things are moving beyond my control.'

Saldas rose and turned away, not wanting him to see in her eyes her disdain for this pitiful vulnerability. 'So you would rather risk your place at the Spear-God's table over the possible loss of your kingdom?'

'My place in *Valhöll* is for Odin to decide. He knows the battles I've fought and the men I've sent to him ahead of me.'

She smiled to herself. For suddenly she saw it, saw it all, opening up before her like a vast horizon on a glorious new day. Now that it occurred to her, it seemed so beautifully simple, so pitifully easy that she felt almost cheated. 'I have a way for you.' She turned back to him. 'A way you can bind Autha's line to peace and still spare all you have created from destruction.'

'How?' In his eagerness, he thrust out his grizzled chin.

'Speak, my love! Speak!'

'Join your two houses together. Offer Lilla to the Wartooth for his son.'

The king's weak eyes searched hers to see if she was in earnest. 'Give my own daughter to my enemies?'

'You wish to make peace with Harald, no? But if it's to last it must be sealed with a bond that will not break. Harald has no daughters. Even if he did, Sigurd would fight you over this – we both know how it stands with him. But Lilla... you need only ask and she will obey.'

Sviggar put his head in his hands, his long fingers pressing his skull till the knuckles turned white. 'You counsel a hard thing, my love. Doubly hard. To give up my daughter to those who have hated me so long, who even now ready themselves for war against me. And then to crawl to them asking for peace and offering her as terms. It's shameful. A father shouldn't play whore-master to his own daughter.'

'You want to stop all this now, don't you? It's not just their side. The appetite for war grows every day among your own people. What higher price can be paid for the hand of your daughter than the security of your whole kingdom? Is Lilla not worth so much?'

'Of course she is, but... Such an offer might be taken as desperation. It might encourage them to strike even more decisively with the sword.'

'Well then – what have you lost?' Her voice rose with impatience. She paused, composing herself. 'You're in the same position now. But if they accept, you gain all that you wish for and you bring this feud to an end.'

'What if they play false?'

'Meet them on your terms. Invite them here to wed Lilla and to parley and swear the oaths.'

'They would never come. They would think it a trap.'

'They *would* come. Or the whole world would know them for cowards.'

Sviggar worked his fingers at his temples as though he wished this were a problem he could just rub away. 'Afterwards – if Harald broke his word? I would have sacrificed my daughter for nothing.'

Gods, the old fool was wearying. 'Just persuade them to come. Trust *me*. I will see in their eyes whether betrayal hides in their hearts. And if I do... you must act without mercy. Not one of them will leave these halls alive.'

'Treachery.'

'Not treachery.' She caressed the lobe of his ear. 'You offer peace. Only be wise.'

His gaze drifted, lost in thought for a while. She could almost hear the scales inside his head creaking first one way, then the other, until finally he expelled a long breath.

'Very well,' he growled. 'If it will serve this realm, I will give up my daughter. But if you see deceit in their eyes, then the feud *shall* end. With the Wartooth's blood.'

'My king.' Smiling, she took his withered hand and pressed it to her lips. He looked up at her, perhaps thinking how beautiful she was, what a loyal woman he had chosen for his queen. Not knowing that inside her, black scorn writhed like a deformed child, and that with his 'Very well' a cry of triumph had sounded in her heart.

CHAPTER EIGHTEEN

They said she was with the other women in the Weavers'
Hall.

The morning sunbeams were pouring through the smoke-
hole in a cataract of light. A circle of women – wives of thanes
and house-karls, freeborn maids with their servants – sat pulling
needles, adding touches to their tapestries or embroidered
garments. Against the walls, thrall-girls worked their homespun
looms.

Sviggar couldn't remember the last time he had been in this
little hall, though it stood not a hundred paces from his own.
Doubtless, his appearance would cause a flutter. But there was
a time for a king to summon his subjects, and a time when he
must go to them.

He strode into the pool of light and found himself
momentarily blinded. He felt foolish, peering about while his
old eyes adjusted, searching the shadows for her face.

'Father?'

'Lilla? Is that you? You're hiding there in the shade.'

'What are you doing here?' She laughed as she stepped into the light with him. In the shadows, voices twittered.

'I came to find you.'

'You should have sent for me.'

'Can't a king take a stroll around his own halls?' He smiled at her. 'I'm not interrupting, am I?'

'Never! I was only making this. It's nothing.' She showed him a piece of linen on which she had embroidered an outline.

'A tree? The Sacred Oak, perhaps?'

She smiled. '*Yggdrasil*. Nine branches, nine worlds.'

He took her fingers and kissed them. 'Delightful.'

'What can I do for you, Father?'

'Take a stroll with me. Would you indulge an old man?'

She laughed. 'You've been saying that for fifteen years.'

'Well, now at least it's true.'

Outside they strolled arm in arm through the meadow behind the Weavers' Hall. It had rained that morning and the scents off the grass were overpowering. Dragonflies flickered between clusters of cornflowers, flashing in the sun.

'Is something wrong, Father?'

'No, child.'

'You're fully restored to strength?'

He gave a hoarse chuckle. 'I don't know what "fully" means any more. I still have my head to think and a voice to command. That's all a king needs.'

'And a father.'

'Hah! Perhaps you're right.'

She squeezed his hand.

'Your mother loved this time of the year – when spring was turning to summer.'

'You miss her.'

'Sometimes. But I only need look at you and I see her again.'

'What about Saldas?'

'What of her?'

'Does she... make you happy?'

He sighed. 'Saldas is a fine woman. Difficult sometimes, true. But yes, if not for these present troubles, I would be happy. She makes me feel younger. At my age, you can't underestimate that,' he chuckled. 'And she has brought fresh life to these halls – the little ones...'

He saw she understood him. Saw in her eyes such love as he hadn't felt for a long time. Lilla's affection was so pure. More than his other children, she seemed an extension of him. His hopes were hers. His will, hers...

'There is something I must ask of you.'

'What is it?'

'A duty I need you to perform. For my sake, for the sake of this kingdom – which I know is as beloved to you as it is to me.'

'I'll do anything, Father. I know we all must do what we can. Especially now.'

'News came last night. From Dannerborg.'

'You mean Kai. One of the house-thralls said his report was confused.'

'A house-thrall! Gods, is there no discretion any more? Alas, his report was not so confused. It's clear a threat is growing beyond the Kolmark far greater than I had imagined. But war may still be averted if I act quickly.'

'What will you do?'

'I plan to make Harald an offer that will end the bad blood between us once and for all.'

'What can I do to help?'

He took her hands in his. 'I want you to marry the Wartooth's son.'

He watched the colour drain from her cheeks, saw the sinews in her neck tighten. For a second, there was a wildness in her eyes, like the terror of a hind at the hunstman's horn. Of course, he had expected her to have some reaction, but not one so stark. He touched her face, but she recoiled as if scorched by a firebrand.

'But you can't mean it...'

'Lilla, have I not always promised that you're to be the wife of a king?'

'But Ringast is no king!'

'As Harald's heir, one day he will be.'

'But he's your enemy, son of your sworn foe. They hate you. Hate all of us.'

'All the more reason it must be done.'

'But... there must be another way. There has to *be* another way!'

Surprise, he could understand, but not this objection. She had always known her duty. Known her destiny. His voice hardened. 'This is the best way, Aslíf. The only way. And the course I have settled on.'

'What about Sigurd? He's older than me and still unmarried. He'll succeed you as king. A union through him would be stronger.'

Sviggar shook his head. 'Harald has no daughter to marry, nor is there any other woman suitable from his closest kin. The union must last. It must be strong if it is to be at all. It has to be between our children.'

'Are you forcing me to do this, then?'

He stroked her hair. 'You know I've always wanted a good marriage for you, one worthy of your character and your blood, and which accords with your own wishes. No king can guarantee his daughter a husband she will love, but in my heart I made a promise to myself that your husband should be acceptable to you.'

In her eyes he saw a torrent of words. 'And if I wanted another?' was all she murmured.

'*Is* there another?'

She looked away. Her shoulders rose and fell in a deep sigh. 'No.'

It was as he thought, then. He supposed it was no small thing for a woman to be confronted with her destiny at last.

'And what if Harald betrays his oath?' she said suddenly. 'I'd be cut off from all that I love and bound to your enemy. And still there would be bloodshed.'

'We will invite them to these halls for the wedding feast. Then we shall see whether they may be trusted.'

'Tell me you're not using me as bait for some trap!'

'Of course not. My hands are above the table. I deal with them in good faith.'

'Do you swear it?'

'I swear it. Let my life be forfeit if I lie.' Sometimes even a king had to bend the truth for the sake of his kingdom.

'I want to believe you, but—'

'Look at me, child. I wouldn't ask this if I thought there were any other way. Will you not do it for me? For your people?'

He could see her conscience turning like a weather-vane in a storm, but there was only one way this must fall.

'I would like to think on this,' she said finally. 'Or are you forcing me to agree to this now?' Her dark blue eyes fixed him with an accusing look.

'I will give you time,' he growled. 'Time to reflect on your love for me as your father. And your allegiance to me as your king.'

'How long?'

'Two days. Then I must have your answer.'

That night, Lilla hurried through the darkness, her hood pulled low over her face. Her father had retired early again, complaining of his chest. Any other day, she would have been worried about him. Instead, she felt almost relieved. No one else would miss her.

Besides, the burden he'd laid on her made her anxious enough. *Did she truly have the power to stop this war? Had he really just put that in her hands?*

Ahead, light was seeping through the boardings of Erlan's dwelling. It wasn't much of a place, but it had a cosiness to it that reassured her. She muttered a prayer to Freyja as she approached the door, steadied her hand and knocked.

Muffled voices. Footsteps. The door opened and her heart sank as Kai's face appeared around it.

'Look who's here! If it ain't the grand shieldmaid of Niflagard!'

'Idiot,' Erlan's voice called.

She flickered a smile. 'I need to see your master.'

The door snapped open and light spilled out over her.

'Lady Lilla.' Erlan looked her up and down. 'Is something the matter?'

189

There was an awkwardness between them all and it was her fault. 'My new mare,' she said, 'it's her leg. I think it's swollen after all.'

'Oh, is that all? You don't want this fella,' said Kai. 'You should ask old—'

'I need Erlan to see it,' she said in a clipped voice. 'You've seen it before,' she explained. 'You'll be able to tell whether it's any worse.'

The others exchanged glances. 'Fine,' Erlan nodded. 'Tomorrow?'

'Now... Please.' Gods, did she have to be so obvious?

'Very well.' He pushed past Kai. 'Let's take a look.'

Relief washed through her as she led him away. She heard Kai chuckle as the door closed but she didn't care. Too much was boiling inside her. It had to come out.

Erlan knew something was wrong. But when she didn't say a word as she led him to the king's stables, he started to wonder whether there really was a problem with her horse.

He was soon dispelled of that notion. When they reached her mare's stall, she turned and fell against his chest.

'What is it?' He'd never seen her like this.

'Something terrible.'

'What? Tell me!'

'It's my father!'

'Your father? Is he sick again?'

'No,' she moaned, her face buried in his tunic. 'He wants me to marry Ringast.' The words were so smothered he wasn't sure he'd heard them right.

'The Wartooth's son?'

She looked up at him. In the half-light, he could see tears streaming down her face. 'He wants to seal an alliance with King Harald. To secure a peace that will stop this war.'

'You and Ringast?' He couldn't get past that thought. She nodded, her eyes bowed with despair. 'Is he fixed on this?'

'He says it's the only way.'

'The only way that *he'll* pursue,' he returned. 'Did he give you a choice?'

'He said he wants my consent.'

'Did you give it?'

'Not yet. He gave me two days.'

'And will you?'

'I don't know. I don't know what to do.' She covered her face. 'I could stop it. I could stop it all. All that bloodshed. But—'

'But what?'

Her eyes seemed to grow wider. 'But there's you,' she whispered.

Her face was full of anguish, yet still so beautiful. He'd known this feeling before, had tried to quash it, to bury it deep down, where it was safe and unseen. But now it rose again, even stronger than before. Suddenly he wanted her. Not her beauty or her body, but *her*. All of her, all that she was. To be all she needed, all she ever wanted, wretched as he was. The fear that she would be taken away was suddenly unbearable.

Without thinking, he lifted her up and kissed her fiercely. She responded. He tasted the salt of her tears on his lips. They came apart. His forehead touched hers.

'I can't marry him. I just can't,' she murmured. 'Yet I must. My father will never accept my refusal. Too much is at stake.'

'What's at stake is your freedom. If you agree, there's no going back.'

'But isn't it my duty? I love my father. I know he wants to do the best by me—'

'All your father cares about is his kingdom. And he'll sacrifice anything to preserve it. Even you.'

'No. He's thinking of his people.'

'What do *you* want? What?'

She shook her head, seeming confused, unable to answer. 'Too many things... If I can save my people—'

'Lilla, you're too good for them. Can't you see that?' He took her face in his hands and put his lips to hers again, his kisses urgent, almost angry. As he did so, a mad thought rushed into his mind. He broke off suddenly. 'What if you ran away? If you left this place?'

'What? How?'

'With me! We could go far from here. Start a new life. Together.'

'Where would we go? I know nothing but this place. This is my home.'

'Don't you understand? The choice isn't between here and somewhere else. If you do your father's bidding, you've already lost this place. Dannerborg will be your home.'

The thought seemed to strike her like an arrow. 'Then where?'

For a second, his own home of Vendlagard lurched forward in his mind. That seemed the maddest idea of all – to return with this beautiful daughter of a king, to make peace with his father's lie, to take up his inheritance, to live and die in the land of his blood.

But *she* would still be there. The ghost of Inga's memory would haunt every shadow in that place. And so, for the thousandth time, he told himself that there was no going back.

Lilla's upturned face still implored him. 'Erlan – where?'

'Anywhere,' he growled. 'If it means keeping you safe. Anywhere away from here.'

'What does that mean?'

'We leave Sveäland behind. We wander until we find a place to settle.'

'My father would send riders after us.'

'You don't think we could outrun a few karls? We'd be gone well before we were missed. We could ride for the Throat, take a boat and sail across the East Sea to Estland. Or down the rivers into Garðaríki and beyond.'

He could see in her eyes her imagination working, roaming far beyond the horizons she knew. But then her eyelids slowly fell. 'It's a betrayal of my father. Of everything I hold dear.'

'It's he that's betrayed you. He's using you to save his own vanity. Throwing you like a piece of meat to his enemies.' He knew as soon as the words were out that he'd spoken too harshly. She pushed herself free from him and turned away.

'He has *not* betrayed me. He asks a hard thing but he's right. It's no more than my duty. You don't seem to understand what has always been true. This is my destiny.'

'Fine,' he snarled. 'Then take the road to your destiny. If that's what you want, why did you come to me tonight?'

'I don't know... I just had to.'

They stood wordless, looking at each other, the musk of horseflesh and straw in their nostrils. He listened to the sounds of the darkness – the animals' breath, a shuffled hoof, distant laughter on the night breeze. What was he trying to talk her into? Why did he care? And yet, he couldn't stop himself.

'Lilla, don't you understand? You're freer than any destiny your birth has laid on you.'

'I can't run from my duty so easily. Not like you.' Her eyes hardened. He saw she had meant to wound him, and she had. 'You want to reduce me to a fugitive, hunted by those who have been nothing but loyal to me. My name would become a by-word for shame.' She scoffed. 'Maybe that's why you carry that name-that-is-no-name! *Erlan*... What does it mean but that you want to hide? And you want me to become another wandering stranger like you? Maybe there's another kingdom somewhere and another king, who sits lamenting the daughter he lost to your dark eyes and that sad smile!' Her words bit like Fenrir's fangs.

'Well, what do you want me to suggest? You came to me tonight, remember?'

She turned away again and ran her palm down the length of her mare's neck. But he wasn't going to let her escape that easily. He turned her back to him. 'If you want Ringast, take him. If he'll have you. If you want to live among your enemies, go to them. Truly, I hope for your sake it will save your people. Because you'll have nothing else.' He grunted. 'Somehow I doubt you'll have even that much.'

Her face suddenly crumpled in misery. 'I don't know what to do. It's too much.'

'I'm offering you a way out. Don't you see?'

She looked up at him. Fresh tears rose and rolled down her cheeks, leaving silver trails in the moonlight. 'What do you want from me?' she whispered.

'I want to help you.' Soon as he said it, he saw the disappointment in her eyes. 'Listen – if you make that choice – that's it. You'll be bound to Ringast for ever. Is that what you want?' She didn't answer. 'Is that what you want, Lilla?'

'No,' she whispered. 'I want you.'

The words caught him by surprise. The last woman who had said them he had failed. Failed so horribly it made his mind spin to think of it. He felt suddenly frantic, like he was about to lose everything all over again – but this time, he couldn't. He mustn't. Whatever it cost.

He bent his face to hers, fastened his mouth on hers. Her body tensed, almost unwilling, but this was the only answer he had for her that made any sense. And after a few seconds, the resistance ebbed out of her. Her fingers curled into his hair, pulling him lower, backing away into the shadows, stopping only when her shoulders bumped against the wall, knocking the planking.

The horses whickered. His hands were caressing her, moving behind and down over her, feeling her body under the soft wool of her dress, sculpted and firm. He felt a sudden rush of desire and immediately pulled away.

'Do you want this as well?'

Her face was in shadow. But he could see the faint light from the night sky glinting off her eyes, which were solemn and shining. 'Yes... Yes I do.'

His fingers went to the brooches fastening her outer dress and pinched open the pins. The cloth slipped free and crumpled to the ground. She seized his belt and pulled him closer, unabashed by his hardness pushing against her. He felt her fingers, shy and exploring, trace the shape of him. 'Show me what to do,' she murmured.

So he did, abandoning himself to his desires and to hers, seeing only her before him, closing his mind to the world as it was, as it had to be, as if war and blood and oaths and honour meant nothing at all.

When it was over, she was the first to speak. 'I didn't look for this, my love. But it's come to me.' She looked different. Defiant. Resolved. 'If we go together, I'll come.'

'Then we leave tomorrow night.' He pushed a stray curl away from her eye. 'Here's what we'll do.'

CHAPTER NINETEEN

When Erlan returned home, Kai was sitting at the bench facing the door, hands resting calmly on the table. There was a cup of ale by his hand, untouched.

Erlan nodded a greeting and let the drape fall but found he couldn't meet Kai's eye.

'What was all that about?'

'Nothing.' Erlan moved past him, sat down on his bed and began pulling off his shoes.

Kai pulled his legs out of the bench and swung to face him. 'Well, it was nothing about her horse, that's for damned sure.'

Erlan threw his shoes to the foot of his bed.

'Oh, come on, master. I can see it there on your face. Something's up.'

'Nothing's up that wasn't already up,' Erlan returned irritably. 'I'm turning in. We can speak in the morning.'

'Oh Hel,' Kai grinned. 'Now I know something's wrong for sure. What did she say?'

'You really think I'm going to tell you? If she'd wanted you to hear she would have come in here and said it. Anyhow,' he added, 'it was nothing important.'

'Now it's "nothing important", is it?' He chuckled. 'Gods, she must have had something to say to come all the way out here in the dead of night.'

'You're a nosy little tick sometimes, you know that?'

'It's been mentioned once or twice.'

'Look, I'd tell you if I could. But I know you. You'd be blabbing it all over Uppland before the sun was up.'

'Hohoooa! Now we're getting somewhere.' Kai licked his long lips greedily. 'Excuse my indiscretion, master, but it don't take a *seidman* to know something's going on between you two. And now you come in here all shifty.'

Erlan cursed, realizing he should have been ready for this. Kai was like a dog after a hare when there was a scrap of gossip to be had. Maybe half the truth would throw him off the scent. 'It's got nothing to do with me. She just said she can't tell anyone else.'

'Tell 'em what?'

'This goes no further.'

'Of course.'

'I mean it.'

'So I see.' Kai chuckled.

'Sviggar plans to use her as leverage against the Wartooth. He's determined to keep the peace at any price.'

'How?'

'How do you think? By marrying her, of course. What else do kings do with their daughters?'

'Can't say I've made the acquaintance of many kings. Nor their daughters, for that matter.'

'Well, he's given her two days to accept.'

'Or what?'

'Or he'll force her to it, I suppose.'

'Not much of a choice then, is it?'

'No. Not much.' Erlan pulled his tunic over his head and lay back on his bed.

'So what did she think you were going to do about it?'

'I don't know. Maybe she just wanted to tell someone... You know, unburden herself.'

Kai burst out laughing. 'Oh, aye! That's a good one! Unburden herself on Erlan Aurvandil – that renowned sympathetic ear.'

Erlan was growing tired of this. He needed to shut it down. 'Look, I'm tired. I'm going to sleep.'

'I saw that.'

'Saw what?'

'You sly dog! You're lying.'

'What?'

'What? What?' Kai mimicked. 'I knew it. There *is* something going on between you.'

'Are you out of your mind?'

'Am I out of *my* mind? Hel, that's the king's daughter! You're juggling fire there, master, or my name ain't Kai Askarsson.'

Erlan sat up, annoyed now. 'I'll tell you what this is, Kai. This is your over-active imagination seeing stories that aren't there. You've been singing too many bloody songs. What would Lilla want with a man like me?'

It was a fair question, and one he hadn't found a solid answer to yet. But Kai wasn't listening. The merriment had suddenly gone out of his eyes and he was scratching at his brow. 'Wait

199

a second. What are you going to do if the Wartooth says yes?'

'This conversation is over.' Erlan rolled to face the wall.

'By the bloody hanged, it is,' Kai exclaimed. Even so, there were some moments of silence. Erlan could almost hear Kai's brain rumbling like a grindstone. 'Hang on.' Some thought appeared to have stuck. 'Surely you're not that crazy? You can't be. You're not going to run away with her?'

'Don't be ridiculous.'

'Gods, but you *have* lost your mind!'

'No one is running anywhere.'

'Odin's eye! You need a knock on your head, that's what you need!'

'You're going to get a knock in your teeth soon. I told you—'

'Well, I don't believe you,' Kai retorted angrily. 'And you weren't even going to tell me. You were just going to leave. What the Hel!'

Erlan didn't answer. It seemed his denials didn't make the slightest difference anyway.

Kai was on his feet, looking more aggrieved now than angry. 'Have you forgotten this?' He pulled up his sleeve and bared the dark scar that marked his blood-oath.

'Gods, not this again! No one asked you to swear that oath.'

'But I swore it anyway, didn't I? And now we're bound to one another and there ain't nothing you can do about it. Anyhow, master,' he added, switching moods faster than the sky in spring, 'you may be mad, but if you're going, I'm coming with you. You can't toss me out like some rotten turnip on a midden-heap. We're a team, you and me.'

For a second, Erlan felt almost regretful. He couldn't help but be touched by Kai's loyalty. That was too bad. There was no room for Kai in any future with Lilla. At least none that he could see. 'Put your arm away,' he said, more gently. 'You're right. We are a team. And I wouldn't go anywhere without you. So I don't know where you get these notions in your head. You've dreamed up some crazy idea but I'm telling you, I'm not going anywhere. And nor is Lilla. She's ready to do whatever she has to do.'

Kai peered at him, still suspicious, though a flicker of doubt had crept into his eyes. 'I'm warning you, as one brother to another. Don't do it. That road ends badly, wherever you think it leads.'

Erlan yawned and lay back. 'No doubt you're right. But you can keep your warnings till they're needed, little brother.' He chuckled. 'Now piss off up your ladder. I'm going to sleep.'

'Suit yourself. Just remember what I said.' With that, Kai sank his ale and climbed up to his bed.

Erlan rolled over to face the wall, watching the shadows from the last of the fire dance over the grain of the wood. *A strange night.* Strange and thrilling. He felt other shadows dancing in his heart: the shadow of anger, the shadow of desire. And still others: the shadow of guilt, the beast that gnaws. The guilt that, beyond their mad hopes, Kai was right.

No. Hel take Kai and his blood-oath – he hadn't asked for it. Hel take Sviggar and his precious kingdom, take Sigurd and his war-mongering and the whole bastard pack of them. He didn't belong here. There was no point pretending that he did. And nor did she any more. This time there would be no mistakes, no broken promises, no bloody end, no tears.

This time he would do it right.

The next night the moon was hazy.

Erlan stood gazing up at it from under the byre's low-hanging roof. It seemed bigger tonight, closer, like a vast hand of comfort reaching down from the sky.

Earlier in the day, he'd sent Kai to train with Einar who, since their return from Dannerborg, seemed to have taken a sort of avuncular interest in him, at least enough to train him up for whatever fight was coming. While he was busy, Erlan had put his horse Idun in with Lilla's mare. He watched them now, two rumps together, their coats shimmering under the thin light of the moon. He patted Idun, hoping the old nag was up to another long ride. They were fed, watered, laden with provisions, furs, sundry weapons, his mailshirt.

He was ready at last, and impatient to be away. His fingers clenched and unclenched Wrathling's hilt, wondering whether he would need his sword before the night was over. Who knows? Maybe the Norns were feeling kind. Though even if they were, there wasn't much time. Kai was off with Bara right now, but he would return to the house eventually. They had to be away before then.

When would she come?

A phrase had been turning in his head all day long. *A love that can heal. A love that can heal...*

Was this love?

When he thought of Lilla, in his mind her eyes, her hair, every curve, every muscle in her body seemed to burn with something bright and vital like the heat of the sun, blasting to ashes the shadows of his past. Was that love?

His mind drifted to the night before, to the passion that

had welled out of her, so natural it seemed like a glimpse into something ancient, something outside of time, something powerful. He'd seen it in her face, felt it in her body. But then, as if floating down on one of those hazy moonbeams, came that other name.

Inga.

And there were those hazel eyes, full of mischief and life, the ring of that laughter in his ears. His knuckles tightened round his hilt. *No.* He wouldn't be turned. He wouldn't fail Lilla. This time love would bring life, not death. He swore that—

Suddenly he stopped.

Another oath. *Always another.* At every turn, the oaths he made seemed to bind him tighter. An oath to his father. An oath to himself. An oath to his liege-lord. An oath he was about to break...

He kicked at the dirt, making the horses shudder. Would his damned conscience never give him any peace? After all, was Sviggar so worthy a lord? His hold over the kingdom was weakening. His vanity outweighed his courage and honour. Did such a man deserve his loyalty?

He scowled. He could lie to others – he had to – but he couldn't lie to himself. Sviggar was worthy. The oath still bound him. And he was making his choice. Lilla needed him more.

But then, of course, there was Kai.

At the thought of his friend, his heart fell into his boots. He wondered whether he would understand, whether he would ever forgive him. Gods, but he wanted to believe that he could. And when all this was over, he prayed Kai would come out laughing. He usually did. Besides, he was happy here. He didn't need Erlan for that.

No. Tonight was where the Norns had marked their road to split. Kai must stay.

Lilla needed his protection. She needed his—

His thoughts were cut short by the sound of footsteps. He recognized them at once.

'Erlan? Are you there?' she whispered softly.

He stepped into the moonlight, feeling a rush of joy that dispelled any doubts in a heartbeat. Except when she was close enough that he could see her face, he realized something was wrong. She was wearing only a pale dress with a shawl over her shoulders clasped at her chest. She had nothing else.

'Everything's ready,' he said.

No reply. He reached for her, but she didn't respond. His eyes dropped to her empty hands. 'You've changed your mind.'

'I'm sorry, Erlan.'

He was surprised how much it hurt. Like a boulder suddenly rolling over his heart. 'Just tell me why.'

'I owe my father everything. I can't betray his trust.' Her voice was strained, her throat tight. 'I can't give up the chance to stop the killing. Even if it fails. I have to try. I'm sorry.'

'You're choosing Ringast, you realize that? Not your father, not your people. You're choosing a man you've never met – your enemy – over me.'

She clasped the shawl tighter. 'There's another reason.'

'Tell me.'

'I don't *know* you,' she exclaimed with sudden passion. 'You say give up everything to go with you, but you won't tell me who you are. Not really.'

'I can't—'

'Oh, your ridiculous oath!' She peered into his face, searching for the answer she needed. 'I don't understand what you want from me.' She shook her head. 'I gave you too much last night. It was wrong.'

'It wasn't wrong. You wanted it as much as I did.'

'Maybe I did. Then...' She buried her face in her hands. 'Oh gods, I don't know! Is that all you want from me? I don't understand! I don't understand you.'

'It's not all.' He tried to turn her towards him, but she snatched away her arm. 'I—'

'Yes?'

'It's like you said. I want *you*. More than this Ringast ever could.'

'That's not enough.' She shook her head sadly.

'Enough for what?'

'For me! For this! To betray my father. And it's your betrayal, too. You owe him a debt. You're sworn to him. If I left, it would be a double betrayal, just when he needs both of us the most.'

Suddenly the shame hit him like sea-spray in the face. 'I'm willing to break my oath,' he admitted. 'But only to spare you a fate that you don't want. To make you happy.'

'You could never make me happy, Erlan – because you can't let go of your own sadness. And this thing you're hiding, it would kill any happiness we try to build. I can see that now.'

'But you can help me let go. I know you can.'

'No, Erlan. I can't. Because you can't let me in. Or you won't.'

He stood there, wanting to prove her wrong, wanting to form an answer. But instead of words, he felt a terrible shudder through his heart and suddenly he couldn't move, couldn't speak, couldn't breathe. He felt blood crashing in his head. He wanted to scream away the rage that hammered inside it but from his lips came nothing but silence.

'You see,' she whispered tenderly, touching his face. Her fingers felt so cool against the anger burning within. 'It doesn't matter what I want. My father needs me more than you do. You just can't see that yet.' She took back her hand. 'Perhaps one day, you will.'

And wiping away a tear, she turned and ran up the hill, leaving him alone in the darkness.

PART TWO

Blood
and Oaths

CHAPTER TWENTY

Huldir Hoskursson, Earl of Nairka, loved the Black River. Since he was a boy, he had made a habit of rising before the sun to go and sit on its bank for hours, with nothing but a fishing line and an ale-skin for company. This morning he had risen particularly early, his sleep having been disturbed by a bad dream. He had shaken it off. Bad dreams were but echoes of the brutal things he had witnessed over the course of his life. Even so, he needed to breathe clean air. So he had left his wife sleeping and slipped outside without a word to her or any of the servants.

It hadn't been a bad morning: a bream early on when it was dark with the mist still on the water, and a while later a silver-skinned carp. When he was young, to catch two so quickly would have delighted him. These days, though, it was the river that gave him most pleasure. Its flat, fresh smell; its rushing water; its surface, changeable as the sky; the endlessly wavering weeds in its bed. Somehow, he always found a bit of peace here.

Aye – a bit of peace was what he needed.

His temper had simmered for many days after Sviggar had banished him to his hall at Svartadale. *To await his instructions...* Huldir grimaced. Instructions from a coward were never worth the wait. In fact the king *had* sent two messengers some days before, demanding his return for a special council. *Another damned council.* Talking and talking, deciding nothing. They even claimed the king had some important piece of news for him, which could only be delivered in person. But he knew how, for kings, everything was urgent. He sent them back with vague promises of following on after.

Of course, he had no intention of returning to Uppsala. He saw the way the king was swaying, had listened to him prate on about bringing the bad blood with the Wartooth to an end. But he would have no part in that. The Wartooth didn't deserve peace. Not from Sviggar, and certainly not from him. King Harald owed him two sons, and one day there would be a reckoning.

He pulled in his fishing line for another cast.

Aye – he would see to that.

His thoughts were interrupted by voices above. The hall-yard would be waking up about now, but this was different. Someone was shouting.

He looked up towards his hall perched on the rise overlooking the river, its gable in shadow as the first rays of the morning sun spilled around it. He wondered what the commotion was about. Some damned argument between a pair of thralls, no doubt. Gods, they were always at each other's throats.

He gathered up his things and climbed the shallow slope to the hall. For some reason a knot of foreboding was lodged in the base of his spine. Folk were rushing about, running out of the eastern gate.

Was something on fire?

He determined to discover what was going on. No one noticed him until he emerged into the yard itself. Then, one by one, the servants saw him. They stopped running. Just stared at him like he was some freak in a travelling fair.

All very curious. He was about to demand that someone explain what the Hel was going on when a voice across the yard checked him.

'Father!'

He turned. Gellir was leaning with a hand against the eastern gatepost, a lick of white hair loose across his eyes.

'Where were you? We've been looking all over for you.'

'Fishing,' he answered, head shaking. 'Would someone mind telling me—'

'You need to come.' Gellir's soft voice had an unusually hard edge to it. 'Now.' His son's half-grimace, half-smile unsettled him. He had never been able to shake the feeling that there was something of the other worlds about this one – the blanched hair, those flat, pink eyes, the thick lips, half grinning, half sneering. How his wife had birthed such a creature was a question he had asked himself many times.

'What is it?'

The other folk were all silent, eyeing him like some damned bear on a chain.

'Gettir.'

'Is he here? Is he safe?'

'See for yourself.' Gellir beckoned to him, then disappeared around the gatepost. Huldir followed, only too aware of the train of thralls and house-karls and servants who fell in behind him as he passed through the gate into the dawn-light flooding from the east.

He turned south, the way his boy had turned. The sun's rays had lit Gellir's white hair so that, for a moment, it glowed like molten gold. Huldir sensed other folk looking up at something but he didn't see them. He saw only the arm of his boy rise and point at the stockade wall.

His eye followed. There was something up there, something spread wide, bathed in the glorious blaze of a late spring dawn. It was some moments before he began to make any sense of it. His first thought was, *Why is Gettir's cloak nailed up there?* He would recognize it anywhere. The black skin of a wolf he had hunted and slain with his own hands. A present when his boy came of age. And now it was nailed wide against the stockade. And next to it...

At first, it seemed like another cloak. Another skin. Only this time of an animal far less familiar, red and torn, hairless, four limbs and a torso clearly discernible, glistening...

His mind suddenly warped, as if the world had been ripped away to reveal the horrors of some other reality beneath. That was when he lost control, fury breaking over him like a tidal wave. He roared and wept and raved, falling to his knees, grinding his face into the dirt with rage and grief. He hardly knew what he was saying, railing at the gods, railing at his sons, cursing every Dane and every Gotar to the blackest caverns of Hel.

Only when he felt his arms pinned, saw in his swimming vision those strange, pitiless eyes in his last son's pale face, did he stop.

'You're embarrassing yourself.'

Huldir looked around, wild-eyed, and saw his son was right. The whole crowd of hall-folk was motionless, watching him.

'Gettir—' he groaned.

'Save your breath, Father. He can't hear you. But he will be avenged.'

'Swear it!' He seized Gellir's shirt. '*Swear* you'll do it.'

'You need no oath from me. I am your son.'

'Yes,' he nodded. 'We will do it together. Three sons, the Wartooth and his seed have taken from me. Three sons he has. And I shall kill them all. There can be no peace between us.'

'No peace,' echoed his son. 'Only slaughter.' Then Gellir smiled – a savage look that filled his eyes with fire. And despite himself, Huldir shuddered, because in it he had seen the beckoning leer of death.

CHAPTER
TWENTY-ONE

The collar weighed heavy around her neck.

Five circles of gold, wound with golden filigree, each thread segmented by tiny gold circlets in the form of serpents. The same collar her mother had worn on her wedding day. Lilla wondered if she had felt as uncomfortable.

She was at least glad for the breeze teasing her carefully braided hair. But the sun was high, making her and everyone else squint as they watched the column of riders approach on huge stallions under banners of red and white and green.

A splendid sight. But to her, dreadful.

She had an urge to fidget, to pull off the stupid collar and throw it away. To run away herself. But she knew she must be still. Whoever wasn't watching the horsemen would be watching her, eager for some reaction, for some nervousness in her face.

She wouldn't give them the satisfaction.

Instead she waited.

It had been a month since her father had sent riders to Dannerborg with his proposal of peace. He had dispatched them within the hour of her consent with barely a word of gratitude.

Of course, he didn't know the real sacrifice she was making. How could he? He thought only of her duty, of her doting love for him. She was determined nothing on her face would betray her heart, even now, even as she stood like some glittering trinket with which her father meant to purchase the safety of his kingdom.

It had been nearly three weeks before the riders returned with an answer: the offer had been accepted. The Wartooth and his house would come. The vows would be taken on the midsummer day.

Today was the ninth day since that message. Nine days in which the message had gone out to the great lords of Sveäland to come. Nine days in which servants and thralls had been scurrying around the halls like an upturned nest of ants in a frenzy of preparation for the ceremonies and feasting, which would last three days and three nights.

But she had made her choice. Now she must play the part she had accepted.

Around her, the noblest men and women in Sveäland waited atop the Tiding Mound, from which the great decrees of the king were proclaimed. From there she looked west, over the three King Barrows. In each was buried a king – the greatest three of the Yngling line, who had ruled the north before her grandsire had wrested the throne from the last of them – the mad king, Ingjald.

Mad and cruel.

She wondered what generations to come would call her father. Sviggar the Good? Sviggar the Proud? *Sviggar the Weak?*

He sat beside her on his huge oak chair, a dark blue robe trimmed with fox-fur around his shoulders. The sun glinted golden off the band circling his head. Beyond him stood Queen Saldas in a flowing white gown, adorned with golden combs in her hair, golden brooches at her chest, golden lacing around her body, her hand light as a bird on her lord husband's shoulder.

Behind them stood a herd of other worthies – lords and heirs of the largest estates of Sveäland – a gaudy array of polished hilts, gleaming buckles and brooches, embroidered shirts and tunics – and somewhere among them, Erlan. The one name she had tried a thousand times to expel from her mind. The one face she couldn't bear to look upon. So instead she looked ahead.

For her husband.

There were dozens of them, but among them she saw no one who could be the great Danish king. This Wartooth. His banner was there – a boar blazoned on purple cloth – but no proud old man with the bearing of a king. Instead, to the fore were riding three younger men.

These, she realized, must be the three Danish princes. In the middle rode an enormous man with a large head of curly hair, and legs so long they almost touched the ground. On his right, a fresher face – surely the youngest – and handsome, even from that distance. But there was something nervous about him. His eyes flashed at everything and everyone.

The third brother was not like that. He sat tall, his eyes fixed ahead – perhaps on her – while the breeze flicked strands of sandy hair about his face. His garb was the most splendid of the three, with a cloak dyed black as jet-stone, adorned with silver brooches and embroidered with silver trim, over a shirt of crimson linen.

The column halted.

It was he who spoke: 'Greetings, Sveär cousins! We ask the favour of a hearth for humble travellers.'

'Greetings, Danish cousins,' her father intoned. 'Welcome to our royal seat. You must be Ringast Haraldarsson. You've become a man since last I saw you.'

'Fifteen years will do that to a boy. Happily we only spied each other from a distance that day or one of us might not be here to reminisce... Yes, I'm Ringast. My father favours me Lord of Eastern Gotarland.'

'And with the Danish crown hereafter.'

'Could be. Though I find it doesn't profit me to forecast my father's whims.'

'Where is your father?' Sviggar said in a voice hard as flint.

'Why, he sits on his throne at Leithra, far as I know.' Beside Ringast, the larger brother, whom Lilla guessed must be Thrand, sniggered.

'Why isn't he here?'

'Alas, our lord father is old. He cannot travel so far as once he did.'

'Not even for a meeting of such import?'

'You mean to see his son wed?' Ringast replied obtusely. 'Fear not, he sends me with his blessing.'

'Do you make mock of us?'

'Not I, Lord Sviggar.' Ringast bowed his head dutifully. 'We are your guests.'

Sviggar stroked his chin, seeming unsure what to make of this young prince. 'We understood your father is willing to end this feud between our families. Did he not deem his presence necessary to such a thing?'

'Cousin, don't doubt the weight he gives this meeting. But he is satisfied that his sons speak for him.'

'A man's oath is his own.'

'My father has a saying: "My sons are my seed, my seed is me."'

'So your oath binds him?'

'Undoubtedly.'

Sviggar gave an impatient snort. 'Well, if you're the future Danish crown, heed well what happens here. Now – you present your petition.'

'Our petition?' Ringast looked puzzled.

'You have a request, do you not?'

Understanding slowly dawned on the prince's face. He shrugged. 'As you wish.'

He dismounted and approached the foot of the Tiding Mound. He looked up at them, gave a rueful chuckle and set himself to the slope. The climb was undignified – he had to stoop to keep himself from falling – but he soon reached the top.

This is the man I'm to marry, thought Lilla. He would be a king one day, and she, his wife – just as she had always been told. And in that moment, she felt death to be a long and weary distance away.

He had the look of a wilful man, his face not unappealing, a little too broad to be handsome, his nose a little hooked. He wasn't old, though his face was weathered, the corners of his eyes a web of crow's feet as though he had been squinting too long at the sun, and his beard was cut close, very precisely. She had the sense of a man who needed control, and was used to getting it.

Not exactly a relishing prospect in a husband.

Her father offered the prince his ring. Ringast dropped to his knee, took the proffered hand, kissed the ring, fulfilling this high-flown mummery.

'I come to do you honour, Lord Sviggar. It's said you are father to the most beautiful daughter in both our kingdoms. I see now that is true.' He looked directly at Lilla for the first time with steady, grey eyes. She saw intelligence there but little warmth. 'I come to ask her hand in marriage.'

This had been a condition of her father's offer – that the Danish prince formally request her hand. A face-saving detail. A mockery, since all knew the union was Sviggar's idea. Her father looked grave as Ringast got to his feet. 'Do you wish to bind your house to mine by a solemn marriage vow?'

'I do.'

'And bring all bad blood between us to an end?'

'Aye.'

Sviggar nodded.

'Of course, we do no more than accept your most honourable offer,' Ringast added.

Lilla heard a scoff and realized it had come from her brother. She prayed he would hold his tongue. Sigurd's thin skin was not helpful right now. As to the barb in Ringast's voice, Lilla had no doubt her father had caught it, but he said nothing.

'Do you accept my proposal?'

'I do,' her father replied, and a small part of her died. She knew she should be happy. Hadn't she stopped an ocean of bloodshed, after all? She focused on holding her lips steady, fearing that if she didn't, her face would melt into a cataract of tears.

'And do you, princess?'

She could feel the prick of Erlan's eyes at her neck. Even so, she nodded graciously.

'Good. We have gold and silver to mark this alliance, cousin. And you?'

'We give gold and land to my daughter as dowry… But come, you must be tired from your journey. Tomorrow we shall agree on terms for this union and be bound to one another by solemn oath. And the two of you shall be wed. But today, let us feast as friends and kinsmen!' He clapped his hands and the crowds echoed his applause.

Ringast raised a hand. The applause ceased. 'Just one small detail I must address first, dear cousin.'

'Detail?'

'A little enough thing, but my father was quite insistent upon it – he being a man of the old ways.'

'Well?'

'It is somewhat delicate. He asks that he see proof of Princess Aslíf's purity. After the wedding night.'

'Her purity?' her father repeated. But Lilla understood at once. Understood only too well. It was an older custom, to be sure, not often practised those days, except by bondsmen families in woodland backwaters. It held that the marriage bed linen, stained with the flower of maiden blood, should be produced and presented to the husband's kin as proof of the bride's virtue.

'Do you question her honour?'

'Forgive me, cousin – it's a mere formality. But my father was quite insistent.'

'Why, there's never been a father more certain of his daughter's virtue! I would stake my honour on it.'

'Oh, you need not go that far. Just to follow the old custom will suffice.'

Her father turned and looked at her. She was struggling to keep her features still, terrified some streak of colour in her cheeks would betray her.

'Very well,' her father declared. 'It shall be so.'

'Excellent! Alas, our father has a certain sensibility when it comes to his future heirs.'

'Enough! We shall settle our new guests. And then, we feast!'

The crowd of nobles stirred, happy to be released from these stiff formalities. Some were already making their way down from the mound-top. But Lilla found she couldn't move.

Her body was rigid with dread.

CHAPTER TWENTY-TWO ☉

As bodyguard to the king, Erlan had been far closer to the events of the last two days than he could stomach. By the second day, he had a belly so full of bile it was all he could do not to vomit over these highly honoured guests.

That first night, the mead flowed in abundance. But suspicion, too, had stalked the benches like a spectre, in silent mockery of the endless backslapping and clashing horns. Everyone knew that, until the wedding vows were spoken, a misplaced word might see steel drawn and blood spilled.

Erlan hovered at the edge of things as much as he could, brooding over his cup, a watchful eye ever on the king. Sviggar at least seemed in good humour. And why not? He was the only man in the mead-hall who was getting exactly what he wanted.

And all the while, Erlan felt a fool. The things he'd said to Lilla. The things he could not say. And now another man would have her. This Danish prince...

'Surprised they came?' He turned to see Earl Bodvar beside him, rolling a horn cup between callused fingers.

'Aye. After all that Kai said, I am.'

'Hmm. There's plenty about this doesn't make sense.'

'So you don't trust them?'

'I wouldn't trust them further than I could piss.'

'I don't suppose Sviggar does either. But maybe he's right – better to risk a broken oath later than face uneven odds now.'

'If that's the game he's playing. I'm not sure he knows what he's doing.'

'Any word from Huldir?'

Bodvar shook his head. 'Not since two days ago. Seems he's laid low with a fever.' He gave a wry snort. 'Let's hope it's fatal.'

'Why?'

'You wouldn't catch me swearing oaths of peace and friendship with a man who'd flayed the skin off my son's back.'

'Hasn't Huldir sworn to Sviggar? He might not like it, but he's honoured his oath this long, at least.'

'Well, that's it, isn't it? Which is stronger – blood or oaths?'

At noon next day, the nobles of every house – Dane, Sveär and Gotar – gathered before the Great Hall, sore-headed and full of talk, ready to swear the oaths that would end their enmity once and for all.

King Harald Wartooth had sent with his sons near a hundredweight of gold as Lilla's bride price: two large chests carried all the way from Zealand. Sviggar's dowry for her matched this mark for mark, adding to it five bales of the finest furs from the northern forests of Botten.

After thanking Sviggar for his generosity, Ringast pledged ten hides of cleared land as Lilla's morning-gift. A generous endowment, though Erlan had his doubts it would ever change hands. Not if Ringast's first night with his new bride revealed the secret that only Erlan knew.

But what could he do about it? Call a halt to the whole proceedings and confess what they had done? Sweep her away to safety, out from under the gaze of every highborn lord in not one, but two kingdoms? No. She didn't want his help. Didn't want him. She had chosen this and the Norns would soon show what was to be her fate.

Meanwhile, everything unfolded as the king had wished. He and Prince Ringast swore their oath, laying hands on Adils' Oath-Ring, each gripping the ancient circle of iron and reciting their words before Var, the goddess of truth, who was said to bless and bind all compacts between men. After them Ringast's brothers swore with Prince Sigurd, and so on, earl with earl, thane with thane, until the alliance was stitched tight by each and every oath. Thus peace was restored between the two lines of Ívar Wide-Realm; the long-lived feud, which had seen Sveär and Danish blood flow like the spring meltwater so many times, was at last laid to rest. All that remained was to put the final seal on it – the marriage bond between their two lines.

Erlan watched the ceremony with Lilla's rejection lodged like a fish-bone in his throat. Part of him felt anger. But another part secretly longed for her to look at him. Just a glance, to show that she too was hurting, that she too was mourning something that could not be.

But she never did.

So here they were. The sacrifices had been made to the greatest of their gods: a wild pig for Thor, a horse for Odin, a bullock for Frey. Prosperity, victory, fertility. Such were the blessings of these gods. Lilla sat on a throne under the boughs of the Sacred Grove in a gown as white as a swan's new plumage, pale blue cornflowers in her hair, a hammer nestled in her lap betokening *Mjöllnir*. Next to her sat this noble prince. A sneer twitched at Erlan's lips. Yet at the same time, he despised the jealousy snaking through his heart. *Love isn't mine to keep*, he reminded himself. Hadn't life shown him that, clear as water?

Meanwhile, the white-beard Vithar stood as *goði,* propped on his crutch, intoning the final prayers to the goddess Frigg, the mother of marriage, to bless their union.

Erlan suddenly caught a scent on the air, subtle... and familiar.

'Beautiful, is she not?' Glancing aside, he found Saldas's green eyes studying him.

He scowled and looked away. 'That's not for me to judge.'

'Come now. You're not jealous, surely?'

'Why should I be?'

'That another man should have his moment. This Ringast... He's very striking, is he not?'

Erlan didn't answer.

'It's indiscreet of me, I know. But the talk among the women is that he's quite the man. If he sees something he wants, he takes it... Mmm. And tonight he will claim his reward.' Her lips came closer. 'I wonder, will he find her as sweet in body as she is in nature?'

'Better sweet than bitter.'

She laughed through her nose. 'Bitter? I think you remember what I taste like better than that.'

He drew her scent deep down into his lungs, letting it

linger there. *Aye, he remembered.* 'Shouldn't you be with your husband?'

'Always so serious!' She smiled. 'We should be friends, you and I. Isn't this a day for enemies to become friends?'

'Today, perhaps. Tomorrow, who knows?'

Despite himself, he found his mind wandering over her, remembering the press of her body. Lilla didn't want him. This woman had. He snatched his mind back from her. Vithar was calling out the last of his blessings.

'Think on what I said,' she murmured. 'I'm not so ungracious that I can't overlook any little misunderstanding of the past.' Then she was gliding away to rejoin her husband, leaving only the ghost of her presence in his nostrils, while Lilla and her new husband led the crowd of guests back towards the hall.

Custom held that, on the first night of the wedding feast, once vows were exchanged, the bride and the other womenfolk dined separately from their men. So, while they took their places in an adjoining hall, the king entertained his new son-in-law in the Great Hall.

Only the loveliest thrall-maids waited on the menfolk that night, steamed and bathed that day, clothed in fresh white robes, white ribbons circling slender necks, and each maid's hair arranged in the traditional style of the marriage feast.

Songs were sung until every throat was hoarse. There were drinking contests, bouts of arm-wrestling, rounds of story-telling, while a sea of drink was drained away, and still they yelled for more. Despite all this, Erlan doubted any man's mind was far from his blade.

It was late. The weakest drinkers were already slumped around the hall, where they would stay till morning. Erlan had retreated with a half-filled cup to the shadows behind the high table, from where he could watch the king. He was still sober. He hadn't forgotten his own Feast of Oaths when his head had been stewed in drink. Nor had he forgotten the heap of trouble that led to.

He took another modest swig, hoping to detect some sign of fatigue in Sviggar that would mean he too could soon retire.

A serving-girl came over and proffered her pitcher. 'Tempt you?'

'Thanks. I've had my fill.'

'Something else, then?' She smiled – a smile that promised much. She had one of those elfin faces of the folk across the East Sea – high cheekbones, a neat, straight nose that flicked up at the end. But she was tall, her movements smooth as molten silver, and the white ribbon in her hair belied the mischief in her eye.

'I'm good for now.'

'The other girls said you'd say that.'

'Don't they have something better to talk about?'

'What's better than a mystery?' She grinned. 'Anyhow, they think your ankle ain't the only thing of yours doesn't work so good.'

'Don't you believe them?' he asked, looking past her.

'I believe in finding things out for myself.' She stepped closer. So close he could smell the chewed mint-leaves on her breath. 'Want to know something else about me?'

'Not particularly.'

'I don't take no for an answer.'

Erlan glanced at her – saw her pupils were dark and wide as whirlpools. He felt a flash of desire, he couldn't deny it. But somehow it didn't feel right. For other men, maybe. But for him, that was too precious a thing. *Too painful a thing...*

'What are you, an Estlander?'

'A Finn.'

'How did you come here?'

'Sold. Brought here when I was a child.' Apparently that was enough explanation.

'What's your name?'

'Rissa.'

'Well, Rissa,' he murmured, 'I appreciate the offer. But I think there's someone over there wants you more than me.' He nodded at the high table where Prince Thrand was thundering for his cup to be filled.

'That oaf?' She snorted. 'Suit yourself, Aurvandil.' Then a sly smile flicked over her mouth. 'But this conversation isn't over.'

Erlan watched her go, irritated because she had only added to the miasma of frustration he'd been feeling all day. His old spear-master Garik would never have had such qualms. He would have taken her in a heartbeat. After all, what the Hel did it matter? He might as well take pleasure where he found it, same as the next man. Same as all these men...

But somehow he couldn't.

Instead he found himself wondering how Lilla was feeling as she waited to be led to the marriage bed of this Danish stranger. Then he scowled at himself. She was another man's wife now. And she would find out soon enough what kind of a man she had married.

Not far away, Lilla was growing weary of sitting upright, more weary still of all those eyes upon her.

She gazed around at the other noble women, their cheeks ruddy from the honey-spiced ale. Had they felt like this on their wedding nights, she wondered? Had they been weighed down by a heavy knot of dread?

Of course not. They were women of virtue. But she had given her virtue away to a man only too happy to take it. Even though he couldn't say that he loved her. That was too much for him, she thought bitterly.

It wasn't supposed to be this way. Her destiny had always been clear. True, she had sometimes kicked against it, but she wasn't too proud to appreciate her good fortune. She was the daughter of a king, and now the wife of a king-to-be. One day she would be mother to a king, just as her father had promised.

Except now this other man had got in the way. This stranger. *This cripple.* He'd become the splinter under her skin.

She'd been a fool, but now it wasn't only her who would pay the price. Fear bubbled up again, fear at what her husband would say when he found out. Fear at what he would do... And that her sacrifice would have been for nothing.

Her thoughts were interrupted by a patter of footsteps, then a tug on her sleeve. 'Hello, La-la!' squeaked a small voice. Katla, her tiny half-sister, was beside her chair, looking incredibly pretty, her raven-black hair all done up in ringlets, sewn with daisies and primroses. Lilla smiled at her.

'Are you happy, La-la?'

'Of course I am, sweetling.'

'Do you like your husband?'

She cupped her sister's cheek. 'Very much. Now shouldn't you be in bed?'

'Mama said I could watch until you leave.' Her big brown eyes were sparkling with excitement. 'She said that's the most *special* moment of all.'

'So it is,' interrupted Saldas, appearing at her daughter's shoulder. 'Are you nervous?'

'A little.'

'You have nothing to fear, my dear. A wedding night is... well, a sacred thing. What could be more precious than your maidenhead, after all?' Lilla looked away, feeling sick. 'Oh, don't be embarrassed, my sweet! Your innocence will be charming to him.' Lilla thought she caught a trace of something else in her stepmother's voice. Something sardonic, even cruel. But the queen's face was glowing with affection so she must have imagined it.

There was a noise near the entrance to the hall. She looked and at once recognized Ringast's attendant standing in the doorway. The hall fell silent. Not even the servant said a word. He only bowed respectfully, and then, with eyes fixed, strode purposefully up the hall.

'Be brave, my child,' Saldas murmured. 'All will be well.'

Lilla rose.

It was time.

She had expected to see more drink in his eyes.

But Ringast's gaze was clear as ever, his features serious, if not quite severe. She wondered if he was nervous too.

The scent of lavender was overpowering. Some over-eager

230

servant had crammed bushels of the stuff into two large jars on the table.

'Gods, I can't stand this stink, can you? Here, take these away.' Ringast handed the jars to the servant who had followed them into the chamber. The girl took them and then withdrew, pulling the door shut.

Ringast filled a cup of wine from the pitcher and offered it to her.

'Thank you. No.'

'Are you afraid?'

She nodded.

He took a long swig of the wine. 'I believe I am too... A little.' He smiled. 'You've nothing to fear.'

She nodded again.

'Come on, princess. Has your father not taught you how to speak?'

'Of course, I... I know...'

'Am I so terrifying?' Abruptly he reached out and touched her cheek. His fingers were rough. 'So lovely.'

He pulled her towards him. She felt his lips on hers, the velvet bristle of his beard. His breath tasted of wine, but it wasn't unpleasant. 'Are you a willing bride then?' he said, pulling away.

His grey-green eyes were close. She thought how differently he looked at her from Erlan. Still she didn't answer. Instead she unfastened her girdle, letting the strip of leather slide through her fingers. His eyes fell, moving over her body.

'Take off your dress.'

'You have to help me.' She turned and felt him behind her, felt his breath brush past her cheek, his hands on the laces at her back. She felt him slide her robe off each shoulder, felt the cool air rush over her skin as it crumpled to her feet. She stepped out of its folds and turned to him, feeling exposed. But there was no intimacy, nothing complicit between them at all.

Yet he must have felt something, because suddenly his hands were on her, grasping, squeezing, cupping, his mouth biting at her neck.

She felt neither pleasure nor disgust, only the physical sensations as he touched different parts of her. Abruptly, he swept her into his arms and carried her to the bed. She noticed how white the linen was bleached. She should have been that pure.

He stood over her, eyes drinking in her body. She looked down. Her fair skin was shimmering orange in the torchlight. The sleek contours of her breasts gleamed and beyond lay the shadow of hair between her thighs. He pulled off his shirt and flung it aside. Her heart beat faster, but not from desire.

Wordlessly, he undid his belt and let his breeches fall. He looked down, perhaps fascinated by his own arousal. But she looked away.

'Can you not even look at me?' There was disappointment in his voice. Part of her almost felt pity for him. He had married a woman who could never truly be his. Not in her heart.

She opened her arms. 'Come, husband.' He hesitated. 'Come, my love.'

He gave a bitter snort and lay on top of her. His body was hard, bulkier than Erlan's, with coarse hair covering his chest. He pushed her legs apart. She felt the hard bones in his hips squash against her thighs. There was a long pause. She suddenly realized her eyes were shut tight.

She opened them. He was watching her.

There was no love there. She felt none either. *How could there be?* This was a betrayal of love. It had nothing to do with it. Instead, all she saw was raw desire. Hunger like a dog's. He hovered for a moment, then thrust himself inside her.

She gasped.

He began to move. It all felt so crude and ugly, but after a while at least there was no pain. Outside of his motion, she felt nothing. She saw only the rafters above, felt the friction of his chest hair against her breasts, heard his grunts of concentration.

A betrayal of love. That was all.

When he had finished, he rolled onto his back. She lay there, listening to him catch his breath, hardly daring to move.

He turned his head and she could feel his eyes boring into her temple. But she couldn't bring herself to look at him. Neither spoke. It was only when they had lain like that a while that she realized he didn't know what to say.

'Did I please you?' she said.

'You were pleasing enough... I needn't ask if I was pleasing to you.'

'Of *course* you were—'

'Don't bother lying. I've known boars enjoy a spearing more than that.'

An unfortunate comparison. 'I suppose I'm nervous.'

'No doubt. Still, you'll come to like it better. In time.'

Lilla smiled mirthlessly at the ceiling, dreading what was coming.

He released a long sigh. 'Well – I suppose I should see whether the old man got what he wanted.' He sat up and tried to push her legs to one side. She resisted.

'Come on, I want to see.'

He pushed her again. She resisted harder, shame burning her cheeks. 'What's the matter with you?'

'You won't find anything.'

'What?'

'There's nothing there.'

His expression began to change from puzzlement to anger. Suddenly he shoved her so hard she had to roll away. They both looked down. There was a damp patch where the linen had darkened, but of the so-called morning petals, not a trace.

'So the Bastard King has played us false,' he hissed.

'No! No – he didn't.' Her voice was trembling.

He grabbed her arm, yanking her close. 'The proof is there. You were no maid.'

'Ringast, please—'

He tried to climb over her off the bed, but she clung to him, pulling him back.

'Where are you going?'

'Away from here! I'll rouse my men and ride at once. I fear me some foul treachery if we stay. Your father has deceived us!' He tried to shove her off him but she held on.

'It's not his fault. His oaths were true.'

'This whole scheme is rotten with his lies. Never trust a damned Sveär! My father was right.' His nakedness only made his anger all the fiercer. 'Well, sweet wife. Your bastard father will soon know how a Dane pays back such an insult.'

'He doesn't know!' She dug her fingers into his arm. 'He doesn't know about me. About this! No one does!'

'Of course, he knows.'

'He doesn't – I swear it.'

'Doesn't know that his daughter's been plucked?' he sneered. 'Or that he puts me to shame? Then he's as big a fool as he is a liar.'

'He's no liar. His oaths were sworn in good faith.'

He shook his head, but this time said nothing.

'My father wants peace between our families. This isn't his insult. If anyone's, it's mine.'

'His oaths stand on this marriage and this marriage is a lie.'

'The oaths must hold. They *must.* Don't you see? You can't let this bloodshed happen because of my... my...'

Her what? Her wantonness? Her indiscretion? Her stupidity? *Her love?*

'I am the son of the Wartooth. I can't overlook an insult like—'

'You can. Of course you can! It's me who did wrong. It's me who deserves punishment. No one else knows nor need ever know. Let me bear the cost, not my father, not my people. Thousands will die otherwise.'

'There's at least one other who knows,' he said coldly. 'Who is the man who took what was rightfully mine?'

She hesitated. 'I can't tell you.'

'You think you have a choice?' He gave a cold laugh. 'You will tell me. I'm your husband.'

Suddenly a wave of fury broke right through her. Fury at what a stupid, twisted, upside-down world it was that had put her in this corner. Who was this man anyway, with his wounded pride and overbearing manner, demanding to know her secrets? Gods, but wasn't every man a hypocrite on this score? 'Why don't you tell me the names of all the women you've bedded?' she retorted, her nose wrinkled with scorn.

'What?'

'All the whores you've had before you took me... How many was it, hey?'

He gave a brittle laugh. 'It's not the same.'

'Why not? Because I'm a woman?'

'Aye. Because you're a woman.'

'That's right. And you're a man. But where are your morning petals, hey?'

He was about to answer, but hesitated, and instead shot her a quizzical look.

'If you want to punish me, so be it,' she said, sensing he was wavering. 'But I'm begging you, let your men depart these halls in peace.'

For a long moment he didn't speak.

'Isn't that what you want, too?'

'What? Peace?'

'Yes. Why else did you come here?'

He swung his legs round and sat on the edge of the bed. His gaze sank to the floor. After a few, long moments, he spoke quietly. 'I'm not going to punish you, Aslíf,' he said quietly after a few moments.

She pulled her knees to her chest. 'You're not? Why?'

He looked up at her. 'Because you're my wife now.'

Seeing he was in earnest, Lilla began to weep – and with the first tear it was as if some dam had broken, relief washing in floods down her cheeks.

'Here,' he said, reaching out and catching one of her tears on the tip of his thumb. 'You needn't cry.'

But she couldn't stop now, couldn't stifle the sobs that heaved out of her. And he would never know that she cried not for her people, nor even for her king. She cried for everything. For love, for fear, for shame, for the living and the dead.

For Erlan.

Ringast left her to her tears. Instead he took his knife from his belt on the floor and unsheathed it. She watched him, her sobs ebbing as her curiosity grew. Suddenly he jerked the blade across his thumb. A red line welled at once, glistening where the knife had cut. He held his thumb over the bed and squeezed.

Droplets of blood pattered in a dark cluster onto the sheet.

CHAPTER
TWENTY-THREE

K ai was fed up.

Three days of feasting, the most splendid occasion he'd ever get to witness, and he had to stay out of sight.

Erlan had insisted that if any of the Danish princes or their entourage recognized him from his visit to Dannerborg, it would put a torch to these cosy peace talks.

'I'll make myself fleeting as a ghost,' had been Kai's reply. 'Though even a ghost likes to make an appearance from time to time.'

'Don't you dare,' Erlan had growled.

Gods, he could cluck like a hen, that one.

In fairness, his master was probably right. That Ringast didn't seem like a man to forget a face. And no doubt Kai's grinning mug would be an embarrassment to Sviggar's grand plans.

Still, he didn't like it above half. The last and greatest of the three marriage feasts was underway, despite the fact that the midsummer sun was still a long way off setting. But no one was paying the sun much heed. The festivities would run on till noon the next day or even longer. And he was missing all of it.

He scuffed the dirt, gazing enviously at the Great Hall from his spot across the yard, propped against a post, one hand holding a half-empty skin of ale he'd swiped from the brewhouse, the other fondling the ear of one of the hall-hounds that lay with its head in his lap.

They were all in there this time – men and women together. He guessed that signified that Prince Ringast had got his oats last night or something. He gave an indignant snort – not something he was in the habit of doing. Something funny had gone on between Erlan and Lilla, that much he knew. But it seemed to have come to nothing. That aside, Kai still couldn't help feeling kind of possessive over the princess. Especially after all that happened last winter. And who was this Ringast? Some stuck-up highborn lord, maybe, but was he actually worthy of *his* princess?

Anyhow, it was done now. They were all jammed in like herrings in a barrel, toasting each other to happy oblivion and having themselves a Hel of a time. What niggled most was that he'd only recently composed a song to beat all others – full of witty kennings, twists in the story that would have the women weeping, and a hilarious bit about a goat. Tonight would have been the perfect occasion for its first airing. Instead, that lice-riven whoreson Bersi had been given the nod to sing some interminable house-lay about gods and heroes. The man had no art at all. The only way he ever moved a girl was with the fleas he left behind under her skirts.

Ahh – the girls! It was a crying shame to miss them. Course, Bara was his woman now. There was no question of his fouling that game. But still, it would've been a sight and a half. All those others, from the queen down to the lowliest house-thrall, all scrubbed and scraped and primped and preened within an inch of their lives. Yep – that would be something fine to see!

He sighed dreamily and took another swig.

'Still, old boy – we make do, eh?' He gave the hound's chin a tickle. But the hound suddenly lifted its head, ears pricked.

A moment later, Kai heard hooves drumming. He turned and saw a rider coming up the road at a gallop. He got to his feet. The rider pulled up in the hall-yard, his horse in a lather. Kai knew most men around the Uppland halls but this man was a stranger to him. By the look of him, he was someone's karl. At least he was carrying axe and shield.

'Where's the fire, friend?' Kai asked.

The man jumped down and flung his cloak over his shoulder, still catching his breath. 'I have tidings for the king. Where is he?'

'That's mighty high company to be seeking on a night like this.'

'I have urgent news for him. Where is he?'

A bit short on manners, this one. But seeing he was in no mood for jesting, he replied, 'Where do you think? In there – probably pissed as a polecat by now.'

'I must speak with him.'

'What's up?'

'A whirlwind.'

Kai looked up. 'Looks calm enough up there to me.'

'I've no time for fooling. Earl Huldir rides here with fifty men.'

'Fifty men? What the Hel for?'

240

'Slaughter!' The karl's eye flashed. 'He intends to betray the king.'

'How do you know?'

'Because I rode with him. I'm sworn to him. But the way I see it, he rides straight to *Valhöll*'s gates, his oath to the king forgotten. I slipped away last night in the Swallow Wood and swam the Fyris further south. I have to warn the king.'

'Suppose you thought he'd sling you a ring or two for your kindness, eh?'

'He'll cover me head to bloody toe in gold when he realizes what rides this way! Huldir means to put these halls to the torch and butcher anyone who tries to stop him.'

'Has he lost his mind? What's he after?'

'Vengeance, of course! Those Danish princes. Gods, but I've wasted enough time with you! I must find the king.'

He turned to the hall, but Kai grabbed his arm. 'Hold up there, friend! You can't just go crashing into his mead-hall and raising all Hel. Loki's toes! It wouldn't take more than a crow's fart to set the whole pack of them Danes to slaughter.'

'What do you mean?'

'Well, the thing stands on the edge of an axe as it is. You barge in there rattling your shield and screaming bloody mayhem and I tell you, mayhem you will get. And long before Huldir and his boys are anywhere near the place.'

'Well then. You have a better idea?'

'Happens I do.'

Kai chuckled. Perhaps the evening wasn't going to be so dull after all.

Inside, Bersi the skald launched into another verse and Erlan wondered wearily whether his turgid house-lay would ever end. It was still early but the heat was intolerable, prickling his back with sweat.

He had spent most of the occasion determined to avoid looking at Lilla, sat in splendour next to her new husband at the king's table. His anger had boiled all away over the last two days, like a kettle left too long over the fire, leaving him irritable, scorching hot to the touch. The slightest thing would set off his temper so he had stayed out of others' way.

He cast his eyes around the mead-hall. Was it only him who was sick of all this feasting? The place was so full the walls must have been bowing outwards. Every noble man and woman under the king's salt was jammed along the benches, and scattered among them, Ringast's entourage.

Tonight the lower folk were feasting too: house-karls, smiths, traders, freemen, bondsmen and the like, together with their womenfolk – all filling up the smaller halls dotted about Uppsala. Erlan could only imagine the wildness of their revelry by now.

But the king's feast in honour of his daughter was a long way from descending into the usual drunkenness and debauchery. The guests had been promised entertainment: skald-singers, tumblers, wrestlers, mummers, fire-eaters, dancing girls, even a dwarf-bear that could caper a jig. The night would be a long one, indeed. Erlan stifled a yawn and let his gaze drift along the benches.

That was the moment he spotted an all-too-familiar face.

Kai was peeking out from the shadow of a pillar, eyebrows jumping about like minnows on a hook.

What does the little fool want now?

Seeing he had caught Erlan's attention, Kai was signalling him over. Erlan sighed, looked about, but most folk's eyes were intent on the skald. So he eased himself from his seat and slunk back into the shadows.

'What are you doing here?' he hissed when he reached Kai. 'Didn't I tell—'

'Yes, yes. Shut up and listen.' For a change, the lad looked halfway serious.

'What is it?'

And it all came spilling out in feverish whispers – about the rider and Huldir and his men, that he was riding here with vengeance in his heart. Erlan listened carefully. If true, it was a bold stroke. Bold and damned reckless. But from what he knew of Earl Huldir, that was entirely possible.

'How far away are they?'

'He said they had planned to cross at Ulvar's Mill. But it'll take them a while to ride that far north. Even so, they might cross before nightfall.'

'Fifty men, huh?'

'That's what he said.'

'Then we need as many. Go find Jovard and round up as many as you can from the small halls. Check the Smith's Hall and the Brewer's – that's where most of the karls will be. Get them armed and on horseback quick as you can. We'll assemble at the stables.'

'But the fella was adamant the king should know.'

'Leave that to me. Just go.'

Kai nodded and turned to leave.

'Hey!' Erlan caught his arm. 'Quietly, eh?'

'I'll be the soul of discretion, master!'

And then he was gone.

Meanwhile, Bersi had at last come to the end of his song. The applause was tepid, but at least the quiet was broken. Thrall-girls began refreshing cups, people rose from their places, the talk picked up. Erlan scanned the king's table and found Sviggar at its centre, dwarfed by the tall back of his oaken throne.

How could he alert Sviggar without drawing attention to himself and arousing the curiosity of Ringast, who was seated right beside him? Then Bodvar rose and made his way down to the lower section of the hall. Erlan hurried through the guests to head him off.

'Lord Bodvar,' he said, catching the earl's elbow. 'A word.'

'Aurvandil! Good health to you.' But seeing Erlan's expression, his smile flattened. 'What is it?'

It took Erlan a few moments to explain.

'Curses on the fool!' Bodvar snorted when he'd finished. 'No one here can know. Whatever madness Huldir intends, the Danes must hear nothing of it. Nothing! You understand? Else this feast will become a bloodbath.'

'What about the Sveär nobles? There's half a hundred swords in here.'

'We'll have to leave them be. Ringast would notice at once. No – we'll have to make do with karls.'

'Kai and Jovard should be gathering men from the other halls by now.'

'Good.'

'What about you?'

Bodvar grimaced. 'I'll ride with you. I've known Huldir a long time. Might be I can talk the old ox down. He's headstrong, sure, but he's never been entirely deaf to reason.' A frown crumpled Bodvar's brow. 'The king should know of this, of course. Go and ready whatever crew they've assembled. I'll join you directly.'

Erlan went as fast as his ankle would allow to the stables, where Jovard and Kai had already mustered a couple dozen men. Even from a distance, he could smell the reek of violence on them. Most, if not all, would have been well on the road to getting dead drunk by the time Kai got to them. But he guessed, by the time any steel was drawn – *if it was drawn* – they would have sobered up some. Then again, maybe it was better to have a bit of ale-fire in their bellies.

The talk was rowdy as the men threw bridles on horses, pulled on byrnies – those rich enough to have them – or quilted corselets or boiled leather, belted on swords, shouldered axes: the usual fuss before riding for a fight. Excitement laced with nerves.

Ever resourceful, Kai had already fetched their gear so Erlan readied himself. Tugging his belt into place, his mind lurched back to his fight with the Watcher in that dark place under the earth. The belt was a trophy, fashioned from the Watcher's tail. But it meant more to him than his victory. It meant life – the will to live in a world where death often seemed the sanest thing to seek. And as he remembered he felt that strange fearlessness surge in his blood. A kind of reckless certainty. But where it came from, he couldn't say.

The light was fading. Darkness was coming.

He gripped the hilt of Wrathling and squeezed it tight. Between the cold metal of its twin rings he found his comfort. Here was his friend – a friend of iron that had served the long line of his blood before him. Lilla had made her choice. This was where he belonged.

CHAPTER
TWENTY-FOUR

The crossing at Ulvar's Mill lay a league west of Sviggar's Great Hall.

It was a mellow summer's evening. Twilight was settling. Rooks and pigeons were fluttering to their roosts, disturbed by the approaching hoofbeats. Erlan's nostrils caught the smell of the river, of the reedbeds, of the stinking mud where oxen and carts mounted the bridge over the meandering Fyris on their way to and from the seat of the king.

The mead-fuelled fighting talk had dwindled to silence as they drew closer. At the head of the column Earl Bodvar slowed to a walk. A low moon slanted off the surface of the Fyris as it flowed smooth and slick.

The bridge had been built to last – heavy planking and huge square-cut piles – and was wide enough for a fair-sized cart to cross without any fear of tipping over. Erlan wondered how long it had stood there. Fifty years? A hundred? Whatever, he doubted, in all that time, the air had ever hung so heavy with foreboding.

Out of habit, he touched his hilt.

Ahead, just short of the treeline, Bodvar raised an arm, barely visible in the gloom. The column halted. No one spoke. Only watched the bridge and listened.

Panting horses. The rushing river. A jackdaw cawing to the north.

'Seems we're in time,' Bodvar murmured.

'If they're coming this way,' said Erlan.

'It's this or swim the river. And Huldir wouldn't do that. Not with fifty... They must be waiting for darkness.' The earl looked round at the men. 'Quickly now – into positions. If the gods are good, then not a drop of blood need be spilt.' He turned to Erlan. 'You know what to do.'

Bodvar had explained his plan on the road from Uppsala. They would divide their twenty-five riders into three, the middle section astride the road out of sight of the bridge, with two flanking sections taking up position among the alder trees growing up- and downstream of where the bridge touched the eastern bank. Bodvar would challenge Huldir's lead riders in the centre. If they tried to ride on, at Bodvar's signal, the two flanking sections were to attack from the side. Meanwhile, Erlan and four others were to swim the river, staying out of sight of anyone watching the bridge from a distance. They were the stopper in the flask, as it were, the barrier to stop any of Huldir's men escaping back onto the western side.

'How are we supposed to swim the river with a byrnie on?' complained Jari Iron-Tongue, when Erlan led his crew to the bank. 'I don't see why we can't just walk across. There's no one here to stop us.'

'With this moon, we'd be seen from half a league downriver if you stood up there,' Erlan replied.

'You can give your byrnie to me if you don't want it,' said another karl.

'You'd be lucky,' Jari retorted.

'It's not deep,' Jovard said. 'If you can't swim you can probably wade across.'

'Probably? That's a real comfort, that is.' Jari's head suddenly snapped up. 'D'you hear that?'

'Odin's eye, you're a jumpy son of a bitch, aren't you?'

Erlan listened. There was a rustling noise behind them, coming closer. All of a sudden a body came tumbling through the reeds clutching a shield and a long-spear. 'There you are! I can't hardly tell arse from tit in this light.'

'Kai!' That was all he needed. He'd given him firm orders to hang back and see how the thing played out. He didn't want any distractions. 'What are you doing here?'

'I did reflect on what you said, master, but decided you probably needed the extra hand.'

'Gods – won't you do anything I tell you?'

'There didn't seem no point in me staying back there twiddling my toes.'

'It was for your own good, bonehead! Tonight's a killing night. You can smell it. I don't want you getting mixed up in it.'

'I can look after myself.'

'No, you fucking can't! And now I'm going to have to instead.'

'Balls to that! We've got this far, haven't we, master?' Kai grinned. 'So what's the plan?'

'How do you feel about getting wet?' Jari smirked.

'Listen up,' Erlan said, losing patience. 'Your shield and one weapon. Everything else stays here.'

The water was cold and fast-flowing but Jovard was right: it wasn't above shoulder-deep and all of them made it across, half-swimming, half-wading, with shield and blade slung over their backs.

Once across they snuck along the bank towards the bridge until the lattice of thick timber loomed overhead. They lined out in its shadow, lying flat against the bank.

'I feel like a bloody troll lurking under here,' muttered Jari.

'Look like one, too,' said Kai.

'Hey, kid – why don't you go suck a—'

'Shut it, both of you! Not another word, understand?'

Kai gave a sullen nod. Probably pulled a face as well but it was too dark to make out his features. Erlan was grateful for the sliver of moon rising to the east. But for its silvery light, they would soon be able to see nothing at all.

Across the river, everything was still.

He wondered how long they would have to wait. And now they were ready, doubts began to enter his head. Perhaps they were in the wrong place. Perhaps Huldir and his men had chosen another way across the Fyris. Perhaps this was all some fool's game and Huldir was tucked up in his hall at Svartadale nursing a head cold.

He scanned the crest of the riverbank. A line of silver birches stretched south, glimmering like sentinels' spears in the moonlight. He strained his ears for any sound that might herald riders. But for a long time, there was nothing.

And then some movement to the south snagged his vision.

At first, he thought his eyes were playing him false, but almost at once there was a swell of sound to answer any doubts. Clinking bridles, the jangle of armour, the myriad thud of hoofbeats, and then the shadows stirred, taking form.

Riders... *A lot of riders.*

They moved too fast to count them. But he guessed at least thirty were trotting towards the bridge, maybe more.

Approaching the gulley that ran down to the bridge, they slowed, filing into twos and threes. Most were helmed and carrying a spear. In the gloom, they all looked the same, like some army of shadows risen from the mist-land of *Niflheim*. But one rider caught his eye. The man's huge rounded shoulders and his torso, big and shapeless as a boulder, marked him out from the rest.

Huldir Hoskursson. The Great Ox.

Erlan ducked as the first rider mounted the bridge, timber banging noisily. He flinched with the shock of it, then flinched again a few moments later when a voice cried, 'HOLD!' clear as thunder.

There was a squall of shouting. Horses whinnied in protest, hooves clattered to a standstill. Erlan stretched his ears into the darkness.

On the bridge one horse kept on. *Clump, clump, clump...*

'Huldir Hoskursson!' the voice cried. 'I order you to hold, in the name of the king!'

The footsteps stopped. There was a pause, then a bellow of laughter. 'Is that you, Bodvar, you old whoremonger?'

Another pause. 'I'm Bodvar.'

'Come on, man – let's see that ugly face of yours.'

Across the river came the sound of horses advancing.

'A little short on company, aren't you, friend?'

'Perhaps,' Bodvar replied. 'Perhaps not.'

Huldir snorted. Erlan guessed he must be scanning the other side, but from that distance, the other karls would be invisible in the shadow of the trees.

'A fine night for a ride, old comrade,' Bodvar continued. 'But the king would like to know your purpose all the same.'

'Your king, Bodvar. No longer mine.'

'Aren't you and I bound by the same oath? To the same man?'

'My oaths extend only as far as my honour will allow. A man is no king who'll pimp his daughter for gold and a shameful alliance. And he's no better than a dog who would have a man sworn to him ignore his debts of blood.'

'We all have debts unpaid, Huldir. But this way we may have peace.'

'Peace!' Huldir bellowed. 'A curse on this peace! How can there be peace for me when three sons lie slaughtered? And the last of them, skinned like a hog! No – there can be no peace for me while the Wartooth and his sons still live. Every night the voices of my boys cry for vengeance.'

'I'm sorry your sleep is troubled.'

'Don't you dare mock me! You know nothing about losing a son and heir. And not one, but three.'

'Careless old bastard, ain't he?' Kai whispered, earning himself a kick from Jovard.

'I know this much,' answered Bodvar. 'Any chance you had of vengeance is gone. You were betrayed. The Wartooth's sons are warned.' It was a lie but Huldir couldn't know that. The fact was only twenty-five men stood between him and his dream of slaughter. 'Sviggar is a fair king. Give up this madness and he promises the Wartooth will make good your loss. He will see that the *wergeld* is generous.'

Huldir laughed long and bitterly at that. 'Are you whelp to a coward now, Vestmanland? You think I would accept silver for my own flesh and blood?'

'The choice is simple. We offer silver... Or steel.'

The sound of a blade being unsheathed rasped over the whispering river. After that, silence. The air reeked of unspilled blood. Erlan's skin prickled.

'Don't be a fool, old friend!' Bodvar cried, a pleading note in his gruff voice. 'The Norns haven't woven this yet.'

'The Norns be damned!' roared Huldir. 'And you as well!'

'Steel it is then,' said another, softer voice with dark relish, then began to laugh. Something fizzed through the air. There was a bone-chilling scream, then a body hit the ground.

After that all Hel erupted.

Above Erlan, timber crashed, arrows whipped from the far bank, war-cries arced into the sky, then screams as the first shafts found their mark.

'Steady,' he hissed, rising to a crouch. 'Hold till Bodvar's signal.'

'What for?' Kai snapped. 'More of them are getting across all the time. They need us.'

True enough. But Bodvar had insisted. If they were to catch these rats, he wanted them all in one barrel. 'Not till his signal.'

'Piss on that! There'll be no one to give the bloody signal if we wait any longer!'

Above them, someone bellowed to charge, hooves thundered, then a horn split the darkness.

Bodvar's signal at last.

'Happy now?' cried Kai.

'As I'll ever be.' Erlan straightened up. 'All right, lads! Hit them hard!'

Gods – what the Hel was a man supposed to say? Die well? See you on the other side?

If there is one...

In a heartbeat they were out from under the bridge and leaping up the bank. The scene that met them was black chaos. The rear-guard of Huldir's band was already on the bridge, pressing forward. Across the river, horsemen were pouring out of the trees, howling like Loki's son. At the far end of the bridge moonbeams splintered off a forest of whaling steel. Horses' screams mingled with the cries of men.

Erlan felt a rush of exhilaration. This was what he knew – this place of death. The place where he came alive.

He screamed and plunged into the storm of steel and flesh, half-aware of the others beside him, their cries filling his ears. The hindmost riders spun on their saddle-cloths, desperately trying to wheel their mounts. But there was little room and anyway they were too late. Erlan hacked down the first of them, who fell with a shriek to the side. The horse stumbled. There was a splash as the man hit the water.

That was one way of getting a body out of this fight. A good way, in fact. 'Into the river with them!' he yelled.

But the advantage of surprise was gone. Ahead, others had turned, some already dismounted. He pressed forward, working his arm mechanically as Garik had taught him: *slash, cut, lunge; slash, cut, lunge.* But in the cramped space, he struck more horse than human flesh.

Jovard was beside him, and beyond him the smaller figure of Kai. He had meant to keep him close – there was no sense the lad dying for Huldir's folly – but a man's choices narrowed in the battle-fog.

A riderless horse bolted past, slamming him aside. He staggered back, twisting his crippled ankle. Pain lanced up his leg. His opponent lurched forward, spear-point darting wickedly close to his head, but Erlan shifted sideways, taking the blow on his shield. The man over-balanced and hit the planks with a thump. In half a breath, Wrathling's point was through him. The man screamed as Erlan ripped his sword free and kicked him, squirming, over the edge.

Erlan grimaced. This was what he was. A killer. Not a lover, not a husband, not a prince. A thrill, dark and bitter, surged through him. There was blood-work to be done.

The confusion on the bridge had intensified, though Bodvar's plan, it seemed, was working. Although more numerous, Huldir's band of men was being squeezed from both sides. Erlan looked around, trying to orientate himself, and glimpsed a small man clutching a spear.

Kai!

The lad's face was bright with laughter as he hefted his shield with all the strength in his scrawny frame under the belly of a horse. The animal missed its footing and over it went, mount and rider together, into the dark waters. Without a second's pause, Kai scuttled on.

Ahead, there was hard fighting. Erlan moved forward. But then, a huge shout carried through the cries and clash of iron.

'Huldir is dead! Your liege-lord is dead!' Bodvar's voice, over the din. 'Lay down your arms! Give quarter!'

For some moments, the remnant of Huldir's shieldband wavered, looking at each other, unsure what to do.

'Lower your blades, fellas,' Jovard growled. 'No sense dying for nothing.'

Erlan saw the fight draining out of the men nearest him. And now he really looked at them, he realized many were hardly more than farm-thralls with a spear shoved in their hand.

But suddenly another yell, ringing with defiance, arced over the skirmish. 'Never! *NEVER!*' And with it came a horse, vaulting through the remnant of Huldir's men.

The scales tipped. The fighting erupted again.

The rider came on, knocking aside friend and foe alike, fixed on reaching the western bank. Erlan stood his ground, weighing how to take him. But then, to his horror, Kai appeared in front of him. Before he could yell at him to get out of the way, Kai had dropped a knee and lunged. Whether by luck or by skill, his spear sank deep into the horse's chest. The beast reared up, its rider snatching wildly for its mane, his helm flew off and a shock of silver hair flashed in the moonlight.

Erlan knew him at once.

Gellir the White. The last of Huldir's sons.

The horse keeled over with a clatter but somehow Gellir was on his feet. Kai seemed frozen, weaponless, as Gellir's axe cut down. Kai met it with his shield – first one blow, then another – staggering backwards under the savage attack.

Meanwhile, Erlan was dragging himself through the battle-debris towards them. The axe rose again as Erlan launched himself at Gellir with a yell that was half-terror, half-rage. They crashed together. There was a giddy instant in the empty air, then the river swallowed them up.

He didn't know what had become of Kai. All he knew were flailing limbs and curses. Fingers tore at his face. His sword was gone. His mouth filled with water. He scrabbled for Gellir's throat but the man was slippery as a salmon.

As they struggled, the current took them, buffeting them against the wooden piers, sluicing them downstream, turning them over and over in a gouging, butting, biting frenzy. They swept onwards. And then, from somewhere on the western bank, a voice was screaming his name. His ring-mail was heavy, pulling him under, grinding his feet along the riverbed, making every snatched breath harder to come by.

There was a sudden whip of air and Gellir screamed like a wounded hog. An arrow appeared from nowhere, buried deep in his shoulder. Desperate to end this, Erlan snatched at it, ground it in hard, feeling the iron tip grate bone. They both went under, deeper and deeper, dredging the riverbed. And suddenly, out of the murk lunged Gellir's face, white and terrible as the World Serpent. The next moment Erlan's skull shattered into a thousand pieces and he saw darkness…

Only darkness.

CHAPTER TWENTY-FIVE

Cold water fills his lungs, the light falls away, his cry is smothered by a salty abyss. Strong hands reach for him, catching his little fist, pulling him back to life.

'Hakan!' *His father's voice, far away.* 'Hakan!'

But Hakan is dead. And he is another man, with another name...

'Erlan!' someone shouted. A slap in the face. A flare of pain. He opened his eyes.

A man's features swam into focus – heavy jowls, drooping moustache. Before he could connect the face with a name he was throwing up half the Fyris all over himself.

'That's it, lad! Better out than in!' That was the fat man's voice. 'You must have the luck of Loki that Jo was there to fish you out.'

Erlan groaned.

'Up you get.' Whether he liked it or not, Einar hauled him to his feet.

'Where's Gellir?' he moaned.

'Gone.'

257

'But he was shot.'

'So he was. Might be he's at the bottom of the Fyris somewhere downstream. But we didn't get him.'

'He brained you with a rock or something,' said another voice. Erlan lolled his head and saw Jovard nearby. 'You went under. I figured it was more use saving you than killing him.'

'I'm obliged to you then.' River-water was still dribbling down his chin.

'Don't know how you found the lucky bugger, though,' chuckled Einar. 'It's pitch black in there.'

'Was that you on the far bank?'

'He pulled you out on our side of the river,' said Einas.

Erlan grunted, still trying to get his bearings. 'Where's Bodvar?'

They found the earl amid the carnage of fallen men and horses strewn everywhere on the approach to the bridge. The remnant of Huldir's band had either fled across the river or given up their arms and were being sorted into a column to be taken back to Uppsala, there to await some sort of justice. Bodvar was standing over Muldir's body.

'Poor, mad son of a bitch.'

Erlan gazed down at the broken hulk of a man, his beard tilted at an outlandish angle, an ugly gash from armpit to nipple. 'If you were him, would you have done any different?'

'If I was him... No. I guess not.'

Erlan felt a thump on his arm. 'You dropped this.' Kai was standing there, grinning from ear to ear, holding out a twin-ringed hilt he knew well.

Erlan seized Wrathling with a laugh. 'You should be dead,

I swear.'

'Not with my luck, master. Ain't you realized that by now?'

Einar gave Kai a hearty slap on the back. 'Now then, my lads – I've got me a thirst to rival Thor. And back home there's meat, mead and maids enough to content a man till the *Ragnarök*! I, for one, ain't going to miss it.'

You will fall and rise again.

The *vala* had spoken those words over him, a lifetime ago. Erlan wondered how long their truth would hold.

He took another pull on a mead-skin he'd cajoled off a hall-maid. It seemed hardly an hour since Jo had dragged him from the river, yet here he was as if he'd never left, albeit in borrowed clothes. Most of the others were happily installed in the Brewer's Hall. Those that weren't wounded. Or dead.

Only Bodvar and he had returned to the Great Hall, where the fog of merriment was now so thick you could cut it. The air was a swelter of smells – roasted ox, spilled ale, stale sweat, women's scent, wood-smoke, vomit.

Bodvar had returned to his place as discreetly as possible, ready to inform Sviggar of the events of Ulvar's Mill at a timely moment. Erlan, meanwhile, was getting drunk.

His blood was still hot with the battle-fire. He kept clenching his fist to stop his hand from shaking, still heard the rush of the river in his ears. Everything seemed unreal – both there and now here, leaning against this pillar observing the feast. The ale wasn't helping, but he didn't care. His temple throbbed like a curse.

Gellir wasn't dead, he was sure. And something told him the

White was far more dangerous than his father. But it wasn't just that. His eye kept straying to the king's table. Even through the shifting air, she was beautiful – a point of stillness amid all that commotion, but so far from him now. Unattainable. For ever. And meanwhile, he was down here in the mire.

Where he belonged.

He took another swig, spilling beer down his chin, knowing no amount of drink could quench the anger burning in his belly.

There was a flurry in the top corner of the hall and down the steps of the platform ran a troop of dancing girls, clad in flimsy white shifts, slit below their waist a dozen different ways. A space cleared between the hearth-pit and the high table and they ran, bare-footed and almost bare-legged, to their places.

There was a hush and then a drum struck up a beat. The girls started moving to its rhythm as a lyre and pipe took up the melody. The performance was for the high folk, of course, but everyone stopped to watch them. Where he stood the hearth-fire obscured his view, so that, to him, the girls seemed to be dancing inside the flames, pale arms rippling like streams of water, long braids whirling like whips, eyes sparkling like jewels with each spin.

It was a few moments before he recognized one of them was Rissa. His eyes followed her, watched her move, watched the rhythm of the drum pulse through her body, her legs oiled and glinting in the flame-flicker. She had a tattoo coiled up her arm that reflected the light like jet-stone. Like all the others, her face was a mask. Except that once – perhaps he only imagined it – she looked at him through the flames – right at him and no other – and for a second her hard mouth softened.

He took another drink, the heat blurring his vision, feeling his anger slide into something else. Or maybe it was all the same. *Blood and flesh.* Suddenly he wanted her. Wanted her cool, shimmering body to slake the heat that boiled in his head.

'Quite a sight, eh?'

Erlan jerked his head round. Sigurd was next to him.

'Hmm. So long as they keep our guests happy.'

'Happier than they deserve.' Sigurd angled a scornful look at the king's table. 'Look at them.' Thrand was beating his fist enthusiastically in time with the music. 'All smiles. Not a whisper of the army they've been raising to see us all dead.'

'You don't trust them?'

'No, I don't fucking trust them. Do you?'

'For once we're agreed then.' Erlan could hear the slur in his own voice. He clung a little tighter to the pillar.

'You see that old man up there, Aurvandil? That's complacency, sitting there. It's a wonder he can sit down after the sport our Danish cousins have had with him.' He sniggered.

'I suppose he thinks enmity is not always expedient.'

'Bah! A man's a fool who has the wolf's head in a noose and doesn't pull it tight.'

Was Sigurd testing him, picking at his loyalty? 'Your father has his reasons.'

'Reasons? It's all folly. Are we to believe the same men who were raising a host against us a month ago are now our bosom-friends? We speak a few words, share a few cups, and all is forgotten?'

'You don't think this changes things?'

'The only thing that has changed is that tonight Ringast's balls are a little lighter. Do you see how carefully my sister sits up there?' Sigurd sniggered again. Erlan's gall was rising. He looked away, his eyes returning to the dancing girls, to Rissa's body, and took another swig of ale. This time he wanted her to see him. Wanted her to know he saw her. 'And the oaths taken? Surely they bind them?'

'Huh! There's actually something rather touching about how seriously you take an oath, Aurvandil. Ah! Vargalf, there you are. You can tell us what you think.'

Erlan looked back sharply. The prince's oathman had appeared at his shoulder, sly and silent as a wolf. 'Think, my lord?'

'How did you put it before? There's a time for making oaths and—'

'A time for breaking them.'

'Aye!' Sigurd cried. 'A time for breaking them.'

'Why make an oath at all if you break it the moment the knot wears a little sore?'

Vargalf's nose wrinkled with disdain. 'Sometimes words serve a purpose, just like steel serves a purpose. But after all, what really binds you to an oath?'

Erlan found the question discomfiting. Oaths had cost him much. 'A broken oath bears ill fruit. It echoes through the Nine Worlds.' So his nurse had told him, anyway. He suddenly felt naive.

Vargalf's lips curled in a half-smile. 'A man of will cuts his own path and walks it. Oaths need not bind him.'

Something in his words tugged at Erlan's memory. He felt he had heard them before, or something like them, but then the dancers' performance came to the end with a flourish and the crowd broke into gales of applause. The sudden swell of noise made him feel dizzy. He pushed away from the pillar and took leave of the prince, intending to find some clean air outside, moving through the jostling, ale-happy sea of faces, determined to avoid any other talk.

But then a hand threaded through his fingers. He glanced down and saw a slender forearm swathed in a swirling tattoo. He looked up into Rissa's elfin face. Her throat was glistening with sweat.

'Did you like what you saw?' She had leaned in so close her mouth nearly touched his ear. Her fingers were restless in his, toying with his hand, but he left it there.

'Mmm.' He felt stupid. Couldn't think what else to say.

'Have you been drinking?' she asked teasingly, her mouth curling into a mischievous smile.

'A little. Haven't you?'

'I don't drink. I take my pleasure in other ways.'

'Like dancing?'

'Like dancing,' she echoed. 'And other things.'

They stood looking at each other, their faces a few inches apart. Her fingers were still laced round his. She suddenly tightened her grip. 'Come with me.'

She led him through the crowd and he followed, shutting down his mind to anything but that moment: the feel of her fingertips in his palm, the wake of mint in the air that swirled past her. Yet something made him glance back.

Lilla was looking straight at him. *Staring at him* – through all that tumult, her eyes full of sadness. And for a heartbeat, he wanted her to see, wanted her to hurt, to feel what he had felt, even though, deep in his heart, he knew it was he who hadn't fought hard enough for her.

Outside the air was cooler. Rissa led him through the

shadows under the massive buttresses along the side of the hall. His head was throbbing, probably as much from Gellir's blow as the drink. But he didn't need to think. Didn't want to. There were no illusions here. Nothing to hide. He didn't know this woman. She didn't know him. Knowledge like that only led to pain, anyhow. This way she could have him, if that was what she wanted. And he... he could forget the world for a while.

She stopped in a shaded corner between a supporting pillar and the wall and turned to him. It was too dark to see her smile, but he heard it in her voice. 'I told you our conversation wasn't over.'

'Is that all you want to do? Talk?'

She gave a slow chuckle and then he tasted her breath on his lips, felt her tongue slip into his mouth. She moaned and the sound seemed to release something in him. Like a rope being cut, setting adrift all the burdens he had been carrying in his head.

She pulled back, slipped her shoulder out of her flimsy robe, exposing a small round breast, taking his hand and pressing it to her. The nipple tightened under his palm, proud as a rosebud. Then she undid his belt, let it fall, and began unlacing his breeches. Her hand slipped inside, fingers cool around his heat.

'Here,' she said breathlessly, falling back into the dark nook, taking him with her. He saw the glimmer of a long pale leg through the slitted skirt, pushed against her, heard her breathing quicken.

She coiled around him, guiding him into her wet warmth hungrily, nails digging into his buttocks, her head kicked back against the wall.

There was a kind of frenzy to the rest of it, two wolves

devouring each other. And for a time, he did forget; until she was shaking and then he was shaking too, and everything was emptying out of him – his anger, his confusion, his sorrow, the battle-fear, the killing rage, all of it – until he was no one and nothing. Nothing but the fire ripping through him.

Why did he do that? Lilla asked herself, over and over. Each time, the same answer. She had no claim over him now. Yet her mind couldn't leave him alone. His absence from the hall haunted her like a ghost.

It was late. The formal toasts had been delivered long ago, but now came speeches inspired by drink and ill-judged loquacity. The first of them was an embarrassment. Her new brother-in-law, Prince Thrand, took to his feet, apparently to insult every noble, Dane or Sveär, who came into view or mind.

The high folk bristled, at least those that were listening, but her husband eventually cut short his brother's ramblings, persuading him in a word or two to resume his seat and keep his misguided remarks to himself. Instead, Ringast extolled her father for the honour done him and his kin, and the new age between their two peoples that lay ahead. 'Now we are all brothers,' he declared, though she imagined few there believed it.

'Well said, cousin, well said indeed,' her father began, rising to answer, only to be overcome by a violent bout of coughing. Before he had recovered, Queen Saldas stood, slipping her arm through his.

'My lord husband,' she murmured, 'allow me to answer for both of us.'

Her father sank, defeated, back into his chair. 'Very well, my dear.'

Saldas looked out over the heaving crowd and a hush seemed to settle over the mead-hall. 'The dawning of this new age of brotherhood brings great joy, dear prince.' Ringast nodded dutifully. 'But I confess a shadow still hangs over my heart. The sadness of separation from this dear daughter of mine.' Her smile fell on Lilla. 'In four short years, I feel our spirits have become one. Is it not so, daughter?'

Lilla smiled obligingly, wondering what Saldas was up to. The queen never did anything out of whimsy alone.

'And yet there is a way to ease this parting.' Saldas gazed graciously down on the new couple. 'I will ride with you to the border and there we shall say our farewells. I trust this will signal the depth of my love for you and the sorrow I feel in losing you. Do I have your blessing, dear prince?'

'Undoubtedly, Lady Saldas.'

'And yours, my lord husband?'

Lilla looked at her father's weathered face. He was fairly beaming at his young wife. 'My beloved queen,' he croaked. 'You speak of sadness, but it fills my heart with joy to hear you talk like this. I should like nothing better than to accompany you on this journey.'

But Saldas took his hand and pressed his knuckles to her lips. 'My lord, I could wish for nothing more. But, alas, I fear you've played the host too well these last days.' His sweat-flecked brow furrowed with a questioning look. 'Who knows better than I the burden of the sickness you bear?' She laid a graceful hand on his shoulder. 'It is enough. You must rest.'

Her father opened his mouth, perhaps to object, but instead

his chest tightened into a new series of coughs. At length the fit passed. 'A king is loath to admit he needs to retire to his bed. But you are right.' He turned to Lilla. 'Will you forgive me, my child?'

Lilla didn't say anything. The sham of it was all too sickening.

'Of course,' Saldas continued, 'I shall need an escort for my return. If my husband cannot ride with me, let me take the man to whom all of us owe a vast debt – including you, dear prince.' She smiled at Ringast. 'If not for his courage, Lilla would not be here for this happy day.' Her green eyes scanned the crowd until she gave a cry of delight. 'There!' she pointed. 'The Aurvandil! Our own shining wanderer.'

And there he was, half-hidden in the shadows. A space cleared around him. She was surprised how painful it was to look on him. 'Who better to ride with me?' Saldas declared. 'Even our beloved Lilla could think of no better choice. Is it not so?'

Saldas let her smile rest on Lilla while she waited for a reply. The whole company was waiting.

At last Lilla nodded. 'It is a good choice.'

'Then it's settled!' cried her father, beaming. 'And settled well.'

Saldas bowed her head to her husband. 'I drink this toast. To my daughter and her prince!'

The hall echoed her words with a clamorous cheer.

Lilla looked out over their faces, all flushed with ale and goodwill. She saw only one man who did not drink with the rest, and at that moment she would have given all she had to know what was passing through his thoughts.

But no one marked him. They saw only their queen – tall and serene, splendid as Freyja herself, in beauty and grace.

CHAPTER
TWENTY-SIX

In summer, it was a journey of two days to the edge of the Kolmark forest. On the first day, Prince Ringast rode at the head of the column with his two brothers, while Lilla rode her mare a little distance behind. Queen Saldas rode next to her.

They hardly spoke. Lilla didn't want to speak – to anyone. It had been a painful parting from her father, and from her little brother and sister, too. He had sent her off with his love and blessing – though what currency they held in a land ruled by King Harald Wartooth and his sons remained uncertain.

'You've won the peace we both wanted,' were his final whispered words. Aye, she seemed at least to have done that. But what had she lost?

As for the other riders, they let her alone, most of them nursing sore heads. Erlan rode further back, beside the queen's handmaiden, Bara. The girl said little beyond the odd complaint about the rain and – when Saldas was out of earshot – why they had to make this journey at all.

Lilla wanted this journey over too, but for reasons other than the rain. *That look*... That callous look across the hall, in which she saw the vast chasm that had opened up between them.

Part of her wanted to turn around, to look into his face and see – truly *see* – him for the last time. But instead she gazed out over the sodden rye fields that shone like silver in the rain, and at the dripping linden trees standing silently by the wayside as they passed.

The second morning dawned on a damp land, but the sun rose high and hot. Spirits lifted as cloaks and tunics dried out and Ringast's men were soon throwing around jokes as usual. Saldas was content to ride beside Lilla, enjoying the sun on her face. For all her declarations of affection, she offered not a word to lift Lilla out of her melancholy.

At length, Ringast dropped back. 'Anyone would think you were riding to your own execution.'

'I'm sad to be leaving my homeland. That's natural, isn't it?'

'I assure you, your new land is much like this one.'

'But it can never be the land of my blood.'

He snorted. 'Well, if the gods are kind, it'll be the land of your sons soon enough.'

'As you wish.'

'As *I* wish? By the hanged, woman – don't you wish for it, too?'

She didn't answer.

'It's time to drop this forlorn face, my wife. It hardly does me credit.' He touched his horse's flank and trotted back to the head of the column.

Ringast was right. She sat up straighter and did her best to look cheerful. After all, what had she expected? The road was there ahead of her, the road she always knew she must walk.

Wife to a king. Mother of kings.

That other road – Erlan's road – was a road she had forsaken. It had never been hers and now it never would be. And as for her heart... surely it could not ache for ever?

Not if she kept walking.

Early in the afternoon, a line of trees crept over the horizon. The sun wasn't much lower when the track rose to meet it before disappearing into green shadow.

'Lady Saldas,' called Ringast. 'Be ready to say your farewells. My realm begins on the far side of that ridge.'

'I shall ride with her to the end. No one shall say I turned too soon.'

'So be it.'

The canopy closed overhead and they soon climbed as far as the ridge-line, after which the road began to fall away. Ringast called a halt. 'We part company here.'

'If it must be... Will you grant me just a little longer with her? In private?'

The prince levelled his gaze at her, then snapped an order. Two riders dismounted and helped each lady down. 'A hundred paces that way, there's a clearing.' Ringast pointed into the trees. 'There's a rise there. A good place to say goodbye to your land.'

Lilla nodded gratefully.

The mound blistered, small and rocky, out of a clearing that sloped northwards towards Sveäland. Lilla scaled its weather-worn crown and from there looked north. The forest fell away below her. Beyond it she could see for leagues over the patchwork of strip-fields, edged by ditches and blooming hedgerows. The farmland shimmered green-gold where the barley ears had begun to turn.

She heard a trickle of stones behind her, then stillness. She didn't look back.

'You will miss it.'

'Yes.' Tears started welling, but she caught them, swallowed them back. Something settled on her shoulder, so light it was a moment before she realized it was Saldas's hand.

'You mustn't despair.' For once, her voice was soothing. 'This is change, nothing more. Your marriage is only another season in another place.'

Lilla closed her eyes and wished for her own mother. Wished there was someone who could bear to hear the truth from her. But there was only Saldas. Only this moment.

'It's hard... to go to a new place. To be joined to a new lord. One whom I do not love.'

'A woman seldom loves the man she marries. Even so, he is a strong man. You may come to love him in time. You'll find happiness, I am sure. It's only when a woman marries one man but loves another that life proves unendurable.'

Saldas could hardly have picked words more crushing, though she couldn't have known it. 'I feel so weak.'

'You're too modest.' An edge had crept into Saldas's voice, and not a kind one. 'You have much power, my *daughter*.'

'Power?'

Saldas laughed – a metallic click in her ear. 'A woman's body is her power. With it, she can make any man lie down like a dog at her feet.' Lilla tried to turn, to see in her face whether she was in earnest, but the grip on her shoulder tightened. *'But you know this...'* That snigger again. Fingers digging into her flesh. Lilla winced. 'After all, you made Erlan your dog, didn't you?'

Lilla gasped, tried to wriggle free, but the queen's hold was strong. She re-doubled her efforts until Saldas suddenly shoved her forward, laughing with scorn. Lilla fell to the ground, the rock cracking her kneecaps.

'Did you really think you could keep a secret like that from me? What a curious creature you are! You waft around like an innocent flower then fall on your back like a mud-whore for the first man who dares defy your father and show you some attention.'

Lilla felt the blood draining from her face, a hard knot of fury twisting in her belly. Slowly she got to her feet.

'Oh, but it's love, you'll say,' Saldas sneered. 'How disgustingly predictable! How easily you deceive yourself! What you feel is the basest of desires.'

'*You – are – unspeakable*,' Lilla whispered.

'Unspeakable? You should be thanking me, my beloved *daughter*. Someone had to protect your virtue, since you wouldn't do it yourself.' Her voice was acid. 'It was the kindest thing I could have done to persuade your father to give you to Ringast.'

'What?' Lilla choked. 'You persuaded my father of this?'

'It was my duty.' Saldas smiled. 'As your mother.'

'But my father,' Lilla stammered. 'I did this for his kingdom. For him!'

'His kingdom?' Saldas's beautiful face curdled in disgust. 'What is his kingdom worth after his humiliation? Men won't serve a man like that for long. You're both of you fools. Your sacrifice, as you call it, did nothing more than satisfy me. Whether your father stands or falls is of no consequence – though I doubt he'll keep his crown for long. If not him, another man will rise. A stronger man. One who will desire me and will doubtless be as easy to control.'

'You are hateful. I curse the day you ever came to my father's court.'

'A little late for that, my dear. Besides, your father has had his uses. But now he's had all the use he ever will of me.'

'If anything should happen to my father—'

Saldas threw back her head and laughed, her pale neck shining golden in the falling sun. 'Are you going to threaten me? You? Our innocent little flower?'

Lilla grimaced. She suddenly wanted to get away from this woman, away from her cruel face and poisoned words. 'You may heed this warning or not,' she said. 'I care little which. But if I hear you've raised so much as a fingernail against *any* of those I love, I *will* come for you. And there will be a reckoning between us.'

The queen's scornful expression wavered for a second. But it soon gave way to another mocking laugh. 'The luck of Frey in that, dear daughter. The luck of all the gods if you ever dare set yourself against me.'

But Lilla was already stumbling down the ancient blister of rock. At the foot of the mound she stole a final glance northwards, out across the land of her fathers, wondering what thread the Norns might weave to bring her back to her beloved homeland one day. Then she gathered up her skirts. Her husband was waiting. And for now, her road must lead to Dannerborg.

CHAPTER
TWENTY-SEVEN

'May you serve your king well.'

Those had been her last words to him, said in a voice stiff as bark.

'As you have, my lady,' he'd replied. It was unnecessary, churlish even, but he couldn't help it. And he saw in her eyes the barb had caught.

He had watched her ride after her husband, watched the whole column take to the road, watched until all sound of them had faded to nothing, and with it any tenderness, any love he had left in him. The last of it had ridden away in the heart of that golden-headed girl.

Saldas returned a little while after, sauntering through the brush. 'A sad parting,' she had said, though she didn't look sad. 'So now it's just we three.'

They took the road north, three horses in procession, three riders in silence, until a few leagues later Erlan called a halt, saying they should find shelter. 'It's getting dark and the rain may return.'

'It seems a fine evening to me,' Saldas replied, shielding her eyes against the westering sun. The lower half of her face was bathed in its golden colour. Midges danced around her like embers. The edges of her were glowing, as if she might suddenly catch fire.

He shook away the image. 'Wet or dry, we're better out of the wind.'

There was a copse set a little back from the road on a rise. Erlan kicked ahead and led them under the birch and ash trees into a small clearing close to the southern edge of the little wood. Once they had dismounted and unloaded their gear, they set about making camp. Bara arranged the cooking utensils and got a fire lit, humming a tune that was popular about the halls just then. Meanwhile Erlan erected three shelters – insubstantial things, but enough to keep off the rain if it returned. His own he placed a little distance from the others.

'Thirsty work?' He looked up from pinning down the last corner of his shelter. Saldas was offering a horn. 'Honey-wine.'

'I had my fill the other night.' He finished tying off the rope.

'Oh, Erlan,' she replied playfully. 'Are you really too proud to be served by your queen?'

He looked her up and down. 'I guess I'm thirsty enough.' He took the horn and drained it in one, its sweetness sticky on his lips.

'Was that so hard?' She smiled. 'Tonight we lay aside our differences. Agreed?'

He peered at her, still suspicious, but said nothing.

'It's ready, my lady,' Bara called, spooning a steaming broth into three bowls.

The green eyes lingered a moment longer before Saldas turned away. 'So let us eat!'

Bara passed around the bowls, then pulled apart a flatbread and handed out the pieces. Erlan was hungry. He fell to eating at once, tasting fowl-flesh, marjoram and wild chervil. 'It's good,' he mumbled between mouthfuls.

'Indeed,' Saldas agreed. 'Who needs all the trappings of the Great Hall? This does just as well. Better, even.'

'You're too kind, my lady,' said Bara.

'Not at all. Here. A drink to wash it down.' She took the mead-skin and filled a horn for Bara, then refilled Erlan's vessel too. 'Perhaps our escort can amuse us with some tales of his wanderings. Or some song his servant boy has taught him.'

'A song? I wouldn't want to spoil your supper. As to stories... How about we hear your tale, Queen Saldas?'

'My tale?' She seemed wrong-footed, as though the question had never been put to her before.

'Aye,' he said, finding he was genuinely curious now. 'How came you to be wife to a king?'

She leaned back and gazed into the night, amusement teasing at the corners of her mouth. 'Trapped by my own words! All right, I shall tell you, though it hardly makes a tale.' She laughed, almost girlishly. 'Why, I don't even know where to begin!'

'Begin where we all begin. With your birth.'

'Very well. I come from the north. My father was a huntsman of the Sami blood. He often used to say how, long ago, his people came from far, far to the east. From a different world – of sand-blown wildernesses, bright mountain peaks and salt-marsh seas.'

'Was he rich?'

She snorted. 'If you mean in gold – no, he wasn't rich. The Sami don't value gold and silver like the Sveärs. But he was wealthy according to our ways. He owned more reindeer than any man of the Northern Forests. And more slaves, too... My mother was one of them.'

Something must have shown in his face, because her eyes fixed his, challenging him. 'Does it surprise you? That the daughter of a slave should be married to a king?'

'A little.'

'Her parents sold her to my father for twenty head of reindeer. A good price, they thought. But he got the better deal. She was a plain child but she grew into a striking woman. I witnessed it myself. She was only twelve when she had me.'

'And your father?'

'Was forty when I was born.'

Erlan raised an eyebrow. 'An old man for a wife so young.'

'She wasn't his wife.'

'Yet he kept you.'

'My mother said once he saw me, he was smitten.' She snorted. 'I was lucky. He left most of his children out for the wolves.'

'So did he treat you... well?'

'Oh yes,' she said in a faraway voice, staring into the fire. 'I was his favourite.' Her eyes jerked up at him. 'His favourite gift. Saved only for his most honoured guests. After all, a wise man increases his influence with what he possesses.' She shook her head, as if to shake away the dark thoughts picking at her mind. 'Still, he taught me a lot. About our people and the forest and the ways of beasts. Aye, and men. He taught me how different folks hold different kinds of knowledge. And different kinds of power.'

'Power which you now possess, I suppose?' said Erlan wryly.

She pushed aside a lock of hair that had fallen across her eyes. 'Wisdom comes to those who seek it. Power too, I think.'

'And your mother? What did she teach you?'

'Only two things.' She picked up a stick from the ground and prodded at the fire. 'She was beautiful, but simple. My father kept her that way. But she figured out one true thing: if you desire something strongly enough, nothing in the Nine Worlds can stop it coming to you.'

Erlan scoffed. 'Any halfwit child knows that's nonsense.'

'Does he?'

'Yes!' he insisted. 'If you mean I can wake up one morning and decide I want fifty marks of silver, and somehow it'll drop out of the sky into my lap. That's absurd.'

'You misunderstand me. What I mean is, whatever you desire most deeply, whatever you truly believe is your due and your destiny – it will surely come upon you. If it's wealth, it will come. Or love. Or revenge.' The shadows danced over her face. 'Or destruction.'

'So did it work for your mother?'

'This law never fails. It is inescapable as death.' She tired of stirring the fire and threw the stick into the flames. 'Most people are ignorant. They don't see that what befalls them is exactly what they have been drawing to themselves.'

'A cruel law, then.'

'Is it? You know the Norns are much kinder than we think. They weave only the fate that we call upon ourselves.'

'If what you say is true, then we have no one but ourselves to blame. For our misery. For our pain.'

'Exactly. And my mother saw this and changed the fate she was calling to herself. In time she got what she wanted.'

'What did she want?'

'A splinter of bone in my father's throat,' she said softly. 'He choked to death. Face down in a bowl of gruel.'

'She murdered him, then.'

'No!' she laughed. 'That's the beauty of it! She did nothing – nothing but change her thoughts. That was enough to change her destiny.'

'You weren't sorry?'

'He wasn't the kind of man to be mourned.'

'So your mother wanted him dead?'

'She wanted her freedom. And she soon had it. So we came south.'

Erlan nodded thoughtfully, finishing his last morsel of flatbread soaked with the grease at the bottom of his bowl. At length he spoke again. 'You said your mother taught you two things. What was the second?'

Her lip curled. 'She taught me how to nurture my hate.'

'Your hate? What do you hate?'

Suddenly she clapped her hands. 'Enough talk with an empty cup. Another drink and this skin is done.'

'There's another with the horses,' said Bara, rising. 'I'll go—'

'No, no – you sit, my dear. Go on, sit!' So Bara sank back down and it was Saldas who gathered their drinking horns and shook them out over the fire.

Erlan watched her glide into the shadows where the animals were resting, wondering what to make of her candour. He didn't trust her – that went without saying – but he still couldn't help feeling intrigued by this woman who possessed so many faces. He knew not which was her true face. Perhaps one he would never see. One that no one would ever see.

She reappeared, carrying three horns and a fresh skin. 'Alas, we have only this nettle-wine left. Will it suffice?'

'I don't see why not.'

She passed the black horn to Erlan, the grey to Bara and kept the white for herself, then filled all three.

'Well then. I drink to you both.'

The others drank with her. Erlan sank a good portion. Bara took only a sip.

'It's bitter,' he said.

'The first taste of nettle-wine is always bitter. Try again! You'll see it's not so bad.' She reached out and with a long finger tipped his cup right back.

'It could do with some spices,' he grunted.

Saldas threw back her head and laughed. 'Bara will be sure to tell the brewers, won't you?'

The redhead nodded uncertainly.

'Weren't you going to finish your story?'

She sighed. 'Well, what more is there to tell? We came south. My mother drew the eye of an old earl who took her as his mistress.'

'A concubine?'

'If you like.' She shrugged. 'Soon afterwards his nephew begged to have me in his household. So I went, and the following year the fool married me, though I brought him no advantage. But it hardly mattered. He was dead within three years.'

'Another desire fulfilled?'

'Hah! Not in this case. No, he died as he lived. Foolishly. A drunken brawl. He never was much good with either sword,' she chuckled. 'But by then, I'd been to Sviggar's halls. When his first wife died, he summoned me. The rest you know.'

More questions circled in Erlan's mind, but the words he wanted to say seemed elusive, drifting out of reach when he tried to voice them. His eyelids drooped, then snapped open with a start.

'I'm boring you,' Saldas laughed.

'Not at all... I'm suddenly weary, that's all.'

'Well, I never fancied myself a skald, but if I'm putting you to sleep...'

'It was a long day.'

'I'm tired too,' Bara agreed.

'Then your beds await. But first... it's bad luck not to finish the cup.' She smiled and raised her horn. 'From the first ice to the last fire.'

'From the ice to the fire then,' echoed Erlan and emptied the bitter wine down his throat.

'And you, my dear?'

'From the ice to the fire,' Bara murmured and tipped back the horn. The queen drank too, upending hers when she was done.

'So then! A peaceful night to you both.' Saldas rose and went to her shelter. Bara did likewise. Last of all, Erlan hauled himself up. And with a final look up at the smoke spiralling into the night, he ducked into his shelter and sank, heavy-limbed, onto his blanket.

CHAPTER
TWENTY-EIGHT

The fire burned on and soon the flames shrank lower. Around them darkness pressed, squeezing back their guttering heat, seeping round the three shelters like a black tide. Darkness oozing through the trees, smothering the decaying leaves and dirt, darkness gaping like the bottomless maw of death, swallowing every pinprick of light down into its cold belly. And then, after a long moment of stillness, the darkness vomited up those evil things from another realm.

Saldas smiled, feeling the shadows press against her body, the clench in the sinews of her mouth, the tightness over her skin. She touched her lips and felt the ripple of murmured invocations over her fingertips, summoning to her those ancient powers she already sensed around her.

The air grew cold. She shivered. They were here, those spirits from beyond. Her *dísir*. Or *fylgyur*, some called them. Fetches. Shape-shifter spirits. Tonight they would do her bidding.

She undid the leather gourd at her girdle, pulling the stopper. Her nostrils flared. Its smell was acrid. But she put it to her lips, tipped and swallowed. At once the liquid seeped through her body like a winter frost, chilling her. Her lips moved with fresh urgency.

I will have my desire. Of course. Didn't she always in the end?

Soon this man who had dared resist her, soon he would have his greatest desire, too.

A snicker escaped her beautiful lips.

Yes. He will have his desire. That is what she would now become. Those were the words she uttered. And soon she would assume the shape of whomever Erlan desired most in all the world.

She couldn't keep the smile from her face, knowing that soon she would possess him. Her spell became louder, but she was not concerned. They had both drunk down their brews like babes at a nursemaid's nipple. A sleeping draught for Bara. And for Erlan... well, by now his mind would be a-swirl with longing, desire enveloping all his thoughts like a hot wind.

The potion surged within her. She felt its force as invisible hands went to their work. There was pain – there was always pain – and she gasped against it. But she had felt it before and now it only heightened her excitement.

Her eyes burned for an instant, the knuckles in her hands contorted, sending a shriek of pain up her arms. Her scalp flared white hot. Then, suddenly, the pain ceased.

She opened her eyes. At first she felt nothing. But she knew the fetches had finished their work. She ran her hands over her body. It was firmer, smaller, but almost bursting with the vigour of youth. She touched her cheeks and sensed the freshness of many years before.

For a second she felt a pang of jealousy at Lilla. That this was how it felt to have her body. But she quickly laughed it away. Instead, she almost wished Lilla were here now to witness her victory.

But what of Lilla, anyway? It was her moment now.

She seized her hand-mirror and slipped outside. There she stopped to listen.

Not a sound.

Nothing but the ebb of Bara's breathing, and beyond the fire Erlan's deeper sighs. She moved closer to the dying embers of the fire and raised the mirror, excited at what she would see.

But when she looked, she was amazed.

For in its surface she saw nothing of Lilla's honey curls. No dark blue eyes. No feckless smile. Instead, an even younger face stared back at her.

Her hand dropped the mirror into her lap. This wasn't what she had expected at all. Yet soon her curiosity overcame her surprise. She looked again, turning her face from side to side, seeing what Erlan saw in his mind.

Was she beautiful?

Undoubtedly, in a girlish sort of way. Her own hair had softened from raven-black to a deep brown, falling in thick curls about her face and shoulders. She smiled at herself and the large, warm eyes suddenly sparkled with mischief. At the same time, inside she felt mischief brimming, a kind of exuberance, an eagerness to fling her arms wide and embrace the whole world and all it could give her. Of course, she remembered that feeling from her own youth, though it had long ago changed into something else, something more practical. Even so, it was strange to feel its intensity once more, and she couldn't help but wonder whose face this was.

Perhaps it was better Lilla wasn't here after all, she thought with delicious mirth. Her stepdaughter would be sad indeed to learn that another girl had a tighter hold on her lover's heart than she.

Saldas laid the mirror down. Everything was ready. She glanced at Bara's tent, satisfied that inside all was still.

I'll overlook your lethargy tomorrow, my dear. Just this once, she smiled. After the dose she had given her, Bara would sleep well beyond the dawn.

Soundlessly, she stole around the fire, pausing only for a moment at the entrance to Erlan's tent. Her hand was shaking with excitement. Her throat was dry. But this proud fool would soon slake her thirst.

And drawing breath, she went inside.

Erlan knew he was dreaming.

A terrible dream that pierced his heart, a dream from which he never wished to wake.

As soon as his eyes had closed, his mind had slipped into a whirlpool of images, each shifting in and out of focus, each sharp and quick as a spear-thrust. He saw smothering darkness, sea-spray, heard creaking timber and the lash of the wind. Then a snowbound forest, mad, mocking laughter dancing in the treetops; his hands slick with blood, a fearful screaming of horses. Then the smell of wet pine needles and Lilla's face, her mouth biting at his chest, biting to hurt him, while her father appeared over them crying, 'Oath-breaker!' And then many other faces from the past, drifting in and out of shadow, murmuring, moaning, louder and louder till their voices became a single roar of noise.

And last of all, through the crowd of faces, *she* came.

And suddenly there's only one voice. One face.

Hers.

And they are alone.

She is soothing him with soft words. She smiles just like she used to and lies beside him. He tries to speak but his words melt into meaningless sounds. She puts a finger to his lips. And then they are naked and their bodies gripped tight against one another, clinging on as though they must never let go. Her skin feels familiar, smells familiar. Every mark and curve of her body he remembers. Only now she is more urgent. Now passion blazes in her eyes, so fierce it feels more like anger. She claws at his skin, urging him on, riding him in a blind fury, begging for him to please her in ways she never has before, exultant, shimmering, glorious in her ecstasy.

And when it's over, he turns to her. He wants to weep, to beg her forgiveness, to tell her to stay. But she will not. She sees the amulet hanging round his neck and asks what it is. He tells her. *'You made it for me. Don't you remember?'* She smiles and says she must take it now. He gives it up. Her hand closes. She tells him she must go. Her fingers caress his eyes, closing them, so softly he hardly feels her touch.

And then she is gone.

He wonders if she'll notice that her fingertips are wet with his tears.

PART THREE

TWILIGHT
OF KINGS

CHAPTER TWENTY-NINE

King Harald Wartooth turned onto his back with a groan. Gods, even that took most of his strength these days. His hip grated like a rusted hinge.

Old bones...

The council talk made him so damn tired these days. Him, whom men had called 'Tireless' in his youth. How the years had crept up on him.

It was a long time since he'd felt the blood burn in his sword arm or heard the ring of steel. Now it was his bladder that burned and his ears that rang. His once-ruddy fist was a clutch of crumbling twigs, hardly able to stop his mead-cup shaking. He grimaced, feeling age gnawing at his marrow, wishing for the sleep that took longer to come each night.

Age laughs last and laughs hardest.

All other foes he could quell. But this one... this one came on relentless as the tide.

They thought he didn't notice how they eyed him as he shifted his brittle arse on his council seat. But he saw. Saw the scheming in their gaze. Heard the whisper of ambition in their minds.

Wouldn't he have been the same? Wouldn't he have sought to snatch the realm from an old man of five and three score years, to place it in the keeping of stronger hands?

He scraped a palm over the callused brow where a crown had sat for thirty years. He was tired. And his worries would keep for the morrow.

Though how many morrows would there be for him?

Aye, how many?

He closed his eyes and soon, despite himself, he dreamed.

The smells fill his senses first. Spitted ox and boiled venison, the sweet tang of mead. Laughter rings. Around him swirls the feast babble. He looks down. His hands are young again, knuckles smooth as oiled leather. He squeezes and feels the strength in them. Warrior hands. When he looks up, everything shines with a lustre not of the world he knows. Towering pillars of polished stone soar to a roof that gleams like gold over rafters of bronze. No human hands built this hall.

The tables stretch on and on, bowing under the weight of silverware and colossal mountains of vittles and drink. Along the benches sit men. Hundreds of men. Warriors. Heroes.

Einherjar.

He hears his name and turns. Surrounding him are friendly faces. Kinsmen. Men the Spear-God took long ago. Their faces shine.

'Welcome, Harald!' cries one. He recalls his name: Handrik – a cousin fallen in Estland, half a lifetime ago.

'What kept you, kinsman?' roars another – the brother to his murdered father. 'We saved your place these long years.'

So this is Valhöll.

The mighty abode of Odin and his chosen ones. He feels the vigour of youth in his limbs, his heart pulses with gladness and relief as he gulps down the ale thrust into his hand. There's a maid across from him, smiling at him. And such a maid! A face like a goddess, a laugh upon her lips.

She offers her hand and he would take it, only a shadow falls across his place. Another's hand weighs leaden on his shoulder, cold as a Yuletide wind.

He turns and sees a single, staring eye. Beside it gapes a lidless pit so dark that his heart trembles – his, whose heart has never trembled yet. The eye gazes on him, unblinking. He tries to shrink away.

'You have no place here.' The One-Eyed's voice seeps into his mind like a mist.

'But... these are my kinsmen.'

'You have no place here.'

He opens his mouth to protest.

'YOU – HAVE – NO – PLACE – HERE.' The cry is so terrible he covers his ears. But before he can think the One-Eyed has seized him and hurled him to the floor. Scornful laughter breaks over him, wave after wave, scalding him with shame. Suddenly his youth is thawing away. He is a bag of bones again, struggling to stay afoot as Odin drags him from his hall.

He wails, clamping his eyes shut. When he opens them again, he is on the edge of an abyss. Below him, mists swirl, thick and impenetrable. Above them he sees a bridge, arcing to the horizon, shimmering like it's made of the very sky.

'You cannot cross the Rainbow Bridge.' Each word hits like a hammer-blow. 'Your place lies there,' the One-Eyed whispers, raising a baleful finger. 'In the mistlands below.'

A hand pushes him. He hears his own scream and he is falling and falling, down into the grey darkness...

King Harald sprang upright. Sweat chilled the crook of his neck. He looked about the chamber, trying to remember where he was, trying to discern in the gloom something solid that would tether him back to the world of the living. Slowly, his breathing began to subside.

The fear did not.

The dream again. That cursed dream.

'What have I done?' he muttered. This peace his son had talked him into... Was that his last chance, gone? Vanished with the swearing of an oath? 'I've lived too long.' He buried his face in his hands.

No. If death would not find him, then he must find death.

He lay back on his pillow, listening to the air rattle in and out of his lungs. Then something made him stop. Was he still dreaming? He strained his old ears. It was faint, but...

Something else was breathing in his chamber.

Harald lunged for his sword as the shadow peeled from the wall and leaped. Then the world collapsed into a tangle of furs and fists, sour sweat and wicked steel. Some stinking, lowborn churl, he thought even as he struggled to fight off his assailant. Ever the cat's paw of ambition. If someone wanted him dead, they might at least have sent a killer worthy of his death.

Worthy or no, the man had him pinned, fingers clamped

on his throat. But Harald had the dagger-hand gripped tight. He yelled, as best he could. A paltry cry although, with luck, it would be enough to rouse the guards, if they weren't as deaf as he was.

The killer snarled reeking breath in his face, struggling to smother him, but the Wartooth had slain a hundred foes a hundred times more savage than this one. He jerked his head back then bit down hard, his dagger-tooth sinking into sour flesh. The attacker shrieked and Harald tasted blood.

He didn't wait for a second chance. He could still fight like a wounded boar if he had to. He lurched forward, rolling the man onto the floor, his age-riddled fingers clasped like an iron fetter around the killer's wrist.

That was when he smelled the fear on the man. No doubt whoever he was had expected an easy kill. An old man, dispatched without a whisper. But that wouldn't be Harald's end. He hadn't lived this long to die a worm's death. He twisted the wrist, heard it crack. The man wailed in pain. Not that it would do him any good. Harald had his measure now, had him from behind with the man's own blade at his throat, its wicked edge kissing flesh.

The man froze.

'Who sent you?' Harald rasped.

He heard footsteps running.

'If you want to live, you'll answer me!' He pressed the knife closer, yanking back the man's head. 'Who sent you?' he screamed, spraying spittle.

But the man said nothing. His eyes only glared wide with terror. There were voices, a yell and the door was torn open. Light flooded the chamber. Harald looked up for an instant, but an instant was too long. He felt his hand pulled closer, saw the jerk of the man's head, heard the *schick* of steel ripping flesh.

He roared in protest, but it was too late: blood was pumping out over his fist. The cat's paw slumped to the floor, shuddering.

Harald stepped back in disgust. This man's secrets were for the ears of the dead now, and the dead alone. He looked at the other faces arriving in the chamber. Faces full of alarm, bodies crowding round him, mouths demanding if he was hurt. But he didn't answer. Because he didn't trust a single one of them.

Instead he stooped, grimacing at the body on the floor, lungs creaking like old bellows.

I've lived too long, he thought, remembering the One-Eyed's cold gaze.

I've lived too long...

CHAPTER THIRTY

Sviggar was weeping.

Erlan had never seen him weep. Yet tears were streaming down the deep cracks in his face and all for a dead traitor.

'You gave him every chance to give up his madness?'

'Just as you asked, sire,' Earl Bodvar said. 'But he was set on his course.'

The council chamber stank with the summer heat. Stale beer, wood-smoke, burned animal fat, mingled with sweat and unwashed wool. Erlan tugged at the golden torque around his neck. In this heat, it was uncomfortable as Hel but it had been a gift from Sviggar and the king liked to see him wear it.

'Then he died as he lived,' Sviggar murmured. 'A stubborn ox... It shouldn't have been this way.'

But that was the way the Norns had spun it. Sveär had slaughtered Sveär, and all so that Sviggar's precious peace could stand.

'And the son,' said Sviggar, wiping his tears. 'Is there no news of him?'

'He escaped.' Bodvar raised a sardonic eyebrow at Erlan. 'At least we found no body.'

'But he was wounded, you said?'

'Aye,' Erlan said. 'In the shoulder.'

'Hmm. That one could prove a stone in our shoe.' The king took a pull on his wine cup. Suddenly he got to his feet. 'You did well, Aurvandil. Both of you. Better than any lord could wish. You have my thanks.'

Sigurd, standing apart from the other councillors, scowled. 'Perhaps if they'd roused more men, fewer need have fallen. And Gellir would not have escaped.'

'They did well to be discreet. And Huldir's son can do little mischief now our oaths are sealed and the Danes gone. Nevertheless, something must be done about his lands. By law, Huldir's title falls to this traitorous son.' He mulled over the question a little longer, then he cleared his throat. 'A decree, then... Let it be known that Gellir, son of Huldir, is outlaw in these lands. His life is forfeit. As for the lands of Nairka...' He extended a long finger at Erlan. 'I hereby name Erlan Aurvandil the new Earl of Nairka, with all rights and claims of land in that title.'

Erlan was stunned. *The Earl of Nairka?*

'You can't simply override the claims of Huldir's kin,' Sigurd blurted.

'I can do as I like! No man is more deserving.'

No man more deserving? Erlan nearly choked. No man had come closer to wrecking Sviggar's careful plans than he had... Still, he knew how to act the part. 'You do me too much honour, my lord.' That much, at least, was true.

'We shall see! Your title will be confirmed at the Summer

Throng, according to proper law.' He snapped his fingers. 'How many days till then?'

'Twelve, sire,' answered Bodvar.

'Only twelve.' Sviggar scowled. 'Gods – and more damned hosting! It'll be the death of me.'

The king suddenly clapped his hands. 'Enough of this bad business with Huldir. We must look forward.' His spirit had returned and no mistake. It hardly seemed possible this was the same man who had been hunched, hacking, over his wine cup a handful of days before. Perhaps all the Old Goat had needed was a good night's sleep. 'So,' he cried, rapping the table with his knuckles. 'The west is now secure.'

'If you trust Ringast,' Bodvar said.

'We've sworn oaths.'

'Men break oaths.'

'Some men, true. But not this Ringast. Unless I judge him wrong.'

'What about his father?' said Sigurd gloomily.

'The son seems shrewd enough to rein him in. No,' he said decisively. 'To my mind, the west is secure.'

'And the east?' said Erlan.

'Ah.' The king's face warmed with a knowing smile. 'The east, my friends, is where our future lies.'

'What future?' Sigurd sniffed.

'One that glisters with gold.' The old man's eyes flashed. 'We've long known that far beyond the East Sea lie lands that are rich beyond the wildest tales. Great kingdoms, they say, whose halls stand ten times as big as this one and shine like vast white mountains of stone. And across the East Sea are rivers that are ripe for trade, rivers that can carry our ships as far as the Black Sea or even further. Trade,' he repeated, whispering the word like a secret. 'That's our future. Didn't our forefathers once seek their fortunes in the south and east long ago? We will do the same. Think how rich we are in skins and slaves and amber. Think how much richer still we could become! In silver and gold and silks and precious stones, and who knows what other marvels.'

'It's war that makes slaves. But you've rejected war,' Sigurd reminded him.

'So I have. A pointless war that threatens this kingdom for no better reason than to sate the Wartooth's spite! There are far greater horizons to conquer. Look here, if any man would make himself a sea-king and test his fortune across the East Sea, he will find in me a generous backer. Imagine – the great sea-gate of Miklagard! What treasures await there? Bodvar, don't they say it takes a whole day to walk across it – that it's as big as a hundred of our villages? A thousand, even!'

'So I have heard.' Bodvar looked decidedly less transported by this idea than his king.

'Its wealth is quite fantastic. Its markets overflow in silks and spices and oils and wines and glass and fabulously crafted wares. And their roads and temples and houses are adorned everywhere with gold and silver and priceless jewels that hail from every land to the very edge of the world.'

'So some merchants have said,' Bodvar admitted. 'Though whether they are to be believed...'

But Sviggar's imagination was soaring and he was hardly listening. 'Why, we could trade with the Danish isles or with the English in the west for a hundred years and never see the wealth we could glean from the east in ten.'

'And just how do you mean to carry out this trade that will make us all so rich?' asked Sigurd.

'With ships, of course! Dozens of new ships. Longships, strong and sturdy, but light enough to cross the river portages. We will build them, see?' His old face was positively beaming. 'Now the Wartooth's axe no longer hangs over our necks, we will build. And *you* will be the one to make it happen!'

Erlan was astonished to see the king's finger was again pointing at him. 'Me, my lord? But I've no notion how to build a boat.'

Sviggar laughed. 'I don't want you to build them yourself, fool. I want you to oversee the thing. This year we will double our fleet. Then double it again next year! We have the timber and the craftsmen to do it, so what's stopping us, heh? It will be the finest fleet the north has ever seen.'

So this was what happened when kings felt full of the strength of summer. This was Sviggar's great dream. And suddenly Erlan realized, maybe he had been wrong about this king. All the while he had seen vanity in the old man's plans for peace. And the old man had seen vanity as well, but vanity of a different kind: the vanity of war. The waste of it. All the while he had been planning something like this. And for a second, Erlan thought maybe Sviggar was the only man truly not vain among all these herds of strutting stags, the only man brave enough to scorn the censure of honour for something better. Something truly great. And not for his own sake, but for something that was simply, in itself, a worthy thing to do.

'Well?'

Erlan had to admit it was quite some vision. 'I don't know what to say, my lord.'

'Say you'll do it.'

It made a change from killing. And it would take his mind off Lilla. Something had to. 'Very well then, my lord. I'll see it done.'

'Gods,' Sigurd scoffed, loud enough to fill the chamber. 'You might as well pick a swineherd off a shit-heap to do the thing.'

'Peace, my son, peace,' replied Sviggar, his good humour apparently unshakeable. 'I have an even greater task for you.'

'What task?'

'The second great legacy that I mean to leave my people here. A temple, built among these halls.'

'A temple?'

'Aye. But not just any temple. The greatest holy place ever conceived.'

Sigurd looked dubious. 'We already have holy places. The *goðar* have all they need in them.'

'The *goðar*! What of them? They're short-sighted as moles. Oh, they may know all about their sacrifices and runes and prayers and all the rest. They may see far into the other worlds, but it takes a king to see the glory that could be in this one.' He smiled at his son. 'You will build this temple and it shall be dedicated to Odin, the High God, the All-Father. Let it be a hall to rival this one,' he cried. 'Nay – a hall to rival *Valhöll* itself!'

The echo of his cry died away. It was some moments before his son answered. 'Aye,' he murmured at length, 'I do begin to see it. A great hall to honour the Spear-God—'

'Precisely! Any fool can die in battle, but no man has ever done a thing like this. We'll make Odin's name the greatest in the north, greater even than all the other gods of the world.'

Sigurd's face had taken on a strange luminescence, too.

Perhaps the king knew his son better than Erlan had credited.

'You begin at once.'

Sigurd suddenly approached and clasped his father's hand. 'I will, Father. I'll do it. Thank you.' It was the most affection Erlan had ever seen pass between them.

'Good! Then our business is done. We meet again two days before the Summer Throng.'

Erlan made to take his leave with the other councillors. 'A word more with you, Sigurd,' added the king. 'And you, Aurvandil. You guards – you may leave us now with the others.'

Erlan exchanged glances with Sigurd while the councillors and guards quit the chamber. Sviggar beckoned them closer. 'I've one more thing to discuss. It concerns you both.' Sviggar took his pitcher of wine and filled two more silver goblets. 'But first let us drink a toast.'

'What are we drinking to?' asked Sigurd.

'To your brother Staffen. He has been in my thoughts often of late.'

Erlan had never met Sigurd's older brother, the man who would have been Sviggar's heir. Though once he'd had good cause to wish he'd never heard the name. When he first arrived at Sviggar's hall he had come within a whisker of being executed for Staffen's murder. Only a trick of fate had spared him. The king handed them their cups then raised his own. 'To Staffen, then.'

They drank.

'So only you are left to me.' Sviggar sighed.

'You forget your wife's children,' Sigurd replied drily.

Sviggar snorted, half-amused. 'Gods, so I did. How strange! Though I doubt I'll live to see Svein to manhood, nor Katla to her maid's blood. And with Staffen and now Lilla gone... their absence has left a gap.'

'A gap?'

'Aye. Like two trees uprooted in the forest. They leave an empty space to fill. But not, I hope, for long.' He suddenly smiled. 'I have decided. You shall have a new brother. I wish to make Erlan my foster-son.'

He said the words so fast, it was moments before Erlan understood. *Foster-son.* Even to his ears it sounded absurd. As for Sigurd... Erlan expected him to explode with fury. But instead the prince remained calm. 'I see.'

'Is that all?' The king was grinning at his son. 'Come, what more say you?'

Erlan watched Sigurd's tongue run back and forth along his teeth, as if choosing his words with great care. 'Erlan Aurvandil has served you well. No one could deny that. He is lucky. Nay, a true darling of the gods.' A small chuckle clicked in his throat. 'So I say this.' Sigurd held out his hand. 'Welcome, brother.' Erlan was almost too amazed to take it.

'You're not too proud to join yourself to us, are you?' Sviggar exclaimed.

'No, I—'

'Nor yet too old to need a father's counsel?'

But I have a father, was Erlan's reflex thought. *I was a chosen son...* Sigurd's hand was still hovering. 'If this is your wish—'

'It is.'

'Then so be it.' He took it. Sigurd pumped his arm.

'Ha!' Sviggar clapped both their shoulders. 'The north has never seen a finer pair of princes!'

They drank again, this time Sviggar draining his cup. 'But for now, we keep this to ourselves. At the Summer Throng I'll make the announcement and bind the thing by law.'

'I'm only sorry my sister won't be here to see it. Her affection for the Aurvandil is well known.' Erlan shot Sigurd a sharp look, but he saw in his narrow-set eyes no trace of malice.

'Aye. A pity. Tell me, was her parting sorrowful?'

But before Erlan could answer, Sigurd begged leave of his father. 'If you're finished with me,' he added. 'I wish to waste no time in the task you've laid on me.'

'Good man! Go to it!'

Once they were alone, Sviggar wanted to know all Erlan could tell him about his journey to the Kolmark, about his daughter's mood, her words, anything he could recall. Erlan recounted those details that seemed fitting, leaving out Lilla's haste to be away and the queen's strange good humour in the wood, and also one or two other things he didn't quite understand himself.

When he had finished, Sviggar smiled, apparently satisfied. 'A father has to let go one day. Does he not? May the gods take good care of her... Well, my boy, this has all fallen out very well. Don't you agree?'

'It seems so, my lord.'

'Seems, be damned! It's turned out for you best of all.'

Erlan couldn't deny it. But as he made his way out of the cavernous hall, he wasn't sure what to make of it all. First an earl – and now this? Foster-son to the king? He should be pleased. Gods, he should be bloody delighted. But something gnawed at his mind, something he couldn't put his finger on.

The estates of Nairka would bring with them wealth and power – advantages he had never consciously sought, though the Norns seemed determined to thrust them upon him. These were surely good things. But land had a way of binding a man. Land meant a burden, a place that would tie him here for ever... and for ever was a long time.

Maybe that was what troubled him.

Or maybe this last and greatest honour represented the breaking of his final link with the past? Vendlagard had been his home; its land, his inheritance – with its leafy woods and loamy soil under the swirling skies of the Juten Belt—

He pounced on this thought before it took him too far. *That was Hakan's inheritance. And Hakan is dead.*

But even that, he realized, wasn't what bothered him. And slowly his mind teased out his disquiet like a stubborn splinter, feeling its way back to his strange awakening in the little wood...

His tongue had been dry, his pulse knocking at his temples.

He had sat up and rubbed the sleep from his eyes, trying to piece together the shards of memory, still jagged in his head, only for his belly to clench with nausea. He put his hand there and was shocked to find he was naked. He looked down, confused. Another shock. Because all over his chest were marks – scratches, each one purple and livid and long as his finger. On his shoulders he found more of the same.

He examined them more closely. He'd seen marks like this before, red furrows in his skin dug by fingernails seized with passion. But so many? And how?

It had only been a dream. Hadn't it?

Flashes of it replayed in his mind. It had been Inga, and yet...

not her.

Perplexed, his mind had wandered to half-remembered stories from his boyhood – dark tales of witches abroad in the night seeking journeymen on the road, hungry to ride them, to tear their flesh and enslave their souls.

But those were just stories.

Although, he remembered, his kinsfolk had taken them as warnings. His father had even once told him to avoid love-play with a witch at any cost. *'A witch will ride you and leave you with limbs locked and sick of life.'*

Instinctively, he had shifted his legs. They moved all right. But even that made no sense. He examined the marks again. Had they camped in some haunt of malignant spirits that had conjured up *her* soul? To taunt him with *her* again?

None of it made sense. And then he'd heard one of the others moving outside and pushed away his troubled thoughts, reaching for his tunic.

As he pulled it over his head, his mind had been too full of questions to notice that his amulet was gone.

Erlan emerged from the shadow of the hall and gulped down a deep breath of fresh air. The bright and dusty day had softened into a balmy evening, filled with the scent of the nearby pines. He was hungry.

He turned his back on the yard and ambled towards the jumbled roofs to the east. Somewhere at the foot of one of those skeins of smoke, Kai would be cooking. Least, he hoped so.

He hadn't seen Kai since his return, as he'd been summoned at once to the king's council. He found himself looking forward to Kai's idle chatter. Perhaps he would tell him about what happened in the wood. Perhaps his friend would have an opinion. He had opinions about most things. As for the news of the earldom, Kai would turn cartwheels about that.

The dying sun was throwing swathes of pink light through the gaps between the byres and barns as he walked home. He was leaving the shadow of one into another blaze of light when a figure suddenly appeared in front of him.

Half-blinded, he saw only a silhouette, then strong fingers seized his throat. He tried to shout but the hand clamped his cry to a whimper, slamming him against the wall.

Pure instinct had him reaching for the seax at his back, but before his fingers touched the haft a knee drove into his groin. He doubled over, every ounce of air knocked out of him, pain flooding through his body. He still had no clue who was attacking him. All he could do was groan as the hand smashed his head back against the wall.

'Look at me, cripple!' a voice hissed.

Through watering eyes, Erlan saw sunken cheeks, a half-dead gaze over a pale sneer.

'Vargalf?' he moaned, the blow still ringing through his head.

'I have a message from my master.' The fingers tightened, digging deep into his gullet. 'Old men don't live for ever. So enjoy the evening sun. Because for you, cripple... *night is coming.*'

The grip vanished. Erlan fell to his knees, sucking in breath after bloody breath.

When he looked up, he was alone.

CHAPTER
THIRTY·ONE

Bara slipped the comb through the glossy hair that fell to the queen's waist. In the mirror, the pale green eyes gazed back at themselves, lost in thought.

The comb struck a knot. The green eyes darted at her reflection, narrowed with irritation.

'Sorry, my lady,' Bara muttered, gripping the hair higher and picking out the knot.

She loved and dreaded this part of her service. Loved it because she never felt more important than when she was beautifying the queen. Dreaded it because Saldas was no easy mistress, often cutting her down with a word, sometimes even slapping her face. But then she'd get a smile like a sunrise.

So unpredictable...

But tonight Bara had more reason than usual to be nervous. Tonight would be different. Because she knew what she knew. True, she could hardly believe it – but hadn't she heard it with her own ears?

She had guessed the queen was up to something that night

in the wood. By now she knew her well enough to know the woman was only pleasant when she wanted something. Bara had watched her closely that night. And a good thing she had. Saldas could play tricks on other folks if she wanted, but not on her. Bara wasn't stupid.

She'd noticed the little extras Saldas had brought along. A gourd here, another pouch there. And when the queen took all that time fetching that wineskin, she'd suspected something. Again when there was a whiff of something strange in her cup. Oh, ever so subtle – but Bara had caught it. And she knew what to do. The nasty stuff had gone in the dirt where it belonged.

It was a simple enough trick – to look like she was swallowing while she spat the stuff back into the horn. Hel, she could have pretended to gulp it back till the *Ragnarök* and Saldas never would have guessed unless she had actually looked inside. But of course, the queen had to watch Erlan sometimes, didn't she? And when she did it was nothing for Bara to drop her hand and spill a little more on the ground.

So now she knew...

This haughty queen was not so noble after all. Why, she'd been rutting like a doe on heat. And all that while, Saldas had believed she was asleep. Gunn's blood! Whatever was in that brew would have had to kill her if she wasn't going to wake up to that racket.

But that's always the way of things, ain't it? A woman like Saldas always got what she wanted, always reckoned herself smarter than the rest. But she'd been caught out now, good and proper.

It was a weighty question, though. What to do about this choice little morsel? The king cuckolded by his slut of a queen and the cripple? It was pure gold! But what she could make of it was a bit of a puzzle.

Of course, if the queen had taken her into her confidence, it could have been different. If she'd only *trusted* her... Why, she would have taken the secret to her grave. It was Saldas who had played *her* false. Had tried to dose *her*...

No. Bara was tired of being pushed around, taken for granted. Tired of all those years as a thrall-girl, used by this man or that. By anyone who wanted her... Of course, she had learned how to get her way eventually. She had her looks, after all. And when it came down to it, men were like iron – get them hot enough and you could bend them however you wanted. But she'd never had any real power, nothing that could change her lot in life.

Until now.

This was something different. If she played this right, she could get what she wanted for a long time to come.

She swallowed hard.

Saldas was so deep in thought that when Bara suddenly spoke it startled her. The girl began blathering on about the hardships of their journey and Saldas sighed. She did so hate the banalities that had to pass between a mistress and her servants.

Tonight, of all nights, she was in no mood for idle talk. Much to her annoyance, the king's health appeared markedly improved. He had invaded her chamber that afternoon overflowing with affection. Of course, she had played the part of dutiful wife. But the change in him was most galling. She had half-hoped three days of hard feasting would finish off the old fool. But every sickness that took hold of him he seemed to slough off like a snake shedding its skin.

'Course, there are some to be had.' Again, Bara's voice interrupted her thoughts. 'Don't you agree, my lady?'

'Some what?' she said, irritably.

'Pleasures...' The girl's reflection was artlessly blank. 'On the road.' Meanwhile, her nimble fingers continued braiding Saldas's hair.

'Whatever can you mean?'

'Well, it's not all discomfort, is it?'

'The road?'

'Aye! What with summer blooming and the sun on your face...'

'And the rain? I seem to remember you enjoyed that.'

'You have me there, my lady,' Bara smiled. 'Still, I don't think I ever slept sounder than those nights on the road.'

'Perhaps you need more work if you're having trouble sleeping.'

'Now you're teasing, my lady.'

Saldas had been entirely serious.

'Didn't half have some funny dreams, though. And the night in that little wood... that was the strangest of the lot.'

Saldas glanced up at Bara's reflection, eyes narrowing. What was this now? 'Go on.'

'Oh, I couldn't possibly share it, my lady.' She covered her mouth. Her pale cheeks bloomed slightly. 'It wasn't quite decent, you see. But so vivid – especially the sound of... well, you know. Why, like it was happening right outside— oh dear, my lady, am I embarrassing you?'

'What?'

'It's just... your cheeks are all flush. Perhaps I shouldn't have said—'

'You need hardly be delicate on my account.' Saldas turned away from the mirror to compose herself. It only took a moment. She cursed inwardly. She should have been ready for this. Should have planned for the worst. Instead, this brazen slut seemed to think she could play her. When she looked back, the girl was eyeing her carefully – too carefully, she thought.

'And what, pray, are we supposed to make of your little woodland fantasy?'

'Couldn't rightly say, my lady. I know there are some who can read folk's dreams. Still, I'd have to be careful who I told a thing like that. You never know where it might end up.' She chuckled, a little too knowingly for Saldas's liking.

'Dreams have a way of fading.'

'Often. But something tells me this one won't.'

For a while, neither spoke. Saldas was thinking, her mind threading this way and that like a needle on a tapestry, trying to find a way through. Bara had finished the queen's night-braid now. She went back to tucking away the strands of stray hair.

Saldas's hand went to her pendant, fingers plucking thoughtfully at each golden link. As she did, her golden cuff slipped down her wrist.

'That gold becomes you very prettily, my lady.'

She often said drab little things like that, but this time something told in her eye. *So that's it. How pathetically common-place.* Somehow, she was disappointed. If the girl was bold enough to try to extract something from her, Saldas had credited her with a more original motive than simple greed.

311

'What – these things?' True, the pieces suited her well, each of them crafted by the most skilled hands in Uppland, solid gold with delicate filigree in exquisite framing. Such things were for queens or goddesses, not thrall-girls. 'Why don't you try them on?' she suggested.

'Oh no, I couldn't. They wouldn't suit me half so well.'

False modesty. She despised it. She could see the little slut was itching to get her fingers on them. She slipped off the cuffs and handed them over. 'I insist.' Bara put down her comb and pushed the cuffs over her hands. 'Let's pretend, shall we?' Saldas smiled. 'You shall be the queen and I, your servant.' Bara looked at her doubtfully. 'Come, will it not be amusing?'

'I suppose.'

'Excellent.' She pulled Bara in front of her and seated her on the stool. 'Of course we must see how this looks on you, as well.' She removed her necklace and slipped it over Bara's head.

Bara sighed with delight. 'They're so pretty.'

'Oh, we're not finished yet.' Saldas loosened Bara's braids and spread her cloud of auburn hair about her shoulders, fussing with the tresses at the front until just a strand or two fell across her sharp blue eyes. 'Well?'

Bara couldn't keep the grin from her face. She touched the gold around her neck, wonderingly. 'I've never worn anything so precious,' she whispered. And then, apparently remembering her purpose, she added, 'Why, they could make me quite forget about everything else. For a while...'

It was all so painfully transparent.

'How long is a while?'

'Might be weeks. Months, even.'

'And then?'

'Who knows? But it's funny how things we think are long forgotten have a habit of popping up again.'

Of course it is. Saldas smiled. 'Stand up.' The maid rose and let Saldas position her full length before the mirror. 'There,' Saldas murmured, close to her ear. 'See how beautiful you look.' And it was true. The girl looked perfectly lovely, her face shining with admiration for her own reflection. In the soft light of the braziers, the gold glinted against her pale skin, off-setting the shades of her fire-red hair.

Saldas was close behind her now. She reached up and ran a fingertip ever so gently across her servant's brow. 'A girl so pretty has no need of a mind troubled with bad dreams.'

Bara shook her head. Her long hair rippled down her back. Saldas could hear the shallowness in her breathing, could practically smell the excitement on her.

She reached round and slid her hand down over the girl's soft belly. At first Bara flinched. *They always flinch*, Saldas thought. But rarely did they push her hand away. She let her fingers drift downwards until she could feel the heat between the girl's thighs through the brushed wool of her dress.

'Is that what you long for?' she murmured. 'An untroubled mind?' Bara didn't answer. She was staring at Saldas in the mirror, concentrating on her face. Saldas pressed the tips of her fingers inwards. A small gasp escaped Bara's lips. But then she leaned back and slipped her hand over the queen's knuckles as they found their rhythm. The girl was shorter than her, her figure soft and full. Saldas could feel her fleshy rump push against her thighs.

She wondered how many men had had this girl. Whether she always gave herself away like this – with no resistance whatsoever. Maybe she had learned it was easier that way, that to give away her body didn't really mean anything after all. Or rather it always meant something other than itself. It meant power or vanity or spite or anger or vengeance. Just occasionally it meant love.

Saldas had loved a woman once – one of her father's concubines who had been a few years older than her. *Korella*. She had taught her much. Given her much. But then her father had caught them one night and in a rage had sold Korella to a trader from faraway Åland. Saldas had wept for a few nights until her father's beatings dried her eyes. Those were the last tears she had ever wept for love. After that, she had sworn that her heart was dead to it.

There was a humming sound in Bara's throat, growing louder. Saldas could feel the wet heat through her dress. Perhaps she would take Bara as a lover. There might be certain pleasures to be had, certain advantages to keeping her mouth occupied with something other than spreading her little secret. Then again, that sort of thing always became complicated. Always created more unpicked threads that might unravel. No. Better to find a more permanent solution.

The girl was moaning now, her body bucking back against her. There was something satisfying about feeling the climax shake its way out of her, about seeing the tiny quiverings in the flushed face in the mirror, about the half-open mouth, the tongue probing at the air. A kind of victory. A kind of possession. But like all things, it passed away soon enough.

Bara sagged back into her arms, breathless. 'I wonder,' Saldas murmured, her lips brushing the edge of Bara's ear, 'will this help you to forget?'

'Oh yes,' the servant gasped. 'Oh yes, my lady.'

Saldas ran her nails lightly down Bara's forearm till she came to the golden cuff. 'You may keep these then, if they will take your mind off things. And this.' She touched the necklace.

'They're really mine?'

'They are.' But suddenly, without warning, she dug her nails deep into Bara's wrist and caught those fiery curls, yanking them back, hard. Bara yelped. 'So we have an understanding. Do we not?'

A shiver of fear passed over the girl's face. She nodded awkwardly.

'Good.' Saldas softened her grip. 'Good.' She turned Bara to face her. 'A queen's handmaiden ought to be beautiful. I'll be glad to make you as beautiful as you can be... If it will keep you from bad dreams.'

Bara nodded uncertainly.

'Well,' Saldas sighed. 'We may do this again. But I'm tired now. Leave me.'

'Can I at least help you... to undress?' Saldas couldn't tell whether this was a clumsy proposition or else the little thief had at last remembered her place.

'Not now. Attend me in the morning.'

'As you wish then... I trust you sleep well.'

Bara bowed and scurried from the chamber.

'You sleep well too, my brazen beauty,' Saldas whispered when she was gone. 'Though I fear your dreams may bring you more than gold.'

For where gold goes, blood is sure to follow.

Her smile dissolved.

How the scheming little whore had outwitted her in the

wood was of little account now. All that mattered was that she knew. And despite that the girl was a fool, there was real danger here. Gold and a few favours of the flesh might buy her silence for a time, but it would not last. And if Sviggar ever found out, she doubted whether even she could turn aside his wrath.

She cursed.

How dare the spiteful bitch blackmail her? Well, the girl wouldn't live to make any more mistakes like this one. Things would have to move faster now. The time had come to move her plans forward. And this silly servant-girl had stumbled across a part to play in them. Saldas grew calmer as her racing thoughts began to order themselves.

Yes. Bara would play a very special part indeed.

CHAPTER
THIRTY-TWO

A mist grey as iron swirls about her.
Her face is damp. The greyness darkens, then bleeds to crimson.
A noise touches her ear, faint at first, growing louder. Murmurs and moaning become screams and shouts. She hears dire curses and the ring of steel. All around the din of war, the clatter of wood against iron.

The mist swirls again. Another scream, high and piercing, through the wraithlike air. Below blades crash. Dark faces twist in pain and fury through the reddening fog.

Then a darker shadow appears, scything through the bloody vapours. Wings beat around her. She spies an eagle, more dreadful than the monstrous Hraesvelgr who births the winds from the ends of the earth. An eagle, with feathers stiff and grim, and savage eyes shining like emerald stones...

Lilla's own eyes snapped open, staring wide and desperate. Above her, only gloomy rafters. She felt the blanket heavy on her chest, smelled the goose fat burned out in the lamp during the night.

317

The tension melted from her body. She reached out. But there was no one beside her, only the empty furs where Ringast had been lying. It was the third morning since their arrival at Dannerborg and every day he had been gone when she awoke.

She rolled over, closed her eyes again and sighed, pushing from her mind for the hundredth time that look of *his* as she had ridden away. So cold – like a great door closing, never to be opened again. Pushing away also the hatred for Saldas that tried to burrow its roots into her heart. If it did, she knew, she would become no different from her father's wife.

Instead she murmured a prayer to Frigg – the wise goddess – that the Norns would now be satisfied, that their spinning and weaving would only make stronger the oaths that had been spoken and never see them undone.

She wished she could believe the peace would hold. Because now she had seen with her own eyes the army Ringast had gathered. All around his hall were camped thanes and karls, wandering warriors who sold their swords for silver, even lowly freemen who should have been home sharpening their scythes for the harvest. Men of a dozen different tongues from Wendland and Friesland and many others, lands far beyond the horizon. Men who, if they had ridden north that summer, would have butchered her own people.

But the Wartooth's sons had sworn for peace. If their word was true, then what need of these warriors, still infesting this hall like lice? There would be no war. They must disperse. *She* was the peace. She must see to it.

There was a noise on the other side of the room. She sprang upright in surprise.

'By the stars,' exclaimed the intruder, clutching at a bronze basin that had almost jumped out of her hands. 'You nearly stopped my heart.'

'Oh, it's you.'

Gerutha, her new handmaid, put the basin on the washstand. Lilla sank back into her pillow and watched her. She wasn't young, perhaps just shy of forty – but tall with sharp, weathered features. Although it was the shock of white hair that always drew Lilla's gaze.

'Thought you was still asleep, mistress. Seemed to me you liked to sleep late.'

'I don't,' Lilla replied irritably. 'Anyway, is it so late?'

'Sun's near the noon-mark now, mistress.'

'Already?' She swung her legs out and rubbed the sleep from her eyes. 'I don't know why I'm waking so late. Perhaps I'm still weary from the journey.'

Gerutha gave a thin smile and carried over the basin and set it on Lilla's knees. Lilla flicked her hair over one shoulder and doused her hands and face in the warm water.

'Sure would be pleasant to have a morning sleeping late. You know, let others do all the work for a change.'

Lilla looked up sharply. 'If you think I'm lazy, just come out and say it.'

Gerutha at least had the courtesy to blush. 'Oh, it's not for me to judge, mistress. Only Master Sletti said we weren't to expect you to work or do anything much at all.'

'Oh he did, did he?' Her first meeting with Ringast's steward had hardly been propitious. Sletti had uttered a few obsequious words of welcome, but his manner was colder than an eel's and twice as slippery. 'What else did Sletti say?'

'I don't want to get no one in trouble, mistress.'

'If I ask you a question, I want an answer.'

'Well, mistress, when he appointed me to attend to you, he did say a woman with your upbringing was like to be...'

'Well?'

'Difficult, demanding and spoilt were his words.'

'Spoilt, is it!'

'With you being a king's daughter and all—'

'How dare he!'

'I'm sure he meant nothing by it.'

'We shall have to see, won't we?'

'You're not going to do anything foolish, are you, mistress? I mean, you won't get me in no trouble.'

Lilla leaped off the bed, suddenly full of energy, skipped up to Gerutha and cupped her face in her hands. 'He won't know you've said a whisper.' She smiled. 'Now help me get dressed.'

The sun wasn't far past the noon-mark when Lilla glided into her husband's chamber, garbed in a fine dress of black wool with blood-red threads embroidered down her arms, with a simple scarlet girdle.

The men stopped talking at once.

Her husband was in conference with a man Lilla didn't recognize, though the scars on his face didn't need much explanation. Standing in attendance was the steward Sletti, his smooth forehead so gleaming it might have been oiled.

Ringast smiled at her. 'Was there something you wanted, Aslíf?'

'I've told you, call me Lilla.'

'I will. Once we know each other a little better.' He looked at the scarred man and then back to her. 'Well?'

'I wanted to speak with you.'

'Go ahead.'

'Alone.'

Ringast and the scarred man exchanged glances. The latter gave a wry chuckle and quit the chamber, but the steward made no move to leave.

'Three is not alone, my lord.'

'Never mind him. You may speak freely.'

'Very well. It concerns him anyway.'

'What is it?'

'I assure you it's no more than my right as your wife.'

'Well, far be it from me to deny my wife what is hers by right.' He slipped his thumbs into his belt. 'What do you want?'

'Those.' She pointed at the keys hanging from Sletti's belt. The steward bridled instantly. The keys gave their holder authority over the household, practically and symbolically.

Suddenly Ringast burst into laughter. 'You have a usurper, Sletti! Gods, but that's bold of you,' he said, addressing Lilla. 'Sletti here has been steward of Dannerborg for... What is it?'

'Eight years, my lord.' His mouth was a thin line of anger.

'Eight years! Hel, has it been that long?'

'The keys are mine by right,' said Lilla. 'As your wife.'

'So you said. And you, Sletti. What do you say?'

'Is there really any need for this, my lord? Running your household and your lands is no simple task. Forgive me, my lady,' he said, with no trace of contrition in his voice. 'It's no task for a girl of your... inexperience.'

'I've seen twenty summers, yet still you think me a girl?'

'I meant no offence. Only that it takes years to master all that needs to happen here. The timings, the provisioning, the responsibilities. Just to learn everyone's name would take you months.'

'Then it's time I made a start. Anyway, I'm not suggesting your experience won't be useful. Merely that from now on you will report to me. I will have authority over you. And I will hold the keys.'

'But lord.' Sletti's high voice assumed a decidedly whining tone. 'Managing your household is a complicated business. Especially now, with so many—'

'All the more reason to share it.' Lilla turned to her husband. 'I will not be denied this, my lord.'

Ringast shifted a half-amused look between them, rubbing at the hook of his nose. 'No. I believe you won't.' He turned to Sletti. 'You'd better hand them over then.'

'But, my lord—'

'Now.'

Sulkily, the steward loosened the silver chatelaine around his waist and handed it over, keys and all, with a jangle.

'Excellent,' she said, trying to sound more commanding than she felt. 'I shall send for you later. But for now you may leave us.'

A mixture of bewilderment and fury fluttered over Sletti's face. Ringast laughed and slapped him on the back. 'Cheer up, old friend. This day has long been coming. For all of us!'

It was a small victory. Petty, even. But Lilla was determined there would be no more late mornings. No more ruminating on things beyond her control. If she had chosen to be Ringast's wife, she was going to make the best of it.

'Satisfied?'

She nodded.

'It might be prudent to smooth his ruffled feathers next time you meet. He's a useful head to have on your side.'

'The man puts on such airs.'

'He thinks he has reason to.'

'Why?'

Ringast sighed and shook his head. 'If you must know, there's always been a rumour that he's my father's bastard.' His hooked nose wrinkled, as though it were distasteful to dabble in such gossip. 'The old man has never acknowledged him, but still... if enough people say it, folk start to believe it.'

'Surely his mother knows the truth?'

'Doubtless. But she died giving birth to him.'

'Oh.'

'Personally, I don't see the family resemblance. Do you?' It was a moment before she realized he was making a joke.

'About as much as I see it in your other brothers.' She smiled.

'Ha! That's true... So why are we alone?'

'There's something else.'

'Evidently...'

'The warriors you have camped here.'

'You've noticed them.'

'You must disperse them at once.'

He turned away from her and poured himself another ale. 'I'm afraid I can't do that.'

'What do you mean, you can't? Aren't you lord of this place? Your word here is law.'

'True.'

'Then why are they still here? You've agreed a peace with my father. You swore on Adils' Ring, which is sacred to both our lines.'

323

'I know what I swore.'

'Then what need of all these men? You foreswore slaughter. All of you! That's why I'm here.'

'You're right that I'm lord here. But my father is my lord and I gave him my word to do two things. To marry you, and to keep every man here until *he* – and he alone – sent word to disperse.'

'But that goes against all that was agreed!'

'When we rode north we couldn't be certain your father could be trusted. If it had been a trick – what then? Why do you think my father didn't come himself?'

She could see it made some sense. If King Harald's plans to attack her homeland had been real, he was unlikely to let the army that he had taken such pains to gather dissipate like a morning mist in summer. Not until he was sure he did not need it. After all, there had been no trust between their families for long years.

For the first time, she began to glimpse what it must have cost them to come. 'But now you know. There was no trick.'

'*Now* I know, yes. At least, I think I do.'

'So send them away. Men like that thirst only for ale or for blood. It will come to no good to keep them here.'

'Not before I hear word from my father.' He took an unhurried pull on his ale. 'You know, not all men are as you say, Aslíf.' The name jarred in her ear, making her feel the distance between them. 'I sent word to Leithra as soon as we left Uppsala. I expect to hear from my father soon. Until then... not one man will leave this place.'

'But, husband, I beg you—'

He raised a finger to silence her. 'Not one man.'

CHAPTER
THIRTY-THREE

Saldas was losing patience.

The noise of the smiths' endless hammering was getting on her nerves. That and the reek of the place – meat-fisted craftsmen stinking worse than Volund's crotch laced with the acrid tang of soldered metal.

She wandered along the booths lining the western road.

There was an urgency to the industry that morning, every smith and fletcher and spinner working feverishly to prepare their wares for the Summer Throng. The assembly would draw the greatest men in the land, attended by their retainers, and many smallholders and freemen besides. A multitude, and each man carrying a purse – which interested the smiths a good deal more. Kings and earls could worry about wars and laws. These craftsfolk only cared about the silver in a man's pocket.

She looked back towards the halls, trying to pick out the face of the man she was waiting for among the heads bobbing along the road.

'I received your message, my lady,' said a voice at her elbow. She turned, a little startled.

Vargalf's eyes were cold as ever. 'Good,' she said, her composure returning. 'Walk with me.' She took his elbow and led him out of earshot of the nearest craftsman.

When they had gone a little way beyond the last of the booths, she steered him towards the footpath that circled round the King Barrows. The ground was well worn, hard packed by summer and the tramp of sentries' feet. But no sentry would pay them much heed. Folk often took a turn around the royal mounds.

'I trust you had the sense to tell no one of our meeting.'

'Of course. What about the thrall who carried your message?'

'A dullard and so shy she hardly speaks. If she thinks anything at all, she would never dare speak of it.'

Vargalf grunted. 'Well, here I am. What do you want?'

She tilted her face to the sun and closed her eyes, enjoying its warm caress. 'Those smiths over there... They're forever tapping away. Watch them long enough and you'll soon learn – certain tasks need certain tools. A swordsmith takes a hammer weighty enough to club an ox, and at just the right moment with the right force he strikes the blade, to give it the perfect strength and shape. But to craft the hilt, he uses tongs as fine as needles to thread the filigree around each ring. For each task, he has the same purpose in mind, but he must choose the right tool at the right moment. No other will do.' She opened her eyes and looked at him directly. 'This is the moment. You are the tool.'

'You flatter me.'

'I don't believe so.'

'If I am the tool, what is the purpose?'

She smiled. The man was blunt. That was all to the good. 'Your loyalty lies with my son-in-law, does it not?'

He nodded.

'And with the king?'

'I am a subject of his realm.'

'As are we all. But you've sworn no personal oath to him?'

'No.'

'Nevertheless, your oath to Sigurd surely binds you to the king, does it not?'

'That depends on his son.'

'Hmm.' She studied him more closely. 'But I think you care nothing for oaths. Unless I read you wrong.'

He stared back at her without answering.

'Speak plainly, man.'

'Very well. Oaths bind those who choose to be bound. I'm not one of them.'

'Well, that at least is speaking plain.' She gave a mirthless chuckle. 'Another question then. Are you... disposed towards the king?'

'Disposed?' He snorted. 'You tell me to speak plain while you talk in circles. What do you want?'

Saldas laughed. 'Fairly said. Well then... men may live for many reasons. Women too, if you can believe that.' She raised a sardonic eyebrow. 'I live by one law: do whatever best serves myself. I find this the truest way to live.'

'My lady, I gave up such lessons at my mother's knee. Come to your point.'

'I am,' she said sharply. 'Sometimes, to live this way, I must be willing to make a sacrifice. Now is such a time.'

'You still dance around the fire.'

'Come then.' She was annoyed because he was right. Why was this so hard to say? 'A sacrifice must be made. Several times sickness has brought the king to the gates of Hel. The time has come for him to enter.'

'You want Sviggar dead?'

'I do.'

Now the words were spoken, there seemed nothing more natural in all the world. 'If you want reasons, I will give you none. Though there *are* reasons, at least sufficient for me.'

Vargalf gave a solitary laugh – an ugly, clicking sound. 'I do not doubt it. But I need no explanation. Besides, reasons matter less than consequences.'

'I see you're the right tool indeed. As you wish, then. Let us speak of consequences.'

'You mean to take power for yourself?'

She shook her head. 'The Sveär folk are not ready to be ruled by a queen.'

'Then they shall have another king. One who answers to you.'

'Precisely.' She smiled. 'There was a second reason for summoning you, besides your more obvious... talents.'

'My connection with Sigurd.'

'Indeed. Sigurd shall be king.'

'And you will rule through him?'

'Let's just say I will be sure to find my place in his kingdom.'

Vargalf returned her smile, an expression so cadaverous that it sent a chill right through her. 'We understand each other well.'

'Naturally Sigurd must be persuaded. But he has little love for his father. Nevertheless, whatever notions he has of honour must be – how shall I put it? – taken into consideration.'

'We can give him reasons, if he needs them.'

'I've no doubt, with the cunning in both our tongues, that we can lead him to this course. After all,' she chuckled, 'are we not mere stitches in the weft of his fate? Mere tools in the hands of the Norns, used to raise him to his glorious destiny.'

'Now the needle is in my hands, you'll see what I can weave.'

'Good. You shall be well rewarded for it.'

'I ask for but one.'

'What is that?'

'The Aurvandil.'

'Erlan?' She was surprised. 'What have you against him?'

'Like you, my lady, I have my reasons. Like you, I will spare you any explanation.'

'I have plans for him myself.' Erlan was an appetite only just whetted. She had not finished with him yet. 'Is he your price, then?'

'Price?' Vargalf's eyes narrowed. 'How about I put it another way? Agree to this and our interests will be harnessed as perfectly as *Árvakr* and *Alsviðr*.'

Saldas snorted. Vargalf was referring to the two steeds that were said to draw the sun across the sky. For a man who professed to like plain speech these words were most colourful. But she had a better idea. If it was a harness he wanted, he could share one with Sigurd. Indeed, she had a vision of her own – herself as goddess Freyja, riding resplendent in her chariot while the two of them laboured away in front like the Lady's cats. They could mewl for their milk, and perhaps – if they did what they were told – she would let them wet their whiskers from time to time.

'You cannot kill him. At least not until I say so. But I promise you, by the time we reap the harvest of our plans, you will be entirely satisfied. Are we agreed then?'

'We are.'

'Good. Then this is what we shall do.'

CHAPTER
THIRTY-FOUR

T hings were looking up for Kai. His master was going to be made an earl of the kingdom and, unless he was much mistaken, that meant he was well on the road to becoming a nobleman himself. A thane, at the very least.

Of course, it still had to be made official, but how he wished that old whoreson Torolf could see him now! His stepfather had always relished telling him what a steaming pile of horse manure his life was destined to become.

How wrong could a man be!

It wasn't even a year since Kai had abandoned his stinking puddle of a fishing village to throw in his lot with Erlan. But here he was, right-hand man to the king's darling, on the high road to wealth and glory. Of course, Erlan saw things differently. But then Erlan was a gloomy ass at the best of times, and his mood hadn't lightened with all this shipbuilding nonsense the king had dumped in his lap. (Kai knew a man out of his depth when he saw one.)

Still, he wasn't going to let Erlan bring him down. Once they were installed in Svartadal, the grand hall that went with the Nairka lands, there would be feasting and wenching a-plenty. Kai would see to that. And singing! Oh yes! And no one was going to tell him to shut up, neither. Hel, he might even see if Bara couldn't be talked into coming.

His imagination ran on a bit – to when he'd have place of his own. A modest hall with a little lake, some woodland, a few fields. True, it all sounded a bit tame. But then he'd had his fill of fighting for the time being. A damned dangerous business, it had turned out. He supposed his appetite for it might return one day, but just now he had more pleasant things to consider.

He watched a bead of sweat swell below Bara's ear. It grew fatter and fatter until, all of a sudden, it raced down her collarbone, colliding with a tiny splash against a ring of polished gold.

He rubbed the link between thumb and forefinger. 'You got this from the queen, you say?'

'I told you – she likes me.'

'She must like you a Hel of a lot.'

'So she should, the amount of service I give her.'

'If that's what it's for, you should be giving the thing to me.' He kissed her neck.

She giggled. 'You'll have to do a lot more than that to earn this.'

The heat in the loft was suffocating. He propped himself on an elbow. 'Why don't you take this stupid thing off?' He plucked at her dress.

'What about Erlan?' Another giggle.

'Oh, him! He's off seeing foresters or something. Won't be back for ages. Come on – off with it!'

Yielding, Bara slipped her dress over her head. She started to remove the necklace, too.

'No – leave that. Gives me something aim for.' He bit at her neck again, while his hands wandered down her body.

'I'll be getting a lot more like this one,' she sighed, stretching like a contented kitten.

'She can't like you that much.'

'Maybe it ain't a question of how much she likes me,' she grinned. 'Maybe she's got to keep me happy. Just like you.'

He dropped his hand a little lower, his fingertips drawing circles round her hips. 'Why's that?'

'Because she knows what's good for her.'

'Pah! What are you going to do if she doesn't? Stab her with a brooch-pin?'

She took his hand, moved it lower. 'No, idiot.' She closed her eyes. 'Mmm. Keep doing that.'

'You like this, do you?'

'Mmmm… Hey! Don't stop!'

'No more till you tell me.'

'Tell you what? Come on!'

'Not till you tell,' he smirked.

Bara gave an exasperated sigh. 'All I'll say is she knows the value of a servant's discretion.'

Kai's eyes grew wide. 'Gods, you're not blackmailing the bitch, are you?'

'Wouldn't call it that exactly.'

'What the Hel would you call it?'

'We have an understanding.'

'The kind of understanding where she gives you pretty things and you keep your mouth shut.'

'I suppose.'

'Are you out of your tiny mind?'

She blew her lips at him.

'Who was it dreamed up this little arrangement? You or her?'

'Me, I guess.'

Kai shook his head. 'You've lost your wits, Bara.' She began to look cross. 'And you reckon on milking the queen as long as you want?'

'Maybe... Anyway, she likes me. I know she does.'

'Oh dear.'

'Hey, so what if I do a little milking off her royal tit? She can spare it. All day long I do what I'm told to do, whether I like it or not. It's time something went my way.'

'Well, we've all got to do what someone else tells us. Me. My master. Even the bloody king's under the gods, ain't he?'

'You have a choice. You all do. But I'm a thrall. There hasn't been no choice in my life.' She touched her necklace. 'Until now. For the first time, I've got some power in my hands and it feels good!'

'Well, I ain't forcing you to do anything, am I?'

She pouted.

'Well?'

'Suppose not. But with you it's different... I chose you. That's why I like you.'

Kai looked down at her. Her pupils were big as cauldrons. 'You know you're crazier than I am. And that's bad.' He kissed her.

She let his lips linger, responding. But then, abruptly, she pushed him away. 'Do you love me?'

'What do you think? I want to jump you every time I see you.'

'No. I mean feelings and that.' She pointed to her heart. 'I mean in here. Or there.' She pointed at his.

'Oh! I don't know. Should I?'

'I suppose not.'

'Do you love me?'

She shook her head quickly. 'I'd have to be crazy to love someone like you.'

'Didn't we decide that's exactly what you are?'

She started giggling. 'No one's that crazy.'

'Thanks a lot!'

For a while, neither spoke. Just stared up at the smoke drifting through the smoke-hole.

'So what's the big secret?'

'Huh?'

'The queen! What's her secret? Must be a juicy one if she's handing out chunks of metal like that one.'

'I could hardly take her gold, then go straight and spill my guts to you, could I?'

'Go on. I'd never tell.'

'You! You've got the biggest mouth in Sveäland.'

'All the better for kissing you.' He leaned in and kissed her neck. 'Here,' he murmured. She threw her head back with a sigh.

'And here.' A collarbone. 'And here.' Lighter still, the swell of her breasts. She giggled, arching her body.

'You know,' he mumbled, 'there's only so many things it could be.'

'You don't give up.'

'Something no one else knows,' he whispered as the tip of his tongue traced her navel. 'Especially not the king.'

Bara giggled. 'Especially.'

'Only two kinds of secret are worth paying out for. Either she wants someone dead, or else she's giving the Old Goat another set of horns.'

'I'm not telling,' purred Bara, closing her eyes. Kai felt her fingers thread through his long flick of hair. Soon she was gasping and – for a while at least – Kai said nothing at all.

'Well, it can't be murder,' he said, stopping, 'or paying you off wouldn't be enough. You'd be face down at the bottom of some lake. So—'

'Just shut up and keep going,' she gasped, her hand sliding round his head and pushing him down.

He obliged for a few seconds then stopped again. 'Who is he?'

'Don't stop,' she begged in a breathy voice.

'Come on. One little name...'

'You little shit – you're killing me.'

'Just a name. Bet it was one of them lusty northern thanes – or one of our Danish friends, eh?'

'Keep going. I was so close.'

'The name! Then I'll give you what you want.'

She groaned, long and deep. 'All right. But you'd better finish what you started.'

'Oh, I will.' He chuckled. 'First, the name.'

'Fine then! It's your own stupid master. It's Erlan!'

'What? Erlan?' No. He couldn't believe that.

'Now finish me,' she urged. 'You promised.' She gripped his hair tighter, but he caught her wrist and pulled her hand away.

'You're telling me Erlan has been with the queen?'

Bara sat up, exasperated. 'Yes – bloody Erlan! There, I've told you now. I swear I'll wring your neck if you ever tell.' She hit him for good measure.

'Oww!' Her punches were surprisingly effective but he was too distracted to complain right now. If it were true, how did he not know already? 'Where the Hel did they do it? And when?'

'You obviously don't know everything your precious master gets up to, eh?'

'Tell me! When?'

'On the ride back from the Kolmark.'

'And? There must be more.'

'There is.'

'Well?'

'Swear you won't tell?'

'On my mother's rosy backside. Come on, let's hear it.'

So she told him. All of it – Lilla's parting, the camp, Saldas's good humour, the brews she tried to slip them (and how she was far too sharp to fall for that, of course). And the rest of it – the heavy darkness, the figure crouched by the fire, and then the wild sport the queen had off his master.

'Course I daren't look up when she came out. She would have had my eyes out right there and then if she'd suspected anything.'

'But you heard it all.'

'Did I? Hel, they could have heard in bloody Finnland!'

'That's some tale.' Some tale indeed. And if true, then Erlan was in mortal danger. You don't bed the king's consort and wait around for a slap on the back and a gold arm-ring.

Kai had to find him.

337

Yet more alarming was that Bara was witless enough to think she could extort gold out of the queen and skip merrily on her way.

Suddenly, dread knotted in the pit of his belly. He knew Bara. She hadn't a hope of keeping this to herself, not if her life depended on it. And he was almost certain her life *did* depend on it. But she'd already told him. Once out, this would spread like fire through a hay-barn.

Erlan's life wouldn't be worth a heap of chaff.

'Well?'

He forced a laugh. 'My master's a sneaky one, ain't he?'

He stroked the gold around her neck, trying to stop his brow from furrowing.

'Promise you won't tell a soul.'

'I already did, didn't I? Listen, if you want more of them baubles, you'll keep that pretty mouth shut.'

If she didn't, the next necklace she'd wear would be red and bloody and two inches deep.

'I will.' She smiled, her bright blue eyes sparkling with mischief. 'Now then, Kai Askarsson. You've another promise to keep.'

'I have?'

She pouted and pulled him closer.

'I have,' he said and kissed her. But behind the kiss, his mind was racing. He had to speak to Erlan at once.

The scent of Bara's skin filled his nostrils.

There wasn't a moment to lose.

Bara sighed under him.

Well, perhaps he could lose a moment.

A moment or two...

CHAPTER
THIRTY-FIVE

Erlan was glad to be home. It had been a long day. Budli Herkjarsson, the king's forester, was nothing if not an enthusiast. He had taken Erlan through every wood within a league of the Great Hall on the hunt for good timber, marking it as they found it. If Sviggar wanted to double the size of his fleet, that meant sourcing an awful lot of the stuff.

This was only the beginning.

Erlan's head throbbed with the scale of it all. Still, he might have felt satisfaction at a good day's work done, but for the shadows plucking at the edges of his mind.

He had decided not to share his misgivings with Kai. Hadn't wanted to burden the lad. Seemed churlish to spoil his excitement. That's what he told himself, anyway. The truth was he felt ashamed at his humiliation. Vargalf's threat had been real enough, the pain in his groin more so. But still he couldn't imagine Sigurd doing anything drastic. The prince blustered a lot. Acted rather less.

As for that strange dream, the marks on his body… these were best kept to himself.

He went inside. Kai had his back to him, but spun around at once. 'I've been looking for you bloody everywhere!'

'What's up?'

'We need to talk.'

Erlan threw himself down on the bench. 'Not without a drink, I hope.'

Kai scowled and hurried to the corner, rummaging around and soon returning with a couple of wooden cups and an ale-pitcher. He dumped them unceremoniously on the table.

'Not sure you'll be getting a job at the king's table anytime soon with service like that. So what are we talking about?' Erlan poured himself an ale.

'Why don't you tell me?'

'Eh?' For a second, Erlan thought he might be talking about Lilla again. 'You mean the princess? Look, I told you before—'

'Not that. Something else. Some*one* else.'

Erlan stared at him, perplexed. 'I don't understand.'

Kai leaned forward, peered deep in his eyes. 'You really have no clue, do you?'

'How about you stop sniffing round like a dog about to piss and come out and say whatever you're getting at?'

So Kai told him. And Erlan listened, fury drip, drip, dripping like poison into his heart. The boy told of the queen's ruse, of the potion and the darkness, of her clandestine visit and the noises from his tent. Told him everything just as Bara had told it.

The dream. Inga… Her, yet not her. And now, somehow, Saldas possessed her too… had reduced her to a stolen secret.

'That devious fucking whore!' he snarled, his fury finally

340

brimming over, throwing his cup against the wall in a spray of beer.

Calmly, Kai retrieved it, set it back in front of him and refilled it. 'You really remember none of it?'

Erlan clasped his head and shook it, as if that might dislodge the cloak of obscurity that veiled that night. Kai's story gave *some* substance to his dream, but precious little.

'I remember— No, not even a memory. More like a nightmare. She came to me and... I saw someone else...'

'Who?'

Erlan took a swig of ale. 'Doesn't matter.'

'But you knew her?'

'I knew her.'

Kai must have seen a familiar look in Erlan's eyes. He didn't push. 'What else do you recall?'

'The night was full of weird visions. When I woke my head was thick as an ox-hide. But... I found these.'

He put down his cup and stood up, undid his belt and pulled off his tunic. Kai's eyes widened in amazement. Even in the flaring torchlight, the welts and scores from Saldas's nails were a livid purple on his chest.

'Turn around. Hel's teeth! They're all over your back, too... I mean, was she screwing you or trying to kill you?'

'That's not funny.'

'I'm serious!' Kai was staring, bug-eyed. 'So you really did it... Hey, where's your necklace?'

Erlan's hand went to his throat. His amulet had gone. It wasn't valuable – a simple rendering of Thor's hammer. But Inga had made it for him, promising him it would bring luck. *She should have kept it for herself.*

Something stirred in his mind. A memory from that night.

'Saldas took it.'

'What for?'

'How the Hel should I know?'

Strangely the loss of Inga's gift stung worse than all the rest. It wasn't the luck it had brought him. It meant more to him than luck. Abruptly he pulled his tunic back on. 'You learned all this from Bara, you say?'

'I just told you!'

'I mean... *how*? Did she just come out and tell you?'

'Not exactly.' Kai's cheeks coloured.

'You know what, it doesn't matter. Who else knows?'

'Only Bara and the queen.'

'You're sure about that?'

'I am. Only...'

'What?'

'There's something else you should know.'

'Go on.'

'Bara is blackmailing Saldas.'

Erlan swore.

'She says they've come to an understanding—'

'An understanding? With Saldas? You might as well put your hand in a wolf's mouth and have an understanding the fucker won't bite it off. Can Bara keep this to herself?'

'I wouldn't bet my head on it.'

'It'll be my head if it gets out.' He swore again. The whole sordid business could come to light any moment. Even if Saldas paid off Bara for a while, he was certain the queen would use this against him sooner or later. 'Not just mine, either. You don't think Saldas is going to sit back and let Bara

342

put the squeeze on her for as long as it suits her?'

Kai gave a terse shake of his head. 'I know.'

'She's in it up to her neck.'

'If she stays here she is.'

'You won't want to hear this, little brother, but Bara doomed herself the second she opened her mouth.'

'So what are you going to do about it then?'

'I don't know. I can't stay here.'

'What about Nairka? What about your lands and title? Gods, you're the king's bloody favourite! You can't just walk away from all that.'

'It's worth dust if Sviggar finds this out. Or worse, I stay and live under the threat of Saldas exposing me.'

'Why not go to the king yourself?' Kai blurted. 'Tell him what happened. Tell him it wasn't your fault. Beg his forgiveness. You know he thinks you can do no wrong.'

'There's doing no wrong, and there's screwing the man's wife.'

'It was her that screwed you!'

'I doubt Sviggar would appreciate the distinction.'

The irony that Sviggar was only days away from naming him foster-son stuck like jagged metal in his gut. For some reason, his mind flew back to that storm-racked night on the Juten Belt, when Inga's body was hardly cold. A night of terror when he'd been stripped to nothing. No name. No kin. No land. Nothing but his sword and the thinnest of threads still binding him to life. Never in his wildest visions could he have imagined the favour and fortune he had won at Sviggar's court. But it was all a lie. Another lie. And once again everything was turning to ashes in his fingers.

Kai was contemplating the bottom of his cup. 'Then I guess you must go.'

It was odd hearing Kai say it. Kai who never admitted defeat, who always saw a way out. But right now, he looked as downcast as a dog who'd lost its bone. 'You should stay here,' Erlan said, laying his hand on Kai's forearm. 'You'll be fully trained soon. A house-karl to the king of Sveäland. Isn't that what you want?'

Kai's eyes snapped up. 'You are kidding? There ain't a king in all the Nine Worlds I'd follow over you.'

'You're actually serious, aren't you?' Erlan laughed. 'I always said you were a mad bastard.'

Kai grinned. 'That's 'cause I am.'

'It's settled then.'

'Not quite. You're forgetting one thing.'

'What?'

'Bara... Saldas will kill her if she stays here.'

Erlan chewed it over a while. Then shook his head. 'She can't know we're leaving. No one can. Anyway, we need to get far away from here, and fast. She'd only slow us up.'

'I have to warn her at least.'

'If you warn her, this could all blow up. Listen, I know how you feel about her. If you'd rather—'

'No! No. I'm with you. Whatever happens, I'm with you.'

'All right then,' Erlan nodded. 'So just make her understand that Saldas can't be trusted. After that, she can decide her own fate. Stay or go.'

'Where do you think she could go? She's a thrall, for Frigg's sake! She's bound to this place, mind and body. If she ran from here, she wouldn't last a day.'

'Someone would give her shelter. A girl like that won't struggle to find a protector.'

'Piss on that! *I'll* be her protector.'

'I told you. She's not coming—'

'We can't just leave her here! Who knows what that crazy bitch will do to her?'

'She should have thought of that before she opened her mouth.'

'Well, it's open now, so she doesn't have a choice! But we still do, don't we? We could help her.'

Erlan could see the resolution in Kai's eyes. He raked his scalp, his mind boiling with frustration. The boy had a point. And something in his own stupid stone heart wasn't entirely deaf to his pleading. There were any number of ways this could all unravel – probably would unravel. Bara was a walking liability, after all.

Then again, he did owe his friend this much. 'All right. She can come. But *you* are responsible for keeping her trap shut. And if there's any trouble with her, I'll drop the pair of you.'

Kai whooped. 'Thank you, thank you, master! Hohoa! Back on the road again, eh? Just like old times!' He bashed his cup against Erlan's, then slung the contents down his throat.

'Aye, and such merry times they were too,' said Erlan drily. 'Now shut up and listen. We have to be away from here before the Summer Throng.'

'That's seven days from now. So what's the plan?'

Erlan refilled Kai's cup. 'That's what we're going to figure out, my mad little friend.'

CHAPTER THIRTY-SIX

L illa was tired, hungry and exhilarated.

It had been an exhausting day. But a beautiful one. The kind of day that the heat rippled off the hard-packed yard in waves, when the sun felt like an old friend and everyone under it a brother or a sister.

Everyone, that is, apart from Sletti who had yet to emerge from his sulk at her usurping of his keys. But the other folk of Dannerborg had taken to her far better than she could have hoped.

Of course, she still wished away the herds of warriors, loitering in their tents around the hall – a reminder that her homeland was not yet completely safe. But she had at least banished all but the highest born of them from inside Dannerborg's palisade. That Ringast had not gainsaid her orders had surprised her. And she had to admit she quite enjoyed the authority she now wielded as his wife. She meant to use it wisely. Still, she was under no illusions. She knew the respect the hall-folk granted her was merely an extension of the respect they held for their lord. After all, what was she to them but an outlander? Or worse, blood-kin of their natural enemies?

Anyhow, their obedience was welcome since there was lots to do. The reaping-time was fast approaching and all the gear necessary for gathering it in needed preparation. Now was the time to sweep the threshing floors, clear the barns, fix broken cartwheels and axles, sharpen scythes and hand-sickles, wax draught harnesses, repair yolks and pitch-forks. And although there was far too much to do, in truth, the more she learned of how things stood at Dannerborg, the more she thought the harvest could not come soon enough. With so many extra mouths to feed, the grain supplies had long been running low. So low that – as she had told Ringast several times – she reckoned it a matter of days, not weeks, before they would be exhausted. That was to say nothing of the supplies they should be putting aside for the coming winter. But even a bumper harvest would not stave off the inevitable if these men of war continued to infest Dannerborg like a plague of roaches.

She told Ringast as much again when he rode into the hall-yard that evening.

His answer was the same as always. 'No one leaves. Not yet.'

'If they don't leave soon, the rest of us will starve come winter.' She pointed at some children playing in the hay beside the stable. 'Those younglings need food. Not this pack of idle wolves that you insist on keeping like pets.'

'I suggest you lower your voice, my sweet. These wolves are wont to bite.'

'I don't care if they do hear me! I want them gone.'

'Not until we have word from my father.'

'Always the same answer. Can't you decide for yourself?'

He shook his head. 'Look, I didn't come home for an argument. Why don't you take a ride with me?'

'A ride? Where?'

'There's something I want to show you.'

Not long afterwards they were mounted and riding west, towards where the land rose into a belt of woodland. She hadn't yet had time to explore the surroundings of her new home and had no idea what lay beyond it. But she followed him contentedly enough, enjoying the warmth of the evening, her curiosity to know where he was taking her growing all the while.

They didn't speak but the silence between them held no shadows. She had learned that her husband was a man given to thinking at least as much as he spoke. Though it didn't make him dour or brooding. She left him to his thoughts. Instead she let the woods speak to her, and the flaming evening sky above them, and the pigeons and the wood-sparrows and the jays and the jackdaws, all roosting in the trees. The air was steeped with that ineffable scent of high summer. The smell of ripening, of readiness, of the summit of the year, beyond which would begin the long descent to winter.

Approaching the edge of the belt, she could see the blaze of the setting sun through the last of the trees. Then, suddenly, they broke through into the open country beyond.

Ringast pulled up. She reined in beside him, staring. Because spread before her was a sight that stole her breath.

She found herself looking out over a long, shallow valley that fell away to the horizon. It spanned perhaps a quarter of a league side to side and was divided down its length into the narrow, rectangle strip-fields common to those parts. But altogether the valley shimmered like a lake of liquid gold spilling from the cauldron of the falling sun. Acres and acres of barley fields stretching almost as far as the eye could see. A glorious sight, and Lilla's heart swelled to see it.

'It's wonderful,' she murmured.

'Aye. Isn't it?' He jumped off his horse and waded into the crop. Lilla dismounted and followed him.

'See how they're starting to drop?' He ran his hands through the fat ears of barley. 'Another week and they'll be ready.'

'The sooner the better.'

'You can't rush these things,' he answered. 'A plant ripens in its own time.' He was smiling – an innocent, almost boyish grin. 'You see, though, don't you? This valley alone could feed a thousand households. Or an army,' he added.

'An army that will soon be dispersed,' she returned, half-wondering whether he was deliberately goading her for his own amusement.

He laughed. 'I know you're worried, my love. But you'll just have to be patient.'

'Patient! Nothing good can come from waiting a day longer.'

'You really think I would betray the oath I swore your father?'

'I don't know.' She peered at him, trying to see behind the stonewall of his eyes. 'Perhaps not. At least not yet... Though you are stubborn. I know that for a certainty.'

He laughed. 'Well, that much I cannot deny.'

She smiled back at him, despite herself.

He stood slightly downhill of her. The barley crop rose around him, nearly up to his chest. He looked like a man perfectly content. A man where he should be, untroubled, unhurried, in spite of the things which might be but were not yet. In spite of the weight of his responsibilities as lord of this land. She suddenly thought how different his expression was from Erlan's dark aspect. The sun was behind him, garlanding his head with gold. She noticed for the first time that his sandy hair had a reddish hue to it. 'My mother used to say that many a husband starts his married life stubborn. It's a wife's job to bring him to heel.'

He laughed again. 'Do you think you're up to the task?'

'Undoubtedly.' She grinned.

He chuckled. But then his smile faded. His face became serious. 'Do you find me hard?'

'Sometimes. A little.'

'Hmm... Well, if I am, it's because I've had to be.' He looked away down the golden valley. 'I've done things I'm not proud of.'

'Who has not?' she said. 'But you need not dwell on them.'

He turned to her and his face softened. 'You have a forgiving heart. That's a rare blessing for a husband.'

Did she?

She thought of Saldas, of what she had done. Felt a creeping disquiet at what she had threatened to do. Could her heart ever forgive her?

Ringast was watching her, perhaps trying to guess at her thoughts. 'You're still angry with me, aren't you? You think I want to keep these men here because of some unreasonable thirst for war... Because I long to see your father fall.'

'I don't know. Do you?'

He mulled over her question, figuring how best to answer. 'Once the wheel of war is turning, it's hard to break it. Often, when a man stands in its path, it breaks him instead.' He plucked a barley ear and rolled it between his palms, examining the grains before flinging them away. 'Sometimes I think honour is no better than a ravenous beast, swallowing up as many lives as Hel herself. Yet we willingly make ourselves slaves to it, binding ourselves to it heart and soul.' He brushed off his palms. 'When you know me better, you'll believe I care what happens to my people, just as you do... And I mean to make sure what happens to them is good.'

She did believe him. Believed that he could do it, too. If the gods weren't set against him. She looked out over the shimmering fields, feeling the barley-whiskers brush against her knuckles.

'Do you think you could be happy here?' There was a trace of hesitation in his voice.

She turned. 'Here?'

'With me.'

A sigh swelled in her chest. She thought of that other road – that road shrouded in shadow, the road she might have walked. But she had turned from it, had chosen this one. She looked around her – at the trees and the horses and the swaying corn and the heavy, dust-flecked air. Looked at the solid man before her, closed her fingers around the solid ears of corn. These things were real. Not some impossible dream, not some hollow promise that asked her to forsake all reason and turn her heart inside out.

'Maybe,' she replied at last. 'Yes. I believe I could.'

So long as I can learn how to forget.

He came towards her suddenly, the hem of his tunic rustling through the crop, his face at once wild and tender. Even in

351

the short time they had known each other, she had come to recognize that look in her husband's eyes, that sudden flare of longing.

And for a second, she wanted him, too.

Maybe that was why, when they lay together this time, she found inside herself something new. Not love exactly, nor even pleasure much. Something else. Something nourishing, something good – like the grain was good, and the sunlight and the gentle wind.

Perhaps she could come to love this man after all.

Yet afterwards, when they had ridden home and dusk had fallen, and they had supped and retired to their bed, the last thing she saw in the darkness before she drifted into sleep was Erlan's face.

CHAPTER THIRTY-SEVEN

'Come on, come on! Anyone would think you'd never made a fire before,' Saldas snapped.

'Sorry, my lady.' The girl's ruddy cheeks coloured redder.

The price of discretion: enduring a thrall so dim she'd hardly notice if her hair was on fire. Well, she wouldn't have to suffer such irritations much longer.

From horseback, Saldas had watched the thrall-girl's fumbling efforts at arranging rocks to frame a small fire, then lay the wood and kindling, and after an age, get the firesteel sparks to catch.

'Good,' she said, the flames at last crackling to life. 'Now help me down.'

The servant scurried over and saw her safely to the ground. Nearby her children were squabbling. 'Take them downstream a little... ugh, what's your name again?'

'Glamvor, my lady.'

'Glamvor. Take them as far as that inlet. They can paddle, but not above their knees.'

'Yes, my lady.'

'I shall call when I wish to leave.'

'Very good, my lady.' And off this Glamvor scuttled, scooping up Svein and Katla with her. Saldas waited until they were a little distance away before she opened her pouch, carefully extracted the contents and unfolded its covering.

The heart had a good weight to it. It glistened, even in the drab light. The huntsman had done well. It can't have been an easy kill. A wolf never was. But this one must have been well on in years, perhaps even a pack-leader.

All to the good. The more blood the wolf had tasted, the better.

She took out the flat stone that had been weighing down her robes since the halls and laid the heart upon it. Then, unsheathing her knife, she cut the meat into three portions and lay them in readiness on the cloth to one side. Then she placed the stone inside the ring of rocks near the heart of the fire to soak up its heat.

That done, she waited.

The others would be here soon.

Downstream, her children were splashing in the shallows, their laughter tinkling across the surface of the water. She went to the river's edge, scooped up a handful of water and let it cool her lips, her eyes shifting about her.

Along the far bank a row of oaks rose straight and tall. Beneath them, the water flowed past smooth as a mirror until the mossy rocks below the ford shattered its surface into a thousand shivers. At the foot of the oaks, thick roots spilled thirstily into the water, writhing over each other like serpents.

She wiped her lips, listening to the water rush over the smooth-worn rocks. *A sound with no beginning. Nor any end...* Outside of time, far beyond the span of her life. Beyond even the span of her imagination—

She snorted. The water might have the whole of time to work its will on these rocks. As for her, she had to work a little faster.

She heard the thud of hooves and, looking up, saw two horsemen approaching on the far side of the river. She glanced at the stone in the fire and noted with satisfaction the glow to its edges. Quickly she laid out the cuts of meat on its flat surface. They began to sizzle and spit.

'My noble mother!' hailed Sigurd over the noise of hooves stomping across the ford. 'Good day to you!' He slouched atop one of his purebred stallions. A towering beast, black as midnight and broad as a bull. Vargalf sat beside him, astride the stallion's twin.

'Prince Sigurd. And Vargalf... as always.'

'A bit late for breakfast, isn't it?' said Sigurd, nodding at the sputtering meat.

'I always make provision for the occasion,' she replied obscurely. 'And you – out for a ride?'

'Something like that.' He threw his leg over his horse's withers and jumped down. 'Shall we dispense with the mummery, my lady? Vargalf said you wanted to speak with me. Here I am.'

Saldas smiled demurely and crouched beside the fire, turning over the meat with her knife. 'Are you in some kind of hurry, prince?'

'What's this about?'

That was good. She wanted him to be impatient. She carried on turning the cuts of meat until she judged she had made him wait long enough. 'Sweet Sigurd, I am afflicted.'

'Afflicted, is it?' He lifted a wry eyebrow.

'With a terrible fear.'

'You – afraid?' Sigurd scoffed. 'For what?'

'Why, for the kingdom, of course...'

She paused, waiting for him to bite.

His jaw shifted left and right. 'Go on.'

'This business we have concluded with the house of Danmark – it seems fraught with hazard. I mistrust the oaths they have sworn.'

'I'm sorry to hear it,' he replied carefully, but she could see in his eyes the hook had caught.

'Forgive me, prince, I *must* speak my mind. Your father remains in fragile health. And worse, I've begun to suspect he is losing his reason. He is beguiled by this pretty illusion of peace. But I fear the kingdom remains in terrible peril.'

Sigurd's eyes flicked uncertainly from hers to Vargalf's and back again. Suddenly, almost violently, he stepped closer and seized her hand. 'I agree,' he said, voice shaking with passion. 'By the fires, how I agree! This same fear gnaws at my heart.'

'I fear these Danes have gulled your father into a stupor, feeding him oaths like milk to a babe. And now he talks of his lofty plans for the kingdom. But are they not so many mad mutterings? To send ships to the ends of the earth in search of gold and who knows what? And all the while the Danes and their Gotar vassals may fall on us at any moment.' She flashed her eyes wildly. It was important that Sigurd should not doubt her sincerity.

'He's blind to it,' the prince growled. 'Blind and complacent... You're right. Every new idea he has carries him off like a feather in a storm. Do you know he actually means to name the cripple his foster-son at the Summer Throng?'

Saldas had to cover her mouth to conceal her smile. Now here was news! Gods, it was too amusing how her husband played into her hands again and again. 'There, you see. His reason is slipping.'

'That louse-ridden beggar!' spat Sigurd.

His whining was pitiful, of course, though perhaps the prick of jealousy could ease her task. 'It's certainly odd,' she said, 'that this man should have risen so high and so fast in your father's esteem. Yet nothing is known of him. Nothing of his past nor where he is from...' *Although I know one of his secrets*, she smiled inwardly. 'Who's to say he's not the Wartooth's man, sent to usurp you – the rightful heir – like a cuckoo in the nest? He is clever, undoubtedly. Perhaps in his seemingly guileless way, he intends to turn the realm over to his real lord.'

'*Yes.*' It was Sigurd's eyes that were aflame now. 'That makes sense. I've never trusted the man.'

'Of course, I may be wrong,' Saldas demurred, satisfied that the seed had taken. 'Erlan has done much for us, after all. And besides – such a plan could never succeed. You're Sviggar's true son. He loves you. You can't be jealous of Erlan, surely?'

Sigurd scowled. 'When my brother was alive, there was no doubt which of us my father loved more. And now there's this damned cuckoo! But my father's wrong about him. And about me—'

'Of course, he's wrong. *You* were born into a great line of kings. And who is this upstart? A nobody, a nothing, or something worse. But you... you are destined to be a king. The Norns have woven it thus. How else could you explain your brother's death?' She let her voice fill with passion. 'Believe me, you *will* be king – and what's more, a great one. First, lord over all Sveäland, and then – who knows? Surely lord of an even greater realm.' She paused to give him time to imagine it. 'If your father doesn't recognize this in you, then truly he is blind. And I promise you, if he doesn't see it, his people *will*.' She seized his hand, eyes bright and earnest. 'These are perilous times, Sigurd. Our people are looking for a king who will stand up for them, one with the vision to make them great – to make them first among the peoples of the north.'

'The earls and thanes likewise look for a strong king to follow,' said Vargalf. 'Sviggar's peace dishonours them.'

'Not just them.' Sigurd nodded grimly. 'His shame is smeared like shit over all of us. We reek of it. Bah! What good is it to inherit a kingdom that's been made bitch to those Danish dogs?' His mouth twisted in an ugly sneer. 'Each time Ringast mounts my sister, he might as well be shafting every one of us.'

Saldas held her peace. She knew when to let poisoned thoughts do their work.

'No,' he murmured, so quietly he spoke almost to himself. '*I* see a way for the Sveär folk – a way to greatness and glory. But Father would never walk that path. He'd rather slither on his belly this other way, with the rest of us crawling after him.'

'Shame shall not be the fate of our people,' Saldas whispered. 'But if the Sveär are to win themselves a greater fate, it must be seized. By a man of will.'

'Aye, I see a path,' said Sigurd wistfully. 'Maybe I've always

358

seen it. Going before me, showing me the way...' He raised his hand, as if he could reach out and touch whatever it was he saw in his mind. 'My destiny.'

'That's right.' Saldas leaned closer to him, reaching out and cupping his outstretched hand in hers. 'Your destiny. Yours to take.' She closed her hand, squeezing his fingers shut. 'Yours to keep.'

For a while, no one spoke. The only sounds were the water's chatter over the rocks, the children's distant laughter, and the wolf heart sizzling in the fire.

It was Vargalf who broke the silence. 'Destiny comes like a wanderer in the night. When he knocks, a man must open the door, else he moves on.'

Sigurd nodded. 'It's time. I must take hold of what is mine.'

'The sacrifice must be made for the greater good,' Saldas said quickly, still doubting his resolve.

'It's been done before,' Vargalf said. 'The old tales tell how the gods once demanded the supreme sacrifice of King Domaldi before they would restore their blessings to the Sveär people. His nobles did not baulk at the task. To save his people, the king had to die.'

'There,' said Saldas, her voice sweet and low. 'Then it's the will of the gods that guides your hand.'

Sigurd snorted. 'Do you know, he thinks he can honour Odin with this temple he plans to build? The greatest in all of the north, he says. But I doubt the Spear-God cares for wooden idols or cavernous halls. He wants blood. The blood of heroes.' Saldas saw resolve seep back into his face like a rushing tide. 'It could be done. It should be done.'

'If there were any other way...' Saldas murmured softly.

'There is no other,' said Vargalf. Sigurd shot him a look like he'd been slapped in the face.

'I fear Vargalf is right. You must be courageous, dear prince. You bear the future of your people in these hands.' She leaned closer. 'But know that you don't stand alone.'

His eyes flashed in a silent jeer. 'So you're with me in this? You – his wife?'

'Life is about the sacrifices one is prepared to make. This is mine. Vargalf – are you with us?'

'I am.'

'Good. So now we shall eat this together to bind our compact.' She crouched to the fire, stabbing each piece of roasted meat in turn and laying them on the cloth to cool.

'What is it?' Sigurd said.

'A wolf's heart. One heart binding us to one purpose.' She gathered up the pieces and handed one to each man. 'Eat.'

Wordlessly, they did as she bid them. Saldas watched the bloody juices running down Sigurd's beard as he chewed and swallowed, chewed and swallowed, forcing the meat down, the grease oozing between his fingers. She did the same, savouring the wolf's sour taste. Soon it was done. She allowed herself a faint smile, remembering the words she had spoken over the bloodied flesh, knowing now that Sigurd's resolve would never waver, that his heart would become stone in his chest, his ears deaf to all voices but the call of his own ambition. The spell was in him now. It would not be long before it took hold.

As for Vargalf... She scoffed to herself. As if he needed any goading to the work that lay before them.

'One heart,' she repeated, wiping her chin clean. 'One purpose.'

'The death of a king.' Sigurd's mouth twisted in a grimace. 'The death of a husband.'

'And the death of a father,' she retorted. 'Our personal interests cannot stand before what must be if we are to save Sveäland from the Wartooth.'

'I'm sure my father would be glad to know his wife is so selfless for his kingdom.'

She turned away, annoyed at this change in tone. But she bridled her irritation. This next thing was too important. 'You know, prince, death always ends a woman's service to her husband.' She paused. 'But sometimes it marks the beginning of her service to another.'

Sigurd circled round her, studying her like a hunter marking a dangerous quarry. 'Are you saying what I think you're saying?'

She lifted her chin, unashamed, presenting herself to him, proud and beautiful. 'It's your choice,' she said sharply. 'Either I stand behind you in this... Or else, beside you.'

A slow chuckle clicked in Sigurd's throat. 'My father ought to know he shares his bed with a she-wolf. Don't you agree, Vargalf?' He turned to his flunkey, smirking. 'Will you tell him or shall I?'

'If you do, tell him also of the scorpion that shares his salt and his blood,' she hissed. 'Listen, gentle prince, if you can find yourself a more fitting queen than I, then the gods grant you good fortune.'

She watched lust leaching into his eyes as they moved over her figure. How many times had she seen that look? The trick was how to use it. But she could see this battle was already won.

'Well?'

'You must learn to control your temper, my lady. I didn't say I could find any better, did I?' He smiled. 'At least, not yet.'

'So you agree?'

'I could see my way to an agreement. There are certain obvious advantages to what you suggest.' He chuckled. 'But if I were to agree, I have one small condition of my own.'

'Condition? What condition?'

'Come, come, Lady Saldas – you can't have it all your own way. After all, did you not say that we must all make sacrifices?'

'What is it you want?'

'Oh, a simple thing…'

And as she listened to him speak, above the chattering stream and her children's gleeful cries and the crackle of the dying fire, she felt the breath tighten in her chest and his words coil around her heart like the cold fingers of Hel.

CHAPTER
THIRTY-EIGHT

Lilla awoke to the sound of thunder.

The night was still black as pitch. She listened to the crash and quake roiling in the dark skies beyond. Folk at home would have said of a night like this that Thor was laughing. But the storm raging outside didn't seem much cause for mirth. Dannerborg's sturdy rafters shook and the rain beat down like lead hailstones and the wind screamed and whistled through every crack in the walls.

It was awesome, terrifying, humbling. Each sudden splay of lightning that lit the chamber only further proclaimed its power. Ringast awoke soon after her and drew her close, not saying a word, at least not out loud. But she felt the tremor of his breath on her neck.

'What are you doing?'

'Praying,' he murmured softly.

So she let him pray. Though he didn't seem like a man who would humble himself before the Thunder God – or any other – at the first crack of thunder, however violent.

But in the grey gloom of a miserable dawn, he rose early. Lilla awoke to find him clothed and strapping on his sword.

'Go back to sleep, my love.'

'Where are you going?'

'Back up to the valley.'

Only then did she realize her mistake: it wasn't for himself that he had been praying. 'I'm coming with you,' she said.

Thus, for the second time before a day had turned, she rode westwards with her husband. Only this time, there was no comfortable silence. Instead they rode with a growing sense of urgency. Dread, even.

And on the far side of the wood, a very different sight greeted them than had the evening before. Instead of the golden dusk, black clouds hung low and sullen over their heads, seeming to brim with malice.

And below them, devastation.

There was not a stalk of barley left standing in the whole valley. The fields of gold had been flattened to a carpet of grey weeds, waterlogged and pathetic, hardly better than the soiled rushes of a mead-hall floor after a feast.

Ringast said not a word – just stood there, looking down the valley. She watched him, watched the silence lain across his broad shoulders like a yolk. He stooped and snatched a fistful of the broken plants at his feet, squeezing his fingers until water ran from his knuckles. 'Ruined.'

'Surely some may be salvaged.' But looking at the filthy weeds at her feet, that seemed a faint hope indeed.

Ringast suddenly spat a curse, spat it with such violence that Lilla felt a shiver of fear through her heart.

'You see, my wife?' he snarled. 'How man tries to raise

something good, and the gods just laugh and tear it all to pieces.'

She didn't know what to say. She moved towards him, although doubting her touch could bring him any comfort just then. But before she reached him there was a noise behind her. She turned to see a horseman break from the gloomy wood.

'My lord!' Lilla recognized him – a karl called Kari. A strong, reliable lad with a thick scar hanging off one corner of his mouth. But despite the melancholy air this gave him, his eyes were bright with excitement. 'They said I'd find you here!'

'What is it, Kari? Speak!'

'Lord Branni has come. From Leithra.'

'Branni?' The name clearly meant something to him, and just as clear was his surprise. 'Where is he?'

'He awaits you in the hall.'

'Tell him I'm coming at once. Go!'

Not pausing for a breath, Kari hauled round his animal's head and dug in his heels. In another instant man and beast had disappeared into the wood as fast as they had come.

'Who's Branni?'

'My father's messenger. And his most trusted friend. If he's here, whatever tidings he brings must be weighty.' He gave a sudden snort and flung away the broken ears of corn. 'Now, my love – you'll get your answer at last.'

In fact it was a while later before Lilla was striding down the corridor towards her husband's council chamber, keys jangling softly against her thigh, a husk of irritation catching in her throat. Ringast had insisted he meet this Branni alone – at least at first. 'I need his tongue loose. The presence of King Sviggar's daughter may hinder that.'

'You mean the daughter of your ally,' she said pointedly.

He only grunted and told her to dress as she would to meet a king, adding that by the time she was ready she could join them.

She had rushed her ablutions, chiding Gerutha for every moment of delay. But now here she was, dressed in all her finery – for what it was worth. She could hear voices, several different voices it seemed to her, despite her husband having said he would meet the Wartooth's messenger alone.

She hesitated at the edge of the shadows, knowing once she entered, all eyes would be on her and the talk would cease. Perhaps her husband would turn her away after all. So she moved a little closer to the doorway and listened.

The voices were hard. Suddenly a fist slammed on a table.

'Damn the old bastard! How can he be sure?' someone shouted. Maybe her husband, though the voice was so distorted with rage she could hardly tell.

There was a chuckle, deep and languid and gravelly. 'It could only be Sviggar's work. The man was set on murder.'

'It makes no sense. Not after the oaths we swore.' That was her husband's gruff voice, calmer now. She peered around the smoke-black doorpost. The top end of the hall was full of men. So much for a private audience, she thought indignantly. Her husband stood behind the long-table, leaning on his fists. Others sat about or leaned against the walls, some drinking, some picking at their hands, all of them listening intently.

Below the dais stood a tall man in a grey travel cloak, an enormous hand hooked over his sword-hilt. His shoulders were broad and bony, his beard and braids the colour of rust. But most distinctive of all were his eyebrows, which were coarse and thick as straw-thatch. Behind him, standing at a respectful distance, were two others, also dressed for the road, their faces hidden in the shadow of their hoods.

'Your father would never be so trusting,' said the man with the bushy eyebrows whom she surmised to be Branni. 'He knows Sviggar is a two-faced villain. Just like his father Ívar, dog that *he* was.'

At the mention of her father's name, Lilla could hold in her indignation no longer. 'That's a lie!' she exclaimed, emerging from the shadows. At once every eye was on her, sharp as dagger points. But she knew she mustn't wilt. 'My father is a man of his word. And who are you to deny it?'

'She shouldn't be here,' growled Thrand, who was half-sitting, half-lying on a bench at the far end of the long-table.

Suddenly Rorik, youngest of the three, leaped from his seat. 'Lady Aslíf, I'm sorry, but what's discussed here is not for your ears. You there,' he ordered a guard, 'escort her from the chamber.'

'No,' said Ringast. 'She stays.' Thrand moved to make another protest, but Ringast silenced him with a shake of his head.

Another warrior, this one with a scar across his forehead from a blow that had taken off half his ear, cleared his throat. 'Is it wise, my friend?' This was Ubbi the Hundred, who hailed from Friesland. Supposedly a champion of great renown. The Wartooth seemed to collect such men like a boy collects pebbles. 'That a lily so freshly plucked from your enemy's meadow should hear this council of war?'

'This is no war council, Ubbi,' returned Ringast. 'And Sviggar is not our enemy. She stays.'

'Suit yourself, brother,' drawled Thrand. 'But I'll not soften what I have to say on her account.'

'I'm glad to hear it. Come, my lady.' He gestured at the seat beside his. She took it. 'Now, shall we continue?' He turned back to Branni. 'As to my father-in-law, I did not read him as a man with two faces. He seemed to me sincere.'

Branni smiled a thin, sardonic smile. 'Naturally your father values your opinion, Lord Ringast. But you must credit him with having had the longer time to judge the man's character.'

'My father hasn't crossed words with Sviggar for years. Decades even. I tell you, Branni, I've looked into the man's eyes.'

A low chuckle rumbled in the messenger's chest. 'You've a good deal to learn about men – so your father says, you understand? You see too much good in them.'

'I see what is there. Now, you have no proof, have you? Nothing that connects this would-be murderer with Sviggar.' Lilla wondered who they were talking about. Evidently something serious had occurred. 'But if you want my *valuable* opinion,' Ringast added, 'I say my father is not a man without enemies. This assassin could have been ordered by any of a dozen men.'

'I dare say you may be right. But it's your father's word that's final. And he has decided. This was Sviggar's plot.'

Ringast glanced at Lilla and back to the tall messenger. 'I take it then that he gave no order to disband this hungry rabble, as I requested.'

Branni smiled. 'He did not.' There were a couple of sniggers around the chamber.

Thrand suddenly thumped the table. 'Thor's beard, if the old man wants a fight then there was never a better time to attack. The Sveärs will still be gulled by this peace.'

Ringast shot his brother a warning look, then turned back to the Wartooth's envoy. 'Well, Branni. Is it war he wants?'

Lilla's heart rose into her throat.

'It is.'

Thrand was on his feet. Even a couple of the others were sufficiently roused from their indolence to whoop with eagerness. But Ringast's face was thunder. 'Silence!' he shouted. 'We spoke oaths for him. Gave our solemn word, just as he told us to do.' He pointed at Lilla. 'See there! I took a wife for him, just as he told me to do.'

'That seems no great hardship,' observed Branni.

'That's beside the point!' Ringast snarled. 'We did it. And now you tell us he wants us to break our word and cast to the wind all that we've just done?'

'The gods have willed this fight, brother,' put in Thrand. 'You know it in your bones.'

'Have they? And what of your oath and your honour? Do you care nothing for them?'

'Whatever honour we lose with a broken oath, we'll soon win back in Skogul's Storm.'

'You fork-tongued wretch!' Lilla cried, unable to contain herself any longer. 'All of you!' Her eyes swept like wildfire around the room. 'I see Danes know as little of honour as they do of honesty. But I warn you – even if you rode with ten men to every Sveär spear, my people would stand fast against you. They will cut you down like a field of rye.'

Thrand only laughed at her. 'That's bold talk from a bride-whore stood in the hall of her enemies.'

Ringast moved so fast that she hardly saw it. Only heard the crack of his knuckles against Thrand's jaw. Thrand was on his feet at once, towering over his older brother like an angry she-bear. But Ringast didn't back down. Instead he seized a fistful of Thrand's tunic. 'Another word against her and I'll feed your balls to the hounds. Understand?'

For a long moment, the two brothers stared each other down. But it was the bigger man who suddenly laughed. 'Hel, she must be good to get you this riled up!'

'One word,' Ringast hissed.

'All right, all right.' Thrand slumped back into his seat, rubbing at his hairy cheek.

Ringast turned back to Branni, who watched with a look of faint amusement twitching at his bushy brows. 'Now... I'm sorry for this assault on my father. But no one who has sworn on Adils' Ring is about to break his oath.' He looked at Lilla. 'Not on our part, anyway. Not while I hold lordship here.'

Branni began to laugh.

'Something amusing about that, friend?'

'Only that your father said that would be your answer.'

'Did he now? Well, since you seem to know what we are going to say so long before we say it, why don't you share his answer?'

But there was another laugh then – and not from Branni's throat. A great, irrepressible roar that seemed to be coming from under the hood of one of Branni's attendants. The laughter rolled on and on, lusty and unabashed, until all at once the man jerked back his hood.

'He said – you impudent whelp – that he would give you his answer himself!'

The old, scarred man standing below them gave another bellowing laugh and then strode up the hall and sprang onto the dais with the energy of a man half his age. For all that she was surprised, Lilla found she couldn't take her eyes off the man. There was something magnetic about him, about his face, about the unassailable way he stood. As though, had he been surrounded by a dozen dancing bears, her eye would still have been fixed on him.

His cheeks were mottled with age and his hair was white as hoarfrost, shorn close, except on top where he was bald as an egg. And his beard was almost as white, trimmed short, save for two tight braids that hung off each corner of his square-cut chin.

The atmosphere in the room had changed in a heartbeat. She felt these other men, these great captains of war, shrink in submission around her, like little boys caught in mischief.

The man was grinning at her husband, his mouth agape, and now that he was closer she could see within the jagged remains of his teeth. There were few enough left to him but one stood out, jutting sharp and curved from his upper gum.

So this is the Wartooth, she thought. *This is Harald, King of Danmark and overlord of many lands besides.* Her father-in-law and sworn enemy of her father. At least until only days before.

Young Rorik was first to recover his voice. 'Father! What are you doing here?'

'What? Can't a man visit his own kin?' King Harald cried. 'Besides, I was curious to see the woman I sent my son and heir to wed.'

Lilla stirred uneasily as his eye fell on her and he prowled around the table towards her. Seeing no escape, she rose to meet him.

'Let's have a look at you then.' He took her hands and drew them apart, eyeing her up and down, a leathery tongue-tip tracing the length of his outlandish tooth. 'Gods, they said she was a beauty and it was no lie! A pox on your damned whining, boy. I've done you proud!'

Ringast was looking more than a little put out by his father's sudden appearance. 'Haven't you better things to do than play these childish tricks?'

Harald cocked his head at his son. 'No sense of humour, this one,' he confided to Lilla in a loud whisper. Suddenly he dropped her hands and spun away. 'Had you all fooled, though. Even you, Ubbi – eh, old comrade?'

Ubbi the Hundred stirred in his seat and conceded a languid nod.

'You'll forgive an old man a little jest, won't you? Reminds me of the adventures of my youth. Did I ever tell you, old friend, how I disguised myself as a beggar and tricked that back-stabbing whoreson Vesti?'

'Once or twice,' Ubbi returned drily.

'Ha! I'll never forget the look on his face when he recognized me. A second before he felt my blade between his ribs!' He laughed long and loud at that, though no one else was laughing. 'Baah! A good tale is wasted on this miserable brood, eh Branni?'

'Undoubtedly, my lord.'

Ringast ignored them and, taking Lilla by the hand, led her back to her seat. 'So now, Father. If you're quite done... You said you'll give us your answer yourself. What is it? I wed. We swore oaths. And now you say it was all for naught.'

'All for naught?' replied Harald indignantly. 'It's not I who tried to murder a man in his bed!'

'Can you prove it was Sviggar's hand on the knife?'

The Wartooth's mouth twitched between a smile and a sneer. 'Who else would it be?'

'What about Starkad the Sea-King?' offered Ubbi, apparently less cowed by the Danish king than the others. 'We had news you broke with him lately.'

'What! That great lump of seaweed! Hah! You heard right, my friend. He and I exchanged a few words.'

'And lost his three thousand spears in one evening,' said Ringast. 'All on account of you not being able to tame your tongue after one too many ales.'

'Well, if the man can't take a joke,' Harald growled. 'Hel take him! We don't need him or his damn vikings. But this other business – no, it wasn't him. Killing with a cat's paw isn't Starkad's style. If he wanted me dead he'd come at me like a man, bellowing for a *holmgang*, one weapon apiece, and let the *Valkyries* take the first of us to fall! But this mean, sneaking murder... getting another man to do the dirty work. That has the mark of the Bastard King all over it.' He glared disgustedly at Lilla.

'You're wrong. My father is innocent of this crime. He would never break his word. Never.'

'My dear, your father *is* a bastard, is he not? And if I've learned anything in this long life, it's that the word of a bastard is not worth his spit.'

'Base-born he may be, but there is no man more noble in all the north.'

'Your loyalty does you credit, child. And puts these ungrateful cubs of mine to shame. But sometimes a man needs no proof. He *knows*.'

There was no gainsaying him. In that, Lilla thought, he was just like her father. Wear a crown too long and a man was like to take each thought that sprang within it to be indisputable as night follows day.

'And you, Ringast,' said Harald. 'It's not your place to question me. The Bastard King will pay for his affront.'

'The peace is sealed with our oaths. You're too late.'

'Now you listen to me, boy. I didn't give you this land to rule for you to turn it into a den of insolence and treachery!'

'Treachery! How can any of us not fail to be treacherous when your mind is inconstant as the shifting wind? We raise an army. You delay. We seal a peace. Now you want to break it. It's you who are traitor to yourself.'

'Do you dare raise your voice at me? Are you my lord now, is that it?' Arcs of spittle rained onto Ringast's face, their noses hardly inches apart. 'I am your father. Your *lord*! My word is law to you.'

The Wartooth's words echoed around the wooden walls. No one moved. All eyes were on Ringast, but he offered no answer, only the defiance in his eyes.

'I'll ride wherever you command, Father,' declared Thrand, half-rising in his seat.

Harald's long grey tongue ran over his dagger-tooth. 'Aye! Of course you would. You'd jump off the edge of the world if there were some bloody butchery in it.' He shook his head. 'But let me tell you.' He wafted a gnarled fist over the company of hardened warriors. 'Tell *all* of you – there's more to this business than your precious oaths. Or the miscreant machinations of this Bastard King.' He jabbed a thumb into his chest. 'My life began with the All-Father – and with the

All-Father it will end. My mother was barren until she visited Odin's oracle, until she set me apart for him. He gave her me. She gave me back. My life is his.' He suddenly spun and pointed a sinewy finger at Ubbi. 'You! Can you deny that I have his special favour?'

'Not I,' growled the old warrior, in his laconic drawl.

'Nor have I once worn armour in battle. To do so would be to hold the Spear-God in contempt. And always he has protected me. You know why? Because every man I've slain I've dedicated to him. To the great company of *einherjar* who will stand in his shieldwall when the giant Surt unsheaths his flaming sword. And now – the All-Father wants more. He has shown me—'

'By the hanged!' Ringast cried loud enough to check his father's flurry of words. 'You mean these damned dreams of yours.'

'It's Odin's choice how he speaks to his favoured ones.'

'Oh, to be sure, Father, to be sure! It must have been Odin speaking. Nothing to do with the bellyful of rancid ale you ply yourself with every night.'

'Silence – damned chick! No man, dead or alive, has walked closer comrade to the Spear-God than I. I'll not fail him now. He shall have the greatest reaping of heroes ever known. You – and you – and you!' he cried, stabbing his finger at each of the on-looking warriors as if already slaying them in turn. 'If I say you go to Odin's hall, then go you will.' He looked up into the dim shadows of the rafters, as though he might even see the face of the All-Father up there, and his voice softened almost to a prayer. 'I've lived long years. But there comes a time when power and silver and blood and fame all fade to nothing. Only the man remains. And he must face his reckoning in this world.' His eyes snapped down to his son. 'That time has come for me.'

'And so for thousands more with you,' Ringast retorted.

'Yes! If that is their fate. If a host must fall then we shall all sup together by the fires of *Valhöll*. When at last Odin will sit and drink with me from the Asgard horn. As comrades. As shield-brothers! And after I'm gone from this world, my name will burn like the sun. Nay – brighter still! For one day the sun will die and the stars will fall, but the name of the Wartooth will live on until the *Ragnarök*!'

The old Dane's face was flushed with the passion of his own words, his small eyes bright as jewels. Lilla felt a chill shiver through her blood – that such a man could exist. Who held the fate of so many others in his hand and could treat them all as so much chaff, to be tossed to the wind.

When his words had died away, it was Ringast who spoke, his voice unmoved. 'You'd be wise not to excite yourself, old man. You'll give yourself an apoplexy.'

The Wartooth raised a bony finger. 'Be very careful, boy. I'm not so old I could not whip you still.'

'You're welcome to try. But if it's war you want you should have chosen this course before you sent us to swear oaths.'

'Bah! This way is better.' Harald glared at Lilla and chuckled. 'Now we have the best of him. As for his foul crimes and his father's shame – all will be wiped out with him and his seed.'

With the thought of that, with the grim finality of his words, Lilla flung herself on her knees before him. 'Please,

Father – you are father to me now, are you not? – then hear a daughter's plea. Quell this wrath in your heart, I beg you. There have been many wrongs on both sides.'

He looked down at her, kneeling before him, his eyes brimming disdain. And she realized mercy meant nothing to him. 'The wrongs started with Ívar. They shall end with me. His base-born line must die. Your father's name will be wiped from the memory of men.'

He was still speaking when Lilla launched at him, her hand finding the haft of the knife at his belt as she leaped. There was a sigh of steel and almost before she knew it herself, she had the point at the old man's throat.

'No!' she hissed. 'He will live. It's you who'll die since you love death so much.' She pushed the point into his leathery skin. She could feel his old body tense beneath her grip, hard and knurled as an oak stump. Could feel around her the ripple of alarm as the other men went for their blades.

'Aslíf!' Her husband's voice.

'Stay back!' she snarled.

A chuckle clicked in the Wartooth's throat. 'Like father like daughter, eh? Murderers, both. Do it then, woman – and I'll see you in Hel this day!'

It was only then, with his laugh ringing in her ears, that she realized she could not do it. Or would not, though it might save ten thousand lives. She could not kill him in cold blood. Furious, she shoved him away and instead raised the blade high over her head.

'If this peace is a lie,' she screamed, 'then I am a lie, for I am the peace. So you must destroy me now!' She seized Harald's hand and put it to the haft of his knife, thrusting her chest onto its point. Another chuckle and Harald's knuckles whitened as he tightened his grip.

'You have spirit, girl. I'll give you that. More than you have sense.' His voice hardened. 'But there will be no peace between us. Tell Ívar Wide-Realm welcome when you see him in Hel!'

'Enough!' Ringast shouted, his voice a sudden blast beside them. The blood was racing like wild horses through Lilla's veins, blurring her vision, but she sensed strong arms thrust back the Wartooth and the point vanished from her breast. 'You're both of you out of your minds!' He pulled her back and pushed her down into her seat. 'I gave my word,' he whispered, fixing her gaze. He looked half-mad himself. 'I will not break it.' He spun around. 'You hear? Not for you! Not for Odin! Not for any god or man. I will *not*!'

'Damn you all!' snarled Harald, still breathing hard. 'You're as stubborn a brood of sons as ever cursed a poor old man!'

Suddenly Ringast laughed, a long, ringing echo filled with mirth. 'Gods, you old fool – of course we are! We're stubborn *because* we are your sons.'

'Baah! You defy me,' Harald croaked, baring his daggered tooth. 'But you hear this. Odin has demanded of me a sacred storm. And I swear to you, he shall have it.'

'Maybe,' Ringast replied, his voice steady now. 'Maybe... If the peace is broken. But I swear to you, I will not be the first to break it—'

'Then you are no son to me.'

'Hear me out... If they breach first then I will ride.' Lilla, her heart still thumping hard at her ribcage, opened her mouth to protest but felt Ringast squeeze her hand to silence. 'Another month. These men can stay one more month.'

'But we'll starve come winter,' she whispered.

'We will find a way. And meanwhile we shall know once and for all whether Sviggar means to betray his oath and do us ill.'

'How?' demanded Harald.

'The Sveärs' Summer Throng assembles soon. Is that not so?'

'It is,' said Lilla.

'If your father would play us false—'

'He never would.'

'I said *if* – he cannot break the peace without his earls' levies. For them, he must make his plans known to one and all. We shall send someone to Uppsala to hear him. Someone who will pass unnoticed.'

'I will go,' said a smooth voice. They all turned. Young Rorik was standing in his seat.

'You?' barked Harald with contempt. 'Why are you so eager all of a sudden? Is there some stable-boy you left behind whose arse you long to kiss?'

Lilla felt a pang of pity for the younger brother. His cheeks were burning.

'Leave him be,' said Ringast.

Harald scoffed and turned away in disgust.

'Very well,' Ringast nodded at Rorik. 'If you wish to prove yourself, then let this be your chance. We'll see to it that they will not recognize you. A disguise, then! That's to your taste, is it not, Father? So it's agreed. And if Rorik returns with so much as a whisper of Sveär treachery then – believe me, Father – I'll be first to cry loose the wolves of war.'

'And if not?' the Wartooth growled.

'If not... Then we must find you some other glorious death to die.'

He sank back down into his chair, his hand slipping easily into Lilla's. She felt the reassuring strength in his fingers and her heart began to beat a little slower. Because she knew, while her father lived, there would be no treachery.

CHAPTER THIRTY-NINE

B odvar's long strides echoed down the length of the gloomy corridor. He seldom came to this part of the Great Hall, but today the king would see him in his private chamber.

Bodvar didn't care where he saw him. He was more interested in finding a decent breakfast afterwards. The ride had put him in a foul mood. Three days in seven he'd been on horseback, to and from his hall in Vestmanland. And once the Summer Throng was over, he'd have to make the ride again. His arse wasn't made for this.

At least things should be more settled now this feud was at an end. Provided it *was* at an end. Oaths had been sworn, but he had his doubts whether his sword would sleep for long.

It rarely had.

Still, his kin had come through it all relatively unscathed. He'd lost a nephew, a couple of cousins. But nothing that burned in his heart like the un-lanced boil that had been Huldir's undoing.

Thank the gods for daughters.

Meanwhile, there was plenty to worry about at home. The harvest would be on them soon. He'd have to organize the cutting teams since the bond-families on his estates spent more time bickering than actually planning things through. Then there was a dispute about Karr's broken harness, and his wife still nagging about the rotten beam in the north corner of the hall.

It would all have to wait until after the Summer Throng.

He groaned, thinking of the endless greetings, of headmen and thanes and small lords posturing like stags, of the same tired old exchanges. At least they would hear tidings from around the realm. He was eager to learn how the spring trapping had gone up in Botten. If his yields were good this year, he could trade his surplus for furs and skins. He reckoned that a good way of keeping his wealth – growing it, even. A bale of fox skins could buy a pair of thralls in the southern market harbours like Riba. Up north, it was worth only one.

But it was the formalities he dreaded most: Vithar droning his way through the Sveär law, and then the endless disputes. Most years he hardly knew why they bothered arguing the case. Judgement always went with the man most able to persuade the freemen to support his cause. And 'able' usually meant silver or the like. This year none of the disputes were interesting. Unpaid dowries; nephews and uncles fighting over land; a couple of angry fathers over kisses (and more) stolen from their daughters. No blood feuds. At least that meant the assembly wasn't likely to get ugly. The law decreeing all weapons to be left out of the meeting circle had never been much of a guarantee that there would be no bloodshed.

Then there were the king's announcements, his plans for the year, and of course, his naming young Erlan as Earl of

Nairka. With Huldir's sons all dead or outlawed, who was left to begrudge Erlan the title? Though Bodvar did wonder how he would cope running the Nairka estates. He chuckled. Erlan would soon discover that some problems couldn't be solved by wielding his pretty sword.

Bodvar was nearing the king's private chamber when he stopped. A sudden lick of putrid air rankled his nostrils. He covered his mouth, just as a short-shanked thrall hurried out of the chamber with a basin and a hunted look.

Bodvar went inside.

His eye went at once to the wasted figure lying in the vast bed. Only Sviggar's hands and face were visible above the black fur coverlet. They were grey as stone, his long beard laid out between his hands like an ancient cobweb. Beneath closed eyelids, his eyes darted restlessly. The reek of corruption was overwhelming. Bodvar clenched his throat, holding down his revulsion. He noticed a dribble of yellow fluid leaking from Sviggar's ear. The veins in his neck had swelled to ugly black tendrils snaking into his beard. Still more horrible was the sound of his breathing, scraping, scraping, in and out.

Only then did he notice the queen seated beside the bed clutching a dampened cloth. She looked up.

'Welcome, Lord Bodvar.' Her smile was plaintive. 'You've come directly from Vestmanland?'

'Aye, my lady. I would have come sooner – had I but known... But the king, is he—'

'In good hands. Although his breathing is very weak.' She paused, and the silence was filled with the dreadful scraping air again. 'The best we can do is make him comfortable. I watch over him and pray the gods be kind.'

Sviggar's head lolled towards Bodvar. 'Who is it?' he wheezed. 'Who speaks?'

'Earl Bodvar, sire.'

'Bodvar? Is that you?'

Bodvar moved forward and knelt by the bed. 'I'm here, sire.' The stink off him was unbearable. Sviggar tried to lift himself onto his elbows but the furs might have been made of lead for all he could move.

'Be still, my darling.' Saldas laid her hand on his chest. 'You must let our remedies do their work.'

Sviggar groaned, sinking back. 'Bah! Sickness is the curse of men's bodies.'

Bodvar frowned. He had no words.

'The Norns are laughing, Bodvar. Gods – someone must be! I've fought many men who tried to take my life. But none so strong as this sickness.'

'None yet conquered you. Nor will this.' Bodvar wished he could believe his own words.

'Aye... This is not my end. There is too much—' A sudden hacking swallowed up whatever he was going to say, shaking him like a child's doll. Saldas dabbed at his brow, leaving a glisten to his pallid wrinkles. 'This blight is in my chest – and now my bowels as well, curse them. But it will abate, I'm sure of it.' He smiled. A skull grimacing. 'I must be on my feet... to address my people.'

Bodvar glanced at Saldas. She gave a slight shake of her head. Sviggar uttered a long groan. His whole body shuddered, his eyes clamped against the pain.

He lay like that a while. But soon he began flopping his head from side to side. His mouth hung open – a dark maw from which the vapours of death seemed to rise with each rank breath.

Suddenly he lifted his hands above his head, waving them as though warding off something falling on him from above. His distress was strange, unnerving, his grey fingers clawing at the air. Then they stopped, flattened, as if shielding his eyes from the glare of the sun.

'What's he doing?' Bodvar whispered.

'I don't know. He does it often. As if he sees something there in his mind.'

With a sudden start Sviggar sat bolt upright, shaking his arms. He coughed hard, then words came tumbling over his lips.

'Stand strong on the right, bleed the sky red, my raven-children.' He mouthed a terrible scream but only an eerie hiss escaped his throat, his eyebrows arched, terrible as the Thunder God's. 'No, no! I couldn't stop her, she threw me and ran away.' Now his voice was meek as a child. 'Forgive me, won't you forgive me? ... Fifteen marks? What's this? More, I say! Send the birds, they know where to go, it's too hot, send them to the raven-roads, eastward. Far-off to where he fell.' Suddenly he started clawing at his own face. Bodvar shuddered. 'My word is iron. Heed me, you dogs! We must have more. More!' He yelled the last word then flung himself back against the pillow. Slowly his hands lifted, wrists limp and weak, and again he began picking at the air.

'Is he dreaming?'

'I cannot say.' Saldas mopped his brow. 'He has a fever.'

'But the Summer Throng... we meet in three days.'

'Alas – not him, I think.'

'Will he recover?'

'If the gods are good. We made offerings to Eir for healing. We can do no more.'

Bodvar gazed on the withered figure of his king. His arms had now sunk and he lay still.

'I should leave you.'

'Fear not, good Bodvar. I know how you love my husband.' Saldas smiled. 'We will not forget it.'

Bodvar turned to go, but brittle fingers caught his wrist. 'Bodvar! Old friend...'

He knelt again, ignoring the cloud of fetid breath. 'I'm listening, my lord.' This was death. He could smell it, eating this man from the inside out.

Sviggar blinked at him blindly. 'The kingdom will be great again, my friend. I have such plans... the All-Father will be honoured. My people will be rich... The gods,' he hissed, '... the gods...'

His grip failed and he fell back. The pillow seemed to swallow him, all but the awful rattle of his breathing. Bodvar rose, shaken, not knowing what to say.

'He must rest,' murmured Saldas. 'Make it known that the arrivals need not attend him. Not until he shows signs of recovery.'

'Certainly, his subjects cannot see him like this.'

'You're a true friend of his crown.'

'Good leave to you, my queen.'

'And you.'

At the doorway Bodvar turned and took a last look at the man he had served since boyhood. And he knew.

He was looking at a dead man.

CHAPTER FORTY

E rlan had watched riders come in all afternoon.
They came in their dozens – noblemen flanked by servants
and sons, gangs of karls in summer cloaks with bucklers slung
across their backs, freemen hobbling in on underfed horses, clan
chiefs and their thanes glittering with gold and silver arm-rings.

As the crowd grew, each newcomer was sized up like a bull
at market. Erlan overheard many names: the Gislung brothers
from Gislamark; Arwakki Arvinsson, the Earl of Gestrikland; his
cousin Kafli-Karl, the clan-father of the Bredlung; Egil the Bald, a
champion from King Ívar's day. Every shape and shade of man
from the other famed clans – the Bjarnungs, the Gunnvorang,
the beardless Halvarung, the monstrous Jotnungers, their necks
and arms daubed with tattoos.

Naturally, the talk was about the Danes and whether the
peace would last. Erlan leaned against a buttress, observing,
feeling more detached from the Sveär folk than ever. That
morning he had gone through the motions with Budli the
forester, marking timber for the first twenty ships that would

launch Sviggar's vision. 'A new age of gold,' Sviggar called it.

Maybe he was right. But Erlan wouldn't be here to see it.

He scanned another batch of horsemen, but the face he wanted wasn't among them.

Kai had been gone four days now. If all was well, he should have been back today. Erlan glanced at the sky. A bright afternoon was already softening to evening.

He should be back...

They had debated long into the night about where they should go. North and west seemed too hazardous, taking them only deeper into Sveär lands. Kai's preference was south into Gotarland, reasoning that since its folk were familiar to him they could pass unmolested. But Erlan ruled it out: Kai was probably outlawed there, after all. Although in part, Erlan didn't want to go anywhere near Lilla. That wound was too raw.

They had settled on the rivers of *Garðaríki*, first by boat to the harbour of Rerik. After that south and east, following the long, winding waterways and portages all the way to the Black Sea. Away from the Wartooth, away from Lilla, away from the great Sveär king. Kai had baulked at the idea of crossing the East Sea. The biggest boat he'd ever been in was barely twelve feet long. Erlan was hardly more enthusiastic, but there was no other way by his reckoning.

The plan, then: Kai was to slip away to the harbour village of Sigtuna on the shores of the Great Bay, there to procure a boat capable of the voyage and a guide who could navigate them out through the Throat until they reached the open sea. But before he left, Kai had met secretly with Bara and spelled out – in the most lurid terms he could express – the danger she was in.

'She's coming,' Kai reported.

'Just like that?'

'Well, not exactly.' In fact, Bara had been stubborn as a lame ox, refusing to leave now she had the queen right where she wanted her, that this was her home, and all the rest of it. She'd been especially outraged when he'd suggested they use a few links from her gold necklace to pay for the boat.

'What convinced her?'

'I told her I love her.'

'And do you?'

'Well, I don't want her dead if that's what you mean.'

'Not exactly.'

Anyhow, it had been agreed. Bara was to prepare her things and meet them in the woods south of the Great Hall at midnight on the eve of the Summer Throng. Till then, she was to go about her duties as normal.

Erlan had passed her a couple of times since Kai's departure. She hadn't spared him so much as a glance. Either she was admirably discreet or else she was going to be cold company on the road. Still, that was no reason to leave her to a fate far worse.

Suddenly he heard someone call his name, breaking into his thoughts. And there was Kai, leading the stocky little pony he'd stolen from his stepfather all those moons ago.

'Is everything ready?' Erlan asked eagerly when he was sure no one else could hear.

'A pleasure to see you, too!'

'Well, is it?'

'All done, just as you asked, master.'

'The boat's secure?'

'It is.'

'And hidden up?'

'Loki himself couldn't have done a better job.'

Erlan sighed with relief, but even as the breath was leaving him a sudden commotion kicked up near the hall. They turned and saw the crowd part for a man striding towards them.

'Isn't that the careless beekeeper?'

Kai's name for Aleif Red-Cheeks – a karl Erlan had always done his best to avoid. 'Where's he going in such a hurry?'

The crowd followed after him and the two companions fell in behind.

'What's going on?' Erlan asked someone in the crowd.

'A declaration.'

'By him?' said Kai. 'Since when did the king give that pock-faced prick anything worth the saying?'

A few faces turned back to the hall. A thin sound, high and skirling, was coming from its entrance. But the Tiding Mound was close and Aleif had soon bound to its summit. The crowd swelled with craftsfolk, drawn to the mound from their booths down the road.

'Now hear this,' Aleif began. Everyone fell silent. 'Lord Sigurd Sviggarsson, Prince of Sveärs, son and heir to the crown of this land, makes known these tidings.' He paused, evidently enjoying the crowd's rapt attention. 'Your king... is *dead*.'

There was a ripple of astonishment. Whispers buzzed. Erlan felt an involuntary tremor through his bowels.

'How'd he die?' someone yelled. Aleif ignored him. 'Lord Sigurd further declares this: "We will honour my lord father by vigil this night. On the morrow, we will set his course on the fire-road to take the place the All-Father prepares for him. The

Summer Throng will proceed, according to our law, in three days' time."'

With that, Aleif descended the mound at a run and strode off towards the hall, deaf to all entreaties for more details. Meanwhile, a hundred conversations erupted around the two companions.

'The king dead?' Kai murmured. 'What does it mean?'

Erlan didn't answer. Instead he looked around, at the King Barrows and the Sacred Grove and the looming gable of the Great Hall, as if for the last time. Everything was about to change.

'Erlan.' Kai was tugging at his arm. 'What does it mean?'

'It means we leave tonight.'

Darkness fell at last. In the corner, the brazier glowed. Above it, a torch hung off the wall, its solitary flame twisting restlessly.

The provisions were ready, their weapons arrayed on the table – Wrathling sheathed in leather, waiting to be carried away to some other land, to the service of some other lord.

'It's time. If you want her, you must find her now.'

'I'll find her,' Kai grinned.

'I'll ready the horses. You're sure they're in the same stall?'

'Put 'em there myself.'

'And you fed Idun?'

'As much as she'd take.' They'd considered stealing better horses, but wanting to leave undetected, they finally decided to take their own. Erlan wondered whether Idun would thank him for removing her from her easy life of lush meadows and juicy apples. Indeed he half-wondered whether she would even make it to Sigtuna. But he trusted her. She was lucky.

Kai pulled up the hood of his cloak and went to the door.

'Kai! For all our sakes, be... subtle.'

Kai winked. 'As a snake. And twice as slippery.'

He pulled aside the drape, lifted the hook, and the door swung open but Kai didn't move.

'A bit late to be going out, isn't it?' Erlan recognized Vargalf's nasal twang at once. In an eye-blink, he had thrown his cloak over their weapons. 'Is your master here?'

'What's it to you?' Kai let the drape fall behind him. Quickly Erlan snatched the torch from the wall. If Vargalf came in, he meant him to see as little as possible.

'What I have to say is for his ears only. If you want to keep yours, you'll tell me where he is.'

Before Kai answered, Erlan threw aside the drape. 'What do you want?'

In the torchlight Vargalf's gaze was disdainful as ever, his skin sallow as a corpse. He was flanked by two house-karls. It was the second time that day Erlan had seen Aleif Red-Cheeks. Beside him stood his friend Torlak, his huge half-lit face ugly as a dung beetle. 'The king demands you attend him.'

'Isn't the king dead?'

'Lord Sigurd is king now.'

'Really? I don't know much of Sveär law, but isn't it for the high lords to name your next king?'

'Mere formality. But it will be done. At any rate, your lord Sigurd commands—'

'Sigurd is your lord, not mine.'

Vargalf's lips twisted in a smile. 'For now. Nevertheless, he says his father would have wanted you at his vigil.'

Erlan looked at the two karls. 'It takes three of you to tell me that?'

'Sigurd was anxious lest you got lost on the way.'

Erlan ran a tongue over his lips. Vargalf couldn't know what he and Kai intended. There was no way. 'Isn't the vigil for high lords only – for earls and the clan-fathers?'

'Are you not an earl?'

'You know that Sviggar had yet to seal the title.'

'Ah yes. That is unfortunate. Still, the service you did him merits a place. My lord is eager you have the opportunity to say your farewells to his father.'

The two men glared at each other.

Erlan handed Kai the torch. 'Supper will have to wait. Keep it warm till I return.'

'Better the boy readies your breakfast,' said Vargalf. 'The vigil ends at dawn. And tomorrow, Sviggar will be buried.'

The son of a bitch had him. For now. But he was equally certain that Vargalf was ignorant of their plans. Perhaps he had some of his own. Either way – Erlan had little choice. Fighting their way clear was out of the question. They must slip away by stealth. So they would have to bide their time and watch for their moment.

'Get some sleep,' he told Kai. 'And come to the hall at dawn.'

Kai frowned, but Erlan nodded to reassure him. 'Lead on, Vargalf.'

'I'm afraid you need to dress a little better than that.' Vargalf cast a disapproving eye over Erlan's scruffy tunic and breeches. 'You honour the passing of your lord and king.'

Erlan snatched the torch back off Kai. 'Fine.'

Moments later he returned, dressed in his finest garb: kid-skin half-boots on his feet and a cloak dyed black as a midnight sea around his shoulders; at his waist, the belt he had fashioned from the Witch King's tail, and circling his neck his golden torque, the lavish gift from his dead lord.

'Your sword?'

'What of it?'

'Every man wears steel. Respect demands it.'

Erlan and Kai exchanged a look. 'I'll fetch it,' said Kai and soon retrieved it. Erlan fastened the sheath to his belt.

'Well then, best not keep the old man waiting.'

Outside the darkness was thin. The long days of midsummer left little time for the night. He followed Vargalf up the slope towards the hall, thinking of the stories Tolla used to tell him as a boy. Far to the north, she'd say, there were lands where the midsummer sun never set, where the pale stallion, Skinfaxi, bore Dag tirelessly around the circle of the sky without rest.

But as they approached, the night seemed to grow darker, deepened by the blazing flares that lit every corner of the yawning mead-hall. They walked its length under two lines of dancing flames strung out like a dragon's spine up to the high seat of the Sveär lord. And there, raised high on the platform, was the body of the Bastard King.

They had lain him on a plinth covered with black furs. Around its base figures kneeled, heads drooping, but his eye was drawn to the king. His clothes were splendid – breeches dyed black crossed with oiled leather leg-bands that scattered the torchlight, a finely embroidered tunic bleached white as milk under an ocean-blue cloak. Erlan saw the glint of gold around the old man's head, saw his beard, braided and oiled; and lying the length of him, clasped in his withered grey hands, was the ancestral sword of the Sveär kings, Bjarne's Bane.

As they passed the fire-pits, some of the kneeling figures looked up. He recognized Heidrek, Earl of Helsingland, pallid and sickly from the wounds he'd taken in Niflagard. And others – the Kvenland earl with his snow-white beard; the young Sodermanland earl, his face smooth and hard as bronze. Last of all, he saw Sigurd – head bowed, lips moving, with not a glimpse in their direction.

Vargalf led him to the steps up and there stood aside. 'I leave you to your mourning, Aurvandil. But we will not be far away.'

Erlan offered no reply. He mounted the steps, conscious his uneven gait announced him better than if he'd yelled his name. But few paid him heed. The noblemen knelt in a ring around Sviggar's body. Those nearest gazed up at it, muttering sombre words. Erlan tried to discern what they were saying. He caught a few words – names he did not recognize, places he had not been. Memories perhaps, which Sviggar was meant to carry with him into the next world. *Whichever world that is.* Further back, other nobles knelt in silence, waiting their turn to pay their homage.

Erlan fidgeted with the torque around his neck, unsure what to do. One of the figures rose and came towards him. The shadows brushed over the man's features.

Bodvar.

'What are you doing here?' the earl whispered, turning him aside.

'My presence was requested.'

'Sigurd?'

Erlan nodded.

Bodvar grunted and turned his back on the kneeling figures. 'Our prince has been quick to throw around his authority.'

'Well, he *will* be king...'

'Maybe. By the end of the Summer Throng, it'll be clear whether the nobles accept him. Or someone else.'

'Who?'

'H'm... If it had been Staffen, there would be no question...' The earl trailed off, brow furrowing. It was a little late to be mourning Prince Staffen, Erlan thought.

He looked past Bodvar at the body of his dead lord. The scent of pine resin skirled from the censers around the plinth, mingling with the smell of something altogether more pungent. 'Last I saw him, I'd have sworn he was back to full health.'

'When was that?'

'Two days ago.'

'I saw him this morning. It was grim. He stank. Like something was rotting him alive.'

'Quite a change in fortune. I mean, after the peace.'

'And a quick one, too.' Bodvar's nostrils wrinkled. 'Something in all this stinks worse than that body.'

Bodvar touched Erlan's elbow and steered him another step away from any attentive ears. 'The ground is shifting, my friend. Be sure you're ready on your feet.' An unfortunate remark to a cripple.

The earl squeezed his elbow then moved away, circling to the far side of the plinth till he was out of sight.

Alone, Erlan looked at the mask of Sviggar's face. The hair on his sunken cheeks looked coarser in death than life. For a moment, he thought of his own father. One day he would burn and Erlan would not be there to see it... But if he had put his own father on the pyre, could he have knelt and prayed as Sigurd did now?

He studied the prince, looking for any clue that might betray some darker truth. But there was nothing. If Sigurd had secrets, his features cloaked them well.

Suddenly the prince glanced in his direction and saw him looking at him. He rose and came over. 'So you've come to honour my father, after all.'

'I'm sorry for your loss.'

Sigurd grunted. 'And I, for yours.' The words hung in the stagnant air. 'He wished to honour you greatly.'

'More than I deserved.'

'You're too modest.'

'Your father was a generous man... A great man.'

Sigurd snorted. 'Great men don't die in bed.'

Erlan's eyebrow gave a rueful flicker. They had the same expression where he came from. But back there, people also reckoned it bad luck to speak ill of a father on the day of his death. He let it pass. Instead he nodded at the kneeling nobles. 'What are they saying?'

'They pray to Odin, reminding him of my father's deeds, of the men he's slain, of the victories he's won. And since he didn't fall in battle, they petition on his behalf, asking Odin to choose him for the benches of Valhalla... Idle words,' he added.

'Idle?'

'Odin has no place for a man whose last deeds were lower than a worm's.'

Erlan listened to the earnest prayers of these highborn men and suddenly a memory arose, of those cold words the Watcher had spoken in that cold cavern: *There are no gods. His carcass will rot and his soul will remain in the shadows with us.*

... There are no gods...

'Are you so certain?'

'Why, any child knows as much.'

Perhaps Sigurd was right, and Odin would have his heroes while the unchosen would pass into the realm of the goddess Hel. After all, hadn't the Watcher been a weaver of lies? Why would he have spoken the truth about this? Erlan couldn't say. But one thing he knew: there was a god who spoke no lies. The god of the white wilderness, of the northern sky. The god who did not speak.

The silent god.

'Be that as it may,' Sigurd added. 'We must play out this foolishness. But his body is old. The corruption comes on apace. Tomorrow, we shall burn him.'

CHAPTER
FORTY-ONE

Kai was bone weary.

He shook his head, hoping to shake his bleary eyes into focus as he trudged along with the procession.

Ahead, he could see the top of the dead king's head, circled with its band of gold. A dank mist swirled about the plinth on which they'd lain him in his funeral wagon. A wheel hit a rut. The grey head jerked, but the crown stayed on. Another jolt as the horses tossed their white manes and Kai heard gold clank against the wooden boards that were carrying him to his final end.

His end in this world, anyhow.

Drums boomed through the mist – slow and heavy, shaking the ground like a giant's footfall. Above them a ram's horn sent a plaintive melody spiralling into the sky. Goat skulls, grim and forbidding, bobbed on poles, riding above the flames that burned beneath them like wights of the deep. Among them banners hung limp, their gaudy embroidering dulled by the mist.

Kai yawned. He'd hardly slept a wink, having spent half the night searching for Bara. He'd looked everywhere – the cookhouses, the stables, the dairy, the washhouses, the brewery, though why the Hel she'd be there he couldn't think. He'd even snuck into the private section of the Great Hall briefly until a house-thrall turfed him out. And even she admitted she hadn't seen Bara all afternoon. He'd slouched back to the house tired, annoyed and more than a little anxious for her. Sleep had been next to impossible, what with wondering what had become of her, or indeed of Erlan. But part of his mind had been racing with excitement too – that they would soon be away, the three of them, and on to new adventures. So instead of getting the sleep he so badly needed, he'd sat up all night, wound tight as a bowstring.

'How much further, you reckon?'

'Another half a league or so to the ness,' replied Erlan, walking beside him.

Kai swore. 'The sun'll be past the morning mark by the time we get there! Not that you can see the damn thing in this fog. Hey – how come those buggers get to ride while we all have to walk?' He shot a resentful look at the nine men on horseback, riding escort to the funeral wagon. Their fur-covered shoulders glistened silver with the dewy mist.

'If you ever become a clan-father, you'll get to ride. Till then, you walk like the rest of us.'

'Right now, I'd happily trade places with Sviggar. Least the old bird gets to lie down.'

'You're not the only one who hasn't had any sleep.' True – Erlan's eyes didn't look much better than his felt. Kai lapsed into a gloomy silence, and for the twentieth time that morning wondered where Bara had got to.

The horn fell silent. A man began to sing. Sweet and deep his voice was, swelling from his throat with a sound almost as rich as the horn. After a phrase or two, others joined in until soon most of the mourners were murmuring along to his song. They sang to their king, to the dead fathers who had gone ahead of him. They sang to the High God Odin and his brothers and sons, calling them to gather as the great Lord of Sveäland took to the fire-road.

'Master?'

'What is it?'

'When are we going to – you know – be off?'

'Shh.'

'Why? They're all bloody singing.' Which was true enough.

Erlan dropped his voice. 'We've to bide our time. The Norns have thrown the pieces in the air. Let's see how they'll land.'

'What if they land badly—'

'Look, we need a night's head start if we're to get away clean. Vargalf can't watch us all the time.'

'So we just wait?'

'Aye. Until all this is done. After that, first chance that comes, we're gone.'

'What are you two whispering about?' They turned to see the drooping jowls of Einar the Fat-Bellied, his cheeks blotched a little redder with the morning chill.

'Just trying to answer this one's damn-fool questions,' Erlan replied. 'I suppose you've seen all this before?'

'Well, they burned his son last year, of course. But a king? I never saw that. Ívar Wide-Realm fell into the drink off Estland twenty odd years ago. Before that... it's been forty years since that madman Ingjald went to the dust. Can't be many still alive who remember that – and fewer who cared.'

Erlan looked around at the droves of mourners. 'You think they care today?'

'I'd say so. Don't you?'

'Mmm. Guess I owe him a lot.'

Einar grunted, then dropped his voice. 'You know, there's some talk about.'

'Talk?'

'Vargalf's been oiling up to a few of the lads – aye, and not the best of 'em.'

'To what purpose?'

'Can't say I've heard. Don't suppose I would from him, neither. But whatever it is, it can't mean no good.'

'Things are moving.'

'Well, I wish they'd move a bit bloody quicker.' Kai nodded at the train of mourners. 'We'll all die of old age before this thing is done.'

The road south began to fall away towards the water's edge at the tip of the ness that jutted into the Uppland fjord.

The sun's rays were finally beginning to break through, though thick skeins of mist still lingered. And suddenly out of the murk appeared a ship's prow: a great dragon's head glaring down at the train of mourners with proud and pitiless eyes, its worm teeth cut sharp into the timber. The ship was not large, far smaller than the war-ships Kai had seen in months past, but big enough. A trading vessel by the look of it, hauled up the beach and onto the tufted grass that overlooked the fjord.

A boat like that didn't drag itself out of the water. It must have taken thirty men at least. Even then, it would have taken most of the night.

Someone must know what they're doing, anyhow.

The procession turned off the path and filtered past the ship. The hull lay on great quantities of timber and brushwood – kindling for a king.

The crowd spread about the ship. Meanwhile the clan-fathers dismounted and, lifting the pallet down from the wagon, carried Sviggar into the boat. Inside, a kind of canopy had already been erected, made from swathes of hide and four wooden posts. They laid his body inside.

The air was filled with wailing as the torch- and skull-bearers formed a ring around the ship. But once the ring was formed, the wailing died and there was silence.

'What now?' Kai whispered.

'Why not shut up and watch?'

Kai gave an indignant shrug. But he didn't have long to wait.

A clan-father shouted a command to the thralls attending the wagon. One of them hopped into the wagon and began handing down the articles accompanying the dead king on the fire-road. Arm-rings, brooches of gold and silver, mirrors and basins of bronze, elaborate drinking vessels sculpted in glass, all manner of weapons – spears, shields, axes, war-hammers, great chests containing Kai knew not what, casks of food, skins of drink – perhaps mead or even wine for a king, he guessed. A veritable horde of precious things, and every one was taken to the ship, passed up, and arranged carefully around the fur-covered pallet.

Two large hunting dogs were then led forward to the prow. There a third thrall-boy was waiting, knife in hand. The work was quickly done – two slits and the dogs were kicking and shuddering, dark blood gushing from their gullets into the grass.

Once the dogs lay lifeless, the thralls picked them up and threw them over the gunwale like sacks of grain, each landing in the bows with a bump.

Meanwhile two other thralls had unharnessed the horses from the wagon, mounted them and ridden them over to an open patch of ground. There they cantered them back and forth till the beasts were lathered in sweat, and with their lungs still blowing, the boys rode them to the same bloody spot.

Within moments, both horses were dead, throats slit, pools of scarlet staining their white coats. The thralls went to work butchering them into smaller pieces, tossing each chunk of flesh into the bows after the dogs.

'Grisly business, eh?' Kai's tiredness was entirely forgotten. Instead he watched with morbid fascination as the thralls flung in the final pieces.

Suddenly, a murmur rose among the crowd. Faces were turning, craning back towards the halls.

'She's here,' said someone.

'Look – there she comes,' cried another.

'Who are they talking about?' Kai asked Einar, trying to see over the heads obscuring his view.

'There.' Einar pointed north. Kai heard the rattle of wheels, then suddenly he could see... a chariot, drawn by a huge black horse.

'*Dauðans goðin.*'

The priestess of death.

Holding the reins was a tall woman, swathed in dark robes that billowed in the dissolving mist. A black veil obscured her face. Behind her was another figure, as different from her as day from night. Another woman, this one clad head to toe in white, her dress a simple linen shift. She too wore a veil, which hung like a spider's web over her face.

The driver stood erect, commanding. But the woman in white seemed limp, almost dazed. Then Kai noticed two thrall-boys holding her arms, perhaps even holding her upright. As the chariot passed he saw her hands were bound.

'Who's the one in white?'

'One of the king's thralls. A brave one.'

'Why?'

'She's chosen to accompany him to the realm of the dead.'

'She's going to die with him?' asked Kai, taken aback.

'That's the idea.'

'Another offering to the gods?' Erlan asked acidly.

Einar sucked his teeth. 'More like a companion, really. To warm the old bugger's bed...'

'Sounds more daft than brave to me,' said Kai.

'It's a great honour.'

'One I could live without. What about the other? The priestess of death, was it?'

'I don't know who she is. I never saw a king's burial before now, only heard the talk. When they buried the Yngling kings, she was said to be some old hag, trained in the arts of the other worlds.'

'*Seiðr* magic,' said Erlan darkly.

This priestess of death had halted the chariot beside the ship. The party climbed down and the priestess led the woman in white to the gunwale. Two of the clan-fathers came to the side and lifted them on board in turn.

The thrall-boys clambered in after them while the woman in white was placed fore of the canopy. There they stood, facing the prow. One of the boys was handed a broad shield. He lay it at the women's feet, then positioned the thrall-girl on it, facing south, over the fjord's misty waters.

At the priestess's signal they hoisted her level with their shoulders. She wobbled as if she might fall, but the priestess steadied her. For a long while, the girl gazed away down the fjord.

'What's she doing?' Kai whispered. Still the woman was silent, the white veil lolling to one side. 'What's wrong with her?'

'Probably drugged,' Einar murmured, as engrossed as anyone else.

She still hadn't spoken, but when she was lowered, the woman in black leaned closer. The girl must have murmured something because suddenly, in a sharp, loud voice, the priestess cried out, 'She says, "Behold! I have looked into the world of the dead and have seen my father."'

The thralls lifted her a second time. She gazed down the fjord a second time, was lowered a second time. More mumbling. This time the dark woman cried, '"Behold!" she says. "I see now the line of my forefathers, my own blood gone over into shadow."'

A third time she was raised and lowered. A third time she murmured into the priestess's ear. This time the black-robed woman called, '"Behold!" she says. "I see my master and my king. He calls to me from the realm of shadow. Send me to him."' She turned to the crowd, arms aloft, her robes slipping to reveal slender white wrists. There was something striking about the contrast between her pale skin and the dark shadow of her veil. 'We must honour her wish.'

She seized the girl and spun her round. The boys pulled her under the canopy. 'She must carry with her the seed of the Sveär blood,' declared the priestess. 'The seal of their allegiance to him.'

The clan-fathers formed a circle around the girl. Each carried a long-shield, which they now joined to form a screen around her. Gaps between the shield-edges remained, however, and Kai felt himself drawn through the crowd, curious to see, until he found a spot where the girl's veiled face was just visible through one of the cracks.

From their cloaks, the clan-fathers produced sticks and began beating their shields. The sound jarred the air – rhythmic, relentless, like the panting of some wight risen from the grave.

One of the clan-fathers stepped forward. The girl lay still. The man dropped out of sight, his head coming into view a moment later through the gap between the shields. He was on top of her. Their heads started moving.

It took a moment for Kai to comprehend.

Gods – he's screwing her!

Maybe nothing should have surprised him by now. He felt like he should look away, but somehow couldn't... Didn't. And there was something about the woman's listless profile that plucked at his mind. The clan-father continued humping away, and her head flopped to one side. The veil shifted, then began to slip over the girl's face, slowly, slowly... until at last, it fell away completely, spilling out a rich fall of thick red curls.

Kai's blood froze.

It was Bara.

Her eyes seemed to stare straight at him through the gap, half-dead. Empty and cold.

In a second his body had gone rigid with white-hot rage, his mouth twisting into a snarl. *Bastards, bastards!* His hand was on his knife. He didn't know what he was doing. Had to do something. *Bastards!* Had the blade half-drawn when a stabbing pain snared his wrist.

'Easy, little brother, easy.' Erlan was there beside him. Kai tried to extract the rest of the blade, but Erlan only gripped tighter. 'Not here, brother. Not now.'

Kai was almost blind with fury. 'Don't you see her?'

'I see her. There's nothing you can do for her now.'

'Horseshit! I'm going to fucking try!' He pulled harder, trying to overcome Erlan's strength but getting nowhere.

'You wouldn't even reach her before twenty men had split you like a log. There's no use both of you dying.'

Kai's head was whirling. But somewhere deep down, he knew Erlan was right. The king would have his sacrifice no matter what Kai did. These folk would have their blood.

'This isn't our place,' Erlan was whispering. 'It never was.' But Kai was hardly listening. He was watching, reaching out with his very soul to meet her gaze. But there was no spark in her eyes. Nothing of the Bara he knew.

He had let this happen.

The horror of it twisted in his heart. He tried to tell himself he didn't love her. But with each brutish thrust of the clan-father's body, the pain only drove deeper.

The first man finished. Now it was another's turn and the beating shields went on. Kai's gaze was fixed on Bara. When the second man mounted her, some spark flickered in her eyes that was stranger almost than her stupor. And he saw that, suddenly, she was fully conscious – looking straight at him.

An imploring look, a look smothered in despair. And then a fearful scream split the sky, on and on, towering above the crowd, filling their ears, scraping at their souls.

But no one lifted a finger. Not even him. And he felt ashamed.

All at once her body, till then limp and lifeless, became taut. She began writhing, trying to fight off the man on top of her. In answer, the clan-fathers beat their shields harder, trying to smother her screams. But she was conscious now. Whatever drug they'd given her hadn't been enough, and now there would be no silencing her.

The priestess motioned to the two thralls, who squeezed their way inside the ring of shields and each seized an arm. But even restrained, she thrashed around until the man on her lost patience and hit her hard across the face. She fell back inert, her face dropped, and again she was looking through the gap at Kai. Her eyes were no longer vacant, but lost, adrift in a storm, searching in his eyes for answers he didn't have. 'Look at me,' he mouthed, pointing at his eyes. 'Only at me.' She gave the faintest of nods. A tear of anger rose and rolled down his cheek onto his lips. He licked it away, tasting salt. Perhaps there was magic in it, because he found words forming. 'I – I love you,' he said noiselessly. For a second, the corners of her eyes creased and he knew he mustn't look away.

Another and another and another lay in her, each one filling her with the seed of his clan in honour of their dead king. Finally the ninth and last was done. The man resumed his place and at a signal, the ring of shields opened and the priestess of death went in.

The ring closed behind her. The shields fell silent. At a word from her, four of them lifted Bara onto the pallet beside Sviggar.

Another scream tore from her lips, so savage the crowd sucked its breath, but they forced her down. She was visible to the mourners now, her skin fresh and white against the grey pallor of the king's corpse.

The four clan-fathers pulled her limbs taut while the priestess produced a rope from her robes. She wound it once around Bara's neck. The girl was babbling with fear now. Two other clan-fathers stepped forward and each took an end of the rope.

Slowly, as if savouring the crowd's gaze, the dark woman drew from her robes a long, curved blade. When Bara saw it, she began to struggle. But the men held her tight. The priestess said something. The rope went taut. Bara's body stiffened. She began bucking in desperation, her spine thudding against the pallet with a sickening clatter. The men pulled harder, biceps bulging with the strain, throttling her.

Kai thought of the many kisses he had landed just there on that slender neck. *Such a delicate thing. A thing so far from violence and anger...*

He covered his mouth and moaned with anguish. Deep inside him something else began to well – something animal and wild, like the howl of a wolf, rising higher and higher till he felt it would split his heart and tear his throat apart. He squeezed his own neck hard, holding in the cry, feeling its power.

The priestess raised her knife. It flashed a moment under the bright rays of the sun, then plunged down, again and again – four, five, six times, each blow rising more bloody than the last, until the priestess's black robes were soaked with Bara's blood.

She had long stopped screaming. Instead, the only sounds were the grunts of the clan-fathers holding her body and the gasps of the dark woman. And soon, at last, Bara ceased shuddering.

The priestess was shaking, her head stooped, the black veil hanging limp over Bara's body. And when she turned back to the crowd, the flimsy material caught, pulling the veil from her face.

Suddenly she stood there for all to see.

Saldas.

The Queen of Sveäland. The priestess of death.

Her chest was heaving, her hands quivered, her arms were steeped in blood. And her face – that face so renowned for its beauty – was twisted into a wild, mad mask, her green eyes aflame, her mouth gaping like a ravenous wolf.

The crowd was silent, waiting. But Saldas said nothing, only gazed down on them with the scorn of a vengeful goddess.

The clan-fathers moved away while the thrall-boys slipped the rope from Bara's neck and closed her eyelids in a mockery of peace. Finally, they covered her with a fine white cloth.

'Odin!' Saldas screamed, sending a jolt through Kai. 'Odin!' She lifted high her bloodstained hands. 'The dead are coming to you. They come on roads of fire and blood! Receive them, Father of All – receive your children! Ride forth to welcome this mighty king to your Heroes' Hall. Sviggar son of Ívar, King over all Sveärs, pledges you the seed of his people, to stand with your host at the *Ragnarök*, when the giant's flames will destroy all things. Receive our king, O Heaven-Ruler, and give us in return victory and power!'

With that, she flung the bloodied knife into the hold of the ship. Then, her gruesome work complete, she went to the gunwale and was lifted down.

Kai watched her, hatred writhing in his guts. He knew what he had just seen was no sacrifice. It was murder, stark and cruel. He knew the secret Saldas meant to protect, knew the folly Bara had stumbled into, saw the vengeance burning in the queen's hard glare.

He looked at Bara's broken body, blood soaked through her white dress like a crimson tide.

Poor, sweet, bloody fool.

His gaze returned to Saldas as she wrapped a dark cloak around her blood-spattered robes.

'One day,' he whispered. 'One day...'

Erlan gripped his arm. 'There's a time for all things, little brother. This isn't it.'

He looked up at Erlan, stone-faced. 'But it will be... soon.'

CHAPTER
FORTY-TWO

Any doubt in Erlan's mind that they were doing the right thing clearing out of Uppsala had vanished with that look on Saldas's face. One thing was clear: Saldas was tying up her loose ends.

Erlan had been marking every flicker on Kai's face, ready to seize him at the slightest sign he was about to do something they would both regret. But the lad seemed to have a hold over himself for now. Somehow.

Surely now they would burn the old man and the crowd could break up and drift back to the halls? Afterwards there would have to be a lull, whatever else was coming. That's when they would be away.

Around the ship the flame-bearers stood in a ring, their torches now pale in the growing sunlight. Then a single flame stepped out of the fire-ring and approached the ship.

Sigurd.

Erlan supposed that it must fall to the eldest of Sviggar's line to light the ship and send him on his way.

The fire-road.

He remembered the songs and burning pyres of his own people, and the lonely barrow on the hill behind Vendlagard where his mother lay. It seemed far simpler than these Sveär customs. He felt a sudden pang, because someone else would put the torch to his own father's pyre now.

Sigurd flung his torch high. It spun, end over end, landing just aft of the canopy under which Sviggar and his butchered bed-companion lay. Sigurd bowed low and backed away. When he reached the ring of flame-bearers they all swept forward as one, and put their torches to the kindling under the hull.

At once the flames began to lick the timber, slowly at first, then more hungrily, along the planking, up the ropes, at the canopy. Sigurd's torch flared, catching the cloth draped over the funeral plinth, and soon the bodies were engulfed in a roar of heat – gold and oak and iron, flesh and bone and blood – all swallowed up in the crackling smoke and flame.

Erlan watched the face of his lord burn, watched the grizzled beard vanishing in wreaths of smoke. And with it, he felt the weight of his oath lift. This man had been good to him – surely better than he deserved and for reasons he didn't understand. But he was gone now, and old though he'd been, Erlan couldn't shake the feeling that someone had sped him on his way.

The wailing took up again. A thrall was handing Sigurd his cloak. His face was stone. Beside him, Saldas was clutching the hands of her two children, her own still bloody from her butchery.

Somewhere, a drum sounded.

Heads turned, distracted. That was when Erlan noticed a

line of karls that had taken up position, surrounding the whole gathering, each one conspicuously armed.

'A bit overdressed, aren't they?' he muttered to Kai.

But before Kai could answer, a voice cried, 'Nobles of Sveäland! Worthy folk of these halls!' Sigurd was standing near the burning ship, his sloped figure silhouetted against the backdrop of roaring flames. 'By mourning my father, you honour me!'

'What he's on about?' Kai hissed.

'*Valhöll* has gained a great son of Frey today...'

Erlan scoffed. He knew Sigurd didn't believe that.

'Now I stand in his place. Head of the house of Fafnung and lord of these halls. His work is mine now. And I will do it, safeguarding what was good... correcting what was wrong.' He paused, his close-set eyes ranging over the crowd of faces. 'Today I offer myself as your king.'

No one spoke.

'Do you accept me, or would you choose another?'

If the nobles or clan-fathers had anything to say, still no one said it. They had been wrong-footed, that was clear. There *was* no other to choose. At least, not yet. These high folk had gathered for the Summer Throng, not to bury one king and choose another. But before anyone had gathered their wits enough to object, another voice cried out from the ring of warriors, 'Hail King Sigurd! Hail Sigurd, King of the Sveärs!'

'King Sigurd!' went up the cry around the ring of karls. And soon it rolled inward through the crowd – 'King Sigurd! King Sigurd!' – spreading from voice to voice like sparks from a fire.

Sigurd raised his hands to quiet the crowd, his face grave.

The shouts fell silent. 'You have spoken. I accept your call! So the gods have willed it. So will it be.'

A loud cheer erupted, mainly from the encircling karls. Spear-points punched the air, although Erlan noted in the rest of the crowd many troubled faces.

'I shall hold my first assembly today in the Great Hall,' Sigurd declared when the cheer subsided. 'All nobles and their thanes will attend.'

'Is that it?' asked Kai, confused. 'Is Sigurd king? Just like that?'

Erlan grimaced and looked at the burning ship. Smoke was rising in black clouds where King Sviggar's body had been. A thought crept into his head. No, more like a shadow across his soul. Something bad had just transacted. Though what, he couldn't say. And although he was now free of his oath to Sviggar, perhaps he owed him this much. This last thing. *Garðaríki* and the lands of the Black Sea would have to wait.

'We're getting out of here,' he whispered. 'But not east. We're going south.'

South, to Lilla. To Sviggar's true heir.

Confusion flickered over Kai's face but he nodded. 'Whatever you think best.'

They edged back through the crowd, slowly, so as not to draw undue attention to themselves.

But then he felt a hand grip his arm. 'A sad day,' said a voice in his ear. He turned and saw Vargalf's gaunt features hovering at his shoulder.

'Worse for some than others.'

'The king is most eager that you attend this meeting.'

'I'm flattered. By all means go and tell him I will be.'

416

'Oh, no need.' Vargalf's lips parted in a sneer. 'He's charged me personally to see you to your place.'

'I'm sure he has.'

The hall was a jostle of heads, the air acrid with sour sweat and the musky skins draped over the highest-born men in the land.

Each had found his place, filtering forwards or backwards, according to his rank. The earls stood foremost with the members of the king's council. There was Vithar the venerable *goði* and speaker of the law, and the other *Ældremen* who would judge the disputes at the Summer Throng. Behind them stood the clan-fathers and thanes and other small lords, and then ranks and ranks of house-karls and hearthmen. Further back a motley crowd of freemen, servants and thralls spilling out into the yard, all curious to see what would transpire in this first assembly of the new king.

Erlan stood with Bodvar and the other councillors at the front, wondering what Kai would see watching from the back of the hall.

'The nonsense never ends.' Bodvar's hoarse voice sounded even rustier than usual.

Erlan merely grunted.

'He's moved fast, but not wisely.'

'Does it make a difference?'

'Oh, he'll stay on the throne. For now. But he won't have won many friends today.' Bodvar nodded at the lords around them, dropping his voice. 'Most may go along with it. But I wouldn't be surprised if plans are forming in a few of these heads.'

'And you?'

'H'm! That's the question, isn't it?'

There were footsteps behind the screen that divided the mead-hall from the council chamber, and suddenly Sigurd appeared at the head of a retinue that seemed to swell with every hour. Vargalf Sword-Storm, of course. Aleif Red-Cheeks, Asulf Swift-Eye, Torlak the Hunstman, and others – many who had led the cheering, Erlan noted. They formed a line along the screen behind the high seat.

There was some commotion near the doorway to the hall. Erlan looked back and saw another file of shieldmen push through the crowd and form a cordon across the entrance.

'Suddenly I feel naked.' Bodvar tapped where his sword should have been. The laws of the Summer Throng held that no man could bring more than a knife to any assembly. Erlan's blade was under guard, along with the other nobles' ring-swords.

Sigurd stood before his father's high seat. 'Today you named me your king. May the gods prove your choice a wise one.'

There was a murmur of approval, though Bodvar stayed silent.

'My father ruled this land a long time. In his youth he won many victories. But by the end of his life, he seemed happier to appease men than appease the gods. And by his actions he has brought this great kingdom low.' He glared at the faces below him, challenging them to dissent. 'The Danes consider our swords sheathed. Well then, if the Danes wish this feud to end, then end it we will... With blood!' He brought his fist down on the table and a cheer went up. But it was shallow-hearted.

Bodvar grunted. 'Hardly bodes well that his first decree means the breaking of an oath.'

'But you know, my worthy friends — our grandfathers were masters of a realm that stretched from the shores of the Western Ocean to the great lakes and rivers east of Kvenland, where the sun rises. From the Snow Seas in the north to the forests of Wendland in the south. It is my pledge to you, my people, that together we will restore this kingdom to its former fame. The Wide-Realm of King Ívar will once more bend the knee to a Sveär king.'

There was another cheer – with more enthusiasm this time. The crowd seemed to be warming to his tune.

'For this new age, for this new realm, as king I need a strong queen.' His eyes glared down again, searching for anyone foolish enough to show any glimmer of disapproval. 'I have settled on my choice. She is already well known to you –'

'Surely no,' Bodvar murmured.

'– proven in ability, faithful in duty. There is none more worthy of this seat here.' Sigurd gestured at the empty throne beside him. 'Indeed it is her own.'

Astonishment rippled through the crowd, even indignation, among the older nobles around Erlan. Somewhere further back, someone laughed.

There were other whisperings, few of them flattering, but they were all silenced in an instant when Saldas suddenly appeared from behind the screen.

If the goddess Freyja herself had descended from the high plains of Asgard, she could hardly have a cast a more potent spell. Saldas was garbed in a robe of golden silk that seemed to imbibe every flame-flicker, with adornments the shape of golden serpents spiralling down her forearms. Her hair was drawn over one shoulder, loosely gathered within black gauze, the only sign of mourning for her dead husband. She looked down at the men below her who stood dumb as oxen, her emerald eyes brimming contempt. But no one disapproved – not audibly.

She took Sigurd's hand and knelt before him.

'My lord husband,' she declared in a ringing voice. 'My king.'

Nicely done, thought Erlan. He began to see it all now. Her scheming. Her victory. She seemed to be getting exactly what she wanted, and no one was willing to lift a damn finger against her.

Sigurd drew her to her feet and she took her seat. The crowd uttered not a sound, apparently stunned by the nerve of this new king.

'Now,' Sigurd proclaimed, taking his seat beside her. 'The Summer Throng was appointed for tomorrow, and tomorrow it will be.' There was a general exhalation of breath, as if the spell of Saldas's beauty had been released. Sigurd seemed to be concluding the assembly, saying how much needed discussing on the morrow, and that much would be decided. Erlan imagined the schemes forming in the minds of the men around him, the plotting that would begin as soon as the assembly ended. But, with even a scrap of luck, he and Kai would be away before dawn. This wasn't his land. This wasn't his king. But he would deliver his message to honour the dead lord who had honoured him. After that it was up to Lilla and the man she had chosen to act.

'One final piece of business.' At Sigurd's words there was a loud creaking noise as the huge doors of the hall swung closed, and then a crash as the crossbar fell into place in the massive iron brackets. The crowd bristled. 'Before you leave tonight, each one of you will swear an oath of allegiance to me.'

Vargalf appeared from behind the throne and handed Sigurd a large ring of solid silver. Sigurd held it aloft.

'The oath-ring of Adils – the greatest of the Yngling kings. He who swears by it is bound in all the Nine Worlds to honour his lord. Whoever breaks his oath brings a curse upon his head and his line for ever.'

'This is horseshit,' Bodvar muttered. 'We all swore by the same damn silver to make peace with the Danes.'

'He who swears will find no other lord so open-handed as me. Any man who refuses the oath... he may depart. I want the oath of no man who would not give it freely. And lest you think me a man to nurse grievances, know this: I will not harbour any enmity against him. Indeed, he departs a friend. But think carefully before you choose that way, because in so doing, you forfeit your share of the favour and fortune which we are about to win ourselves. Songs will be sung one day about what we begin here in this hall!' He paused, letting the weight of that choice sink in. 'Now – who will swear first?'

'I will.'

Almost before anyone knew who had spoken, Saldas had risen from her seat and knelt in front of Sigurd again. She bowed her head and took hold of Adils' Ring so that both of them gripped it at once.

Her oath was elaborate, each word carefully chosen. It ended with the blackest of curses on herself if she ever broke her vow.

Sigurd accepted with a nod. 'Who shall follow her?'

For a long moment, the hall was silent. Once the queen was seated, no one and nothing moved. Sigurd looked out over the sea of faces, and for a second, Erlan thought he saw a glimmer of doubt in his eye. But he suddenly cried, 'Heidrek Helgirsson! Will you swear?'

The Earl of Helsingland was standing close to Erlan. He looked sickly and grey-faced. Some said he still had a blade fragment buried in his guts from his last fight. A scrap of metal killing him by inches. He stood there, the corner of his eye twitching.

'Well?' barked Sigurd.

Heidrek's eye stopped twitching and with sudden resolve, he shoved his way past the other men to the platform, every step reverberating through the wooden planks till he stood in front of Sigurd.

He turned to the assembly. 'Today we set a great king upon the fire-road. I have honoured that king for half my life.' He turned back to Sigurd. 'In this I do *him* one final honour. Yes, I will swear to his son.'

A murmur blew through the crowd like wind through barley. Heidrek was on his knees, gripping the cold metal, declaring his oath.

After him, another earl was called and another and on and on – lords of the ancient kingdoms of Gestrikland and Norrland, the young Earl of Sodermanland, even the Lord of Kvenland, the land of a thousand lakes across the sea – they all bent the knee and took his vow.

With each one, the tension in the hall lessened. Apparently by force of will alone, Sigurd was binding the most powerful magnates in the land to his allegiance. Soon every earl had knelt and made his vow. All but one.

'Bodvar Beriksson, Earl of Vestmanland,' rang Sigurd's voice. 'Will you swear?'

Erlan glanced at him. The crags of his rugged face gave away nothing. Until, all at once, with a snort of resignation, he mounted the platform.

'So, Lord Bodvar. You served my father well. Do you kneel to me?'

'I do not.'

The words dropped like lead at Sigurd's feet. The queen looked stung. But to Erlan's surprise, Sigurd only chuckled. 'Is it so distasteful to call me your lord?'

Bodvar didn't reply.

'Perhaps there's another you wish to serve.'

'Neither.'

'You fancy the throne for yourself, then?'

'Anyone who knows me would laugh at that idea.'

'Oh, but I do know you. I know how you like to laugh.'

Erlan realized he was referring to the joke Bodvar had made at Sigurd's expense at the Yule feast. Bodvar had been drunk and had spoken too freely. Sigurd had been humiliated.

'I laugh only at what is laughable.'

'Insolent dog!' Saldas hissed.

'Peace, my lady.' Sigurd waved her down, still seeming amused. 'Let him have his say. If he has the boldness to speak his mind, then let him speak freely before his king.'

'You are not my king.' Bodvar raised his gruff voice so that even those farthest back might hear him. 'My king lies in ashes. My king would never have forced his successor on his people. My king would have left us the choice. A choice that you have stolen.'

'Stolen? I am his heir.'

'Yes you are.' He paused for a long moment. Sigurd's cheeks reddened. 'You know, as I do, that a man is only king once appointed at the Assembly of All Sveärs.'

Sigurd sniggered, then his laughter swelled as if carried on a wave of relief. 'Bodvar! I never marked you as a stickler for the law. What difference would a vote make, now every earl but you has sworn an oath to me, and on this sacred ring?'

'I speak only for myself, not for them. To them... I say only this.' He turned to face the assembled nobles. 'I've lived and fought beside you all my life. You've had my admiration and my loyalty, all of you. Until today. This path you've chosen will be a road to your ruin. But now it's too late. Your words have bound you to it.' He shook his head sadly. 'The sun has set on a great king, whose memory shall be all the nobler for the shame of the days to come. As for me and my blood, we will go another way.'

'You cannot let him speak to you like this, husband,' said Saldas.

'Peace, Saldas – I told you peace.' Sigurd smiled. 'Let us not sour a day that has been sorrowful enough. Did I not say he was free to make his choice?'

'To choose, yes – not to insult you.'

'Well then – allow me to show how gracious a king may be. I will overlook the more pointed of his words as those of a man whose sense is clouded by grief. I know my father meant much to him.' Sigurd rose, a wolfish smile on his face. 'Earl Bodvar, may your lands be plentiful and prosper. You are free to go.'

Bodvar hesitated. But then, apparently making up his mind, he turned to descend the stairs.

'No, no,' Sigurd said. 'Please—' He gestured at the doorway to the council chamber. 'You may leave through my own quarters. You'll find your sword that way, too.'

Bodvar stared at him.

'Well, you know the way, don't you? I'm afraid we don't have all day to listen to you.'

Bodvar's jaw tightened and he threw a last, scathing look at Sigurd, then stalked away into the council chamber.

'So,' barked Sigurd. 'Shall we continue?'

But with Bodvar's refusal, a shadow had fallen over the hall. The clan-fathers went forward, one by one, though none of them refused. As for the rest, Erlan knew questions would be circling their minds, just as they were in his. Were they really free to refuse Sigurd's oath? Most of the small lords, their thanes and freeholders, and the host of shieldmen and karls, were sworn to an earl. Could they refuse when their overlords had submitted? Why should they, anyway? A man would be foolish to join himself to one earl against the rest, even if that earl was Bodvar.

Nevertheless, some did refuse.

For every three or four who swore, one would follow Bodvar's lead. And, which was more surprising, Sigurd was true to his promise, sending them on their way apparently without any ill feeling. He went further. After the first handful of refusals he promised them a final feast in the Coopers' Hall that evening. Another demonstration, he said, of his boundless generosity.

Yet with every new oath, Sigurd's strength grew. Great men swore, proven men, named men. Rothgar Iron-Claw, Faldur the White-Eye, Karolf Bear-Gripper, Ulf the Barker.

Yet still Erlan was not called.

And all the while he wondered, what would he do when his time came? He could swear and still be away that night. Indeed, swearing might make their escape all the easier. Only then he would be an oath-breaker, cursed by his own mouth. Such a thing had a way of following a man like a wolf with the scent of blood on its tongue, hunting him down until the debt was paid in full.

'Erlan Aurvandil.'

He felt the weight of hundreds of eyes on him. But one pair pressed closer than the rest, green and bright.

He limped his way through the throng of nobles and up the steps, his mind banging back and forth like a gate in a gale. *He would swear and escape. He would refuse and... what? Walk free, like Bodvar?* Somehow Vargalf's cold threat suggested little chance of that. Aye, that was a darker way. But he had been in darkness before and found a way through.

'Erlan.' Sigurd smiled sourly. 'Dear, brave Erlan. You came to these halls a beggar, almost. Ha! A crippled beggar. Yet you've won a bright name for yourself. *The Shining Wanderer...* Who knew my father had a poetic turn in him?' He gave a sharp snort. 'So then – do you kneel and swear?'

Erlan cleared his throat. 'Lord Sigurd,' he began. 'I—'

'Silence, wretch!'

The cry hit him like a slap in the face. 'Not another word from that false tongue,' Saldas snarled.

The vast hall behind him was absolute stillness. Erlan stood frozen too, trying to read in her face what she was doing. But already she had pulled Sigurd close, was pouring some sort of explanation into his ear. Erlan watched Sigurd's expression change from surprise to bewilderment to fury.

'Seize him. Now!'

The nearest guards had obliged before Erlan had even reached the hilt that wasn't there, twisting his arms behind his back. The crowd broke into a hubbub of confusion. Someone kicked the back of his legs and he fell to his knees.

'This man is denounced.' Sigurd was on his feet. 'He is charged with villainy of the foulest kind. If true, he shall not live. Where are the *Ældremen*?' Erlan listened, bent-double, as Sigurd called out the names of the four white-haired judges. Whatever he was supposed to have done, it seemed he was to be tried at once.

In the tail of his eye he saw four white heads moving towards the platform, the sound of old Vithar's crutch hammering the floor like a knell of death.

CHAPTER
FORTY-THREE

Moments later, Erlan was flung down in front of the council table. Sigurd and Saldas took their places, flanked by the four *Ældremen*. Behind them lurked Vargalf, his eyes never leaving Erlan.

Sigurd opened proceedings. 'The queen brings this charge. Let her tell the truth of it.' He signalled for Saldas to continue.

When she stood, the power-hungry look of earlier was gone. In its place, an expression dignified, almost demure – a mask Erlan had never seen before. After her blood-soaked arms, her screaming mouth, this face of virtue was all the more disturbing.

'My lords of the King's justice,' she began softly, 'forgive my outburst before. But once you hear what I have to say, you will agree that anger is the only response to what this man has done.'

'What could merit so sudden an interruption to the assembly?' said Torstig Snow-beard, in a grating voice.

'Sudden is hardly the word. The wrong this man did me was some time ago. It has weighed on me ever since. But...'

She faltered, apparently composing herself. 'But for the sake of our new king's honour, I could not let this *man* utter his oath.'

'He has wronged you, my lady?' asked Vithar, leaning on his crutch.

'Did I not just say so?' Her voice was trembling. 'Yes – he has wronged me. More than any man ever has. And not only me. He has betrayed my late husband, his oath-lord. Those filthy hands have dishonoured us both, though my husband never knew it.'

'He's an oath-breaker, then?' Torstig interjected.

'More. No man is fouler in all the kingdom.'

'Why not denounce him before now, my lady?' This speaker was Leidolf, the youngest of the *Ældremen*.

'Why? Because my husband's honour was worth more to me than justice for myself. How could I let his good name be made a mockery while he still lived? How could I break his heart with anger? And I was right to wait. His sickness took him and he was spared the distress of dying with poison in his heart against this man.'

'You did right, my queen. No doubt of it,' Sigurd interrupted. 'But let us hear this man's crime.'

'It's not long in the telling.' She shot Erlan a dark look. 'All here will recall how, after Princess Aslíf's marriage, I rode in company with her to the Kolmark. There, we said our farewells. And, fool that I was, I had suggested that this... this *fiend* accompany me. After his deeds of the winter, I thought him a man of honour. Brave and skilful. How wrong I was! He knows nothing of honour. Sviggar thought he sent a protector. In truth, he sent a wolf.'

Erlan listened, weighing up his predicament. He was buckled forward on his knees, but through his tousled hair he could see his judges' faces. This was a game of wits with Saldas and already they were lapping up her story. All except Leidolf, maybe, who looked like a man not to be led by the nose anywhere.

'On the road home, we camped in a wood where he wasted no time putting his plan to work. He made shelters for each of us and then we ate. My handmaid was tired and went early to her bed.'

As she spoke, Erlan was trying desperately to piece together the hazy recollections of that night. But they were scattered and splintered like a broken pitcher. Even so, if he was to answer her, he had to remember.

'Since she slept late,' Saldas was saying, 'I can only imagine he drugged her with some sleeping draft to put her out of the way.'

'That's a lie,' he growled, earning himself a kick.

'Silence, cripple,' Sigurd snapped. 'Your turn will come.'

'No lie, my lord,' Saldas said, with a fragile smile. 'What reason have I to lie? My handmaid took to her bed and soon afterwards I, to mine. In any case, this man didn't wish to talk, and—' She stopped and touched her brow, looking affected.

'Pray continue, my lady,' croaked Vithar, like some kindly old bullfrog.

'I didn't like the look I kept seeing in his eye. I lay down in my shelter, but listened to hear what he did. For a long time, I heard nothing but his breathing, though I knew he was still sitting by the fire. Now and then I heard the sound of an ale-skin being lifted. By then, he must have drunk nearly the whole skin.

430

I forced myself to stay awake, refusing myself sleep before I was sure he was settled. At last, I heard him rise and crawl into his bed. After that his snoring, and only then I closed my own eyes.'

She seemed to falter again.

'It's clear the recollection is hard for you.' Sigurd reached out and pressed her hand. 'Simply tell what happened.'

'I... I fell asleep... And the next thing I knew, I awoke with a start and fingers around my throat. I was terrified. For a second I was disorientated, not knowing who or what it could be. Then he hissed for me to be quiet and I knew it was him. I felt the prick of a knifepoint under my chin. Then he pulled away my blanket and... I'm almost too ashamed to tell.' Her head dropped, her shoulders curled forward, wilting like a flower. But then, forcefully, she lifted her head. 'He began tugging at my skirts. I saw he meant to have me and I began to fight back. I didn't care about the knife or even whether he killed me. I just knew he mustn't have me. I tried to scream to rouse my servant but his fist was fast over my mouth. Besides, I now know she was unconscious from his sleeping draft. I could have screamed all night, it would have done me no good. Instead I fought all the harder, tearing at his clothes and his body, trying to force him off me... But... he was too strong...' Her voice cracked. 'Too strong for me.'

Erlan had to admit, it was a flawless performance. She went through the same pretence of wilting, then composing herself, as if a welter of emotions roiled inside her.

'He was strangling me, harder and harder till my mind filled with blackness. I kicked and scratched but what could I do? Alas, I am only a fragile woman. I began to weaken, to lose consciousness. I must have stopped fighting because

431

then I felt him. He was...' She pressed her hand to her mouth. The judges' grizzled faces were watching her intently, but their expressions were stone, even when a tear shone on her smooth cheek. 'He was inside me,' she said. 'Raping me... Raping his queen.'

Saldas had finished her story. Through his tousled hair, Erlan watched her resume her seat.

'She's lying,' he said, careless of the blow it drew. There was only silence.

Finally Torstig Snow-beard spoke. 'A terrible ordeal, my queen. This man will pay for his wickedness.'

'He will,' Leidolf added quickly, 'if this is true.'

'Of course it's true,' Sigurd said. 'Why would the queen humiliate herself before us all for a lie?'

'I have not accused her of lying, my lord. But the Sveär law holds sway over this matter. No man accused is not allowed to answer the charges – even ones as grave as these. That is, after all, why you have us sit here in judgement, is it not?' Leidolf raised an eyebrow at Sigurd.

'You'll get no truth from him,' said Saldas. 'His tongue is crooked as his heart is black.'

'That is for us to judge, my lady,' Leidolf replied.

'Very well. Let the villain speak his lies. Though it only wastes our time.'

'Speak then, Erlan,' Vithar croaked.

'Like this?' The guards still held him buckled over on his knees.

'Let him kneel upright,' said Leidolf.

But the guards held him until Sigurd snapped his fingers. The strain in his shoulders was released and he felt blood flow back

432

into his arms as he sat back on his haunches. For the first time, he could look his judges in the face.

'This woman can't speak a word but it's a lie. This story of hers is just the same.'

'Slanderous cur—' Sigurd exclaimed.

'Tell us only what occurred,' interrupted Vithar. 'Keep your opinions to yourself.'

'Very well. We left Ringast's company earlier that day and made camp, as she said. I put up shelters. We ate, we drank. Only it was she who took care of the drink. She insisted on that. I drank what she gave us, as did her servant.'

'Who is this servant-girl?' Leidolf asked.

'Her name was Bara, Balli's daughter. We drank what the queen gave us, and the last I remember clearly was a sudden weariness coming on. Too quickly to be natural in my opinion, but I don't know for sure. After that, as I recall, we three went to our shelters at the same time. And when I lay down to sleep, my mind was filled with strange thoughts... A jumble of memories.'

'Strange thoughts! A jumble of memories!' Sigurd sniggered mockingly. 'Do you hope to convince your judges by proving you're mad, cripple?'

'I speak what I recall.'

'Let him go on,' said Torstig.

'I'm not mad. I mean only to show why I believe the queen drugged the drink she was so set on serving us. I recollect nothing of her shelter. I deny completely attacking her or harming her in any way. As to laying with her—' He broke off, choosing his words carefully. 'If your law demands the truth, then I will tell you the truth. I don't know whether I lay with her or not. I certainly can't recall it.'

'He doesn't even have the decency to deny it,' Saldas gasped.

'This is absurd,' said Sigurd.

'How can a man not know whether he has lain with a woman?' Leidolf demanded in a steady voice. 'Were you drunk?'

'Not drunk, but drugged. Of that, I *am* certain.'

'Then why do you even admit the possibility?'

Erlan hesitated. 'I... I have a flash of a memory.'

'A memory. Of what?'

'Of a coupling. But not with her... With another.'

'What other?'

'One of another time and another place. Not her.'

Torstig cleared his throat. 'Yet you admit a coupling did take place?'

'I told you, I don't know. I can't say whether the memory is of a dream or of something real.'

Leidolf scoffed. 'Young man – you can hardly expect us to judge a thing on your dreams.'

'I well know it, my lord. But this is the best I can tell. If it did happen, it was under some craft of hers. I have no memory of her. There was no rape.'

'See how he insults me,' Saldas snorted. 'He rapes me and claims it was my doing. For the sake of decency, how much more of this must we hear?'

'You know the truth, Saldas.'

'I do,' she said, returning his glare. 'That is why you will pay for what you did.'

Erlan knew he had one more arrow to shoot. Bara. But he couldn't figure how to use her witness without also dragging Kai into this mess. If he told them what Bara had told Kai, Saldas would know immediately that Erlan could only know what had happened through him. And if that happened, his little brother wouldn't outlive the day.

'Her servant Bara must have known something,' he said.

'How could she when you had drugged her?' Saldas retorted.

'Who is this Bara?' asked Leidolf in a level voice.

Saldas touched her lips. 'She was my personal maidservant.'

'Well, we must fetch her here at once,' Leidolf replied.

'You cannot, my lords.'

'If the justice lords summon her, she must come,' insisted Vithar.

'Summon her from the halls of Hel then,' Erlan said grimly. 'She's dead.'

'Dead?'

'You saw it yourselves.' He threw a damning look at Saldas. 'Your queen butchered her this morning.'

But Saldas's face was steady. 'Such cruel words. Bara had the high honour to be King Sviggar's companion in death.'

'What, this same servant?' The shock in Leidolf's voice was evident.

'Yes.'

'You murdered her because she knew what you are,' Erlan snarled.

'Murdered her?' Saldas laughed. 'How ridiculous! The poor girl was distraught at my husband's death. She was on her knees before me, begging that she might accompany him out of love and loyalty. And now you defile her sacrifice with more of your desperate lies!'

Erlan laughed a hollow, bitter laugh. 'Convenient that the

one person who could prove you a liar sacrificed herself under your butcher's blade.'

'It seems we could go back and forth a long while to no purpose,' said a deep voice. It was the fourth lord of justice, Eirik, who so far had not spoken. 'With no other witnesses, we have only the word of Queen Saldas against the word of the Aurvandil.'

'Surely the word of a queen carries more weight,' Torstig said.

'Perhaps,' Eirik returned. 'But this man has not been proved a liar before.'

'If the queen says he attacked her,' Sigurd said impatiently, 'what possible reason have any of you to doubt her? Let's just get on with this.'

'I had hoped for the same courtesy, my lord,' Saldas said, glaring pointedly at Eirik. 'But I see now my word is not enough for these venerable ears.'

'Eirik *is* right, though,' said Vithar. 'Without witnesses, the word of any two adversaries carries equal weight, unless one is already a proven liar.' He shifted his weight on his crutch. 'Or else there are further proofs.'

'Very well,' replied Saldas. 'I had thought I should not need them, but I do have such proofs.' She stood and proffered her fist, waiting until she was sure every eye was on it. Only then did she open it. And in her palm was a tangled leather thong. She lifted it so that it hung to its full length. 'This is his.'

Erlan scowled. And in his mind, he heard that soft voice in the shadows: *I must send you out, my love – into the wild winds of the All-Father's will.* The winds were wild, sure enough, and right now they were blowing him onto the rocks.

'What is it?' Leidolf asked.

'An amulet,' she said. 'After he had taken what he wanted, I found this on my blanket in the morning. I must have torn it from his neck as we struggled.' She tossed the scrap of silver and its thong onto the table. 'There's your first proof. Ask him. See if he denies it is his.'

Leidolf leaned forward and picked it off the table, turning it over in his fingers. Suddenly he looked at Erlan. 'Do you deny it?'

'It's his,' said Sigurd. 'I've seen it around his neck.'

'Do you?' Leidolf repeated.

'No.'

'Then explain how the queen should come by it.'

His memory was a fog. All he remembered were shattered fragments of the dream. Inga. The pleasure. And the pain. 'By some trickery of hers – how else?'

'Trickery? But how, exactly? And *why*?'

'I don't know. She took it somehow. But not like that.'

Sigurd scoffed. 'See how his lies run dry.'

The chamber fell silent.

At length, Eirik spoke, in his quiet, deep voice. 'You called this your first proof, my lady. Are there others?'

'I believe there are – though I don't know for certain. I fought wildly with him, tearing at his skin with my nails, even as he was... Well, you examine him. His own body will bear witness against him, I'm sure of it.'

The stern gaze of the four *Ældremen* settled on Erlan. He felt a vertiginous chasm opening up at his feet.

'Strip him,' said Leidolf.

In a moment the guards had ripped off his cloak, pulled his tunic over his head and flung them on the floor.

There in the dim and flaring light, his pale torso was streaked black and purple with the fading welts that Saldas, in her runaway ecstasy, had raked over his skin. The marks were still there, marks that told of a struggle, though whether made in the grip of passion or of fear, they were silent.

Torstig sucked his teeth. The others leaned forward, looking closer.

Erlan knew it was over now. They would never believe him, even if he told them what Bara had witnessed. And if he did that, Kai would be taken. So he kept silent.

'Do you have anything to say?' Leidolf's expression was hostile now.

Erlan shook his head. He only prayed Kai was getting out, getting far away from this place.

'Then I believe we are ready to pass judgement. Are we agreed?'

The other three *Ældremen* nodded. Sigurd was smiling. Saldas looked calm, almost serene, as though she had resumed her place high above the tawdry business of dispensing justice.

'Your decision, Torstig?' rasped Vithar.

'He is guilty of a most heinous violation against our beloved queen.'

'Eirik?'

'The same.'

'Leidolf?'

'With these,' he gestured at Erlan's torso, 'and no explanation... Guilty.'

'That is my verdict as well,' Vithar said. 'Erlan Aurvandil, kneel before your judges.' The guards shoved him to his knees. 'Any man who lies by force with a woman not lawfully his own is in violation of the law,' he intoned. 'If she is married, his life becomes forfeit to her husband and his kin, unless the husband accepts lesser compensation for this crime. In this instance, you have been found guilty of rape. Rape of this, our noble Queen Saldas, the wife of your oath-lord and king.' The words shivered through Erlan like the tolling of a mighty bell. 'You are hereby declared an oath-breaker, outside of the law. Since King Sviggar no longer lives, his claim passes into the hands of his son and heir, Sigurd, King of Sveäland. Therefore, your life is forfeit to him.'

Sigurd rose and walked around the council table with measured strides. 'A wise and just decision. I will give careful thought to the fate of the man who has disgraced my father's trust and violated the honour of my queen.' He stopped in front of Erlan. 'As for the gifts my father bequeathed on you...' He reached down and took hold of the golden torque that circled Erlan's neck. 'They are yours no longer.' He tore it off. Erlan gagged as the metal wrenched his throat. 'Take him away.'

But before they did, Saldas snatched the amulet from the table, with a glance at him in which was a flash of triumph so fleeting only he could have seen it. 'I'll take this. It hasn't brought you much luck, after all.'

Erlan was hauled to his feet, and a sibilant whisper sounded in his ear.

'You're mine now, cripple. All mine.'

Then the world went black.

CHAPTER
FORTY-FOUR

With bile souring his gut, Kai had stood at the back of the hall among the thralls and freemen and watched. Watched the earls bend the knee, watched Bodvar make his stand and vanish, watched others do the same – too few but worthy at least of some respect. Watched Erlan denounced and dragged into the council chamber. And then, along with every other man, highborn or low, he had waited.

Eventually the upstart king and his black-hearted queen had emerged and Kai had watched some more as Sigurd bound the rest of them with their oaths. A few more refused and were ushered away to this last feast that Sigurd had promised them before they were free to leave the halls.

When at last it was the turn of the lowest folk, in which Kai was numbered, they were to declare an oath in unison. Kai had moved his lips but hadn't spoken. They'd have to slit his throat before he swore allegiance to that bloodthirsty bitch and her hound.

Afterwards the gates were opened and they had been free to go. Kai had slipped out innocuously among the throng with little doubt of what had just happened: Erlan had fallen into the queen's hands, and that meant no good.

But sure as he was of that, he had no clue what to do now. His mind was a fog of dark words and darker foreboding. So he drifted along with the crowd, feeling rudderless.

What the Hel was he supposed to do?

He tried to think, but every time he began to settle on some sort of plan his thoughts sifted like dust through fingers and he heard that terrible scream again, saw those terrified eyes, begging him, accusing him.

He had done nothing. So what if cold reason told him that had he tried to save her they would now both be dead?

I just watched her die.

His footsteps wandered as his mind wandered. And as the sun fell and the sky began to purple, he found his steps had brought him, by hazard, close by the Coopers' Hall on the south-eastern edge of Uppsala. A swell of voices roused him from his gloomy reverie. A group of men were going into the little hall, overseen apparently by a handful of Sigurd's karls.

Of course. The Coopers' Hall was where those who refused Sigurd's oath were to be supped before they quit the halls. An idea occurred to him. What if Bodvar could help? If anyone could be trusted for his good judgement it was surely him. He'd know what to do about Erlan... If anything could be done.

Kai couldn't see the earl among the stragglers entering the hall. Perhaps he was already inside. But Kai could hardly go striding in there past those karls, bold as Baldur, and demand a little chat with the earl. Instinct told him the less attention he drew to himself the better. Instead, he slunk away, and keeping to the shadows he circled to the back of the hall where everything was sinking into twilight. There, he found a gap between the planking in the east wall and peered inside.

He could see men taking their seats along the tables that had been pulled into place. Cups and pitchers were being handed out, apparently to quell a thirst before supper was served. He tried to pick out Bodvar's rusty braids among the others, but couldn't see him. There were more men off to the right, hard to see with the planking and the dim light. Closer to him, a few feet from his peephole, a few men were settling at a table and passing round a pitcher. One man, hunched over his cup with his back to Kai, seemed familiar. When he glanced to one side, Kai recognized him immediately.

Jovard.

That's right, he remembered. *Jo refused, too.*

Perhaps he might help. After the scrap at Ulvar's Crossing, they were practically comrades, after all. Kai put his mouth to the slit. *'Psssst!'*

Jovard went on drinking and talking.

'Pssssssst!' Louder this time. 'Jo!'

At the sound of his own name, Jovard turned, looking puzzled.

Kai called it again in a forced whisper.

Jovard squinted at the wall, then rose from his seat. None of the others paid him any mind. He came to the wall. Kai called again.

'Who the Hel's that then?'

'It's Kai.'

'Kai Askarsson?' Jovard said. He put his eye to the crack. Kai stood back to show himself. 'What are you doing skulking back there? They've taken Erlan.'

'I know! I'm looking for Bodvar. Is he in there?'

'Haven't seen him.'

'Hey, Jo,' someone crowed. 'Who's out there?'

'Give me a second,' he called back.

'Some frisky filly, is it? Hey, Jo? Hey!'

'I said give me a fucking second,' Jovard snarled. The other man shrugged and resumed his conversation.

'I must speak with him!' said Kai.

Jovard nodded. He stepped back and craned his neck. 'Not a whisker of him in here. What do you think he can do?'

'I don't know. Something...'

Jovard gave a low whistle. 'Reckon he'll have his own problems soon enough.'

'Maybe... Hey – why did you refuse?'

'Just seemed the better bet. Going with Bodvar.'

'So will you ride with him to Vestmanland?'

'If he'll take me. If not, I've some kin down in Gotland.' He shrugged. 'Either way, I'm done here.'

There was a sudden noise behind him. Jovard turned away. 'Hang on – something's happening.' Kai watched his eyes narrow. 'They're closing the doors.'

Beyond him, Kai could see the men nearer the doors. They were on their feet. There was a second noise: a crash of wood and iron. 'They've barred it!' someone yelled. The first to reach the door began beating on it, shouting at the guards on the other side.

'What are they playing at now?'

'I'll go take a look,' said Kai.

But just then a man standing on a bench near the door cried out and pointed at the roof.

'What is it, Jo?' hissed Kai. 'Jo?'

'Smoke,' murmured Jovard, as if he couldn't quite believe it.

Then the hall erupted in a roar of alarm.

'Fire!' someone screamed.

And immediately men were leaping on tables, knocking over benches, others gaping upwards as more tell-tale wisps coiled through the roof. Already the crackle of burning thatch was audible over the growing clamour, louder and louder, the fire's hunger growing with the eating.

'Is there another way out?'

Jovard shook his head as if in a daze.

The men near the door had seized benches and were battering the wooden frames as hard as they could. The crash and splinter of wood only added to the din, but the doors held fast.

All at once Kai caught the sound of voices coming round the corner of the hall. Quick as a startled hare, he sprang away from the wall and shot across the grass, reaching the cover of the trees just as men appeared. They were carrying torches. Kai ducked into the bracken, fearful that they had seen him, but he soon realized they weren't interested in the trees. They were four – three carrying a torch in each hand, a fourth toting a pail and a large brush. While the first three lined along the wall, this fourth began daubing it with black arcs of pitch or whatever it was in his pail. As he passed each man, they put their torch to the wall. The fire took at once, streaking up the timber. And then, at a signal from one of them, they tossed one torch at the foot of the wall, the other they lobbed onto the roof.

'Can you hear them?' the karl with the bucket sniggered.

Some of the shouting inside had become screams now.

'Shitting 'emselves,' laughed another.

'They deserve it. Walking in here like babes to their mama's tit. Halfwits.'

'And traitors,' said the first.

They moved on, soon disappearing around the far corner. Cautiously, Kai rose from his hiding place. The flames seemed to have deepened the darkness, licking higher and wider up the wall all the time.

Poor bloody bastards. He ran to the crack – which was still clear of the flames – and ignoring the swelling heat around him, he peered inside.

It was another world in there now – a swirling maelstrom of fear and panic. Burning thatch was falling from above, showers of sparks exploding off the rafters, seeding more deadly flames below. Upturned tables, men raving, hurling themselves against the door, some on their knees praying, others trying to tear at the walls, for all the good it would do them.

Jovard was still standing nearby, frozen, still apparently unable to grasp that this was really happening. Kai put his mouth to the crack and shouted his name. That seemed to jerk Jovard out of his daze and he suddenly flung himself at the wall.

'Help me! Kai! *Help – me!*'

Kai was shaking. What the Hel could he do? But Jovard had already dug his fingers into the crack and was yanking at the timber, ripping the flesh off his knuckles. 'A lever! We need a lever!'

Kai pulled out his knife and started hacking at the wood from his side, trying to wedge it between the two planks – but what use was six inches of steel against solid oak? Each plank was a foot and a half wide and sunk at least four feet into the ground. 'Harder,' cried Jovard. 'Pull harder!' Behind him there was a crash and billow of smoke and sparks, hard followed by howls of torment.

Kai tried not to look. It was as if the fire-world of *Muspelheim* had ripped up out of the earth and was rolling in great gouts of flame towards him. He gave up on the knife, instead shoving in his fingers, shaking and tugging at the wood with all his might. The heat was growing all the time. He could see Jovard's bared teeth on the other side, his face a savage vision of horror and desperation, bloodied fingers scraping the wood.

But it was no good.

The heat was pulsing off the walls now. A roar of flames beside him filled his ears. Instinctively he covered his face. Then, astonishingly, the board seemed to give. Hardly a fraction of an inch, but Jovard's hope flared with the tiny movement.

'It's coming. The bastard's coming! Wait! There – the trees behind you!'

'What about them?'

'Fetch a branch – as a lever, damn you! Hurry – for Frigg's sake, hurry!'

Kai looked behind him. Where was he going to find a branch that could rip open a wall? With hope dying in his heart, he ran into the woods and scrabbled about for something – anything – that might serve. It was dark now, and unless someone had helpfully left a ten-foot iron bar back there, he knew it was pointless.

His foot kicked something in the bracken. He picked it up. A branch fallen from the spruce tree above him. But it was curved and pliable, still almost fresh. *Useless.* He swore. But it was all he had.

He ran back to the wall, brandishing the thing like a spear. The roof was a furnace now, roaring and snapping like some angry fire-worm. He reached the crack, shoved the end of the branch in far as it would go and heaved. 'Jo!' he yelled and the bleeding fingers appeared again. He pushed and wrestled, imagined he saw the board give, pleaded with it to break, somehow. But it was no use. He stopped and knelt at the crack. Jovard was already stepping back, his face a wound of despair. All around him was a squall of smoke and screams.

Kai saw his lips move but could hear no words above the furnace. A curse perhaps, or a silent prayer. Then there was a cracking noise above. Jo looked up, blinked twice, his face pale as the dawn. And then he was gone, swallowed up in a flume of fire and ash.

Sparks and searing heat blasted the wall, throwing Kai on his back. He lay there winded, ears ringing, watching orange embers dance up into the night sky.

It was a few seconds before he dragged himself to his feet, deaf to anything but the roaring flames. He tried to reach the crack one last time, but the heat was too much now, holding him back like an invisible wall. His skin was burning. The wool of his tunic was searing hot.

That was it.

He wilted backwards, retreating deeper into the shadow of the trees, until the screams of the dying and the roar of the flames had merged into one long wail of anguish rising up into the night, each sound indistinguishable from the other.

Not far away, Erlan was pulled down and shoved forward. His shin cracked against something hard. He staggered over.

'Get up, arseling.' A spear-butt jabbed in his back and he straightened up in pain. That was when the stink hit him – stale piss, fouled straw, putrid meat.

The hood was removed. For a second, he couldn't see. Then slowly shapes coalesced. One of the guards held a taper, the only light in the dingy chamber. The air was damp and rotten as the inside of a beggar's mouth. The floor was hard packed and strewn with a few piles of old straw. The walls were simple, round piles driven into the earth and in the middle of the chamber there was a rectangular area, stone-lined, that must have once served as a fire-pit. Low down on one wall was a tiny entrance-door. The threshold he'd just tripped over, he realized. He looked up. Above him the roof was heavy thatch, solid apart from a small square smoke-hole at its pinnacle. He guessed the little structure must have been some kind of smokehouse once, where meat and fish were cured and smoked and stored. Except those were usually clean and dry. This was filthy, cold and dank.

'Your new home,' said Vargalf.

Erlan said nothing.

'Take his arms.' The guards seized his elbows. Vargalf cut the ropes securing his wrists. 'Strip him.'

Moments later, he was naked and the guards had tossed his things against the wall where they landed in a heap of rotting straw.

'Hands.' His fists were yanked forward. Vargalf snapped shackles over his wrists. They were so tight the blackened metal bit into his flesh. 'Hold him.' Vargalf reached up and took one end of a chain that was hanging from the main beam overhead. He fed the battered links through the rings welded to Erlan's shackles, then flung them back over the beam, catching the end of the chain and dragging it over to the wall where he began hauling it tight. The tension grew, Erlan's hands rising higher and higher, until his arms stretched their sockets, lifting him onto his toes. Vargalf grunted with the effort of hooking the chain on a bracket bolted to the wall. Then he stepped back and considered his handiwork. Dissatisfied, he told a guard to help him and Erlan was hoisted a couple of links higher, till he could barely feel his weight on his toes.

'Better,' smiled Vargalf. 'Comfortable?'

Hardly. The shackles were burrowing into his flesh and his shoulders were snarling in protest at the dead weight of his body. He tried to relieve the pain on his toes, but could only hold himself a few seconds before he had to drop again.

'It's a good thing that fool Sviggar can't see you now. I don't suppose he'd like to see his favourite pet stripped like a common thief.' Vargalf stepped forward and peered at Erlan's body, examining the queen's fading scratches on his chest. He circled round him and Erlan felt a sharp fingertip trace other welts on his back. 'Then again, he might have thought you deserved it after he saw these. A man can be quite particular about whom he allows to fuck his wife.'

'It wasn't like that.' Erlan's lungs were struggling against the weight of his body. 'She—'

'I just hope it was worth it. But knowing what we intend for you, I very much doubt it was.' He looked up, almost sympathetic. 'Do you know, for all the pleasure you may have given her, Saldas really hates you?'

'She's a lying bitch.'

'No doubt. Anyhow, she was most insistent that you receive a memorable welcome to your new... situation. So, would you like a taste of what you can expect here?'

Erlan glared down at him.

'Undecided? Then I shall choose for you.' He went to one of the murky corners of the smokehouse. 'I know how you prefer people to speak the truth, so I won't hide anything from you.' In the corner of his eye, Erlan saw him take something long and thin, and flex it between his hands. Then he returned where Erlan could see him.

'Do you know what this is?'

It seemed like a kind of whip – three thin switches, each nearly four feet long, but firm and straight. About a foot from one end, they were tied together by a woven-leather handle. The other ends were loose. Vargalf flicked his hand and they swished menacingly through the air.

'Birch wood. Very strong. You'll soon see why.'

Without any warning, he took two quick strides, his foot slapping the floor as his arm followed through. A sharp crack snapped the air as the whip lashed against Erlan's chest. He tried to scream, but his chest seized, choking it off in his throat. Vargalf circled round. Erlan scrabbled desperately on his toes, sucking air to ease the pain lancing through his body.

'See? Good as new. Strong as ever. I find they last a lot longer than the men we use them on.' He approached and examined the three bright welts across Erlan's chest. Already they were filling with blood. He traced a finger down one and held it up, red. 'I'm afraid, my hobbling friend, that however the queen gave you those other marks, these ones will be considerably less pleasant.'

Erlan closed his eyes, snorting at the foul air like an angry bullock.

Vargalf paced round him. 'You do fascinate me, though, cripple, I admit. You and your dogged insistence on the truth.'

The foot slammed and the whip cut the air like a blade. Erlan's back erupted with fire, the heat racing to his fingertips. This time his scream filled the chamber like a breaking wave. As it sank back into a moan, his back muscles began to spasm.

'The truth doesn't matter. Who controls what folk call the truth – that's what matters. And right now, Saldas holds that power.'

The switches cut again, this time slicing his hips and buttocks. His body kicked forward, spinning crazily on its chain. He clamped his mouth shut until the worst of the pain had passed.

'The truth—' Erlan gasped.

'Yes?' Vargalf leaned in.

'The truth crushes those who twist it... in the end.'

'Oh, in the end?' Vargalf laughed. 'You shouldn't concern yourself with whatever may come – in the end, as you put it. The only truth you need know – in the end – is that you will not live to see it. No. You'd do better to focus on what is here. What is now.'

By the time Vargalf had finished demonstrating Erlan's present reality, he was gasping out short, savage breaths, while droplets of Erlan's blood fell like red tears from his birch-whip into the filthy straw. He reached up and seized Erlan's throat. Erlan groaned.

'I'd say we've made a good start, h'm? But we've plenty more time to discover how much you can endure... Starting tomorrow.' He tapped Erlan's hollow cheek. 'A happy thought for you to sleep on. If you can.'

He threw the blood-flecked whip into the corner. 'Oh – as to happy thoughts, you might spare one for your young friend.'

'Kai?'

'The boy has gone the way of the fire-head, I'm afraid. Gutted like a Gotar swine.'

'You fucking weasel. What harm could he do Sigurd or his murderous bitch?'

'None. If he's dead.'

The wooden door slammed shut and the smokehouse was left in darkness.

Erlan hung for a while, blocking out the pain in his wrists, struggling to breathe, telling himself not to believe his tormentor. And at length he felt strong enough to take his weight again. His eyes followed the chain up to the beam above him. If he could just get over that, his pain would ease. Only a few feet, but he might as well have wished to touch the North Star as have any hope of getting over it.

A chain clinked in one of the shadowy corners. 'Erlan.'

He recognized the hoarse voice. 'Bodvar?'

'Aye.'

'I thought they let you go.'

'Then you're a bloody fool. Like me.'

'Are you... all right?'

'I've been better.'

'Can you move at least?'

452

'No more than you. They chained me here before they brought you in. After they'd worked me over some. Did you refuse the oath, too?'

'Many did after you. But I didn't get the chance.' His ribcage suddenly spasmed painfully and he sucked the air. 'I'm here because the queen wants revenge,' he said when it had passed.

'Revenge? For what?'

'I offended her vanity.'

'Hah! Then certainly you must die.' The chamber fell silent. When Bodvar spoke again, his voice was grim as death. 'It's an evil tide that's rising, mark me. And with it comes a flood of the raven's wine.'

'Do you think Kai is really dead?'

'Well, if he is still alive, only the gods can help him now.'

'And who'll help us?'

'I don't know, lad,' Bodvar muttered. 'I don't know.'

CHAPTER
FORTY-FIVE

Kai stood still in the dark.

But his eyes flicked from corner to corner, restless as his mind. He knew the shape of the house, knew its smell, knew where every object lay. But something had changed. That morning, this had been their home. Now it felt like a fist closing around him.

He listened to his fingers drumming on the table.

Come on, think!

He had to clear his head. Anger still burned hot inside him, its billowing smoke smothering his reason. He knew what he *wanted* to do – imagined sneaking into the Great Hall, slipping into the queen's chamber. Imagined the pulse of alarm in those green eyes as his hand closed over her mouth; heard the sob of fear when his knife touched her skin; felt the panic as the point went in. Afterwards he would slip away, like a grave-ghost that was never there... That was what he wanted to do. But that was just rage calling. It served him nothing. He must use his wits.

Staring into the darkness, he saw Bara's pleading eyes,

the flecks of red spattered across the clan-fathers' beards, the roaring flames snapping at her blood-soaked shift.

My beautiful little fool!

But what use his anger? For her, it was too late. She was dead. He must live for the living. That meant Erlan. At least, he hoped it did, though he acknowledged the very real possibility that his master was already dead.

And he knew: if the queen was tying up loose ends, it wouldn't be long before her attention fell on him. He had to stay clear of Vargalf's clutches.

Vargalf...

Suddenly, it was clear as water. They would come for him. They would come for him tonight. He had to get away. If he was to be of any use, if he was to find out anything, he had to get away. It didn't matter where.

His fingers stopped drumming and his hand reached out for the cloak sprawled over the table. He snatched it away. Even in the gloom, the axe-blade murmured with a dull shimmer. These were Erlan's weapons but they were no use to his master now. He would take them, would see them safely back into Erlan's hands, if the gods were good.

He swung the cloak over his bony shoulders, the wolf pelt warm against his neck. The thing was too big for him, but Erlan wouldn't mind if he borrowed it a while, would he? Besides, Kai needed the eyes of a wolf now. Needed its nose, its claws, its teeth. He smiled grimly in the darkness. He could see more now. The table, the stools, the jumble of pots and pitchers; the shields, the long-knives, the pair of spears arranged on the table.

Only Wrathling was missing. Kai figured the king must have

that now. He snorted. That was too bad. He would just take what he could carry and be away.

He slung a shield over his back and pulled the strap tight across his chest, then slid the long-knife into his belt and picked up one of the spears in his left hand. Lastly, he seized the axe in his right.

He felt strong. Felt like a killer.

Felt like killing.

He pricked his ears at the darkness.

Silence.

He laughed – a low, mean rasp in his throat. Nothing like his normal laugh. He took a look around the little dwelling that had been their home. He knew it would be his last. Then he turned, poked aside the drape with his spear-point and opened the door.

The air was cool on his face. He stopped, sniffing the air like a fox emerging from its den. He took a couple of strides, waited again, his eyes scanning ahead. All was stillness. He turned west and began stalking up the slope, keeping to the thicker shadow. But a few more paces on he heard a noise. He stopped and waited.

Two figures appeared, silhouetted against the gloom, coming down the slope. His eyes narrowed, seeing.

He smiled. Maybe he did have the eyes of a wolf.

In each man's right hand he saw the slender outline of a sword. In the other, one had a spear, the other an axe. Kai recognized the slouched shoulders and bowed legs of Aleif Red-Cheeks and beside him the other, bulkier man with Vargalf the night before. Torlak, wasn't that his name? Torlik?

What did it matter?

He could hear their muted talk, then a brittle laugh. He backed away, taking care not to knock his weapons, and he'd soon reached the door again and slipped inside.

His own breathing seemed loud as thunder. The *lub-lub* of his pulse thumped in his ears. He edged back from the doorway, not taking his eyes off it for a second. Outside, their footsteps drew closer.

Silently, he slipped back under the loft where the darkness was thick as tar, slipped back until his back jarred against the wall with a soft thud. Deep shadow enveloped him. His breathing steadied. Gently, he laid his spear on the ground and drew out the long-knife with a thin scrape of steel.

He was ready.

Bare moments later he heard voices approaching the door. He couldn't make out the words but suddenly the voices stopped. A series of blows to the door shattered the quiet.

'Open up in the name of the king!'

Silence.

'Kai Askarsson – we're here on king's business.' Kai recognized the nasal lilt of the careless beekeeper. 'Open up.' More banging.

'He's not 'ere,' said Torlak.

'He might be,' Aleif hissed. 'He's a tricksy little fucker, that one.'

Kai raised an eyebrow in the pitchy dark. *You have no idea.*

The latch lifted. The door flew open. The drape crumpled and then a spear-point appeared. A moment later the men were in the room. They trod cautiously, as if unable to see what was around them. Torlak's bulk caught against the bench and he shifted sideways, knocking Aleif's sword arm.

'Watch it, you dozy bastard.' Aleif shoved him and the big man bumped even harder against the table, making the weapons Kai had left behind clank.

'It's darker than Hel's arse-crack in here,' said Torlak.

'Quit your bitching,' snapped Aleif, who had moved apart and was turning around, trying to see into the shadows.

'Well, where is he?'

'He must have known we were coming.'

'What do we do then?'

'We find 'im, don't we? If he doesn't come easy, you know what Vargalf said.'

'Slit the little worm's throat,' the other chuckled.

Kai smiled. If this pair of whoresons wanted to hunt a wolf in darkness, they should've known better than to come to its lair blind.

Still, Aleif saw better now. He went to the table and looked down at the weapons there. 'Check all this,' he muttered, prodding at a spear handle with his sword. 'The lad reckons he's a killer, does he?' He sniggered. 'He'll probably stab himself and save us a job, the silly prick.'

'What now then?'

'Take a look round the back. I'll check the rest of this place.'

Kai watched Torlak find the door while Aleif looked around. He must've seen the shape of the ladder to the loft because he went to it and put a foot to the bottom rung.

'He can't be that much of a halfwit, can he?' Aleif muttered to himself. 'Hey! You up there, you dopey arse-nut!' he called. Silence. Kai listened to the reassuring drumming of his heart.

Outside he could hear Torlak's footsteps shuffling through the grass. Aleif hooked his axe in his belt and began climbing the ladder. He was soon up it and Kai listened to him scrape his sword across the straw-covered planks. Kai stole two steps away from the wall. There he stood, wrapped in shadow, one pace to the side of the ladder.

Aleif cursed and down he came again, rung by rung, to the floor. He reached the bottom and stopped, one hand still on the ladder-rail, straining his eyes into the shadow where Kai had just been standing. Kai let his axe-handle slip through his fingers, feeling the roughness of the wood scrape his palm. He squeezed. The axe stopped.

Aleif shook his head, frustrated.

Kai hissed. Scarcely more than a wisp of air through his teeth, like a wind-gust teasing the treetops in some distant wood. But Aleif heard it and turned.

Kai was close enough to see the blotches on Aleif's cheeks, close enough to see his eyes widen in alarm as he stepped out of the shadow. Aleif's sword was rising, a cry forming in his throat, but too late.

The axe slammed home. The sword fell instantly as Aleif's blood began to flood onto the floor. The blow had knocked Aleif against the ladder, where his body now jerked and shuddered. Kai ripped his axe free. More gouts of blood welled darkly from the gaping rent which used to be his mouth. Then, slowly, he slumped to the floor, a heap of broken limbs.

Immediately Kai downed his axe and shoved his knife in his belt. He wasn't sure how much noise had been made. But whether or not Torlak had heard anything, he would be back any moment.

He seized Aleif's ankles and dragged him under the loft. Blood seeped out of him in an ugly smear, but there wasn't time to do anything about that. Not now he could hear the big man's footsteps approaching.

The hem of Erlan's cloak was heavy with blood. Kai looked around for the axe but the door was already opening. He was out of time. By pure instinct, he took three steps towards the doorway, positioning himself to its left. The door rattled open. The drape stirred.

'There's no one there. Didn't I tell you? The little turd's run off.'

Silence.

'Aleif? Are you there? Aleif?'

Torlak was in the room now, the drape fallen behind him. His head turned, blinking blindly into the thicker darkness inside the house.

He's a big bastard, thought Kai, standing directly behind him now, the long-knife drawn and in his hand. It felt good. Sharp. *Sharp as a wolf's fang.*

'Aleif, stop pissing around.' Torlak ventured a couple of faltering steps forward.

Kai followed him, marvelling at this ogre's stupidity and his own stealth. He could see everything now – the table, the ladder, the bulky shoulders ahead of him, the clumsy feet shuffling across the floor. Could hear everything, too – the scrape of the spear-butt along the ground, the brush of the man's clothes, the fear in his breath, the beating of his heart. He could smell the sweat and stale shit seeping off his clothes, the beer and rotten teeth on his breath.

But Kai... he was the wolf. Silent. Seeing. Deadly.

He could have put the knife into him by now. But that would be too easy. He wanted him to see his face. Wanted

460

him to recognize his killer.

Torlak took another step forward. The sole of his shoe slapped something wet. Another step. Same sound. He looked down.

'Aleif?'

Kai smiled. This was a dead man.

Torlak stepped level with the ladder. He bent over, leaning on his spear, peering into the darkness. At last he saw it, swearing violently, recoiling from the bloody heap, wrenching round his body, lifting his sword. But even as he turned, it seemed to him as if a shadow had risen out of the very earth. A face pale as the moon, grinning like some mad demon, teeth bared to the gums. He hefted his sword, but the shadow was already past its point. He lurched back from the fierce teeth and the flashing metal, too scared to scream. But the knife was already plunging deep into his terror-stricken heart.

Kai struck again and again, not a whisper in his throat, despite the savage scream of triumph ringing in his head. Torlak tottered, then crashed backwards over Aleif's body. For a few seconds, a weird rattle clicked in his throat, his body twitching, and then he was silent and still.

Kai's mouth was locked rigid in a grimace. Slowly he backed away, sliding the knife back into his belt. His foot kicked against something. He looked down and saw his axe. He picked it up. It was slick with Aleif's blood.

He felt strong. Wild.

I am the wolf.

The wolf had fed well that night. But now it was time to run.

461

CHAPTER FORTY-SIX

Dawn seeped into the dismal chamber.

There had been little sleep. Little true wakefulness, either. Dreams and reality had swirled together like muddy clouds in the stream of Erlan's mind. He was thirsty, each breath scraping his throat.

The light revealed chains bolted to the wall, a squat black brazier and next to it a stack of iron rods, filthy with grime. Vestiges from the smokehouse's days of curing meat.

Erlan shifted. Pain raced down his arms.

The noises of the new day were filtering through the walls: cartwheels' rattle, the low folk's distant chatter, dogs barking, the first muffled hammering from the smithies' booths, even busier than usual in anticipation of the Summer Throng.

'Bodvar?' he croaked. 'Are you awake?'

'I don't know what I am,' came the weary reply.

'At the Throng. D'you think the earls will accept whatever Sigurd tells them?'

'Till yesterday I'd have said no. But—'

'There must be more like you.'

'Maybe. But the high lords are sworn to him now.'

'Some may break faith with him.'

'Depends.'

'On what?'

'What he intends... But who can tell? Men draw their lines in strange places.'

'There's some hope then.'

Bodvar grunted. 'I fear any hope is small.'

In truth, so did Erlan. 'Why would he keep us alive?'

'Maybe leverage over the earls. Though more likely...'

'What?'

Bodvar grimaced. 'To make a show of us. The fate of traitors.'

They fell to silence. The day wore on. Erlan hung, joints straining, mind drifting in and out of consciousness, his head rolling back and forth. Rolling back and forth...

Rolling...

He hears the ropes creak through the fog, the hull pitching under him. His back aches as he heaves his oar – shoulders burn, hands sting. He looks up. The sky is red. A battle-dawn. Ravens caw and turn on salt-laced winds. He hears a roar and sees his father, his blade wet with the *Valkyries'* tears. Next all is stillness; his shoulders throb, rolling, rolling. There are his shield-brothers, gone to the mead-bench; under their stiff bodies the raven's wine has turned to crimson ice on the frozen deck. His hand trails in the water. The salt stings his wounds and he gazes into the murky deep. He thirsts. He thirsts... A wave crashes in his face.

Erlan jolted awake. A guard stood in front of him, holding an empty bucket. He felt water running down his body.

'Your drink, arseling.'

Erlan was already licking thirstily at the dirty rivulets running over his lips. A few drops, but to his parched tongue, each drop an ocean.

The guard went out, slamming the door behind him. Erlan looked up. The light had changed, though he had no clue which marks of the day had passed. Outside the noises had died some. Then he heard another: someone approaching.

The door snapped open and Vargalf stepped inside, followed by a guard dragging in a well-built man with a sweep of fire-red hair. The redhead's hands were bound. Another guard entered after them and shoved the man to his knees.

The prisoner's face was swollen. He was bleeding from a slash to his forehead. Blood was smeared in thick streaks over his eye and down his cheek. Yet, despite these disfigurements, there was something familiar about him. Apart from the swelling and his wound, the man's face was well proportioned, young, handsome even, with a fine straight nose, high and wide-set cheekbones, a strong chin. But the red beard and flaming hair didn't match the rest of his face somehow. His cloak was filthy and so ragged it was more hole than cloth; his tunic, barely rags. And he stank.

Vargalf looked up at Erlan. 'Feeling neglected, cripple? It's been a busy day. And eventful. Eh, friend?' He gave the prisoner a kick. 'I'm afraid our guest here will be needing your place.'

The chain lurched, jerking Erlan's wrists. He winced, then collapsed to the ground with the chain falling after in a heap.

He was dragged to one side. Another chain-rattle, another tug and he was pulled tight against the wall.

It took them bare moments to strip the redhead and hang him in Erlan's place.

'Fetch it,' Vargalf ordered. Whatever *it* was.

A guard disappeared.

'Who is he?' hissed Bodvar from his filthy corner.

'Excellent question! The very question I must answer, in fact. So then,' Vargalf barked, 'who are you?'

'I've told you. My name is Aksalf. I'm a swineherd from the coastlands.'

'A swineherd!' Vargalf laughed. 'You certainly stink like one. Let's try again. Who *are* you?'

'What else can I say?' The prisoner was twisting on the chain like a fish on a hook. 'Please!'

'Perhaps you're too ashamed to recall who you are in your present condition.' Vargalf grinned. 'We'll soon overcome your coyness.' He drew his sword and without a moment's hesitation smacked the flat of it across the beggar's hamstrings.

The beggar yowled like a kicked dog. 'My name's Aksalf! I'm a swineherd. From Nordshamen by the East Sea.'

'Nordshamen! I dare say such a place even exists.'

'I swear to you—'

'Swear what you like. I only want to hear your own name from your own lips.'

'Aksalf. It's Aksalf.'

'As you wish,' Vargalf sighed. 'I guess we'll take the long road.' So saying, with horrifying deliberation, he began beating the beggar's legs till they were swollen with scarlet welts, so raw they glistened.

'Njord damn you with a black and lonely drowning death, you sack of swine spunk,' the beggar gasped when Vargalf gave his arm a rest.

'A curse! Ha! So our swineherd has some bollocks on him after all.'

The door flew open and the guard returned wearing heavy leather gauntlets and carrying a brazier brimming hot coals, with an iron rod thrust in it.

'There,' Vargalf pointed. The guard placed it in front of the beggar. 'Perhaps this will get us where we want to be a little quicker.' He stirred the rod among the coals. When he pulled it out, its point glowed orange.

'Now then – your real name.'

The beggar's eyes widened with fear. 'Aksalf, a swineherd from—'

'Nordshamen,' interrupted Vargalf, losing patience. 'Yes. I tell you what,' he held up the glowing point to the beggar's nose, 'you're going to answer my question. Because if you don't, by the time I'm done with you, there'll be nothing left of you but a stain on this fucking floor!' His voice had become a shriek. He snatched away the iron. 'Let us begin.'

Erlan would always wish he could blot the hours that followed from his memory. He did his best to bury his face in the wall while the smokehouse filled with the reek of burning flesh and the echoes of the man's screams. How long it went on, he couldn't have said. Too long. But the wretched beggar proved of sterner mettle than he first seemed, doggedly refusing to say more than his name and his village.

'I begin to believe you're slow-witted,' Vargalf said at last, scowling in frustration and shoving the rod deep in the coals.

'Except that I've heard folk speak highly of you.' He sniggered. 'True – folk say other things about you, too. That you're not like other men. You are a man of... different tastes.'

The other only whimpered.

Abruptly, Vargalf seized the iron and circled behind him. Then he lifted the point and simply laid it against the man's naked buttock. The beggar uttered a soul-shattering scream.

As it died away, all it left was Vargalf's ugly snigger. 'They say you enjoy a bit of heat around the backside. In fact, they say best of all you like something hot and hard right up it!' He roared with laughter. 'Shall we find out?' He signalled the guards. 'Hold him.'

But it seemed that was enough to break the man. 'Stop!' he sobbed. 'Stop! I'll tell you – I'll tell you who I am. Please.' He was gasping in his panic.

'Go on.' Vargalf's face creased into a vulpine sneer.

'Rorik. My name is Rorik. I'm a Dane.'

'A Dane called Rorik,' Vargalf crowed. 'Imagine that! And your father is?' The point still hovered near his branded backside.

'Harald,' he snivelled. 'My father is Harald, King of the Danes.'

Vargalf expelled a long breath and lowered the point. 'Release him.'

The guards let go and the young Dane swung gently on the chain.

'That's enough for now.' Vargalf tossed the iron onto the brazier. 'So we have restored you to your noble name, young Rorik. That's a start. But I'm afraid tidings like this must be brought before the king at once.' Rorik made a pitiful figure, eyes clamped shut in agony and shame. 'And don't worry, my other dear friends, I've not forgotten you.'

Vargalf went out, laughing, and the guards with him, toting the brazier and with it any hope of warmth. The bolts snapped shut.

'Why are you here?' asked Erlan when all was quiet.

'Someone had to come,' Rorik wheezed. 'Ringast had to know... Someone had to come... I had to... had to show my father...' His voice filled with bitterness. 'Would he not be proud to see me now?' His body was pink and red where ugly blisters bubbled on his skin.

'How did they take you?' asked Erlan.

'I trusted in that disguise... like a fool. It worked for my father. Of course it worked for him! Everything works for him. But never for me. I'm cursed. A man born with no luck.'

'How did they take you?' Erlan repeated.

'That devil recognized me.' He spat out a long string of saliva. 'May every god curse him! The first I knew of it something smashed my head. I was dazed but tried to fight, though I had only a knife.' He gulped awkwardly. 'I remember staggering, taking another blow... Then they were dragging me here.'

'Did you witness what happened at the Throng?' Bodvar asked.

'I saw all I needed to see. This Sigurd is an oath-breaker. My father was right about this house of the Bastard King.'

'Tell us what you heard.'

Rorik sucked in a hoarse breath, as if so much talk was too wearying. But after a time he did speak. 'Your law. Disputes. Judgements. After that came Sigurd's boasting. He made much of his kingship and the destiny of the Sveärs.'

'What did he say?'

'He harked back to the Wide-Realm – so he called it.'

'Ívar's rule.'

'Aye. He'd have you believe his grandsire ruled half the world.'

'Ívar was your forefather, too.'

'So he was. To my shame. Sigurd thinks he can restore this Wide-Realm. He plans to raise a host.'

'When?'

'Immediately. He's already dispatched riders to every chieftain, every king, every sea-lord who might rally to his banner. And with them, any man who can hold a spear.'

'For whom will he send? Be specific.'

'For whom won't he? Finns, Norskmen west beyond the mountains, the Western Gotars, Sami raiders and forest-men, the Estlander lords, and more.'

'Who, boy? Tell us!'

'Kurslanders, Gotlanders, the Rus of the northern marshes, Kvenlander riders. Besides this, he means to levy every axe and spear in these lands. The riders carry with them promises – of gold, of slaves, of land for the outlander lords and the sea-kings if they come.'

'The Niflagard hoard,' Erlan murmured, remembering the gold they had found that winter deep under the earth.

'He's gold enough there to pay every hero in Valhalla,' said Bodvar.

'And blood, of course,' Rorik continued. 'He promises plenty of that. Aye, he's fond of talking of Danish blood. But he'll find it's not so easily spilled.'

'And the earls and other nobles? Are they with him?'

'Most. But some oppose him.'

'Who?'

'One called Arwakki.'

'The Gestrikland earl.'

'And another, Kafli.'

'The Earl of Sodermanland.'

'They spoke up. But there were others who supported them.'

'What did they say?'

'They argued with Sigurd. Said he couldn't make them break solemn oaths sworn on that sacred ring.'

'Adils' Ring.'

'That's it. And more. They said it's too late in the year to raise a host from lands so distant, that even Sveärs would be loath to leave their harvest.'

'How did he answer?'

'He said it was a little late to change their minds, that they'd already sworn to him as their king, but they only shouted the louder – as long as the Danes kept their oaths, then so shall they. Said the Spear-God would never bless a war built on broken faith. Sigurd railed at them, called them traitors, said he'd dispatch riders to the four winds then and there, whether they were with him or not.'

'Did they reply?'

'Arwakki protested that they were loyal, but that in this, they couldn't act. Sigurd mocked them for cowards. Arwakki said Odin knows they're no cowards, that they do but honour sworn oaths. He ended saying only if we Danes break faith first will they support a war.'

'Gods! This all sounds better. For them and perhaps for us.

470

If opposition to Sigurd grows, one of the earls may challenge his crown.'

Rorik scowled. 'Enough seem willing. They hang off his every word – especially this "Wide-Realm" song he likes to sing.'

The three fell silent.

'But now they have you,' Erlan muttered at length.

'That changes nothing. My father and brothers will fight without me. And they'll win!'

'That's not what I meant. I don't doubt Ringast is strong. And your father too. But how strong are you?'

Bodvar's head jerked up. 'You think Sigurd could use him to unite the earls.'

Erlan nodded. 'Aye. Whether what he says is true or false, Sigurd has only to make him talk.'

CHAPTER
FORTY-SEVEN

K ai Askarsson stalked forward on all fours, the earth crumbling under his fingernails. He could taste the dusk in his open mouth. His fingers squeezed the shaft of his spear.

Ready.

A moment more. Wait for night to settle a little heavier. The dark would cloak his movement, just for a second. Long enough to loose the spear.

The deer lowered its head. Another heartbeat and the spear was lancing through the dusk. There was a quiet thud and five foot of ash lodged, quivering, in its flank.

It tried to run, buffeting the spear crazily in its panic. Four steps, five, six... then it stopped, keeled over, dead as a stone.

Kai hissed in triumph. His belly growled in anticipation.

Moments later, he was dragging his kill to his new home. He had found a hollow under the crooked roots of an old oak tree that teetered on the edge of a bank of earth. There, he had dug and dug, scooping out a hiding place, a den, a place of safety from Vargalf and his dogs. He was safe in the earth, safe and warm. The earth was his shield, his womb. There, he slept all day, curled in the bracken that lined the floor like a nest. Only at twilight did he wake. At twilight his work began.

He gutted the deer a short distance from his hole, then dragged it back to the oak where he skinned it – enough to take the meat he needed – then sat cross-legged carving out hunks of flesh. Those first days in the forest, he had wanted to build a fire. But he dared not risk it. By day there was smoke; by night, flame. Someone might see. Someone might come. And now he was used to feeding on raw meat when he could catch it. On earthworms when he couldn't.

He bit greedily into a glistening lump of flesh. Blood and fat ran through his fingers, down his chin. He wiped his hand across his cheek, feeling grateful. He still hadn't got used to the way the worms would flick around in his mouth, even after he had bitten them in two, or the metallic taste of their slime. This was better.

His face was black, caked with dirt and blood, just like his hands. His blond hair was a crust of mud. Wrapped in Erlan's wolf-cloak, he looked more beast than man as he shuffled around his hole.

He could feel the meat's heat in his belly, feel the power of the deer seeping into his limbs as he rocked against the chill.

Gauta's hounds rise from the mud,
Jaw-swords drip with fresh-flow blood.

He shook his head. His thoughts came more and more like that. Snippets of songs that he couldn't place. Had he heard them long ago? Or did some voice come to him now? The mad mead of the One-Eyed God's words, whispering to him from the flesh of the forest.

Shadows speak and spirits cut through sleep,
Beast and man bound by the dreams they keep.

Strange phrases that didn't fit together – like pieces of a broken rune-stone, its meaning scattered. He didn't know what to make of them. But he kept listening for the next.

Ancient roots delve deep through ice and fire,
Driving one who sees to his desire.

The more he listened, the more he heard other sounds. The silent voices of the dark. The mocking prattle of the birds and the wind whispering to the weary trees stories from far away. Was this what Grimnar, the old *seidman,* had heard under his hanging friends? When Kai ran, the branches seemed to bend, stretching out to touch with shy and crooked fingers. But when he turned and looked, they stood mute, blind, waiting, waiting... *for something.* But what, they wouldn't say. Among their tangled limbs, shadows danced, living, urgent, bursting with the burden of their knowledge, like children desperate to tell the secrets they must keep. And each night, he saw a little more, heard a little more, smelled a little more. With each kill, as he fed on the forest's flesh, it seemed to draw him tighter to its bosom and, seeing in him one of its own, began to give up its secrets.

His belly was full. His work must begin. The moon was bright, cutting through the trees with shards of silver. He knew the way to the edge of the halls, had been there every night, scouting the shadows, searching out his master. *No* – his friend. His oath-brother. Hadn't he sworn with his own blood in that freezing wilderness? A lifetime ago... So until he'd found out what had become of Erlan, he had to keep returning. And so he had. Seven... eight nights? Ten maybe. In the forest, a man's reckoning was like to fail him.

He ran through the undergrowth, his footfall light as a ghost. The outlying buildings were still half a league off, but he ran hard, ignoring the burning in his lungs.

Stop! A voice within. A scent on the wind. The outline of a shadow. He obeyed, slowing first, then all at once, he halted. Ahead in the gloom he saw a familiar shape.

Wolf.

Its head was broad, its black ears pricked forward. But as the creature advanced cautiously towards him he realized it was no wolf, but a dog. A hunting dog, a wolfhound, with long shaggy shanks and a beard that glistened with the dusk-dew. It came closer until it stood face to face with him, not three steps away, its eye glimmering in the shadow, wild and cold. Only when its head ticked to one side did he see that one eye was all it possessed. Its twin was nothing but a maw of shadow.

A sliver of fear went through him. There was something preternatural in the hound's unblinking stare. Still they looked at each other, and as they did, Kai saw something else in its eye. A kind of respect. A kind of understanding.

'*Whither farest thou, brother?*' Kai heard.

'*I run to the call of my blood. And you?*'

'*I run with the moon. I run the silver way.*'

'*Alone?*'

'*Aye, alone, thither to the place where the white mother calls – to life, to the never-dying life.*'

'*May you find it, brother. Run long and well.*'

'*And thee, brother. Now go to thy blood. I hear his cry.*'

All this passed between them, though not a sound was uttered. The wolfhound curled its lips. Its fangs gleamed white and fierce but to Kai it was only a smile. Then it backed away, its one eye never leaving his. Kai smiled back and it was gone.

The moon was not much higher when Kai reached the edge of the woods. He darted from shadow to shadow, closing on the halls and smaller dwellings like a *draugr* returning from the halls of the dead.

He'd seen much since the Summer Throng: the herds of low folk departing, the lingering of nobles and their karls. And over the following days, more had come. At first only Sveärs, but then outlanders – painted men with shaven faces, others shorn-headed or strangely garbed. The gathering of warriors grew and the halls resounded with their drink and song. But despite all he'd seen creeping through the shadows, he'd found not a hair of Erlan.

Pale wisps of cloud drifted across a waxing moon. Midsummer's Eve was long past now and the nights were growing longer. He skirted the hall-yard, slipping under the buttresses along the north side of the Great Hall. Squalls of laughter flurried inside, the murmur of voices. He pressed an ear to a crack, trying to make out the talk, but caught nothing but scraps of idle banter.

Nevertheless, he listened a long while, until the eating was done and most had taken to their beds. His nose wrinkled in disgust. He'd learned nothing, again, and it was time to move on. Except just then he noticed a light moving through the darkness beyond the end of the hall. He watched it float away from him in short, even arcs. He realized it was someone carrying a torch.

Curious, he crept after it, taking care to remain in shadow, closing the distance only enough to discern two figures and also a steady rattle. The taller figure held the torch in one hand. By its light, Kai saw that in the other he carried a pick. He was hooded. The second man was squatter, broader, with an unruly shag of hair. Creeping closer, Kai realized he was pulling a handcart, and so the rattle.

He followed them across the flood-meadow towards the beech wood known as Budli's Grove, but holding back, staying low, tracking the bank of the stream.

On the far side of the meadow, the men skirted the edge of the wood and walked on another three hundred yards or so before they cut into the dark trees. Kai followed them, eyes fixed on the flame as it bobbed through the trees, until, all at once, it stopped.

What the Hel are they doing?

His scalp prickled with curiosity. He circled round carefully until he came to a spot perhaps thirty paces downwind of them. Satisfied that he could see them but that they would need the eyes of an owl to have any clue he was there, he stopped.

The taller man had his back to him. He muttered something to the other, who bent over and grabbed whatever was on his cart. He pulled and a long, slender bundle slid off onto the ground with a thud. Then he did the same with a second, slightly smaller bundle. Another thud. Something about the shape of them gave Kai a flicker of unease.

The squat man chuckled. 'Suppose this pair were bound to end up 'ere, heh?' he said in a whisper they could have heard in Danmark.

'Shut up and dig.' The other flung down the pick.

The squat man gave a disgruntled shrug, then grabbed the pick and set about it. He soon loosened the soil. Then he dropped to his knees, scooped out a double handful of dirt and flung it into the darkness with a splatter.

At the sound, a pigeon fluttered in the trees above Kai's head. The tall man's head snapped round and, for a second, the torch lit the hooded face.

Kai crushed his body to the ground and held his breath.

Because Vargalf stood glaring into the night.

CHAPTER
FORTY-EIGHT

Far to the south, sun-rays splintered off the surface of the lake, winking at Lilla like elven glass. A lazy afternoon breeze rustled through the shore-rushes and up the slope, rippling the folds of her dress.

She sat on a bench looking northward. Homeward. She'd been counting the days: eight since the Summer Throng. Fewer since they had expected Rorik's return.

With each passing day, her nights had become more restless. For the first time in a long while, she had seen her mother in her dreams. Last night was the third time she had come, her face gaunt, the lines of her mouth severe, not like Lilla remembered her. She was trying to tell her something. Each time, she reached out and lay hands on Lilla's shoulders, drawing her close, about to whisper in her ear, about to tell her why she had come. But each time, Lilla had awoken.

'You all right, my lady?' Gerutha's voice broke her thoughts. She looked at the unfinished embroidery in her hand, the needle poking through the weave.

'Just thinking of something from long ago,' she lied.

Gerutha twitched a sympathetic smile. 'Need help with that, my lady?'

'No.' She tugged the needle and continued her stitching. 'And please, Gerutha, how many times have I said? Call me Lilla when we're alone.'

'Lilla, then. Doesn't quite seem right, is all.'

Gerutha's gaze lingered on her a little too long and it annoyed her. The older woman seemed to see right through her, just like her mother had done. Seemed to hear what she couldn't say. 'You miss your home.'

Lilla smiled. 'How can I when there's so much to do?'

'It's still soon,' Gerutha sighed, ignoring her deflection. 'Memories are bound to linger. They're no bad thing. Anyhow, I've a feeling you'll do well here.' She squeezed Lilla's knee. 'Folk are already saying their lord's made a good match.'

'H'm! They don't even know me.'

'And when did that ever stop folk passing judgement! Matter of fact, they say it's thanks to you the harvest'll be coming in. The talk was all of war. Now it's all crops and yields and how you're Thor's answer to their prayers.'

Lilla thought of the fields of flattened barley. Was that Thor's answer too? 'They have some foolish notions.'

'Sometimes... though I ain't so sure they're wrong on this one.'

Lilla sighed and stopped her work. 'The truth is I don't know what will happen. It seems that everything is hanging by a thread.'

'Aye. But then don't life always?'

Lilla gazed out over the lake. Her mind began to float

away again, like a house-marten seeking the safety of a familiar nook: it wanted to return to *him*. Suddenly she shook herself. 'I owe you thanks, Gerutha. So much has changed. But with you I feel... I don't know... like there's something to hope for.'

'Things change, you find a balance, they change again,' Gerutha shrugged, 'and we flap around like a flock of hens till everything settles again.'

'Is that all it is? Change.' She looked north again. 'Still, I miss my father. And—' Not him. She couldn't speak of him. 'And the children, too.'

'Your father's little ones?'

'Mmm. They looked so sad when I said farewell.'

'They've got their mother, haven't they?'

Lilla snorted. '*A* mother.'

'That bad, eh?'

Lilla shook away the thought. 'No matter. My father will see they're cared for. Anyway, I don't mean to be gloomy. It's so beautiful here.' She turned to Gerutha and forced her face to brighten. 'Tell me more about you. I want to know!'

'Me?'

'Don't you have a family? Or a man, at least?'

'I had a good one.' She gave a rueful laugh. 'Oh, he was a brute... But he was always gentle with me.'

'Where is he?'

'Gone where I can't follow. The Heroes' Hall, I guess.'

'What happened?'

Gerutha shrugged again. 'He was headman of our village. A wise man, in his way. But he had a wild streak in him – a roving streak. A few summers back he got himself a share in a boat and

481

went raiding east... That was it. He didn't come back.'

'That must have been hard.'

'At first. But I'd seen other women suffer that and go on. Didn't see why I should do any different. Life's hard enough without spending it grieving. And it wouldn't have been fair on my son.'

'Oh, you have a son!' Lilla was relieved to turn the conversation in a more cheerful direction.

But the lines around Gerutha's mouth tightened. 'No. Not no more... You know bad things happen often in this world. But just once in a while, something truly evil happens, too. That night, when those brothers came... No mind with any whit of goodness could have imagined it...' Her words faded into a dark memory. Lilla watched the wind pluck at the loose wisps of her hair and wondered what she saw. 'Anyhow,' Gerutha forced a smile, 'they can't hurt my boy no more. I'll find him again one day – in Hela's halls.'

Lilla reached out and squeezed Gerutha's hand. 'I shouldn't have asked. I didn't mean to remind you.'

'It ain't you reminds me. I see that night every time I see my own reflection.'

'What do you mean?'

She touched the white streak in her hair. 'Afterwards, next time I looked in a mirror, I had this. It was the fear, I suppose.' She gave a snort. 'I told you memories ain't no bad thing. Well, there's one memory I'd happily forget.' Her voice dropped to a murmur. 'That devil's eyes – red as fire. His whispering voice. I tell you, whenever fear stalks my dreams, it wears his face.'

'Who was he?'

'It's no matter,' Gerutha said hastily. 'Let's talk no more of it.' But, despite herself, Gerutha's eyes glazed and drifted north. 'Everyone was killed that night. Everyone except me. That's why I came here.'

Lilla didn't know what to say. What could be said to lighten such a terrible burden? So instead she put an arm around Gerutha. At first, her maid resisted. But Lilla persisted and finally Gerutha's stiff body softened.

'I hope we can be friends.'

'I should like that.' Gerutha smiled. 'Lilla.'

'Am I disturbing you?' They both turned. Ringast was hovering behind them, one hand propped against a birch-tree.

'We were just talking.' Lilla stood to greet him.

He nodded, but didn't speak. He looked hesitant, which wasn't like him.

'What is it? Is there word from Rorik?'

He shook his head. 'Not yet.' He suddenly scowled, evidently uncomfortable. 'We have other news.'

'What? Speak.'

'Your father. We heard that... that he may be dead.'

'Dead?' Lilla's ears filled with the sudden pounding in her heart. *No,* someone whispered. *Not so soon!* The ground seemed to lurch and she felt herself falling, her mind spinning like a sycamore seed. But strong hands caught her waist. Her head slumped against his chest.

'Aslíf?' She blinked up at him. 'Aslíf!' His face was a blur. 'It's not a certainty yet. Just a rumour.'

'A rumour?'

'Aye. Come with a merchant who crossed the Kolmark.'

'From Uppsala?'

'Not himself. But—'

'Then there's hope?' Her heart couldn't bear this new sorrow so soon. Old men die, even old kings, but somehow she had believed she would be spared this for a while longer.

'If you mean is there a chance he's still alive, then yes, I suppose there is... a chance. Maybe he's only sick, or maybe it was some other lord, or—'

'Or what?'

'Or maybe it's true, Aslíf!' He seemed irritated, angry even. Lilla suddenly realized she had no idea if Ringast cared whether her father was dead or not. Maybe he welcomed this news. Or maybe he just didn't like bringing it. 'When my brother returns, we'll know the truth.'

'And if he never returns?' she blurted, voicing the silent fear that all of them had shared these last few days.

'He will return.' But even as he spoke, his granite eyes, always so certain, betrayed his doubt.

'So meanwhile we just wait?'

'No. Meanwhile we prepare.'

'Prepare? For what?'

'For the worst.'

Kai watched the squat man dig.

If anyone but Vargalf were standing over him, Kai would have crawled closer, but he knew better than to test those ears. Instead he stayed low, motionless, just another shadow in a sea of darkness.

The breeze had stilled, the only sound the slice and crunch of the pick, punctuated by the splatter of soil being flung out of the hole. At last, the pick-man stepped back, content his work was done.

Vargalf peered in, muttered something. The other threw down his pick and lay hold of one of the bundles beside the hole. He gave it a pull and a shove and it fell in with a thud. The man seized the smaller bundle and hauled it in after the first.

Kai had no doubt now. Those bundles were bodies. Two bodies. And he could only think of two of Sigurd's enemies who hadn't been turned to ashes in the Coopers' Hall.

The squat man set about filling in the hole. He was soon done. Vargalf grunted with satisfaction but didn't linger. He set off back for the halls at once, the other hurrying after him with his handcart bumping away behind.

Silence returned to the wood.

Kai remained still, only his eyes moving, following the torch until it was a pinprick, and finally extinguished. Only then did he rise and creep through the moon-shadows towards the fresh mound of earth.

He circled round it, scuffed his toe against it, sniffing the air, feeling a kind of dread creep through his limbs. A wreath of cloud drifted in front of the moon, cloaking the wood in deep darkness for a second before moving on.

Kai's axe dropped and suddenly he was on his knees, scrabbling at the dirt. The loose soil shifted easily. He dug and dug, curiosity burning through his hands as he willed the ground to give up its secret. Then his fingers hit something solid. He cleared more earth, traced contours, felt coarse material – homespun or hemp – and beneath it, some *thing*, lumpish and hard.

His hand recoiled. It was cold as ice.

He took a deep breath and forced himself on, clawing at the earth until two shapes jutted clear. Then he took his knife, sliced the sacking between them and reached inside.

He snatched his hand back at once, knowing exactly what he had touched.

A foot.

Except that it was a small foot.

A child's foot.

Relief and confusion rinsed through him. This wasn't Erlan. It was just some kid. But who? And why the Hel was Vargalf out here burying children in the dead of night?

It made no sense...

But suddenly it came to him, clear as a comet in the sky.

The witch-wolf feasts on the ring-slinger's kin,
The black earth barrow that he flung 'em in.

He scrambled to the other end of the grave and sank in his fists, tearing at the dirt until he had uncovered two more lumpish shapes, these ones round. He pulled out his knife as a bank of cloud rolled across the moon, bathing everything in shadow. Feeling his way, he lifted the sacking and sliced it open; first one body, then the other. His heart was beating hard. He tore away the first shroud. Above him, the cloud bank drifted on its way, pouring silver light through the branches.

He froze, seeing the smooth, arched forehead of a young boy. The infant eyes were wide with terror, dark curls plastered against his head. And yet, he was the image of his aged father.

Svein Sviggarsson. *The Spare Heir.*

'Poor little tyke,' he murmured, eyes already moving to the other body. The sacking still covered the other smaller face, but he knew whose it was.

Sproutlings slaughtered, seeds crushed,
The Bastard's bairns all gone to the dust.

He pulled away the sacking anyway and gazed down on the small, round face. Katla's eyelids shone white in the moonlight, luminous and peaceful, as if she had just been lullabied into her dreams.

Kai's hands went to work again, scraping and clawing, unearthing more of Svein's slender frame. He touched the stone-hard chest, touched something else that was rough. His fingers slowed, tracing the thing higher and higher until, suddenly, they stopped.

Jerked away.

The noose around the boy's neck was savagely tight.

CHAPTER
FORTY-NINE

Outside a cartwheel jolted. Then another.

Erlan's eyes stayed closed, his body curled tighter against the wall, but his ear followed the sounds out through the cracks into the late summer air.

'Bodvar.'

The heap of shadows in the corner stirred.

'There's more... Outlanders.'

Bodvar lifted his head. There were more noises now. Clinking bridles, the jangle of weaponry, the thud of hooves, and over them the murmur of voices, all wafting into the gloomy smokehouse.

'You hear their tongue?'

'I hear it.' Bodvar listened some more, then added, 'Finns.'

The carts and the hooves kept coming. 'Plenty of them.'

Bodvar grunted. 'If one Finn sniffs blood, the whole pack of them come running like hungry wolves.'

'Finns!' Erlan muttered. 'Piss on it! How damn long must it take for word to reach Finnland and for this crowd to come back? Have we been here that long?'

'Long enough.'

Long enough since they had been chained up. Long enough since each day had started bleeding into the next in a smear of boredom and pain. Long enough since he'd lost his reckoning of time. *Another thing they stripped me of.*

He shifted his weight, feeling now familiar flares of pain about his body. His skin was a patchwork of sores and cuts and bruises, his wrists swollen, reeking of pus, his hair a thatch of black straw, his beard thick as felt.

'The Finns came,' he muttered. 'Who else now?'

'Estlanders. And Gotlanders before them.'

'And the Norsk.'

'Aye, and the Western Gotars... and Kurslanders.'

'He must have hundreds. That's not counting the Sveär hirds.'

'Hundreds? The little shit's got thousands by now,' Bodvar growled. 'If the Wartooth can match this host, then the Slain-God will be licking his lips.'

Erlan glared at the bloodstained chains hanging empty where Rorik had been. 'Poor bastard,' he added, with a nod in that direction. 'I wonder what happened to him.'

'Nothing good.'

Vargalf had come for him a few days ago. By then, the young Dane was a wreck of a man – beaten, burned, lacerated, abused. 'Softening him up for his moment to shine,' Vargalf had joked. And his moment had come. With Earl Arwakki and his companions still refusing to levy their lands, Rorik had become a necessity. He would be the thorn that would shift these stubborn nobles off their backsides.

Rorik had gone to his fate. But what was to be theirs? Erlan looked at his wasted hands. His body was slowly devouring itself from hunger, despite the worm-riddled scraps thrown at them to eat.

Bodvar was worse. Erlan could smell the rot coming off him. The reek of shit and shame.

But if Erlan's body was broken, his will had grown harder, like a blade tempered in the flames of his hatred. Love had taken everything from him. Hatred at least offered the promise of watching his enemies suffer as he had suffered. Hatred was real. Love was nothing but a fading dream.

And yet his greatest fear was that his mind would crack long before any chance of vengeance appeared. Most of the time, he hardly knew waking from dreaming. The damp, close walls dissolved into a black abyss, vast and empty as the *Ginnungagap* out of which all things had come. Voices spoke to him out of the darkness in sibilant whispers. The words of the *vala* came often, echoing through his mind till they drove him nearly mad.

You will bear much pain, but you will never break.

Never break. *Never!*

Many times Inga was there, murmuring soft words: that he hadn't protected her, that he had broken his promise, and now he was paying the price. With eyes closed, he sensed her standing there before him. Many times, he had lifted his head, peeled back his eyelids to see her, but there was only shadow.

Often he felt his father's hand on his shoulder, the gruff voice whispering in his ear: that here was the price of folly, that he could have been his own lord in his own land. Instead, his pride had chosen this path.

Sometimes Garik came, laughing that he was a sullen fool, that he thought too much, that life was but a joke, a riot of feasting, fighting and fucking. Wasn't that what awaited him in the Hall of the Slain after all?

And sometimes there was another voice, one he didn't know. A stranger's voice that told him all these other voices were lies. A voice that belonged to some other shadow moving in the dark, that wouldn't come close. Couldn't – not yet. And somehow he believed it.

But what did any of it matter a weasel's cock? Which voice true, and which false? The chamber was real. Whenever his eyes opened, there it was in all its grimness. Then he would feel his aching body again, grit his teeth and resolve to hold on...

The bolt snapped. The door slammed open. Erlan's head jerked up. Shadows fled to dank corners as Vargalf entered, holding a torch.

'Good news, friends! Your time is close.' He aimed a kick at Erlan. 'Still with us, cripple?' Erlan groaned. 'Excellent! And you, old man?' He bent and struck a blow across Bodvar's face. 'I bring tidings of our Danish friend. We asked him to sing and sing he did. Like a skylark! The boy had skill, who knew? Arwakki and his friends were most moved, I must say, when they heard his lurid tale of a Danish plot to betray the kingdom into the Wartooth's hands. A remarkable performance, really. I would have believed it myself had I not fed him every detail.'

He laughed. 'I'm afraid you were both implicated. Yes, dear cripple.' He prodded Erlan with his boot. 'It turns out you've been cat's paw to the Wartooth all along. Sent here to inveigle your way into the old king's bosom, murdering his bodyguard Finn Lodarsson along the way so you could take his place – all so that you could gull Sviggar into this false peace. There was even suggestion of an understanding between you and the fair princess, who meant to usurp Sigurd's succession as the rightful heir. She was won over of course during your heroics of the winter.' He gave a pained look. 'I'm sorry to say the earls were only too ready to believe the worst of a cripple. Such malice! Still, they always were a mistrustful bunch of whoresons.'

He went to Bodvar and yanked back his head. 'And you... Sviggar's most loyal subject – oh my! We learned that in your ignoble breast lurks such falsehood, such betrayal as may scarce be believed. Rorik told us that gold is what you crave. Gold and land. In return for your cooperation, the Wartooth promised to raise you to your own vassal kingdom – with him as your overlord to be sure – but a substantial realm nevertheless. And all of it sealed with a union between your daughters and the Wartooth's other sons. Rather neat, don't you think? Of course, Sigurd wants me to pay your girls a visit. Such lovely young things, too.'

'You fucking snake!' snarled Bodvar. 'You touch one hair on their—'

Vargalf lashed down his fist, stifling Bodvar's threat. 'Did I say you could speak, shit-slime?' he screamed in a shower of spittle. Bodvar groaned, rolling his head in agony, while Vargalf calmly licked away the phlegm on his lip. 'You should consider yourself lucky. By the time Rorik had finished, Arwakki was ready to rush down here and butcher you himself.' He gave an empty laugh. 'So of course, all opposition to Sigurd's plans has now evaporated. The levies are being called and will be assembled within the fortnight.'

'What have you done with Rorik?' Erlan murmured.

Vargalf gave a wry snort. 'You have an imagination, don't you, cripple? Suffice to say, he served his use admirably. Indeed, it's been an altogether useful few days for Sigurd. Word arrived that Starkad the Sea-King is on his way to add his strength to ours.'

'Starkad?' rasped Bodvar. 'That old viking?'

'The very same. With a hundred ships, no less, packed to the gunwales with his black-hearted killers.'

'Starkad would never join Sigurd. He's one of the Wartooth's oldest allies.'

'You know the Wartooth's talent for turning friends into foes. So,' exclaimed Vargalf, clapping his hands together, 'I'm pleased to say the prospects are looking good for this king that you scorned. Considerably better than for either of you.'

'What do you mean to do with us?' croaked Bodvar.

'Isn't it more interesting if you *don't* know?' Vargalf flashed his vulpine smile.

'You're going to pay for all this, you sick son of a whore. You do know that? You and that incestuous arse-tick you serve.'

'Oh, don't be like that, old man. Besides, you'll find out our plans for you soon enough.'

The door opened and two guards struggled in, carrying a squat cauldron.

'Ah. Perfect.' Vargalf stood aside as they hefted the cauldron to the centre of the chamber, a thick, oily liquid sloshing over its rim.

'And the rest.' The guards hurried out, returning a few seconds later with a shallow metal bowl filled with glowing lumps of coke. They set it down in the fire-pit under the chain, then took the cauldron and placed it on top.

'Now him.' He pointed at Bodvar.

The guards unchained the earl, dragged him to the middle, then fastened the hanging chain to his shackles.

'Up with him.'

Bodvar moaned as he was hoisted off the ground. When they were finished, he hung there, naked and twisting and three feet off the ground. His skin, already marked by dozens of battle-scars, was caked with filth, blood oozing from the freshest welts that streaked his body.

'Now I have you where I want you, as they say.' Vargalf's mouth curled. 'You know, it's amusing to think what a fool you proved to be in the end, old man. What did you imagine you would gain by rejecting Sigurd? Did your pride really demand so much?'

'Not my pride.'

'Your honour, then.'

'Neither are worth wasting on a lump of dog-dung like Sigurd.'

'Huh! For a lump of dog-dung, Sigurd has raised one Hel of an army.'

'It's one thing to gather an army, another to make it fight. Few will stand true when the testing comes.'

'Well, now you come exactly to my point!' Vargalf cried delightedly. 'You see, this is where you – both of you, in fact – can finally be of service to your king. Once our new friends have seen exactly what becomes of traitors to his cause, I've little doubt they'll do everything that Sigurd tells them. Now,' he said, peering into the cauldron, 'I believe we're ready for our little game.' The bottom half of the cauldron was glowing with heat. Inside, the liquid was bubbling away. Steam rose in billowing clouds around Bodvar's filthy feet.

'Such ugly things – feet,' said Vargalf, with a casual slap at them. 'Ungainly, aren't they? They stink. They ache. We hide them away in shoes. Yet without them, we can do very little. A man won't achieve much sitting on his arse all day.' He gave them another slap. The noise was blunt and ugly. 'A man should be grateful for them.' He peered up at Bodvar's haggard face. 'Are you grateful for your feet, old man?'

Bodvar said nothing, only looked down, grim-faced, eyes filled with defiance.

'No? Perhaps we can teach you some gratitude, eh?' He nodded at the guards. They unhooked the chain and, inch by inch, lowered Bodvar's blackened toes into the billowing steam. The earl bucked crazily, trying to escape the fierce heat, but Vargalf held him steady.

Then the smokehouse was filled with the hiss of flesh and oil.

Erlan had heard many men scream, but nothing like the strange strangled groaning that rose on and on from Bodvar's throat. His body spasmed, but Vargalf only gripped him tighter, oblivious to the heat, his grotesque laughter mingling with the bubbling and the scream and the sigh of the oil.

'Up!'

The guards hauled on the chain. The smell of boiled human skin coiled into Erlan's nostrils.

Bodvar's russet beard, now a filthy black, drooped down his shit-smeared chest. But his feet were spotlessly clean, bald to his knees, *glistening*... and even as Erlan watched, huge bubbles of skin began to blister and burst all over his shins. His toes were quivering, the nails scarlet and pushed up at crazy angles by the swelling flesh beneath.

Vargalf peered closer at them, fascinated. 'Well?' He looked up.

'What do you want from me?' sobbed Bodvar.

'Want?' Vargalf smoothed down his beard. 'Only that you suffer. You think you can do that?'

Bodvar didn't answer.

'Shall we go again?'

CHAPTER FIFTY

I t had taken him days to find. Weeks, even. But now Kai knew. Those innocent, lifeless faces had jolted him. Made him see the time for skulking like a wild animal was over. He had to learn the truth. If Erlan was dead, he would go far from this place – where, he had no idea, but he would survive. The moon and the forest would show him the way.

But if Erlan was alive...

Lately, the old dream had come to him often. The bloody rain, the screaming. He would awake wild-eyed, ready to strike, only to see he was alone. Alone with a thousand spirits and ten thousand stars.

After his grim discovery, he'd begun watching beyond the dawn, venturing out before dusk. Days had turned into weeks. All the while Sigurd's host grew. He'd had to be sly as a fox, lying up at a distance until darkness settled, drawing him nearer to the halls and the one great secret they had kept from him.

The secret he now knew.

He winked up at Yngvi-Freyr, grateful for the crumb the luck-god had tossed him. The night before, Kai had spotted a figure he knew at once. Knew from the way his blood ran cold.

Vargalf.

Kai had followed him, skating from shadow to shadow as he marched through the halls, trailed by two men struggling along with a cauldron of some kind. They had gone well beyond the last hall, beyond even the wattle-and-daub houses scattered beside the East Road that ran towards the coast.

There, Vargalf had entered an old smokehouse, while the guards went for another container – this one full of coals. The smokehouse was unremarkable in itself, with crude-cut planks for walls and a turf roof that sloped nearly to the ground, standing a little distance from the other buildings. Kai had never even noticed it before and wondered what Vargalf could want with a hovel like that.

The question had barely formed before he knew the answer. Erlan.

It must be.

He waited, not daring to creep closer for fear they would suddenly reappear. Much later, when the night was at its blackest, Vargalf and his men had left. Then all had fallen silent.

He lay there in the dark, watching and waiting. But it was a night like none he'd ever known. Strange signs appeared in the sky – a shimmering green mist rose out of the horizon, snaking up into the air, glowing like an emerald sunrise. Kai watched, his mouth agape in fear and wonder, as the light shifted and gathered, forming a river that flowed with great sweeping curves into the black abyss. Then, somewhere in those emerald waters, clouds of crimson began to appear, until the green flood throbbed red as if stained with blood. He watched the shapes dance and twist like a living thing, a wild fascination seizing his heart. Never in his life had he seen anything so beautiful, so awesome.

So dreadful.

Were the gods speaking to him? He had learned to hear the spirits of the forest, but not yet these mighty spirits of the sky. He listened hard. But they didn't speak. And yet somehow his heart was strengthened, and at last, with the dawn's onrushing light, the vision had faded and then disappeared.

Figures began to stir in the dissolving darkness.

Kai shifted his weight, his hip numb from the hard ground. His back was damp from the soaking dew. He shivered. But he didn't have long to wait. He could already smell the first fires of the smithy-boys.

The sun was hardly past the mid-morn mark when two men appeared from the direction of the Great Hall. They wore swords and one clutched a rag of sorts. They went inside. Kai crawled closer. But the little door soon snapped open and the men reappeared, dragging between them a third man, his head covered in a hood.

Erlan.

Alive, but... at once Kai saw that the figure slumped between the guards was a ruin of a man. He was garbed in rags, head lolling – and his feet... there was something queer about them. They were naked, white as flour, trailing limply in the dirt.

Was this really him? Not the man he knew. Hardly a man at all.

Kai cursed violently, cursed the time he'd wasted in the forest, cursed his damned caution. He was too late. His brother

499

had needed him and he had failed him. Seeing what those bastards had reduced him to, rage clawed at his throat.

The men were dragging Erlan towards the Great Hall. Kai followed, keeping his distance, until he could get closer under cover of the other byres and dwellings.

As they went along, more people followed them – warriors mostly, from their dress, and outlanders of every kind. But there were many Sveär men and women too, all headed for the hall-yard.

Kai didn't like the look of this. Nothing but trouble could come from another of Sigurd's assemblies. The guards dragged their prisoner on through the throng, yelling at them to make way.

Around the hall-yard a crowd was already forming. Kai wanted to get closer. But how? It was all happening too fast.

Looking skyward in frustration, his eye was drawn to the Sacred Oak. It stood tall as a watchtower, looking down on the Great Hall and its yard. Of course! Up there, he would see all and, more importantly, no one would see him.

He peeled off the crowd, skirting the dark rectangle of earth where the topsoil had been scraped for the foundations of Sigurd's new temple. The place was deserted, curiosity having called away the workers, so that he passed unnoticed.

A minute later, he was breathing hard, his cheek against the cracked bark of the ancient oak. He looked up into the branches overshadowing him like a giant's hand. He could hear them, the soft chorus of spirit voices: whispering, sneering, sobbing, some wrathful, some plaintive. Echoes of the sacrifices that hung each year from the blood bough. Nine of every creature – man and beast. Nine for the Nine Worlds. Was this where all those spirits were now, trapped in the limbs of this ancient tree? He shuddered.

Nevertheless, stowing his cloak, he swung himself onto the lowest branch and began to climb. Higher and higher he went, shutting his ears to the murmur of voices until, some forty feet up, he was able to move out onto a branch strong enough to hold his weight. He inched out until he could see down through the foliage onto the assembly.

Below him were all the great men of the kingdom. King Sigurd stood with his back to the hall, a gold band crowning his head, one of his father's finest cloaks hanging off his sharp shoulders.

There were others. Men whom Kai didn't recognize, hailing from any of a dozen lands around the East Sea. Some had the Norsk look about them – white-blonde with many-braided beards. Others with faces and arms marked by swirling tattoos of blue and black – perhaps Finns or Estlanders. All of them looked like killers. Doubtless many named men, renowned men, about whom many songs had been sung.

Behind these warrior-lords, and oddly out of place, were two of the biggest horses Kai had ever seen; lean and muscular, with coats gleaming like jet-stone in the slanting sun. Kai wondered why they were there. Then one of them dropped its head and he saw Vargalf's hateful face between them. Instinctively Kai shrank back. But Vargalf didn't look up his way.

The crowd of karls and lesser folk was four or five deep, ringed around the middle of the yard. Erlan's guards advanced through the crowd, the hemp hood drooped between them. People moved aside as they dragged him into the circle and threw him at Sigurd's feet. There, he lay still.

The crowd's murmurings quickly died. Then, painfully, Erlan seemed to muster enough strength to drag himself onto his hands and knees.

'Sveär lords,' Sigurd began, 'and lords of the many lands that have heeded my call. I summoned you today to show you, to show all of you, the fate of a man who sought to betray his people and his king. The fate of a man who betrays *me*.' He pointed at the wretched figure. 'Many of you know this man. Those who don't, I shall make him known to you now.' He gave a nod to the guards. The hood was ripped off.

Kai nearly fell off his branch.

Instead of the dark mop he was expecting, he saw a tangle of rusty blond hair. He was so surprised it took several moments before he recognized him.

Bodvar. Crouched like a dog before its master, his feet laid out behind him in a butchered, bloody mess.

'Bodvar, son of Berik,' declared Sigurd. 'Earl of Vestmanland, that was... A man highly honoured by my father. But now, he is marked a traitor – alas, my father ever was a poor judge of character. Now we know this man for what he is. Look at me!' Sigurd suddenly barked at the broken figure. A guard stepped forward and yanked up Bodvar's head. 'Many here witnessed your prideful display the day I was chosen king. This man wanted us to believe he was a man of integrity with his refusal. But now we know the truth. You already served another master. You'd already taken another oath.'

Sigurd began prowling around him like a lynx circling its prey. 'The Danish spy confessed. You all heard him. Rorik, son of the Wartooth, no less. Alas, one son Harald will have to do without.' He allowed himself a joyless chuckle. 'Rorik confessed that you were sworn to his brother Ringast. Even as my father lay dying, you plotted to put his kingdom in the hands of his enemy.'

Kai was confused. Where the Hel had Rorik sprung from in this miserable weave of events?

Bodvar said something but his voice was weak and didn't carry.

'It's folly to deny it,' interrupted Sigurd. 'You're a traitor. However,' he paused and shook out his blood-red cloak, 'a king should make room for mercy in his rule. Should he not?' He grinned. 'You like a good laugh, don't you, Bodvar? Well, then... Laugh at this. You are free to go.'

The crowd drew its breath.

'Go, you fool! You're free.' He shoved the kneeling Bodvar, toppling him onto his side. For a second he lay like a corpse, but then, slowly, he pushed himself round on his belly, dug his fingers into the dirt and clawed himself a few inches forward. He pulled again, slithering like a worm away from Sigurd and his nobles. Kai could see the bone scraped clean on his feet. He watched as the earl, groaning with pain and defiance, pushed himself onto his knees. He shuffled forward a couple of steps then collapsed in the dust. Someone in the crowd laughed. Then another and another. And suddenly the whole pack of them found their voices: jeers and hoots of derision filled the air while Bodvar clawed his way, inch by dogged inch, to freedom.

When he reached the centre of the ring, the noise reached its loudest. But abruptly the heckling ceased, because Vargalf had led one of the massive horses into the ring. Those were Sigurd's stallions, Kai suddenly remembered. The 'midnight twins'. Of purer stock than any horseflesh in the north, dwarfing even a man as tall as Vargalf.

Together, man and beast advanced slowly. The crowd was hushed, as though under a spell, waiting to see what he would do.

Suddenly he ran at Bodvar, the horse trotting after him. He hissed, the beast reared up, hooves big as buckler-shields, towering ten feet over Bodvar's head. Then it fell like a breaking wave on his back. Bodvar's head bucked backwards, his limbs shot out flat, dust billowed under him, as the hooves pounded him again and again. A few jeered. Most just gaped, eyes thirsty for more.

Vargalf pulled the horse off him and circled round, his eyes never leaving the prostrate body. Kai wondered whether Bodvar was dead just like that. But then he moved. A twitch, then again, until he managed to roll onto his back.

'Stay down,' Kai whispered through gritted teeth. Though even that wouldn't help him.

Vargalf led the first horse back and was exchanging it with the second when a voice, strong as thunder, bellowed:

'A curse on you, Sigurd! A curse on your blood, a curse on this crown, a curse on your filthy bed of incest! A curse on this fair kingdom that you have stained so foul!' Bodvar paused, gulping down the dusty air with the effort. Sigurd was already striding towards him. 'Murderer! These folk may not know it. But I know. I know what *you* are. Murderer! You killed—'

Sigurd's boot smashed against his head.

Bodvar didn't move. Sigurd stood back, nodded, then kicked him again. Bodvar's head jerked stupidly. Sigurd was breathing hard. 'Silence,' he said, then again in a murmur. '*Silence.*' He turned back to Vargalf. 'Again.'

Kai's eyes were welded to Bodvar. He thought he saw his

eyelids blink, but that was impossible. Except then his head flopped. He was still alive, just, but all he could do was lie there.

The black hooves thundered and then they were kicking about his limp body like a sack of grain, again and again. Eventually there was a sound like snapping wood. Vargalf circled round to make another run, but Sigurd growled, 'Enough.' Vargalf looked over. Sigurd shook his head. 'Away with him.' The guards scuttled forward and seized the battered corpse, then dragged it out of the yard, leaving a trail of blood in the dust.

'Thus the fate of any man who betrays his own blood under my rule,' Sigurd declared. 'He was traitor to the Sveär folk, traitor to his own honour, traitor to me. Mark it well.' The outlander lords and the Sveär nobles looked on, but their hard expressions cloaked their thoughts. 'Tomorrow you shall witness the fate of another man, guilty of outrageous crimes. His end will be no less final.'

He turned with a flourish of his cloak and strode off towards the hall. The nobles followed. The rest of the crowd began to disperse, their appetite sated, at least for one day.

Kai slid back along the branch.

One night... One night to save his friend. There was nothing beyond this night.

Nothing without Erlan.

CHAPTER
FIFTY-ONE

E rlan groaned and opened his eyes.

No one had come today. And Bodvar, he was gone, the only remnant of him a stain of shit and squalor in the other corner.

It wouldn't be long before they came for him, too.

The deep gloom in the smokehouse meant darkness had fallen. *For you, night is coming.* Night had now come. Maybe his last.

He chided himself. This was what he had chosen when he left the wind-swept strands of Vendlagard, shrouded in tears and sorrow. The Norns had brought him here – first to crest him high on a mounting wave, only to smash him down on the rocks of shame and ruin. He snorted, remembering how Sviggar would have named him foster-son. *Who could deny those fate-weaving bitches have a sense of humour?*

He shivered. At least he'd only have to endure the cold for one more night.

Then it would be over.

A chain rattled. The door-latch gave a metallic click. He lifted his head. The door swung open. A pool of light flooded the floor. A murmur. A footstep, this one lighter than any he'd heard before. He looked over, dread lodged in his throat at the prospect of Vargalf's hard features appearing out of the darkness.

Then a dark, shimmering robe stepped out from the recess of the doorway. Saldas straightened up, peering into the shadows, a firebrand gripped in her hand. A guard entered behind her.

'Where is he?' she said, her eyes still adjusting to the murk.

The guard pointed. She held up the torch. Erlan felt its light spread over his body, stealing away the blanket of darkness to reveal his bloody and filth-encrusted limbs.

She gazed on him. Her brow wrinkled, not with concern, but something closer to disgust. 'Fix this,' she said, proffering the torch.

The guard took it and slotted it into the nearest sconce.

'Is he secure?'

'Aye, my lady.'

'Then leave us.'

The door clapped shut. Erlan uncurled from his huddled position, spreading his legs with his back to the wall. She stood in front of him, unfazed by his nakedness. He noticed her nostrils flare slightly at the stench of excrement and piss-soaked straw. Beneath her cloak, she was wearing the same dress she had worn the first time he saw her. It clung to her like jealous hands, its dark colours shifting with each flick of the flame. One half of her face was shadow; the other, pale and beautiful as a waxing moon.

'Look what a man's pride brings him to.' She shook her head. '*Tsk, tsk*. You're a fool, Erlan. How easily you could have avoided all this. You only had to do what I wanted.' She laughed. 'Gods, you wanted it yourself! But instead... Well, now you know the price of your defiance.'

'Is that all you came for?' he whispered. 'To gloat?'

'H'm. To gloat would suggest the end was ever in doubt. No – I came to make you an offer.'

'An offer?' He glared at her, mistrustful. 'You mean my freedom?'

'Freedom? Mmm – of a kind. Yes, why not? Your life. And your freedom.'

'If Sigurd wants to make me an offer, why doesn't he come himself?'

'Sigurd doesn't even know I'm here.'

'Is he not your lord? The son you now bow to as husband and king?'

'My lord?' Her green eyes hardened. 'No man is my lord. I follow my own will.'

'As Sviggar discovered to his cost.' Saldas glared at him, but gave no reply. 'This offer is from you, then?'

'You think I'd come as errand-boy for anyone else?'

A chuckle rattled his throat. 'I don't suppose you'd do anything for anyone else, come to that. So why give me my life?' He looked down at his wasted limbs. 'If you want my body, you've left it a bit late.'

Her lips twitched with a smile. 'I could restore your body. If I chose to.'

'Why would you?'

'Why?' She stroked a finger under her chin. 'Perhaps it amuses me.'

It amused her. That was her answer. Erlan looked at her,

tried to see through her. Why was she here? He couldn't flatter himself that she wanted him as some sort of plaything. There had to be more.

'I don't believe you.'

'Why not? It amused me to reduce you to this,' she twiddled her slender fingers at him, 'this pitiful animal sitting before me in a puddle of his own shit. It amuses me to lift you out of it. To take your life or to save it. That power is mine.'

'And what do I have to do, to receive such mercy?'

'Simple.' Her mouth hardened. 'Submit to me. Do that and I'll raise you up again.'

'And Sigurd?'

'Puh! Sigurd is nothing. I put him where he is. I can remove him just as easily. But whether I should raise you to his place – I haven't decided. Though I could do it. Like that.' She snapped her fingers.

And with that sound, he suddenly understood. This wasn't amusing to her. It was everything. She felt it like a blade at her throat. It possessed her like a maddening thirst. She needed him to submit to prove her power over him, to prove that, in the end, everyone and everything *must* yield to her will. That she was nothing less than a god.

And in that instant, he saw the only power left to him – stinking and slimed as he was. The power to refuse, to deny her the one thing she craved above all else: his submission.

'Well?'

'I admit it,' he said, voice breaking, 'often I've felt you like a ghost in my soul. A murmur in my head that won't let me rest.' Her lips curled in satisfaction. 'Even though I've hated you, I've always... wanted you.'

'Hmm,' she purred. 'Once I restore you, we can enjoy each other as much as we want. I already have a plan for Sigurd's downfall and for raising you to the kingship with power over every soul in the land. Except mine, naturally. Only bow to me, and everything else shall be under you.'

'You mean it?' he said, tears welling with relief. 'You'll take me away from this place?'

She smiled at him, painfully radiant, as foreign to that dank place of suffering and misery as a shining sun. 'You'll find me a most loving lord, Erlan.' She moved closer. Reached out and touched his face with the tip of her finger. He jerked away, but she persisted. It was the only tender touch he had felt in that foul place. For a second, his will wavered. Why shouldn't he do as she wanted? *Why?*

'Rule with me,' she murmured. 'Together we might do great things. Let me save you now and the kingdom shall be ours.'

'You'll get me out? If I say yes, I mean.'

'In a moment,' she whispered, her mouth close enough for him to smell the sweetness of her breath.

'What about Vargalf?'

'Vargalf is mine. They're all mine. Oh, Erlan, just say it and I'll take you away. You'll forget all about what has passed here. You'll have learned your lesson. And you'll soon forgive me, I promise you.'

Her hand was cool against his cheek. 'What must I do?'

'Swear to me.' Her voice tightened with excitement. 'Swear your loyalty to *me* and no one else, and in a moment you'll be gone from here.'

He dropped his head. He was so tired. He felt his hair, lank with grease and grime, brush his face. Slowly, he nodded.

'Go on. Say the words and I'll take you away.' She tilted his face to hers. 'Go on – *speak!*'

The chain suddenly rattled and he had her wrist. She flinched, but didn't cry out, though his blackened fingernails were digging into her skin. A jagged laugh clacked in his throat. 'It's killing you, isn't it? That it wasn't you I wanted, that I wouldn't submit.'

She tried to pull away, but he held her. Only when she stopped struggling did he throw away her hand in disgust. She stood and backed away from him.

'You're actually mad.'

'Because only a madman would reject you and your promises of power?' he snarled. 'You may think yourself a goddess over men. To me you're nothing but a venomous whore.'

Saldas's mouth twisted. 'Do you know what they're going to do to you?' she hissed. 'Sigurd is going to have those horses of his rip you in two. The last thing you'll feel in this world is your spine snapping.'

'So be it,' he replied grimly. 'Now run back to your son's bed, little whore.'

She looked down at him, hate cascading from her eyes. 'You're a strange, stubborn man.' She gave a mirthless snort. 'I confess I was intrigued. To feel your adoration. To know your sweetness... But you have none.' She smoothed her dress. 'You'll not see me again.' She slowly raked the phlegm from her throat, squatted down and spat in his face. 'Goodbye. Cripple.'

He felt her spittle running down his cheek. 'I'll see you in Hel.'

'Hel?' she chuckled. 'Oh, you have a world more pain to suffer before you reach there.'

With that, she was gone, leaving him with nothing but the guttering flame and the echo of her warning.

Kai ran through the forest, his shield jarring his back. But he didn't care. It had to be now. Whatever happened, this was Erlan's last chance.

The moon urged him on. *Run faster, my child, run for your brother.* The spear and the axe felt strong in his hands. Dawn would not break before both had tasted blood. The trees flew past in the darkness, their branches clawing at him, holding him back.

Why do you hurry so? they murmured. *Your life changes nothing. We will stand here, unmoved, till the last of you is crumbled to dust. We'll be standing here still when the world is swallowed in fire.*

'NO!' he snarled and ran swifter, his heart pounding in his chest. Ahead, he spied the meadows beyond the trees. Another fifty strides. Only then would he slow.

He reached the treeline and halted.

I need your stealth now, he murmured. But to whom, he couldn't say. To the wolves, to his brothers of the forest? To the shadow-spirits that swirled about him? To the mist that hovered over the midnight dew?

He crept forward, eyes fixed on the hovels lining the dark horizon like shield studs, and finally there was the smokehouse, and above it smoke whorling into the sky.

At the sight of it, fear washed through him, cold and stark.

He stopped, hesitated, his heart full of doubt and terror, words jabbering in his head. He could slip away, could flee the kingdom. Forge another life somewhere else. Find someone else to serve. Something else to do...

He looked up into the sky where, only the night before, he had seen that awesome river of blood. But this time there was no blazing message from the gods. Only emptiness and silence.

He gripped the haft of his axe tighter, clamped his long lips into a hard line.

What was another life, after all? There was only one life for him. Only one thing for him to do. And it was here.

It was now.

CHAPTER
FIFTY-TWO⊙

H is head had barely dropped when the door opened again. Light spilled into the chamber. This time the footsteps were familiar.

'You're not an easy man to fathom, cripple,' said Vargalf, while the guards fixed fresh torches into the wall. 'Whatever Saldas offered you, you should have taken it.' He stepped closer and peered down at him curiously. 'Still that defiance in those eyes. *Hmm*.' Impulsively, he swung a fist. Pain exploded through Erlan's skull. 'Her touch was gentler, h'm?' Vargalf turned away. 'Hang him up.'

A few moments later Erlan was suspended from the chain.

'No. Tonight we need him higher.'

The guards strained away, hoisting him in painful jerks upwards. His feet were five feet off the ground before Vargalf growled, 'Enough. Now fetch the rest.'

The guards left them.

'The low folk say a man must live by the choices he's made. I can't say yours displeases me.' He came closer, dropped his gaze to Erlan's feet. 'You know Saldas is entirely indifferent whether you survive tonight's activity.' He said it almost absently, his interest taken with Erlan's left ankle, the spur of bone visible beneath the skin where the break had healed so badly. 'I've a free rein, as they say.' Suddenly he squeezed the bone, hard. The old jet of pain raced up Erlan's body and out through his mouth in a violent, visceral scream. Vargalf's thumb and fingers bit like hot needles, deep into his bone. Erlan twisted and thrashed, in vain.

Vargalf released him. The pain eased, leaving Erlan gasping.

'Interesting. Yes – I see your problem. Oh, by the way,' he added casually, 'I've something to show you.' He threw his cloak over his shoulder to reveal a sword-hilt at his hip.

He drew the blade and held it up for Erlan to inspect. 'Recognize this?' Despite his exhaustion, the length of steel was all too familiar. He felt a pang, as though suddenly looking into the face of an old friend.

Vargalf cut at the air. 'You call it Wrathling, don't you? A fine name for a fine blade. But what was yours is now mine. A gift from Sigurd.' Erlan looked down with burned-out eyes, thinking of the long line of Vendlings who had bloodied that steel in Odin's storm. And he had lost it. He was the fool. His throat contracted with shame.

Vargalf re-sheathed it. 'Poor cripple. Ignorant of so many things. Well, at least tomorrow you will learn something. A new kind of pain. You know I have the honour of overseeing your dispatch from this world.' His nostrils flared. 'And afterwards, when you find yourself wandering the halls of Hel, then at last I'll have had my revenge.'

'Revenge?' Erlan's eyes darted. 'What wrong have I ever done you?'

'I suppose you think you're innocent?'

'No one is innocent.'

'Ha! Something troubling your conscience, is it, cripple? Well, fear not. By the time I'm through with you, whatever it is will be well paid for.'

'Why do you hate me?'

'That's another question. A fair one. And you will know the answer. Soon.'

Vargalf circled around him. 'Of course, besides my own, more *personal* reasons, your death is part of a much greater work now. Indeed,' he whispered, 'you might even call it my master work.'

'Yours?' Erlan scoffed. 'The Wide-Realm is Sigurd's vision.'

'Who do you think gave it him? Who do you think cleared the way to make it a reality?'

'Cleared the way?' For a second, Erlan was confused. Did he mean the king or... 'Not Staffen?'

Vargalf smiled at his own cunning. 'His brother was the first step.'

'But he was killed by a stag. No – by the Vandrung shape-shifters—' Suddenly Erlan's thoughts were confused again. After the dark deaths of winter had ceased that had been the explanation he had accepted, along with everyone else.

'Yes?'

'That was you?'

Vargalf raised an eyebrow.

'Wait, so you're... you're a shape-shifter.'

'Are you so shocked?'

Erlan thought of Grimnar, the strange *seidman* in the forest, remembered the jay that had guided them to the caverns of

Niflagard, and then the horrors of that black night when the shrieks of the Vandrung had split the air. Such things were possible. He'd seen them with his own eyes... but *Vargalf*?

'You murdered Sviggar's heir.'

'I removed all obstacles between Sigurd and the throne.'

'And Finn the archer?' He could still see the grotesque contortions on the face of the king's bodyguard as he writhed and choked on the mead-hall floor. His murderer had never been found.

'Sviggar's guard dog had to go. Too loyal. Too effective.'

'You poisoned him.'

'A mercy!' protested Vargalf. 'I spared him a broken heart, after the loss of his wife and such.' She had been one of the nine women sacrificed and hung from the Sacred Oak.

'And the king? You murdered him, too?'

'You look surprised! But the old fool insisted on staying alive for so long. It was rather simple in the end. Hardly more than a nudge in that direction. Of course, Finn would never have let it happen. But you – your mind was so often on other things.' His mouth curled sardonically. 'And now the harvest ripens for the greatest slaughter the north has ever known. The Wartooth has his thousands. Sigurd has his. And there is nothing anyone can do to stop the coming deluge of blood.' A hard, cruel edge had crept into his voice as he spoke, and his eyes glinted with a kind of bleak joy.

It sent a chill through Erlan's heart. 'Your master work?'

'Indeed.'

'For whom? For the Wartooth?'

'That old boar? No, no! Oh, it's taken some goading on the Danes' side, to be sure. Harald survived the man I sent to kill him. A shame, since his sons would have been sure to seek revenge. But the effect was the same. He blames the Sveärs and dreams of *Valhöll* and a glorious death.' Vargalf sniggered. 'I fear when death finds him at last, he'll be sorely disappointed.'

'Who, then?' Erlan demanded, so urgently that he twisted on the chain. 'Who do you serve?'

There was a noise as the door opened. Vargalf glanced over. 'Another fair question. And you shall know that answer, too.' The first guard shuffled in awkwardly. 'Ah – at last!'

Erlan watched, dread squirming like a snake in his bowels. First they brought in two large caskets: one heaped with firewood, the other full to the brim with lumps of coke, the special fuel the smiths used to make a flame hot enough to temper steel. After that a water butt with a wooden ladle, and last of all, a large metal basin full of glowing coals, which they emptied into the fire-pit directly below him. At once, the heat off the coals coiled like ivy around his legs.

'Are you familiar with the process of smoking meat?'

Erlan had become so used to the cold and dank that his skin had almost forgotten what it was like to be warm. But pleasant as it felt, he knew this wasn't for his comfort.

'The trick is controlling the temperature and the timing. The coke gives heat. The smoke gives flavour. The water slows it all down. It's really quite a skill.'

Vargalf told the guards to wait for him outside.

Once they'd gone, he began prowling back and forth, muttering to himself, throwing dark glances up at his prisoner. Erlan shifted awkwardly. Pain snarled through his wrists. The heat was becoming more intense, yet still not unpleasant.

Those of Vargalf's words he caught he couldn't understand.

Another tongue, perhaps, making him wonder whether Vargalf was from another land entirely. And yet... there was something familiar about the sound of it – how every word was hard-edged and guttural.

The heat was growing. Erlan looked up. The beam was only three or four feet above him, but it might as well have been as far as the moon. The soles of his feet began to prickle.

Vargalf ceased his mutterings, his gaze settling on the glowing coals.

'There's something honest about a fire.' Vargalf snorted. 'Perhaps the only kind of honesty I respect. In the fire, nothing can hide. Everything is peeled away to its hardest, irreducible core. And if it's strong, it endures – is made stronger even – tempered by the flames. And if not... then even the strongest part of it is destroyed for ever.'

He looked up.

'I wonder what you will find – at the core of you. And will it endure?' He flashed a wicked smile, then turned and seized a couple of lumps of coke and tossed them onto the coals. For a while, they remained unchanged, but soon the heat began to seep through them, making them glow, the air above shimmering as the temperature rose.

Erlan flinched with the lick of stronger heat. His calves began to smart, yet still it was bearable. Vargalf's dark eyes were glowing orange in the flame-light.

'Too soon for more?'

Erlan braced himself as Vargalf tossed more lumps of fuel onto the fire. He'd witnessed Vargalf's skill too many times now. Had seen how he could draw an ocean of pain out of a man and still keep him alive, if only by a hair's breadth. He clamped his jaw tight. There were no more choices to be made. All he could do was endure, and see where the fire would lead him.

The rising heat slithered up his legs, whispering of the pain to come. He sucked in sharply.

Vargalf sighed. 'So we've begun at last! Let your body drink in the heat. The fire will speak to your bones, take you to what is real. You're lucky. Few will ever see what you will now.'

Erlan tried to shut out the pain building in his feet and legs, focusing instead on the parts of his body not yet enveloped by the stifling air.

'One thing I see clear enough,' Erlan rasped. 'Saldas rides you like a man.'

Vargalf's face curdled and he snatched another lump of fuel and tossed it onto the fire. 'Again – your ignorance,' he snarled, angrily. Erlan felt new waves of heat rise around him. Sweat was running in rivers down his spine. 'It is she who does my bidding, though she hardly knows it. The same as Sigurd.'

He tossed a piece of firewood into the flames. Quickly it began to smoke. Then he threw another and another and the smoke grew, billowing upwards, forcing its way into Erlan's eyes and nostrils. He coughed, feeling the heat climb a notch, squeezing a groan from his throat.

'Good,' soothed Vargalf, in a languorous voice. 'Perhaps we'll muzzle that insolent tongue of yours before much longer.' The wood was burning hungrily, cracking and popping as the flames bit into it, the smoke seeping like a smothering fog down into his lungs.

'Sigurd has been mine since I came here. It was simple enough to turn him against his father. A little flattery, a word to prod here, a reminder of some slight there.' He chuckled. 'Every man has his darkness. One needs only to draw it to the surface. With Sigurd – resentment of a father, jealousy of a brother. Once I knew that, I could make him do whatever I wanted. Murder, betrayal, incest... and soon slaughter on a scale never before imagined.'

But Erlan was beyond answering – the heat consuming his feet and legs was overpowering, turning every vein, every sinew in his body to fire.

'If Sigurd lives, I'll make him drown the world in blood. To the furthest horizon and beyond. Fire, slaughter, rape, pillage... *Death!*' Erlan looked down. Vargalf's face was flushed, his eyes inflamed, the outline of him wavering in the smoke and burning air.

He closed his eyes and focused on the pain.

'Slowly, slowly,' he heard Vargalf say. 'We mustn't rush you.' There was a sizzle and blast of steam, which scalded his skin, stole his breath, but the ratcheting heat stalled, just a fraction. The ladle rattled as Vargalf tossed it back in the bucket.

He knew Vargalf could play this game for hours, keeping him just beyond the breaking foam of death. He felt his skin blister, felt the fire inside him like a living thing – seeping through him from his feet, through his thighs, into his guts, closing around his heart like the fingers of some fire-wight.

His mind turned inward, pain swirling like a fog. And suddenly in it he saw his heart burst into flame, saw layer after layer peel away, ignite, curl and crumble to ash, each one bringing with it memories, flashing like ghosts through his mind.

The steam and smoke and stench all vanished. He saw Sviggar's body, stiff and cold; felt his temples throb the morning he awoke in the wood; saw Lilla, regal and white under her bridal veil; tasted the muddy water of the Fyris; heard the awful howling in the darkness and the bite of winter on his hands. He tasted the Watcher's blood, its iron tang, felt its searing fire as dark magic rushed through him. There was Kai's laughter, the crushing cold of the lake; vomit and sea-salt on his lips; the musk of his father's sweat in his nostrils; and then he saw *her.* Her face under the silver surface of the water, the crimson clouds, the swirling brown hair, and last of all that hideous, gaping wound.

He looked down and saw the knife in his hand.

In his own hand...

That was when the scream ripped out of him like a slaughter-yell, shattering his ears. His body thrashed wildly, the chain a shriek of grinding metal. He opened his eyes.

The chamber was different now, the shadows alive, slithering, swaying, writhing in every unlit corner, flitting across his vision through the billowing smoke and steam. And all around him, Vargalf's laughter rang.

CHAPTER
FIFTY-THREE

K ai heard the scream.

It turned his blood cold, summoning him to his destiny. Or his doom.

He was close. He could see the guards' silhouettes beyond the hard-packed road across the tufted grass. They hadn't even turned their heads.

He slipped over the road and went to ground, his shield-rim jabbing into his back. He bit his lip to stifle the pain. It was too unwieldy. He'd have to do without the thing. He slid it off his back and stowed it in the grass.

He eyed the guards. Maybe he could just rush them. But there were two of them, both bigger than him. Together they'd squash him like a toad. No. A little cunning was needed.

His gaze happened to alight upon the eaves sloping off the smokehouse roof and suddenly he had an idea. He foraged around beside the road until he found what he was looking for. Two stones – smaller than his fist, but big enough to make a decent noise. He slipped them into his pouch, then crept round to the back of the smokehouse, where he took off his cloak. The roof edge hung level with his chest.

Right, my lad. Here's where you earn your bread.

He shoved the axe into his belt, propped the spear against the eave, then hopped onto the roof, digging his fingers into the thatch, pulling himself higher till he'd got his whole body up there. Satisfied, he lay flat to catch his breath and listen.

No alarm. No running footsteps. The thatch was warm. He put an ear to it, but couldn't make out much. Some muttering. A sort of panting.

I'm coming, brother.

But first there were these other bastards. He hauled up his spear beside him, then squirmed higher up the roof until he was just below the swirling smoke-hole. Carefully, he drew his knees under him so he was almost sitting and looked through the smoke down the other side.

There were the guards, crouched on their hams. He waited and listened. Now and then, one of them spoke and the other replied. He waited a little longer until both of them laughed at some joke, then quickly shuffled round the smoke-hole so that now he was directly above them, hardly twenty feet away.

He held the spear tight, the thatch even tighter. His axe was digging into his back. That wouldn't do. He wriggled his feet, wedging his heels deeper into the rushes to take his weight. Then he reached behind and pulled out his axe.

I need another bloody pair of hands, he thought, jamming the axe-head under a foot so that he could extract one of his stones.

Here goes nothing.

He held his breath and lobbed it high into the air. A couple of seconds later, there was a thud as the stone landed in the darkness somewhere off to the right, out of sight of the guards.

He waited for a reaction.

Nothing. *Brilliant. Deaf as fucking posts.* He pulled out the second stone and was about to throw it when one guard nudged the other.

'Hear that, Orn?'

'What?'

'A noise. Round there.' The guard nodded round the side of the smokehouse.

'Go take a look then.'

Kai waited for the first guard to stand but instead, after a bit, he shrugged. 'Bah! Probably nothing.'

'You're a lazy turd, Dofri. Anyone ever tell you that?'

'No one's stopping you going.'

Kai launched his second stone. Another thud in the dark.

'There you are,' said the one called Dofri, getting to his feet. 'You must've heard that.'

'I heard it,' nodded Orn. But still neither moved. 'Well?'

'What?'

'Well, off you go then.'

'What about you?'

'Someone's got to stay here, 'case that crazy bugger wants something else.'

Dofri cursed and slouched off into the shadows.

Kai's heart quickened. From his perch, he watched Dofri disappear and smiled. Below him, Orn had his back to him, facing into the night, still crouched on his hams.

Kai squeezed his axe, drew a deep breath and began to slide. His backside scraped the thatch, faint at first, but louder as he gathered speed; the bottom edge was fast approaching, the axe was ready in his hand.

Orn must have heard him. He began to rise and turn. But it was too late – his doom was falling, hard and heavy as Thor's hammer. He looked up. Kai saw the surprise in his face. He went for his hilt, but Kai was over the edge and landing on his feet, neat as a tomcat.

For a heartbeat, they stared at each other, the surprise in Orn's face turning to fear. But Kai's axe was already falling. The edge sank deep into the guard's neck. Kai ripped his arm back and Orn's head flipped over in a spray of blood.

Orn slumped to the ground, fanning the grass with his blood, but Kai was already moving. He dashed away from the doorway into the shadows, the spear still gripped in his left hand.

Fifteen paces. No more. Out of sight, in range. He stopped and turned.

He hadn't time even to catch his breath. Dofri had heard the noises and appeared at the run, brandishing his spear.

Kai grinned.

He saw Dofri stand over Orn's body, saw his head snap up, searching the shadows for Orn's mysterious killer. The guard waved his spear blindly. 'Who's out there?' he called, voice trembling. 'Answer me!'

Kai answered with a snickering laugh, a laugh born in the shadows and holes of the forest, a laugh no longer his. Dofri stood rooted like a rock, uncertain, his spear lowered. But Kai had no intention of going forward to test it.

. . . .

Dofri felt afraid. His guts were water. He peered into the blackness, eyes straining. And suddenly he saw: two eyes, pale and wild, then a glint of metal – a pinprick lancing out of the night.

The spear was halfway through his neck before he realized what it was. But it was much too late. He was on his back, blood already filling his throat. He blinked, disbelieving, clutching at the shaft. His legs were shaking, but he couldn't do piss-all about it. And then a shadow appeared over him.

He saw the face, streaked with filth, hair jutting everywhere in dirty yellow spikes, eyes pitiless as a wolf. The mouth was a gaping hole of rage and savage madness.

It was the last face he ever saw.

CHAPTER
FIFTY-FOUR

'Look at me, filth!'

Erlan raised his head. Through the writhing air, he saw Vargalf, his long sharp nose, his hollow cheeks, those cold, sneering lips. They were moving.

'You make much of forswearing your past, don't you, cripple? Of refusing your father's name? And now you have another – the *Aurvandil*.' He spat on the floor in disgust. 'A name you won at great cost.' His eyes darted upwards, sharp as spears. 'A name that cost me much, too.'

Erlan heard the words but didn't understand. He saw only a sea of shadows, felt only the burning air.

'*The Witch King was my father!*' Vargalf hissed. 'Do you hear me, cripple? You – killed – my – father!' The words were a shriek now, driving into Erlan's brain like a blade. 'Blood calls for blood vengeance! I mean to have it, and more. I want your pain, your will... Your very *soul*.'

A memory leaped from the depths of Erlan's consciousness. *The Witch King. The Watcher.* Suddenly Vargalf's pale face shattered into a thousand pieces and he saw again the towering Watcher's strange and fearful beauty.

Vargalf was spawn of the Witch King? An overlord?

There was a new dark edge to his voice now. 'You killed my father, cripple, but his lord – the one I serve – can never be killed. In his thrall is a host more numerous than the stars and they will carry on his work – in every land, among every people. And I mean to finish his work here. I'll see every tribe of the north in thrall to him before I'm through.'

This was the way the Watcher had talked – of lords and tyrants, of wars and rebellions that Erlan didn't understand. Yet at the memory of him, something stirred in him, something beyond the pain. A kind of strength, a kind of rage, waking like a vengeful beast that had slept untroubled a long time. And suddenly out of him ripped a monstrous, mad, swaggering laugh.

For a second, Vargalf looked wrong-footed. His face darkened and then he snatched up more coke. 'Something amusing you, cripple? Let's see if you can laugh this off.' He slung it on the fire.

'I – drank – his – blood,' Erlan hissed slowly, like some black-souled *draugr* in a saga-tale.

Vargalf watched him and gradually the hard lines around his mouth knotted into a smile. 'Is that so, cripple?' he murmured. 'Then my father is in you now, too.'

The dry heat suddenly surged through Erlan's head like a red flood. His sight was changing, shedding veil after veil as it went deeper, and the more he saw, the more he screamed. He saw shadows fuse into solid things that shifted and moved. Living things with limbs and sinews, black as coal; feet and claws, pointed and cruel. He saw figures clinging in dark corners, figures hanging from the smoke-stained rafters, figures peering at him from atop the beam. They slavered at the burning air, black tongues licking black lips until they shone.

He knew not what he saw, only that they stared at him, hard and cruel, with yellow eyes. His vision darted from one to the next. The more he screamed, the more he saw.

He felt shame looking on one – a twisted, clutching creature, curled on itself, gnawing its knuckles. Another had a face drooping and sorrowful, its skin diseased and pitted as though poison corroded its flesh from the inside, a foul drool spilling from its cracked lips, and Erlan tasted bitterness on his own tongue.

His screams rose upward to the biggest of these shadow-fiends that paced along the beam, eyes fierce as lightning, lips peeled in a snarl, teeth jagged and broken. Staring at it, Erlan thirsted for blood and vengeance.

Another – the ugliest of these creatures – squirmed near the doorway. Its nose was cut away. Mucus streamed into its jutting mouth. Its eyes were crossed and its ears monstrously wide. His heart twisted, wringing out self-pity like a fetid slime for all the wrongs done to him.

There were others. One, sleek and smooth, pawing itself, eyes big and round and grasping. Another whose lips never ceased murmuring, with powerful hands circling its tail like a noose. Overwhelmed, Erlan tore his eyes away and looked down at Vargalf. But he too was changed, seeming taller, and his mouth gaped in strange yawning motions. The stench grew ranker still until Erlan became aware of another figure behind him.

A heavy cowl covered its face. The shade bent low and began to whisper. Vargalf listened, intent, while long, white fingers crept like spiders along his shoulders, up his neck, suddenly gripping his head and jerking it backwards. The shadow bent still lower, as though to kiss Erlan's tormentor, but when their mouths were not quite touching, the shadow convulsed and began to vomit. Wave after wave of crimson slime gushed from the shadow's throat and Vargalf swallowed it down like milk, swallowed it till it overflowed down his beard and ran down his chest. And then the shadow was spent and drew itself up tall again.

Vargalf was speaking, but Erlan heard only the roar of the flames and the sound of his own screaming, yet as he watched he saw clouds of scarlet smoke billowing from Vargalf's mouth.

Erlan sensed the other shadow-creatures closing in, along the beam, down the chain, scuttling like roaches. They clung to him, swarmed over him, plucked at his eyes, squeezed his chest, snorted phlegm in his face. And always the heat of the fire was crushing him and crushing him. He longed for death, but more than anything feared that death would bring no relief.

Then, far above him, he saw something so bright it seemed to burn right through these shadows and brand his eyes with its blinding image. A pure light poured in through the smoke-hole, white as winter, driving back the darkness. The black creatures shrank back, their bodies dissolving into the retreating shadows in craven fear.

Erlan stopped screaming. At once the walls and rafters of the smokehouse returned to his vision. Even the bright light grew dim, shrinking into something solid. Something real.

For a second, it hung from the thatch engulfed by clouds of surging smoke. Then suddenly, it dropped, landing on the beam. The wood groaned in protest, and Erlan saw within the fading light the outline of a man.

'Erlan!'

He stared, unable to believe what he saw. A man shouting his name. Or something like a man. It looked almost as wild and strange as the shadow-creatures it had driven away.

'Erlan!' He saw the ragged mess of hair and cursed the fire because he knew its heat had only driven him into a new place of torment, one where phantoms of relief came to taunt him.

That boy is dead. He saw only another shadow.

But then he heard Vargalf's yell. 'You!'

'Erlan!' the phantom cried again. This time he recognized Kai's voice.

A stab of hope penetrated the heat and the pain and the torment. The little madman looked like he'd sprung from some grave but there he was, flesh and blood, a wide grimace cracked across his face, and bristling with steel.

From below came a long scrape of leather and iron as Vargalf unsheathed Wrathling.

'Where did you spring from, weasel-shit?' Vargalf snarled.

'From Hel!' yelled Kai. 'She calls for you, devil!' His arm fell like a hammer. The spear whipped through the roiling air. Kai bayed in triumph, sure he'd found his mark, but at the last blink, Vargalf lurched right. The point shot clean through cloak and tunic, slicing his shoulder.

Vargalf shrieked as the point impaled the floor behind him. He staggered backwards. His cloak was dangling from a single clasp. He tore it away angrily and readied his sword. But the boy was quicker.

Kai hit the ground hard, rolled, then found his feet before Vargalf had even taken a stand. Kai was screaming, a feral yell to rouse the dead and freeze the bones of the living, and before Vargalf had time even to raise his sword, Kai was on him, axe-blade scything at his bleeding shoulder. The overlord threw up a desperate guard and Wrathling rang with the blow.

Erlan was shouting Kai's name, his pain forgotten. He saw only the fight below. Rage welled inside him – not the bitter, self-pitying anger of before, but a ravenous fury – at his tormentor, at the man turning his own ring-sword against his oath-brother. He thrashed around, helpless as a fish on a hook, his blistered legs kicking at the burning air. He hauled on his wasted arms, scrabbling to get a grip on the chain, ignoring the blood flecking his face and the blinding pain in his wrists. But his nails tore at the metal in vain.

Below, Kai threw himself at Vargalf. He was close enough to smell the bastard's sweat. The axe was no bloody use this close. He dropped it and slammed his shoulder into Vargalf's belly. The two of them went over, Vargalf winded. Kai went for his knife, grinding his fist into the other's bloodied shoulder. Wrathling flew clear. Their feet kicked frenziedly at the box of firewood, knocking it over, scattering the logs with a loud clatter. Kai felt fingers strong as stone circle his wrist, holding his dagger-point in check.

But his other thumb had found Vargalf's wound. He drove it in deep. Vargalf screamed. Kai thrust his head forward, snarling like a rabid dog, still unable to drive home his blade. Instead he lunged for the pale throat. Vargalf craned his head, trying to

533

escape the slavering jaws, but then Kai's tongue scraped stubble and he snapped his jaws shut.

Vargalf shrieked. Blood fizzed like rust on Kai's tongue. He bit harder as they rolled across the floor towards the fire-pit. The heat surged beside them. He jerked his head and felt flesh tear. The overlord screamed again. Kai spat blood and sinew, baying with savage delight, his eyes whirlwinds of killing hunger, but Vargalf's fingers were in his hair, winding into it. His scalp suddenly flared with pain as Vargalf tore away a clump of knotted strands. But Kai didn't care. What was pain to him? He was a killer now, born for this.

They bumped against the edge of the fire-pit. Vargalf's grip was unyielding, pushing Kai's hand into the flames. Kai screamed at the scorching heat, dropping the dagger into the flaming coals.

Steel was gone. This would be settled by blood and bone now.

Kai bucked his scrawny torso, mad as a wild ox, smashing his skull into Vargalf's face with a satisfying crunch. He grinned a bloody grin, sensing weakness, and lunged forward, hungry for more blood, and to finish this.

Above them, fury coursed like ice through Erlan's veins. The air was filled with screams from below. But there was only one way to reach his brother.

Up.

He writhed so hard he bit his tongue and tasted blood. And with the taste a memory came, of the blood he had swallowed far below the earth in the Watcher's cave. And suddenly his arms seemed to fill with darkness – with some primal strength dragged from the depths of those black caverns, the strength of the ice-giants of old, the strength of the wind and the earth and the ocean. A roar began far away in the lightless places where things long forgotten to the minds of men still dwelled. It swelled within him till his chest nearly burst and it broke from his mouth in an inhuman howl.

He reached for the chain, got a grip and, hand over bloodied hand, began to climb.

Kai was in a clawing, snarling, gouging fight for his life. His boots scraped the floor, scrabbling for a hold, his scorched hand clamped on Vargalf's throat. His nails had grown long and sharp. If he could hook a thumb under this bastard's jawbone he'd rip it clean off, but still he couldn't lose the overlord's grip.

Vargalf's nose was a bloody stream; his neck, a bloody maw. Kai snapped his teeth, looking for more, when Vargalf's elbow slipped and their heads banged together. Kai saw his chance, lunged, felt cartilage between his teeth, jerked back. There was a ripping sound and he came away with an ear in his mouth. Vargalf shrieked and Kai spat bone and blood and spittle, spraying the overlord's milk-white skin scarlet.

But Vargalf was far from done.

And suddenly Kai was on his back beside the fire, the wind knocked out of him. Vargalf got a knee up, pinning his right arm. Kai struggled in vain, his left hand still gripped in the iron fingers that had never let go, but the other hand was on his face. He felt a thumb close over his eye, saw only blackness, felt pressure build sickeningly inside his socket, braced himself for the pain...

Erlan reached the beam. Everything was red – his hands, the chain, the fire, the darkness. He hauled himself up. The chain went slack. From below came a sudden, heart-rending cry, answered by a thick, guttural laugh. Erlan looked down and saw Vargalf throw back his head in triumph and bury his hand in the fire. In an eye-blink, he'd ripped it clear, a shard of metal flashing in his hand. Flesh sizzled. Erlan jumped, but even as he fell he saw Vargalf burying the blade into Kai's side.

Once.

Twice.

Then Erlan crashed onto them, knocking Vargalf away, sending the dagger skidding for the shadows.

Erlan thought nothing of his burnt skin, his mauled wrists, his wretched nakedness. His only thought was to grind the life out of that man. He leaped on him, his shackled fists smashing into Vargalf's blood-slicked face. The overlord fell back, then rolled aside. Erlan scrambled after him, dragging his chain like a fire-worm's tail.

He snatched his tunic and yanked hard. Vargalf flopped over. Erlan jammed his shackles under his chin, the metal biting into the wound Kai had inflicted. Vargalf groaned. Erlan answered with a madman's laugh, filled with a strength he didn't understand. Snot bubbled bloody from Vargalf's nose and his dark eyes widened, panic-stricken.

But there was a sudden force crushing Erlan's neck, cutting off his breath. He saw the chain in Vargalf's hand. The overlord pulled. Erlan's head snapped back, breaking his grip, his neck twisting crazily. He rolled with it and flipped onto his back. Vargalf was under him now, hands hauling like an ox on the metal noose around his neck. There was no air – only pain, only animal grunts, only pressure, as if his skull would explode any moment in a shower of brains and blood. Vision began to blur. His fingers tore at the links, his blistered heels raking at the hard-packed floor. The strange surge of strength was leaching out of him. It would be over soon. All Vargalf had to do was hang on.

Erlan kicked and skidded, desperate to get a grip. His sight was fading, the smoky rafters shrinking to blackness. He heard an ugly cackle, thick in Vargalf's throat.

'The – end – comes – fast – *cripple*!'

But this couldn't be the end. This wasn't the end. The strength that stretched from the dawn of men did not die here.

With one last, colossal effort, he smashed one heel and then the other into the packed mud. His crippled ankle shrieked with pain, a river of fire racing to his skull. But the floor gave and now he had a foothold. He shoved, shoved like he had to topple a mountain, shoved like he had to uproot Yggdrasil and every one of the Nine Worlds hanging from its boughs.

His head smashed like Thor's hammer into Vargalf's face. The choking pressure round his throat vanished and then he was beating back his head, again and again, smashing down with all his waning strength, driving the overlord's nose back into his brain. He heard teeth splinter, cheekbones shatter and split. The chain hung slack and now, his throat freed, a scream of primal rage broke from his lips, a scream for survival, a scream for vengeance, a scream for thirst, for blood, for savage pain, for death.

He spun around and brought down his shackled fists with a crash, pounding again and again into the red pulp of fractured bone and blood and gristle that had once been Vargalf's face. He pounded for Bodvar, for Rorik, for Sviggar, he pounded for Kai, pounded for himself, until his fists beat at nothing but the wet, red mud while the sound of his own mad scream rang in his ears.

'Erlan.' A weak voice. 'Erlan...' again. 'He's dead. Leave him. He's dead!'

Finally the words penetrated the fog of blind fury. His fists slackened, making limp, wet slaps against the ground, and then... ceased.

He slumped back, pain crashing in on all sides at once. His head hung like a dead flower. His face was a black and red smear, his hair a snarl of sweat and blood and filth.

'Erlan.' He shook his head, eyes blinking as if he saw nothing. 'Erlan!'

He looked over at Kai and at last he saw him. The lad was on his back, head tilted, a dark scarlet smear daubing one cheek. Where his eye should have been, there was only a sunken black hole, brimming thick clots of blood. The other – unnaturally bright and blue as a spring sky – stared at him, eyelid flickering. Erlan felt weak. His skin stung like he'd been flayed to the bone. But he knew he had to reach Kai.

He slid off Vargalf's faceless corpse and crawled over, the chain strung out behind, his blistered feet dragging through the filth. Reaching Kai, he sat up.

Only then did he see the floor on the other side of Kai and his heart sank. A lake of blood fanned from the wounds in his side, shimmering black and orange in the firelight.

The raven's wine... Enough to slake an army.

'Let me help you.' He lifted Kai's head into his lap.

'Ain't no helping me now.' Kai's voice was faint and ragged.

Erlan shook his head. Kai's face looked strange in the fire's flicker – half living, half already dead. Like the face of Hel herself. 'You came back for me.'

Kai grimaced. 'I had to.'

'Vargalf said you were dead.'

'Bet he wishes I were now.' He tried to laugh but it stuck. 'You look terrible.'

'You don't look so good yourself, little brother.' Erlan grinned, pushing Kai's fringe away from his good eye. 'Where were you all this time?'

'In the woods... They never caught me.' He closed his good eye and sighed. 'Is the fire dying?'

Erlan glanced over. It was still burning strong. He shook his head.

'Funny... So cold.' He clutched Erlan's hand. His fingers were like icicles. 'Is there water?'

The pot in the corner was empty, Erlan knew. He shook his head again. 'I'm sorry.'

'Doesn't matter... It'll be over soon. For me... But you must live.' He gave a sudden suck at the air as a spasm passed through him. 'Listen... there are things I must tell you. Things I saw.' His voice was so quiet. 'Bodvar is dead.'

'I know.'

'They trampled him. Sigurd's horses...' He tried to twist his head to see Erlan better. 'They'd have done the same to you.'

'Stay still, brother.'

'They meant to kill you.' Erlan squeezed his hand. 'But now – now they can't.'

'We'll leave this rotten hole. Should've a long time ago.'

Kai almost smiled. 'Think I'll stay here... if it's all one to you.'

'No. You go where I go. That's what you always told me.' The words sounded hollow as a reed.

'Listen to me. There's more. Sviggar's bairns... That son of a whore strangled them.'

'Svein and Katla?'

'Buried them in the forest,' Kai choked. 'I saw him.'

Erlan swore. He tried to picture the two younglings, but found he couldn't without seeing them in the folds of Lilla's skirts. But they weren't hers. They were the queen's, and now they too were dead.

His body was too weak to feel more hate. He felt only a kind of weary acknowledgement: that nothing as innocent as children, not even her own, could exist alongside Saldas.

'Sigurd is bringing war,' Kai muttered. 'There's an army about these halls... every tongue I ever heard and more. Like he's ready for the fire-battle that'll end it all.'

'The *Ragnarök*?'

Kai snorted. 'Would've made a fine song... Too bad I won't be there to sing it.'

'I'll make a song for you.'

'You?' Kai smiled. 'You haven't got the rhyme of a dead goat.' His breathing came quick and shallow now.

Erlan looked down, a lump swelling in his throat.

'Reckon I'll take my leave now, master.'

'Stay... Stay, brother. Just a while longer.' He felt his eyes welling up.

'I'll try, brother... if you tell me one thing.'

'If I can—'

'You can...' Kai's cheek was cold as stone against Erlan's

hand. His one eye gazed steadily at Erlan. 'Tell me who you are.'

At first, Erlan said nothing, but his mind began to swirl with his past, the past he had tried so hard to lock away. The past he had sworn he would share with no one.

'My father named me Hakan. My name is Hakan, son of Haldan, son of Haldor the Black, Lord of the Vendlings and chief of the Northern Jutes. I am the chosen son of my father. I was to be lord of my people.' They were simple words to say, yet why did they stir in him such muddy clouds of shame? His eyes dropped.

'Hakan? That's your name?'

He nodded.

Kai smiled. 'It's a good name. And you're a good master... A good brother.'

A tear slipped from Erlan's eye and ran in a grimy trail down his cheek, then dropped onto Kai's face.

'Hakan, son of Haldan. If you love me at all, do this for me.'

'Say it and it's done.'

'Swear to me...' Kai's voice faltered, but his hand gripped like a vice. 'Swear you'll be revenged on Saldas. For Bara's sake... And for mine.'

'I swear it.'

Kai released his grip and let his head fall back. Under the streaks of mud his face was very pale now, but his lips wore a wide and peaceful smile. 'That's an end then...' Erlan could feel the pool of blood spreading wet against his knees. 'Go, Hakan. You're free now. Go!' Erlan's tears were falling freely onto Kai's face. 'Don't weep for me, Hakan... I can see it all clear now. I did what I was here to do.' He smiled, his ice-blue eye twinkling one last time. 'You must do the same...'

His head went limp in Erlan's hands and his bright eye now dimmed with the final shadow of death, leaving only a frozen smile that cut through the dried blood that had welled from his broken eye. Gently, Erlan closed the other for the last time.

He sat like that a long while, his heart so heavy he thought he might never rise from that spot again. But he had sworn an oath. To see it done, he must live.

At last he shuffled backwards and laid Kai's head on the ground. Then, with every bone aching, every inch of skin stinging, he climbed to his feet. The chain still hung from his bloody wrists.

He looked around and his eye fell on the iron rod that had been left against the wall. He recognized it with disgust: remembered it, red with heat, branding Rorik's ravaged body. Swallowing the pain, he wedged it between his knees and jammed the end under one of the cuffs. His wrists screamed in protest, but he pushed on, twisting the shackle against the black iron. Twisting and twisting, growling in agony and effort, till every sinew in his arm was about to snap. But there was a sudden crack, the rivet-heads popped and the shackle flew off.

He gasped in relief, not daring to look at his ruined flesh. Instead, he jammed the rod into the second shackle and strained again. Moments later, there was a merciful popping sound and the rivets spat like apple-pips against the wall. The cuffs fell to the ground.

For a few seconds he waited, rocking back and forth until the worst of the pain had ebbed away. Then he looked down. Black and purple bruises circled his wrists. The skin was a mangle of red and pink and grimy white shreds of flesh, running with pus. They throbbed. But they would heal.

He gazed on the ruin of Vargalf's face: his wounds would not.

Erlan grimaced. He was free. He looked around and saw Wrathling, discarded to one side. He hobbled over and picked it up. Vargalf's possession of it had been short-lived.

What did the son of a bitch expect? The runes on its hilt cursed the hand of anyone but its rightful owner. Vargalf should have known this.

He peered into one of the murky corners. The miserable heap of clothing was still there where they'd tossed it when they stripped him. He went and picked them up. Damp, rotting, ragged. But they would serve. As he dressed, he found under them his belt, cut from the Witch King's tail. Gnarled leather, crudely worked – no man would envy him this. But he was sure it carried with it some dark strength. Fastening it, he then gathered up the other weapons and cast a final look around the scene of so much torment.

Better that it burns. All of it.

He snatched the torch from the sconce and held it to the wall till the flame took and began to creep up towards the thatch. Then he tossed the remnant of the torch into the fire.

Kai lay beside it, still as stone... peaceful. As though only sleeping next to a warm hearth.

'Let the fire carry you home, little brother. Wherever that may be.' That said, he went to the door and slipped outside into the darkness.

After the smokehouse, the air smelled sharp and clean.

He was about to move off into the shadows, but he hesitated. A solitary, glinting eye was peering at him out of the gloom. He saw movement and a shape detached itself from the darkness.

Long limbs loped towards him, then stopped.

A dog. A wolfhound, its long pink tongue hanging low, tasting the air. One eye gazed at him, cold and questioning. Its twin was nothing more than an empty shadow.

For a moment, man and beast stood motionless, watching each other.

Inside the smokehouse, the flames crackled, taking hold of the timber and thatch. The noise distracted the hound. It turned to the door, lifting its nose at the smell of smoke and blood and death.

When it looked back, Erlan was gone.

PART FOUR

THE PLAINS OF BRAVIK

CHAPTER
FIFTY-FIVE

G ellir the White had found it at last.
Dannerborg. Seat of his enemies.

He pulled his hood low over his brow. The gods had given him a face that folk remembered. Now, more than ever, he needed to be invisible.

He had approached from the west, abandoning the horse he'd stolen, flitting from cover to cover like a fox, closing in, till he reached the woods carpeting the hill above Dannerborg. There he stopped and waited and watched – the gate, the guards, the palisade – watching folk coming and going.

The place was awash with men of war. Most were idling or practising strokes or wrestling or drinking. He quickly saw there were far too many for anyone to note an unfamiliar figure moving among them, especially not in the dusk-light.

It was simple enough to slip through the gates on the tail of a hay-cart without even a blink from the guards. And now he sat in a gloomy corner of the hall-yard, whittling a piece of wood.

Waiting. Watching under the brim of his hood, his pink eyes bathed in shadow, thinking of the great Lord Ringast.

The excrement who had flayed his twin brother.

The Wartooth's son would pay for what he had done. They all would.

Gellir rolled his shoulder to test the wound from the arrow. The muscle was stiff as bark. He squeezed it, feeling the ache as the blood rushed into it.

After his escape from Ulvar's Crossing, he had crawled out of the river a quarter league downstream. He had managed to stem the worst of the bleeding but the fever must have been in him by then. He walked for leagues, avoiding all villages and hamlets, until the throbbing in his shoulder and his head had reduced him to a stumble. At last, he came across a lonely homestead, far from any other place – the dwelling of an old woodcutter and his young wife. He collapsed on their doorstep.

She hadn't been scared of his face. They had taken him in, tended him, though the fever gripped him for weeks. All the while his mind drifted through strange visions. Faces mainly, dozens of them. People he had killed, their pitiful, pathetic pleas frozen in the instant of death. Faces that might have tormented another man but he found them only ridiculous.

Eventually the woodsman's wife's poultices and brews began to tell and he became strong again. The time came to leave. They had a horse. He needed it. Things got a little ugly when the old man objected. And then that business with his wife...

Well, what did they expect? There were only two types of people in this world: hunters and their prey.

And now he had found this place.

His older brothers were dead. His twin, dead. His father, dead. There was nothing in him now but revenge. Blood called for blood.

He settled down under his cloak and waited for the dead of night, nursing one thought and one only:

The Wartooth, his sons, their seed... All of them must die.

Erlan Aurvandil slipped his feet into the water and sucked in sharply. The skin wouldn't heal for days, maybe weeks, but salt water seemed to ease the pain a little. Bubbles chuckled between his toes as the boat cut through the firth waters.

Shapes slipped by in the pre-dawn gloom: ragged islets blanketed with spruce, ringed with rocks, bloated and smooth, tumbling into the dark water. By his reckoning, the mouth of the Great Bay must be close. After that, the open sea, and Sveäland would glide, along with everything else, into his past.

A north-easterly wind sighed. He tasted salt and breathed a little easier. In three days he'd come many leagues and hardly a moment had he felt safe. Every jar of his bones, every chafe of his legs, every needle-prick of pain, he'd expected the shout of pursuit. But it never came.

He had hobbled away from the nightmare, fleeing on the first horse he found before the hall-folk had even awoken to the flames devouring the smokehouse and its horrors. Once clear of the halls, he flung himself into the first stream he came to, washing weeks of filth and blood off his wasted body, soothing his fire-raw limbs. But the water couldn't wash away what he had seen. Or what he had done.

Are you a man or a monster, my son?

His mother's question.

He knew not the answer. Something monstrous had possessed him by the end, some ancient rage. Was that him or something else?

He found the boat where Kai had said it would be, hidden half a league east of Sigtuna in a craggy inlet, under brushwood and bracken. A sturdy little *knarr* of the kind merchant-men used to come and go across the East Sea. He made her ready, then pushed off into the fjord, leaving the horse grazing near the shoreline.

He was heading east through the Throat and out of the mouth of the Great Bay. Yet long after pursuit by land was impossible, he still found himself looking over his shoulder, half-expecting riders to break from the treeline and cry his name.

But the only sounds in the night had been the breeze trembling against the sail and the trickle of the clinker-hull over the surface of the moonlit water. Darkness gave way to morning. Only with the first taste of salt air did he allow himself to believe he had escaped. Only then did he ask himself where he was headed.

Kai was dead. His best friend. *His last friend.* As for the others... they were dead or scattered.

So where should he go?

He felt the sea surge under the tiller. The salt-spray flecked his wrists, stinging his wounds. A good pain, he thought. *It means I'm alive.*

Aye, he was alive. But Kai was dead.

A pang of sorrow rose like bile in his throat. Kai could have lived. Instead he had come back. Yet hadn't the Norns woven him that fate long ago? Hadn't he seen it in the burning flames and bloody rain of his dream?

Erlan wondered what those dark sisters were weaving now, for him. His *urðr*. He could almost hear the click-clack of the Norns' needles. But so far as he could read their pattern, they wanted only to strip him: of fealty, of friendship, of love. Of anything of light or goodness that touched his life, sucking it all down into their black well of tears and giving him nothing in return.

So where should he go?

He knew little of the lands beyond any horizon. The white lands of winter to the north were a mystery. He knew the great market-harbour of Rerik lay somewhere to the south. He might find service there among the lords of Wendland, or even further south in Frankia. Or he could go east, to Estland and beyond, to the great rivers of which Sviggar had spoken. Behind him lay only darkness. Yet the roads that lay ahead seemed just as obscure.

He was free to choose.

Maybe freedom is darkness. The future, an emptiness, vague and shifting as a mist. But looking inside himself, he found only one thing of any substance. His oath to Kai. No, it was more than an oath. It was a debt. He owed Kai his life, owed him his revenge.

He thought of Sigurd and Saldas, of their foul betrayals – betrayals not only of him. What evil they had wrought on Sviggar, his oath-lord? Didn't he owe him vengeance as much as his friend?

And Lilla?

He tried to imagine sailing on, leaving the whole pack of them to devour each other like rabid wolves until there was none left standing. But the realization came to him stark and certain: he would have no peace until Sigurd and his queen were destroyed.

The clouds of Odin's storm were gathering, the *Valkyries* readying their steeds. The great slaughter that was Vargalf's dream seemed inexorable now, unstoppable as time or tide.

So where should he go?

The first ray of morning broke the horizon, stabbing his eyes. Dawn was come, pouring out its golden fire over the glistening water like the mead of the gods. He spat sour phlegm over the gunwale and suddenly the image of Kai's ruined face came tripping over the waves, calling him, demanding his answer.

He sighed, deep and long, then pulled the tiller towards him, letting the wind fill out the sail.

The bows swung to the south.

CHAPTER
FÍFTY-SÍX

L illa rolled over. Her head was pounding. She had gone deeper than she meant to, and for longer too. Night had now fallen.

As her eyes grew accustomed to the gloom, shapes began to materialize: the gnarled old rowan tree, the glade of oaks corralling the stars above. The air was heavy with the smell of silverweed and sorrel, and above that the lingering whisps of Urtha's Weed, still smoking in the little pan.

Ringast would be angry that she was late. But she didn't care. She had needed to be alone, needed the solace of her mother's world for a while.

The circle remained where she had drawn it in the earth, the four runes marked in its centre.

Fehu – Freyja's mark – for luck. For the change that was coming. A shifting of the world when things would reveal their true nature, including her. Then *eihwaz* – the yew-tree – the mark of Heimdall, the whitest of the gods. A mark for strength and steadfastness. She would need both before the leaves of autumn fell. Above these, she had drawn *laguz* – the mark of water. A mark for purity of thought and sight. To help her see the way ahead and what she must do. And last of all, *dagaz* – the dawn-mark. A mark to summon the light to break through the darkness of confusion and dispel the evil that seemed to be closing in on her and all she loved.

But the runes had done nothing. Urtha's Weed had led nowhere. All she had seen was a chaos of faces, all she had heard a tumult of voices crying out in fear and anger – and closer to her whisperings that seemed to portend much, yet were too soft to discern.

She cursed in frustration. Half-wise, her mother had called her. Half-wise she was, unable to grasp fully the gifts her mother had bestowed on her.

Her throat was dry. The taste on her tongue was smoky and bitter. Her senses were still unsteady, still caught in that twilight place between this world and the eight others that adorned *Yggdrasil*, the Tree of Worlds. She had hoped to see her father. Hoped that the grief in her heart might call him to her while his spirit was not long departed. When he didn't come, she had let herself believe it was because he was still alive. But then she found even that too much to dare. And of all the rest, only one face stayed with her, etched in her mind like runes on a barrow-stone.

To think of it turned her blood to ice.

It was a child – an infant really, no more, with its back to her. She had reached out and touched its shoulder, not knowing whether it was a boy or girl. The child turned and she had recoiled in horror. Its face was half-formed, warped and bloody, its mouth a shapeless maw.

She tried to wipe the image from her mind. When she couldn't, she tried to explain it away instead. This was fear, nothing more.

A mother's fear...

She had told no one that she had missed her moon-blood, not even Gerutha. She had hardly dared admit it to herself. But the quickening of life inside her was undeniable.

The mother of kings.

So she was destined to be. It seemed her destiny had wasted no time reaching out to her. Already it had been several weeks since her marriage-night. That first strange, loveless coupling. She had taken Ringast's seed, nonetheless. And if the goddess Frigg meant to bless that marriage bed, then she was carrying a Danish child.

But if not...

She refused to name the alternative, even to herself.

She got shakily to her feet and tried to expel the dizziness from her head in one long breath. Her keys jangled. She touched them and suddenly felt irresponsible to have hidden herself away in this wood when she might have been needed. Gathering her things, she stumbled through the trees along the worn old path back towards the hall.

She could smell the campfires burning before she left the wood, could see their dancing orange flames. The tents of five thousand warriors were spread along the lakeshore. Idle men, with only one object. *War.* That was why they had come. To slake their thirst for fame, to sate their hunger for a glorious death.

She had sacrificed love in order to save them from this madness. But now that sacrifice looked ever more futile. If her father was dead, then her brother must now hold the crown. She knew only too well what he would do with it. The Wide-Realm had been his long-cherished dream. But in the mind of a king, even a dream that vain could become a reality. And many would die in its pursuit.

She looked about her – faces looming and disappearing in the darkness. Walking among them, she felt their eyes on her. The bolder ones called out a greeting – their words a good deal more respectful than their gaze, which was sure to follow her long after she had passed.

She pulled her cloak tight about her shoulders. She had been careless tonight. The effects of the smoke were still heavy on her senses. She had inhaled too much and now she was late and having to return before they had worn off.

Once inside the gate, the yard was quiet. A few forges were still glowing but the hammers had long fallen silent for the night. Folk had already retreated to their hearths, or even to their beds.

She wasn't hungry. She wanted only to lie down in darkness so that her whirling mind could settle. She could change nothing tonight, anyway.

Half-stumbling her way along the dim corridor, her heart fell to see Sletti gliding towards her.

'Might I get you anything, my lady?'

Only my bed. And a night untroubled by irksome thralls, she thought unkindly. 'Nothing... Although you can send Gerutha to me.' Her handmaid was discreet and, unlike Sletti, didn't peer at her with that false obsequiousness. These were welcome qualities, given her state.

'I shall go and find her, my lady.'

'I'll be in my chamber.' She pushed past him before he could see her bloodshot eyes.

The oil lamps were already burning low. The shadows seemed to close in on her, making her feel giddy, so that she had to palm the walls to keep her balance.

How could I have been so careless?

She half-hoped her husband was sat up drinking with Thrand or Ubbi or any of the other so-called champions. But when she slipped through the drapes and entered their chamber, the furs on the bed stirred.

She felt the colour rise to her cheeks as he rolled over and sat up. The flame-flicker made his torso gleam like bronze.

'Where have you been?'

She went to a sideboard and set down her pouch with her back to him. 'In the wood.'

'Again?' Her practices were no secret from him, but that didn't mean he liked them. 'I'll never understand why you can't just leave all that for the *goðar*? It's not fitting for a highborn woman.'

'It was good enough for my mother.' She sounded more defensive than she meant. The pulse was thumping in her temples like Volund's hammer. 'The gift of the far sight shouldn't be denied.'

'The far sight,' he scoffed. 'You haven't seen my brother in your... whatever you call these visits.'

'No.' A thousand other faces. But not the one her husband wanted. Nor the one she wanted to see.

'So what use is it?'

'The gods reveal what they reveal.' She shrugged.

He grunted. 'Perhaps you need to be a little more persuasive.'

She shuddered involuntarily, remembering nine frozen bodies hanging from the Sacred Oak. That was how Saldas had wooed the gods. And worse, they had listened.

'Look, I don't want you going there any more. Staying out after dark with Hel only knows what characters prowling around looking for sport? It's madness. Do you realize what sort of men are camped down there?'

'Well, you invited them here, didn't you?' she snapped, a wave of dizziness rocking through her. She steadied herself against the sideboard. 'Besides, they wouldn't dare touch your wife.'

'I'm glad you have so much faith in their restraint.'

'You're over-reacting.'

'No more of this, understand? I forbid it. That's an end to it.'

'You can't stop me doing what I've always done.'

'That's exactly what I can do.'

Suddenly the drapes parted and Gerutha appeared. For an awkward moment none of them moved, other than Gerutha's bright eyes flicking between her lord and her mistress. Ringast sank sullenly back and rolled towards the wall, leaving the handmaid to her work.

Lilla let Gerutha busy about her, trying not to catch her eye as she unpinned her head-cloth, unfastened brooches, removed her belt and keys, lifted her short outer dress over her head and helped her out of her robe. At last she stood before the mirror wearing only her linen shift, while Gerutha's fingers fussed over her night-braid. She closed her eyes, enjoying Gerutha's lightness of touch, trying not to let her anger boil any hotter against her husband.

'Finished, my lady.'

Lilla's eyes snapped open. She felt suddenly embarrassed – to be caught dozing off on her feet. She thanked Gerutha and hastily gave her leave.

Her maid removed the last remaining torch from its sconce and went out, leaving only a small oil lamp burning in one corner. Lilla slid under the fur next to her husband.

For a while they lay next to each other in silence. She felt the heat of his body, heard the masculine pitch of his breath. She stared at the rafters. They seemed to sway like rushes in a wind. She palmed her brow, wishing the pounding would go away.

'I'm sorry,' he whispered. 'I married you. All of you. Even the things I don't like,' he chuckled. Not many men would admit that, thought Lilla. He tilted her face towards him. 'You understand I'm just fearful on your behalf.'

'I know.'

He blew out a long sigh. 'If I'm honest, it's my kid brother that's nettling me. Thrand is all guts and gristle. But Rorik – he's young. Soft-hearted. I shouldn't have let him go.'

For a long while, Lilla didn't know how to reply. But she wanted to give this man something. Something good... anyway, he was bound to find out sooner or later.

'I have something to tell you.' He rolled over and looked her in the eye. 'I hope it will cheer you.'

'What is it?'

'I'm carrying your child.' She watched a smile dawn slowly on his face. It was no lie that she wanted the child to be his. Even if it were born with dark hair and dark eyes... it was his.

'A child, already?' A grin broader than she'd ever seen there before formed on his rugged face. His hand slid over her belly.

'It seems Frigg was in a hurry to bless us.' She laughed nervously. 'Are you pleased?'

'Pleased? Gods, I'm delighted!'

She laughed again, feeling a little giddy, as if she were hovering above the bed, watching herself, prompting her replies. 'Then so am I.' And why not? Wasn't this her destiny? *The mother of kings.* That had always been her future. Now it was her present. Or soon.

He was murmuring sweet words, moving on top of her, praising her as the best of wives. Perhaps she was. She let him make love to her, riding the wave of his passion, and never once thinking of ...*him*. At least, not until it was over. And then, with Erlan's face in her mind, she let her husband caress her belly, let him savour the promise of his own life-blood, secure now, flowing on down the rivers of time.

Ringast fell asleep with a smile on his face. She soon followed into a weary sort of oblivion. But Freyja was mocking her. The far-seeing goddess of *seidr* had no intention of giving her a dreamless sleep. Instead, Lilla felt the wind of the beating wings again against her cheek, then a noose squeezing her throat, squeezing the breath out of her, and she saw the figure again, the stunted, stooping figure with its tousled hair, and her hand moved out – full of dread – and touched the child's shoulder, turned it towards her. And when she looked upon it, its little features seemed to melt away like tallow in a stream of blood. She tried to scream but the noose was too tight —

Her eyes lurched open. She sat up. Her mouth was wide in a silent cry with her tongue sticking out, dry as bark. She was just thirsty – and her mind was playing games with her. That was all. There was no truth in it. It was only thirst... and the echoes of Urtha's Weed.

Beside her, Ringast slept on. She slipped out of bed and fumbled her way to the stand in the corner where a pitcher of water stood. She was already halfway across the room when she noticed the oil lamp had gone out. The shadows seemed darker than before.

She shivered, telling herself it was from the cold, not wanting to admit to the whisper of fear in her heart. She felt her way to the table, groping, half-blind, till she found the jug, filled a beaker, poured it down her throat, refilled it, drained it a second time.

Gods – but she needed sleep.

Slower this time, she drank a third cup, at last feeling her thirst slaked. Then she tiptoed back to their bed and slid under the covers.

She lay back and gazed up into the lattice of rafters. For what seemed like hours, her eyes wandered among the beams, sleep always just beyond the grasp of her weary mind. She could hear her heartbeat and her husband's breathing. Beyond that, the mead-hall and all under its roof were swathed in silence.

She felt a ripple of air over her face. There was a soft sound like the sweep of a brush – hardly a sound at all – and in the crook of her eye, a flicker. She looked over at the drape. It was so dark she could hardly see the doorframe, though she thought she perceived a slight waver of shadow. She looked harder, only now all was absolutely still.

Perhaps she had imagined it.

She imagined so many things...

She closed her eyes, pushing away her fears and her worries and her regrets... But it was no good. Sleep still escaped her.

She opened her eyes, and found herself looking into the most terrifying face she had ever seen.

Skin so pale, hair so white that her mind flew like a comet to the nightmares of childhood – a *draugr* – one of the dead returned from the halls of Hel holding a long blade, deadly sharp, poised above her husband's face.

Without a second thought, she threw herself at him. Her head and shoulder smashed into his torso, sending them crashing off the bed in a snarl of limbs. She heard a curse, her head butted the ground, then a lean hand was over her mouth stifling her scream.

She bit down hard, tasting blood and dirt and wood-smoke. The killer hissed in pain. On the bed Ringast was stirring but not nearly quick enough. The seax blade flashed. She lunged for his wrist, stopping the edge bare inches from her eyes, but his other arm was round her neck, squeezing tighter, pulling her back on top of him.

A growl sounded in her throat as she fought desperately to hold off the blade. If she were stronger, she could have prised off his arm or crushed his groin or... something! But he was too powerful and his sinewy forearm was squeezing the life out of her.

For a second, she wondered whether she was asleep and this was just another nightmare. But there was another cry. Then a foot slammed into the man's skull.

He rolled away, groaning and she wriggled clear, gasping, her throat burning. Then a shadow seemed to fall on him. She heard a squall of grunting and scuffling and butting and curses. Ringast must have hurled himself bodily into the fight. But what chance did he have, naked and unarmed?

Arms. Weapons.

The word jolted her brain. Of course! Ringast's sword was in the corner, as it was every night. If she could get it, she could end this fight. She forced herself to her feet. At once the giddiness hit her again like a slap in the face. She practically fell into the corner, cursing the darkness, throwing her arms about until at last her fist struck something solid, its shape familiar. The sword clattered to the floor. She threw herself down, fingers scraping at the floorboards. Behind her there was a cry of pain and a horrible laugh she knew was not her husband's.

Then she had it, her hands scuttling apart till she found the hilt. She felt strength surge through her as she began to drag it free. But suddenly the roots of her hair screamed, her head yanked back and sharp steel kissed her throat.

'No – no – no, my lady,' hissed a sibilant voice in her ear. 'Leave it where it lies.' The wicked edge pressed deeper into her skin.

It didn't feel real. Any of it. She hesitated.

'Do as he says!' That was Ringast's voice. 'Lilla!'

She let the hilt drop. The half-drawn sword hit the ground with a clang. Immediately the killer pulled her to her feet and spun her round. In the gloom, she saw her husband on his knees, clutching at his chest. Wounded, but alive.

'You should have gone for your sword instead of your woman,' sneered the killer in his grating whisper.

Ringast made to get up. At once Lilla's head was pulled back harder and the pale man's bicep tightened.

'Not another move, Dane. Unless you want the floor painted with your wife's blood. Call for help, it'll be the same.'

'Who are you? What do you want?'

The man didn't answer at once. Instead he toed the floor till he'd found the sword and kicked it behind him. 'Who am I? Aye – that's the question, eh? But you ought to know.' He chuckled – a thin, hissing sound. 'A man should know why he's about to die.'

'Do I know you?'

'Not so well as you knew my brother. Gettir the Black.'

Lilla saw Ringast's shadow stiffened. 'You're the White... Your brother was a murderer. So are you.'

'You had him flayed alive.' That's a lie, thought Lilla. Her husband would never do something so cruel.

'No less than he did to dozens of my people,' replied Ringast. Lilla could hardly believe her ears. 'No less than you did yourself.'

'So now you know why I'm here.'

'If it's me you want, let her go. She's nothing to you.'

'But she's something to you, isn't she?' His lips were close enough for Lilla to feel the heat of his breath. 'The Danish dog got himself a new bitch, didn't he? Everyone knows that.' He gave an ugly snigger.

Ringast said nothing, only shuffled forward on his knees.

'No-no.' The White pressed the knife closer. Ringast froze. 'I'm the only one left now, thanks to you and your father. There's a blood debt to be paid.'

'We'll give you silver.' Ringast was trying to sound calm, but Lilla could hear the alarm creeping into his voice. 'However much you want. Just let her go.'

'She must be a good ride, huh? Or is there something in here you're worried about?' His fingers spread over her stomach. Lilla shuddered. 'That's it, isn't it? More spawn of that crooked old cocksucker!' Suddenly he shoved his hand down between her thighs. She struggled, tried to pull away, revolted by his touch, but the steel edge only bit deeper, this time drawing blood. 'Still wet with your muck.' He scoffed. 'Ain't no amount of silver can buy what I want.'

'What *do* you want?'

'The blood of the Wartooth and all his seed. All of it. Down to the last fucking drop.'

Lilla felt his grip on the seax tighten. Her husband cried out. There was a short, sharp sting as the knife began to cut into her neck.

She blinked and suddenly blood was gushing down her chest over her breasts, soaking her shift. There was a strange gurgling noise in her ear, a sucking sound, a clatter and something heavy slumped against her back, almost pulling her down to the floor. Then a thud.

How painless death is, after all, she thought, feeling nothing.

Everything was slow as if moving underwater. Her husband was lurching to his feet, pulling her tight to his blood-slicked chest. Her vision was a blur of shadows. She turned, wondering why the *draugr*-man had let her go, but where he'd been stood a woman instead, trembling like a sail in a squall, her eyes mad and staring, a streak of white in her hair.

That was when Lilla knew she must still be dreaming. She looked down and saw that other face, the pale face, shining up at her like a fallen moon, and jutting from his neck was the bloody haft of Gerutha's work-knife.

CHAPTER
FIFTY-SEVEN

Sigurd's reflection in the mirror stretched, threaded his fingers behind his head and leaned back against the wall.

Saldas could feel his eyes roaming over her body while she combed out the final tresses of hair. She put down her comb, drew her dark mane over one shoulder and turned towards him.

He was regarding her with the same thirsty expression she had often noted in his eyes since she first came to these halls. Before it had been clandestine. Now he wore it brazen as the sun.

She let her shift fall to the floor.

'Come to bed.'

She moved towards him, lithe as a serpent. Soon as she was in reach he pulled her down and rolled her onto her back. She drew in a deep breath and purred, her breasts swelling against his chest. He slid his hand up her stomach, then cupped her soft orb of flesh. She felt her nipple tighten. He bent down, circled his tongue around it.

'Hard as an acorn,' he whispered.

'Just what your father would say.'

He looked up sharply. 'Why did you have to say that?'

She glared at him, feeling little but contempt, then shook her head. 'Forget it. I don't feel like this tonight.' She rolled away.

'You're my queen and my wife.' He gripped her arm. 'You'll do as your king demands.'

She jerked round. 'Do you know how pathetic that sounds? Oh, I certainly would do as my king demanded if the king was any kind of man.'

'What are you talking about?'

'How is it you still dawdle around these halls while the cripple lives?'

'Erlan?'

'You let him slip through your fingers. He's made a laughing stock of you – of you and that... *slave* of yours.' To say Vargalf had proved a disappointment was a towering understatement.

'We hunted for him for days. We don't know which way he went.'

'There's only one way he could have gone. South, you dolt! To the Danes. Into the arms of your enemies... and his love,' she added acidly.

'His love?'

'Your sister! Gods, were you blind to that as well?'

'Bah! If he loves my sister, he's the fool. Besides, he'll find no friends among the Wartooth's sons. Those he has left,' he sniggered. 'No. The cripple has fled for good. By sea, like as not.'

'Evidently, you don't know him as I do. He has gone to them, and by now he'll have told them all that's gone on here. Ringast will know your strength is growing. You must strike at once, without delay. That's what a king would do. Instead, you lie here, pawing at me like a little boy.'

Sigurd scoffed, though she could see the insult had struck. 'You heard Rorik crowing like a cockerel. Ringast will sit on his arse waiting for news from his boy-loving brother. Ha! He'll be waiting a long time. Meanwhile they'll stick to their oaths.'

'You think they haven't guessed the worst for Rorik by now?'

Sigurd considered this. 'That's soon fixed. We send a messenger, purporting to be from him, telling them to await his word.'

'It's too late, you fool! Erlan will have carried the truth to them by now.'

'We don't know that.'

'You're as blind as your father. First you let this man who... who *violated* my body and your honour escape justice – aye, and the man you told your earls was a traitor in the pay of the Wartooth – and now you sit back and hand the initiative to your enemies. Do you think your earls will tolerate such weakness in their king?'

'No one can call me weak with the strength I have now. With Starkad's ships, we have ten thousand spears. We will defeat any foe that stands against us. Starting with these sons of Autha's line.'

'It's not enough to defeat them. You must slaughter every one of them. Grind their bones into the dust, soak the earth with their blood.' She watched her fervour spark in his close-set eyes. 'And your sister must die as well.'

'Lilla?'

'Of course.' She reached out and traced a nail down his chest and around his nipple. 'Your crown will never be secure until every possible seed of revenge is destroyed. After what you've done, Lilla's sons must come for you.'

'We did it together.'

'I merely served your will.' She squeezed the hard nub of flesh, heard his intake of breath. 'It was your decision to take the crown from your father. All the more reason that you'll never win my love nor peace of mind until you've cut out your sister's womb.'

'You are a pitiless she-wolf, aren't you?' he snorted. 'Lilla's out of the way. We need only defeat her husband. She can do us no harm now.'

'Do you dare baulk at this when I didn't spare my own children to serve your ends?' It had been a dark deed – perhaps the darkest she'd ever done – but she had steeled herself to it. It had been the condition on which Sigurd had insisted, on which everything had hung. Having now met it, there was no way she would let Sigurd pay a lower price than her.

His grey gaze flicked between her eyes. 'Very well. She dies. Are you happy?'

Her lip curled in a shallow smile. 'Not quite. There's something else I want.'

'What?'

'The Aurvandil's heart.'

'And how the Hel am I supposed to bring you that? He's probably halfway to Miklagard by now. Or else – if the gods are good – at the bottom of the East Sea in whatever worm-eaten tub he stole.'

'The bones say otherwise. The cripple lives.'

'Well then, my gentle queen, if it's in my power, I'll fetch his heart for you. You can even eat it, for all I care. I know you have a taste for such things.'

'To see it will suffice.'

'Satisfied?'

'I will be – if you move, with all your men... tomorrow.'

'Tomorrow? Out of the question. We've not yet mustered our full strength. And Starkad is not yet—'

'If he doesn't come this far north, we can save time,' she interrupted, weary of his excuses. 'Send word to him. We march with the strength we have and meet his fleet somewhere south of the Kolmark.'

'Like where?'

'Gods, must I lead you by the nose every step like some dumb ox?'

'Well? Do you have a place in mind?'

'Why not Bravik? It's a large fjord – large enough to shelter Starkad's fleet – and the road south passes close by to the west.'

'Bravik,' Sigurd repeated. He nodded. 'Very well. Bravik it shall be.'

'And we move tomorrow.'

His nostrils wrinkled with doubt. 'More spears arrive every day. It would be hasty—'

'You already have the largest host ever gathered in this land.' She smiled playfully. 'If you delay any longer, waiting for men who may or may not come, I fear you risk looking faint of heart.'

'Are you calling me a coward?' he flared, his pride touched, as she had meant it to be. But she knew how to stir other sensations in him, too. She let her eyes fill with heat and saw his expression change, heard the thickening in his breath.

With exquisite slowness, she slid her hand down over his belly until her fingers furrowed through his dark curls and closed around his manhood. She felt the rush of blood under her fingertips as she began to move her hand in long, lazy strokes up and down his growing length.

He was hard as steel in no time.

'I know you're no coward, husband,' she murmured. 'What I'm saying is, you're ready.' She let her fingers rise and fall with the rhythm of her words. 'Ready to mount up. Ready to ride hard. Ready to fight. Ready to take what is yours.'

She looked down at him and let a soft moan of pleasure escape from her lips for effect. 'Only reach out and it will fall into your hand,' she whispered, squeezing a little tighter, moving a little faster. 'Only close your fingers and all of it will be yours.'

His hips were shaking. 'You're right,' he murmured. 'It *is* mine to take. The Wide-Realm belongs to our line... To *me*.' His voice was trembling. 'I will go.'

She brushed her lips against his. 'On the morrow?'

'On the morrow, then.'

'So be it,' she said, letting his shaft flop onto his belly and rolling away. 'And once you bring me your sister's womb and the cripple's heart, then I'll show you how grateful a queen can be.'

CHAPTER
FIFTY-EIGHT

Erlan arrived at Dannerborg after dark, perched on the back of a cart, footsore and exhausted from a long and confusing journey, let alone from his numerous wounds. At least he had reached his destination. He was directed to the steward, a strange character who seemed to hold sway in the yard and immediately took him before the high seat in the mead-hall.

There, draped across the seat's ornately carved arm-rests, was not Prince Ringast, as he had expected, but his brother Thrand, who looked like he was the wrong side of a barrel of beer.

When Erlan tried to explain who he was, that he had come from Uppsala, Thrand ordered him seized and disarmed at once.

'There are too many damned strangers skulking about this place. Lock him up!'

'The princess will vouch for me, at least. She must hear what I have to tell. You all must.'

'Unfortunately for you, my brother's fair wife isn't receiving guests just now.' Thrand's beard cracked into an ale-soaked smile.

'But I'll be sure to pass on your message in the morning. Now tell me – Aurvandil, wasn't it? How do you feel about pig-shit?'

They slung him in a byre that had until recently served as a sty, one that no one had thought to muck out. There were at least no animals in it and Erlan scraped together enough clean straw to sleep better than he had in a month.

He was awoken with a kick long after dawn had broken and, surprisingly, he felt well rested, albeit ravenously hungry too. And nervous – at the thought of seeing Lilla again, at how she would receive the ill news he bore.

'Has the princess been told I'm here?'

'Princess?' the guard sniffed. 'Don't know about no princess. But Lord Thrand has a mind to see you.'

They put him in irons. Erlan locked his jaw against the pain as they clamped his mangled wrists. That these were his new friends was a depressing thought. Nevertheless, he followed them without a word of complaint.

Inside, Thrand was sitting in his big chair, upright this time, palming his brow. He looked ill-tempered and, frankly, unwell. On either side of him was a dangerous-looking crew. Some were clearly outlanders, especially the broad-shouldered woman lounging against a pillar. She was taller than he was, with cropped white-blond hair, a boiled leather tunic and a spear-straight nose.

A shield-maiden. He hadn't seen one of them since his boyhood days at Vendlagard. *Odin's Daughters*, the skalds called them. This one was peering at him as though he were worth rather less than a mummer's fart.

Hovering at Thrand's elbow was the steward, his bald pate gleaming like polished amber.

They stood him in front of Thrand.

'A battle wound?' said the prince.

Erlan snorted. 'Which one?'

'The foot, man – the foot!'

'Oh, that. That was my father.'

Thrand let out a bellow of a laugh. 'Well, we all know what damned whoresons fathers can be, huh?'

'Did you really summon me here to discuss family?'

Thrand pulled at his long beard menacingly, his eyes shifting. 'I suppose it was the Bastard King who sent you.'

'No one sent me. And Sviggar is dead.'

Thrand's expression changed, but not as much as Erlan had expected. 'So it's true. Well, if that's all the news you came to tell, it's been a wasted journey.' He stood suddenly and ranged an accusing finger at Erlan. 'You will tell me this, though – where is my brother?'

'Where's Ringast?' retorted Erlan.

'Never mind about him.'

'This is his hall, isn't it?'

'Listen, you stinking pig's turd. I'm the one gets to ask the fucking questions.'

'Well, you'll get no answers until he is here. Him or the princess.'

Thrand glowered at him a while, then turned to the steward with a scowl. 'Where is she, damn it?'

'Attending your brother, my lord. She has been sent for.'

'Go see to it yourself. Quickly!'

Erlan watched Sletti gather his robes and hurry off towards the shadowy passageway. But when he reached the doorway he stopped abruptly and backed away with a servile nod.

And suddenly, there she was.

She seemed taller than he remembered, and she was dressed more simply than she would have been at the Sveär court: a pale green apron fastened with bow-brooches over a coarse-wool shift the colour of cream, and her hair tied in a work-wench's braid. At her belt was a bunch of keys. But his eye found its rest on the bandage at her throat, dried blood staining one side.

She carried her head high, perhaps to armour herself against the implacable gaze of the crew of hardened warriors. He guessed it was their gaze that made her seem nervous. She still hadn't noticed him as she approached and then she actually looked directly at him. Still nothing. It was only then that he realized his own appearance must have changed, at least beyond her recognition.

'How fares my brother?' growled Thrand.

'His wound will mend.'

'Let's hope so, for your sake. It wouldn't do for you to be left here, a widow among strangers, would it?'

'His wound will mend.'

'So you said.' Thrand snorted. 'But we have other things to discuss. Do you recognize this man?'

She looked directly at Erlan a second time. It was several moments before there was any spark in her eyes, followed at once by shock.

'Erlan?' The disbelief was blazoned on her face. 'But... what's happened to you?'

'I could say the same. Been shaving too close?'

She touched her bandage abstractedly, still staring, but offered no explanation. Instead she went to him. As if by instinct, she pulled him close. He smelled the sweet scent in her hair. 'You're so thin,' she murmured. 'Your face.' She touched the hollow of his cheek. He felt ashamed at how filthy he must be.

It was only then that she seemed to notice his irons. 'Take these things off at once!' she exclaimed, rounding on Thrand. 'You should be honouring this man, not treating him like a common thief!'

'He was a stranger. What else was I supposed to do after your uninvited guest the other night? I didn't know he could be trusted. I still don't.'

'Remove these immediately.' Her voice carried a new authority, one he had not heard in her before. And for the first time, he glimpsed her father in her. Thrand rolled his eyes and nodded to Erlan's guard. Moments later the irons fell with a rattle at his feet and the guard dragged them away.

Lilla took his hands at once and pushed back his tattered sleeves. She gasped. 'Where did you get these? What happened to you?' In truth, his wounds were far better than he could have hoped. His feet, his legs, the lacerations and bruises about his body had all begun to heal remarkably quickly. He knew that was strange, but had no explanation for it. The same had happened when he had taken wounds far worse from the Witch King.

'I was a prisoner. Of your brother.'

She looked up at him, confused, a thousand questions fighting behind her eyes. 'But how came you to be here? Where's Kai?'

'Kai is dead.' She uttered a long moan of despair. Tears at once sprang from her eyes and Erlan thought, not for the first time, that her heart was far too soft for a world so hard.

'I'm so sorry,' she whispered. 'I know you loved him.'

Three simple words, words he had never said to himself. Had never seen were true until now. *He loved Kai.* The realization struck him in the heart like an arrow. All that time... he'd had someone after all, someone he trusted, a brother he had come to love, in his way. But now he was gone.

He tried to speak, but his voice failed him as a wave of grief came crashing over him. Perhaps she saw it in his eyes. She stepped away, giving him time to compose himself. 'Go on. Tell us what we must hear.'

So he began to tell her, tell them all, delivering his litany of murder and betrayal and bloodshed. Name after name, deed after deed, he listed the crimes of Sigurd and his queen, and their wolf of a servant. All of them listened with faces of stone. Lilla's was the hardest of all. He had expected her to rage, to wail, to weep. Anything but this blank wall. It was only when he told of the children's murder that the wall broke.

'O vile serpent! Faithless, false, traitorous black-souled whore!' She fell to her knees. 'O my father, my father! What a fool you were to press this snake to your heart! Gods, her own children,' she wept. 'What mother could do such a thing? If only I had been there—'

'Then you too would be dead,' said Thrand.

'He's right,' said Erlan.

She looked up at him, and he watched the anger sink into a mire of sorrow. She suddenly seized him and buried her face in his chest, weeping, oblivious to his filthy clothes. Instinctively, Erlan drew her closer, feeling her shudders of grief echo through his own body. He was surprised how good it felt. How natural. To hold someone. To hold *her.* He closed his eyes.

There was a shuffling noise. Erlan looked up. Thrand was hauling his considerable weight to his feet. 'Brother. We were told you were abed.'

Erlan felt a hand on his shoulder. He turned. Ringast stood there, his frame stooped in a dark robe, a heavy bandage patched across his chest, stained black and yellow. His face was sallow as a corpse.

'She's another man's wife, Sveär.'

Lilla suddenly let go of him and turned to Ringast. 'Come, husband. You must sit.'

Ringast continued to glare at Erlan, but he allowed Lilla to seat him.

'I'm no damned Sveär,' growled Erlan, glaring back.

'I don't care what you are. She is not yours to comfort.'

'The Aurvandil was telling us news from the north, brother,' said Thrand. 'I think you should hear it.'

'Where is Rorik?' demanded Ringast.

'Dead.' It was the first he'd mentioned the youngest prince.

Thrand erupted, flinging his cup against the wall, roaring, 'Bastards! Those shit-eating bastards! Why, I'll drink Sigurd's blood for this!'

'Save your fury for the storm coming, brother,' Ringast said in a voice of iron. 'It's as we feared, then. How did he die?'

'I don't know, exactly. Only that he was better off dead after Sigurd's oathman had finished with him.'

'Did they dare to break their oaths so soon?' hissed Ringast. 'Have they no respect for the gods north of the Kolmark?'

'Sigurd used your brother to unite the earls to his purpose. Vargalf forced a confession out of him that painted you as the oath-breakers. He said you meant to take the kingdom by deception.'

'We've kept our word.'

'I know that. But it doesn't matter now. Rorik confessed and the earls believed him.'

'So the Sveärs never meant to keep their word.'

'Sviggar meant to. But not Sigurd.'

'We will avenge these deaths.' He looked at Lilla. 'All of them.'

'All of us seek vengeance now. But Sigurd will not be so easily taken. He's been gathering a host to match any that you have. Vargalf said a man called Starkad was also on his way to join him.'

'Starkad?' Ringast swore. The name caused a ripple among the other warlords.

'Aye. And with him, three thousand spears.'

'That's my father's doing,' Ringast scowled. 'Even so, Sigurd may have many, but so too have we – between here and Leithra.'

'Your armies are no use apart. How far away are your father's men?'

'Too far. I'll send him word at once to join with us as soon as he can.' Ringast looked around the chamber, from face to granite face. 'Well, Ubbi my friend,' he growled to the oldest and hardest of all, 'your patience is about to be rewarded.'

'The Norns wove this long ago,' Ubbi replied gruffly.

'A sacred storm, my father called it,' said Ringast in a wistful murmur. 'And you, Aurvandil? You were sworn to Sviggar. Will you fight now for a Dane, against your oath-lord's blood and banners?'

'I'll fight with you.'

'Then swear to me now – as your lord.'

'No. I've sworn too many oaths. Besides, the oath of vengeance I am under is enough. But I will fight with you... until Sigurd and Saldas are no more.'

Ringast eyed him carefully. 'Very well. But if there's treachery in your heart, I'll rip it clean from your chest at the first whisper.'

'So be it.'

'Oh, stop it! *Stop it!*' Lilla suddenly cried. 'All of these oaths and blood-drenched threats! This is all too horrible. There's been so much death already.'

Ringast made to comfort her, but she shoved him away. 'How many more are now to come? Death after death, until we are all drowned in an ocean of blood!' She stabbed Erlan with a piercing look. 'I've done everything I could to stop this. Everything! And still this storm is coming.'

She backed away from both men, tears of boiling anger streaming down her cheeks. Suddenly she threw her arms to the skies and cried in a ringing voice, 'Oh, Freyja, sweet Freyja – help me! Show me how to end all this death!'

With her cry still resounding in their ears, she ran weeping from the hall.

As her footsteps died, there was a long rasp of steel. Thrand was on his feet, brandishing a huge, double-handed blade.

'There's only one way this ends,' he snarled. 'With steel.'

CHAPTER
FIFTY-NINE

The arrow smacked into the sacking with a thud.

Lilla grunted with satisfaction. It had been a year, maybe two, since she had picked up a bow, but it had only taken her half a morning to regain the knack for it. She drew another shaft from the quiver.

Prepare for war, her husband had declared. All around Dannerborg the encampment had finally come alive, every warrior shedding his cloak of idleness in exchange for the hard byrnie of war. Every man was to make ready to move out, although in which direction they would march, no one yet knew. The Kolmark presented a vast frontier and her brother's host could come south by any of a dozen ways. Besides this, Ringast had yet to agree with his father where their hosts should unite.

Wherever they marched, Lilla had no intention of remaining behind. Naturally Ringast was insisting she stay at Dannerborg, safe from the worst of the danger, but if every man was preparing for war, why should she do any different? Did she not have more cause than any one of them to fight? No one had a greater debt to repay now than her.

She nocked the arrow, drew it back, held her breath, just as her father had taught her as a girl, then released a narrow thread of air, slowly easing the pressure in her fingertips until – *thrumm* – the bowstring snapped and the arrow shot straight and true, striking so close to the previous arrow that it tore off a fletching feather. An old thrill passed through her, and she remembered with sudden fondness how her dead brother Staffen used to stir her into a lather of competitiveness when she was a young girl and desperate to impress him with her skill.

'Imagining Saldas's face?' said a voice, only too familiar.

She jerked round to see Erlan's lean frame propped against a tree, his arms folded, his gaunt cheeks creased into something like a smile. 'How long have you been there?'

'Long enough to see you've more of your father in you than I'd known.' He nodded at the arrows. 'I once saw him shoot a pigeon on the wing. Hel of an eye, he had.'

'You shouldn't be here.' Angrily, she pulled out another arrow and turned back to her target. 'I can't be alone with you.'

'Where else would I be?' She heard the tread of his uneven footsteps limping closer as she nocked the arrow and drew the bowstring. 'Everyone else is dead.' She felt his hand on her shoulder. His touch went through her like a shock of lightning. She spun around, pointing the arrowhead straight at his heart. 'Stay away from me,' she whispered. 'Please.'

Above the tip she saw his dark, fathomless eyes, intent on hers. There was no fear in them. Instead he reached out and pushed aside the point with the back of his hand like it was nothing. She felt the resistance drain out of her. He stepped inside the point. Her arms dropped and the arrow thudded harmlessly into the earth. Before she could utter a word to hold him back, he was against her, pressing her into his chest, which was harder than she remembered. Then his breath was on her lips, his mouth against hers. She let him kiss her, not even caring if anyone did see them, her senses gulping him down like cool water for her parched heart.

'We only have each other now,' he murmured when their lips parted. This directness surprised her. This urgency. Maybe his suffering had stripped him of any pretence, of any patience for taking the longer road. He pushed her back till her shoulders butted against a tree. A shiver of desire peeled up her thighs as his hands began to lift her skirts.

'No,' someone said. It was a second before she realized the word had come from her own throat. 'No,' she said again, firmer this time.

'Don't you want me?'

She pushed him away. 'You know I do. But I can't... I won't.' She slid her hands around the trunk behind her, clinging to it as tightly as she could to stop herself from reaching for him. 'I mustn't.'

He stepped back. In the thin lines of his face it was plain that she had struck a wound. *Another wound*, she thought. As if he was in want of more.

'You need me, Lilla. Who else will see you through all this? Who else can you trust?'

'My husband,' she said softly, feeling a deep sadness well out of the gulf that was breaking open between them.

'You mean your father's enemy,' he said in a bitter voice.

'He's a good man.'

'But you don't love him.'

'He's a good man,' she repeated. As if those words alone could protect her heart.

'Lilla, I came here for you.'

'No, you didn't. You came here for revenge. And you shall have it. But it's too late for me. Too late for us.'

He shook his head in frustration. 'Ever since I've known you, obedience has made you a slave, Lilla. Obey your father. Obey your husband. Submit to a woman like Saldas, who has taken everything from you. Is that what you're always going to do? Always surrender? Always lie down and take whatever fate the Norns have handed you?'

She had hurt him. But there was no doubt he knew how to hurt her back. 'I'm not going to lie down. I'm going to fight. I'm going to fight because the blood of my father's house must be purged. Because the stain of my brother and that viper who warms his bed must be wiped away for ever.'

'Sveäland is already lost to you, Lilla. You should give it up.'

'No. I won't. *I won't!* I owe it to my father. Who else is there but me? Someone has to stand up for my people, someone who knows their true heart, even if it means fighting against them now. Renewal must come. And it must come through me.' She thought of the life being knit together in her womb, and looking into Erlan's gaze, she wondered whether another with those same dark eyes would rise up one day to re-take her father's rightful place.

But even if Erlan was the father of this child, he must never know it.

'Maybe you're right,' he said at length. 'For what it's worth, I'm sorry about your father.'

'And I'm sorry about Kai.'

His eyes dropped to the floor. 'Mmm. I failed him once. I won't fail him again.'

'I know.' For some reason, she felt compelled to add, 'You will see him again, you know. One day.'

'Huh! Maybe we all will. And sooner than we'd like.' He turned away, apparently with nothing more to say, and left her clinging to her tree.

She watched his figure retreating through the wood, forcing herself not to call him back. Only when she was certain that he had gone did she loosen her grip on the bark and stoop to retrieve her fallen bow.

That night she had the dream again. The swirling mist; the eagle, its eyes flashing with hate.

She rose quietly, wrapped her fur about her and crept outside. The cut on her neck was throbbing, but the floor felt pleasantly cool under the soles of her feet. She padded through the shadows, leaving her husband to his own dreams and secret fears.

Outside, everything was still. There was not a breath of wind, as if some vast and ancient spell had been cast over Dannerborg and all its folk, turning everything to stone.

She climbed the staircase that clung fast to the north wall of the mead-hall and led up onto a gallery that looked out over the palisade towards her homeland. There, she slid down into the crook of the wall and gazed up at the night sky. There was no moon, only a splendid canopy of stars scattered like seed across the vastness of Ymir's Skull.

It was beautiful. And yet she shuddered.

Everyone was dead, like he said. Her father, her mother, her brother Staffen, Katla, Svein, Kai... Everyone she loved. *Except for him*. And suddenly she had a hateful thought – hated herself for having it. Because she realized it would be easier if he were dead, too. Realized that while he lived she could only ever love him. That she could never love her husband.

She covered her mouth, choking back the moan that suddenly rose in her throat. But the wave of sorrow quickly gave way to anger. This was Saldas's doing. All of it. She had been deceived. They all had. Yet everything had fallen out just as Saldas had wanted.

And the more she thought of it, the more she saw something fearful in the irresistibility of Saldas's will. How was it that the world seemed to bend itself to her every desire, however much destruction she left in her wake? Lilla's throat burned with outrage and she was suddenly seized with an urge to cry out for justice, cry to the stars and the darkened moon.

She dug her nails into her palm in frustration, welcoming the pain that shot up her arm. How easy it would be to fight Saldas's hate with hatred of her own. Was that the only way a woman like that could be stopped?

There is a power stronger than hate... These had been her mother's words, uttered long ago. One of the many lessons Lilla had only half-understood. *Nothing in all the Nine Worlds can overcome the power of love.*

Lilla remembered how she had thought that insipid at the time. Childish, even. But maybe her mother was right. Maybe there was a deeper wisdom hidden in her words that Lilla could use to put steel in her will. Yet almost at once, another voice

586

spoke, mocking her. *Who are you?* it sneered. *Don't you know you're too small for this? Too weak.* Hadn't Erlan spoken the truth? She was nothing but a slave to the will of others. Nothing but a slave to her fate.

'I can't do this,' she whispered. But no sooner had she spoken than she heard an answer.

You're not alone.

She gave a start, so audible was the voice, its tone so soft. Soft, yet strong as iron. She seemed to know it, though it was certainly not her mother's.

I will be with you, my love. You have the power within.

I? What 'I' was that?

She waited with stilled breath, longing to hear more. But the shadows were still and silent, and high above her, the stars stared down, cold and unmoved.

Yet in the silence, she was suddenly sure of one thing: Saldas must fall.

She must...

After that, there could be a new beginning.

Lilla lay back and let her gaze drift among the stars. A memory came – of her mother standing beside her father. Two lives that had given her life. She wondered where they were now. In the halls of Hel? In Valhalla? Or some other place? Maybe they lived only in her now. Yes. In her and in the life within her.

Instinctively her hand moved to her belly.

There is no one else. Only she was the true heir to her father and the true queen of her people. She must take up her crown. And with that resolution sealed in her mind, her eyelids grew heavy and a peace settled over her, as wide and gentle as the dew.

Soon she knew she was dreaming, because she was climbing higher and higher, spiralling upwards on the still air like an eagle until she could see out across the land, over forests and fields and lakes and heaths and hills.

As she looked, she heard the sigh of the sea. She turned to the east and the stars began to stir, hardly at first, but then more until the chinks of light began to ripple and roll, as though she no longer gazed into the sky but upon its reflection on the surface of the sea.

As she looked it seemed like the waves grew, the stars climbing and falling, swelling into foaming breakers. Then she saw a long spit of land that split the waters like a dagger. Around it thick forest skirted the shoreline, and a bleak, bald hill rose out of the darkness to the south. She heard noises: ropes gnawing, the rush and chuckle of a clinker-hull over water, the buck and spray of bow-breakers. She saw ships, oars pounding the swell, sails thrapping in the building wind. Dozens of ships now, hundreds, surging towards the dagger-spit of land. Men's laughter seasoned the air. She saw linden shields, banners whipped by the sea-spray, steel points and ash-shafts.

An army was riding the wind from the east.

Then her gaze turned north and everything changed. She smelled barley fields, heard the thud of hooves. She looked left and right and saw a thousand horses flanking her, galloping riderless. Black and brown, white and grey – beasts of every colour and marking, muzzles foaming in a killing froth. She was galloping herself now, thundering through the fields towards a shadow spread across the horizon.

'Lilla!' she heard as the shadow loomed into a wall of trees.

'Lilla!' again, as she broke through the treeline and into the forest.

'Wake up, Lilla.' Her eyes suddenly opened. Above her, a face slowly took form. 'What are you doing out here?' Her husband's voice.

She reached up and clasped him. Pulled him close. 'They're in the forest,' she whispered. 'They're in the forest now.'

'Who are?'

'Sigurd – and his army.'

'What?' Ringast looked confused but he must have seen the certainty in her eyes. 'Go on. Tell me what you've seen.'

'I saw a host of horses swarming through the forest. And a fleet of ships carrying an army with the wind.'

'Where were they? What else did you see?'

'I don't know – I—'

'Think!'

She closed her eyes, remembering. 'I saw a twin fork of sea – a spit of land sharp as a spear-point surrounded by forest. And a hill – yes, a hill – bald as your father's head, rising to the south.'

Ringast stared at her wide-eyed, then fell back on his haunches. 'The fjords of Bravik,' he murmured in wonder. And then he nodded, the lines of his mouth hardening with resolve. 'Bravik, then. So be it.'

CHAPTER SIXTY

'Bravik? You're sure?'

The voice was coarse. The speaker was Branni, a man whom Erlan had learned was the Wartooth's eyes and ears. The man he trusted above all others, so Thrand had told him. He was tall, thin, bald as an egg, and possessor of the most unruly pair of eyebrows Erlan had ever seen – one of which was arched doubtfully at Ringast.

Branni had arrived at Ringast's camp the night before, mud-spattered and weary from his journey, which had taken him first to Dannerborg, where he had discovered Ringast had already moved his army north and east. He had then ridden onwards like the wind, another twenty leagues, until he had overtaken their motley host.

'I'm sure,' replied Ringast, palming his sweat-slicked brow. It was warm in his tent, but not excessively so. The Dane's face was pallid. He looked ten years older than the fine-fettled prince who had approached the Tiding Mound at Uppsala in such splendour on Midsummer's Eve. The air in his booth was musty with the furs serving as his bed, and through the tent flaps wafted the smell of churned-up mud and horse droppings. But there was another scent lacing the air – subtle, but which caught in the nostrils like the smell of rotten meat. Erlan wondered what the wound on the Danish prince's chest really looked like under Lilla's dressing.

'Your wife's dream, you say.' There was no concealing the scepticism in Branni's voice. 'Has she a *vala*'s sight?'

'It seems to me she has.'

'Can you prove it?'

'I believe her. That's enough.'

'Oh, *you* believe her. In that case, I'm brimming with confidence, my lord.' Erlan wondered what part this man really played that he could speak to Ringast in such an insolent tone.

'Damn you, Branni, I believe her. And that's an end to it. Gods, you have no trouble believing my father's dreams when it serves his bloody purpose.'

'True.' Branni's wild brows furrowed. 'But that's a different thing. Your father is a friend of Odin and has been since the cradle. The All-Father has told him much down the ages that has been shown true.'

'Who's to say Odin is not friend to my wife also?'

A deep growl rumbled in Branni's throat as he chewed this over. 'Very well,' he said. 'Let's say she's right then. And these two forces she has seen will join at the Braviken fjord. Then the sea-borne host can be none but Starkad's, and we know he has three thousand spears. That means your army here could be outnumbered two to one, at least, when he joins with Sigurd's force.'

'All the more reason my father must hurry.'

'He planned to set sail with his full host at dawn yesterday.'

'If Sigurd's army are already in the Kolmark,' said Thrand, 'they could reach the Braviken fjord in two days. Maybe even by nightfall tomorrow.'

'Father's fleet should be well at sea by now,' said Ringast. 'Which means he'll have reached somewhere—'

'Just south of the Gotland straits,' offered Branni.

'It'll take them two and a half days to reach Bravik, so long as the wind doesn't turn against them.'

'But the old man still thinks he's coming to Dannerborg,' pointed out Thrand, stooping to refill his cup from the ale-bucket.

'Hmm. Thrand's right. He'll land too far south. Then he'll never march north in time to help us stop them at Bravik.'

The tent fell silent for a while.

'We must send him another message,' Ringast said at length. He looked at Branni. 'Will you go? If you leave at once you can intercept him. I'll give you my swiftest vessel.'

'I'm sure you shall,' smiled Branni faintly. 'And if I reach him, what would you have me say?'

'Tell him to sail further north, to the fjord at Slätbaken. From there it's less than three leagues to Bravik by land.'

'And where, pray, shall I tell him to meet you?'

Ringast knuckled the hook of his nose. 'There's a low ridge that rises along the southern edge of the Bravik plains. I know that ground. We can stop them there.'

'They could be ten thousand to our five, brother,' Thrand said.

'I know that. If Father can reach that ridge by dawn the day after tomorrow, then we'll make a stand. If he can join us, if we can concentrate our forces,' Ringast looked earnestly from face to face, 'then they'll never get off that plain.' The grit in his voice gave Erlan some confidence. The grim pallor in the prince's cheeks, less so.

'What if he doesn't reach us by then?' Erlan said.

'Then they'll cut a bloody swathe through this land like a scythe through barley.'

Thrand suddenly laughed and gave his thigh a thunderous slap. 'With or without Father, we'll stop them on the plain. Oh, we'll give them a merry time of it, brother! Never fear!'

'I should be away,' Branni said, rising wearily to his feet, indifferent to the younger prince's swagger. He bowed and made to leave, only to hesitate one last time. 'Is there anything else I should tell your father?'

'Yes,' Ringast nodded. 'You can tell him Odin has granted him his chance to die.'

CHAPTER
SIXTY-ONE

Einar Fat-Belly had been in a foul mood for a long time. Never fouler than tonight.

After a long day in the saddle, what he wanted was a decent night's sleep. What he got was the watch falling after the midnight mark.

No one was bloody coming, not if they had any sense. Besides, he doubted anyone south of the Kolmark knew they were even there. The king had sealed the Sodermanland border days before to stop any news heading south. Although they'd find out for themselves soon enough.

The shadows were dense enough to touch at first. Everywhere the spruce branches blotted out what little light there was from the stars. Still, he was always surprised what a man could see once his eyes grew accustomed to it. Back through the trees he could see the pinprick fires further north where his Sveär clansmen were camped, asleep on the pine needles that carpeted the ground and filled the air with their scent.

Lucky buggers.

Somewhere either side of him would be the next man on the picket line, probably leaning against some tree, bored as he was, dreaming of whatever pair of tits he'd left at home.

The rest of Sigurd's army fanned west from his position. Outlanders, a lot of them, although the Sveär levies were near full strength. His own crew, the Bredlungers, had mustered to a man, led by their headman Kekli-Karl and his cousin, Arwakki, Earl of Gestrikland. He would have thought this late in the summer most would be loath to leave their barley fields uncut, but men often seemed willing to drop whatever needed doing if there was a whiff of silver or slaves in it for them.

He was easy either way. He didn't fancy this new king above half. Not even that much. But he was sworn to Arwakki, who was sworn to Sigurd now. So it goes.

Einar hawked a gobbet of phlegm into the gloom, then resumed his watch south. The shadows were still as ever. The wind barely tickled the treetops.

Gods, he needed a piss.

That meant unhitching everything again. He was in full rig, with a leather corselet halfway down his thighs and several buckles fastened under his copious belly, securing the various blades about his person. He propped his spear against a spruce, put down his shield and groped about until he eventually got to the drawstring of his baggy hoes.

There was a flutter in the branches. For a moment, his fingers stopped. Somewhere above him, a bird cawed.

'Bloody crows,' he muttered, rummaging in his breeches till he found what he was after. He gave a contented sigh and flopped himself out—

And at once froze every muscle.

There were shadows creeping in the dark. He stayed absolutely still. They were a little distance through the trees. Even with the scant light, he saw the glister of a wicked-sharp blade, then more shadows stealthing at a crouch towards the Sveär line.

He scanned the darkness directly ahead of him. Still nothing there. It was a few seconds before he heard the distinctive *fizz, fizz* of arrows being loosed, and then the first muffled clash of iron and warning shouts.

'Guess someone's found us out after all,' he mused to himself.

Still, just now nature's call was more pressing. He turned back to his tree and felt a rush of relief as he unburdened his bladder. There were more shouts off to the west and beyond them the sounds of other skirmishes breaking out further down the line.

'Here we bloody go then,' he muttered irritably.

And after a long and satisfying piss, he re-fastened his buckles, picked up his spear and shield, and bellowed the alarm at the top of his lungs.

CHAPTER
SIXTY-TWO

Erlan closed his eyes. A light wind licked his beard. Spots of rain spat upon his cheek.

'A grim day for grim work,' said Thrand.

Erlan opened his eyes.

The hulking prince looked more than ever like a murderous bear, his woolly hair jammed under his ring-eyed helm, rugged fists resting on the handle of his long-axe. 'There'll be heavy work on the right today.'

'It's yours if you want it,' said Ringast. 'Take the Rus berserkers with your two hirds. Keep your right flank tight against those reedbeds. Close to the lake as the pimples on your arse – understand?'

'Oh, aye,' returned Thrand with a yellow-toothed grin at Erlan. 'Good killing to you, Aurvandil. And mind you've a brew waiting if you reach the Slain-Hall before me.'

Erlan nodded.

Thrand bumped down the rocky outcrop onto the plain, buckles jangling.

'A steel arm, brother,' called Ringast after him. 'For Rorik.'

'Sure! We'll settle a few scores for the lad before the day is done.'

Erlan watched Thrand wade through the sea of men below them on the right, shouting orders. A crowd of warriors clad in bearskins hefted their gear and stalked after him into the murky dawn.

Berserkers.

These ones from the rivers of *Garðaríki* and the Rus tribes beyond. Shield-biters who cared little for armour or mailshirts, who loved the madness of slaughter like a babe loves its mama's teat. He'd seen them before, that red morning on that blood-soaked fell, where he'd stood in his father's shieldwall.

That day he'd fought to live. Today he fought to kill. One man in all these thousands, who must die by his hand and his alone.

Sigurd.

He looked north from the outcrop of rock, which swelled from the earth like an ancient tumour. The road that had carried them northward from Dannerborg rolled on, dipping into the plain below them, then rising again, up the shallow slope to a low ridge of pines on the far side of the plain.

That way lay the Braviken fjord where Starkad's fleet was anchored bobbing on the grey waters. Beyond it, the Kolmark forest. That way, Sigurd's army had come, which even now Erlan could see stirring in the gloomy wood.

The previous night had been a dark one. Those same woods had flared with bloody skirmish as the two vanguards first met. That opening exchange of blood and steel had been short-lived. It served neither side to be scattered in the darkness. Instead, after the two armies had touched, Ringast had withdrawn his forces to their position along the southern ridge overlooking the Bravik plain.

A quarter league west another wood bordered the plain, this one of ash and beech, not quite turned to autumn rust. Ringast's left wing stretched to its edge under a forest of spear-points. The prince had placed his berserkers on his wings. Better to direct their madness at anyone trying to outflank him than have them scything down his own best men in the centre where there was sure to be confusion enough.

Those berserkers were Hedmarkers, led by the cousins, Grim and Geir. Inside them were the Skanskar hirds – thralls levied from the farms of Skania – five men deep under the banner of the twin thanes, Alfar and Alfarin.

Closer in were Ubbi's Frieslanders – tall and slim, with long limbs and long reach, battle-hardened from their never-ending wars with the Franks. Next to them, immediately below Erlan, were the men under Ringast's direct command: two thousand men with four thousand killing blades, mustered from all over Eastern Gotarland. Earls, thanes, piss-pot clan chiefs, farmsteaders and the freemen they could levy. All stood under Ringast's raven banner.

A thousand yards to the east, where Thrand had gone, were the waters of the Snow Lake, grey in the dull morning. Its western edge was choked with reeds, eventually giving way to firmer ground where Thrand would take his stand. Any flanking attack would flounder in the marsh-mud like flies in honey to be picked off by the Wendish archers positioned behind Thrand's Gotars and Rus. With him stood named men, champions – Haki Cut-Cheek, Dag of Lifland, and Toki the Fair whose face was so ugly it'd seal a whore's cunny. So Thrand had said.

Inside them, Ringast had placed the Wendish. Shorter than the northern men, but strong and stubborn as mules. They carried long-swords and smaller buckler-shields, and fought under the banner of Duk, Visma's husband. She, however, had begged to carry Ringast's standard and he had granted her the honour.

The dark before the dawn had dissolved to a dirty grey. There was no bright morning sun, no gleaming mail, no glinting helms. Just a sea of heads, black and brown, rust-red, white-blonde. Many wore simple iron helms and boiled leather. The richer ones, mailshirts, dark as slate. Above them, felt banners twisted in the wind.

A storm of blood and iron waiting to break.

'Still no word from my father,' said Ringast, eyes moving from the far treeline into the wind blowing from the north-east.

No one answered.

'The wind has been against him for two days now.'

'He must come today,' said Visma.

'Today, aye. But it's a long road from sunrise to sunfall.'

'We don't need your father,' Ubbi growled from inside his helm. The old warrior looked the very soul of war, faceless behind the mail that hung from his helm to his chin. He was bristling with steel and over his shoulders hung a blood-red cloak, pinned to his mail by gilded bear-head brooches. 'Just look, my friend! Was ever such a host assembled in all the north?'

'Never that I've known. But let's see what comes out of those trees.'

'*Click-clack. Click-clack.*' Visma threw back her head and laughed. 'Can you not hear it? The rattle of the Norns' looms, weaving the cloth of all our fates, ready to dye it red with blood?'

'My fate's in the hands of Odin, not those blind bitches,' Ubbi answered.

'The *Valhöll* benches are being cleared, the hall floor swept,' muttered the youngster Kari, his youthful voice half-singing under his breath.

Visma recognized the song. 'Odin's maids make ready to welcome home his heroes.'

'Not for you, woman,' Ubbi cried. 'There's men to please before they look to you!'

'If I kill like a man, why shouldn't I take his maids like one, too?'

They both laughed at this.

Erlan listened, fingers drumming impatiently against Wrathling's hilt, still nested in its sheath. He cared little for this talk. Odin's favour, Tyr's skill, Thor's strength. He'd heard a bellyful of it these last days as each prepared for the coming slaughter. It was supposed to fill him with fire. Instead it left him cold. He didn't know these gods. Only the silent god meant something to him. Those others were tricksters and liars. But the silent god did not lie. *Could not.* And he prayed now to that silent god to grant him his revenge.

'The time is near.'

They all turned at the softer voice. Lilla stood there, and even in the morning murk, she was something bright in a world of grey. She wore a pale yellow dress under a grey travel cloak, the hood shadowing her face, and under it, just visible, the dressing around her neck.

There was something fey in her eyes as she looked from face to face. Erlan felt a pang in his chest, like the jarring of an old wound, and turned away.

She gazed up at the drab clouds, letting the rain sprinkle her face. 'The *Valkyries* have ridden hard. Sweat falls from their horses' flanks.'

'Sweat or no, the rain is no good for our archers,' said Ringast.

'Nor for the shieldwall's strength,' said Ubbi.

'It's the same for them.' Erlan stared ahead. He wanted this to begin. There had been enough talk.

As if in answer to his thought, there was movement along the ridge.

'There,' Kari pointed excitedly.

And in that moment their breath stopped as men seeped onto the plain like a dark tide from the shadow of the trees. Three deep, four, then five – hundreds of warriors – they kept coming. A mass of men and above them a thicket of spears, stretching from the western edge of the plain along the ridge and beyond the lake to the east.

Erlan glanced at Ringast's silent host below. Even a blind man could see they were outnumbered, and badly.

'There are more in the trees,' Ringast said. Beside him, a laugh boomed from Ubbi's helm. 'Something amuses you?'

'What else can you do but laugh, my friend, when you see a death as beautiful as that?' Ubbi swept his spear along the battle-line.

He's right, thought Erlan. It was an awesome sight. *If the Wartooth doesn't come soon—*

He broke off the thought. It changed nothing. He was alive because of Kai, here for only one reason: to discharge his oath to his brother. *Aye, the mad little bastard would have liked to see this.* This plain was about to become a sinkhole of death, a butcher's field. Songs would be sung later.

Now men would learn what luck they had. Now men would pray to their gods – pray to live, if they had a good enough reason for living. But if he was to kill well this day and keep his oath, it were better to think himself already dead. The silent god had given him back his life once before. Perhaps he would again.

Banners swayed over Sigurd's Sveär hordes like drunken giants – great towers of cloth, black and red, blue and gold, green and yellow. Skulls of oxen, of rams or wolves or bears, pinned atop them, staring across the plain, each a pitiless face of death. One rose higher than the rest over the heart of the huge host, on its face a great black beast, lined in scarlet thread on a bright blue background. The eagle with a wolf's head: Sigurd's standard, crowned with a wolf skull, its crossbeam draped with silver pelts. Beneath it, Sigurd would be standing. That was where Erlan must go, into that ocean of men.

The Sveär king's army had unfurled itself at least ten men deep with its back to the trees. But now a moment of stillness settled over the plain.

A figure stepped out of Sigurd's line, strode a few paces forward, slung down his shield and drew his sword. The man wore a cloak of white lamb's wool, distinguishing him from the battle-line like a snowdrop on a dung-heap.

'Someone fancies himself,' said Ubbi.

'Let every man hear this,' the white warrior cried.

'And woman, needle-prick,' hissed Visma.

'I am Adils, son of Arag, son of Arnalf of Norrland,' the man declared, brandishing his ring-sword. 'From this day my name will be sung in every hall to the four winds. I swear by Arnalf's blade, before the sun falls, I'll lay Ringast's head at King Sigurd's feet.'

This prompted a cheer from his own side, while an ironic jeer rolled up towards him from the south side of the plain.

'Archers,' Ringast called to his right. 'Put that fool back into line.'

Another terse order was given and a neat volley of arrows whipped into the sky, thudding all around the boaster an instant later, one piercing the shield behind him with a crack. He didn't wait for another volley, but shrank back into line to the hoots of Ringast's men.

'Are you going to answer that?' asked Ubbi.

'He'll get his answer if he gets through today.' Ringast touched his hilt. 'I'll waste no words on that pack of dogs.'

'What about your own men?' said Lilla.

'They'll fight without any pretty words from me.'

'They will. And they'll die,' she returned. 'But if they're willing to waste their lives for you, surely you have words enough to waste on them?'

He held her gaze, then nodded. 'You're right.' He stepped forward to the edge of the mound. 'Hear me, you raven-feeders!' His voice rose like a wolf-cry over his host. 'We come from many lands, born of many fathers. But today our paths are woven together. Today we stand as one.'

Erlan looked down on the sea of grim faces upturned to their captain and wondered whether his words kindled fire in their hearts.

'Kingdoms will rise and kingdoms will fall until the Nine Worlds burn in the final flames. But this day on these Bravik plains will never be forgotten. Every one of us shall live long in the tales of men.'

The sound of drumming began to the east, rolling in like a

breaker down the Danish prince's battle-line, men hammering spear-shafts and axe-heads against limewood shields.

'Be the Spear-God's wrath against this oath-breaking king! Be the very blood and fire of the ancient earth! Arise, death! Arise, darkness! Arise now, Sigurd's day of doom!'

Their shields shook like thunder, ringing through Erlan's head, swallowing the last of Ringast's cries in a roar that broke from every mouth beneath his banners.

The cheer was answered at once by a bellow of fury yet louder, that might have come from the very bowels of Ymir, the first giant of the earth. The shout washed across the plain, and with it a single, blue arrow loosed from the heart of Sigurd's host.

'Do you see it, lord?' Kari cried. 'Odin's arrow!'

'I see it.' Ringast calmly watched the blue streak sail high overhead and land harmlessly behind.

'The offering is made to the High God's altar,' boomed Ubbi, pointing his spear to the sky. 'Let's go find our places in his hall!'

'There's time enough for that, old man,' Ringast answered. 'How about we win ourselves a victory first?'

'Their line is moving!' Visma was pointing across the plain. The Sveär line was closing up, their shields locking into a shieldwall with a great clatter.

Ringast turned to Lilla. 'We must take our places. You must move back from here. Now!'

'I too have my part to play, husband. The best place for me is here.'

'Damn you, woman! At least promise me you'll ride south if they break through. Ride to my father's protection.'

'How can I promise that? My fate is bound to you. To all of you.' Her deep blue gaze scanned the war-hard faces, lingering just a moment longer on Erlan's. 'If all of you must fall, what is my life worth beyond this day? No! I stand with you.' Her words recalled to Erlan the *vala's* prophecy, spoken over him the day he became a man.

A greater hand is on you. You will fall and rise again.

His lips moved silently. *Rise again…*

'My lord,' cried Visma, 'you *must* take your place.'

'Hel take your stubbornness then, woman!' Ringast snarled at Lilla in frustration. 'Stay wherever you please!'

Lilla suddenly laughed, face bright with a preternatural light. 'Oh, sweet husband, save your fury for your enemy! They deserve it far more than me.' Ringast seized her and kissed her passionately, as though it were certain to be for the last time.

Erlan looked away, looked down into the sea of slaughter about to break. His place was down there. His *urðr*. His fate.

He hefted his shield and went to find it.

CHAPTER
SIXTY-THREE

'You need to finish this soon,' Saldas murmured into Sigurd's ear.

The king dropped his voice. 'What troubles you now? Is it not plain we have the greater strength?'

'Do you see the Wartooth's banner among them? Where is his boar? There must be another force.'

'If Harald doesn't stand against us today, we'll finish him on another.'

'Fool! He may be close by. You have to end this quickly and then ready your men to face another army. Maybe even before sunset.'

'You forget yourself – presuming to advise me on matters of war. Anyway, our numbers will tell soon enough.' He turned away but she pulled him back.

'Can't you see the ground he's chosen? He's bottled you in. You can't outflank him, unless your wolf-warriors there can swim.' She pointed towards their eastern wing. 'He's forcing you to break his centre. But there, he has the higher ground to fall back on. They might hold all day.'

'Against the men I've gathered? Against these champions?' Sigurd replied, raising his voice to the man stood a little way forward. 'There's no host but Odin's hall of heroes could stand against all these. Starkad – what say you?'

The huge warrior turned. This was Starkad the Sea-King, who had brought with him three thousand spears and shields. Born in far-off Hordaland, and renowned in every land of the north. His hands rested on the pommel of his long-sword with a lightness that belied their strength. To Saldas's eye, he might have been cut from a mountain. His mailshirt bulged with the hulking muscle beneath. But, she wondered, had he the brains to match? He stank of the sea, yet men seemed to follow him.

'We'll soon see what luck the Wartooth's son has,' Starkad answered, his voice strangely soft. 'But he's no fool. Nor is he stood among fools. I've seen the banners of Ubbi the Hundred, and those Hedmarker lads, Grim and Geir. It'll be a fight, all right.' He said no more and Saldas was none the wiser as to his brains, though that fearful blade did give some assurance.

'Victory's in the rain,' said another called Egil, his shorn head a motley of black tattoos. 'When the plain turns to a mire, the day will be ours.'

'It's Odin's will how fares the day,' Saldas said. 'There's a battle to be fought and won both here and there.' She pointed to the sky. 'I'll do my part. See you do yours.'

'What is your counsel then, my queen?' said Sigurd irritably. 'Perhaps you'd like a place in the shieldwall with us.' He allowed himself a snigger.

'Puncture his centre like a dagger through the heart. Form your line into a spear-point. Attack with no mercy.'

'A spear-point?' Sigurd looked sceptical. 'That will weaken the shieldwall.'

'Not with your best men at its point, and behind them Starkad's *víkingar*. Then drive with all strength and speed at Ringast's banner. Cut him down, cut their line in two and our greater numbers will swallow the rest.'

Sigurd looked at the hard faces around him, judging what they made of this.

'It means breaking the strongest part of their line while their arms are still fresh,' said Starkad. Then his rugged face broke into a laugh. 'But we have to kill them one way or another before sunfall. May as well set to it.'

'Very well. Send forward the sons of Alrek and their hird. Egil, add your Kurslanders to the point of attack. Starkad, your men will form the second wave. Strike hard and swift.' He lifted his voice and cried, 'Sound the horns!'

As a gale of noise rose around them, Saldas touched his arm. 'Remember, my love... if you see him... I want his heart.'

Sigurd snorted. 'Patience, *my love*. You'll have it soon enough.'

She nodded, satisfied, her hand moving absently to the crude-cut amulet hanging from her neck. Sigurd's face curdled. 'I begin to think you have a fondness for this cripple.'

She dropped her hand. 'My heart is yours, husband. You know that.'

'Do I?' He scowled and turned away.

She reached out and turned his face to her, softening her gaze. 'Fear not, my love. I told you – I've seen your return to me. I've seen you come to me in the Kingshelm. *Victorious*. I've seen it.'

'So I must trust to your dreams, must I?'

'And my love.' She smiled.

He looked at her, trying to read whether she was in earnest, but she saw the doubt in his eyes. So she kissed him, engulfing his senses with all the passion she knew. After all, even the meanest thrall needed encouragement from time to time.

'The Wide-Realm, my husband,' she whispered. 'It *will* be yours.'

'Aye,' he growled, resolutely. 'The Wide-Realm.' Then he lifted his voice over the heads of his champions. 'The Wide-Realm!'

Saldas turned away, her face setting into a mask, while Sigurd's war-cry rolled away down the line.

Einar rested his hands on his belly.

At least he had a full stomach. One thing to go into a fight with no sleep, sore feet and little faith in the man leading you, but on an empty belly? That was plain stupid.

Still, much good it would do him if he took a length of steel in his gut. And truth be told, he was scared shitless. There were enough mad buggers within pissing distance to bring the whole world to an end. And all of 'em seemed like they couldn't wait to make it happen.

He cursed. He needed to piss. Again.

At least it wasn't the other. The place already stank enough, of vomit and piss and excrement, nerves voiding warriors' bodies of anything surplus to the pure business of killing.

And dying.

Einar tried to think of something else. He'd had his share of fights, raiding here and there. Even stood in the Sveär wall more than once. But this was going to be butchery on a scale none of them had seen. Odin's bench and all the rest of it seemed a far throw away. Dying face down in agonizing pain, an awful lot closer.

He belched and wiped his hand across dry lips.

'Pass me some more of that stuff, eh?' he said to the man in a wolf-skin beside him.

The wolf-warrior took a gourd from his belt and tossed it to him. Einar caught it and put it to his lips. The fiery liquid warmed his innards and put flames in his skull, blinding him to his surroundings for a merciful moment.

'Frey's cock!' he gasped, handing it back. 'That gives you a kick in the pants harder 'n my wife! What the Hel d'you put in that?'

'Wolf's blood for one,' answered the other, with a snicker. 'The rest ain't for telling.' He flashed yellow teeth, revealing the grooves he'd filed across them. 'Makes you a fierce fucker, though!'

'If it makes me half as fierce as you look, that lot should be shitting themselves.'

They both laughed at that. Although Einar had been deadly serious. Suddenly, behind them, Arwakki's bannerman started blowing his horn. The earl roused his men with a shout.

'Here we go then,' grinned the Sveär wolf-warrior.

'Aye,' muttered Einar, picking up his shield. 'That's what I'm afraid of.'

The wolf-warrior started howling.

Erlan stood ahead of Ringast's banner. Ubbi, a little to his left, with the best of Ringast's oathmen ranged behind them under the raven banner fluttering above Visma's head.

The plain was ringing with horn-blasts heralding the slaughter. Wendish ox-horns, Norsk goat-horns, Gotar ram-horns, all joined together in a cacophony of noise with mad berserker howls, Sveär war-cries and the weird yells of the Skanskar vassals.

Erlan watched silently, his tortured body now forgotten, his hand shaking on his shield-grip.

The storm is here.

All a man could do was try to outlive its blast.

Sigurd's shieldwall came on. Then suddenly its centre folded forward into a point, so that the whole line aimed like a spearhead straight for where Erlan stood. The Gotar centre, meanwhile, stood stolid, in a flat line to receive them.

'Ringast!' Erlan cried.

'I see it!' shouted the prince through the din.

For a second, he seemed uncertain. Then he was yelling orders left and right, which were bellowed down the line. It seemed an age before anything happened, until, at last, Thrand's berserkers to the east and the Hedmarkers to the west began to advance.

Seeing this, Ringast ordered his centre to fall back fifty paces. The Sveär shieldwall was two hundred paces off, but a colossal cheer went up from them, perhaps thinking Ringast's centre had quailed before their overwhelming numbers. They came on even faster. But suddenly Ringast's men turned and took their stand. His shieldwall was ready, open like the jaws of a wolf, inviting in their enemy.

'Archers, loose!' screamed Ringast. The spitting sky went dark as five hundred arrows sped through the air. They plunged to earth and the first men fell, black fletching jutting from their bodies.

Sigurd's bowmen were quick to answer. A deadly cloud rose behind the Sveär shieldwall.

'Cover!' shouted someone. The front rows dropped to their knees and raised their shields, Erlan with them. Behind, men lifted shields above their heads. Then the first arrows were raining all around. Erlan heard arrowheads slit the dirt, the clatter and ring as they pierced limewood shields or bounced off iron helms. Then other sounds – the rip of mail and flesh, awful screams. His arm shook against the impact – once, twice. Through the shield-gaps, he saw the first men in the Sveär wall approaching fast – shields locked, eyes aflame, mouths agape, spear-points bristling. The man next to him fell out of line, an arrow buried to its fletching through his chest. His mouth bit vainly at the air, blood bubbling through his teeth over the white braids of his beard.

'Close up!' men screamed as the dying Gotar was yanked away and shield-rims rattled back together.

'Stand up,' someone yelled. Erlan glanced left and saw the crimson cloak of Ubbi stalking behind the shieldwall. Another slew of arrows fell, but now they had to take their chances. Erlan stood, raking his spear down his shield, snapping off the arrow shafts. Blood thundered in his head, the tramp of two thousand feet sending tremors through his body. He looked ahead, glimpsing Sigurd's banner.

'I swore it,' he whispered, and in that last moment Kai's face, with its bloody smear of crimson tears, flashed through his mind.

The two walls came together in a rending, roaring, grinding crash of wood and metal.

Erlan's feet slewed as a weight like a mountain slammed against him. Behind, men braced him to hold the massive surge, crushing him from both sides. Spear-points thrust like viper heads through gaps in the wall. There was no time to think. His arm thrust and stabbed and thrust again. Men were screaming as the first ones were cut down. Others leaped over them to take their place. A filthy face appeared above a shield-rim. He lunged, his spear-point gripped, he ripped it back and came away with half the man's face. Erlan thrust again, saw the point vanish into the man's neck, twisted, pulled. The man crashed to the ground, clutching his throat. Another filled his place.

Shapes flashed past Erlan's head, javelins from behind hurled point-black into the Sveär ranks. Men cursed and growled and shrieked and he smelled the stench of viscera for the first time that day.

Overhead arrows zipped, long-spears flew – a deluge of death, throwing screams from the men behind up into the sky. A sea of raging faces writhed and jostled behind Sveär shields. But Sigurd's attack had been checked and Ringast's wall had given little ground.

A huge long-axe crashed into the Gotar wall a couple of yards to Erlan's right. There was a shattering thud, then an arc of blood sprayed the air, spattering his face. The press was too tight for the headless body to fall and the blood-shower spurted ever weaker over the swarming warriors until it was spent.

'Death! Death!' a voice was bellowing to his left. He glimpsed a crimson figure driving forward into the Sveär wall. *Ubbi the Hundred*. For a second, Sigurd's line bowed inwards as

Ubbi's Frieslanders piled forward in a gale of steel. Erlan heard Ringast's shout behind. 'Cut off the head!'

Cut off the head?

Left and right the Gotar wall surged and suddenly he understood. Ringast meant to puncture their wall and sever the point of Sigurd's attack. Like a wolf ripping off the snout of a boar – if the jaws could close, Sigurd's best men would be trapped and destroyed.

Erlan heaved against the mountain of men, his throat raw with a scream. A blade flashed. A stinging pain streaked his cheekbone. Steel rang as a point struck his helm. He felt blood stream down his face into his mouth.

He swallowed it, tasting iron. At once, a searing heat tore down his throat, coursing through his body like liquid fire. He gasped, trying to steady himself. The heat sucked back into a tight ball inside him that felt like it would burst out of his chest. Then his limbs cooled. They felt stronger, harder, as if now made of metal. The fire burned but he was in control again.

At least something was.

Only now he thought nothing of tactics or position or even victory. Now he thought only of the slaughter – a fierce flaming rage inside him – the battle-song, the blood-cries, the killing joy! Faces and limbs and heads and helms were nothing but a red harvest to reap. And he laughed a mad, dark laugh that rang in his ears and echoed in the caverns of his wounded heart.

The man who cut him tried again, thrusting his spear. Erlan roared and, with a deft flick of his wrist, sent his long-spear straight for the man's head. The other slumped like a sack of rocks, his face caved in, the spear-shaft swinging wildly at his comrades.

Erlan's hand was already on Wrathling's hilt. The fields were high. The harvest before him, bountiful. With a yell like a fire-wight, he set to making Wrathling sing.

And sing she did.

In the mad whirlwind, the Vendling sword went to its bloody work. Fear crept into the eyes of the men around him, as he opened rifts of flesh in the Sveär wall. And slowly Ringast's line pushed forward.

Through his red fury, he spied the whip of Ubbi's crimson cloak. There was a crack, a shower of splinters, then a wild shout of triumph.

'They're broken!' a voice bellowed. 'Their wall is broken!'

Erlan saw Ubbi vanish into the gap, his Friesland oathmen plunging after him, and he flung himself in their wake.

An axe struck at him. His shield parried the blow. He stabbed and felt steel pierce leather and flesh. The old warrior was bellowing for champions to face him.

Suddenly the air filled with the whistle of arrows.

Thuk, thuk, thuk – they fell around Ubbi but his luck stayed with him. The old champion just shrieked with savage laughter and plunged on.

Erlan was now close to Ubbi. Just ahead he saw Sigurd's standard. His mouth was filled with mad words, his head with mad thoughts. Two bull-headed brutes leaped into his path.

'Hold, Gotar! The sons of Alrek will not let you pass.'

'No Gotar, me!' he screamed. 'I'm the night and the nowhere and the black abyss of Hel!'

Two strides and he'd knocked aside the first man's spear, roaring as Wrathling scythed into the man's face. He heard a raging howl as the brother flew at him. But Erlan only laughed. Did this fool really think he could kill him?

Something flashed between them and the brother's severed arm squelched in the dirt. He screamed until Erlan silenced him, sending him crashing on top of his dead kinsman.

He looked up, grinning, his thirst unslaked. Not twenty paces forward was the wolf-eagle banner and under it surely Sigurd. Ahead, Ubbi's axe was flying like an iron wind. Then a shout went up.

Starkad! Starkad!

The crush of men parted for a moment and down the channel came a monster of a man.

Ubbi was closer. He turned. If he wanted a champion to face, none was bigger than this bastard. He stood wide as a mountain, tall as the sky. Starkad the Old, the Bloody Ox, the Giant's Bane. No shield – only a massive long-sword gripped in both fists.

Ubbi bellowed his war-cry of 'Death!' – eyes glinting with savage glee.

'If it's death you want, I'll show you to his gates,' roared Starkad.

Ubbi laughed. 'You can try, villain! Come – my blade is thirsty!'

The champions closed, striking out blow for blow, while the battle broke around them like storm-waves round two pillars of rock. And who could say which would fell the other? None but the Spear-God himself.

But Odin had other fates for each of them.

Erlan's eyes, meanwhile, were fixed on Sigurd's standard. The Frieslanders had driven a wedge deep into the Sveär line, but there was no sign of any link-up with Ringast's men from the other side. And now momentum was waning. Limbs were tiring. Breath was short.

Rallying cries rang amid the Sveär host. A heave of muscle, a clatter of shields, and the wall closed once more. Erlan yelled in frustration. One man couldn't break a shieldwall, after all.

Then suddenly he glimpsed a splendid bronze and iron mask. The ancient Kingshelm, forged an age ago for the Yngling kings. Wearing it was the man he must kill. He hurled himself at it but the Sveär ranks seemed to have multiplied again, as though every man slaughtered had risen from the dead.

Then another war-cry sounded.

Kursland! Kursland!

Ahead, a mass of men surged towards the shieldwall and was driving back the Frieslanders. Arrows fell thick as hail. Erlan looked for Ubbi and saw a flash of crimson a distance off.

There, Starkad and Ubbi were trading blows and trading wounds, but even they couldn't withstand the Kurslander flood. The fresh waters swelled about them and broke them apart.

Ubbi raged, cheated of his chance to fell the man-mountain, as Starkad was borne away, leaving Ubbi surrounded by a mob of blue-black tattooed faces. And from their number stepped a bald brute with a face half-black like the split face of Hel.

Ubbi grimaced. 'So death has come for me at last, eh?'

'Egil Seal-Head's come for you,' the painted man cried. 'And death with him!'

'Damn you – I've a taste for life yet. Come! I'll have that black head off your shoulders!'

Egil roared, lurching at the old champion. Ubbi met spear with shield-rim. The shaft scraped wide and Ubbi stepped in, putting his boot in the other's stomach. Egil reeled back, feet slipping, scrabbling to land another thrust. But Ubbi hadn't lived so long giving second chances. His sword swept over Egil's shield-rim and bit into his skull, splitting it open like a boiled egg. Egil slumped to the ground and the old man roared in triumph, shaking the mail that covered his face, baying for his next victim.

But instead came a shout of a command. The line parted like a curtain and behind was a line of archers. For an instant, Ubbi glared. He'd seen many sights during the *Valkyries'* song but never this. A row of stars – arrowheads and eyes, twinkling. He opened his mouth to cry one last shout of defiance but the first of the arrows was faster, piercing his face-mail and plunging into the back of his throat. He shuddered, blood bubbling from his mouth as a dozen arrowheads slammed into his body. He swayed, stumbled, tripped on his cloak, and finally crashed over into the mud.

Ubbi the Hundred had found himself a glorious death at last.

CHAPTER SIXTY-FOUR

A cheer burst from the middle of Sigurd's line, loud enough to turn Lilla's head.

She strained her eyes, scanning the writhing bodies to see what it meant. But it was too far, too many heads and arms and weapon-shafts to make out one happening in the ten thousand unfolding before her.

From her vantage point behind Ringast's centre, the plain was a roiling sea of carnage, a bloody, dizzy swirl, banners and standards tossing like ships on its surface.

She had watched Sigurd's line advance, watched it met and held as the shieldwalls crashed together, watched Ringast's banner snap back the point of her brother's attack, then drive into the ranks of the Sveär host. But that too had been checked.

Her hands were shaking. She looked down. Her knuckles were white, tight around her staff. There was fear in her blood – fear and wild excitement. Both rose like a vapour off all those warriors, imbuing each breath she inhaled.

She re-doubled her chanting. Since the first arrow, she had

been invoking spells of protection over her husband, over Erlan and all the rest. Her bow and arrow-quiver lay at her feet, should the unthinkable befall her husband's army. Next to them in the dirt was a patchwork of runes: *seidr*-magic to blunt the weapons wielded against them, words to strengthen their blades and shields. And now, both of them were lost in a maelstrom of steel. Her husband. And the man she loved.

She scanned the plain to the west. On the far left of Ringast's line, she could make out the whirling bearskins of the Hedmarker berserkers. To their right, the Skanskar bondsmen led by Galdalf's sons. Against them, she saw the banner of the Jotnunger – the tallest Sveär clan from the north who took their name from the giant race of old. Shrieks and bellows carried to her as the animal-warriors hurled themselves against those men of stone. Those still alive were butchering each other over an ever-growing pile of the dead.

In the centre, she searched for Sigurd's standard – the banner of her own house. She found it, blue and black, rising from the centre of his line. At first, it had been pushed back. But the ranks behind it had swollen as more and more men appeared from the trees to fill the places of the fallen. And for the first time it was gaining ground as Ringast's banner slipped back.

How could he have gathered so many? Sigurd's reserves were so numerous, while her husband had none – save for the waning hope that his father would come.

To the right, the crush of warriors stretched all the way to the marshland. She fancied she saw the figure of Thrand laying about him with his deadly axe, wearing no armour, like the Rus berserkers around him. They and Thrand's Gotars had been pushed back but were holding still, despite the Sveär onslaught.

She recognized the standard of Arwakki among the Sveär wolf-warriors and near that the banner of Harling Snake. She knew them both – men tempered in the fire of many battles. Thrand would have no respite. Howls mingled with death-cries and screams, swirling towards her with a mist blowing off the Snow Lake in ever-thickening skeins.

Something about that mist was wrong...

She glanced behind at the other *seidkonur* lined along the rise: old women and some younger ones, her handmaid Gerutha among them, singing their *galdr*-songs around a blazing fire, their charge to protect Ringast's forces from sorcery, securing him victory in the unseen places while his warriors held the battle-line.

The mist swirled closer. Lilla felt her gaze drawn to the treeline behind Sigurd's host. There was evil there. She could feel it.

Saldas...

That moment she heard a piercing screech overhead. She shuddered, recognizing the sound from her dreams. She strained her eyes among the banks of cloud chasing overhead. The cry sounded again. Closer now, above her. But after a few more seconds of scanning the sky, she gave it up, dread weighing heavy in her chest.

The mist was swallowing up the eastern end of the line. She looked at the flask in her hand: a gift from one of the *seidkonur*. Her mother had forbidden her this deeper magic. But she had to see more. How else could she stop Saldas? If not now – when?

She moved closer to the fire, pulled the stopper from the flask and poured its contents down her throat.

. . . .

Somewhere towards the eastern end of the Sveär side, Einar Fat-Belly was wishing his by-name was Hard-Head or Stone-Skin. Least then he might have a chance to live through this madness.

His wolf-warrior friend had fallen in the first volley of arrows. So much for brave talk. By now, he'd be well on the road to *Valhöll*. Einar might have been happy to join him, sat on the Spear-God's benches, with a frothy ale and a soft tit or two to fondle. But these things had their time and place. He wasn't quite done with this world yet.

The other Sveär lads weren't faring too badly. Madmen, most of his kin, for sure, and Arwakki was maddest of 'em all. Just as well, since some big Wendish bugger was trying to take his head off.

That much he'd gathered anyhow, glancing away from the yellow-haired savage gaping at him right now. The berserker's whiskers were stained red and he had the battle-mist in his eye, but fortunately for Einar the man sorely lacked brains. Einar lifted his arm, sidestepped left and deflected the berserker's blade into the mud.

They should call me Einar Elfin-Toes, he thought, slamming his shield-boss into the berserker's shoulder.

'Silly boy,' he snarled, jabbing his spear-point under the man's beard-braids. Blood gushed over his fist as he ripped it clear.

Einar stepped back, letting two of his mates go ahead. He was blowing like an ass. All he really wanted to do was sit down. Slim chance of that. He wanted to be sick, too. That was more likely.

To his left, a Gotar, big as a troll with a bare chest slick with gore, was bellowing like a skewered ox. He looked vaguely familiar but Einar let the point slide.

Reckon some other hero can deal with him.

He looked for Arwakki's banner and spotted it away east. That was when he noticed the mist, curling round its flapping hide. It was thick and moving fast, so that even the carnage around the Gotar troll-man was becoming obscured. The first tendrils slipped past Einar's face. It felt cold. Strange sibilant whispers seemed to join the battle-babble.

He didn't like this one bit, and there was already plenty else not to like.

'Come on, you fat son of a whore!' someone cried. 'Lend a hand!'

He snapped his head and saw one of his Bredlunger kinsman straining against the wall.

Einar tried to grin away his terror. 'Better 'n that, my lad – I'll lend you my belly!' He flung himself against the line of linden shields. 'Right, you bastards, heave!' he roared. And the world grew darker.

The stink was worse than Hel's own shit-pit. The ground was littered with piles of the fallen. Erlan's world had shrunk into a chain of moments, lurching forward through the blood and bodies. There was no memory of the past, no thought of the future. Only this terrible, awesome present.

Was this the *Ragnarök* – when the world of men would be sucked down in a whirlpool of pain and fury and slaughter for all time? Was this the destiny of men? To burn till the end of time with the savage rage of battle, to kill or be killed for ever? Rising, only to die again and again.

Sigurd's banner was too far to see now. So many fresh waves

had been thrown into the Sveär line that Ringast's centre had started to bow backwards. Slowly the Sveär tide was starting to tell, and like a rudderless boat on the ocean, Erlan was carried wherever the flood took him.

Blood streamed into one eye. He recognized the battle-yells of Ubbi's Frieslanders – those still alive. On the left, the Hedmarkers and Skanskar levies were falling back under the weight of Sigurd's right – huge men with huge hammers and long-spears. More men were pouring into the centre, pressing the remaining Frieslanders left and Erlan with them.

Then he glimpsed the standard of Galdalf's twins: red cloth with two black serpents entwined around a spear, jerking crazily above the fray. That meant he was among the Skanskar hirds, ragged bondsmen with hardly a spear and shield for each man. Some were giving ground, some running away, but enough still stood against the big Jotnungers and were dying, mostly, for their efforts.

A stocky man in a russet cloak was yelling to another just like him. Erlan recognized Galdalf's twins, Alf and Alfarin, though only the gods could pick them apart. 'Fine weather for giant-killing, brother!' cried one.

'The bigger they are—'

'—the bigger their bloody swords!' his brother finished for him, and they laughed like devils.

Wrathling was a long streak of gore. A man in a crude iron helm came at Erlan, snarling through rotten teeth. He lunged his shield-rim. Erlan dropped his shoulder, lifted his shield and scythed Wrathling from the right. An instant later the man landed with a splash in a lake of blood and began screaming, his leg hewn clean off.

Two Skanskar bondsmen rushed past Erlan, headlong into a maw of Jotnunger spearmen. Next to him, another man screamed, pawing at an arrow-shaft in his arm. Suddenly, arrows were falling everywhere. More men fell.

'Alfar!' cried his twin. 'Those lads ain't too fond of you!'

'Stand close, brother! If one is meant for me, you'll do just as well!'

Still, the twins both ducked under their shields. Erlan did likewise. There were rattles and thuds all around as arrows showered shields and bodies. A cold mist was blowing among them now, its damp air chilling his lungs. Erlan stole a glance at the sky, the first since the shieldwalls had met. He blinked, unable to believe his eyes, knowing his mind must have cracked. Because what he saw was far beyond the sight of ordinary men.

The air was alive with winged creatures.

Lilla fell to her knees, clawing at her throat.

She gasped, feeling liquid fire swirl through her, pricking at the inside of her skin like a thousand needles. Her arms shook. She was losing control. Her breath came in short, desperate pants. It was too intense.

And too late.

She opened her eyes, but her vision was dissolving, the grey sky above darkening like a bruise. Beside her the fire crackled. She felt a sudden crushing pain all over her skull. She cried out, afraid – but she couldn't stop now even if she wanted to. The roar of battle grew louder, but the cries outstripped the clash of metal until all she heard was one long scream.

She dropped her staff, clutching at her belly, the pain more than she could bear. Only then did she realize it was her screaming. She tore at her hair, nails raking her head over and over till suddenly she fell back on the ground. She lay there, staring at the sky, and the pain began to recede, giving way to a new strength that flooded through her shoulders and down her arms. Her screaming stopped. She closed her eyes and listened.

The battle sounds were changing. Instead of the shapeless welter of noise, she heard ten thousand sounds, each sharp as a pin. She found she could pick out any one at will: the sigh of a man's last breath; the *schick* of a knife being drawn; the ring of a sword edge slicing mail; the snap of a banner in the wind; men's voices – screaming, choking, praying, pleading; the rustle of leaves in the distant wood; the mist slipping through the air. And above her, cruel laughter.

She opened her eyes and sat up. So she thought, at least. But everything had an unreal quality, every line was sharper, every colour more intense, and she found she could perceive every movement in the battle as though time itself was hers to sift. Shields blocked, spears parried, swords thrust, axes hacked, and somehow she knew how each weapon would find its mark. She saw runes graven on blade edges, saw a serpent-tongue tattooed on a warrior's neck, a thread of wool tied around the wrist of a severed hand for luck.

Clearest of all, she saw blood. Blood bespattering everything like scarlet rain, flung by the furious tempest that was swallowing this multitude of men and vomiting them out again in red death.

All at once the ground fell away beneath her and she rose into the sky, up and up, till she was far above the tumult of battle.

She experienced a violent surge of joy. She was amazed, confused, exhilarated – except at once she saw the sky was swarming with other creatures. Hundreds of them, swooping and screaming, shrieking like demon-gulls. As she looked, at first she thought they had the form of women, trailing long black hair like banners of mourning. But the likeness went no further. They wore ragged robes that billowed at every turn, and butchers' aprons, gleaming wet and red, with wasted arms stretched longingly to the chaos below, sinews twisting, and their hands — their hands were horrible. Crooked like talons and dripping with gore.

She knew she was no longer in her body and wondered what strange vision this was.

One of them swept close in a rush of air, turning to look at her. She saw its face was all shadow, its grimace a gaping laugh beckoning to oblivion, and in its eyes some dark, cruel joy.

She watched the thing dive into the frenzy below like a hawk snatching a hare. Immediately it was climbing away again, except now it held something in its terrible hands.

No sooner had Lilla the wish to know its prize than she moved closer. And she saw there in the creature's grip a man, or something like a man. She only doubted because it was such a wretched thing – a husk of a once-proud warrior, all strength and life sucked out of him. His scream was loud enough. So loud and long and desolate that it wrung her heart. The creature climbed higher, clutching the man jealously to its blood-soaked apron, heading for the clouds above.

Lilla looked away, horrified, wishing she had the power to drive these things away. Were these the *Valkyries* – the wish-maidens of Odin, fetching his chosen ones to ride in glory to the Slain-Hall?

But these were no maids. They were monsters.

She watched as others plunged to earth and climbed away, shrieking with laughter as they carried off the dead, each soul – or whatever it was – more wasted and wretched than the last, writhing in those bloody talons. In vain.

She felt sick, but steeled her pity. She couldn't help the dead. But the living – perhaps she might help them.

Then she heard it again, the sound that pierced through every other. She knew it at once. Looking, she thought she glimpsed a shadow cutting through the clouds. But it was so fleeting she wondered whether it wasn't just fear taunting her imagination.

But there it was again, only for a heartbeat but long enough to know it was real. The shadow she dreaded from her dreams. *Himinns Freki* – the wolf of the skies. The black eagle.

Saldas's eagle.

And then a huge pair of dark wings broke from the clouds and swooped down along the battle-line, skimming the surface of the spreading mist.

She watched, and all the while all she could think of was Saldas, wondering what dark magic she was weaving to bend the fate of all these dying thousands to her will. Lilla looked within herself, determined to find a way to counter Saldas's power. But she hardly had that thought than the black eagle climbed again and banked towards her. She felt suddenly pinned, caught in its sight, unable to move, her will somehow frozen. She could only watch with growing horror as the long smooth shadow swung onto a line straight at her, the cruel hook of its beak looming ever larger until it tore straight through her, ripping through her abdomen as she screamed and screamed, her belly shrieking with unquenchable pain. Her mind insisted it was still a vision, but her body knew the pain was real, and suddenly she was falling. Down and down she fell, spiralling in an ever-shrinking world of agony to the ground below...

CHAPTER
SIXTY-FIVE

'You see that?' shouted Erlan.

'See what?' yelled back Alfarin.

'Those things – swooping from the clouds.'

Alfarin shot a look to the skies. 'Can't see nothing but rain and arrows!'

'I'd keep your bird-watching for another day,' his twin cried. 'If you live to see one.'

Erlan suddenly wondered where Lilla was in all this mess. He felt a sharp stab for her but scowled it away and spat blood. She was another man's concern now.

Through the mist, he saw Ringast's banner had fallen back beyond where battle first joined. Sigurd's banner was surging on. He cursed, seeing hundreds between them now. And the Sveär numbers never seemed to thin.

'Here come those giant-spawn again!' cried Alfarin, as a group of Jotnunger reformed their wall. He felt doubt stall the men around him, mostly Skanskar farm-boys. *Bondi* – probably wondering what the Hel this fight had to do with them. They had fought well in spite of that, but now they were flagging. And dying.

Erlan's eye caught another man standing motionless in all that movement, staring into the sky as though in a trance.

Another who can see! Maybe he wasn't losing his mind after all. The temptation to look up again was instantly unbearable but then a Kursland spearman slipped through and ran screaming at the seer. At the last moment, he glanced down, saw the danger, but the spear was through his chest before his shield had even moved.

Erlan turned back to the Jotnunger line.

Let gods and demons and witches and who knows what fell things fight their battles above. He could only fight like a man. Fight and kill. Or be killed.

The Norns must choose which.

Einar Fat-Belly saw it in their eyes first. The fear, and the flood of Sveär reserves pressing behind him reflected in their stricken gaze.

Harling Snake had thrown in his hirds now, and the Finnish archers and short-spearmen were hard behind them, too. He was damned glad it was Sigurd's side that had the numbers.

It was the fog that tipped it, though. No one liked to fight in it. But the Wendish had a fear of it. Which was why, when they broke, they ran like Hela's hounds.

It was moments like this Einar was glad he was no runner. Besides, all manner of madness was occurring up ahead, most of it swathed in the mist.

A sudden, eerie quiet had settled over his sector of the plain. Apart from the groans of the dying, of course. Even the arrows had thinned almost to nothing. To the left near the marshes, he could still hear the berserkers' shrieks.

His throat was dry as sand. He'd give his right arm for an ale-skin, he thought, then wished he hadn't. You never knew when some vindictive god was within earshot.

His eye happened on a Gotar spearman face down in the mud and there, across his back, was indeed a decent-sized skin. Einar had it off him in a second and found it wasn't quite empty.

'My thanks, old Aegir,' he chuckled. The god of brewing had always been his favourite. They had an understanding, after all.

'And thanks to you too, friend.' He slapped the dead man's rump and set to glugging down his ale like Thor on a hot day.

There was a sudden *zipp* and shudder as an arrow punctured the skin, stopping a whisker from his chest. He stared stupidly at it, mouth agape, beer dribbling over his knuckles.

He wasn't a superstitious man by nature, but he was nevertheless captive to a strong feeling that the Spear-God was trying to tell him something. He let the skin drop and squashed his helm tight on his head. There was heroes' work to be done. And wasn't he just the man to do it?

'Hold up, lads!' he yelled. 'I'm right behind you.' And off he jogged after his blood-baying kinsmen.

Where is my father? thought Ringast Haraldarsson for the hundredth time that day.

They were losing. That much was obvious. Ubbi had fallen; his Frieslanders were scattered. To the right, Thrand must still be holding their flank, though Ringast couldn't see a damned thing. As for his western wing, he prayed those murderous cousins, Grim and Geir, were good as their reputation.

Then the Wendish hirds bolted out of the mist.

'My lord – see there!' screamed Visma. He saw all right, cursing them for cowards as they fled.

'So much for your countrymen,' he snarled at the shieldmaid. 'We have to shore the hole. Now!'

But what with? He had no reserve.

'Let me go, my lord,' Visma begged. 'Let me salvage some honour for my kinsmen.'

'Take half these men.' He jabbed his sword at the Gotars holding the centre right. 'Close the gap. If you fail, the day is lost!'

'Give me the standard,' cried Kari.

Visma tossed the young warrior the raven banner and drew her sword. 'Odin keep us all! For Wendland and Ringast!' Then she ran along the line, yelling, 'Who wants a hero's death?'

Men broke off to follow her but Ringast harboured little hope. He could see almost nothing through the fog. His flanks had held so far but what use was that if the centre crumbled?

They must hold!

Victory. He wanted victory, no less. No glory, no seat at Odin's table, nothing but to crush these oath-breaking devils – for Lilla's sake even more than his own.

Is that love, then? Gods, what a place to find it!

He lifted his voice and bellowed into the mist. 'Ringast still stands, you hear? Your lord still stands with you!'

His words might give his men some backbone to stand and fight, but only the weight of steel could force back the Sveär tide.

Where is my father? he thought again. And then a voice roared out of the mist. 'RINGAST!' His own name rolled up to him like thunder. '*RINGAST!*' In the swirling vapour a towering figure took shape, his hulking limbs slathered in blood.

'Starkad,' Ringast murmured, recognizing the champion who had turned coat from his father's hearth into the ranks of King Sigurd Kin-Slayer.

The Sea-King continued to bellow his name like a war-cry, hewing a path towards him. Men who had stood all day were thrown aside like rag-dolls. Ringast readied his shield and sword, thinking ruefully that his day may end quicker than he thought.

Starkad roared at the other Sveär warriors to stay back.

'A curse on you, traitor,' yelled Ringast. 'You betrayed my father.'

The big *víkingr* grimaced. He was soaked in blood. A piece of his beard hung off his face, cut clean along the jawbone, which flapped crazily when he spoke.

'I'm here for your head, boy.'

'You'd better come get it then,' Ringast snarled, bracing himself.

'In the north, they know me as—'

'Shut up and fight, you towering sack of shit!'

The smile slid from Starkad's face. His licked his ruined lip and hooked the grisly flap of beard between his teeth.

The two men began circling each other like wolves. Suddenly Starkad's point drove at Ringast's face. He blocked it, slashing low with his sword, but Starkad was at full stretch and the tip swept by clean.

In another eye-blink the massive blade crashed down. Ringast lurched under the falling arm, slamming into Starkad's bloody torso. It was like tackling an oak tree. Their bodies jarred and he felt the wound in his chest rip open.

He sucked back the stab of pain, but the old champion also groaned and fell back a step. A thrill rippled through Ringast as he realized the Sea-King's strength was nearly spent.

'You've found your last fight, Starkad.'

But the turncoat was far from done. He whipped round his arms in another deadly blow. Ringast slewed the wrong way and too late. He could only wrench up his shield in desperation to cover his neck.

There was a crack, a shower of splinters and blinding pain screamed up his arm. His shattered shield fell in pieces to the ground. Starkad's blade was lodged in the mud. Ringast lurched backwards to get clear for a second's respite. His hand was agony. He glanced down, seeing only his thumb, a finger and a bloody stub. Half his palm was cut away.

Starkad laughed through teeth still clamped down on his beard, kicking away the broken shield. Ringast grimaced. His shield-hand was in spasm. All around them Sveär warriors were rushing past. But they knew better than to cheat Starkad of his prize. Ringast's foot knocked something hard. He recognized the shape and weight of a spear.

Starkad growled, unable to speak, great bulging arms whaling at Ringast's exposed left side. But he too was fading. Ringast caught the blow above his head. There was a grinding of metal as Starkad crushed down the weight of his two arms against Ringast's one. The prince sensed his last moment fast approaching. With one last desperate lunge, he released all resistance and flung himself forward, crossing the sword-line.

He should have been a dead man. But Starkad's strength worked for him, whipping his sword round his wrist and an instant later he felt it carve into sinew and muscle.

Starkad gave a long, low sigh. His huge sword fell, his big hands pawing at the steel buried in his neck. Ringast left it there and calmly picked up the spear at his feet, gripping its shaft in the crook of his ruined arm. Then he drove the point hard into the champion's belly. The ring-mail burst and Ringast felt metal grind against Starkad's spine.

The Sea-King fell to his knees, eyes wide and confused. Ringast twisted the shaft deeper, turned it like a screw, then with a single, violent wrench ripped it clear... and Starkad the Old, champion of ten kings, fell on his face. Dead.

Dazed and breathing hard, Ringast tugged his sword free of Starkad's lifeless body. Blood was welling from his cloven hand.

'I'm with you, lord,' shouted Kari, his new bannerman.

'Glad somebody is, boy,' he gasped, clutching his arm to his chest.

He looked right. The fighting there was thicker than ever. Visma seemed to have rallied a remnant of her Wendish swords and was fighting under her husband's banner. Ringast glanced behind. Not fifty yards back, the ground rose sharply to the outcrop where they had stood before dawn.

He swore. Had they really been pushed back that far?

His men were fighting bravely but there were fewer of them every second. If his father didn't come now then this day was lost. And in his ear, he felt the breath of Odin's whisper... calling him.

'Not yet,' he growled through gritted teeth. 'Not yet.'

Lilla came to with a sensation like a red-hot comb raking her insides. She tried to close her mind to the pain, determined not to slip back into unconsciousness. How much time had passed, she had no idea. She sat up and looked across the plain.

From her position, the mist lay in a blanket between her and the far ridge, obscuring all but the closest butchery. The fighting was close now. So close she could have tossed her staff and hit her husband's banner. Someone to the right – the Wendish, maybe – had broken and were streaming past the outcrop. Forward of them others were trying to plug the gap, but the shieldwall was haemorrhaging like a breached river-dam.

This was the moment, she realized. When everything hung by a thread. When her husband, if he had a second to spare her any thought at all, would be willing her to go, to flee, to find safety somewhere. Anywhere.

But how could she leave now?

Suddenly she heard the eagle's cry. A shiver of dread shot through her. Her gaze turned east, seeking the dark shape against the steel-grey clouds. And then she saw the soaring shadow away over the marshland. As she watched, he fell like a black thunderbolt and swept along the bloody seam of slaughter, speeding up the plain towards her.

Seized by a sudden impulse, she groped for her bow and quiver beside her in the dirt. For a second her hands floundered and then she had it. A second more and she had a shaft torn free. She nocked the fletching and drew back her arm, her eyes now sharp, tracking the dark wings up the battle-line. 'Father, help me now,' she murmured, taking aim, her eye boring down the length of birch past the needle-sharp arrow-tip.

Except that Freki, as if sensing danger, pulled up suddenly, beating at the air with all the power in his wide-spread wings. Up and up he climbed. Lilla shut out everything but him. No sights, no sounds, no smells. No sensations – not even the pain that was rinsing her insides like a boiling kettle.

She took a snatched breath, swung through her hips like her father had taught her, and loosed the arrow.

For a frozen moment, there was nothing. Only the pinprick shaft speeding away into the grey above. Then there was a small, crumpled sound, so faint she could have imagined it... but that the huge bird jagged off its track.

She watched, hardly daring to hope, as the eagle began to fall, one wing buckled out of shape. But the proud head was still up. She had winged him only. Still, that was enough to pluck him from the sky. He half-fell, half-dived in a black streak across the plain – one wing out strong, trying to grip the air, the other flapping uselessly. And then he disappeared with a crash into the tops of the trees in the far woods.

She let out a strangled whoop of triumph, answered at once with a fresh wave of pain through her belly. She dropped the bow and fell to her knees. The pain seemed to know, seemed to sense its release, throwing her back like a tidal wave, breaking over her with all its force.

Arms closed around her. Someone was with her. She recognized Gerutha's voice. Her vision fading, she looked out one last time. The mist covered the whole plain now, east to west. Above it, the clouds still drifted. But something in the air had changed. Some presence had receded.

'Saldas is broken,' she whispered.

'What?' exclaimed Gerutha, voice frantic. 'What did you say?'

But Lilla's consciousness was slipping away. And then she felt it: a breath of air from the west. And the breath became a breeze, building, and then a wind whistling past her face, driving the mist before it.

Saldas is broken...

The air filled with a new sound then – the blast of a hundred horns. Lilla looked west. Men were spilling out of the trees – men of war, spearmen, shieldmen, archers, warriors in their hundreds. *In their thousands!*

She sank back into Gerutha's arms, surrendering to the sweet darkness of oblivion closing over her.

Because the Wartooth had come at last.

CHAPTER
SIXTY-SIX

Shield-rim trees, the skalds called them. And the kenning never fit so well. The western wood had come alive.

But these trees were deadly, bearing shields of every hue, steel of every shape, under banners blazoned with every kind of beast. And as the Danish horde fanned from the trees, a low-slung wagon emerged in its midst, drawn by snow-white horses. Above it, whipped by the westerly wind, rose a banner – a scarlet boar on a cloth of white: the mark of the Wartooth. Under it stood Harald, King of the Danes.

'Behold the impudence of sons!' the old war-king cried, his bristly face alight with mischief. 'Where's a father's respect, I ask you?' His old companion-in-arms, Branni, stood beside him listening, his grey hood pulled forward, one tufted eyebrow raised sardonically while he surveyed the plain. 'They're making a fine cowpat of the business, by the look of it. Brat – you Irish rogue!' he called down to a loping killer with the slaughter-thirst in his eye. 'Can you hear me – you deaf son of a whore?'

'I hear you, Wartooth.'

'Just look at 'em! To think the young whelps would start without me.' He roared with mad laughter.

The Irishman pressed a long thumb against one nostril and emptied the other into the grass. 'Sure, they've barely got things going. Still plenty of them Sveär bastards left.'

'Let's see what mischief an old fool and his friends can make, eh? Onward, my children!' he cried left and right, a maniac grin glazing his face. 'There's your feast by Odin's eye!' He drew his sword and shook it at the killing storm ahead. 'To slaughter, my younglings! My most buxom wench to the first man who wets his boots in those far waters. On, my beauties! The Wartooth's tusk will bleed those Sveär wolves white!'

His wagon rolled onto the plain. Beside him, Branni stood tall and grim, while his bannerman Tyrfing the Skald whipped up the reins. Danish horns split the air anew and the Wartooth's motley army surged forward in a flood of fury.

Under the creak of the wagon wheels, Tyrfing heard his lord's soft mutter: 'Now, old friend, is this enough? Ah, my bones are weary. It's time we meet, eye to eye.' Then the Wartooth's throat opened in a boundless laugh, fey and fierce. 'Meet me in the storm, you Lord of War! Hahaah! I'm come to seek you out!'

The horses' hooves pounded onwards.

At the horn-blasts, every man on the plain had stopped. For a heartbeat only, but long enough for those plaintive notes to pierce his mind.

Around Erlan, the wall of Hedmark berserkers and Skanskar spearmen was buckling backwards. But the horns filled the air with new terror and new hope. Now Odin would have his full reaping and the day would be won and lost.

'You hear that, brother?' cried Alfarin, still near enough for Erlan to hear. 'Sweet as mead, that sound! Let's see the last of these big bastards fall and then on to their king.'

And suddenly a great crushing flood of Danes, Gotlanders and Irish was on them, sweeping everything before it. Grim and Geir, slick with the battle-slime, took their vengeance on the Jotnungers then, joined by Hedinn Slim and his men. On the Danish left, Veborg the war-queen and her Gotlanders swallowed up the Telemarker bowmen, who had rained down death all day.

It was a massacre.

Harald's men surged on, mangling the Sveär right into a charnel house. At their head was the Wartooth himself with his father's sword, the Flame of Danmark, swinging about him. The snow-white horses thundered down the corpse-strewn plain while Harald cut red swathes left and right, shieldless and seeking death, crying to the High One to accept him home.

Then Sigurd's right broke, fleeing eastwards to escape the closing jaws of the Danish onslaught. Erlan saw the wave come and he was ready. He had not forgotten his oath to Kai. And now he saw his chance revived. One man could never have cut his way through to Sigurd. Now, though, a thousand men were carving a path and he went with them. The writhing wave of slaughter rolled on, blood frothing like the foam of the deep.

Time was as nothing. He knew only madness. Faces flashed and fell before him. *Cut, hack, turn, scream... run on!* Yet each face seemed more familiar, each aspect darker, each beard blacker, until all the flashing faces dissolved into one:

The face of his first lord.

His father.

Again and again, it was his father's face. Again and again, his sword struck the fleeing figures, but it was his father who fell. He wanted to shut his eyes, to shut out the horror. But it was no good, because the horror was inside him. The horror at what it made him feel.

The horror of savage joy.

Further east, one man's voice rang over the tumult with laughter in his words.

'Run on, my brothers!' cried Ringast. 'This day will be ours! Drive them into the mire – and give quarter to none!' His face was ashen and his body a bloody wreck, but his words stirred the weary hearts of the Gotar hirds.

The Wartooth's wagon raced on, its wheels daubed red from the blood-soaked soil. Yet as Harald flew east with the wind, two men stepped from Sigurd's fleeing host and stood their mark. Grettir the Evil was one; Svein Reaper, the other.

They raised their long-swords high and brought them down as one. The blades bit deep. The horses reared up, screaming. The wagon lurched. Tyrfing the Skald was flung wide, knocked senseless. The old war-king and Branni went over with the wagon.

The bloodied wheels spun. The dying beasts pawed at the dirt. King Harald dragged himself up, winded but still unblooded. When he stood, Grettir and Svein Reaper were waiting.

Moments later, Tyrfing opened his eyes. His head was

pounding. Groggily he looked up and there saw his lord fighting for his life.

Harald roared defiance, laying about with sword and spear. He was old but still had some speed and skill in him. He needed it, for these two knew their business, probing him, keeping him at distance, making him work. Tyrfing tried to get up, but his head swam and he collapsed again and could only look on through dazed eyes.

Then Branni was there, in his long grey cloak with the hood so far forward that Tyrfing saw only the flash of a single eye. And in his hand, a long ash spear. He seemed taller, though, and as the Wartooth fought his foe, Branni did nothing.

Instead Svein Reaper made his move, darting left, snapping over his hands. The blade cracked Harald's wrist. His sword fell but he didn't cry out. Now Grettir came at him, was past his spear, and drove his point deep into the old king's thigh. Harald dropped his spear and staggered, clutching his leg.

Branni now stepped forward and the two Sveärs, seeing him, strangely shrank back. Harald looked up into Branni's face, which was hidden from Tyrfing's view. His mouth gaped, awe-struck. 'So, old friend,' the skald heard Harald mutter. 'It's you.' Branni nodded.

Harald fell to his knees. Branni spun, his grey cloak whirled, steel flashed. And the Wartooth's head bumped into the dirt.

Tyrfing moaned and sank his face into the mud. When he looked up again, the king-killers were gone and Branni with them. And afterwards, although the skald looked for him among the living and the dead, Branni was never seen again.

This is how it was later told that Harald fell to the Spear-God himself that day. That his old shieldbrother Branni had been lost at sea and the One-Eyed had taken his place. They said that Odin walked amid his battle-storm of heroes that day.

But who knows the truth of it?

All that can be said for certain is that the Wartooth was dead.

And in all those thousands, this one death was not unnoticed. The cry went up that King Harald had fallen. The Sveär cheered. It even seemed they might rally around their own king. With Harald dead, perhaps the Danes would lose heart.

But there was another to lead them, and the Wartooth's son roared vengeance when he saw his father's banner fall.

Erlan was ahead of him, his mind a blizzard, face after face the same. Until he saw it – at last a face that was not his father's. This one was cold and dead as the metal on which it was stamped. The Kingshelm – his second sight of it that day – spattered with mud and gore.

He drew a deep breath. This was why he was here.

'SIGURD!' he screamed with every sinew, remembering the torturous heat, the blood tears streaking Kai's cheek. 'SIG-URD!'

A shout beside him. The twins were there. Sigurd's bannermen turned to face them. 'We'll have these!' Galdalf's sons leaped ahead, each taking a man.

He yelled Sigurd's name a third time, his voice a fearful howl. This time Sigurd turned. 'Hel has come for you, brother!' Through the sight-holes of the Kingshelm, Erlan saw Sigurd's eyes flare with dread.

Erlan threw off his helm, heedless of the storm around him. 'You see me clear, kin-slayer? The blood you've spilled cries for you from the halls of Hel!'

The Kingshelm shook with cold laughter. 'Come then, cripple. I promised Saldas your heart. And she shall have it.'

'I have no heart, you fool!' snarled Erlan madly.

He shifted Wrathling in his hand. His shield was a ruin, splinters and rags flapping at its edge. He flung it down and drew his seax.

Sigurd took his guard. Around them, the twins' war-cries howled, but Erlan saw only this man, this death, without which nothing that day mattered a thrall's fart.

The first move came suddenly: Sigurd's blade cut upwards. Erlan parried with his knife. Wrathling swept low but Sigurd dropped his shield and at once resumed the attack.

He moved at surprising speed. Erlan's dagger had to work fast, up and down, blocking a hail of blows. Twice, Wrathling rang the Kingshelm like a bell, but glanced away unblooded. He tried to get wide of Sigurd's blade to attack his open side, but the king dropped back on distance, then sprang forward even stronger.

Rage was no good for this fight. Erlan needed to use his head. Sigurd was fresher, faster, a match for his strength, and he had a shield. But Erlan noticed one stroke Sigurd made repeatedly: a high cut from the right for the gap between seax and sword, which so far Erlan had parried.

Sigurd went high again. Erlan left a gap open. Sigurd took the bait, but Erlan was ready. He ducked down and left under the falling blade. A fool's move if you didn't know it was coming, but it worked. He punched Wrathling up and right, deflecting the blow, then cut down hard with his seax, feeling the metal bite ring-mail and sink into Sigurd's wrist.

The kin-slayer screamed but Erlan was already driving his

crippled ankle into Sigurd's knee. The old pain flared as Sigurd went down.

But the king's flailing edge caught Erlan's calf a lucky blow. Erlan screamed, fresh pain shearing up his leg, and he went sprawling too. Sigurd was already struggling to get up. Erlan was a dead man if he did. He flung himself forward, grabbing the king's belt, dragging him back down. Wrathling was gone now. But Erlan was on him.

The Kingshelm was inches away, weirdly impassive, while Sigurd writhed under him like a wounded boar. Erlan got a hand round his neck, then a knee over his shield arm, close enough now to hear his rasping breath. Sigurd sliced at his back again and again, but so close his edge couldn't bite through his mail. Erlan slashed his seax.

Sigurd screamed. His sword fell. Erlan snarled, sensing triumph, bloodied fingers squeezing the king's throat while Sigurd squirmed in vain to break free. The Kingshelm jerked loose, revealing half the face beneath, girning with fear and fury. Gold flashed under Sigurd's chin.

Erlan tried to stab him in the face, to end this, but Sigurd caught his wrist, his gauntleted fingers digging like iron nails into Erlan's half-healed wounds.

Erlan snarled, spraying Sigurd's beard with spittle, gripping his throat tighter and tighter. The pain in his left wrist was unbearable. His fingers flexed and the seax fell.

At once Sigurd slammed his fist into Erlan's side. He felt ribs crack while his hand scrabbled frantically for the knife, but in vain. The Kingshelm flew off. Sigurd's eyes were bulging. And now Erlan recognized the gold round Sigurd's neck. It was *his* gold. His mark of honour. The torque that Sviggar had given him.

Well, if Sigurd wanted it that bad, he could choke on the fucking thing.

Erlan seized it with both hands, crushing the gold into Sigurd's windpipe. Blood vessels slithered like snakes in his eyes. Erlan pressed harder, laughing madly, his revenge surely a few strangled breaths away.

'Die, you murdering bastard!' Erlan whispered, twisting and grinding the gold. '*Die!*'

Then everything happened at once. A flash. Sigurd's arm whipped up. A voice cried, 'Erlan!' and a spear slammed down inches from his face.

He glanced left. Sigurd's forearm was skewered to the ground, and in his hand, the long seax. Sigurd heaved with fury. But Erlan, seizing his chance, threw his full bodyweight on the golden torque. There was a crack. Sigurd's head snapped forward. His body shuddered briefly, then his eyes grew hard and still as glass.

Erlan sank, exhausted, onto the dead king's chest, not caring what came beyond that. Maybe he could lie there for ever.

'Ain't time for sleeping yet, boy!'

Erlan looked up at the silhouette standing over him, confused.

'Want a hand up, traitor?'

He knew that voice. 'Fat man?' he murmured. 'What are you doing here?' His mind was muddy, unable to form coherent thoughts.

'Bit of killing,' replied Einar Fat-Belly. 'Like everyone else not busy dying. Or already dead.'

Erlan blinked up at him like a man waking from a long sleep.

'I'd say two dead kings is enough for one day, wouldn't you?'

Erlan could only stare. It was all enough. Enough for a day. Enough for a lifetime. Enough until the Final Fires and the end of all things.

'Hold, you barrel of Sveär snot! Your fight's not over yet!' Suddenly the bloodied sons of Galdalf were there, on guard and glowering at Einar.

'Not him!' yelled Erlan, snapping out of his torpor.

'What's he to you, Aurvandil?'

'A friend.'

'He's a Sveär.'

'Touch him and I'll split you like a log.'

'What? From down there?' chortled Alfarin.

'That's fighting talk, that is!' his brother laughed. He dropped his guard. 'As you like then, Aurvandil – your fat friend lives.'

'Wise choice, fellas,' said Einar, lowering his spear-point. 'Now then, lad. Are you done rolling in the mud?'

Erlan took Einar's proffered hand and was duly hauled to his feet. The fighting had swept on towards the lake. The two men gave each other the up-and-down. The fat man looked different. His heavy jowls were ghost-white beneath the mud and filth, the muscles in his face stiff as bark in a rigid grimace.

'You look bloody terrifying.'

'You don't look so pretty yourself.' Einar turned and gazed down the plain towards the sounds of the routed Sveärs and the ravaging Danes. 'That's it then,' he said simply. 'No sense the rest of us dying now.' He pulled out a goat-horn slung on his back and put it to his lips.

The first note rose high and smooth. Then others followed – six sweet notes, rising, falling, repeating over and over in a tune every warrior on the plain would know. It meant a man's luck had held. It meant the battle's end, the closing of *Valhöll*'s gates and the *Valkyries'* ride for home.

A strange stillness radiated outwards from Einar with each note, the groans of the wounded and dying lending sombre harmony to the horn's music. In the distant marshland, the fighting continued.

Some warriors approached. Erlan recognized Ringast among them. He looked half-dead, slathered in blood, his arm clutched tight to his chest. Around his hand was wound a clump of bloody rags.

'Who told you to sound the battle-end? Who the Hel are you, anyway?'

'Einar Fat-Belly, some call me.' Einar sat the horn on his prodigious gut. 'Guess that's better than Einar Horn-Blower, if you catch my meaning.' He gave a husky chuckle.

'You have no right to end this fight.'

'Then end it yourself.'

'Why would I, when victory is nearly ours?'

'It's already yours.' Einar pointed to Sigurd's lifeless corpse. 'Your feud just died with him.'

Ringast looked where Einar pointed and, seeing Sigurd, his face changed, a welter of emotions stirring just beneath its surface. 'Who did this?' he said in a trembling voice.

'I did,' said Erlan.

Ringast nodded. 'So the gods granted you your revenge.'

'And you, your victory.'

Ringast heaved off a deep sigh. 'Aye.' He looked about him,

surveying the bloody plain. 'At what cost?' The dead were strewn in every direction, piles of broken bodies scattered as far as the eye could see. Erlan thought of Vargalf – of his dark words in that stinking smokehouse. This was the carnage he had been planning for so long. *His master work.* Erlan recalled his words with a shudder. And looking at the thousands dead, no one's victory seemed so complete as Vargalf's.

'My father also found his death in the end. I hope he's satisfied now.' Ringast fell into a brooding silence.

'There's yet a king who lives,' said Einar.

'What king?' muttered Ringast bleakly, staring down at Sigurd's body.

'There.' Ringast looked up. Einar was pointing at him. 'There's my new king.' He dropped to his knee.

The sons of Galdalf were leaning on their shields, blood leaking from a dozen wounds between them. Alfar looked at the fat man and then at his brother. 'Aye. Hail King Ringast, Lord of Danish Mark.' He too fell to his knees.

'Hail Ringast, King of the Sveärs,' declared Einar.

Ringast looked down at them like they were ghosts risen from the grave, as if he only half-heard their words. But all around him, men were kneeling, relieved, exhausted and muttering their allegiance.

So rises another king, thought Erlan. Hel, these men would kneel to a billy-goat if it meant an end to this slaughter. But not him. And despite the pain throbbing up his wounded calf, he stayed standing.

'Victory then,' said Ringast. Then louder. 'Victory! Call off the slaughter! Victory!'

And the cry rolled eastward. Horns echoed Einar's call, riding the wind towards the lakeshore. Everywhere men collapsed. And soon the ring of steel had fallen silent. The wailing of the wounded and the dying would take much longer.

Erlan felt sick. Something wet ran into his mouth. He drew his tongue along cracked lips and tasted salt.

Tears...

The battle was over. And Ringast was King Over Them All.

Lilla felt the wind brush against her face.

The rain had stopped. She opened her eyes and for a moment knew nothing but the serenity of the white clouds speeding overhead.

White on blue. *So beautiful.*

She tried to move and felt something nettle her belly.

'Be still,' a voice hushed. *So soft.* She wondered what had happened to the battle din.

'I didn't know whether you'd be coming back.'

Lilla tried to lift her head. 'I'm thirsty,' she whispered hoarsely.

'Drink this.' A gourd touched her lips. Water dribbled into her mouth. *So sweet.* She looked up and saw gentle eyes – gold as ripe corn with dark speckles – and a flash of white hair.

'Gerutha?'

'I'm here, my sweet.'

Lilla looked at her, confused. 'Why is it so quiet?'

'The fighting's over. The battle's won.'

'Won?' She tried to sit up. Too sudden. She gasped as pain pricked low in her abdomen.

'Easy, girl, easy.'

Lilla looked down. Her dress was drawn up over her knees. A bright red stain spread like a sunrise over the pale yellow cloth. Suddenly she became conscious of the wetness against her thighs. She looked at Gerutha and noticed a white cloth soaked red in her hand.

'Whose blood is that?' she murmured.

'Why—' Gerutha shook her head gently. 'It's yours, Lilla... It's yours.'

CHAPTER
SIXTY-SEVEN

Night had fallen.

Saldas had waited for word in a fever of agitation, but none had come. Dark thoughts swirled in her head. The break in her arm throbbed in time with the beating of her heart.

She rolled the bones. Again they told her nothing. She had tried to see within herself what had happened. But that sight was now a blur. Broken like her arm.

Once Freki had fallen, she had quit the battlefield, not even staying to see what had become of him. She had been complacent – she knew that now – had sensed the danger too late. And now her arm was badly cracked and needed better care than anything in Sigurd's baggage train could avail. So she had ridden north with a single escort who was now keeping watch outside her tent.

The man had had the nerve to ask why they were fleeing when the day was almost theirs. She told him his next question would cost him his tongue. He had held his counsel after that.

She lay back under the rustling canopy, listening to the waves flopping onto the Braviken shore. Out on the firth the prows of Starkad's war-ships bobbed: sentinels awaiting the return of the men who had sailed them there.

But none had yet returned.

The throbbing in her arm was relentless. Under her instruction the escort had bound it – a temporary dressing that would have to serve for the time being. But she was also tired and, despite the pain, sleep crept over her like a shadow, bringing with it dark dreams. And so it went on, weariness and pain wrestling her in and out of consciousness while she drifted along its border.

Until a sound made her open her eyes. She called her escort's name but there was no reply. Irritated, she was about to sit up when a breath of wind snapped at the tent-flap. The oil lamp's flame flickered. She called the escort's name again. No answer.

The fool must be asleep. She ought to rouse herself and admonish him, but it all seemed too torturous. Better to sleep. Or at least rest. She closed her eyelids and listened to her own breathing and the lap of the firth waters...

Suddenly a hand, rough and hard, closed over her throat. Her eyes snapped open. She tried to sit up but was stuck fast.

Her gaze moved up the arm pinning her, willing her face not to betray her fear. A figure was kneeling by her bed. In the flame's flicker, she saw a face, a mask, its features lifeless. All but the eyes, which glinted at her, cold and bright as stars.

The Kingshelm.

'You're alive,' she sighed, relief flooding through her as she sank back into the blankets. If Sigurd was alive, that meant victory.

The metal face gazed down on her. It was unsettling. She could hear his breathing, but he said nothing. She suddenly had a horrible fear that he was there because he had fled.

'Were you victorious?'

He nodded. Another wave of relief. She reached out to the Kingshelm, suddenly remembering: *she had seen this*. Had seen him come to her. So her sight had been correct.

She wanted to see his face. Her fingertips touched the cold iron. 'Take it off.'

The mask shook.

'You're angry with me.' She heard the trace of shame in her voice. 'I didn't flee.' She was speaking too fast. 'My arm – it's broken.'

The eyes in the Kingshelm were unblinking.

'But see now!' She managed something like a laugh. 'The All-Father gave you victory! My work had done enough. And you doubted my tellings were strong! I told you. The Spear-God favours the strong. Always.'

He moved not a muscle. Only stared at her.

'Spare me your anger, husband.' She poured honey on her words, as well as she knew how. 'Forgive your queen. Forgive your wife.' She smiled. Nothing. His silence was discomforting. 'Well, if you can't forgive me yet, then I must win your forgiveness.' She reached out with slender fingers and found the buckle of his belt. 'Soon, my love, there'll be nothing you won't forgive me.'

He caught her wrist. She winced as he turned it over. But before she could object, he had placed something in her palm. It had a weight to it, soft yet solid, wrapped in a rag that glistened.

Her chest tightened with excitement as he peeled away the wet cloth and she saw—

It was a heart.

A human heart. The flame-light shimmered red and gold on its surface.

A shock shivered through her, delicious, tingling her blood. 'Erlan's?'

The Kingshelm nodded.

'Oh, my king! My lord!' She squeezed the grim gift in her elation. Blood oozed through her fingers. 'My love. You've outdone yourself.' It was no flattery. Perhaps this man would prove useful to her after all. 'And Lilla?'

He made no sign, only reached out and took back the ugly thing, then dropped it on the floor with a slap. His eyes glared out from their dark recess. She saw danger in them, the violence of battle too. But then, they released hers and moved over the rest of her. His breathing deepened. She knew that change. Had heard it often enough in other men.

'It's better you don't speak. Better the silence and darkness cover us both.'

He reached out and pulled at the fur that covered her. She made no move to stop it, embracing the cool air on her body as the fur fell away. She lay back.

This, she knew.

She let the disquiet of his silence dissolve away. Men had different reactions to the storm of battle, after all. Some grew hot and fierce and hungry as fire. Others grew quiet, so quiet – as if their minds had never left the field, like the bodies of the dead and the maimed.

But here, she was in control. She stirred, letting tiny

movements snake over her body, drinking down his lust.

He stood, and then, stiffly, he went to the lamp and blew it out. *Perhaps he is wounded.* Most would be. But questions could come later. For now, the darkness was enough.

She heard his cloak fall to the floor, sensed him return to her bedside. In the darker shadow, she saw a movement, felt a finger trace over her belly. Her muscles stiffened. His fingertips were rough. But soon she relaxed, enjoying his touch, feeling his hand brush aside the loose strands of hair that spilled over her chest. For a moment it hesitated. She felt him toy with the little silver amulet nestled between her breasts. 'Don't stop,' she urged, not wanting him to be distracted. The metal dropped onto her chest. Then his palm slid around her breast, his leathery thumb tracing over her bud of flesh.

'Take off your helmet,' she murmured.

He leaned away. She heard a thud as the iron helm hit the floor. For a second she caught an outline, then the shadow bent over her; his warm breath was on her skin, his lips on her breast, his teeth biting, sending sparks of pleasure through her nipple. The heat was building inside her. Looking down, she could only see the shape of a man. Hair black as tar, matted with sweat. He stank of it. She inhaled the sour tang deep into her lungs and desire welled through her. Ordinarily, she didn't find this man to her taste but the reek of victory on him was irresistible. His victory.

And hers.

'I want you.' Her fingers threaded the tangle of his hair, gripping his skull, pulling him closer. She felt his hand slide around her wrist, then close tight, crushing her veins. 'You're hurting me.'

Something slipped over her hand, something rough. It pulled tight with a jerk and she realized it was a rope.

'What are you doing?'

But before she knew what was happening, he yanked her broken arm straight. Pain raced up her arm into her armpit. She cried out, tears springing to her eyes.

'Sigurd – it's broken! What are you doing?'

Still no answer. She tried to wriggle free as he bound her, but that only sparked more pain so she lay still, his full weight pressing down on her chest.

'Are you mad? Please, Sigurd... Stop! I beg you.' She had pleaded for nothing in her life. She hated the pathetic whining sound on her tongue.

He pulled the rope till her wounded wrist was secured as tight as the other. All she could do was suffer the burning in her arm.

'Are you still angry with me?' she gasped. 'Sigurd – please. Answer me!'

She felt his hair brush her face as he bent close to her ear.

'Sigurd is dead,' breathed the shadow, his hand closing over the amulet between her breasts. 'And this—' The leather snapped. 'This is mine.'

CHAPTER
SIXTY-EIGHT

Erlan watched smoke rising into an autumnal sky above the King Barrows.

The new king and the remains of his army had made weary progress. There wasn't a shieldman or shieldmaid who didn't carry some wound. Most carried many. And the ruined flesh and cracked bones, the cuts and bruises all lingered a good deal longer than the thrill of victory, or even the relief of being alive. Of course, blood poisoning would reap more lives before the autumn leaves fell or sooner. So each looked to his wounds.

Nevertheless, the sight of Sviggar's hall roused a cheer that rolled down the column of riders. A few hall-hounds approached, sniffing suspiciously at the warriors and their unfamiliar scents, running alongside, barking warnings that their masters would never hear.

Erlan rode among them. His revenge was almost complete. But now doubt gnawed at his guts.

Was it enough? Enough for Kai? Enough for him?

His belly growled. Empty like his heart. He had feasted on blood and what had it come to? An emptiness inside him. Nothing more.

Vargalf. Then Sigurd. Two deaths, and the third to come.

He looked ahead at Ringast's sloping shoulders rocking with the motion of his horse, his broken hand cradled in his lap. He was the King Over Them All now. The Half-Hand Lord. A worthy lord, and beside him rode Lilla. His queen. His wife.

Erlan scowled. *How the Norns love to weave their knots. And we little men writhe and wrestle, only making them tighter.*

There was hardly a fighting man left in Uppsala. Sigurd had taken every man who could hold spear or shield. Few who had ridden away were riding back among the victorious Danes and their allies.

'A different sky today, brother,' called Thrand. The big Dane's face was pale, a seam of dried blood streaked across his nose and down one cheek. 'No bowing before kings this time.'

'Not for me, anyway.'

Thrand gave a begrudging smile. 'Suppose I can stretch to that... So then, which hall suits you and that kingly arse of yours? Leithra or here?'

'There's no mightier hall than this in all the north.' Ringast nodded at the Great Hall, which rose majestically before them. 'And this is the land my queen loves the most. So you take Leithra and the Danish mark. You'll answer to none but me, as your king.'

'Gods! Father would choke on Odin's mead if he knew his hall fell to me,' laughed Thrand. 'But I'll serve you true, brother. For his sake. Aye – and yours!'

'Good. Meanwhile, there are new lords to make and lands to distribute. Our Sveär cousins died under our blades, but I mean to make a good peace with them.'

There was an audible scoff beside Erlan. Saldas rode sullenly next to him astride a shaggy cart-horse, her wrists bound, and garbed in nothing better than a heavy cloak – all Erlan had allowed her the night he had dragged her back to Ringast's lines, spitting and cursing and writhing like a wildcat. Her hair was a dishevelled tangle, the bandage under her cloak soiled and ragged.

'You have something to say, Saldas?' called Ringast.

'Children and fools talk of a good peace,' she said scathingly. 'Peace is nothing but a bloodless war. It awaits only the first head to fall.'

'Well then. That head will be yours.'

'Kill me and you kill any chance for this pretty peace you desire. The Sveärs will not stand for it.'

'We shall see.'

By evening, a crowd of low folk had gathered, huddled and murmuring in the dusk of the day. A breeze had swept clean the slate skies, unveiling a horizon bruised purple and a falling sun that glistered like gold.

King Ringast stood atop the Tiding Mound, ready to address his Danish and Gotar lords, those Sveärs who had bowed to him, and the Uppsala folk. Beside him stood Lilla – his new queen, Aslíf Sviggarsdóttir. They were already calling her the Eagle Queen. The liege-lady of Gotarland, Danmark and her beloved Sveäland.

Facing them was Saldas, flanked by the Skanskar twins, Alfar and Alfarin. She wore only a linen shift, her hair tied back in a simple braid.

She looks almost innocent, thought Erlan, looking up from the foot of the mound. *Like a maiden on her bridal night.*

Then he remembered: *she looks how it serves her to look*. Even death was to be a performance. Though in truth she looked utterly natural.

'Saldas, you stand accused of murder,' Ringast declared. 'Murder of your husband. Murder of your children. Murder of your handmaid.'

'Murder of my handmaid? You are joking!' Saldas laughed, hard and hollow. 'Look at you all – with your solemn, self-righteous faces. And now you charge me with the death of a thrall?'

'You had your own children murdered,' Lilla exclaimed, unable to contain her emotion.

'Peace, my wife,' said Ringast.

Saldas snorted with contempt. 'By the gods, what is this? You want to kill me? Then kill me. Why stage this mockery by claiming any right or invoking some law? Sviggar died. His children died. That conceited slut died. And now I must die. So be it. I don't need to explain myself to you, nor suffer this ridiculous pretence of justice. There *is* no justice. There's only the last one holding the knife. That is the only law.'

'Do you condemn yourself then?'

'Who else is there to condemn me?'

'The Aurvandil.' Ringast beckoned to Erlan. He stepped forward to climb the mound.

'Him? What proof has he?'

'Vargalf,' Erlan called.

'The words of a dead man! A man *he* murdered. What proof is that?'

Erlan gained the top of the mound.

'The Aurvandil is a man without honour. I'll not be condemned by him. You need no witnesses.'

'It is the proper way. According to your own law.'

'The proper way? Then here is your witness! Yes – I killed them. Yes – I would do it again. I would kill all of the seed of that vain old dotard if I could.' Here she glared at Lilla.

'So you admit it.'

She tilted her mouth at Ringast in a mocking sneer. 'Look at you with your *proper* ways. The new king. But what is a king without sons, eh?'

'What do you mean?'

'Ask your wife there. You'll get no fruit from that.' She pointed at Lilla's belly. 'That womb is barren as the northern wastelands now.' She laughed. 'The King Over Them All? Ha! Aye – but a king without an heir. You may as well spill your seed in the dust for all the good it'll do in her.'

Ringast reached out his good hand to Lilla, a searching look in his eye. Erlan saw a pained shadow pass over her face. But she touched her husband's outstretched fingers.

'Are you so sure you're done with me, Ringast?' said Saldas with a sly smile. She smoothed a hand over her stomach. 'Put your seed in here. It would be no hardship, my lord, I promise you that. I can still give you sons. But you'll get none from her.'

Erlan could see in Ringast's face how the words rankled. But his reply was hard as an anvil. 'You have admitted your guilt. You shall die for it. Nevertheless, in recognition of your rank, I give you a choice. To be hung from the Sacred Oak until you are dead. Or else the same death you gave your lord and husband. Poison.'

A grim look settled on Saldas's beautiful features. For a while, her mouth worked and her green eyes raged. 'You think I am afraid to die?' she said at last. 'You think I favour a quick death? That I would refuse the pain? Hel take you, Ringast. Hel take all of you! I choose poison.'

'By your own hand then.' He signalled to a boy at the foot of the mound. 'Bring the draught here.' The boy approached, holding out a vessel in front of him as though its very vapour reeked of death. 'This was found in your chambers. Doubtless of your own making.'

The boy held out the vessel to Saldas. She hesitated.

'Will you not drink, murderer?'

'I'll drink it,' she murmured. 'But first you will hear me.' Abruptly she snatched the cup and lifted it high. The wind caught her hair and for a moment it shone with a dark lustre, her green eyes dazzling, bright with the fire of the falling sun.

'I drink this,' she cried. 'And I drink it to your deaths. You!' She raised the cup to Ringast. 'You who are called King Over Them All! You hope for long years, but your rule shall be numbered in days. With your death, your realm will be cloven, clean and bloody as your hand. Autha's line ends with you. Dead seed in that dead soil.' Ringast met her words with a stony glare.

'My darling daughter,' Saldas sneered, 'your womb is dead. I curse your heart as well. It will be for ever sick and empty. I see years of loneliness. I put envy on you, to gaze upon the fruit of other wombs and choke. Your father's blood dies with you.'

Lilla's eyes stormed as Saldas turned to Erlan.

'And you – the wandering cripple! You shall bear the blackest curse of all—'

'Does your pride make you so blind, Saldas?' he said. 'Your words have no power now. You are broken. Lilla defeated you.'

'Believe that if you like. It won't stop my curse binding you. Darkness lingers over you. Lives in you, making you its slave. You will run and run, but never be free of it.'

'You're wrong,' he replied. 'A deeper magic overshadows me than any you can conjure. Not even the All-Father's words can bind my fate. It was seen. It was spoken – by one with farther sight than you.'

He shuffled closer, peering deep into those emerald eyes, knowing it was for the last time. 'And what do you see for yourself? Can you see far down the road into Hel's dark world?' He snorted. 'I can tell you what awaits you in this world. They mean to feed your body to Sviggar's hounds. Soon all this,' he reached out and touched her shimmering hair, 'will be nothing better than dog-dirt, ground into the dust... Your glory turned to shit.'

The certainty in her eyes wavered.

'You once told me we all receive only what we're calling to ourselves.' He moved closer still, so that only she could hear him. 'Is this what you were calling? Is this what you wanted?' Her lips moved as if to speak. 'What? No oath? No more curses?' He shook his head. 'Then go to the black Hel that's calling you. That's always been calling you.'

The blood drained from her face. She was paler now than he'd ever seen her. But somehow she found her voice again. 'Listen to me, all of you, listen!'

'No!' Lilla's voice cracked the air. 'There's nothing more for you in this life. Nothing.' She was trembling, but she approached with steady steps. Erlan moved aside.

With the sunfall at her back Lilla was wreathed in an ethereal glow. She put her hand against Saldas's cheek. 'Do you not doubt, my sister?' she murmured. Saldas stared at her, a kind of dread dancing in her eyes. 'Did you *never* doubt?'

Saldas's mouth opened, but nothing came.

'You see. There are no more words to speak.'

Saldas stared right through her, her body stiff, her eyes suddenly dim. And then her gaze fell, leaden, to the cup.

She looked at it so long that Ringast signalled to Alfarin beside her, but she stopped him with a shake of her head.

At last, she looked up into the skies above. And as she looked her expression changed. A smile formed on her face, sly and cruel. Her head snapped down and she glowered over the crowd one final time, the pride in her eyes bright and hard as a diamond, not a trace of fear in her face. And putting the cup to her lips, she drank the poison down to its last drop.

Her hands fell to her waist. Then, violently, she lurched forward and flung away the cup, sending it bouncing over the lip of the Tiding Mound. She fell to her knees, trying to retch, trying to scream, only managing a small, stifled gasping noise. She tipped onto her side, fingers tearing furrows at her neck as her body bucked and stiffened. She gave a single, sharp cough and a cloud of dark droplets sprayed from her mouth, staining her shift red. Her eyes bulged and rolled, the green pools turning scarlet, as blood welled through her lips. And finally death passed like a shadow through her, and she lay still, her beautiful lips pared wide into a hideous grimace.

No one moved. No cheering. No jeers. Nothing. Not a sound.

'It is done,' said Ringast, breaking the silence. He turned to Lilla. 'Your loved ones are avenged... Are you satisfied?'

She was about to answer when a long, screeching cry caused everyone to look up. High, high overhead, an eagle was circling the King Barrows. A dark shadow. Dark wings. It cried again, and Erlan saw a shudder pass through Lilla.

'They're avenged – yes,' she answered her husband. 'As to satisfaction... I feel none.'

Ringast grunted and turned to address Galdalf's twins. 'You know what to do with the body.'

They nodded and, without further ceremony, seized Saldas's shoulders and feet.

CHAPTER
SIXTY-NINE

The night-fires were lit. The councillors had been recalled. Lilla had long grown weary of their talk. The wound inside her ached. She needed air, needed to get away from the closeness of the hall and the thoughts that had plagued her every day since Saldas's death.

Wrapping herself in her cloak, she went outside into the night, hardly giving a thought to where her steps might lead. It happened they took her away from the smoky halls, beyond the byres and the barns, and the dwellings huddled about them, out onto the river meadows.

The night was clear. For a long time she gazed up into the sky, letting it fill her with its silence. She walked on a little until she could hear the stream running off to join the river, could see its silver spray scattered by the ancient stones. Her gaze followed the glimmers downstream until it was checked abruptly at the sight of a figure seated on the bank.

She pulled the cloak about her and glanced back at the halls. Whoever it was seemed deep in thought, tossing stones, one after another, into the water. As she watched, the figure turned, seeking another pebble, and she recognized his silhouette.

'My husband says you're a hard man to persuade,' she said.

Erlan lurched to his feet, his hand reaching automatically for his knife. She pulled back her hood and his hand fell away. 'Shouldn't you be nursing him?' he replied. 'He's a sick man.'

'He's in council.'

'Still? It must be midnight.'

She shrugged. 'There's much to be done.'

He nodded. The strands of his hair fell in shivers across his face. She could see the cut across his cheek, vivid and dark. 'I hear he's changing his name.'

'He is,' she answered. 'He wants to bridge the divide between Dane and Sveär any way he can.'

'With a name?'

'Among other things.'

'Only a fool changes his name.'

She came a step closer. 'Your father didn't name you "Erlan", did he?'

'See? I should know.'

She watched as he tossed another stone into the stream. 'Why won't you stay?' she said quietly.

He sniffed. 'He's a good man, that husband of yours. Your father chose well for you.'

'He did,' she said, letting him avoid the question. For now.

Another long pause. 'Is it true?'

'Is what true?'

'What Saldas said.' He turned to her, half his face bathed silver in the moonlight. 'That you're barren.'

671

'I don't know. I—' She didn't want to tell him. Didn't want him to know about the child that was lost to her. The heir that was lost to Ringast. That one last life which Saldas had stolen from her. Stolen from him, too. Better that he never knew. 'Time will show.'

A growl hummed in his throat. 'I'm sorry.'

'Ringast told me he gave you one night to think about his offer.'

'I don't need another night.'

'A night may change a man's mind. And so his destiny.'

'Not mine. I'm resolved.'

This all felt so stiff and cold. She touched his shoulder, softened her voice. 'Why won't you stay? Tell me.'

There was a long silence. She saw in the gloom his brow crumple. 'Isn't it obvious?'

He suddenly turned to her, fixed her with those dark eyes that had so struck her when her father first summoned him to their table. She dared not admit what she saw in them. 'But I – I want you to stay.'

'That's exactly why I can't.'

'But we would be good to you. We owe you a debt of—'

'You owe me nothing. All debts are paid.'

'Is there nothing I can say to make you—'

'I'm in love with you, Lilla,' he said sharply. 'Don't you know that? *I love you.* Just like I did before.'

She couldn't answer, couldn't look away. The words sort of thrilled her. But she knew they shouldn't.

He shook his head. 'If I stay here, it will destroy me. Destroy us both.' He looked at her again. 'Wouldn't it?'

She still couldn't speak. She knew he was right. Why else did she care whether he stayed or not? 'Yes,' she whispered. Her hand sprang to her throat as if it had betrayed her.

'Hmm.' That same pensive growl. 'If he didn't so clearly deserve you, it might be easier. But there it is. He's the better man. And you chose him.'

'That's not fair. I had no choice.'

'Of course you did. And you did choose.'

Her heart twisted. If he only knew how many tears she had shed at that choice.

'What I offered you wasn't enough. Maybe what he can will be.'

'But I don't love him.' The words escaped her like a moan.

'Still… it's done.' Abruptly, he turned away and tilted his face to the stars. 'Our fate is woven.' Suddenly he scoffed. 'You know I can't figure it out. I've been sitting here trying to. But I can't. Sometimes it's easier to think we're all just slaves, after all.'

'Slaves?'

'Aye. Bound by the fate the Norns weave for us, the strands of their web hard as the bars of a cage.' He turned to her sharply, his dark eyes bright with intensity. 'Or maybe we're free. Dangerously free. Free as the gods and powerful enough to change the world. To change *everything*.'

'Maybe it's both,' she said softly. 'Sometimes we're forced to make a choice we don't want to make.'

'Like now,' he growled, casting his last stone into the chuckling stream. 'To stay or to go. To keep looking…'

'Looking for what?'

He gave a weary sigh. 'I must find another kingdom. Another king.'

'There are many kinds of kings in the world. Ringast would have been a good lord to you.'

'Wherever I go, men demand an oath. Some good like Ringast. Some wicked, like your brother. Or the Watcher.'

A chill passed through her at mention of that name. 'Why do you think of him?'

'I – I think of him often. I don't know why. So many threads lead back to him, I suppose. Do you not?'

'Sometimes,' she admitted. 'When I've wished things were different. But then I remember what might have been, if you hadn't come for me. But he's gone now,' she added. 'His power is broken.'

'Is it, though?' he said darkly. 'Or will there always be another lord like him? In all lands and all ages, just like he said. Calling folk to him, as he called me. As he called those wretched Nefelung all those moons ago.' He gazed up, his mouth agape, transfixed by the beautiful abyss above him. 'The curious thing is, people will listen. They will fall under that thrall. And all this – Vargalf, Sigurd, Saldas, the slaughter of all those men – it will all happen again and again and again.' His gaze dropped and he scuffed his toe at the ground. Seeing something, he stooped and picked a flat stone out of the grass, turned it over in his palm. 'Seems to me this is our only real choice. There are two ways to live. By power. Or by love.'

She hadn't wanted to interrupt his thoughts. She was remembering that moment under the blood-beech, the falling rain. How she had thought that life *was* love, but she couldn't explain that to him. Seeing he had finished, she murmured, 'We all want to love. It's part of life.'

He suddenly rounded on her. 'No – I don't mean the stuff of

the skalds' songs and sagas – shining moons and aching hearts and all that. I mean love that fights. Love that stands, that's strong.' He clasped his fist between them, his dark eyes burning like coals. 'I mean a love that bleeds for you. A love that will *die* for you.' As abruptly as it had come, his passion subsided. 'Kai showed me that.'

'You miss him.'

'Of course. He's the reason I came back. As you said...'

His face was clouded and sad. But there was a rugged beauty to it as well. She wondered what it must look like if it were shining with joy. Almost without thinking, she lifted her hand and traced a fingertip under the stitching across his cheek. The muscles in his face flickered.

'Your wounds will heal,' she whispered.

He reached out in turn and laid his palm against her belly. It was a gesture of astonishing intimacy – crossing a line. Yet she let it rest there. 'And what of yours?'

She felt brittle inside, but his hand was warm. She drew a little closer, not taking her eyes from his. Quite naturally, his hand slid round to the small of her back. When he dropped his head, her lips rose to meet his. They kissed. He tasted sweet, like honey-wine. She closed her eyes and parted her lips, feeling the love that she had hidden away so deep, that she had bolted and barred, suddenly break free. A flood of light and hope and desire rushed out through her mouth, whispering into his soul as her tongue touched his. She grasped him tighter, fearing – knowing – that she would never hold him this close again.

But then he pushed her gently away, a shudder passing through him. 'I can't lead you into another betrayal. Not of him.'

She nodded. That way only led to sorrow. To sorrow, and blood. Her hands fell. His dark eyes were still on hers. Seeing them, she couldn't help thinking of that other life that had died within her. *That part of him.* So she believed, anyway. Soon there would be nothing to link them at all. Nothing but her memories.

'Then you must go,' she said. 'But let me give you this much to take with you.'

She saw he thought she meant to give him a gift, since he looked at her hands. Instead she laid one of them on his heart. 'Close your eyes.'

He did as she said and she began to speak, to murmur, to summon that power that had spoken to her in those visions of the night. His eyes were calm. She knew he hated the hidden mysteries known to her and Saldas and few others. But this time he seemed to trust her. She let her eyes fall shut and felt heat flooding through her neck, felt her eyelids flicker.

'Aurvandil.' Her voice seemed to resonate more richly. 'Go, my love. Go and find your kingdom. Go and find your king. But carry these words with you. Wherever your path leads, wherever your feet shall wander, my blessing shall carry you closer to love. A love that holds the world. A love that has no end, that lives even beyond the Final Fires when all things must die. A love that sets you free.'

He put his hand over hers and slowly opened his eyes. 'Your hand burns like fire.'

'May its heat stay with you then, wherever you go.' Her voice cracked. 'My love...' She blinked away the tears she felt welling. 'I must go. Ringast will soon miss me. I must go.'

676

. . . .

Sleep took Erlan quickly that night, but lightly.

Sounds stole in and out of his ear – from the shifting recesses of his mind or the whispered taunts of night-spirits, he couldn't say. The cries and yells of slaughter, pleadings in the darkness, murmured curses, muffled laughter. He turned over and over, trying to find some peace. At last he sank into a deeper sleep and dreamed of a breeze blowing from the east. A sea-breeze that licked saltily at his lips.

He is running. He's run this way before, but this time his legs are weak and unwilling, as if they dread what lies ahead. He feels the hard-packed path beneath his feet, familiar as a pair of old soles. Then he hears the wailing, clawing at the sky. There is the pool again, its surface smooth as amber, and the kneeling figures. He stops, unable to approach. Then a darkness surrounds him and the wailing grows distorted, as if far away. A weight crushes his chest. He can't breathe. He is underwater. Above him, something stirs. He sees waves of oak-brown hair, wafting folds of crimson. Scarlet billows swirl past his face.

Blood.

He cries out but the water seals him in silence.

It is *her*.

She begins to turn. He sees her pale cheek, the smooth line of her jaw. And then her eyes, lifeless beads of hazel brown. Her hands drift down to him, her fingers touch his face. They are cold with death. The waters chase away a wave of hair. He sees the wound. Blood beats from it in pulses. Her lips form the shape of his name and cold fingers close around his neck.

Hakan.

Suddenly he is choking and her face is gone. Bright, emerald eyes glare down instead. Sensual lips curve into a frigid smile. He feels nails dig hard into his neck, squeezing the life from him. Brown hair darkens to midnight black, laughter bubbles through the water. The hair billows again and the beautiful face cracks, fissuring again and again until it is shattered into a thousand pieces. Her hard beauty withers. The lines of her face grow old. Now her lips are pale as snow and her green eyes glow hotter, till they are burning red flames. The grip tightens and it is the Watcher's sneer that mocks him as he fights to break free. But he cannot. His eyes grow dim, the cruel face blurs, his lungs are bursting, and he knows that soon the end must come. But then...

A hand appears around the Watcher's pale throat. The hand jerks and the Watcher is wrenched from the water. The hand reappears, reaching for him. It is rugged and callused, dark-skinned, its back covered with coarse hair. He takes it and is pulled up and up until his face is about to break the surface. Beyond is the shadow of a man. In a moment, he will see...

Erlan awoke with a start, gasping for air. In the darkness around him the hall-folk's sighs swelled soft and gentle as a distant sea. He lay back, his gaze lost in the shadows of the rafters.

He had to get away from here.

Tomorrow.

Tomorrow he would leave this land of ghosts far behind.

EPILOGUE

The wind licked hungrily at the sail.

The shallows of the Uppland firth were slipping behind now. The channel would soon open into the wider mouth of the Great Bay. Beyond that lay the East Sea. And then...

Ringast had known Erlan was set on leaving. At least so he'd said at Erlan's final audience. Nonetheless, the Dane had been as good as his word, furnishing him with a sturdy *knarr* and filling it with all he needed.

And now, stowed in the bottom of his craft was everything he owned in the world: Wrathling – the sword of his ancestors; a spear; an axe; a new linden-shield; his seax and half a dozen assorted knives. All of it lay at his feet. Beside them rested a sea chest filled with enough salted pork, herring, flatbread and cheese for three weeks, together with a couple of good cloaks, a helm and mailshirt – Ringast's gift – oiled and cleaned since the carnage of the Bravik plains. And finally a fresh tunic – Lilla's parting gift.

She'd given it to him as he stood before her husband. A beautiful shirt spun from lambs'-wool, embroidered with scarlet thread. 'It was my brother's.' She meant Staffen, whom Vargalf had murdered. As he took it from her, she had reached up and kissed his cheek. 'Farewell, my Erlan,' she whispered. And that was all.

In the bows were wedged a large cask of water and a smaller one of ale, together with two skins of mead. 'If it was me going, I'd need a dozen of those things,' Einar had said, as he helped Erlan load his gear. 'Yaah! You're still young. Next time I see you, maybe you'll have learned to drink like a man.'

'If not, you can teach me yourself. At the All-Father's table.' It was something to hope for, even though he didn't believe it.

'Aye. We'll drink there, if not before.'

'See it ain't too soon, fat man.'

'And you, boy.'

Last of all, Erlan had said farewell to his old horse, Idun. He took her an apple, of course, which she devoured in a second, then plucked at his hands for another. 'Be good, you old mule,' he whispered in her ear.

And so here he was, with enough food and drink for three weeks. Three weeks would take him to any horizon of his choosing, Ringast had said. After that, he was on his own.

He tried to imagine what lands lay ahead, what folk dwelt in them. Was there some hearth beyond the horizon with a place for a wanderer? A stranger like him?

The bubbles giggled under the clinker-hull. He'd just settled against the tiller when his eye caught a shadow skulking along the shoreline. It wasn't quite evening and when he looked he could make out an animal of some kind.

A wolf, maybe?

Curious, he pushed the tiller away from him and eased the

boat towards the shore. He soon saw it was no wolf but a large dog. He let the wind spill. The hull sank lower in the water. Drifting closer, he made out the shaggy limbs of a wolfhound, loping along. The dog slowed too, as if waiting for him to close the distance to shore.

Something about the animal was familiar. When he was near enough, he saw a single eye gazing back at him, bright and bold. The other was missing. Suddenly he recalled where he'd seen that eye before – staring at him then, silent and grim, as he emerged from that smoky pit of death and devils, while the flames devoured the body of his friend.

Strange, he thought.

He turned the prow into the wind and the boat came to a standstill, the sail gently ruffling. The wolfhound sat patiently by the water's edge, and for a while, the two just looked at one another.

'I'll live to regret this,' he muttered at last. 'Hey, you!' he called. 'Are you coming?' He whistled. In a second, it was in the water and paddling for the boat. Moments later, he was hauling a dripping bundle of thick fur and scraggy limbs over the gunwale. The dog scrabbled to its feet and immediately shook himself dry, soaking his new companion.

'Gods – you filthy mutt!'

He grabbed it by the scruff of its neck to have a look at it. The dog's one eye stared right back. There was something odd about that eye. The more he gazed into it, the more it seemed to draw him deeper into its stains and swirls.

He broke off abruptly. 'I don't know who sent you, mutt,' he said, scratching behind the wolfhound's ear. 'But I guess I won't refuse the company.'

The dog began licking his hand, then, without any warning, cocked his leg and sprayed the nearest thwart. 'Piss on it,' Erlan swore. Then realizing what he'd said, he laughed. 'There's no doubt what to call you, is there, you scruffy little bastard?'

Later, as the sun kissed the western lands, the mouth of the Great Bay fell further behind and the little *knarr* began to rise and fall on the first rollers of the East Sea.

A breeze blew fresh from the north-west. He pulled the tiller and the bows swung south. The sail cracked as the following wind surged the hull forward. He shuffled his feet wider, bracing against the roll of the waves, the tiller steady under his arm. The air tasted sharp with salt. To the west, the sea was shimmering, reflecting myriad shards of amber light across his bows.

A lord worth serving. A love that can heal.

Could the steps of a wandering cripple ever lead to these?

He hooked his hand into his belt, rubbing at the dark hide. And suddenly a sharp stab of hope rose in his heart and ran his doubts right through.

A lord and a love.

He felt like screaming the words, hurling them like a spear at the dying furnace of the sun. He closed his eyes, enjoying the warmth on his face, remembering the lightness of Lilla's kiss. His tongue ran over dry lips. He could still taste her, still smell the last trace of her on him.

'A lord and a love,' he murmured.

And opening his eyes, he looked to the south and smiled.

HISTORICAL NOTE

If *A Mighty Dawn* was set in the realm of myth, *A Sacred Storm* has progressed us into the realm of legend.

Is there a difference? Well, I think there is.

Although we don't have any contemporaneous written records of the events fictionalised in this novel, we do have several written sources that refer to some of its characters, and at least four separate accounts that identify and describe in varying detail a large battle that took place in what is now Sweden at some point in the middle of the 8th century.

The Wartooth:
Harald Wartooth, King of the Danes, was almost certainly a real person – *Haraldr Hilditǫnn* in Old Norse – so named either because he lost a couple of teeth in a battle which then miraculously grew back, or (as I have it) because of the rather odd setting of his front teeth.

One of the more striking characters of the Old Norse sagas, he is identified in all the sources that refer to him as the son of Autha (or *Auðr*) the Deep-Minded, who herself was the daughter of Ívar Vidfamne (which roughly translates as "Wide-

Realm"), the king who ruled over a territory that stretched from Eastern Scandinavia (modern-day Finland and Estonia) as far west as Northumberland in northern England.

Several of the sources – though not all – agree that Harald's father was Rorik Ring-Slinger (*Hrærekr slöngvanbaugi* in Old Norse). The treachery of Ívar Vidfamne against Autha (his own daughter and Harald's mother) and her husband King Rorik is recounted in some detail in one surviving fragmentary piece of a saga, known as the *Sögubrot*. (Just as Earl Bodvar explains to Erlan in Chapter 3.) King Ívar's scheming to gain direct control over the kingdom of Denmark seems to have been the main cause of the feud between himself and his daughter Queen Autha, which I have taken as the premise for this novel.

The many stories and escapades spanning the entire life of Harald Wartooth were eventually compiled into one place as part of a much larger work called the *Gesta Danorum* (the Deeds of the Danes) by a 12th century Danish theologian and historian called Saxo Grammaticus. (Incidentally this work is also where Shakespeare found the original version of the story about a Jutlandish prince called Amleth – better known as Hamlet.) In order to steer clear of all the contradictory accounts of who Harald was and what he did, I have taken this and the *Sögubrot* as the two main sources to plunder.

The episodes about Harald in the *Gesta Danorum* are many and colourful. Even from his birth, the Wartooth was special, his mother only conceiving him after a visit to an oracle of Odin and dedicating the life of any resulting child in service to that god. (Remarkably similar to the story of Hannah and Samuel in the Bible, in fact.) As Harald became a man, he enjoyed confounding his enemies with a good disguise, which he did on more than one occasion, and apparently the strength of his glare alone was enough to overwhelm some of them.

Saxo Grammaticus recounts that, because of the favour that he enjoyed from the war-god Odin, Harald Wartooth never wore armour in battle – suggesting perhaps that he was also a "berserker". But according to Saxo, Harald survived as king over Denmark and several other lands and vassal kingdoms until the ripe old age of 127 (which, of course, stretches the bounds of credulity). This being the case, with the infirmities of age, as I described in this novel, he really did seem to develop an acute paranoia that his more ambitious and unscrupulous underlings were trying to dispose of him. Indeed, there were several attempts to murder him, one of them in his bath. His resulting determination not to die such an ignominious death, but rather to see out his days with one last, "glorious" battle, becomes the main driver – again according to these sources – for "arranging" a battle with a man called Sigurd Hring, the king of Sweden (or Svealand, as I call it) and a younger kinsman of Harald.

This battle, probably the earliest described in such detail in the canon of Old Norse literature, became the stuff of legend.

The Battle of Brávellir:

This great clash of arms between the Danish king, Harald Wartooth, on the one hand, and his vassal – the Swedish king, Sigurd Hring – on the other, is described in both the sources mentioned, as well as The Saga of Hervör and Heidrek, and The Saga of Bósi and Herraud.

Saxo Grammaticus describes the set-up of the battle rather

in the manner of one king organising a football match against the other. A time and place were arranged, and it was agreed that each side should have seven years in which to assemble the largest host that they possibly could. One of the saga accounts puts a bit more weight on the fact that the Wartooth spent those seven years continually goading his kinsman Sigurd with provocations that the Swedish king couldn't ignore – which rings a little truer than the idea of a sort of glorified prize fight, convened as a handy and high-profile means of despatching this long-lived Danish king once and for all.

Be that as it may, the battle is alleged to have involved all the greatest champions of the age, and my account of the multitude of different tribes and people-groups from lands as diverse as Russia to Ireland, is no exaggeration. Several of the champions, but by no means all, mentioned in the various sources appear in this novel: Starkad the Old, Ubbi the Frisian, Einar the Fat-Bellied, Grim and Geir of Hedmark, the shieldmaiden Visma, Arwakki, Kekli-Karl to name just a few. Perhaps most notable, the Wartooth's own banner-bearer, named Bruni (which literally means "bushy-brows" in Old Norse) was reported to be the man who struck the death-blow to the old and blind King Harald – at last giving him the glorious death-in-combat that he was seeking, setting him on his road to Valhalla and, incidentally, thereby bringing the battle to a close. I have changed Bruni's name to Branni, for obvious reasons. But there is a footnote to the account concerning him: that Bruni was never seen again, and thus the legend grew that he was in fact Odin himself – the Wanderer – walking amid Skogul's Storm.

The location of the battle is not known for certain. *Brávellir* is the Old Norse name for the central plain of Östergötland

(Eastern Gotarland) – which is a large area, and consequently this name for the battle is vague, at best. But Saxo Grammaticus places the battle more specifically, at a site just south of Kolmården – the large forest that separates the old Swedish provinces of Södermanland and Östergötland, which I call the Kolmark – and nearby the fjord of Bråvik. I was content to go with his conclusion.

I must confess to having taken a couple of liberties with some of the details of the battle. I'm afraid that historical (or at least textual) accuracy has been sacrificed at the altar of fictional expediency, for which I apologise to the sticklers amongst my readers. I have brought the battle forward in time several decades from the mid-to-late 8th century into the early 8th century, in order to fit with the chronology of the rest of the Wanderer Chronicles and Erlan's story. Although it is true to say that pinning the battle to any one particular year is now impossible.

Perhaps more reprehensible, I have slightly altered the outcome of the battle, slewing the victory in favour of the Danish army when the saga accounts hold that the field was won by the Swedish king Sigurd Hring – or at least that he called the battle to an end when it was known that King Harald had fallen.

In my defence, my Sigurd, although sharing one of his names, is not supposed to be Sigurd Hring. Indeed, there is some suggestion from various other sources that Sigurd Hring is a mistaken conflation of two separate men: one called Sigurd; the other, Ring. Hence my invention of Ringast, son of Harald, who in my retelling is the last king standing, as it were, and thus takes the crowns of both Denmark and Sweden: King Over

Them All, at least for the time being.

With the cast-iron truth about the lives and deaths of these ancient kings and warriors now lost in the mists of time and legend, I can at least justify these contortions to myself, if not to you. But I hope you will nevertheless indulge me in the small licences I have afforded myself with the accepted facts.

The Burial of King Sviggar:
A final word about the burial ritual played out in the despatch of King Sviggar to the afterlife. Viking and Old Norse enthusiasts will probably recognise this as a re-working of a well-known account, by an Arab traveller named Ahmad Ibn Fadlan, of a king's burial that he witnessed in a land far to the south and east of Sweden, on the banks of the Volga river in what is now Russia.

Those familiar with his description may, quite justifiably, jump on the fact that his account dates from some two centuries later than the setting of this story. However, I've made the assumption that, since the people whom Ibn Fadlan encountered were Rus, formerly settlers from the north and probably having their origins in Sweden, it is not unreasonable to suppose that their rituals and burial practices might reflect those enacted by their ancestors in their distant homeland. I have added no details of my own to the rather shocking ritual that he describes. In fact, I have left some of the stranger details out.

Yet even these are not as strange, nor indeed as wonderful, as many things that Erlan Aurvandil will encounter as his adventures continue...

ACKNOWLEDGEMENTS

A bit like Monty Python's song about Eric the Half-a-Bee, *A Sacred Storm* began life as half-a-book – the second half, in fact, of the very lengthy first draft of *A Mighty Dawn*. One swift chop to that beast and it became the raw material for the sequel, which then lurked in a drawer for, I think, just over two years before I was ready to renew work on it.

The old adage that writing is rewriting has never been more true. And, it being a long book, I had created for myself a fairly hefty editing job. So hefty, indeed, that there were considerably more 'Oh-what-the-Hell's-the-point!' moments than I had experienced in writing *A Mighty Dawn*. There are several people I need to thank for seeing me through those and for keeping me on track right to the very end.

First and foremost (at least in a literary sense) is my editor at Corvus Atlantic, Sara O'Keeffe. She has been and is the rock on which I have had to lean a good deal harder this time round. Her sage advice has made this book so much better than I could have hoped and I am very grateful to her for her expertise and enthusiasm and friendship.

My thanks, also, to the team at Corvus. In particular, to

Kate Straker and Jamie Forrest, and to the rest of the marketing peeps. Also to Will Atkinson and to Clive Kintoff and his sales team for spreading the book far and wide.

Thank you to Sophie Hutton-Squire, my copy-editor, whose eye for detail and nuance in the text is quite bewildering. Not to mention her speed at turning around a document.

I am also very grateful to Charlie Campbell, my agent at Kingsford Campbell, for his encouragement along the way. I never fail to feel a thrill when I see his name flashing on my mobile screen. (For all the right reasons, of course.) His clear-headed counsel continues to be invaluable.

Once again, I am indebted to Neil Price for his insight and scholarship, in particular his vision of what battle must have been like in those early days of the Viking age, which appears in his wonderful book, *The Viking Way*, and which was so helpful for writing the climax to my own book.

Mark Twain said that he could live for six months on a good compliment. I would like to thank all those friends and strangers who have got in touch to say nice things about *A Mighty Dawn*. It's pathetic how good it makes me feel, but no less welcome for that.

My family, as always, have been a great support. My parents, Olaf and Dibby, my brothers, Christian and Alexis, and their wives, Christina and Abbie. Their love and encouragement is unwavering.

My two daughters – the Teen and the Tot – thank you for keeping my feet firmly on the ground.

Lastly, and most importantly, I must thank my beloved wife, Natasha. You are wise, thoughtful, gracious, long-suffering (through the tough bits) and altogether generous of heart and spirit. I would not have been able to bring this book in for such a happy landing without your love and support. On to the next one, my boo...

T.H.R.B.
January 2018

Read on for a sample from

A
BURNING
SEA

also by

Theodore Brun

CHAPTER ONE

ERLAN

However many times he berated that damn dog, it still pissed all over the bows soon as they were underway.

Erlan Aurvandil rose with the weariness of a man repeating an action for the hundredth time and snatched the battered bucket from the middle of the hold. He held it over the gunwale long enough to fill it with freezing river water, then clambered past the mast to douse the steaming puddle, the acrid smell of urine sharp in his nostrils.

'You dirty mongrel.' He flung the bucket back down into the strakes. 'I ought to skin you and sell your coat for arse-rag.' Not that a tongue-lashing ever did an ounce of good. That gimlet stare from the dog's remaining eye always seemed to throw him off, seemed to be laughing at him no matter what he said.

He scowled and hauled himself back to the stern to resume his place by the tiller.

At first, Erlan had called the wolfhound Kai, after his dead friend. Well, in truth Kai had been a mere servant, in the beginning. But by the end the lad had sworn blood brotherhood to him, loyal to the death. And he had been, too... loyal to the death. He had sacrificed himself to save Erlan from agonising torture at the hands of a man who was mad – or something worse. And this one-eyed hound had stood by and witnessed it all, silent and solemn as the Slain-God. Now the boy was gone and this dog was his companion instead.

A poor trade. But he would take it.

In his more wistful moments Erlan wanted to believe that the instant after death his friend's departing soul had turned aside from the Hel-road and instead come to dwell in the body of this animal. It was a far-fetched notion, he knew, born of whimsy or more probably loneliness. In any case, Erlan had soon found it too uncanny to address the hound by his friend's first name so he took to calling it Askar instead, the name of Kai's father. That suited better, and then Erlan shortened it to Áska, which meant "ash" in the Norse tongue. Ash was the colour of his coat and that's the name that stuck.

'You know your piss will rot right through that strake one day.' He took a swig on his ale-skin. 'And when it does, this tub will sink like a stone. Us with it.' Áska scratched behind his ear, apparently untroubled at the idea of disappearing into the depths of the great Dnipar river.

Perhaps he trusted that it was a good boat, despite that it exuded the whiff of his stale urine. After all, the little *knarr* had carried them a vast distance now. It had been the parting gift of

King Ringast – the King-Over-Them-All they had called him, in the days before Erlan had departed Sveäland. The victor of that bloody day of butchery on those Bravik plains. That awesome day, when the destinies of many men had been settled.

Mine too...

Erlan had slain Sigurd the Kin-Slayer that day, the prince who had murdered his own father, King Sviggar, and stolen his throne. Sviggar had been Erlan's oath-sworn lord. By killing Sigurd, Erlan had seen his dead lord avenged, seen his oath to the wizened old warrior satisfied, his duty discharged. Yet here he was, a world away, still serving him.

He could have gone anywhere once the shores of Sveäland had slipped beyond the horizon. The four winds could have carried him anywhere in the world of men. But one name kept coming back to him. One place.

Miklagard.

The Great City.

It had been Sviggar's vision. His last vision, it turned out. Some of his underlings called it an obsession, since few of them caught the taste of it. The old king saw gold flowing like a river out of the south and east. He had started building a trade fleet to realise his dream – ships to find a way through to this near-mythical kingdom of which only the most far-faring merchants brought news. But Sviggar's dreams of gold and glory had been answered with butchery and murder, ground into a mire of blood-feuds and betrayal.

Sometimes, however, one man's dream can become another man's destiny. And the more Erlan had thought on it as he left behind the bitter shadows of the Sveär halls, the more he wondered what this mythical place might hold. This

Miklagard. What riches could a man make for himself if he pioneered a trade route between the north and this mighty kingdom that lay beyond the southern sky? He had grown weary of swearing oaths that bound his sword-arm to another man's troubles. Weary of slaughter and the black horror-dreams that came in its wake. What if he built something... *good*? Something that did honour to his dead lord's dreams?

Well, he'd already paid a high price to answer that question. Him and his dog.

Their voyage across the East Sea had been the simplest part of their journey. He'd arrived in the market harbour of Rerik within four days of leaving Uppsala. The place swelled like a pimple off the arse of the East Sea. He disembarked full of hope that, with all these sea-skippers gathered in one place, surely one of them could give him passage to Miklagard. But his enquiries met only with laughter. His pouch of hack-silver availed him only disappointment.

Plenty had never heard of it. Of those who had, none had any intention of trying to reach it. Still, he had his boat. He had hoped to sell it for more silver, but if no one wanted to help him, he would try alone. One weather-worn skipper – a man grey-bearded and wolf-eyed – had at least told him the best route to make a start on his voyage. 'You'll find the mouth to the Visla river a hundred leagues east of here. Follow the river south. After that you fork up a tributary they call the Boog.'

'Queer name.'

'Queer folk named it,' the skipper shrugged. 'You need crewmates, too. Unless you can row a damned sight better than you can walk.' Erlan ignored the jibe. 'You're mad, by the way.

I'd wager my ship you'll get stuck in that ice and freeze to death. Else someone'll cut you to pieces.'

'Don't suppose any man would take that bet.'

'Suppose not,' the skipper chuckled. 'Still, if you want to know, the Boog's your best route south. And after that, the Dnipar. They say it's the greatest river in all the wide world.'

Then perhaps the greatest city lay at the end of it.

Erlan found himself a couple of crewmates in a small hamlet along the coast. They cost him a third of all his silver, too, which irked him. They were a pair of thralls aged fourteen and sixteen. Brothers, who were more bone than meat and hardly said a word between them. Still, they pulled hard enough. And after the days turned into weeks the rowing made them strong. Made them all strong, because Erlan took his turn at the oar. They drove deeper and deeper into the fathomless landmass, snaking with the winding river, cloaked by the pine forests and firs that crawled up to each bank.

It felt strange owning this pair of brothers. They were his chattels. His property. In essence, no different from the sea chest stowed against the strakes, or his axe and spear and shield. Yet he treated them as he would have any shieldbrother, giving them an equal share of any food they came by when they hunted at night, or any fish they pulled from the river. He didn't see why he should have done any different.

Poor buggers…

They had reached somewhere near the headwaters of the Boog just as winter began to stretch its brittle fingers across that strange land and bring all life to stillness. On the river, the ice had been spreading for some days until one dawn they awoke and the hull was stuck fast. They managed to break it out that time. But Erlan had realised it wouldn't be many more mornings before they would be stuck in the ice for good, for the whole winter, and these empty hills were no place to linger. So he had taken the younger brother and headed inland to seek out any signs of life.

Before long they had come across a kind of settlement. More like a large steading than a village, scraped out of the hard, black earth into a miserable little enclave of shacks and hide-skin tents. The headman was suspicious at first. But they managed to avoid any serious misunderstanding, and his suspicion soon gave way to curiosity. Erlan led him and some of his men back to the river. The headman grasped their predicament quick enough: his servants – or his slaves, for such they undoubtedly were, the way he treated them – proved strong as mules, dragging the little *knarr* up the river bank.

'Dnipar? Dnipar?' Erlan had said a hundred different ways, gesturing and repeating himself over and over. The headman's gaze was blank until at last light dawned on the old crooked face. 'Pryp!' he cried, pointing east, not south. 'Pryp!' Another flurry of gestures, grunts and other signals, gave Erlan to understand that there was indeed a portage to another waterway, but whether this was the river the skipper in Rerik had told him about or some other the gods only knew. The hilly country round about at least suggested some kind of watershed.

But portage or none, what soon became clear was that no amount of persuasion, by silver or by steel, would convince the headman to help them this side of winter. So Erlan and the brothers had found themselves reluctant guests of this man and his kinsfolk – although to call themselves guests was putting it generously, for the miserable old buzzard had all of them work every joint and knuckle to the bone, even as the temperature dropped still further, until it seemed the very ice-world of *Niflheim* had spread its deathly mantle over all of life, nevermore to give it up into the hands of the green gods of spring.

Erlan had never passed a harder winter. The wind whistled through the steading like the breath of Billingr, the great ice-giant, screaming in the ears enough to drive a man to madness. The sad, beleaguered community huddled around sad, beleaguered hearths, buried under voluminous pelts which weighed them down so heavily that they came to resemble beasts themselves, shuffling about, sifting and grinding what meagre grain they had drawn from the earth into stone-hard loaves that nearly broke the teeth.

The cold had been constant, seeping deep into a man's bones, benumbing his flesh, slowing his blood to an ice-flow, gnawing at his joints like a wolf. Every morning Erlan would awake to an aching body. At first, he thought it was from the hard pallet the headman gave him for a bed. Eventually he realised it was because every muscle in his body shivered its way through the night, leaving him stiff as bark and exhausted come morning.

When the nights were longest, the older of the brothers had started coughing. And gone on coughing and coughing until the blood started to stain his lips. After that, he didn't put up much of a struggle. It was as if the splinters of ice that encrusted everything outside had infiltrated the boy's chest and were bleeding him to death from the inside out. Erlan did what he could for him – which wasn't much – but he died even quicker than Erlan could have guessed. The younger brother wasn't long following him to a shallow grave. He got himself mauled by a bear when he was out hunting. He didn't outlive the night.

But Erlan clung on, and on, out of sheer bloody stubbornness. And at last, the winter had broken, the river ice cracking up with long, yawning sounds which echoed up the shallow valleys like the moans of wood-spirits luring a man to his doom. Then, one day, the headman had appeared with two yoke of oxen.

'It's time,' he croaked. Erlan – who by now knew something of their tongue – needed no second telling.

The portage was Hel. But even Hel was better than a day more in that sad and hopeless place. It took them five days to drag Erlan's boat by sled and by makeshift runners over the fast-dwindling snow to a boggy valley head where, the headman assured him, the river Pryp rose from the depths of the earth. 'The river carries you towards the rising sun for a long time. Afterwards comes the big river.'

'And then the sea?'

The old man shrugged his bony shoulders. 'The river will take you where it takes you.'

Erlan had wondered whether the man even knew what the sea was. 'Thank you,' he said and meant it, then bundled Áska over the gunwale and shoved the little boat out into the current…

That was three weeks ago.

The Pryp had looped north and south like a serpent writhing on a hook, growing wider all the time until, as the headman predicted, it had emptied into another body of water, but one so wide that at first Erlan took it for a lake. But he soon discovered that it, too, had a current and his hopes rose: that this was indeed the great Dnipar river of which the Rerik skipper had spoken. They travelled onward, speeding by sail when the wind was with them, or else simply letting the current carry them south. Many times the ride splayed out so wide that Erlan was sure they had at last reached the river mouth and the open sea. But always it funnelled again like the neck of an ale-flask and soon Erlan gave up trying to predict what lay ahead.

The land was vast beyond imagining. So vast it troubled his mind. If this world of men was so wide and endless, what of those eight other worlds that hung from the boughs of *Yggdrasil*, the World Tree. And what kind of place must this Miklagard be – if indeed he ever found it – and what kind of people filled its halls?

Sometimes he saw villages on the riverbank. Twice he spied places that looked like strongholds, but his *knarr* went shooting past before anyone could have stopped him. He encountered hostility only once: he rounded a bend in the river and passed close to a handful of men standing knee-deep on a sand-bar. They had yelled at him, then followed up their insults with a spear and two arrows. One of them even pierced his sail, though it arced overhead harmlessly enough.

But for that, and for the uncertainty of where this river would finally carry him, he had to admit the journey had been altogether peaceful. Even the late winter sun on this particular morning shone with a gentle sort of a light, softening up the land in preparation for the exertions of spring, when the last of the snow would melt and life would erupt in earnest.

He slouched back against the tiller, tipped back his head, closing his eyes to the sun's thin caress, listening to the stream of bubbles under the clinker hull. He smelt the river air, its muddy scent mingling with the sweeter smell of pine sap drifting across the water from the surrounding woods.

Peace.

It seemed so alien to him. To all he had known in his twenty-odd years. Yet out here it was easy enough to come by. Out here where there were no people. Was that all it took? The absence of the whole world. No wonder few folk found it...

The change must have come a little while back, without his notice. But then it touched his conscious mind. A change in the sound of the river, a change in the run of the water under the hull. The bubbles ran faster, louder, a little more urgent. He opened his eyes.

The river was narrowing some distance ahead. Not again, he thought, exasperated. He got to his feet, trying to see further. Then he climbed onto his sea chest, balancing himself against the mast, shielding his eyes against the dawn-light sparkling off the water. Áska lifted his head.

They were definitely moving faster now. The banks were drawing in closer. He noticed more rocks breaking out of the silt along the shoreline. Further ahead on the western bank the treeline seemed to shrink, then come to an abrupt end. It just disappeared. It was a few seconds before he realised why. The land was dropping away. He swore and turned back to the tiller.

But everything was happening faster now. Without warning the boat suddenly slewed to the right till the bows were pointing flat across the stream. The force of the water against the side-strakes rolled it over to its larboard gunwale. For a second, Erlan lost his balance and stumbled, twisting his ankle. The old wound – the injury that made him a cripple – shot a sudden streak of fire into his groin.

He gasped in pain, but forced himself onwards to the stern till he had hold of the tiller and shoved it away from him. The bows began swinging back parallel with the stream, but the noise was growing now, the water beneath the strakes bucking and roiling like the sea. At least he had control of the boat. Áska was standing in the bows, muzzle sniffing at the air. Suddenly he began to bark. That was when Erlan heard the roar of water ahead of them.

Under him the boat buffeted even more. Until now he had thought only to keep its course straight ahead on an even keel, but a sudden fear flooded his body, a sense of something powerful and dangerous ahead. He needed to reach the shore – except the banks were closing in, rising up about them in a great grey casing of rock.

There was a sudden bang, a scraping, a listing of the boat over to the larboard. Rocks! He swore again, trying to peer ahead but feeling suddenly powerless as a bairn's twig in a spring torrent. There was another glancing blow, careening the boat the other way, the current was sucking the little craft forward, pitching them downwards.

There was no going back now. No turning for the bank. No escape from the frothing cauldron dead ahead. The noise was growing, spray was kicking up, the smooth surface of the river fracturing into breakers and white-foaming gulleys, pitching and tossing the boat all over. By pure instinct, Erlan scanned his belongings. His ring-sword, Wrathling, was within reach as always. His shield and axe a little beyond. The food, the salt-barrel, the cloaks that served as his bedding, all stowed up in the bows.

He snatched the hilt of his sword. 'Áska, to me! Now!' The dog's head turned at his cry, then everything seemed to move in slow motion. The bow-post rose up, almost gracefully, Áska's shoulders hunched, bracing against the soaring timber, there was a giddy weightless moment, and suddenly the bows plunged downwards with the force of a hammer blow. Down and down, as the waters thundered about them, a hurricane of spray blinding him to everything – the crash of waves, the cracking of timber – his grip on the leather sheath his only reassurance, and then everything heaved upside down.

He was flung headlong into the boiling flood. Splinters of wood spat like thorns in his face. He took blows to the body and shoulders, felt the looming shadow of the *knarr*, the rapids lifting it up as though it were light as a toy in the hands of a god. And then for one breathless, frozen moment, it hung above him. His heart sprang into his mouth and the next instant he was underwater, whirling in a maelstrom of foam and rock and wave, over and over, smashed and pummelled again and again till he knew not up from down, and his lungs were screaming for air…

Praise for Theodore Brun

'Evocative prose and the brutality of the Viking world, it's all here, woven with a deft touch into a tremendous tale.' Giles Kristian on *A Mighty Dawn*

'Brun writes with passion and his recreation of this bloody, fascinating world is convincing.' *The Times*

'A hugely impressive effort, this is a rip-roaring blockbuster brought to life in vivid detail. You can smell the smoke of the Viking hall, taste the burning desire for revenge. With Brun – there's a new heavy weight writer on the medieval block.' Justin Hill

'Just when you thought the brilliant Giles Kristian had the Viking crown for good, along comes another fine contender for the throne… Engrossing, spellbinding, *A Mighty Dawn* is exactly that.' Jon Wise on *A Mighty Dawn*, *The Weekend Sport*

'A masterly debut. … If Bernard Cornwall and George RR Martin had a lovechild, it would look like *A Mighty Dawn*. I devoured it late into the night, and eagerly await the sequel.' Antonia Senior on *A Mighty Dawn*

'At the point where history and myth blurs, Theodore Brun has crafted a thunderous epic of blood and fire, love and loss that will keep you reading deep into the night.' James Wilde